# A·N·C·I·E·N·T L·I·G·H·T·S

# Davis Grubb

# A·N·C·I·E·N·T L·I·G·H·T·S

The Viking Press  ·  New York

c. 1

Library of Congress Cataloging in Publication Data
Grubb, Davis, 1919–1980.
Ancient lights.
I. Title.
PS3513.R865A84    813'.54    81-51881
ISBN 0-670-12262-9 hardcover    AACR2
ISBN 0-670-12263-7 paperback

Grateful acknowledgment is made to the following for permission to reprint copyrighted material:

*New Directions Publishing Corp. and David Higham Associates Ltd.:* "Do not go gentle into that good night," from *Poems of Dylan Thomas.* Copyright 1952 by Dylan Thomas. Used by permission.
*United Artists Music:* A selection from the song "Over the Rainbow" by Harold Arlen and E. Y. Harburg. Copyright © 1938, 1939; renewed 1966, 1967 by Metro-Goldwyn-Mayer, Inc. All rights administered by Leo Feist, Inc. All rights reserved.
*Warner Bros. Music:* A selection from the song "Lady Be Good" by George Gershwin. Copyright 1924 by New World Music Corporation. Copyright renewed. A selection from the song "Dancing in the Dark" by Howard Dietz and Arthur Schwartz. Copyright 1931 by Warner Bros. Inc. Copyright renewed. All rights renewed.
*The Welk Music Group:* A selection from the song "Lovely to Look At" by Jerome Kern, Jimmy McHugh, and Dorothy Fields. Copyright © 1935 by T. B. Harms Company. Copyright renewed T. B. Harms Company (c/o The Welk Music Group, Santa Monica, CA 90401). International copyright secured. All rights reserved.

Cover design by R. Adelson
Printed in the United States of America
Set in CRT Caslon

*For my beloved brother*
*Lou—and all the debbils—*
*Susan and Rosie and Eru and*
*all the rest.*

I wonder whether the Girls are mad,
And I wonder whether they mean to kill,
And I wonder if William Bond will die,
For assuredly he is very ill.
—William Blake, "William Bond"

# P·A·R·T
# O·N·E

Sweeley Leach preaches the new gospel,
the Criste Lite, in his battle against
the devious forces of our computerized
planet in the year 1992.

# O✦N✦E

The tear shall melt the sword of steel,
And every wound it has made shall heal.

For the tear is an intellectual thing,
A tear is an intellectual thing . . .

When Satan first the black bow bent
And the Moral Law from the Gospel rent,
He forg'd the law into a sword
And spill'd the blood of Mercy's hord.
                              —William Blake

The world discernes itself, while I the world behold,
By me the longest yeares, and other times are told,
I the world's eye.
                    —Ovid, *Metamorphoses* iv, 226–28
                    (*translated by Sir Walter Ralegh*)

3

Now. Right here. Yes. You're touching it—this tiny flowershaped freckle between my legs, a few centimeters from my vulva, in the soft ribbon of white skin between hairline and thigh.

Straighten up now and listen well. For I am no lying wench as I warn you that, in this world as in the real one, your life will most surely depend upon your understanding what follows: the testament of my father, Sweeley Leech, who art in heaven and whose book (yes, one day you may come across a rare copy) was written, as it were, in tears of Joy run down from the cheeks of the laughing Jesus.

It is, of course, a freckle transplant. In 1989 it was one of the first in modern medical technology, though now they have become extremely common and are often performed in hospitals where Love is not considered carcinogenic. Smaller than the petal of the tiny sundew that grows among the moist mosses of the Gallimaufry, the freckle first appeared on the face of a strawberry blonde named Dorcas Anemone, daughter of a dedicated and devout neo-Nazi in Clarksburg, West Virginia.

As Poe so prettily put it, Dorcas loved and was loved by me, back in the late and rather unlamented nineteen-eighties. We parted—as earthly lovers really always should e'er they "do the winged life destroy," as Uncle Will Blake warned—and she made me the sweet legacy of her freckle, as a tender souvenir to be kept always in my closest, though not necessarily most secret, regions.

The morning of our parting she came up foaming in lace among her satin shoulder straps like Saint Bridos from the surf of musk and seareeking quilts where we had twined and tossed in love the moony night through. Her dark eyes shone like those of the nine-year-old Tutankhamen. Her tiny navel was the mark a silver spoon tip makes in thick cream. I kissed the shreds of cracked, peeling Avon Sweet Orange polish on her nails. Her pubes were a salad of geranium lettuce. She smelled of the tartness of dreams and of warm milk. Now she sat back, pressing her soft little buttocks into her boyhard heels and—not really masturbating herself, but touching, as if in mnemonic reverie, the soft, wet braille of scalloped labia. She seized my right hand in hers and moved it up and down— stroking the tiny freckle on her face with my fingertip. Her eyes closed and trembled, the lashes glowed soft burnt copper, and her

4

mouth looked parched and she bit her lip—moving my hand in that sensuous, sacred cadence as though the freckle were her tiny clitoral surrogate, or my own.

This silly mark you love beside my mouth, she whispered into my bangs. Fifi, I want it always to live where my mouth was always so happy!

O, my precious and delectable Dorcas! She could say something as loving and sweet as that; could, in fact, conjure up the idea of the transplant itself—and then say something that made you wonder if she had a grain of sense. O, but she had more grains than the sea. And she was not mad. She was wise as the stars.

After a marvelous cold salmon and a monologue in which she discussed the vision of the City of God as it appears first in Bellay and then in Spenser, she paused, stared down, eyes crinkled with joy, at the bit of potato on her fork.

*Pommes de terre,* she crooned. I adore them, Fifi. And I have decided—from now on I'll call the little darlings *pommes* for short.

And she did: asked the scented little waiter for *pommes,* and when he brought her sliced baked apples with a Midi sauce, she raved over them as the finest potatoes in Christendom.

But her funniness was often conscious. And when she was about to utter something she *knew* was especially wicked and audacious, she would turn her face a little and talk to you round the corner of it—peeking round the corner of her cheek at you, through curls and high lace collar, eyes flashing with turquoise disingenuousness, her mouth twitching as it fought back laughter.

To the modern religion there is this Moral: Bryant's an eater— and Roberts is Oral.

The sweet morning of our parting she willed me her freckle with a great and formal act of lovemaking on my happy though amazingly passive body. I lay akimbo and sprawling while, as she devoutly devoured me, she chanted snatches of the songs we had jukeboxed together with—and wept in a loud, female voice. Then she called on the partyline and got hold of a new doctor from some island called Seychelles—a cosmetic surgeon—and arranged for him to transplant the freckle that morning. He was—obviously— fascinated as Dorcas described rapturously what she wanted done, where the freckle was now, where she wanted it to be forever, and then went into some detail about the good times the freckle had already had in that neighborhood.

That afternoon was a pulsing yellow-and-scarlet day in Indian summer. We hiked and hitchhiked out to the young doctor's tiny home and office, where he performed the simple operation quickly and without pain. Afterward we turned on with some marvelous Apply County grass and packed a huge luncheon in an old wicker picnic hamper from his pantry. We all piled into his muddy and buttsprung Mercedes and smoked another joint from my stash and drank red Málaga from Lake Chautauqua from a tawny leather bottle with a beautiful golden nipple on it, fashioned by some unremembered Alhambra Cellini into the tiny suncolored penis one sees on Cinquecento cherubim.

We drove down the Ohio River till we found, at the forest fringes of the Gallimaufry, a small grove of lindens around a spring-fed pond. After we had stripped and swum and fell upon the luncheon with ravenous appetites, we separated. The young doctor lay nude in the sour grass and wintergreen watching me and Dorcas as we pattered about, picking and feeding to each other the warm, delicate raspberries growing in the shuddering shades around the pool. We were naked, too. And still hungering—even after our huge lunch and the wine and the grass. Hungering for something more. Every few moments one or the other of us would turn a laughing, burning glance toward the young Seychellian. Hungering. For something else. Then we would find some more of the fruit—breathing in its somehow feverish, pulpy fragrance —and laugh and tease and feed each other, smearing the crushed juices all over our faces and breasts and fringed, flat bellies and pretending that the raspberries were what we actually hungered for. Dorcas, a petite, laughing Pascin; and I, lanky and rosy and lean.

The young doctor watched us until he could endure it no more and with a great, thrilling roar sprang up and gave chase. He caught Dorcas first and was soon wet with her. I joined them. And we were together: O, so together. Until at last he gave us each that something we had hungered after so—a lovely teaspoonful apiece! O, the memory of love that day in that place—amid the bright persimmon wind and the pawpaw and black walnut psaltery of a West Virginia September, while the leaves clashed in the taut air like tiny wedding sabers above our heads, calicoing our shameless Joy with lemony two-bit pieces scissored out of sun and leftover moon.

Therefore to begin at the beginning, as dear dead Dylan Thomas said before he died trying, vaingloriously, to get his other wing into paradise. Here. In this hotel bedroom. In the enormous John L. Lewis–size bed with the sexy ceiling mirror in the tenth-floor Executive Suite of the Daniel Boone Hotel in Charleston, West Virginia. It is six-thirty on the morning of September 4, 1992. You will in full term discover that this was to be the morning I would helicopter to Manhattan from Echo Point, traveling with my father to assist him in carrying out the most extraordinary bank holdup in world history, and certainly—as history and bank holdups go—the first Christian one, too.

And I begin my true and astonishing story by exposing to your inspection, by having you actually stroke and, in sweet Criste's name, enjoy, this minute romantic adornment. Here. In this bedroom, as I have said. Though I have not said until now the sad reason for my being in Charleston, West Virginia, at all: the death of the real writer in my family: the late Davis Grubb. I'll explain all about that in a minute—I mean how his name and not mine is given on the cover of this volume as its author. He was not the author. Except at the very beginning. The book—this story and all the true things that happen in it—they are mine.

But back to my tiny love relic and its meaning to the beginning of the story.

This is me you see here wrestling in the snarled, me-fragrant bedclothes beneath the big mirror, strutting my long legs out like sanitary straws bobbling out from the mocha ice-cream soda of my leafbrown Valentina negligee, hulaing my arms to unimaginably trite Don Ho raw coconut milk Muzak in the hotel hallway by the elevator banks. No Gillespie, no Benson, no Fuller or Miles or Mac Davis! O, ye of Percy Faith!

I see me capsuled in the tousled light above my morning eyes. I arch my pelvis and grind merrily into my finger—that slim axis to the jolly millwheel of the Holy Universe. I joyously survey the livid, distant miracle of me there, seeing my secret adored body, secret as the oystered seas: church and chapel of the womb, seeing the tender

7

furry portal as it labyrinths into the catacomb of my warm, cathedraled sex. I make inventory of my other self: from the laureled black ogive of my cunt to the fleeing cherubim of legs akimbo and all the stained-glass wink of eye and lacquered toes and butterfly fingers. Adoring myself, I still make feverish inventory as the obsessive fear deepens that Dorcas's freckle—that precious, adorable bookmark between the leaves of the book, as it were—that this badge of love has been stolen from me, pirated frivolously from that little private wildwood between my thighs. I will be less rhetorical. To be blunt, I figured that the freckled treasure had been stolen from between my legs by that infernal fairy whom I permitted to be intimate with me in the Labyrinth last night at Echo Point.

Fairy. A most troublesome word. Fairy.

Suspend, if you can, all connotations of sexuality connected with this abused and most misunderstood word. Know that when I speak of a fairy I mean precisely that, nothing less, that I imply nothing else, that I desire you to infer no more. Fairies are exciting and lovely to the eyes—but mischievous and lusty beyond belief. They are perfectly formed, not gnarled and lumpish like the gnomes and elves—the tiny girls like tiny, elastic Dresden goddesses: nipples like specks of red pepper, and tiny pubes like wisps of milkweed floss or like a fleck of chimney soot. The tiny boys are not as sexually aggressive as the fairy-women, but they are little imps of horniness with almost perpetually raging, red, minuscule hard-ons. For a girl to seek sex with this really habituating little lover is not wise if pursued too ardently, too often. But if you would seek love with a fairy, go into the Gallimaufry, your body freshly bathed and perfumed, and wearing your sweetest, gayest Pucci frock and a dab of musk between the thighs and behind each ear and in the sweet hollow of the knee. Usually this is enough to attract one. You should—despite the thorny, rocky floor of the forest of the Gallimaufry—be wearing pumps with high heels and straps to your calf. No hose. No lingerie whatsoever. Some fairies are turned on by red-painted toenails and a gold ankle bracelet. Do I seem to your tired Christian mind too utterly depraved? So be it. Both I and my father, Sweeley Leech, know a truth—that in these furious times we must appeal to what you consider the lowest part of your human nature because it is in that region that your highest human nobility has taken refuge. Until the spiritual revolution which is coming, you will—unless you are a member of the Children of the Remnant—remain staggering and baffled and choking in the brimstone pollution of this dying age.

But more of the how and why of having sex with fairies. I have described how a lady who is feeling sexy in that area should adorn her body. She should determine her spirit and bravely set her mind to a state of complete abandon during this fairyfuck. She should seek a glade where the falling moonshine is of a specific blue intensity. She should close her eyes and breathe deeply through the nostrils from time to time. When, sweet and unmistakable upon the breath of the lilting night wind, she suddenly smells the faint scorch of fireflies on the shuddering violet air, hears faintly the sizzling kindle of the glowworm as it brushes, by chance, against the nautilus of the silver-tracked snail as it mucuses its sweet, cowhorned way up a stem of wild ginseng; when a girl senses in the night air's breathing breath the sweetness of murdered clover, she knows that a tiny, turgid lover is approaching through the night-nodding weeds and wild flowers and mists. You know—the smell in the air after a hay harvest—like tonka bean—the sweet aroma as of a spice ship caraveling in from Zanzibar or Mauritius and wrecked suddenly on the silver plow of shore, its treasures spilling out among the oysters and sea urchins so fragrantly. But also a smell, like a thin, tiny counterpoint, mixed in with this always—sharp and pungent as the pinch of turmeric in green tomato pickle—this is the fairy's rutting scent. One waits—one's inhibitions crumbling like the walls of some pink-tinted Troy—feet spread apart, thin white ankles stained with crushed grass and glowing, perhaps, with the blood of glowworms. One can abandon oneself to one of these fiery, hotblooded, prurient creatures as one rarely does with a mortal. By now—usually, that is—the scent of one's swollen and weeping vulva is enough to draw one of the insatiable creatures of the night. The flowing skirt is held high; the bared pelvis is thrust forward into the light of the lascivious moon. At this point the insertion of a lacquered forefinger into the labia—an interval of self-titillation or conversation with one's waking clitoris—this will produce the first tiny come, which rather takes the edge off one's incredible desire. This—all of this, of course—should be done only in certain hours of star and phase of the old and constantly prurient moon. One is

backed up against a young sycamore or sugar maple or in the bole
of an old, loving willow—thighs exposed and thrust lewdly out into
the moving air, the curls of one's love hair like infinitely small antennae sounding the prescient night air. One's lathering finger is by
now gone mad. And then the soaring rocket bursts faintly, staining
the summer violet with smeared gold. And a moment later, he—or
she—is there. With a tiny lusty cry a little hand grabs the patent-
leather strap of your pump and clambers up the slippery flower
stem of your thigh. How tiny the creature is! How perfect! And in a
moment he—or she—is pulling aside, with tiny fingers no bigger
than the blossom of the wild flower called Indian corn, is pulling
aside, as I say, the brier patch of your pussy. The creature is clothed
in tiny Levi's and, quite often, a torn jacket, salvaged from a Barbie
Doll some child threw into the junk. Now the heavenly part begins.
Before one knows what absolutely divine thing is happening, the
little fellow has stirruped a tiny Ked-clad foot into the lower V of
the vulva, and sometimes, delightfully, with a foot insinuated gently
into the twinkling, clean asshole—a part of the body I always view
like a jolly Christmas tree ornament or a tiny starfish from oceans of
which I can only bathe in dreams. Now and again the little sprite
will seize a wispy strand of pubic hair and swing both legs and torso
deep into the vagina. And begin gently wiggling his toes! O, sweet
Criste—Master of all love! There is a word in the fairy language for
such a coming but there is no human tongue can shape it.

As a mortal woman, twenty-six years old and above average in
sexual capacities, I speak of that human rarity—sex with a fairy—
with temerity and reverence. There is nothing like it in the range of
mortal sex acts. One is never quite the same after it is over. And let
it be said—without the stigma of carrying tales—that I was quite
thoroughly fucked by a fairy in the Labyrinth at Echo Point last
moonlit night. And, much as a wandering hillbilly guitar player
stole my driver's license and credit cards from a motel dresser doily
last month in Steubenville, so I suspected on this morning that the
little lover of the night before had stolen Dorcas's freckle. I search
misty-eyed with fear through the tremulous morning light. I sigh.
My hips and legs slump down. I have seen the dear freckle—it is
safe. O, Dorcas, I simply would have died if he had stolen it!

✦

Now follows what Sweeley Leech always terms a Causal Liaison. You think of someone you haven't thought of for years, you pick up your pencil, and for no reason apparent, write that name down. A moment later the mail arrives and there is a letter from him. Not coincidence, not even ESP, nothing like that, nothing that connects people in thought as much as it connects them like gears in the invisible and heavenly Patek Philippe of an eternally moving universe.

The Causal Liaison on this morning was as follows: after a full hour of preoccupation with Dorcas Anemone—an adored name I haven't really thought about for maybe a year—there was a sudden, short, shy knock on my bedroom door. I lay still, thinking it was the housemaid. But the light in the sky in the window was all sundown: a sunset like a stained-glass window had been dynamited, with fragments of saints' eyes and lips and blessing hands surviving among the boughs and leaves of incandescent trees. The knock came again—a shy knock, an about-to-give-up-and-go-crying-back-to-the-elevator knock. Somehow I knew.

She was terribly pale, and paleness always made her prettier, more glowy and intense-looking. I could tell that a bad love affair had been recent: she was dressed so badly; that was proof because Anemone was always the zingiest when it came to clothes. As intimate as we had been before, I felt shy in front of her and went into the bathroom and put on a negligee that wasn't see-through.

She sat suddenly on a stool, looking so very much like Miss Muffet in a black frock with a Peter Pan collar and small appliquéd flowers—O, very Methodist, somehow—and, of course, I felt exactly like some rather awful spider about to sit down beside her.

Fifi, you mustn't touch me, she began.

I went over and kissed her softly on the neck.

No, Fifi. You really mustn't touch me.

I understand, I said. I *want* to understand.

No, you don't understand, love. It's not us. It's not even you. It isn't even really me. It's—it's La Machine.

You mean the food blender?

I rolled a thin joint—lovely, midseason, homegrown—Grass à Dieu, Dorcas used to call it.

No. I mean La Machine. La system. La whole fucking world.

Maybe you can explain, I said.

I can't—Fifi, I can't touch another human being anymore.

You're touching me—touching me very deeply.

I don't mean that way, I—

Are you hung up on your vibrator?

Not even that personal.

I passed her the joint, but she shook her head sorrowfully.

La Machine, she sighed, has finally reached out and dragged me into its meshes, Fifi. I can't even love without it.

Explain. Really, Dorcas, you are being absolutely—

I am a captive of it, she said, her voice rising a little. The way your father says that Christ is the prisoner of the Church.

Are you into the Church?

Fifi, you're really an intuitive soul. But you're not being one now.

I stared lovingly at her, yet wanting not so much now to make love to her as write about her. An eagerness to record all her life's most exquisite moments—both mundane and heavenly—obsessed me. I could suddenly smell in memory's nostrils the tart reek of the sticky green ink of my nursery printing set. But suddenly I wanted to understand.

I'm ruined, Fifi, she said forlornly.

Then it is time to be re-begot.

I know, phoenix from the ashes. But the ashes of me, Fifi— they've all blown away.

I toked a couple and held the cigarette out toward Anemone. She shook her head and looked more miserable.

I sighed, osmosizing some of her growing melancholy. I stared at her a soft, melting moment and I guess it was too much.

You really mustn't touch me, Fifi. And you are touching me, you know—with your thoughts, your memories of us. It's as though you were searching me out with your tongue and your tongue has eyes. And you mustn't. You might catch IT.

I know you too well, Dorcky, I said. I know your fastidious and hygienic self too well to make the guess that you caught VD.

No, she said. O, no. Last year I lived with a man in Paterson, New Jersey. He slept with everybody. I means lots of girls besides me. But I knew he couldn't catch anything.

Couldn't?

O, no. He discovered this marvelous prophylactic.

What?

He wore a Sergeant's flea-and-tick collar around his penis.

So then what could I possibly catch from you, dear?

Her voice fell to a whisper.

ML, she sighed hoarsely at last.

ML?

Media Labia, she said. It's when a woman's libido gets hopelessly entangled in the machine. There are other names for it—horrid ones. Coaxial Clit, for example. But it all revolves around La Machine.

Say it again, I implored.

La Machine! TRUCAD. La ultimate world economic order. La whole fucking system that has us all prisoner.

She began to weep into a large blue bandanna with small white overall silhouettes of Elvis Presley's death mask.

The phone rang sharply. Dorcas moaned sensuously, her teeth grating. I couldn't prevent my hand from reaching for her—my fingers brushing an erect nipple under the black crepe de Chine bodice.

It was the hotel housekeeper saying that the maid on my floor wanted to go home unless I wanted my room done. I sped the poor little soul home to her boyfriend and kids. I turned back to Dorcas. My fingers still were ginger-ale bubbles up my arm, where they had brushed her. Dorcas had incredible breasts—like inverted Haviland teacups. One felt that if a fingernail were flicked against such a soft, ceramic dome it would give off a deep, soft chime—like bells beneath the sea.

Your nipples, I said, without looking at her. They are hard as little pussy-willow buds.

Naturally, she said.

Should I take that as a compliment?

No, she said, O, I still have the very deepest feelings for you, Fifi. It isn't that. I mean they get erect—*whenever the phone rings.*

She bit her lip.

Perhaps if *you* went away somewhere, she said then, in a strange, dreamy voice. And called *me* on the phone—

Is this rather oblique desire to have me go away and call you somehow connected with ML?

It *is* ML, Fifi.

How did you first detect that you had ML?

Well, she sighed, I am between love affairs now. This was about six months ago. I didn't notice it at first.

What? What were the first symptoms?

O, getting off alone, she said. During the Carson Show.

You have a thing about that poor old man?

No, not Johnny, she said. His guests. Candice Bergen. The Muppets. Robert Redford. Anybody. It didn't matter whom he had on—I made it with them—through the TV.

Well, darling, millions do that, I suspect.

Well, they don't know what they're getting into, that's all I can say.

ML, huh?

You bet. And when it hits you—well, you're just—just wasted. Screwed.

Wasted?

So far as a normal love life goes. Yes. Wasted.

How do you mean? Dorcas, you know I call any kind of a love life okay so long as it has real love in it. Even the nightblooming variety that changes into a sweet, drifting memory in the morning, like campfire smoke in the air. How did the ML—I mean, how does it affect you?

It enslaves me to sexual relationships only through the agency of the Media.

I see. Well—

I lit a straight cigarette and paced the closet space, picking out the clothes I was going to wear back to Echo Point.

It began this way, said Dorcas. I might as well tell you my boy-friend in Paterson, New Jersey, didn't work. Didn't do anything but the things he did very well and he didn't often get paid for them. Except by me.

You were keeping him.

We were sharing. I like that better. Sharing. I shared my money and he shared his body and we both shared Love.

What were you doing?

Working in Union City, she said. In a bar. As a topless, bottom-less dancer. The two other dancers I worked with were both perfect angels—one of them a transsexual who, the night after she got out of the Albuquerque hospital, was picked up in male drag. I guess we're never satisfied in this world. Anyhow, I was making out with both of them and with Officer Lemley at home. O, he knew, all right. I think he kind of liked it.

Officer? He was a policeman?

No. Officer was his first name. I guess his Montana father thought it would always give him respect. Officer J. Lemley. He was no policeman. O, no. Far from it.

I can see how that would be awkward, I said. I mean they'd have to call him Officer Officer J. Lemley. Which would look like shit on a traffic ticket.

What? O, yes. I guess they would.

You broke up with Officer Lemley?

Yes.

A nice break? Or a messy one?

Well, it all began the night I came home and the flat was empty and the phone rang.

Just like now—a moment ago, I said.

Yes, she said, her lashes shimmering against her cheek; she bit her lip. It makes my nipples erect. It makes me wet— My legs like rigatoni too well done. The phone.

The phone rang again. Dorcas pressed her thighs together and moaned softly.

Make it stop. O, Fifi, do make it stop!

I grabbed the phone off the hook and stuffed it under a large lavender cushion on the floor.

By now I had hurriedly dressed. I might say that dressing is usually for me a kind of ritual of love. I adore my body and I like to regard it as a pleasing gift I am wrapping to be opened by somebody later. Or maybe just opened by me. Times when it's just me, I'm always somehow in a swoon of delighted surprise—maybe at just finding everything still there, and in such adorable order! I had gone into the bathroom and left the door open so I could watch and listen to her while I tugged on a pair of Pucci slacks over my really best black lingerie. I put on an off-white linen artist's blouse and a pair of loafers.

The phone rang, I said. After you got home to the empty flat that night.

Yes. And it was to be the bell of my doom.

How? Who was it?

It wasn't a Who yet, she said. So far it was only a What.

Which was—?

An obscene phone call, she said.

I *adore* them, I said, handing her her purse and grabbing up my own tawny shoulderbag. Let's get breakfast and shock the hotel staff. I adore obscene phone calls. And you know—I never got one.

Well, normally, I don't care much about them, Fifi. I'm not a student of people like you are. They do sometimes get on my nerves. But this caller—he—he—

He had style? What?

Fifi, it was like getting a dirty call from Billy Graham.

What's funny about that? He makes them to God all the time.

He had hardly spoken into the phone for three minutes till I got off.

Came?

One of the kind that wrings you out, Fifi. Absolutely divine.

So you hung onto the phone for a while?

Why, no. That's just it. We made a date. Obviously, he had gotten off, too, and well—obviously we were *made* for each other.

You met.

He had reserved the wedding suite at the best hotel in town. Champagne. Caviar. And French fries. I think I told him I was mad for French fries and catsup.

And afterward—paradise, I suppose.

Hell, you mean. Sheer hell. We couldn't touch each other. No way!

Were you—undressed?

Totally. And ready. I was wet to my knees and he—

But what—?

She covered her face with her fingers for a moment, steadying herself before going on.

We never saw each other again, she said. And, as I told him last night, I hope we never do.

Wait a minute, Dorcas. You never saw him again. And you spoke just last night.

O, last night and the night before. And every night in the foreseeable future, to coin a phrase. But only on the phone. We never see each other.

What a fascinating *ménage à trois!*—with Ma Bell in the middle. Is she a good lay?

Divine, sighed Dorcas.

Let's get something to eat, I said.

In the cidery, underwater deeps of the hotel dining room she pointed out one of the young, dark, Lebanese waiters, flitting from table to kitchen like dacoits in some dope-reeking Suez alley.

There, she said. That's the kind of young Bedouin who raped D. H. Lawrence.

T. E., T. E., T. E., I corrected.

Don't laugh, Fifi, she pouted. You always make fun when I'm being *literary*.

I laughed like a fool. Darling Dorcas. I would never change you and I would never make fun.

A blond singer was accompanying herself at a baby Steinway. She sang angrily, as though directing a tirade at someone invisible in the audience. The effect was as though a separate person were playing the piano behind her—and doing it maliciously, with cruel wit, undercutting the voice with mean and scornful harmonies.

A ten-dollar bill to the chef had persuaded him that it was possible to produce ham and eggs and red-eye gravy later than ten a.m. Dorcas finished hers in a hurry. I sensed the encounter was almost over.

Do you have change for a twenty, darling? I asked Dorcas. I want to leave the waiter a large tip.

Why, Fifi? I thought the service was awful.

It was, I said. But I think how unhappy I always am when I do something badly. Maybe the extra tip will cheer him up.

You're a good person, Fifi, she breathed. Good-bye. I'm due back in Room Eight-fifty.

I know, I said.

I waited a beat.

You're expecting a phone call.

Fifi, I hope you understand. I haven't gotten off all day.

I adore you, Dorcas.

And I you, Fifi. And—what is it you always say when you part from a lover?

I smiled.

I always say, "Remember me—but promise to love others, too."

Yes, yes! That's it! And I say it now to you, darling. Good-bye. Good-bye again. And again and again. Good-bye always, dear Fifi Leech, and forever Hello.

I was a little hurt after she left. She had never once asked if the freckle transplant had lasted. O, I know I'm a sentimental fool. But in the dark, under the tablecloth, through the slit of my fly, I touched it in its steamy, fragrant valley. After another cigarette, I had a glass of good domestic champagne and tipped the ecstatic waiter another ten dollars to bring me an extension phone on a cord. I dialed her number. She was quick to answer.

Fifi?

Yes, Dorcas. Make it, baby.

O, Fifi, she shrilled into the receiver. At last we're alone together!

I held the phone until her marvelous orgasm had subsided and kissed the mouthpiece and hung it gently in its cradle. It was the least I could do for an old lover.

That was when I glanced up and saw my father, Sweeley Leech, at the reception desk in the lobby. He had all the Manhattan luggage with him and I had a hunch he was looking desperately for me. I paid my check and slung my bag over and headed toward him. Guiltily, I might add. I knew all too well I was half a day late for the most incredible bank caper in human history. Sweeley's face—a little aureoled with gold the way Bruce Dern the actor's is—that face knew it, too.

Over the long cracked leather settee in the hotel's American lobby a TV set showed Auschwitz on the screen—I paused, forgetting about my father for a moment: seeing Auschwitz on a cold gray 1992 morning. I felt I could breathe the air there that now so artfully smells of nothing. My eyes filled with tears at the face of a French Jewish singer who had survived it—a face out of which flowers had been hammered. It seemed a curious augury of something waiting up ahead.

I moved swiftly toward the face of my father. Sweeley Leech moved swiftly toward mine.

# T✦W✦O

Are you ready, sir?

I could hear him up in the bungalow, making last-minute preparations for the flight to New York City. The small copter sat squatly, craning its blades amorously moonward.

Are you ready, Sweeley Leech?

In a minute, dammit. In a minute!

Sometimes I called him "sir"—more often by his Christian name. Side by side we looked like brother and sister—or lovers, which, once, we were. Lovers once; father and daughter always; equals always, too.

The gleaming tip of new autumn moon fanged out from a purple cumulus like the tooth of a fox from a hen's throat—beyond which the hanged, holy galaxies and luminous Northern Lights scattered their white feathers like chickens frightened in a violet yard.

Beyond the bungalow, down the lilting lip of the meadow, shone the river—its pooled, placid surface gleaming like blackberry jelly in a silver spoon. Behind the house, against the lit latitudes, soared the burial mound of the Adena and behind it, refulgent, green, and carved like an empress's lace collar, lay the great stone Labyrinth, Bebo, which had been there, legend held, even before the bungalow, before the mound itself, a thirty-foot-high mouth-shaped preeminence, its grassy teeth clenched as it holds back skeletons, shards of glory, and slumbrous secrets.

Are you ready, sir?

He hurried to a casement window, flung it open with a woody cry, and glowered down at me through the smoke of the moon.

Will you, for Christ's sake, be patient, woman? I am making one last desperate search through the house—my safe, my strongboxes. My ledgers. There is always the chance that I have overlooked something here or there.

I bit my lip, concerned and frightened for him. If he—if we, that is—pulled off the bank job, it would shake the Western World as no other crime in any annal. And Sweeley Leech would, in vengeance, be destroyed. His mind was into mine at that moment.

If I—if we, that is—he said, his voice soft but carrying across the lit mists like the wings of an owl, if we pull off this bank job, it will shake the Western World like no other crime in any chronicle. And if I succeed and—

I love you, Sweeley Leech. Your mind is my own.

Well, dammit, Fifi, I love you, too, but you must learn patience.

Be patient toward my impatience, then. You have had thirty-nine lifetimes to learn patience, sir.

Don't remind me.

Why? Do you regret them?

It's not that. I regret all of them—except maybe this one—because in each one I failed. But maybe in this one I'll succeed.

I walked over so as to stand directly beneath the open casement sill where he leaned—his fingers with the single big gleaming amethyst ring just a foot or so above the crown of my hair.

Fifi, Fifi, do you believe in me?

You know I do, dad.

I know. O, I know you do!

He turned away with what could have been a sob or could have been only a knot of light undoing itself in the lambent air.

My God, he cried, and he scurried off into the latched darkness of the bungalow. I just remembered another quarter million in Xerox I had hidden in the hamhouse!

I smiled and plucked a bud of sweet shrub near at hand and crushed it in my fingers and then held it to my face, breathing in its sweet little death.

He was gone again and one could not guess for how long. I heard his cry as he found the shares of Xerox and a beat of silence before his other, and more demented and anguished, outcry, as he remembered some shares of Polaroid hidden in one of the cameo cabinets in his jewelry room. I felt a tickle against my ankle. I stared down, my eyes drunk with moon and firefly shine, and saw this perfectly matchless little fairy with his doublet open and his tiny codpiece dangling and the most charming and pretentious little hard-on. His glans glowed like a tiny ruby.

No, I said quite firmly in the language of fairies (which I shall not confuse you with here). He pouted and rode cumbrously off on the back of a snail, masturbating himself moodily against one slimy little horn.

I felt a pang of pity.

Later, I whispered after him, down into the jungles of the grass. Another night—we have a great and holy scam to pull off in the morning, my father and I! When it is over and we are back home rejoicing in the Criste Lite, I shall let you do anything you want with me, sweetie chum!

He seemed to take cheer and, ready for a lovely come, sprang off the snail's back into the lap of a bawdy, maidenish wisp of light at the root of a dogtooth violet nearby. I heard her sharp whistle of reciprocation as her lithe, lit legs clasped him round. And then I was alone with the night and the moon and Echo Point, listening and wanting both to laugh and to cry at the sounds of my father, my oldest lover, turned into a madman—or perhaps a true debbil—a demon burglarizing his own home.

And can ye drink of the cup! I heard him roar in a voice like a bull of Catalonia.

My father is the gentlest man on earth, with a voice that can quote Shakespeare, Lenny Bruce, or Blake—Uncle Will Blake, late of the New Jerusalem and Felpham, England. But when Sweeley is full of anger he has a voice that could shatter a glass beaded curtain, and a face like World War V.

One thing is lacking, I heard him sob. Those were Criste's words. Just one thing is lacking. And I know what that thing is!

Have you seen shadows move in moonlight and suddenly become a figure? Well, at that moment, some ribbons of light took shape and moved from out the doorway of the small stone building up the lane toward Glory, where fingers of poplars meet the wind from the river and glitter in sequined elegance. I saw that it was my father's lover, Loll. I scarcely know what to say about Loll. I would rather have you see her and make up your own mind. The trouble is that there are so many of her. If you were to spot her in the calico light of the noonday sunparlor, all the chamber aflutter like a Klee watercolor, you would see an old twisted black woman, with a face blackwrinkled as a Bible—or a purse—a drone carrying on a silver tray a sweating silver pitcher of chiming lemonade and carved crystal tumblers that look like part of the ice. She is smoking a Salem Light and reeks strongly of Madame Jovan and marijuana. She is a witch. Nobody knows her age except herself, and all she ever told me—I know nothing of what she may have told my father—is that she was the daughter of a blackhearted scoundrel of a Christian named Morrison and his mistress, Loll's mother, Queen Traganina of Tasmania (last of her race). She is gnarled and misjointed and almost malignant-looking by day, but at night— Ah, that is another story! I stared at her now—a slim, full-breasted night girl with fingers like fresh, clasped stalks of flowers. They fumbled with the half-burned butt of a cigarette, then threw it away with a curse.

Fifi, have you got a Salem Light? she asked in a voice like a clinking glassful of something cool and sweet.

I gave her my pack. She took one and lit it thoughtfully from a firefly she plucked rather ungratefully from the darkling air. She threw that dead, lightless insect body into the grass and inhaled, blowing smoke through her slender, almost chiseled nostrils.

Shit, honey, she said. Sweeley's in a mood tonight.

I know him, too. O, God, I know him, she rambled on. And he makes me—

She snickered.

—Proud.

Why, Loll? Why don't you leave him, Loll? You know you've always been grief to him.

Because he makes me Proud, she iterated.

Proud of what, Loll?

O, maybe just me being the lover of a twenty-century man.

Sweeley is anything but a twentieth-century man, I scoffed.

I said twenty-century man, she said. A man who remembers twenty centuries of Isness. Shit, these moonmists—my Salem's gone out.

She tossed away the sullen smoke and stood with her back to me. She seemed lit more by the starlight than by moonshine. And something else, a frightening, ill-boding thing, it seemed to me then. The moon was behind her, behind the bungalow, behind the Labyrinth named Bebo and the river. But her shadow fell toward the moon—dark as a cut-voile pattern upon the luminous wind-dimpling grass.

In the Celebes—in 1896–97, she mused, more to her demon self than to me, I had me a grip on a fifteen-century man. But he got converted by a wrong kind of missionary and ended up in Wasness.

She paced through the gemmy, wet grass to the arched-hedge entrance to the Labyrinth. She turned and smiled at me. The delicate arch of her slender foot—like a panther, bowbellied to spring.

Still afraid of the Labyrinth, aren't you, Fifi?

I turned away.

Aren't you, Fifi?

She did not ask the question again: I had answered it with my stillness. I was afraid of the Labyrinth, and as to the dangers or nondangers of exploring all its ways and alleys, Sweeley Leech would never tell me one way or the other. He swore that the end of the Labyrinth, the innermost chamber, the Chamber of the Stars, it is called, was the most holy and perilous spot in all of Apple County.

At this moment I heard a hounded howl from my father somewhere in the deeps of the house. He had mislaid fifty shares of Occidental Petroleum and had given in to his deepest fears that the stock had increased a thousandfold since he'd bought it.

But back to my fear of the maze.

The odd thing: I remember in my childhood going in and out of the maze at will, without any dark thought, without any fear. Going, yes, to the farthest chamber itself—through the Lane of Spiders—and without fear. Then, as I grew older, I learned that the last room was Sin, and the Labyrinth, even in its simplest outer recesses, became formidable and threatening to me. Though I must report that my father sometimes spends days or even weeks back in there and perhaps beyond it—in the Gallimaufry: that astonishing and miraculous fragment of glacial rubbish that I will tell you about later.

Loll moved toward me again, her face wet with lipframing smiles.

Say something religious, I said rather mockingly.

Back of every small-town faggot, she said, stands a good church alto.

That's true. But it's your religion talking, Loll. That's not Sweeley Leech's kind of Criste.

O, I know his kind of Criste, she sneered. That's the Criste that got him locked up in the Glory jail overnight last spring.

How dare you mention that, Loll? You were in that congregation that pressed charges.

I ain't say I am and I ain't say I wasn't, she said. See how good I talk darky talk, missy?

Lay off, Loll. I'm not a bigot.

No, but your father is. He is a bigot against the Christian Church. That's why he went out deliberately and with malice afore-thought to our Congregational Presbyterian baptism and com-pletely created a riot by moving a mountain.

A hill. A small one, too.

A mountain, I say.

It wasn't more than thirty feet around—and ten feet tall.

Do you deny that Sweeley Leech said a prayer blaspheming the Church and moved it?

I do not, Loll. But that's not the point—

Suddenly I heard my sister, Lindy, in the kitchen, rattling the skillet. Lindy has awful insomnia and is constantly coming down to make scrambled eggs at the most secret, twitching hours.

One thing is lacking, said our Lord to me! wailed Sweeley Leech, his voice seeming to come now from the small but lapidarian library where he kept his sweetest treasures. I wondered if the Dürer *Tyndale* was still there. I adored that little fat book, priceless, beyond appraisal—still clasped in its old black lamb and sterling buckles. It was an earlier *Tyndale* than the 1526 and every other page was an adorable first-state woodcut by Dürer. Sweeley knew I doted on that little Bible, still reeking, it seemed, of the sweet fumes of its cremated author, and so it was that when I was three years old and he came in to find that I had, with crayons aforethought, colored the Adoration of the Magi and the Whore of Babylon (almost indistinguishable in my skyblue veneration from the Mother of our God), he had, as I was about to say, encouraged me to color a few more of the spidery, wild little pictures, but I soon wandered away into the tall iris to trade jokes with a mushroom-sheltered friend or foe.

One thing is lacking! cried my father again. "Sell what thou hast and give to the poor." But, God help me, I know there are at least two hundred million dollars in wealth hidden about Echo Point and I cannot find them all. And so—and so—

His voice almost broke, in the heart-wringing falsetto of Tagliavina doing a Naples street song.

One thing yet is *still* lacking! he thundered again, and I caught a glimpse of his young blond head hurtling past the French doors to the parlor, and I thought again that he was so much a look-alike to Bruce Dern, the actor.

I could not see Loll now, the moonlight had grown too bright. Yet I heard her sneering voice.

Sweeley Leech moved that mountain, she was yelling. And the godly members of the Congregational Presbyterian Church got him fined under the Apple County statute for Alteration of Real Estate. Fifty dollars, if I'm not mistaken. And a night in the Glory jail.

Oh, go away, Loll! I answered, and there was nothing but a spiral of molecules where she had been, though I heard her sensuous groan as she lay down on her pallet just beyond the door of the dark stone outhouse.

Why did you ask me to go away, Feef?

Lindy's voice floated plaintively through the good smells of her bacon and eggs.

I ran into the lamplit kitchen. I stared at her a minute, smiling, then threw my arms around her. She smelled so good. She was the only member of my family I hadn't made love with, and maybe that made me adore her the more and yet grow filled with dismay at everything she believed in.

I was telling Loll to go away, I said. Not you, Lindy, love.

Want some eggs?

Mmm. No, thanks. I've still got Loll on the mind.

Lindy sat eating her eggs and bacon ravenously at the Georgian breakfast table. She daubed a suncolored glob of pawpaw butter Loll had made. She crunched it into her mouth with her toast but she did not look up at me as she spoke.

You're going through with this pagan, un-Christian, immoral insanity?

Is that what you think of what Sweeley has decided to do in New York tomorrow? Obscenity, you said?

I said insanity—but thanks. You're right. Obscenity *is* the word.

I stared down at her, defensive again; it seemed my life with Sweeley Leech was always spent in love among the barricades.

The thought comes to me, Lindy, that when the Imagination pokes its way through the placenta of the provable and decides to be on its own, the result is either Genius or a Presbyterian.

She ruminated, stopped chewing entirely for a moment.

I'm attacking your Church, not you, love, I said.

I am my Church.

I know, I said. Forgive me, dear.

I suppose there are the weapons for your mad crime in that luggage out there by the copter?

Yes. I suppose that's what they really are, Lindy.

I thought of our Lord's blessed whips coiled like sleeping cottonmouths in some ancient bag like ours.

You plan to take this bank by main force?

I hope, I said, and thought unaccountably of Edwin Newman.

You know you could both be killed.

I don't think so, I said. I think rather that when they know what we're doing to their bank they'll be too stunned to do much but look—watch—listen. For all I know—and Sweeley Leech would know this—it may be something waking amid the opium cribs of their most secret wishes—to do themselves. To make one small gesture that could—like ripples becoming tidal waves—alter the whole economy and not just of that bank, but—

You don't seem to understand, Feef, she said, turning to face me now, her face looking pallid and drained in the flocculent, quivering lampshine. Shaw put it best. Poverty is a crime. Wealth is Goodness.

Artie's always given to such pronouncements.

Lindy began to hum "Indian Love Call." She hummed it nervously. I looked down at her, loving her, thinking how small and pretty and neat she was and how infinitely sad and—cloven. Yes, cloven in twain.

The kitchen extension rang. I picked it up. It was Dorcas. She was free again. Free of La Machine. A detective from the C&P phone company had come with a protest because of the intercepted obscenities. Dorcas had gotten him to bed; they made it three times, they were in love. She promised we'd sleep together next time we met. Darling Dorcas. She put her repentant, Dorcas-converted phone dick on and he said all seven of the prohibited FCC words. And hung up. I felt a little of my faith in Goodness flowing back.

You think this book thing of father's is really on the up and up?

I stared at her, warm with pity, and hating myself because I hate pity.

Well, yes, Lindy. I do.

You believe this about his—his twenty reincarnations?

I believe in all our reincarnations. It's just that Sweeley Leech remembers his.

Going back to—to—

You can't say his name, can you, Lindy?

Crist-ee, she said, spitting it out, rhymes with feisty. He calls Him Crist-ee. And that is *blasphemy,* Fifi.

No, it's not. It's an adorning endearment. Like you call Jim Jimmy—

Christ is my Lord and Saviour, Lindy said. Not this Criste.

I was silent, respecting the blind, as she tapped her white cane through the conversation.

And you think father *knew* Jesus Christ?

I am sure of it, I said.

And lived in a rooming house with him and the woman Maggie and—

Yes, all of it. You can't shame me into denying it, Lindy.

O, but the patent falseness of it. Living in a rooming house. Imagine Christ living in a rooming house. It's so anachronistic.

And the Weirton part, I said. Be sure to mention the Weirton part. You always do when you're doing a number on Sweeley Leech.

Well, I mean, after all, Feef. Everybody knows there weren't rooming houses twenty centuries ago, and there certainly wasn't any Weirton. That ugly, reeking steel-mill town, Weirton!

Don't you understand, Lindy?

What?

That Weirtons create Criste. Every time.

She whirled on me then.

Well, for Christ's sake, why can't he call him Christ, then? Jesus Christ. Not Criste—like some locker-room good old guy.

O, Criste would never be that.

I imagine he would. Father's Christ certainly sounds that way. Will you tell me the reason for the fake Middle Ages spelling—C-r-i-s-t-e?

Because he needs a new name. A cleaned-up name.

Cleaned up?

Yes. The name Christ won't do anymore. It must be Criste. This name Christ has been disgraced. The name is a cliché—not a metaphor, as it first was. Criste is a metaphor. Christ is a word like fuck and cunt and cock—good words, holy words, once. Now soiled, scuffed clichés that we use awkwardly, sorrowfully. Fuck and cunt were once prayers in men's and women's mouths, Lindy. Don't you know that? As was Christ. And now all of them—all the once holy words: Christ and Fuck and Cunt and Jesus—they won't do anymore. They're solid-gold amulets that have been made into foot-scrapers for the world's doggie doobies—all the way from the cowshitted brogans of the county TV evangelists to the Vietnam-stained Gucci loafers of the Popes and Billy Grahams and the blighted bat-infested belfries of the pealing Norman Vincents.

You ought to get up a club act. You really should.

It's ending though, Lindy—your Christian Era is ending as it should—as it always has.

Christ only came that once, she said. And one more time.

She did a Joe Williams voice when she did the "One More Time."

He's always been coming, Lindy. Always. And he always will.

But in Weirton, she said then. Really, Fifi. Weirton. How *déclassé*. Not even a real Anglo-Saxon slum. Really now, Fifi. Our Saviour would have more panache!

I sulked across the tile floor and huffed out the lamp beneath my cupped right hand.

Why did you do that, Feef?

I somehow trust the moonlight more tonight, I said. We'll be flying through it soon—father and I.

She came and laid her fingers on my arm. The moon cast a light and shadow from her face that made me want to crush her in my arms with compassion and sorrow: something ineffably sad lay ahead for her, I knew.

I'm sorry, Feef, she said. It's not easy to be a Christian. I try—but it's not easy. I—I forgive you and father for doing this thing.

She paused.

You know we'll be dreadfully poor after it's over.

Yes. Day-old caviar at least, I said.

I whirled on her again in the swarm of moonmotes from the gingham curtains standing briskly on the wind.

Don't you know that the man has tried through nineteen centuries to remember that book? I said in a broken voice. Can't you see what it means to him? Every lifetime half remembering—like an old lost kiss or a half-remembered dream that hangs on all day and won't show itself to us! Nineteen centuries! Thirty-nine lifetimes almost getting it. And now—in this year of our Lord nineteen ninety-two—he has but one thing left standing between him and that memory's full realization.

This one thing—this mad thing you propose doing together? This spit in the face of our nation's God?

In the Labyrinth called Bebo, I said, Uncle Will showed himself to Sweeley last Friday night and smiled and joked awhile, and then he told him frankly that Criste had told him there was one thing lacking.

I feel dirty just listening to this, you know, Feef. Lord, you are a trying person.

O, I am trying, Lindy. Trying desperately. Because I know the kind of Faith you profess and the kind of life you lead and that these two disparities are tearing you apart. They are stressing you, breaking you into awful two-celled things, not Life. O, give up this hypocrisy, Lindy, and admit—

Admit nothing, said Sweeley Leech, striding into the kitchen with a large Kroger shopping bag full of a fortune in bonds and shares. You are a good girl, Lindy.

Are you ready, sir? I asked again, feeling all his holy fool.

Almost, he said. With hard work and diligence this night—I have, goddammit, succeeded.

He held himself up, proud in the weltering moonshine.

We are penniless! he said, with a smile of profound relief. Now, let's check everything out again in the Mark Cross valises and take off. Beurre, you could have checked our weather while I was up there.

(I might point out here that "Beurre"—French for butter—was Sweeley Leech's love name for me. He said I looked like a pat of salty butter on a tea towel when he first saw me, fresh from Rinsey's sweet breast.) Did you?

But Lindy saved the night for me, but with a cruel jibe at Sweeley.

Why don't you let a little Jesus into your life, father?

A little Jesus is a dangerous thing. Who said that? And besides, daughter, Criste is *in* you—not *outside*—waiting to be freed. Like the trumpets beginning the "Gloria" of Beethoven's Mass in D. O, they do free him! Those horns!

He slapped his knee and I caught a glimpse of what he was wearing for the trip: ragged gray flannel slacks from Bloomie's, a five-hundred-dollar blue Manx tweed sportcoat from Saks Fifth Avenue, a scarf from Sears, and a T-shirt reading: ALMOST HEAVEN—WEST VIRGINIA.

No, Lindy, love, Criste is within you. The Lite of him is within you, too.

He snatched a Ming bowl from the cupboard, its fierce glazing glimmerous in the moonlight like blazing apricot. He filled it with Product 19 and a half pitcher of cream from his Druid cow.

A foreign sportscar—there is hardly any other kind of car in 1992—roared past along the dusty road to Glory with its hi-fi blasting. It was one of the popular macho songs of the time.

> Ain't no semen on mah mustache,
> Ain't no 'gasm in muh beard.
> Ah'm a macho baby,
> Nothin' need be fear'd.

I was out in the yard again, my eyes on the dark, vertiginous opening to the Labyrinth. Lights more than fireflies seemed aghast and moving in it. I felt frightened. I climbed into the spacious cabin of the copter and checked out our instruments. The CB was quacking—some horny housewife named Ronny McDonald was working up a date. Outside, the autumn galaxies seemed more crackly and like a Christmas tree than ever. Something was in the air; all my psychic energy seemed drained by the North Star. Or was it Saturn? Even before I had switched on the broadcast band I knew something was wrong.

Back in the kitchen, Sweeley Leech's voice had risen in one of his politically oriented tirades against the very-right-wing Lindy, poor misguided child.

Don't you see? There are no more nationalities. Peace has finally come to the world. Men finally discovered that the dollar, the yen, the Swiss franc, and the ruble were more important than ideologies. They have banded together into a government over governments themselves. TRUCAD, my sweet baby, TRUCAD. That's what it's called. Any war now is nothing more than an interoffice squabble. Hasty, hot memoranda flash back and forth. But with the merger of world finance with the United Nations—war was over.

He paused.

And so was the Individual.

I came into the kitchen, my heels kicking up comets of glowworms from the wet and sleeping grass.

Are you ready, sir?

Why, Beurre? he asked, suddenly grave and concerned for me. You look like you want to leave at once.

I do, I said. And I don't. I want to see it happen—but I don't want to be in it. I mean—

I leaned against him.

Sweeley, do you really want to leave for New York City tonight?

Yes, why?

Because you better hurry, I said in a half-hysterical giggle. It may not be there when we land.

He kept staring, waiting.

I just picked it up on the broadcast band, I said. It may be a hoax and it may be on the level.

Well, for God's sake, spare us your suspense dramatics, Feef, wailed Lindy from the corner by the refrigerator. She was watching television on her wrist. Dick Van Dyke was giving his usual sense of sneaking up on you with a bomb.

Take your time, Beurre, Sweeley said, laying his arm around my shoulder. What did you hear about New York City?

That a half-dozen kooks—terrorists—have built two homemade neutron bombs, I said. They're going to explode the first—to show they mean business—somewhere within a five-hundred-mile radius of the Verrazano Narrows in New York Harbor. There is a second neutron bomb—built, they claim, for less than a thousand dollars—in a midtown office building.

Manhattan?

Yes, I think.

How much do they ask?

Twenty million dollars.

Hell, snapped Sweeley Leech. We've got three times that amount in those bags out there. Bearer bonds and some cash—at least twenty-five million.

You're going to *bail out* New York City? asked Lindy, aghast with outrage. Those Jews?

Yes, those Jews, snarled Sweeley Leech. Because most of them are better followers of Criste than you or I. Go on, Beurre.

There's nothing else. I said—it may be a hoax.

It isn't a hoax, Sweeley Leech said. It isn't Armageddon, either. And I wouldn't miss it for the world.

Why, father? sneered Lindy.

Because in New York City this autumn night, two things are going to happen: one of them very ugly—that's TRUCAD—and another thing—a bigger thing, a beautiful thing—a truer thing— that's the People. Dem debbils! They're going to do something as beautiful as the moon.

Lindy didn't even kiss us good-bye. Poor little soul—so wormed into the cocoon of something that would never wake to be butter-flies. Not unless some strong and beautiful shining of the Criste Lite came to change her.

I didn't really know what lay ahead. Adventure, surely, and ad-venture is always sacred. I was a little uneasy, but Sweeley Leech looked placid and at peace behind the controls as we soared up into the very cool womb of midnight and looked down, like God, to see the sleeping lands. Wheeling. Pittsburgh. Brownsville. The Pleiades were steady as ITT—hell, steadier. The Susquehanna River was out hustling her glisteny, glamorous ass to the moon. Everything—all the vibes from both star and leaf and mankind—they seemed steady. Cool. So was Sweeley Leech. I knew we would live to see the wonder and dismay and secret joy on the faces of the Citibank guards next day at ten. And we might see the souls of some of them saved. Really saved.

We flew on in silence for a long while. I mean we didn't speak. All the stations were talking about the Big Apple Bomb Rip-off.

My freckle began to burn between my legs. I smiled—the sign was unfailing. O, transplants like that are so very psychic. Dorcas Anemone was making out with her phone company dick.

I know one thing, father, I said, nestling into his shoulder.

What, Beurre?

I know that with this bomb rip-off—and our bank job—all within twenty-four hours—little old New York will never be the same.

I fingered my freckle through the folds in my Pucci slacks.

Maybe the whole world will change, said Sweeley Leech. Maybe they'll fall in love again. Maybe they'll really get it on with God.

# T✦H✦R✦E✦E

I don't know what made me think of it—skimming through cumulus and moonlight five thousand miles above the Catskills—but I did find myself pondering the West Virginia State Home for Agelasts. Sweeley founded it—bribed important politicians to get it through, for there was (and is now), I think you will admit, a crying need for a home for Agelasts: an asylum where they are protected from the scathing wit of life outside, where they will not be made fun of, where, in many cases, they may be protected from themselves.

The Home, as they affectionately call it, is not a cheery place—that would defeat its purpose. Little solitary blobs of people—of all ages and sexes—sit alone, gloomily staring at television sets which feature reruns of *Gilligan's Island* and other sober, somber projects. Agelasts? They are, according to the Oxford English Dictionary, people who never laugh, but I think in the main I would call them unfortunates without any option but to look on the universe realistically.

Sweeley Leech's dear face, all gold and ocher shadows from the foxfire of the instrument panel, told me he was not yet ready for conversation. Sweeley is such an intense talker when he does it: he races over your own words sometimes like Cheat River white water over a small canoe; yes, he has this habit of talking while you talk, so that when he stops and suddenly falls silent, listening, the effect is disturbingly like eavesdropping. Not that he doesn't hear everything you say and absorb it. Now he sat, eyes fixed on his burntumber reflection in the aquarium of the Plexiglas window; he was sensing things out in dimensions of his own. Bored, I picked up a copy of *The New York Review of Books* and read the provocative title of the lead article: "Don Ho and the Influence of the Hawaiian Guitar on Vladimir Horowitz." I yawned and dropped it back into the litter of maps and magazines and skycharts on the floor.

The night out there was sheer dream: all azures and moonstained aquamarines and flecks of emerald. Light among the clouds spilled and spurted like white semen across a vast white belly. The stars bore down with blowpipe flames—these pinpoint plenipotentiaries of all our ticking existences. I wanted to stretch my arms and thrust my pelvis and nipples windward through the windshield, to fly ahead of our skimming little old Lockheed-Datsun helicopter. A star caught in my eyelashes, swam loose in babbling light for a little aeon, and then burned free of infinity itself and dropped into Weehawken. We were almost there. From this height, the tiny windows of houses, the firefly swarm of the roads and streets, did not even suggest frightened people—for man of the late twentieth century is somehow beyond fear. But he is not quite yet beyond the will to live and the will for life in others. The light-glistering firechains in New Jersey below us looked like flaming gold leaves caught in branches along the reeking, shipshod shore.

My freckle began to burn and tingle in my lace panties again. I smiled—Dorcas Anemone was at this moment coming—with her telephone company cop. Out at sea, the lights of ships and other copters shimmered and flamed and failed and wandered—like stars that couldn't make up their minds.


How shall I describe Manhattan from the sky that fateful night? City and sky seemingly miles beneath us and all woven into wondrous one. Imagine a slightly smudged sheet of violet paper between you and the light of the blazing mind of God. Okay. Now imagine that a divine seventeenth-century Venetian silhouettist—and an absolute wizard—has scissored and pinked that paper into a crazy lace of both wise and mindless intricacy. It looked that way.

I knew we were going to get there. And I think I knew we'd live to pull off our bank job the next day—the one that would give Sweeley Leech the book he had been seeking for so long and one that might shock some sense into the world. The alternate option was incineration in a few hours within the cool canyons of the loveliest city on earth. Sweeley Leech looked happy and at peace behind the controls as we soared into the very cunt of wonder and looked down, like parents, on the sleeping nightmared child called Manhattan.

The radiophone buzzed. I picked it up. It was Lindy from Echo Point, naturally worried about us—but for the wrong reasons.

You know, Feef, she said, that New York is virtually under atomic attack. And that if you do manage to survive this night, in the morning the bank thing will be your nemesis.

That's very shrewd, Lindy—discussing a thing like that on the radio. How generous of you.

O, Feef. Like I prayed for you last weekend, You know: "The Lord is my shepherd—blah blah blah blah blah blah blah." Remember?'

It loses something in translation. I prefer the King James.

The broadcast-band radio was quaking faintly among the dazzle of the instruments. The announcer was spelling out the terms of the terrorists. Twenty million in cash in small bills; two eighteen-wheel trailer-trucks were waiting in an unspecified Manhattan garage, ready for the getaway. No attempt must be made to stop the rigs on their way through either the tunnels or the bridge or the bomb will go off. In midtown.

Feef?

Yes, Lindy.

TRUCAD is very very harsh on people who offend against the Creed.

Fuck TRUCAD.

Feef?

Yes, Lindy.

I do love you and father. I only pray you'll be converted before it's too late. Good-bye, Feef. Good night, father.

Good night, Lindy.

She was right, of course. The act we had planned next day was, in effect, more than just a parable, more than the mere making of a metaphor. It was a divine blow at TRUCAD.

Sweeley Leech had taken a small pink envelope out of the pocket of his tweed jacket. The envelope had come in that evening's mail. I watched as Sweeley Leech read it and began to laugh—his laughter was always like a firework and lit everything for yards around. He handed me the note—on expensive, scented stationery. It was from a woman named Puddintame who ran a whorehouse on the high-road to Glory called the Jew's Harp House. She had had father bounced several times.

This note, for all its official sternness, was actually a billet-doux from a sensitive and good woman. I read the words and knew not only why Sweeley had laughed so hard, but that his laughter was that of love and admiration.

"Dear Sweeley," it ran. "I don't give a D—n and I swear to G-d it's true—whether you fuck my girls or not."

*Damn* and *God* had dashes but *fuck* didn't. O, God, how lovely people are in certain queer, strange lights.

What did Lindy want? Sweeley asked.

I think she wanted to get us busted.

Why?

Well, discussing things about the bank on the radiophone. The way things are in the world.

TRUCAD would find nothing amiss in this helicopter, he said. Six pieces of luggage—five of them packed with bearer bonds and large-bill cash to the amount of twenty-five million dollars. It is my money. I have spent the past month gathering it from my holdings all over the world. I got most of it through the Swiss Bank, Crédit Suisse, and Union Bank. I had the perfectly legitimate assistance of Kuhn Loeb, Lehman Brothers, Glore Forgan and Company, Merrill, Blyth and Company, and First Boston Corporation. It is—as I say—all mine, to do with what I please. I broke it up among different companies so that the largeness of the amount I was accumulating would not attract the attention of TRUCAD. And apparently it hasn't.

He hesitated as we approached the heliport atop the Plaza Hotel. Park Avenue South looked distinctly irritated. The Pierre Hotel's neon was positively pouting.

I looked down now at the glistening black face of the Plaza's roof porter directing us in for a landing. I always get dizzy when I am this close to the earth. Miles up is so unbelievable. I saw a couple of officers—obviously, TRUCAD men—on the roof. Sweeley read my thoughts.

If they do go through our bags—what of it? There's nothing illegal here.

Except that TRUCAD does encourage credit—tends to discourage cash. And except that it would let it be known—the night before our crime—that that much money was around the place.

We'll take that chance, Fifi.

I started thinking about TRUCAD. It had come into being out of the old Trilateral Commission and the Bilderburg thing, but they were small compared to what TRUCAD became.

It was the great—and thankfully short—depression of 1988—directly following the so-called Closet War at the close of the eighties—it was this that gave us TRUCAD. It was the inevitable moment in Time when a world of businessmen suddenly came to their senses and realized what they were. They were moneymakers. Wars were waste. Wars were over relatively worthless ideals. Wars were over money, too, but they cost so much. And you couldn't always buy the enemy off. And so—in 1990—TRUCAD came into being. It dissolved boundaries, healed old hatreds, merged men in their common love of wealth, made nationalities odious, and united all the nations of the earth—the big ones, the ones that mattered, that is—into one great economic brotherhood—and the greatest and most relentless tyranny of the mind which the recorded earth has seen. TRUCAD replaced Fraternity with the Interlocking Directorate, it replaced Equality with Parity, Patriotism with Good Business, and the Ultimatum gave way to the Intergalactic Memo. I suppose it represents the most apocalyptic victory of the Liberal in Government—a Liberal being one who believes in every human right under God (in whom, however, he does not believe). TRUCAD changed Patriotism into Boosterism—legislatures, houses, and senates into sales forces, statesmen into district supervisors, and politicians into country drummers. The territory is Man.

Take a card, Sweeley Leech said to me after we had jumped down to the tile of the port. He held out a deck—obviously cheap magic-store junk—and eyed me hopefully.

I took a card, the ten of clubs.

Put it back, Feef.

I did. He shuffled. He hurled the deck onto the floor at the slightly bored black porter's feet—all save one card. He held it up triumphantly. It was the seven of spades.

Seven of spades—right, Feef?

Wrong, father. Really, I won't indulge you in this obsession of yours.

My brother, Mooncob, is an accomplished magician, he whined.

He is also a charlatan of the worst kind, I said. He isn't even that good a sleight-of-hand artist. And what if he is? Father, you can work miracles. Miracles! And you want to do card tricks.

Miracles don't count, he said moodily, examining a gaudy wooden egg he produced from the pocket of his jacket. I want to *fool* you, Feef.


We were on the elevator, riding down to our suite two floors below. A cute man was a few feet away. I fell in love instantly with the lovely nape of his neck. O, I do so want to live forever, I dreamed. Is Sweeley Leech correct when he swears we all do—every living thing lives on and on into the broken-down sundowns of forever? I wished we were far away from Manhattan—probably doomed Manhattan. I yearned to be in the country below the Gallimaufry in the spring. I kept my eyes on the lightly curling nape of hair at the divine boy's neck. I dreamed I was in a cove below the Labyrinth, on the tumbling meadow with my lips all buttery around a golden country cock. I remembered how those hills thrust up like lovers to love the sky and then, when the act was done, fell down in tousled slopes and meadows, all passion spent, and stretched, gasping, at last among the goldenrod and wild garlic. I spoke to the young man with the heavenly hair at his nape. He turned, eating with a plastic spoon from a small container of banana yogurt. My voice is slightly husky, slightly contralto, and, I am told, sexually arousing. As it should be, for it is a voice made liquid by love, without a polyp of guilt in it, or a bad tonsil of shame: a timbre drenched and dripping with all of Love's lovely and lovable humors. He smiled at me. There was a fleck of yogurt in his mustache. I wanted to lick it off—still cold and sweet from his cup. He is Jewish, I thought. I remembered Dorcas's curious, low-key anti-Semitism—echo of her mad father, I suppose.

C. C. Anemone, her neo-Nazi father, had become the notorious antiporn, antisex, antilife firebrand who, among other achievements, had proven to the Harrison County Court that King James I was a practicing homosexual and gotten the Authorized Version banned in all Clarksburg schools and churches.

The Jews, she warned me one day, in addition to cutting off all those lovely little foreskins—Jews are even *born* different, Fifi.

Really? In what way? I always thought Jews were born like anyone.

Her voice fell to a thrilled horror. O, no, she said. It's something called B'nai Birth, Feef.

The elevator stopped while a small white Shitzu leading a small white fat woman got on. Sweeley Leech held out a rose to me. In his other hand was an aluminum cup. He instructed me to take the rose, tear it up, and put it in the cup. I sighed, loving him madly, and complied. I looked at his marvelously young and handsome face. He looks thirty-five. He is—well, considerably more than that. I stared at his mind—there in his eyes—and marvelled at all it has survived. Not just the slammings around of twenty centuries—but the little rough assaults of his present life. Months in hospitals, months drunk or drugged, his mind slashed and sundered and put back together again after the lightning bolts of fifty shock treatments, years on pills or God knows what. Years rich, years bitterly poor. The Establishment has gratefully assisted him all along the paths of self-destruction: the Establishment early recognized my father as its mortal enemy. He looks like a Soviet sinner staggering back from brainwashing years in Samarkand. He is a survivor. I reached over to feel the cock of the handsome, darling guy with the yogurt in his mustache. Last look he had a hard-on. Instead, my fingers closed on the leash of the fat woman's Shitzu, who sweetly bit my ankle and then licked it furiously, as if in repentance. The divine boy was gone. We got off at our floor at last. My fingers folded cockless and lonely and a little damp with fear, because, instead of Muzak, the loudspeakers in the hotel were all broadcasting the flat, droning voice on the Emergency Broadcasting System. It was somebody named Smith. I had always thought what a perfect voice Walter Mondale had for the Emergency Broadcasting System. A lady came down the carpeted, Gothic hallway outside our gilded door. She was smoking a Havana cigar. Her face was as frozen and immobile as the 1986 Mount Rushmore Steinem.

She passed and went into another doorway, slammed the door, and began singing an air from *Ruddigore* in a clear, glucose soprano. Sweeley draped a green silk kerchief over the cup into which I had deposited the ruins of the rose. He snapped his fingers and snatched away the scarf. The rose was not, as he had hoped, restored. He sighed and turned away.

I never get to *fool* anyone, Sweeley Leech said. Not the way Mooncob does.

But you can make miracles, I said. You can give eyesight to the blind.

No, I can't, he said. They find it themselves. I only help them get the Criste Lite out from under their little bushels. I only let out that imprisoned splendor.

Well, anyway—you *do* do miracles. You moved a *mountain.*

So will you someday, Fifi, he said. We all will. Dey's all debbils!

He laid his tape recorder on the bed, and the small leather case containing the new computer cards. For the bank job. For the great Sweeley and Fifi Leech unprecedented and Christian unrobbery.

Didn't leave any fantasies lying around back at Echo Point, did you?

No. I looked around, father.

You often do leave dreams around to trip over—or worse. You imagine something vividly—too vividly—girl. And you forget about it and leave it there in the twinkling sunlight of the veranda. And I come along and stumble over it—sometimes a tyger! tyger! burning bright—and have to conjure it away.

I don't meant to be careless, sir.

I love you despite that, Fifi, said Sweeley Leech, and gave me a nice, nostalgic feel through the silky cloth of my slacks.

Let's get a drink, I said. So much is happening in New York tonight. I want to be out with the debbils.

On the elevator a lady's pregnant belly was singing softly. I recognized it at once—that hideous new product of the media called

41

Fetaphone: a miniature hi-fi with a tiny vaginal speaker to pipe music to an unborn baby. I glanced knowingly at her.

Great thing, Science, huh? I said.

Yes. And with the anal extension, I give him stereo.

We got off in the opulent and faded candy-box hotel lobby. Through the doors I could see children with neon yo-yos on the edge of the Pulitzer Fountain on Fifth Avenue. I loved them, thinking: In the midst of Death we are in Life. But the streets were full of anything but Death—yet.

A mob of conventioneers swung uncertainly down the pavement along Fifth from Fifty-ninth Street. The doorman was eyeing them unpleasantly.

Real Americana, I said. Shriners.

Not even the old Americana, he snorted. They look more like the Taft.

Sweeley was talking to a group of cabdrivers down on the curb. I caught his eye and waved.

It's so warm, love, I shouted. I'm going back up and change. Will you wait?

He nodded and bent again, gossiping with a group of his beloved debbils. I swooped up to the room in the Patou-reeking elevator and ran to the suite and shed every stitch except my high heels and gold ankle chain and slipped into my leopardskin coat, drew it tight around my waist with a sash of boa, and swooped back down to the Plaza lobby again. The coat was not at all uncomfortable. Little delicious drafts kept blowing up between my legs like the most heavenly naughty thoughts. I got wet and puckered just from kissing wind.

Sweeley came swinging back to me up the stones of the paveway.

What's the latest on the bombs?

He smiled and grimaced.

Poor little city, poor little debbils. It isn't just two bombs. It's three. The first is scheduled to be detonated at eight p.m. The second—closer—at ten. And at eleven—if the money isn't there—the third will go off somewhere in midtown Manhattan.

Is it a bluff?

No, Beurre, he said. I don't think so. It's being run by experts—teenagers who practiced shoplifting for a year and then paid visits to nuclear power plants. They got the knowledge from a dozen or so books from the Donnell Branch of the library. And they owned a couple of old fishing boats and now they're in business.

Do you think the city government will come up with the twenty million?

There is no real city government anymore, Beurre. TRUCAD will be the force to decide whether these lives here are worth that much.

Do you think they will?

He seemed not to hear me. He was staring at a small and bombulating band of fundamentalists—trumpet, drum, and flute.

Curious, Beurre.

What is, Sweeley?

That tune, he said. That dance of the dead from Gilbert and Sullivan's *Ruddigore*. Nobody ever plays it. And you heard that woman singing it upstairs not an hour ago.

Yes, I know it.

I began to hum along.

Causal Liaison, said Sweeley Leech.

A poor distraught woman with a bandage on her arm was watching and listening to the little band. She glimpsed Sweeley then, through tears of obvious frustration, and ran to him.

Sir, you look like you'd *know*. Why can't I love God?

What *do* you love, you darling? asked Sweeley Leech, laying his left hand on her bandaged forearm.

Why, it's really shameful, she said. I love my cat, I suppose, best of all on earth.

Then go home to your cat, you darling, said Sweeley Leach. Because that is God.

He didn't think I noticed, when she hurried away smiling and daubing away her tears, that she was, at the same time, balling up the unwound bandage from her arm—healed now—where my father's Cristeed fingers had just lain. He tried to hide these things, not wanting me to know. Yet, I know. O, Sweeley Leech, I know that you call the ones you love "debbils" and seem to scorn the wrath of every god, but love, O, love, I·know you like the Golden Book you are trying to write.

He seemed to be reading my thoughts. What do I mean, "seemed to be"? He always was!

Thirty-nine lifetimes, he said. Each goddam one of them me trying to remember the first—the dream one—the one that would never quite come back to me. Like the perfume of a girl we once held who has gone away. We smell that smell on a city street or in a circus alley or in a bar and we turn and our eyes try to pierce the dark and see that girl. But it is only the scent. Or music we heard—the most beloved tune in the world and we can't quite remember it.

Did you talk to Criste in the Labyrinth, father?

I never talk to Criste, he said. I haven't talked to him since the day they lynched him. In Weirton. Twenty centuries ago. But he made some marks—words—in the dust with his finger. I can see him now. The most adorable man. Laughing generally. Cutting the fool. O, the medievals knew. I can see his slopping huge eyes and his snub nose and moonish face and one tooth gone, like so many of the poor. He wrote in the dust—

A story?

Not exactly. Not a story. And yet every story. He made up thirty or forty big symbols in the sand. Runes. And I think he knew I was watching. Wanted me to watch. Wanted me to remember. If it took forty lifetimes. And sometime to put those symbols into a book. A cosmic, comic combination they were! O, Beurre, they really were.

Who did appear to you in the Labyrinth, then?

Uncle Will, of course, said Sweeley Leech. Will Blake of Felpham and the New Jerusalem. He talks with Criste all the time. And he told me—

In what part of the Labyrinth, sir?

The Corridor of Light, he said. When you pass through the Lane of Spiders, past the Inca Emperor's Death Chamber.

I remember, I said. I faintly remember.

At any rate, he said, Criste told Uncle Will—between jokes and laughs and general, joyful kidding around like Criste and such men and women always do—he said I almost had the memory. Almost had the book of the Criste Lite. But one thing was lacking—

Strange, sir, I said. I know what you're going to say. "One thing is lacking." Those were the Criste's words to the bad little rich boy in Saint Mark. "One thing is lacking."

One thing is lacking, said Sweeley Leech. Sell what thou hast and give to the poor. Hence the unrobbery. Once I achieve—forgive me, love—once we imprint that metaphor upon the ledger page of the world, the book will come to me all in a rush.

I know it will.

We were walking down Fifth Avenue among groups of some somber, some apathetic people. Leaning against a building was a young black drunk with a fifth of Nighttrain Express in a paper bag. As Sweeley passed he stopped, bowed, took the bottle from the young man's hand, took a swig, and before the man could really know what was happening, Sweeley had slipped a ten-thousand-dollar bill into his bag and given it back with the wine.

I know it will, too, he said. It's so close, so near, so beautifully near to me. Only once before—in Polynesia, in the sixteenth century—did I ever come so close. It was before Captain Cook or any of those Christian rapists, and the people were so pure, so Cristelike in their love of both flesh and spirit—a love held between a lifted cock and the stars, so to speak. But now—

He looked at me and snuffled away a tear.

Lindy doesn't understand, he said. She doesn't know that her Church is run by the Anti-Criste himself. And that Criste's dear, free spirit is dungeoned in chains in the basements of those churches!

I squeezed his hand.

Don't think about Lindy, dad. She'll come round someday.

Yes, he said. Dey's all debbils!

I glanced at my digital.

It's ten past eight, I said. The first bomb—out at sea, you said?

I didn't say. He smiled. You told me. Seven hundred miles off Ambrose Light. Of course, they didn't say in what direction. And the second—

Five hundred miles off the Verrazano Narrows.

I waited a beat.

So maybe it's all a hoax.

Maybe. We'll see. Remember, these are amateurs—and amateurs are rarely careless.

The mood in the street seemed lighter now that the first deadline was past. It was a warm night. A pride of kids like tawny summer lions was draped across the hood of a Land-Rover at Fifty-seventh and Fifth. We cut across to Madison. A man was doing sleight of hand in the moonlight. Sweeley's eyes glistened and his tongue moistened his lips.

God, I wish I could do that.

Shall we wait, darling? I sang out. And see if he can move a mountain at this great Presbyterian picnic?

You're good to me, Beurre, he said.

And then we ducked into the awninged, candlelit deeps of a charming coffeehouse on Fifty-fifth off Mad called the Thé— tucked in between a store full of Finnish Modern furniture, called, ambitiously, the Chaise Manhattan, and a Colonial-style branch of Citibank which looked, architecturally, like a mixture of a funeral home and a woman's exchange (which, now that I think of it, a funeral home is).

We ordered an enormous communal bowl of really first-rate bouillabaisse—I swear it was chock full of Mediterranean seabeasts old as Sappho, and as sweet to the tongue. We had a nice red wine. Sweeley used to drink horribly. Now he has a little wine to mock the Angels, as he says.

The candlelight was like yellow smoke. It flamed in the fresh, clean hair of lovers at tables. The air smelled softly of sex. I saw an add in the *Times* drama section of a concert that night at Alice Tully Hall. Alicia de Larrocha and Maazel doing De Falla's "Nights in the Gardens of Spain." I swore I'd have to go. I needed sex with music that night.

My father looked happy. Grave and happy at the same time.

TRUCAD may already know about my unrobbery tomorrow, he said.

You mean from Lindy talking about it?

No, he said. There is no secrecy anymore. They're tapping the soul now. The spirit world is their next colonial venture. Criste alone can stop them.

He paused and gobbled a divine fragment of clam, licking the tart marine broth from his upper lip and grunting.

They have a way of shooting—quite painlessly—a small, really microscopic, quasar ensemble under the skin. The blemish is scarcely visible—yet it records a fairly accurate report of the subject's thoughts. It's in its infancy now but they're using it.

The candles all seemed to die as the lights went on in the room.

46

But they hadn't gone on in the room, they had gone on in the street outside. The city was washed with a queer and melancholy quicksilver, as though everything—trees, grass, cats, and children—had been splashed with a cheap molten silverplate, the kind you'd see on a gangster's loving cup. The light had come from seven hundred miles off Ambrose Light—fleeing ahead of the sound, which had not yet reached us. There was a halt in the living in the air: an audible rustle of eyelids and perhaps of folding labia and wilting penises—and then the talk and laughter seemed to quicken and increase. There was no sound of the bomb yet. But my mind was racing with what my father had just said.

What kind of blemish, sir? What did you say it looked like?

On colored skin it works best because it is invisible. On a white skin it would appear as a small blemish. A freckle.

A whattle?

I didn't hear you, Beurre.

I mean, a What?

A freckle, he said.

My thighs were like heavy cold marble. My cunt felt like a broadcast satellite.

A freckle, sir?

A freckle. Why, Beurre? Have you acquired one recently?

Yes.

He searched my face, smiling, a little concerned.

Your face is—as always—matchless, Beurre. I see no freckle.

Yes, but I have a freckle. Two or three years old now. I wish you'd told me this before. It casts someone I love very deeply in a most terrible light. I can't believe that she'd—

Wait, he said. I don't think you fully understand. This ensemble of quasars that comprise the blemish or freckle—they aren't, in any way, a transmitter.

Then how does it work?

It stores up memories—memories of your thoughts, feelings, intentions, perhaps your plots.

And how does the—enemy—how does TRUCAD get it?

They leave the ensemble in the skin of the subject until they feel it's stored up enough information for the removal—

The removal?

Yes, he said. It's done with hardly any pressure of the finger of

47

the investigator. Just a certain skilled practiced twist of the finger—and the little instrument is free, a freckle on the tip of his finger.

I squeezed my thighs together, yearning for the friendly little flash of Dorcas Anemone's many comes. I couldn't feel it anymore. Now I had three networks an inch from my clit.

I think I had such a freckle, I said. The kind you're talking about, Swee, but I think it's gone now. And the little thing has been near the fingers of at least seven men and three women in the last twenty-four hours. And one of them—

I fished into my sling purse for my compact mirror. I opened my coat in the candlelight and moved it to the edge of the checkered tablecloth. I spread my legs and held the little compact mirror down. The freckle was gone.

Then they have it, I sighed.

The light in the street had wasted, like some dying firework. But now the bomb's sound came. The sound rolled in with all the low decibels working overtime. It wasn't a boom. It wasn't a roar. It wasn't even a rumble. It was more like the great bass organ note—sustained, holy, exquisitely unbearable—at the opening of the mighty Bach Toccata and Fugue.

I hardly heard it, so tumbling down in the nursery of my fancy came the gay-colored block castle built by myself and a fair child named Dorcas Anemone—now, obviously, a TRUCAD spy.

The dishes and silver were still chattering like the teeth of someone very old and ill when we paid the check and hurried out into the scorched night. And the next bomb closer and about an hour and a quarter off.

Dey's all debbils, Beurre, roared Sweeley Leech and did a cartwheel ahead of me up toward Sam Goody's. Dey's debbils, every one.

I loved him, loved his antics, loved his voice, but I wasn't listening. A wind was rising from the harbor, from the sea beyond: the Atlantic hymen ruptured at last.

Maybe, I said aloud to myself, my heels clicking slowly in the night air, maybe she never knew. Maybe they shot the freckle into *her* cheek—my love, my darling's cheek—and she never knew, and willed me the freckle unknowing what a dark thing she was giving.

But I knew better.

48

Why would TRUCAD plant a freckle on Dorcas Anemone? Just to get it to me? Balls. I felt old and cynical and dreadfully wise.

Dey's all debbils, Beurre—sacred, holy, and eternal debbils!

And I knew suddenly that even if I found out that Dorcas was one of them, I would always love her. And I would forgive her. I would even forgive TRUCAD. Sweeley Leech says forgiveness is the only thing that makes Criste's Lite different from Plato's. O, I should adore to know Plato, incidentally.

I simply have a thing about seducing gay men!

# F✦O✦U✦R

The second neutron bomb exploded four hundred miles east-south-east of the Verrazano Narrows. It didn't frighten people as much this time because by now they were rather used to it and because the second one exploded a half hour early—at nine-thirty. No fall-out ensued, the winds being variable but strongly south-southwest-erly. Everyone was lighthearted now but underneath was a feverish sobriety.

I walked a few feet behind Sweeley Leech now on our way up Eighth Avenue. I had a good six ounces of primo hash in my suede sling bag. I had rolled a thin joint. I took three or four tokes, snuffed the roach out against a newly planted tree, whose boughs brushed my forehead gratefully with wet leaves, and put the extin-guished but still smoking butt back into the stash, which was a Dow plastic bag. Sweeley stood under the marquee of a porn shop, caressing the lovely and varicolored beavers with his eyes.

A black passed me. His face was mulatto and clean-shaven. On his chin were tattooed six hairs.

Down the street came a man with ten inches of bandage atop his head—and on top of the turban of Johnson and Johnson rested a sports hat.

Two queens outside a delicatessen waited fuming in line. One stamped her high-heeled foot and turned to the other, the little beads on the tips of his/her eyelashes glittering like tiny antennae.

Well, I simply told *her,* darling—I'm not letting *anyone* spoil *my* happiness!

I caught up with Sweeley under the glittering jockstrap marquee of a men's gay theater, the Adonis.

I stared at the tumescent and slavering posters.

Poor Lindy, I observed, I always get the psychic signal just before she calls me about some nonsense regarding sex. Wait, now. The radiophone will buzz any minute.

Sweeley stood enraptured, staring up into the littered air at something. Was it a star? O, he knew how to conjure a star into his fingers. I looked, following his gaze. Up into the soured neon stain of light above the squalid, pissy avenue with its reek of stale semen drifting in holy sadness from theaters and rent-by-the-hour gay-cribs. I stared hard into the wounded galaxies. And I saw it—more incredible than a star: a firefly that had wandered from meadows into the choked and strangulating air of Eighth Avenue, screwing its tiny wings into the acidulous vapor of the night, its cold little fail-safe lamp stuttering a golden burn and indemnifying faith in God, in all that foul, airless bandage of pollution and stink. The firefly circled my father once, then lighted on his nose and gathered itself, burning more fiercely than before—a veritable death throe of cold fire. Sweeley's eyes caught its light and kindled. He smiled gravely, as in a sacrament, lifted his forefinger, poised it for the tiny insect to mount, and then held it up. The firefly became a star soaring to rest, a few inches into eternity, above the MONY building.

My radiophone buzzed.

Echo Point here, snapped Lindy's little voice. Feef, I know what you and father are doing. You're probably standing in front of one of those porn theaters.

Yes.

Who is it, Beurre? called Sweeley.

It's Lindy, father. Yes, Lindy.

Has the bomb gone off yet? O, I know it couldn't have. You wouldn't be talking, Feef.

Pause again.

Unless you're ghosts.

*Two* bombs have gone off, Lindy. If twenty million dollars isn't delivered to the terrorists by eleven, the third is scheduled to go off in—

I glanced at my digital.

—forty-two minutes. Of course, they've all been off schedule a bit—so it might go off at any minute.

Pause.

Feef?

Yes.

Do you think maybe TRUCAD will refuse to pay the ransom?

I don't know, Lindy. There's been a depression. The dollar is scarce.

Come home, why don't you? Forget this madness tomorrow.

I must ask you—please don't discuss this on open air, Lindy.

Okay, you'll do what you have to. Father's insane. Everyone knows that. Certifiably. All I can do is *pray* for you both.

Don't pray for us, dear. We know your God. When you've learned to pray to Criste, then you may pray for us.

I love you, Feef.

I love you, too, Lindy.

Good-bye.

She clicked silent. We headed north and boarded a Broadway bus, which was flatulating diesel smokily like Uncle Will Blake's farting and belching God—the one he called Nobodaddy—the God of Lindy, the God with no scintilla of good Criste's mercy. Sweeley ran over and grabbed my arm, my suede bag swung—lazily tendriling fumes, though I wasn't aware—in the urine-tinted neon stare of the street. We got a seat in the back. A large Texan and his lady were eyeing four Hasidic rabbis across the aisle. The Westerner wore a T-shirt lettered TEXAS SCHOOL BOOK DEPOSITORY FAN CLUB. The rabbis were animatedly discussing—in English—the possible forces back of the Begin assassination in 1984, which precipitated the Closet War. They saw the Texan and, inured to such scathing surveillance, went on talking about the most ancient of conundrums—the John Kennedy assassination in Dallas.

From the Bay of Pigs on, asked one, what could be kosher?

I smiled and sniffed the air. Someone in the bus was turning on—a comparatively common event on municipal subways and buses in the nineteen-nineties, but this time with something that smelled suspiciously like hash. Sweeley seemed oblivious. The smell was getting stronger—harsh and acrid, without the stealing, seductive sweetness of grass—almost as if someone were smoking it in a leather bong. Which is what it was. A leather bong: my suede sling bag! I saw the white fumes curling up, curling ravishingly around my shoulder and arm, and dissipating sweetly, sharply into the air. I began to laugh. I snatched open my purse and plucked out, with scorching fingernail polish, the smoldering plastic stash, and dumped it, causing billowing clouds of rich fumes to rise from the plastic floor. O, darn. Five ounces of simply heavenly Algerian primo hash and everyone on the M104 bus getting turned on. Sweeley began to sing.

> When the footpads quail at the nightbird's wail,
> and black dogs wail at the moon!

Four Sha Na Na characters—a fifties vogue back in full force— sprang out of their seats, struck formation, and began to harmonize.

> Then is the spectres' holiday—
> then is the ghosts' high noon.

We struggled a pathway through the knots of swaying, dancing, singing passengers. We almost fell as the bus lumbered joyfully sidelong and collided with a city garbage truck. The garbage-truck driver stormed boisterously aboard the bus, took one breath, stared at the ballet, and groaned.

Jee-suss.

He began to hum and neck with a nun.

As we descended into the sweet ruins of the night—the gold and the green of Needle Park, below Zabar's—the bus driver, a plucky lady from Flatbush, was in her bra and panties now, backing the bus off from the encounter and lumbering a stony way up the middle of the garlanded traffic island on Broadway in the seventies. The Texan was sitting on the lap of one of the happy rabbis, fingering

his *payess,* singing the old Eddie Fisher standard, "Oh, My Papa."
The green night bowed its sweet hair down around us. Sweeley was
not stoned. A swarthy Dominican ballet dancer pranced through
the night—obviously a recent passenger of our anointed carriage.

I am estoned. Estoned. Estoned, he chanted happily.

Dominican, I bet, said Sweeley Leech.

No. Estonian.

We laughed and ran like children past the Hotel Empire toward
Fiorello's and a new music club called Fast Forward, where the
ageless Mabel Mercer was singing a night of Johnny Mercer.
Brotherhood!

A flock of kids in an open car stuttered up Broadway in the
smoky wake of the M104, which, a moment later, could be heard to
nose its way splinteringly through the show windows of a men's
shop called Charivari. The motor farted amiably and blew up with a
flatulent thud.

Ain't no semen on ma mustache! blared a hi-fi wristradio. Ain't
no 'gasm in muh beard. Ah'm a macho baby—

Damn them, I said. Damn the machocists. Damn the homoso-
cials.

Dey's all debbils, Beurre, chanted Sweeley Leech, standing now
like a yearning child in front of a tiny magic and parlor-trick store
next to the Lincoln Center Deli. I breathed in a cloud of kosher
corned beef that was a meal in itself. The hash had made me ravenously hungry.

Ah'm a macho baby—nothin' need be fear'd!

Damn them!

Dey's all debbils, he admonished me again.

A loudspeaker began to stutter and wail with feedback in the
plaza in front of the New York State Theater. A small mob was
gathering anxiously. It was only thirty-two minutes till doomsday—real or apocryphal. I came out of the deli with a bag full of
roast beef sandwiches on Jewish rye with schmaltz and two contain-
ers of Dannon's red raspberry yogurt.

Sweeley, like a hungry schoolboy, saw, smelled the food.

Quick, gimme, I'm starved.

I gave him a large roast beef—oozing with rapturous sweetness.

I giggled, stoned—not waste-high, but stoned.

I cheated, I said. I ate first in the deli. I cheated, Sweeley.

What did you eat?

I had a small tin container bearing the label Heinz—from which I ate two hundred and sixty-three and a half baked beans.

I love you, said Sweeley Leech. Did we ever sleep together, Beurre?

Aw, that would be telling, I cooed, flicking open six inches of leopardskinned nakedness and lowering my lashes coyly. But I am an exceptionally easy lay in the case of fathers as handsome and young as you.

The loudspeaker was the TRUCAD West Side Deputy Mayor explaining that the third bomb had been found and dismantled and the conspirators all shot and—an inconsistent moment later—explaining that TRUCAD's Civil Defense Council had determined that the third bomb was all bluff and had never really existed. TRUCAD comforted everyone.

Amid all this a sound truck with loudspeakers playing the third movement of the Bartók Fifth Quartet alternating with a bearded voice explaining that the TRUCAD announcement was a rip-off— that the bomb *would* go off in sixteen minutes but that TRUCAD had figured up the loss of human life (no real-estate loss, of course, with a neutron unit) and weighed it in the scales and decided that sixteen million people simply weren't worth twenty million dollars. Modern political candor! The sound truck paused in front of the TRUCAD speaker's hastily assembled stand on the State Theater plaza. Some men ran out and overturned the sound truck. Sweeley Leech's eyes filled with tears and he turned away, eating his yogurt sadly with a little plastic spoon.

Ain't no semen on mah mustache. Ain't no 'gasm in—

Something else was weeping sweetly on the offended air. Music was leaking livelily out of Avery Fisher Hall—music seeping, wisping out like the good Jewish Baghdad, Samarkand, Oz smells leaking out of Zabar's, up Broadway. I saw a fairy moping under a discarded Schlitz Light carton along the curb. I picked him up, consoling, and kissed him and put him back, restored and singing, amid the mud and scum of things. Sweeley had been in the magic store. He came out with a purple wooden egg, flourished it, dropped it, and watched, horrified, as it rolled down a storm drain on the corner.

I want to fool people. Mooncob *fools* people.

I thought of Mooncob, my hideous uncle. He seldom appeared at the bungalow at Echo Point. He was on the road—in the South and Middle West most of the time—doing evangelical radio and television shows. How can I describe him? Picture him. He looks like Edward Andrews on the old Hitchcock shows. See him at our kitchen table eating an egg salad sandwich. He is talking excitedly about Salvation and Jesus and his special God, the God of Thou Must Not and Emperor of You Must. A piece of egg salad flies out of his teeth and lands on my cheek. He never pauses, skims it off my skin with the tip of his finger, puts it back in his mouth, eats it—eats me, in a way. A fly is walking down his temple. It pauses at his left eye—a staring, evangelical orb—then walks across that naked eye, and Mooncob does not even blink. O, horrid little man with your sleight-of-hand tricks! O, dreadful little creature whom—for God-known reasons—my father, the miracle worker, worships!

But, as I have said, something else was weeping out into the false twilight of Broadway, on which soon, barring miracles, there would be a broken light for every heart.

Do you hear it, Swee? I crooned, beginning to dance to the strains.

It was De Larrocha and Maazel and the Philharmonic doing De Falla's "Nights in the Gardens of Spain." O, I must have it!

Wait, father. Wait here.

Where you goin', chile?

Over to the music, I said. I want to be fucked by music. I want to feel that divine De Falla thing on my neck, shoulders, between my legs, father. Wait now.

I met a charming lady usher. The ticket window was closed. The concert—the Falla—was drawing to a close. I stood in the back— far back in the shadows behind the last row. It was so full of the music, that sepulchred cornice in the theater. I stared at the orchestra for a moment, breathed deeply, then wriggled out of my coat and stood nude against the wall—O, bared to the succulent bullets from the Guernicad *volupté* of the Spanish firing squad. The music was palpable, like blows, like tiny blows of fairy wings against my nipples, knees, calves, and cunt. I lay fainting back against the wall, swooning and panting with the rapturous sweetness of it, all crumbs of fear of what lay ahead washing from me in the mad joy of violins, the plangent roller coaster of Alicia's piano, the haunting soul kiss of the horns. The Alhambra was my hot, panting lover. O, music should always be *felt* with the naked, praising flesh. I opened one eye! The first violin—he alone of all the orchestra had seen me. He was playing to me, too—his tightening adagio of sweet Cremonad passion was bringing me to a glorious come. And maybe him. I felt the wetness a moment later—the hot collapse of thigh muscles—the shuddering, drenched clitoris back again into its holy, cloistered nun's cowl. I went back into the street—after tipping the astonished little usher a thousand-dollar bill—and found Sweeley. It would be ten minutes till it happened. If it were going to happen. And I felt unreasonably, illogically, happily certain that it never would happen, that the marvelous people in their marvelous city would never, *could* never, die.

Sweeley seemed to share my optimism. But I did have the obvious thought.

Would it be doing the right thing, I asked, not looking at him, if we paid off the terrorists with our twenty million for the unrobbery?

No, he said. That's pandering to Force. No. It must be done in the way which Criste described to Uncle Will in the Labyrinth.

But the city! I stammered, my eyes tearing, scalding and salty. The most miraculous, beautiful city on earth, lovely Manhattan. O, I love New York City like a woman, sir. Because that's what she is! A woman, a personlady—a fine, fierce, fickle, fuckloving ladyperson. A girl having her period (a long one) and fucked up with a dose of clap—and, God knows, needing a bath. Her armpits stubbly and rank, too, but who cares? She's, O, my loveliest of loves. The people mustn't let them kill my lady Gotham. They've got to give her time to make the Big Comeback! O, Lord, that's only fair! A ladyperson shouldn't ever be crowded.

Believe, murmured Sweeley Leech. Only believe, Beurre.

Believe? In God, you mean.

In people. In debbils. It's the same thing.

It was a lovely September night. In the glistening yellow-striped black air the doomed wasp thrummed his way through the stunned autumn. The wind was suddenly like the wisping, good-bye kiss of rubbing alcohol as it leaves the skin.

How can the people save New York when TRUCAD says they can't?

Sweeley Leech said nothing, a faint smile flashing upon his lips.

Because at that moment we both heard: a whisper, a susurration, a smothered, clamorous motion, a wild Something of movement and fear and devotion and coming together. It seemed to emanate from every latitude and longitude—a migration of iron fragments to a lodestone held in some huge fingers: inexorable and devout. A beech tree waves its wild hair in the tide of air and a leaf strikes my face faintly and I am suddenly most deeply moved by its impact: furious and weighty with Time. But it was manifest that the particles rushing to their irresistible nucleus were human and not mere dumb grit and inanimation.

Is it the Revolution, sir?

It is one, he said. But it is also a lynch mob.

Who's the victim this time? I sighed wearily.

Death, I thought I heard Sweeley Leech chuckle as he moved away from me into the moonstained shadow of an old elder, but I couldn't be sure. I followed him, lonely and anxious, O me of little faith! Groups of people, like small birds hurrying to the execution of a falcon, thumped resonantly past along the flagged pavement, stonewalled against Central Park's cramped, intense verdure and scattered midden. The trees lining the light-standard-studded walk were like windhaired women against the pale magenta stain of the nightsky. O, somehow trees seem to me always as feminine as safety pins.

Death? I called to my father. Is Death about to get himself wasted again? Is that what you said, Sweeley Leech?

Whatever his answer was, as he dragged me down the pavement through the cunning, clumping, furious knots of men and women and children, his voice was lost, ripped up by the wind and scurrying leaf.

The moon sails serene into a scudding cluster of cumulus. I perceive that there is indeed pie in the sky—that it is blueberry and has scorched and bubbled over onto the gasburners of the galaxies. I glance at my digital in the pale dusk. Eleven-ten. Maybe the third bomb has already gone off and me and Sweeley Leech already in heaven and these mobs of singing people souls on their chanting way to their own.

Abruptly, Sweeley Leech pulled me abreast of him and, drawing me close, kissed me on the mouth. I laughed and drew back from his tongue.

Whenever you laugh like that, Beurre, he said, it means you're scared.

I admit it, I laughed. O, I am scared.

Sure, Beurre. Sure you are.

Aren't you scared, Sweeley Leech?

Deliciously so, he admitted. Relishing it, too. In the old human nosethumb at Death.

It merely confuses me, I said, staring at the stream of humanity all around me, all of it seeming to center its pellmell reflex toward the plexus of the threatened city.

What confuses you, Beurre?

If the third bomb is going to go off in mid-Manhattan, why aren't all the people running *away* from that center—instead of toward it? Is it some kind of doom instinct, father?

They are bringing something, he said. To the center of the city. The center, in its way, of the universe.

What? Bringing what?

Again his answer was dragged from his lips by the wind and I did not catch it. But I thought he might have said the words *Love* and *Hate.* Was it really the Revolution, then?

What are they carrying, Sweeley? What are they bringing to town?

Did he say—? Was the word he used *Honey?*

A radio sneered past in a racing car. A newrock tune that sounded like a stoned mohel circumcising a jew's harp. I looked for Sweeley's sweet face.

It could *still* go off, I said. At any minute. Remember, the first two were off schedule.

It could, he said.

And we'll be dead.

We would be dead, Beurre. Vegetably so, at least.

I breathed twice for a beat.

I kissed his ear. He smelled like pennies and pipe tobacco and whiskers like daddies always do to little girls. I ran ahead a pace.

The radiophone squawked like a tiny frog on my goldhaired wrist. I snapped on Receive. It was Lindy—anxious, of course. But O, so very ubiquitous.

59

Yes, love.

Has the bomb gone off yet, Feef?

Two of them have, I said.

O, my dear, were you wounded?

Obviously not, darling.

I paused.

The terrorists announced three, I said. Two at sea. They've already gone off. They threaten a third here in midtown Manhattan as of about now, love. That's about all I can say.

Are they going to pay off the beasts?

TRUCAD has figured out that the twenty million dollars the terrorists ask is far in excess of the computerized and *real* human value of the human life involved. No *real-estate* damage will result *if* the third bomb goes off—it's a neutron—and the population *will* replace itself. That cold. That candid. It's rather refreshing, don't you think? I mean after all the twotalk of the past.

I'm glad they're not catering to such elements, Lindy said. TRUCAD has refused to pay, eh?

Right.

And justly. Why should they pay?

Well—human life. Ours, for instance. There is that factor, love.

Still, we must be toughminded, as Uncle Mooncob says, Feef. In the long run, worse loss of life would result by giving in.

Dear Lindy. She rambles on. Do you care what else she says? Listen as I tell a little more about her. What sort of woman is this who, when her two nearest and dearest kin face incineration, speaks of principle? Listen.

There is a God, Feef, she said once. There is a Providence. I mean, Fate takes away a George Gershwin and a few years later gives us Paul Anka. All the great composers aren't Jewish. O, by no means.

Pause, while her father and sister maybe wait to die.

I mean, I'm so into music and literature now, Feef. O, it's all part of my awakening in Christ, I know. I *feel* literary, I *dress* literary. I have a new scent that even *smells* literary!

Yes, I know. Bard of Avon, darling Lindy.

What, Feef?

Nothing, love. I was just musing meanly.

It's all right, she said. You're *not* mean. Not cruel. I know you,

Feef. You don't believe in all this blasphemy of father's. You are not mean that way, Feef. I know you. For example, you would no more toss a lighted cigarette into these dry autumn woods than you would set fire deliberately to the little Communion dress of a Catholic child. You are not mean, not cruel.

Thank you, Lindy. I adore you. Now excuse me.

She rang off. But I knew she would be back—the soap-opera, *Policewoman* thrill of our predicament is irresistible. And I can return to the task of helping you know this woman who is, in her dear, negative way, so crucial to this story.

Lindy is a grub, almost a chrysalis. Now, we all know the natural history of grubs. They become the chrysalis, and then the painted butterfly that flutters by and stains our gladsome eyes. She is unformed, inchoate, like fingers clawing and not yet gathered into Dürer's enduring praise Fingers that grope. She is not yet beautiful—yet all the elements of beauty lie programmed in the sleeping mulch and mast of her forest floor. Someday—later in the story, perhaps—you will not turn from her as you do now. You will adore her, desire her, seek her as you now—who knows?—may seek after me.

Lindy is twenty-one, five years younger than I. Because she is so incomplete I think father loves her more, though I think I am his friend more than she.

She has married four times. Always men of wealth. It is her argument that it is as easy to fall in love with a rich man as with a poor one. And so much more—well, American.

Providentially, all this pastry-cake Betty Crocker piety is leavened with certain bittersweet ingredients of Sin. We all need Sin in our lives. It is our contraries that make us alive. Sin and Love warring. O, Sweeley Leech will tell you how we all need Demons within us to season and dress the even, suffocating fabric of unvarying Piety. He has his lust for Loll—and money—and, formerly, drink and drugs. I have my lust for Sex—with, well, almost Anyone. Lindy lusts after Salvation and gay men and old-style Mafioso gangsters. She cannot resist them. Only members of the old Calabrese—the Palermo-style gangster, I mean. Not the sleek, gray-flanneled, Yves St. Laurent–sweatered, WASP gangster—the only kind since TRUCAD's criminal arm bought out the old Cosa Nostra. Lindy is a Romantic. Decades after the last Spanish pirate was hanged and had rotted in chains at London, girls loved any dark, swarthy man with an impudent earring wisping and winking about his neck.

I pause in this reverie. My hand stole to the vent of my leopard-skin coat. I fingered with fond and fatal grief the place where the freckle transplant had so lately been. More than a bit of pigment was gone. For a while my trust in any woman's love or pledge of loyalty was gone. And then I remembered the gangster that Lindy actually married. And lived with in Newark for almost a year.

I must gossip a moment about this remarkable man and his fate. The greatest city in the world might be about to sprout a most deadly mushroom, but I insist on telling you of this extraordinary executioner—Lindy's third husband—Garbanzo Valenzuela. Actually, he was not Italian, not Sicilian at all—he was Bolivian. He was first into drugs. He was arrested for selling tranquilizers to teenagers—telling ardent young devotees of American Lit that Thoreau invented Thorazine. Later he became the skilled, oiled, noiseless hit man he was when he died.

He met Lindy. Lindy was into Catholicism that season. est, TM, and Methodism were passé. She convinced Garbanzo he should make his peace with God—confess all his sanguinary sins to a priest. After weeks of harangue he agreed. The priest listened silent in the confessional for almost three hours as Garbanzo confessed all his murders. Leonardo-skilled murders, Michelangelo simplicity to his executions. The excited priest sent him to a monsignor, who heard even more detail. Impressed, the latter sent Garbanzo to the archdiocese, where a bishop heard the confession—even more detailed by now—and breathlessly the bishop hastened Garbanzo to Rome on the fastest jet to the Vatican. There he was listened to by the head of the College of Cardinals and, at last, it was discovered wherein lay the hot interest of the Church in this man of sorrows.

A lay-priest, very high in prestige among the Cardinals, spread the cards, as it were, on the velvet table to the astonished assassin. He would be forgiven all his sins by the Church—on the condition that he commit one more. It was explained that such expiatory crimes were frequently resorted to by the College. The final crime—the one which would expunge every past transgression, however incarnadine—was simple: to hit, to waste, the Pope. This was an incorrigible and impenitent rebel whom no amount of politicking could expel. The project is described in certain secret Vatican archives even now. It is called the WPA (Waste Papa Arrangement). Of course, it never came off—not by the hand, at least, of Garbanzo Valenzuela. The Pope, as you will recall, did die suddenly, as John Paul I did, back in the seventies, after a few weeks aloft. But Garbanzo fled, shocked and half-crazed, to the arms and solace of poor Lindy, and died three days later in East Orange from salmonella after a Burger Chef Special.

After weeks of inconsolable grief, Lindy rallied. She gave up her Catholicism and went back to the arms of the Presbyterians. She decided to tour Europe. She had never been there, and it was a lifelong ambition of Lindy's to visit Europe so that she could see, firsthand, the actual settings of all her favorite films. I can see her strolling the chiaroscuro of the Louvre, among Matisses, humming Lara's theme from *Zhivago*.


It had begun raining now. The drops fell warm and heavy with the autumn savors on one's lips. The warm drops plucked and puckered the placid surface of the Pulitzer pond, before the looming up of the sometimes alarming gray and jeweled dowager bosom of the Plaza Hotel.

Sweeley drew me near, his face rapturous with pleasure.

Did you hear what is happening?

No, Swee.

They have come from every borough. On foot, in cabs, in wheelchairs. They have paid the city's ransom out of their own poor, mean little pockets. Dollars, nickels, food stamps, jewelry.

He sprang away from me, hiding his quick tears of emotion. The tears mixed with the gathering rain down the gutters of his most eloquent gargoyle face. We moved among returning, penniless, but somehow jubilant, mobs toward a charming and new little pub beside the miracle jewel basket of a store called À La Vieille Russie.

The threatened atomic destruction of Manhattan's blustery, easy-fingered children had been called off. Now all that remained was Apocalypse.

A *paparazzo* was darting around among the starched white tables, flashing his Nikon over shoulders and into cleavages. An occasional lush nipple, a flash of pubes, was caught with f/7 at a five-hundredth. The television wall was on. The Astrojets–Dallas football classic. I decided I would be for Dallas tonight because I think Tom Landry has cute ears. Sweeley ordered a three-hundred-year-old wine and paid for it with a bank note marked by a five and three zeroes. He was so anxious to be poor again. Poor baby. Only ten minutes ago he had discovered five hundred overlooked shares of Texas Instrument in his shaving kit.

The air was upbeat. People were broke and happy and scared—but scared of living now, not of dying. In the back a portable wrist-radio was playing an old Charlie Parker thing called "Barbados."

Sweeley darted out and squatted next door before the show window of À La Vieille Russie. He stared in longingly, remembering old, rich, winter days when he bought the toys of crown princes, the thingamajigs of emperors, the dainty Fabergé Cracker Jack prizes of Rasputins, and snapshots of nude grand duchesses with shaved and mouthless pubes. He came back, lit up with the memory-possession of a silver sow with an uplift nose holding a whale-oil wick. For Russian cigarettes. For Turkish cheroots in the gardens of Sarajevo before Apocalypse's first ringing crack of Christianity's rooftree on that Saint Vitus Day, 1914.

Are you scared?

You mean about tomorrow? The unrobbery?

Yes.

No. I am excited. Like before my first fuck.

The atomic scare, the money demand, he said then. I could have saved the city myself.

With our money?

No. That is pledged to Lord Jesus. No.

How, then?

I could have sneezed a Screod of a time-shift.

A miracle, I said. Yes, I believe you could have.

It would have saved the People, he said, smiling.

I lighted a legal joint and inhaled.

But the People saved the city, he said. That is as beautiful as a thing can be. The city-hating, pollution-choking, garbage-fed People saved their dear old New York. Beautiful. Beautiful, Beurre.

He mused.

Dey's all debbils, Beurre, he crooned. Debbils every one.

A child with a tiny live monkey ran sappy with happiness past us.

Sweeley was holding something toward me into the luminescence of tallow wick and Steuben crystal. It was a folding silver coin. I was not supposed to know it was folding. He dropped it into the empty wine bottle, shook it a little, swooped it out onto the tablecloth again. He tried to palm it and to substitute a real Kennedy half-dollar—and dropped it into my saucer of guacamole. Long, sad sigh from poor Sweeley Leech.

The world turned slowly onward, on the axis of great Hamlet's mill. The stars shone down. The moon was a gaudy, gay serendipity of quiet. I squeezed my father's dear, disappointed hand.

You always fool me, Sweeley Leech, I said. You fool me into thinking—now and then—that you are only the second-wisest, dearest man who ever walked amid Galilee's laughter-roaring hills!

# F✦I✦V✦E

Any man who has a vision and publicizes it is a hustler.
—Lenny Bruce

It was morning and I was on the edgy side. Not about the bank unrobbery facing us. About Lindy. She haunted me this morning; she seemed, these days, so—so *fatal*. I knew in the marrow of me that something involving her fate was looming among the Pleiades of Sweeley Leech and me.

It was 7:47:30 on my Taiwan digital on the morning of 9:5 1992.

Sweeley Leech and I were at a small oval bamboo table in the rear of an Arab-style pizza parlor across from our target. It was a stunningly clear and dashing autumn day. The air was peppermint on the tongue. Tiny clouds scudded back and forth across the sky, blue as a majorette's eyes, like invisible waiters with invisible bowls bearing lovely, fluffy whipped cream. I watched a girl in a Givenchy frock crossing Madison Avenue. Her ass was talking brightly of the succulent moments it spent in a backseat the night before.

I am a great ass-reader. Ladies' asses are visible, intelligible diaries—more candid by far than the asses of men, who are busy hiding their ass-thoughts, and certainly more revealing than the diaries of Nin or Woolf. See that other ass—moving down past the bookstalls on Fifty-fourth? A perfectly charming, lovable ass, but nothing, nothing happened there last night. Or the night before. Not for weeks. And the ass is complaining about that: stiff-cheeked and sucked in with resentment.

I looked across at our target. The newly renovated Madison and Fifty-fifth Street branch of Citibank. White-painted, quartered windows, a fanlight over the doors, Paul Revere fixtures—polished to blind the eye and absolutely fainting with history.

Poetry, Sweeley Leech said suddenly, after long thought, may only be the power to remember the Future.

I sipped at my small glass of morning rosé. I gobbled the last crumb of scrambled egg from my fake Haviland dish.

Father, I said, a little testily. Here I am facing my—our—first bank unrobbery and you speak in metaphors.

Hell, yes, he said. Because it is a metaphor we are making when we do this thing. Stealing—that's a boring cliché!

He lapsed into meditation again. My thoughts swung back to poor dear Lindy. What was in the wind, in the stars for her—that dark, gold vein in the agate which I could discern even from this post in Time.

The really cute young waiter was looking at Sweeley Leech, his wine-eyes sleepy with sod. Earlier, when he came to the table I gave him the softest of feels, and for an instant, the light of his eyes came out at me: woman; held for an instant, then went back to Sweeley's crotch. Sweeley waved his long hand toward the walls—murals of Nureyev dancers with Shirley MacLaine gypsies.

You like?

I pursed my lips, rolling my eyes at the taut, tulle asses of the ballerinas at the bar.

They give me a sense of Degas vu.

I sipped my old, good wine.

And the wine, I added thoughtfully, a sense of déjà bu.

✦

The bank would open in eight minutes. Sweeley Leech yawned, yet showing not the slightest indetermination or lack of intention.

Sensitive as he was, Sweeley Leech seemed often not to possess a nerve in his body.

Lindy. Her face. Shimmering in a slot of morning sunlight from the bamboo-shaded window. Twained. Twinned. Tearing itself in half somehow: the spirit behind that face.

Six minutes to go. The valises of booty were in the backseat of the old '82 Mercedes Sweeley Leech had rented from Honda-Avis the night before. The seven valises. Sweeley's ham came. It was the only breakfast he ever ate—a thick slice of ham that was a Polish joke. But he respected it—do you know what I mean? Sweeley respects food more than he loves it. I heard his voice now, murmurous and satiny in the stillness of the pizza parlor.

> I praise this meat because it meant
> Some dumb beast's soul to heaven went.
> Such as stood round Criste's crèche
> Now resurrected in my flesh. Amen.

Most of my nerves were for his safety, not mine. O, I know he is a candle whom Society will and must blow out—but, God, don't let it be soon. His hair gives off a soft, clean light; his blue eyes are active and pondering as he chews his meat and sips a glass of cold water. I envisioned the small strawberry birthmark he has at the base of his spine. I longed to kiss it for luck. And for love.

Lindy persists in my mind's receptors. So tormented. I think how sad it is when a person likes to fuck and hates the opposite sex. Lindy just hates other people. She doesn't hate us—her family— because to her, family is not people but surrogates of herself. That is why she is always so angry with us when we don't do what she would do.

Beurre, I think we can cross the street now and begin this holy thing, he said then.

He winked and grinned.

The whip round my waist, under my light batwing-sleeved green wool coat, felt heavy. I watched as Sweeley reached inside the

Greek boiled-wool caftan he wore and adjusted his own. They were intended more as symbols, as show biz, than as actual weapons. The whole thing had a mad Alice in Wonderland air about it. I giggled and shivered at once.

Sweeley Leech handed the dumb, astonished waiter a thousand-dollar bank note and bade him keep the change. The boy flushed and gaped and wilted a little, his eyes like tiny cups of mocha feasting on father. Sweeley was aware and—without any passion save kindness and general love—drew the boy against him and kissed him on the cheek. We left the place with a flourish. Nobody noticed us as we jaywalked to the Mercedes. Nobody notices anything odd in New York City. A light delivery truck almost clipped me. The driver smiled and waved. I read the sign on the panel: STORK DIA-PER SERVICE. "Your Baby's Shit Is Our Bread and Butter." Advertising hasn't mellowed much in the nineties. There was a funeral parlor next to the bank we were about to hit. A very costly mortuarium. With an angle, according to a modest framed statement which I stopped long enough to scan. Hair, as it is well known, continues to grow after death. This service included funeral, burial, and the whole bit *with* perpetual monthly shampoo, wave and set, and blow-dry.

Beurre?

Yes, father?

You keep to the lobby, near the doors. I want you to control the guards. I'll handle the bank manager.

He seized my hand and said a touching thing.

Try not to hurt anyone, he said. I don't want anyone really hurt.

Take care of yourself, darling!

The seven valises were heavy as stone. The two armed TRU-CAD bank guards at the door watched us with sharp curiosity at first and then relaxed, having assumed that the caftan clothed another Arab, still curiously carte blanche anywhere in the Western World—curiously, I say, since Arab oil is rather passé as a fuel and the Arabs no longer have any political clout. Sweeley arranged the valises—salved and glowing richly with opulence—on the beige-carpeted floor beside the desk of the rather surprised bank manager, Mr. Horn.

Horn looked like a Catholic Woody Allen. He looked not *over* his horn-rimmed glasses but somehow *under* them. He wore a silk-

wool-Dacron pullover V-neck sweater of the color of a cigarette ash
and a loose Italian suede jacket from Battaglia. Backtrack. What
does a Catholic Woody Allen look like? He lacks the marvelous
Jewish guilt that gives us *Annie Hall* and the Concerto in F. Mr.
Horn had no sense of humor that was manifest. He looked at the
expensive and obviously bulging luggage. He looked at Sweeley
Leech, who was sitting at his desk, smiling at him. Sweeley Leech
looked rather gravely back at Mr. Horn. Horn cleared his throat.

I know you have business with me, he said. But first I have a
favor to ask.

Anything.

Mr. Horn edged closer; his voice fell.

There was an Italian American who lived in Red Bank and ran a
small grocery with his wife. The wife had given him four sons:
three dark, as he was, and the fourth—well, rather like Sean Cas-
sidy, light and rather Gaelic. All his life the Italian American worried. On his wife's deathbed he could hold back no longer. "Tell
me," he said. *"Cara mia,* I must know. The fourth boy—is he
mine?" And, failing fast, the happy woman winked. "Yes," she said.
"But the other three aren't."

Mr. Horn's voice fell even more.

My favor, sir, he said, is for you to tell me why such a catastrophe should be considered a joke. I simply don't get it. Here's a
good, staunch Italian American Catholic whose wife cheats. By the
way, sir, are you Catholic?

With the small *c,* please, said Sweeley Leech.

No matter, said Horn. But I feel like a jerk. Masterson, the
chairman of the board, told that story yesterday, and everybody
laughed but me. You see, I look at the wife like one of our women
depositors.

Certainly, Mr. Horn, it is a most solemn story, said Sweeley
Leech.

At any rate, said Horn, it is a so-called pleasantry. Citibank policy is to start off every interview with a pleasantry. I've tried to
comply.

You've done marvelously, said Sweeley Leech. Under normal
conditions I would have wet my pants laughing.

I wondered whether you wore any under that robe—you know,
one wonders about under kilts and all. Are you Arab?

West Virginian.

O, hell, I was in Norfolk once.

Norfolk, England, you mean.

No, Virginia.

Never heard of it.

You came about a loan? asked Mr. Horn.

Not exactly, Sweeley Leech replied. In fact I might say exactly the opposite.

You want to make—

The horned eyes ogled the lustrous luggage.

—a deposit?

He chuckled.

Since the oil-embargo days we are used to seeing caped and robed gentlemen such as yourself bringing in large deposits like this.

Well, no, sir. It's not exactly a deposit. You see, you don't know my name. And when I've finished here, inserting—the word I prefer—this money into your bank you still won't know my name. You'll never know my name, Mr. Horn. Name isn't involved here. Gesture is involved. Metaphor is involved.

How do you mean?

I mean, said Sweeley Leech, that there are over twenty-five million dollars in bearer bonds and securities in those valises, and with them—

Yes?

—with them I plan to unrob this bank.

I was within earshot of all this, busy as I was at the doors passing out—like free literature in a church—five-thousand-dollar bills. Three out of five people, you might like to know, kept them, and some even came back and kissed me, but there were others who—suspecting, I guess, that this was some kind of government hoax—tossed theirs into the street.

Could we run through that again? asked Mr. Horn.

Gladly. I have a great deal of money here. Money that I am forcing into the safes and files and computerized tapes of this institution. I hope you realize that this is the world's first recorded crime of its nature—the first bank unrobbery. And there is nothing you can do to stop it. You are in thrall to me, sir.

Already there was movement in the room: small movement, forest movement, leaf and shadow and sunlight movement. And the patter of very small feet. Clerks and tellers and junior management persons began to high-step and look between their shoes as if avoiding treading on fragile creatures.

How do you plan to do this? Horn inquired, his eyes shining.

Would you believe fairies? asked Sweeley Leech. And the anger of the living Criste?

Horn seemed to stagger a little; he buried his face in his hands. He reached for a phone and dialed.

Effie? This is Front Control. Could we have something a little lighter on MusicCom, please? I mean George Crum before lunch is a little— Thanks. Maybe some musical comedy or light opera.

Almost instantly the aggressive chords of avant-garde music froze in the loudspeakers. A moment later, and thrillingly, the unmistakable strains of the song from *Ruddigore* Sweeley and I had overheard the night before. O, the Causal Liaisons were thick and fast that day. Mr. Horn looked distraught. I felt that if Sweeley Leech had at that moment, cruelly, told the man a joke he would have burst into tears and run for the Person Room washbowls.

The Philosophy-Religion Committee has been warning of this for years, Horn said.

Philosophy and Religion Committee of TRUCAD, you mean.

Of the government, Horn said. No one ever refers openly to TRUCAD these days.

You knew we were planning this, my daughter and I?

Yes, said Horn sadly. Though we didn't know which day you were going to strike. We knew you'd picked this branch.

How did you know?

Horn fished around inside a small teak box on his desk and took out a tiny glass vial with an ivory cap. I pattered over close enough to see what it contained—a small dark fleck, like a scale of rust, no bigger than the petal of the sundew that grows in the Gallimaufry.

On the surface, Horn said, what you are doing is merely— deranged. Forgive me, but that's the word. Deranged. But that's only where you're concerned. I know you're not a fake. I know you are in dead earnest. When people hear about this crime, they will know that, too. Where the public is concerned, what you're doing could set a dangerous, radical example. Namely: promiscuous, premeditated, and unreasonable giving. Don't you agree—

He paused and leaned forward.

—Sweeley Leech?

Sweeley took it gracefully; nodded.

How did you know my name, Horn?

Again Horn held up the little vial and shook it.

From this minute, almost microscopic quasar ensemble—which has for the past three years been implanted in a most personal and private, I should hope, area of the skin of that young lady by the door who, I might add, has been coming on to Laidley, the bank guard.

Laidley was cute, though. He was an Irish cop who looked like the actor Pat O'Brien and was perpetually aggrieved that nobody remembered what Pat O'Brien looked like.

From this unit, government authorities were able to pick up enough of the young lady's thoughts—your wife, sir? girl friend?

My daughter.

Your daughter. Really? You look about her age. Remarkable. Anyway, that speck of chemistry and physics contains every thought your daughter has had in the past three years.

He paused.

Fortunately for your plan, Sweeley Leech, not more than six percent of one one-hundredth of what the lady thought was of any use to us. Almost all of it was about sex. As for that part—well, when the wife of Agent Laurel heard an hour of it, she made a dive for the fly of the technician who was airing it. We did get enough to know that you were planning an—as you call it—unrobbery. And we began to figure how to forestall you.

I'm doing nothing illegal, said Sweeley Leech. Forcing money on a bank—without a deposit slip. Nothing illegal—because there are no laws, as such, against promiscuous giving.

But why are you doing it, Leech?

Because of the words of a friend, given to me long years gone by in Weirton: "It is better to give than to receive." And again: "It is easier for a camel to pass through the eye of a needle—" Hell, you know it! And my friend's advice to the rich young man: "Sell what thou hast and give to the poor." Cornball, huh? That's why you smirk and raise your eyebrows, Mr. Horn?

No. No. It's not that. I'm just realizing how dangerous those sayings are. For the first time—realizing.

New Yorkers never see things. The fairies and elves of the Gallimaufry were busy in the room—among the valises, in computerized catacombs of the business area. Large metal information centers began to smoke—the blue, curling tendrils of it like vines from the bowels of hell. Of course, being a believer, I could see the fairies. No one else in the room did. One was cruelly crushed under a high heel from Bloomie's. Another drowned in the water cooler. But they were doing their work so marvelously. New computer data were being fed—new amounts to new names programmed in. The money changers were being flogged from the temple. I thought of the whip round my waist—I smiled at not having had to use it. Yet.

You know how nutty all this is? Horn asked then. Aside from the philosophy. You know as well as I do that banks have millions—billions, trillions, probably—that are never claimed. Estates unsettled. Insurance payments unclaimed. Interest never collected. You are spitting in the ocean, Mr. Leech.

You don't understand, Sweeley Leech said, with the owlish solemnity which I always cherished. All of this money is going to *people.*

Really? How will you arrange that?

My small court is arranging that. The Fairy Court.

Horn saw then the spiraling smoke from the computer banks. He saw the wallets of deeds and bonds shuttling through naked, shimmering space. He heard steel drawers open and close—unaided by any visible hand.

But riddle me this, then, Leech, he said finally. If you think money is so filthy and dirty, why do you want to force it on others? It may corrupt them.

I don't think money is filthy and dirty. I think it is holy—it is a sacrament where it is needed. I just don't like it idle. Money is blood of life to a mother with hungry, cold children. Money is also cancer in a rich man's liver.

Horn was frightened. Moreover, he suspected that something genuinely funny was happening and, as usual, he was missing the point.

What will you live on? squeaked Horn. Have you ever really *been* poor?

Unfortunately, I shall discover when I get home that I've hidden away a few thousand shares of Occidental Petroleum or three thousand preferred of Minnesota Mining. And as for being poor—yes, I have. In several lives.

In several lives? God, man, are you into *that?* My daughter Jenny thinks she's Alice B. Toklas.

Sixteen million dollars—all backed by Swiss francs in the event of another crash—is being programmed into the computerized balances of sixteen hundred small checking accounts.

Horn sneezed.

The frolicking, rollicking music of Gilbert and Sullivan danced through the room: tinseled and sequined with morning and autumn light. The air seemed to dance with atoms and molecules and all the primal brilliance of the cosmos. O, I do wish the TV cameras in every crevice of the room had been recording our little friends from the Gallimaufry. A tiny Jewish fairy from out on the street came to the window once, stared in horror, and fled for a subway, his *payess* trailing. A bagel no bigger than a Life Saver lay, uneaten, on the walk behind him.

My Pat O'Brien bank dick came over to Horn then.

Mr. Horn, is everything A-okay?

Yes, Laidley. Go back to your stale black coffee. And for God's sake, man—

What, sir?

Well, your fly is open, for starters.

Laidley came over and squeezed Sweeley's hand.

Sir, you got one helluva woman there.

Thanks. Enjoy.

Laidley came back to me.

You say sixteen million, Horn resumed. Going into the bank accounts of horse players, food-stamp cheats, welfare scroungers, junkies, and whores.

Let him who is without a sense of humor cast the first pie, said Sweeley Leech.

He indicated the four bags which were still unopened.

That, he said, is really special. And I don't think you're going to like it, Horn.

Is there some—some joke in all of this that I'm missing? whined Horn.

He popped three Rolaids and chewed disconsolately.

75

I should get jokes, he said. I am Jewish. Jews are funny people.

Score a big one against ethnic stereotypes, I thought. And come to think of it, Laidley looked like an Irish Luther Adler. I was keeping him distracted, shall we say, in the shadow of an authentic Rubens on the bank wall above the water cooler.

It is a joke, said Sweeley Leech. That's why news of it will spread like an autumn grass fire among the windrows. It will become a myth—which is a kind of joke that lives. It will be felt in that secret kingdom of the human memory that bears the name of Sherwood Forest. People who hear of it will never be the same!

You see yourself as a kind of Robin Hood, then, Mr. Leech?

No. Just a man who wants to get to the City of God intact.

You may be called there sooner than you want, Horn observed grimly, if you pull this scam off.

I know when I shall go, said Sweeley Leech. You won't hurry it—or stay it. But enough of that.

This is really deranged, Horn said, fighting for reason. You realize, of course, that the originals of all these computerized statements are intact—across the river in Jersey. And another set—

You really *should* try to believe, Mr. Horn.

In what? Fairies?

Them. In the Invisible World. It's all around you. And if you were on Riverside Drive right now, looking across at a window of that building below the Palisades where your computer information is stored, you would see curls of smoke issuing from it, too. And you might see small brown debbils darting into the deeps of those steel minds and altering their memories—their thoughts—making them change, for example, the checking account of Mrs. Pilar Lopez of 312½ West 105th Street, Manhattan, to a spanking ten thousand dollars instead of five dollars and thirty-eight cents overdrawn, plus five dollars bank charge.

And the money that's in these remaining four bags?

That goes to settle what I believe your files call the Steloff Mortgage.

Horn stared, trying to bluff with his eyes.

You don't know anything about that. Nobody outside Citibank and the government knows about the Steloff Mortgage.

I do, said Sweeley Leech. It is a big redlining campaign you guys have on now. Two city blocks in the West Forties—all very poor tenements—being held up and the mortgage about to be fore-closed. A mortgage worth twenty million dollars, which you don't want paid off because then you can't grab those blocks, evict those people, keep them down, kick them out. To make room for some monument to Christian Liberalism like Lincoln Center.

Isn't Lincoln Center better than what was there? Stinking slums are what was there. Doorways for junkies to hide in and knife old women.

I would prefer the music of children's laughter, said Sweeley Leech, to all the world's philharmonics. Because I know that laughing children grow up to be Beethovens and Harold Arlens and George Bensons. You guys drove out the laughing children, Horn.

Damn you, Leech—TRUCAD *wants* that land. They don't want the Steloff Mortgage paid off! You can't pull this off.

Too bad, said Sweeley Leech, and rose, heading for the doors, heading for me.

The gay music of *Ruddigore* stormed like Halloween corn hurled across a sleeper's window at midnight. I felt marvelous. Sweeley looked marvelous. Something buzzed on my wrist. It was the radio-phone. Inevitably, guess who.

Feef?

Yes, Lindy!

Feef, I hope I'm not interrupting anything.

Just the bank unrobbery, Lindy.

O, Feef. I did hope there was time. Feef, I wanted to beg you both again to give it up.

Sweeley grabbed my wrist.

Lindy, ring off. We're making our getaway, goddammit.

Hush, father. Feef is my sister. I won't be shushed. Feef, I wanted to ask this, then. If you and father won't give it up—if it's too late for that. Feef, father, when you come back to Echo Point and write your book, will you let me enter it in the Nobel Prize Contest?

I rang off. Two bank guards, followed by Horn and a gray-haired type with a microphone and small CB unit were approaching. We undid our whips. Suddenly the gaudy, Victorian fairyland disap-peared. The strains of the Ghost's Dance from *Ruddigore* were brutally interrupted by a voice.

You won't get away with this, Sweeley Leech! We have your

name and number! You shall pay for this unnatural intrusion into the affairs of commerce, this insult to Christian business!

The voice seemed godlike on the excellent hi-fi. Sweeley looked at me.

It sounds godlike, I said.

That's because it *is* God, he said. The God of money. God-amighty, if you want. The God Uncle Will grabs by the giant ears and calls a farting, belching Nobodaddy!

Sweeley snaked out his whip and flicked a cocked .357 Magnum from the hand of the guard—not my dear Laidley. He thunder-cracked the whip in the golden air above the Rubens. The fairies cheered and scattered.

Belch and fart on high, you God of a Nobodaddy! Who need fear God when he has Criste for a friend?

We sprang into the street, Horn on our heels. He grabbed the hem of Sweeley's caftan and held it for an instant.

Your opinion, then, at least, he said. Please, give me that at least. Of what?

My Italian friend. Was the fourth boy his?

And then miraculously, gay and pulses pounding, we were both away into the people and splendor of a blowing autumn noon on America's loveliest isle while the Mercedes, with a fart that might have been from the ass of God himself, self-destructed in the aston-ished light behind us.

We grabbed a hansom cab on its way back to the park. Sweeley had dumped his boiled-wool Greek caftan in the back of a dilapi-dated old fruit truck at the corner of Fifty-seventh. He now wore a light flannel winter suit by Bill Blass. With a divine red tie on a blue shirt. Police sirens were yodeling like castrated Dobermans in the astonished streets behind us. We got out at the corner of Fifty-ninth and Fifth and walked toward the fountain. The sirens seemed angry at being so far off the trail. Sweeley ran ahead of me toward the shop of the Tsars, twinkling like a faience cigarette box in the razzle-dazzle of solstice light. Sweeley was declaiming, from his fa-vorite, next to Shakespeare, Uncle Will Blake:

> And there to Eternity aspire
> The selfhood in a flame of fire
> Till then the lamb of God . . .

It was one of Uncle Will's lovely little unfinished things. Sweeley ran across to the fountain, took off his shoes, and, unobserved, let the cool waters kiss his naked feet.

I could see in his face a newfound land: a radiant grace that had only glimmered faintly there before. He had stamped his metaphor in bold letters upon the gold day. He was chanting again now, lacing up his Tretorn buckskins.

> Was Jesus Chaste? Or did he
> Give any Lessons of Chastity?
> The morning blush'd fiery red:
> Mary was found in adulterous bed . . .

Leaves blew like droplets of blood across the dun-gray paving stones of the square. Little children, not yet dumb or blind, talked to fairies by the Sabrett's hot-dog wagon and shared choice tidbits with elves among balloons. The blue sky rang like struck crystal with a pure and lambent light, and birds chased up and down the stunning azure firmament like black skaters upon a frozen sea. Crows heading south scissored out clouds of absurd white cardboard and stacked them gainward the sun.

> The Vision of Christ that thou dost see
> Is my Vision's Greatest Enemy; . . .
> Thine loves the same world that mine hates,
> Thy Heaven doors are my Hell Gates . . .

He had his shoes back on now and was moving toward me with a red silk scarf—divinely incarnadine in the slipping, quivering light—and a small black silk hat.

Beurre? A trick—please watch. I think—I have it now.

I ran away down Fifth Avenue toward FAO Schwarz. God, I adored my father at that moment. I was so proud of him—proud of me because I was part of him, in love with myself because he had helped make me. I knew he would write the Criste Lite now. And I thought, shuddering, my eyes full of Schwarz teddy bears and toy tin-drum sets, of Lindy's idea—the entering of that holy book in the Nobel Prize Contest. The opulent black glass of the Nobel computer bank dilated dully down the avenue. Criste save us all: to have bestsellerdom of his book would destroy it—cancel out its good. The last thing Sweeley Leech wanted for the Criste Lite was fame and glory. He wanted joy out of it—the joy of understanding Something so long, long forgotten in the lonely ways of man. Yes, it was a book to be shared along lonely roads of man.

I longed to get back to the bungalow at Echo Point. Sweeley's book of Criste was not even down on paper yet, and I was afraid for it. And the fear had to do with Lindy.

I longed to get back to the chopper and leave. But Manhattan was not done with us there. Not quite yet.

My father held the red scarf out to me. I took it—but not before I had seized his dear face and kissed him hard on the mouth.

# S✦I✦X

I wandered alone in the theater district. It was late afternoon. I meandered up Sixth Avenue, which Sweeley's friend Ring Lardner had once called "the Avenue of Small Pretensions." I cut into the diamond district. I mused on the theater poster I had seen on a Forty-seventh Street theater—the Ethel Barrymore, I think. It reflected the eighties so perfectly. Edward Albee and Stephen Sondheim had adapted the Works of Otto Rank into a musical. It was called *The Perfumed Catheter.* I tarried on the corner of Forty-sixth and Sixth, eyeing the headlines. The evening papers were surprisingly restrained in reporting the unrobbery. Accounts were scattered and confused. In a bygone day of international rivalries, now coalesced and appeased by TRUCAD, the panicked supposition would have been that the currency forced into the economy of New York City was Soviet or perhaps Cuban. A man and a woman were being sought. The man's name was not given. This was immediately curious. Horn knew it. But perhaps Horn, overcome by one of those occasional lapses in cupidity and flights into grace, had de-

81

cided to protect the perpetrator of this extraordinary act of perverse generosity. Who knows? Perhaps Horn even believed that Sweeley Leech was the one man alive kind enough to explain to him the point of the story about the Red Bank Italian. The *Times* was unusually arch and aloof; the *Post* played up the event for all the psychiatry that was in it: Frederick Hacker, the great Los Angeles authority on terrorism, explained the gesture as relieving a long-suppressed desire to shit on daddy's carpet. I mused over this. Good enough. Maybe it was that. "Everything capable of being imagined," as Uncle Will wrote, "is an image of Truth."

The terrorists of the Manhattan Neutron Bomb Ripoff had escaped in three eighteen-wheel trailer-trucks down the Jersey Turnpike—and had not been apprehended, thanks largely to a local of terrorists in the Teamsters that had turned three gasoline rigs sideways in the middle of the southbound Maryland Interstate. There was autumn fog, so choppers were useless.

A few other stories that made the front page, each reflecting something about our times: an assassination attempt; on *The Muppet Show,* Andrew Klein, of Prospect Avenue, Brooklyn, a puppet technician, lost the tip of his thumb—when asked about the likelihood of a conspiracy by another network, Gerald Ford, aging former President and member of the celebrated Warren Commission, said, "I'm not guessing. We were mistaken before."

I was frittering away Time. I knew it. Sweeley Leech, with a great bag of Fritos, was catching a Doug Henning magic show at the Helen Hayes. We were to meet after the show, catch a bite at Le Pot Noir (a divine little Provençal restaurant in the Fifties near Tenth), then take the chopper back that night to West Virginia.

I munched the edge of a steaming, crisp taco. I thought of this amazing man: my father, my lover, my own dear Sweeley Leech— a mortal who had, I believe, just stared eyeball-to-eyeball with Jesus—now sitting amid small, softly farting children with their Julie Andrews nannies, and Weight Watcher matrons from Fort Lee and Livingston, watching a strange child do illusions. Illusions! O, my darling Swee, you see through every illusion. But that you bother is more reason for me to love and adore you. Do you wonder, love, that I wandered (happily) from bed to bed seeking your image?

A pleasant-faced American Indian in a buckskin tuxedo went past singing arias from *Tosca* and leading five saucy, butt-wagging, officious Pekingese.

An elderly James Mason type in Old School tweeds and a walking stick of undressed furze hurried toward me. Under his white locks, into his ear was pressed a blasting eight-track tape deck. The old man was cursing and shouting. I detained him an instant. He turned down the volume violently and glared at me.

You obviously hate that rock, I said. Then why do you listen to it?

Because I love to hate it! he snapped, flicked up the roar of the Moogs and Fender basses, and padded off into history.

The world is full of such extremes in these curious nineties. Very tender souls move side by side with those who love to hate. You see, under TRUCAD there are no wars, no depressions, and no patriotism. Patriotism has been replaced by Solvency, with a Bill of Rights rewritten in the Constitutional Revision Act of 1988 to equate solvency with virtue. Money is God, they tell us; with their vast money, TRUCAD is splitting God like they split the atom. Or so they claim.

I stood in the sundown shadow of the candy-striped awning of a lovely little art gallery called La Mère de Cézanne, run by a very ancient Frenchwoman who may very well be. I stuffed my newspapers into a cement receptacle, narrowly avoiding injury to a small fairy from Santo Domingo whose ancestors, the night Columbus landed, ran to the beach bearing gauze bags full of great luminous fireflies. I picked him up, kissed him, and put him back in the receptacle.

I dove into the art gallery and sank to my knees, in prayer, before an absolutely mouth-watering Renoir. Tiny as a book jacket. Framed in candy and gold whipped into hard, glittering lace. But my eyes were on the ankles—the well-shod feet—of an apparently mouth-watering man standing before a fake Modigliani. Advertised as a fake, of course, for such are the times. For example, in a window of Knoedler's this morning I had seen, side by side, Andy Warhol's *Campbell Soup Can* and a simply edible little still life of strawberries by Chardin. The Warhol was five times the price of the Chardin. This, I believe, is what Art Circles now refer to as the Weight Watcher Principle in Art.

The ankles stirred. I adored his shoe buckles. I was sure he was some divine lost pirate. I wanted him to take me captive. At once. He did not see me there in the jelly of orange and yellow shadows by the corner. Neither did Mère de Cézanne. He was doing something. Obviously furtive—obviously criminal. I adored him the more. Out of his briefcase came a painting—identical in every way with the phony Modigliani he had been studying. The shift was done in a sleight-of-hand gesture which would have charmed my father.

I stood up. He saw me. He knew that I had seen. My face must have been flushed and my eyes bottomless and glittering. Under my eyes it always gets a little puffy when I'm turned on sexually. He stared at me, and our eyes said back and forth what we knew the other had seen or been seen doing. He shrugged and a little smile quivered in the corner of his lips. I went over to him slowly, feeling warm perfumes wafting up from the various gardens of my flesh, counting on them, too!

You saw, then, he said.

It doesn't matter, I said. The whole material world is based on theft. Do me a favor.

Anything.

Take me somewhere, I said.

I folded thumb and forefinger around each lapel and looked up through my bangs.

Because I want to suck you off, I said.

His eyes saddened. With a fine gesture, modest and respectful, he pointed into the shadows, where something of lace and Shantung silk sulked like an enameled Klimt icon. I made out the form and face of a charming young girl—of no more than nineteen—who stood smiling at me.

She just has, he said. I'm awfully sorry.

Blown you?

Divinely, he said. Though I'm sure you would have done as well.

Then I quote Juliet, I laughed. "Ah churl, drinke all, and leave no drop for me."

With a laugh like a bell the girl came through the pale, transcendent light with her arms stretched to me. I could see the milky glimmer on her full lips, and I shivered with anticipation as she pressed her pursed mouth to mine. Our breaths stormed for a moment before a small warm flood of my new friend's semen passed out onto my tongue. She kissed him then, too, and ran out into the evening. His sperm tasted like hot butter and Clorox. I smiled a moment, eyes closed, culling its sweetness into my throat, and he came over and laid his hand on my arm.

Since we have all three communed so sweetly, he said softly, I feel that you and I are very old acquaintants.

I smelled the salt-tang, seafroth smell of a fine bouillabaisse simmering somewhere in the rear rooms of the ancient French lady's quarters. She did not miss a trick. She had, I am sure, seen every unzipping, every bit of sucking, and the final coming between two loving mouths. Her eyes twinkled like snails upon an affable old log. But she had not spotted the theft.

We began walking slowly toward the Fifth Avenue Brentano's. He smelled like strawberries and copper—rubbed copper. I wanted to stop him and bite his earlobe.

So you're an art thief, I said, however.

Among other things, he answered, knocking a V-8 can into the gutter with his blackthorn stick. I am also—

The pause made me feel not that he was quibbling with himself over telling me but rather how he would tell it.

I am also a TRUCAD agent. And you are Fifi Leech, Sweeley's girl.

I'd rather talk about your art thefting, I said. Politics bores me.

I appreciate that. I won't dwell on it. I just want to get first things first with you right off. Politics. The fact that I was sent out of headquarters this morning with the instructions to waste you.

What was her name? I asked after a moment, sauntering a few steps ahead.

Who?

The girl who went down on you at La Mère de Cézanne. The one who made us a kind of trinity of desire.

You heard what I said, Fifi. I mean, you did hear me say I was sent out to kill you? Aren't you afraid of death?

O, squeamish about getting it over—but not even a squeam about surviving it. Are you?

Am I what?

Going to kill me?

No, he said, walking faster now.

Then tell me about art thefting, I said. I've never stolen anything, but I adore crime stories. And some criminals. Most, I'd say. Not like my sister. She simply devours Mafia gangsters—the old Calabrese style, not the new white-collar WASP Mafia.

Such as myself, he laughed. Name: Adonis McQuestion. Age: thirty-two. Religion: Methodist. Ancestry: Irish and Scotch-Irish.

Sex: Let me count the ways, I said.

No, he chuckled. Male. Not a machocist. Not a homosocial. Just a really average nice guy. Believe me, Fifi. I'm not going to kill you.

He harrumphed, and hammered on his pleasant palm with a seasoned old billiard-ball briar after much stuffing of tobacco from a small sealskin pouch. The smell of his blend, rummy and acrid and male, mixing with the taste of his seed, began to turn me on to sex again. A slow tear coursed wistfully down toward my knee.

I never killed anyone, he said. I'm new at this. I don't even like it. If I didn't have my—my art hobby to support me, I don't know what I should do.

Poor baby, I said. But tell me—what will you do with this original, now that you have it? Throw it over the fence? Is that the phrase?

First, he said, I must correct a false impression.

Yes?

He indicated the open briefcase; a broken gemmy light glittered in its deeps.

This isn't the original, he said. This is the—

His voice fell and I smelled his darling breath.

—this is the priceless Vernor Forgery.

I don't understand.

Aren't you into art?

Well, no one ever cut off his ear and gave it to me. But I adore painting.

I bit my lip.

Besides, I said. You didn't answer me. What was her name?

Soleil, he said. My adorable, edible Soleil.

Let me be clear, I said. I am not jealous. We shared—she shared you with me. That was beautiful. I love her. It's just that I want to know the names of people I love, Adonis McQuestion.

You have perfectly enormous eyes, he said. And lashes so long I bet they wear holes in your glasses.

I do wear glasses sometimes, I said. But never mind that. You say—you mean to say you replaced the original of that exquisite Modigliani with a forged—no, it's the other way round, isn't it?

Entirely, he said. But perhaps I must explain something. Something about art in 1992.

Please do.

Forgeries are in, he said. Really great, inspired forgeries. This is fairly recent. Back in the fifties only a few eccentric old professors began to collect Thomas J. Wise and other literary forgeries. The Folger, Princeton, Huntington Hartford, even the Library of Congress. Then painting forgeries. The great Dutch forgeries of the unknown Brueghels are in the Louvre today, you know.

I didn't realize that.

Today the art world bows at the feet of some of the greatest technicians the world has ever seen—forgers, of course, but no doubt geniuses all. Last month in Antwerp I saw the literally indescribable Lowenstein Forgery of *The Last Supper*. I tell you, even the little dabbles of updating didn't upset or offend me—the Burger Chef dish, almost unnoticed, by Saint John's elbow, the Diet Pepsi peeking out from behind Judas Iscariot's sleeve.

He shook his head sadly.

Poor Mère de Cézanne, he said. She knows I steal from her. She puts up priceless imitations in her gallery, knowing that she will be preyed upon by scum such as me. She knows all too well that the forgery which I steal from her is worth a king's ransom, but she is happy with the little, fading, dusty, fly-specked—and relatively worthless—originals. I hate to think of cheating her so. But if I am to get out of TRUCAD I must have some respectable line of endeavor.

I understand you, Adonis.

Do you, Fifi? O, I am really a much misunderstood man. I was desperate the day I swore in with TRUCAD. It was the day after a rival—right out from under my nose, at the Whitney—made off with the unbelievably esteemed Brickman fake of Picasso's *Les Saltimbanques*. I was—well, let's not talk about it, please.

But why did TRUCAD send you to kill me?

Not TRUCAD. Their police arm—the League.

What League?

The League of the Red Green Confusion.

I don't know about it.

I'll explain in a minute. Back, however, to the reason for hitting you. It was to hurt—unbearably hurt—your father.

Why?

TRUCAD has computed him, Fifi. They've calculated that he is about to write something that will shake the world. A book, they say.

I fluttered my eyelashes.

Don't give me that eyelash thing, he said. You know perfectly well he's planning a book.

Well, if I do—you tell me. Then I'll say maybe if you're right. Just maybe.

The League thinks it's some kind of religious or philosophical treatise. A very dangerous one.

That was close to home. I winced.

All right, I said. That's miles from it, but at least it's relevant. And this—your League thought that my death would upset father so much he wouldn't be able to write?

Right. I know. It stinks. I know enough about your father and his—his outlook to know that your death would just make him write the book all the faster.

Right, I said. So what else is new?

I think I love you, he said, and kissed me on the neck, in the warm shadow between ear and shoulder blade. I leaned into him. New Yorkers went around us. When a fat bulldog, wheezing and strumming on his catarrh, tangled his lead round both our legs, we broke up laughing into each other's breaths. A moment later we were heading up Fifth.

Let's go to Rumpelmayer's for sodas, I suggested. I have time. I have to meet father at seven, but that's nearly an hour and a half. I think I love you, too.

Nothing permanent, he sighed. Just eternal.

Everything is permanent, I said. Everything we love, we touch, we fuck—everything is part of us and permanent. And beautiful.

I fished in my stash.

Broadway Specials—that's the soda I like. Chocolate and coffee ice cream. O, God, I am ravenous. Got a light?

I held up a legal joint and we shared.

An eight-track came squalling past in the cradling arms of a young Hispanic wearing a sweater reading ORAL ROBERTS UNIVERSITY SCHOOL OF ORAL SURGERY. We tittered into the fading light and hurried on past Rizzoli's. I saw one of Cousin Davis's books— *La Voce de Glory*—amid some open Léger and Marino prints and felt a warm, sad love for someone dear but gone.

> Ain't no semen on mah mustache,
> Ain't no 'gasm in muh beard.
> Ah'm a macho baby—

What do you feel about the future of American music, Fifi?

Well, we survived the Tijuana Brass.

You know the smoky haze deep in a topaz—that's the way the hour was: the late garden of the day, and light slanting and slashing hard Georgia O'Keeffe affirmations upon the slotted stone and steel walls of the city. I breathed in the winy air and smelled the good male smell of him in the aura of us both as we wended up the avenue.

Two cabbies in the Plaza drive were discussing how the northward trek of the dread Brazilian fire ant had been checked with a remedy simple and folkish as penicillin. A spray composed of a mixture of Fresca and Colonel Sanders' chicken batter. Ants had been seen in clumps, floating back to the Antilles on the naked Gulf: riding freighters, oil tankers—anything—to escape this dread insecticide Vomex.

Adonis squeezed my ass and clumped his pelvis sideways at me, throwing me deliciously off balance.

I stripped raindrops off the leaves of a branch and threw them, laughing, in his face. We clung. I could feel the sweet, aching hardness of his cock through my dress. We started over toward the St. Moritz.

How does this League know so much about my father?

The League, he said, is directly under TRUCAD's scientific development program. I don't know whether you know how far ahead of us the Soviets were back in the eighties in parapsychology. Then,

with the Unification of Nations Treaty back in 'eighty-eight—after
the Closet War—West and East pooled their psychic wisdoms.
There's dark talk now about their actually having discovered how
to program into an afterlife. Marvelous, eh? When you consider a
theory that I have heard of—a theory the League's developed, after
an old pupil of Hobiger's—that may mean such control of the afterlife will take place. And that a man might be sentenced not
merely to death but death plus a season in hell. Frightening, eh?

Not really, I said. When you know the antidote.

Religion?

The Criste, I said. His Lite. Sweeley will tell you. Don't hold
back dear Sweeley's book.

Somehow, said Adonis McQuestion, I don't think I could.

He mused on up Central Park South, pondering and solemn beside me.

I really doubt—he laughed—that anybody could. Because—you
know why? Because it's—it's in the air of the world these closing
years of the two millennia. It's a sweetness. If Sweeley Leech were
destroyed tonight, I think someone else—somewhere—would write
the selfsame book.

We were at the St. Moritz now. We meandered up to the Café
de la Paix—still open on the sidewalk, under the tinted Swiss aw-
nings and tables with tinted Swiss francs. A lovely couple sat at the
corner.

These are bad times, said Adonis. But the new sexual freedom in
the air—the lack of shame—it is really beautiful.

Yes. It is the beginning of the New Age—the Age of God's
Love—as manifest between our simple selves.

Watch, he said, a twinkle in his eye.

He drew me to the table where the black-haired boy in the wintergreen blazer and the luscious little blonde with the auburn eyebrows were sitting. Adonis leaned and whispered something to the
couple.

Brown! cried the girl with delight.

More of a chestnut hue, insisted her boyfriend.

Brown, darling, pouted the girl.

A little reddish, he amended. Show him, dear.

The girl pulled up her scalloped skirt to the limits, round her waist. She wore no panties. Adonis and the escort stared with approval at the neat diamond of chestnut hair. Adonis led me inside Rumpelmayer's.

A Broadway soda?

Yes, O, yes. O, I'm fairly dying for it.

Anything else?

Yes, something else. Dying for that, too! But we can't, Adonis. I have to meet father in an hour. O, I do wish we could fuck. I adore you, really. Can I take a come-check on it?

John, the counterman, mixed our Broadways. Adonis had a watercress and turkey salad on rye. I licked some mayonnaise off his lip. I love to redd up lips.

If TRUCAD, I said slowly, wants to stop father's book—why hit me? Why not—and I go mad at the vision of it—why not hit him?

They're scared of him is why, said Adonis after thinking it over a spell. They're scared he might be—well, they have a theory that Billy and Oral and all of them had it right, that the Second Coming is due. The thing that mixes them up, the issue they can't fathom, is why, if your father should be the—the Second Coming, why he is so set against the Church.

Because he knows that the Church has become the citadel of the Anti-Criste.

I suppose so, said Adonis. Still, it's not the Church that is bad—it's the people in it.

Sweeley calls that the biggest lie of our time. Of course the people are good. It's the thing they make together when they forsake their individuality and become presbyters and false prophets. So you have it backward. The people in the churches—people everywhere—have a need for spiritual truth as strong as their need for food or sex or water. Can they be condemned—the fundamentalists, the Catholics, the Jews, the whatevers—for drinking polluted water if all the world's water has become polluted?

We could get a room at the St. Moritz, he said.

No, I said. No no no no no. I told you I have to meet my father. We can't fuck tonight.

He nodded, this time with rue on his upper lip. I kissed it away, too.

You see, he said, they really are suspicious that Sweeley Leech might be the Second Coming. And if they killed him—well, you know what happened the last time. Two thousand years of lousy residuals.

I seized his face as gently as I'd seize a flower and turned it toward my eyes.

Listen, Adonis, I said, Sweeley Leech is the Criste. But so am I. And so are you. And everybody. Jew. Muslim, Sumerian, Aztec, Ife, Babylonian—whatever. He is inside us all. Sweeley just tore out a bigger hole in his bushel to let the Lite stream out.

He smiled at me as I flipped his lip with my finger.

What will you do now? I asked. Now that you no longer can carry out your assignment to waste me?

Follow you, he said. And that won't be hard, love. I know what comes next, you see. The League will program another person to do the job. My job, from here on out, is to get in between.

Thank you, Adonis McQuestion. I do love you.

Me, too, Fifi. So from here on out, I'm shadowing you.

I stroked the hairs on the backs of his beautiful hands.

> All women shall adore us, and some men
> And since at such times miracles are sought.
> I would have that age by this paper taught.
> What miracles we harmless lovers wrought.

He touched my left breast, through the cloth.

But explain me something, Adonis. The League. You mentioned it: the League of the—what did you call it?

The League of the Red Green Confusion.

He fumbled in his briefcase and came out with an Ishahara deck—cards for determining color blindness. They were cards a little larger than a playing deck—each with a circle, looking something like a thriving germ culture, of varicolored dots the size of peas. Picked out in a mosaic were the numerals 73—or 45—or perhaps merely a big 2. If you were red-green blind, you saw one number. If you had normal vision, another.

Realize the power, he said, of an agency that can speak—via television—to a scant seven percent of the world's men, and less than three percent of its women. Think of the access an evil government agency would have into those minds. Quite secretly, understand?

And a nice exclusive little ready-made group of people who are al-most wholly subject to your orders.

How? Subliminal television, you mean. I had heard TRUCAD was using it.

Exactly.

I wrinkled my nose.

But how—I mean I don't understand how flashing a card subli-minally on television and making one person see seventy-three while the other person, the color-blind viewer, sees forty-five—how could that change anyone's—? O, I think I see.

I stared at him, blinking.

Not numbers, I said.

Exactly, Fifi. Smaller dots. More intricate designs. Not numerals but words. Sentences. A color mass as intricate as the dots in a news photo. And spelling out one sentence to the color-blind, and an op-posite sentence to another, normal-visioned person.

So that, I said, a man, color-blind, and his wife and children, nor-mal color perception, could be sitting watching TV, and— whoosht—he gets one thought flashed subliminally to him, and the wife and children get another.

Exactly. He raced on: You see how deadly a power is held here. People begin to come in—to sign up—not knowing why, not knowing what they expect, not what they may be expected to do.

And up-to-date new messages being subliminated all the time.

It is strange, he said. The League is almost a hate organization, a police group which is unaware of itself. It makes for such really fear-beholden members.

What if the color-blind receptor tells his wife and children what he has read?

He doesn't know what he has read. He can't know. It's flashed subliminally.

Are you a member of it?

No. I'm with the new Mafia—government-controlled now, as if it always weren't. As you probably know, the WASP Jimmy Carter, Rockefeller boys bought out the old Sicilian Mafia back in the late seventies. For a reputed two trillion. I don't know; I've heard that much.

He sucked loudly at the last of his Broadway and then ate a glob of ice cream.

The irony is this, he concluded. The old Godfather Cosa Nostra is dispersed—drinking, sniffing coke, and getting blowjobs from Palm Springs call girls—

Working girls, I corrected. "Call girls" is not beautiful.

I kissed his chin.

I did it once, I said. In Los Angeles.

You were curious?

Very.

About what working girls were really like?

O, no. I knew that. I wanted to be a whore—that's a perfectly legit word—because my sister, Lindy, was thinking of becoming a nun. I wanted to understand that. Nuns.

You became a whore to understand nuns?

O, yes. Don't you see how much alike they are? Identical, really. Women who spend almost all their time with other women—hating men, loving a Gothic, abstract cock called John. Or Jesus. Whores are really very ethical people. So are nuns.

You're a sphinx, Fifi, an oracle of Delphi. I never quite agree with you, but I know I adore your pretty head.

He pushed a bang back out of my left eye.

Did your sister become a nun?

Of course not. She got scared off.

How?

Well, she learned that she'd have to become the Bride of Christ, and she remembered promising her second husband when they broke up that she'd never marry a Jew.

Jesus?

Of course. A rabbi.

Well, it's an abstraction.

Yes. So is all prejudice.

You know, said Adonis, I think I know why I suddenly realized not only that I couldn't ice you but that I owe it to you to see that no one else does. Maybe owe it to myself.

Thank you.

And Sweeley Leech—does he need my protection?

No. He has a higher one. But thanks, lover.

Yet I think—I think I would lay down my life for him. And that's a dumb, romantic, ass-wipe thing to think.

No, it isn't. Sacrifice is one of the liberators of the Criste Lite.

I spotted a flame of geranium Shantung in the light from under the pastel awning—a bolt of ribboning red hair and white teeth flashing from under the birdwings of a laughing woman's mouth. It was Soleil. She had followed us, I suppose. Or perhaps it was old Causal Liaison again.

May I join?

You already have, darling. Back at Mère de Cézanne's. Please sit beside me. We three are really One.

What is your name?

Fifi Leech. And you're just Soleil.

Do you want to order? asked Adonis.

No. I'm not hungry. Yes, just Soleil. Is it too—well, seventies-ish?

I love your name, Soleil.

Fifi, don't you agree that Adonis looks like Warren Beatty?

No. He's himself. Why Warren Beatty?

Because I just sat beside Warren Beatty when I went into Gaspard de la Nuit's for a raspberry brandy. He hit on me.

Wanted to make out with you?

Yes.

Why didn't you let him? He's adorable.

Because I think I fell in love with you back there at Mère de Cézanne's, Fifi. Do you mind terribly?

I—

O, you do. Aren't you bi? I was sure you were back there when I kissed you.

I hate bi. I hate hetero. I hate homo. I hate little tokens like food stamps to get you laid. No. If I'm anything, I guess you'd have to call it multisexual. I think, you see, that there are three hundred million people in America. And every one of them a different gender.

O, God, Fifi, now I know I adore you.

Yes, and I could so easily reciprocate, darling—except that I think I have the hots for Adonis just now.

Soleil slumped, disconsolate, her flame of silken hair dropping over the blazing flower-hue of her low-cut dress. I could smell her aroused state—clean, saline, faintly sour, and with the malty, heavy overlay of *odeur de femme.*

I glanced at my watch—the digits blazed like fireflies. I had twenty minutes to meet my father. Fifteen, if traffic wasn't bad, in the cab down to Forty-fifth. I decided to chance it. I fished in my purse for money. Three nickels, a transportation token good in Philadelphia, six dimes, and a bank note left over from the unrobbery. Woodrow Wilson's mean, ascetic, lifehating face on it. One hundred thousand dollars. I ran out to a pleasant-faced black standing beside a roomy Checker cab—one of the new Chevrolet-Datsun make.

Please, I said. May I buy your taxi?

Say what?

I want to buy your cab. It's good. Here. Take it in to the desk clerk in the hotel. They're experts.

The man turned the bank note over and over in his fingers in the heavenly, rippling light of early evening.

Say—what are yuh? Flaky?

Then Adonis stepped in. He gently unfolded his crocodile-skin ID folder. The man saw something—a League identification, I guess.

The bill is good, Adonis said. You can see who I am. With the government. I'd know counterfeit.

The shield alone cost eighty thousand dollars, said the man. The cab is worth maybe eight thousand, used. There's three of you. And I'm going to play half this hundred thousand on the Futura at Belmont tomorrow—third race. Thanks, ladies. Thanks, fellah. Any trouble with the cab, contact me through Dow-Jones. 'Bye.

O, I felt awful—standing up father even as much as five minutes. But I was faced with a dear friend in need. And I know what Sweeley Leech would have bade me do.

In a moment we were doing it. No one looked in the cab window at the billowing, laughing tangle of naked legs and flashes of laughing teeth and crisped, moist hair.

Adonis's erect cock looked like a women's lib statue with a cervix on top. Soleil and I took turns doing him, our lips meeting like electric things over the gentle, jolly, soft mushroom cap. When his come began—the semen strutting and roping out into the warm light from the café—Soleil caught most of it. I let her, and she smiled at me with doped, ecstatic eyes, his milky seed latticed and clinging between her sweet, fluoride-bright teeth. She had not come yet; I had, twice, and her face was puckered with want as my fingers separated the blessed, rosy petals of her sex and began to love her. O temple, O playground, O tavern and tabernacle of womanness—how I adore the taste of girl. My nose was quivering with the marvelous scents of what was happening—the bright, bitter sting of the semen smell and the oceanic tartness of the feminine. Soleil began to chant when I began to rim her darling little buttercup of an asshole. My hands, which are large for a woman's, almost met around her waist. Nobody was doing me. Nobody had to. I was at my happiest, gloriest, holiest—giving pleasure, lovely pleasure.

Against my probing finger and my lips I could feel Soleil's labia begin to gather and shudder and flood as the orgasm swept like a Texas tornado through her Gulf Coast. Her chant fell to a drowsy, grateful, happy whisper. We got our clothes back together and sat up. Nobody was looking in the window of the cab at our Joy and the miracles we harmless lovers wrought. As I slipped my feet into my loafers, I saw Sweeley Leech over the edge of the window.

Father, I'm sorry.

It's all right. The miracle has come.

I glanced down at what he was carrying—a Red Apple shopping bag. He held it open so I could see: a plain yellow ruled pad designed all over and on both sides in cola. I saw the glimmerous, ghostly shine it gave off. And yet the bare glimpses of it filled me with such Joy that I laughed in spite of myself.

O, father, have you started the Criste Lite?

I have written it, finished it—it was more simple than I thought.

By the way, father—Sweeley Leech, this is Adonis McQuestion and Soleil.

I love you, smiled Sweeley, and went on.

Adonis and Soleil got out the other side of the cab and wandered around to where they could stand beside father and me.

I wrote it in the light of the aisle light—during the magic show.

All of it?

O, Fifi, if you knew how simple it is. And yet how difficult to remember. But I have done it—I have remembered. And it's here. It's here.

He smiled and kissed me.

Say good-bye to your friends. Then we'll take off.

Soleil threw her arms around me, her lips pressed mutely into the hollow of my throat.

97

Remember me always, darling, she breathed. But promise to love others, too.

That's what I always say, dearest Soleil. O, how did you know?

Your mouth taught me, your fingers, Fifi—your insane little tongue between my legs. O, I do adore you, Feef. Please remember me as something besides just a crazy little redhead in a green Shantung dress.

I drew back, smiling, alert.

Green?

Yes, darling. Paris green. Grass green. Shamrock green.

It's *red,* dear, I said. Geranium. Rust red. Autumn red.

O, I know. I'm—

You're a member of the League—I smiled—of the Red Green Confusion.

You guessed. Adonis isn't. But I am, dear. Does it matter?

I don't care.

O, Fifi, it *won't* make any difference. Adonis and I will be like your shadows. Protecting you and your father from whatever. And inevitably—during our long windings through adventure—I know another night of love lies ahead of us. Somewhere.

She and Adonis both kissed me, and then, to his infinite pleasure, they kissed Sweeley Leech and ran off together, young and adorable, toward Sixth Avenue.

Did you find Joy? asked Sweeley Leech, and we drove my new Checker toward Fifth on our way to the Plaza Hotel, atop which our chopper was fueled and waiting.

Unbelievable Joy, father.

It shines all around you. I can see the light of your having given Joy—the Criste Lite.

The shopping bag seemed to give off moonrays. I kissed my father.

We got out of the cab and said good-bye to it on Fifty-ninth in front of the hotel.

An aged Broadway chorus-line dancer—old and wild in the face and with better legs and ass than mine—came over to Sweeley Leech and pointed to the shopping bag.

Your flashlight is on, she said.

I know, said Sweeley Leech. And it will light the world, dear.

And before he grabbed my hand and raced for the elevator, he gave the old gypsy a kiss, and a feel, and a ten-thousand-dollar bill—another of those which, unfortunately, had been overlooked that day.

My radiophone buzzed. I flicked it on.

Feef?

Yes, Lindy.

Is it over?

O, no, darling! I screamed happily back into the little case on my wrist. Over? Darling, it's just *begun!*

Is father—well—inspired?

More than that. The book is finished.

Finished? What do you mean, finished? It takes months, years, to write books.

And all of them—if they told just the Truth—could be written in fifty pages. In an hour.

There was a puzzled, probing pause.

You mean—father has written his book in New York?

In the aisle light of the Helen Hayes Theater. On both sides of the pages of a yellow pad.

Well, slender volumes have been known to do well. Gibran. Benton. McLuhan. Yes, I think for a book of inspiration it should be short.

Inspiration, shit, I said. This is the Criste Lite, Lindy.

O, I know, Feef. And I want you to know I'll do whatever I have to do to get it published. Anything.

She rang off then. Leaving me uneasy. *Anything.* I knew she meant just that.

I smiled, though, thinking: Every book could be this short—if only the writer had two thousand years.

# S·E·V·E·N

There never was a time when I did not exist, nor you,
nor any of these kings.
Nor is there any future in which we shall cease to be.
*—Bhagavad Gita*

Violet sky. Crumpled, mauve infinities pierced with sharp, silver hatpins of moon. Stars frozen in flame, and planets flirting and flickering their nebulous eyelashes over the coquette's fans of cirrus. Below, the endless American land—a great dark dish of beaten pewter and the dark floss of forests, gleaming with autumn glory like oily, Gothic salads, tossed by heroes in death throes. The death of summer down there. Death: the joke of Time, who keeps the ace of springtime up his frosty sleeve, the white rabbit of comebacks in his silk hat.

The black Ohio River shone and shimmered and wound like a dark, sullen torrent of Coca-Cola sewering into the rotting teeth of little children; those dumb, phallic monoliths of smoking industry squandering the air, souring the dear light: Mobay, Solvay, and Consolidation Coal. The cooling towers of Research Cottrell, now Arab-owned, hunkered like a white hen above the blood of April martyrs. Blake's Satanic Mills. We swung over the place where the river, at the Devil's Elbow, coils back like a hog-harried blacksnake and skeedaddles for Sistersville and Friendly. The small, sweet lights of Echo Point pricked the black veil beneath us. We landed in the great meadow below the Gallimaufry. Sweeley lumbered up toward the bungalow, where the pantry shine showed Lindy was probably up making eggs. I caught the shadow of something tiny in the grass beneath my feet—was it one of the Fairy Court? No, it was a disconsolate cricket—angling lamely through the frost, amid the fading green columns of his crashing summer palace. I thought of the desolate little hearts down there in the September grass: each little innocent imagining that, with this chill, like none within his memory, the world is ending. Everything is programmed into his little mind but faith in resurrection: spring that would surely come again. Aren't we like such incredulous crickets, anxious ants, and pessimistic beetles as we swing back and forth, godless, between aeons? Sweeley knows that this age is going to end in tumult and blasphemy and chaos within months from this tiny Now. He knows it. But he knows that it will be no more than the crisping in flame of an autumn leaf to make the good mulch for May when she comes hungering.

Man is Eternal. Individual, thinking, conscious Man is Eternal. But what of little Us in our Big Now—fucking, loving, eating, sleeping human beings in our little nineteen-nineties, nineteen-eighties—even the crazy seventies and sixties, I'm told—a beetle crushed by a rolling stone, artists afraid of art scrambling back into their cozy little anti-war holes; and among poets, a batch of pale, lifehating godhating naysaying bookclub avatars, scuttling and hopping back and forth in the liberal, cautious, cynical safety of their rabbit-pen warrens.

I didn't go right back to the house. I had a small, friendly visit to pay to a hippie friend living in a small stone cottage a half-mile from the bungalow. Her name is Donna—Donna Agar. She is from California, around Monterey. Today is her birthday, and I was bringing her a present fresh from the Big Easy—a sponge. Well, you know, we didn't have much cash left after our trip and a sponge is nice for the bath. And really quite costly.

Donna is mad. But she is mad in that daft, sweet California-girl way that I think only Mark Twain and Raymond Chandler ever wrote about. All California women are mad. Maybe so much of the Criste Lite streaming and flaming invisibly up from the San Andreas Fault does it. It affects their dear minds. This is not sexist—it is statist, I guess. Anyhow, I adore her—even though I'm always doing numbers on her. We have never fucked. I am a little afraid of California fucking. I hustled out there long enough to be that wise.

Donna was having a party. She was dressed as Florence Henderson in her decline. There was an eight-track playing country and western—a rather lovely song called "April Girl–November Man"—a thing about a young fox and an old dude. Sweet. Everything was done in Appalachian style. Donna and her analyst boyfriend came here in 1988. They seemed born for mountain living. I don't know what would happen—and I'm making no Appalachian apologia—what would happen to mountain culture if it weren't for the old hippies from Haight-Ashbury and Dreamsville, Nevada, and Sweeley knows where all. The natives can't stand the gingham and calico and corn likker myth. They dress like Rhoda or Julie on *Days of Our Lives*. They drive Ford-Toyotas and live in mobile homes. While the sojourners from afar—they come in and pick up the old things and keep them alive. O, well, someday the government will be having that last old Burger Chef declared a landmark.

Hi, Feef.

Hello, Donna. I brought you a sponge. Happy Birthday.

A sponge. You dear. Look—a sponge!

There was a brazier of good Nicholas County marijuana smoldering against the log wall. A luncheon table with checkered tablecloth contained all the goodies. In mad fantasy, Donna (or perhaps David, her consort?) had lettered cards with names above each delicacy. Over the smoked cocktail sausage tray was the sign DEVIL DOOBIES. Over the wine tray, ANGEL PISHY. I was helping myself to a stone mug full of a punch made of crushed raw pawpaws and Yoohoo. I put the half-filled mug unsteadily down, spilling most of it, and wended back to Donna.

Her boyfriend wore dirty, thick-lensed glasses like petri dishes

full of some benign but pale-flowering culture. He inched over to
me. He had a black, untrimmed beard with a face so sweetly infan-
tile as to make the whole effect one of a baby emerging from the
packed, black, cunni-maternal hair. He winced, not liking country
and western all that much. He had a large collection of Brubeck and
Don Cherry sides. Forty-fives. The tragedy of his life was carved in
his liberal, Hunter College face, and that tragedy was the defeat of
George McGovern. David had worked in the California primaries
for Moto, the first foreign-born American President since the early
eighteen-hundreds, was really a fine, loyal executive, true to TRU-
CAD's aims. This was in 1988.

Hallo, Fifi.

Hi, David.

Sorry to hear about your cousin. David—same name as mine.

O, yes, Cousin *Davis.*

I was his analyst for a while.

He pressed his lips together, as if saying: No, you're not going to
get one inch of professional confidence out of me. Think of Cousin
David what you will.

You don't approve of analysts, do you, Feef?

I went to one once. She was so funny. Smoked long black cigars
like Freud did. Wanted me to stop cigarettes.

Cigars, eh? Well, as they say now: A cigar is *also* a good smoke.

And a cock is still a good fuck, I said.

He laughed, but he backed away. Donna's sister came over with
Donna.

We wanted Lindy to come, said the sister, whose name was
Olay.

Yes, Donna said. It seems like all you Leeches do is shuttle back
and forth to New York City.

Lindy didn't go with us, I said.

No, I know, said Donna, but she said she was chopping back tonight.

Really? I said. No, really?

I felt suddenly panicked—things were fitting into place way back
in the sewing room of my mind: stitches holding together a fabric
that seemed ripping, a quilt that was coming apart here, together
there.

Really?

Yes, said Donna. Didn't you know? Something about entering a book in the big Nobel Prize Contest.

Well, she's full of shit about that, Donna.

Well, she sounded determined.

I heard the chopper gunning up then—the blades cutting through the dewdrops of the shimmering moony mists.

Where are you going, Fifi?

The Queen Anne's lace lay like crocheted place mats across the still, flat meadow. I ran hard toward the copter—seeing the shimmer of the micalike disc above it now as it tested the air with its weight, lifted and hovered above the flagstone yard for a moment. Lindy was waving—her face fiendish with righteousness—in her hand a Red Apple shopping bag which I recognized as father's. Yes, I saw that, too—the glints and warm sparkles of light which emanated from its coarse paper mouth.

Lindy, no!

It will win the Nobel Prize! she was yelling to me on the bullhorn from the cockpit window. It will win the prize! It will make father rich again. O, Feef, it must be published.

And I will bet my life, I bellowed, that you haven't even read it! You wouldn't *dare*.

I haven't, she said. I *wouldn't* dare. Not till it's printed. I hate manuscripts. Besides, I want to see the reviews first. The *Times* ratings!

You're *afraid* to read Sweeley's book, I yelled. *Afraid!* If you read it, it would *change* you and you wouldn't be *stealing* it like this. O, Lindy, the Criste Lite wouldn't *let* you if you'd *read* it.

Stealing? O, no, dear Fifi, I'm giving it to the world!

The copter gunned louder then; the dying sunflowers curtseyed and flattened under the downthrust of air. The faint coal of Lindy's Salem Light mingled with the equinoxes. I turned to the bungalow. Loll was watching from the shadow of the grape arbor. It was night and she was so beautiful—beautiful beyond my first-book powers of description. Naked. Breasts like warm mounds of custard. Pubes that glistered like dark, wet endive. And her eyes—cruel with manhate like eyes above the harem veil of an Ashanti slave.

She laughed.

Lindy got your father's book. Lindy has an eye for fitness, I should say.

Get away from me, Loll. Where's father?

In his workshop. Where is he always, when he ain't between my legs, learning about the Light of the World?

There was usually a fragrance about Loll. Now she smelled like Death—not rotten, but empty of anything save hate. The air about her, as I passed within her aura, smelled like a bedroom where they've just redded up after somebody died. She slipped into the mists.

The long lane down to the river highway was pastoral and leafy-shadowed—lambent in that moonshine as it had been for centuries. The river road was the Interstate—a strip as naked and thick and unadorned as the hairless, big wrist of a Good Old Boy. Down the deep night someone was playing a guitar and singing. Probably Loll. She had a sweet contralto that was almost too rich for a woman. The song was "April Girl–November Man." I pushed through the kitchen amber—the holy old lamp haloing the air above the oilcloth-covered table where Lindy's dirty scrambled-egg dish waited for me to rinse and wash at the pump.

My thoughts, as they so often do, wandered down between my legs. I was wet. Panicked as I was about what was happening all around me, I was thinking of Dorcas Anemone. I was sure her betrayal with the quasar-ensemble freckle had led to this. It was a mad, unconnected thought, but it made me horny. I often get horny when I'm scared. Thinking angrily about Dorcas, thinking back. Adorable Dorcas—who got high and ate linguine with her Afro comb in Cavanetti's on Broadway. Who plucked her eyebrows at Sardi's with my roach clip. Who swore she came from a childhood so poor she had her tonsils out two years apart. With a hometown so impoverished that when it rained all the colors ran. Poor baby. I want to know who in the League of the Red Green Confusion or perhaps the TRUCAD Mafia had forced her to do it to me.

Sweeley was standing in the doorway. With a guitar. Singing. It was his singing I had heard, not Loll's. My eyes blurred at his dear image—his head slightly bowed to the remembering of the words, his eyes soft and the blue of a many-laundered denim workshirt, his hair luminous with a queer and newfound grace.

You know what Lindy's done, father?

He kept on singing. Sure. He had to finish the song before he answered so tragic a question.

Yes, he said. Didn't you expect her to?

No. No. No, and I usually have precognition about Lindy.

She's an organizer, he said. She wants to organize the Criste Lite—take it out of the foolish hands of the individual—mass-produce it—church it—temple it—best-seller it—until, just like the last time, it dies a stained-glass death.

Can't you remember it? Can't you put it all down again?

Visions have no sequels, he said. No Xerox in the brain.

It was a vision?

It was. A vision I had half glimpsed for—and when I say the time of it, I say it knowing that only you are listening—for two thousand years.

He smiled.

Maybe, he said, in another forty lifetimes—

I paced the moonlight, counting the flagstones.

I'll go after her. Tomorrow morning. On the New York Greyhound.

For what reason?

To stop her. To get the Criste Lite back. Father, Lindy isn't worthy of the Criste Lite.

Don't say that, love. She needs it so badly.

She hasn't even read it—hasn't even looked at the pad inside that Red Apple shopping bag.

Of course she hasn't.

But why? I'd think she'd be curious.

You heard her. She wants to get the reviews first.

Reviews! Of something like the Beatitudes?

Lindy will come through all this, Beurre. Pray, though. And be gentle with her. Forgive her. She is like so many of her sad multitude. Her God *is* dead. They killed him a long while ago with piety and money and pity and shalt-nots. He's got to be born again.

*Tell* me about the book, then, father.

O, it was everything—so short, and yet it was everything.

Can't you remember any of the words?

It wasn't words. Can you understand that? No words. In heaven, Fifi, there is only form and color. And movement. The Criste Lite had that. It was the—well, it was the damnedest, most godawful *funny* book I ever read. Funny. And horny. A real stroke book!

Horny, beautiful, and funny. For a while there, while it was coming to me in the light of the theater aisle during the Magic Show, I could *hear* again the hills around the town where Criste and Maggie and I lived. Near Weirton. O, I know you find it hard to believe—

No, I don't.

Sure you do, girl. Incredulous of a Weirton two thousand years ago. Yet Weirton *is* that old. Older. I can take you to the pews of the Greek Orthodox Church in Weirton or Wheeling tonight and show you the old shawled women. Of Split. Of Budapest. Of Sarajevo. They brought ten thousand years of oldness to that church, to that Weirton.

What was it like then, father? I mean, say we were there now, and off behind the Gallimaufry, Criste was coming down the old stone road with a bunch of his friends—Maggie and the men.

Let me remember.

Prayers? Hymns?

Prayers, hymns, hell. Laughter. Jokes. Bawdy jokes, too. Drinking songs. And other kinds of prayer.

Criste did comedy?

Hell, he was a clown, honey. Kings know this: None is more sacred than the clown. But Beurre, you *mustn't* try to stop Lindy. It has to be.

But the Criste Lite!

Causal Liaisons, Beurre, Causal Liaisons. Be sure that somewhere else on earth tonight—or in that world elsewhere—a man or woman is getting it down in another yellow pad.

Father, whatever—I'm going to New York City in the morning.

But not to stop Lindy, he said. Please. Not to use Force to save a book whose only meaning is no Force.

He leaned the guitar against the honeysuckle and put his arms around me and we stood swaying back and forth in the wind and the moon, not as lovers but as lonely humans on an incommodious earth.

Lindy would be shocked if she looked at those pages, he chuckled presently, letting me fall back onto the stone bench at the verdant and dewglistening archway to the Labyrinth. She would call it some kinky kind of pornography, I think.

Is it—?

Why, yes. Maybe. I don't know. The feeling you get from it is like a great orgasm that has been frozen and cloned into endless variations and all within the split divinity of a moment.

Yes. Yes.

Beurre, there are ecstasies ten million–fold the ecstasy that you and I knew that night— That you have known with so many, bless your loving woman's heart.

He paced away from me; stood.

Ecstasy of the spirit, he said. It is the final mode of the undiscovered melody. I heard it in the Helen Hayes Theater that night during the Magic Show. It was during the tank escape. No—the levitation act. Anyhow, I wrote it down—

But you said it wasn't words—

It was images—form, as I said. Pictures, they would be to you. I had dozens of colored markers in the shopping bag.

Is it something that could be published?

Yes. With very special color processes. Even then, the Criste Lite, which is found only in original copies, wouldn't be there.

Then there is a chance—?

That she'll enter it in that infernal, fucking Nobel Prize Contest? That it will be chosen from all the other manuscripts from all over the world? Yes. And that it will be published? Yes.

Do you think it will happen?

I will not say. I will not tamper with the spider threads of Chance. Hell, I try to tell you—and I sound like some roadshow Gibran.

He tousled his flame-pale hair with his fingers.

I know, he said. My trying to tell you about what I got on paper in the theater that night—I can't do it. You want words and there were no words—only form. And color.

Can just a few hieroglyphics hold so much magic, father? A few pages of symbols?

The oldest magic, he said. The magic that was one with the Word in the Beginning. And don't misguess the power of a few symbols. I knew a simple Japanese scientist who read four numerals on a scrap of Viennese notepaper and knew that within decades a Japanese city would be incinerated—as it happened, his own.

He kissed me again, this time with passion; I could feel his hard excitement against my leg and I pressed into him. Loll intervened.

There is, she said gently, a New York City Express leaving Echo Point tonight at twelve-oh-two.

Dey's all debbils, Beurre, said Sweeley Leech.

That settles it, I said. I'm going. Tonight. Father, won't you come?

No way. I will do nothing to stop Lindy. To stop anybody. That's interference and hence Satanic. And you mustn't do it!

He held me a moment more, the erection subsiding. I looked at Loll, her lovely mouth curved like a Parthian bow which had long since sent the killing arrow to all men. Father ignored her. But I knew that ten minutes after the bus pulled out for Glory and points north, Sweeley Leech would be like a strong smoothbarked tree wrapped round in the sucking, sweet vines of Loll's voluptuous limbs.

I threw a few things in a bag, found a hundred and twenty thousand dollars Sweeley Leech had overlooked. It was in the Fig Newton jar in the pantry. I tossed in some dresses, my vibrator, best lingerie, pills, a half pound of good Gallimaufry grass, and a tattered, beloved old copy of *The Doves' Nest* by my first love, Katherine Mansfield. Of Auckland. Of Menton. Of the mind of God.

I ran toward New Zealand, up the moon, up the Gallimaufry road to town.

Kathleen, Katherine, I chanted. I would have loved you better than that awful J. Middleton M. O, my dear Miss Beauchamp.

I heard the Greyhound sneezing like a fat elephant round the clump of willows beyond the country's electric cross.

I bought my ticket, one way, and sat brooding over Dorcas and the loss of a freckle that was now nothing but a tiny scar between my legs.

And I slept all the way into Hagerstown.

It was chilly on the bus—too early in the autumn for heat. I had my old mink over me, hunkered up like a boy in the rear seat. Somewhere out of Baltimore I felt a hand under the robe. The seat was perfectly dark. I could make out the shape of a man.

Your hand is very nice, I said softly, after he'd gotten my skirts up. But I really must know to whom I am indebted.

The free hand flicked on the flexible ceiling light. Instantly light flooded the tousled, genial countenance of Adonis McQuestion.

I got on at Baltimore, he said.

He inched up a canvas edge of a tarpaulin, and I caught a glimpse of lustrous browns and golds and cherry. In a gold, old frame.

Peale's best portrait of Washington, he said. In the Peabody. I stole it tonight. The Lebow Forgery—one of the pinnacles of the art. I dread to think what the curators will be saying in the morning when they find they're stuck with that scaly old original.

How did you know I'd be here?

What do you call them, sweet—synchronicities?

He lighted a joint, inhaled twice, passed it to me. We were making out under the wraps. With fingers and things.

That's not why I had to see you tonight, he said then.

Why?

I don't know how to tell you, Fifi.

Something's happened to Sweeley Leech! O, Adonis, where is my father?

He's all right. He'll always be all right, I suspect. It's your sister.

Lindy, I said. The chopper has crashed.

No, Fifi. Nothing that climactic. And in a way—worse.

What, Adonis? O, what?

She's been hijacked. When she landed at Pittsburgh for fuel. In the airport. They kidnapped her—with whatever it was she had with her—and flew on to New York. It must have been valuable. Was it your father's manuscript?

Who are *they?*

I told you once—and you probably knew—that the old Cosa Nostra has been bought out lock, stock, and barrel by the Establishment. A three-trillion-dollar payoff, I'm told. The old Mafia boys are living it up at Roslyn, Palm Springs, Palm Beach, and Havana. A few fag hitmen on Fire Island. But the women—

What women?

The women of the old Mafia. They're like the women from *Lysistrata*. A more fierce, savage bunch the world has seldom seen.

He sighed.

The Cazzo Nostra, they call themselves, mnemonically.

And they have Lindy?

Yes. In New York City.

Then there's a reason for this trip, I said. I wasn't sure at first—now I know. It was meant for me to go to New York tonight.

I think I understand.

To save Lindy, I said, then laughed. Or maybe to save those women from her.

Well, he said. There's nothing you can do right now.

Yes, there is, I said, slipping out of my panties. Come back in the shadows, love, and I'll show you.

I thought you'd never ask, he said, and immediately he was inside me and moving.

But it was far from being a lovely fuck, such as I had hoped for the first time with my Adonis. While he was doing it to me my mind was all a-love with darling Katherine Mansfield in her cold London flat and my high heels were kicking the Greyhound midnight clean into New Jersey. But my eyes were crying themselves dry for poor dear Lindy.

Kids farther up the aisle had a radio—not loud, but bleating, thrumming softly.

It was playing one of the new Love-Spirituals:

> Rockin' in my arms, rockin' in my arms,
> I love my Jesus best way I can.
> I love my Lord like I love muh man,
> Make love with Jesus ever' chance you can.
> Yes, He's rockin' in my arms, rockin' in my arms,
> Yes, I'm rockin' in my lovin' Jesus' arms.

I cried myself to sleep with my head on Adonis's spent shoulder all the way into Philadelphia.

# E·I·G·H·T

He who bends to himself a Joy, Doth the winged life destroy
He who kisses the Joy as it flies, lives in eternity's
    sunrise.
                                                    —William Blake


            The world was all revenge and thou hast said:
            "It is a seething sea!" Earth had no room
            For walking, air was ambushed by the spears;
            The Stars began to fray, and time and earth
            Washed hands in mischief . . .
                    —Firdausi, *Shah Namah* (*Book of Kings*),
                    (translated from the Persian by Warner)


Lindy in Moscow drinking pee-colored Polish vodka and eating
Colonel Sanders' fried chicken and humming "Sventytski's Waltz"
from *Doctor Zhivago*. O, would that she were there!
    Lindy in Leningrad at the Hermitage, shoplifting ideas among
Novgorod icons and the pastry-gold of Romanov presentation

repeater-watches by Paul Burré. Lindy cribbing themes for a speech reporting her tour to the Echo Point Christian Endeavor. O, Criste, that she were there.

But I was on the New York Express, hurtling through the Allegheny night beside a new lover, who smelled like ozone and peppermint and wiry chest hairs, agonizing into the light-freckled and neon-veined midnight after the poor lost Lindy— hardgripped in the fist of the merciless Cazzo Nostra. Was she now safely projecting herself into the Ida Lupino role in *Road House?*—Lindy has a way of astral-projecting among the stars in old films.

They were repairing the Jersey Turnpike. I could smell the smarty-pants tang of asphalt; gravel brightly shotgunned into the bus underbelly. Adonis took my hand.

What are you looking at?

I held up the Polaroid snapshot in the spear of seatlight.

It's a picture of me, I said. Surrounded by fairies. It was taken in the Gallimaufry.

He examined it, smiling. He arched his bunkers at me quizzically.

I see small figures. But they are only tricks of light and shadow—sunspots and speckles among the grass and leaves. It's an optical illusion, love.

That's like saying the stars of Van Gogh are only daubs of oil and pigment. *The Bridge at Arles* an optical illusion. And it is!

I snatched my snapshot back and tucked it reverently into my shoulder purse.

You are a flower, he said, kissing me sweetly. My nipples, through the thin, shawl-collared blouse of spidersilk, tingled against the hairs that foamed thinly through his deep-cut shirt. I would kiss your petals one by one, my love.

The moon divined our intentions and crooned across the sill. The stars set up a great giggling. He lowered his mouth, freeing my left breast from its encumbrance of silk, and mouthed it for a moment, tonguing the nipple in a dance of double-talk that sent top-priority messages clean down to my panties.

I turned on my Sony wristradio. I dialed the Library of Congress recording R-QT-7119F—the Ravel Quartet. It is a new service— hundreds of thousands of recordings in government catacombs, all playing simultaneously and micro-broadcast on specially dialed frequencies. I looked at Adonis. His eyes were closed—into the pizzicatos of the fast movement.

Industry, not infamy, I said.

He quizzicked me again with his marvelous eyebrows.

FDR's speech. After Pearl Harbor. It sounds like he said "a date that will live in infamy." But he really said "industry."

Adonis kissed my cheek again.

It doesn't matter now, he said. There is no Japan. No America. No Russia. No anywhere or anypower but TRUCAD.

I agree. Why are you staring at my ring?

It is beautiful beyond reason, he said. I am afraid to touch it.

It is very old.

How old?

I know it sounds dreadfully institutional, but it's a Late Minoan carved gem from the Sir Arthur Evans Collection—most of it in the Metropolitan. It's from about fifteen hundred B.C.

It looks, he said, like a tiny gold cup full of seagreen Jell-O.

My mind strayed from his interest; I forgot the ring. I forgot Lindy, and the sneezing, elephantine Greyhound.

Is your father, Sweeley Leech, the revolutionary they say he is? Adonis's voice broke into my reverie.

What?

He said it again.

O. Yes. He's been in many revolutions. For example, he played the viola da gamba in the 1729 premiere of the *Saint Matthew Passion* by Bach. And he had another close call when he was tympanist in Paris in 1913 when Diaghilev hurled *The Rite of Spring* at everybody and his uncle. Now, Adonis, do let me meditate for an instant. I'm into a reverie.

But your ring, Fifi. It's—

Hush, love.


It is suddenly a month from now. Thirty days into Time and October—tawdry as a Minsky Magdalene in her sublime rags, rotting in the riot and ruin of summer, and rife with cheeky hints at resurrections. The picture of it upon my receptors is bold as the tinted membrane of a decal on a child's smudged, lunchtime hand. I am stepping out into the patterned flat stones of the court at Echo Point. My feet are naked. The flags are stained and fluttering with the laughter and beckon of leafshadow. Pools of suncoins flutter round my lacquered toes.

I heard Adonis's sweet, low voice somewhere: Fifi? Your ring is twinkling strangely.

I ignored him, deep in autumn nocturne. It seemed so urgent with beauty.

Pools of suncoins spendthrift and spin between my legs. I walk on, as though wading in lights, as though placing each pulsing foot upon the throbbing golden artery of the sun. My toes curl in thousands of delighted Babinskis, yet with guilt, for I know I am crushing fairies to death beneath the whorled print of my simian pads.

This is the suncoined morning that Sweeley Leech will tell me about the man named Judah Samphire. And for some reason, upon this night of strange nights he, Judah Samphire, is into my realms of feeling. But why?

What did you say, Fifi?

I—? Adonis, what—?

What did you last say, love? Sapphire?

No. Samphire. Judah Samphire. Did I say it out loud?

Yes. What does it mean?

He is the short, squat man in a black bowler hat and black suit and beetle-black shoes.

Who does what?

Who invariably appears at the house or cottage of whatever family Sweeley Leech is about to be born into. And points out to them the folly of even considering another name for their child save Sweeley Leech. Who also appears to announce when Sweeley is about to die.

I lighted up a thin joint of Old Field Blossom. I toked, held, and blew out blue heavens. My eyes shortly thereafter fell in love with each other, made love, and produced lovely children. Visions. Metaphors. I wondered how to explain Judah Samphire to Adonis McQuestion.

A mother, I said, is sitting in the shadow of the grape arbors, nursing her new baby boy. She is pondering names for him. Her father's. His father's. Grandparents' names, perhaps. Names of famous statesmen. Caesar. Alexander. Maybe a nice writer. Pliny. Catullus. Suddenly—and mind you, this may be on a morning during the second century—suddenly she sees a tiny black figure on the horizon. She watches. Something in the parallax of the road—something warns her that a man of import is approaching. The figure grows larger, discernible. She sees the black bowler, the black suit, shoes; she hears his chattering tambourine.

Tambourine?

Always. When he comes to announce either Death or Birth he comes clangoring like a Gyptian.

I paused.

He is the Yoke-bearer.

What else?

He brings a small pastry box of pasteboard, tied with butcher twine. Ravishing smells emanate from it. The senses of the new mother are dazzled. Inside the box, which she greedily unwraps, is a fragrant spice cake. It is very special: strewn and scattered with succulent, rare bits of fruit, laced with wines of Cathay and vanished Araby, laughing with spices from the Old Route to Samarkand. It is irresistible.

She eats it.

O, yes. Who wouldn't! And the magic in it takes possession of her soul, spirit, mind, flesh. It prepares her for what Mr. Judah Samphire has to say.

What does he say, love?

"You have a child here. Have you a name for him?"

The mother ponders, her mouth full and exuberant with the delicious cake; though its essences and magic are already taking possession of her soul.

"Sure," she says. "I think we may call him Junior. Frank Junior. After his dad."

"And his last name?"

I snuffed out the roach after one last deep toke. I held my breath and exhaled.

"Smith," says the lady. "After his daddy."

"Wrong," says Mr. Judah Samphire. "His name is Sweeley Leech. Is that clear?"

The cake is finished, gone; but its tonka-bean and wild-vanilla savor haunt the tongue.

"Why, I suppose you are right," says the young mother. "Sweeley Leech. Yes. Yes. It does have a certain ring. I don't know— Yes."

She pauses.

"But why?"

"If it's any of your business," replies Mr. Samphire, "Sweeley is the dear corruption of the word *Seely*—of the Fairy Court. Leech is—and you should know this—a Healer. Any more questions?"

A sweet languor steals over the woman's flesh, invading her loins, making her nipples to stand and her petals to sweat attar of roses.

"Why, yes," she breathes. "Is he, by chance—a Son of God?"

"We are all that," says Mr. Samphire, his eyes dreaming in the morning light, which is the first yearning, molten morsel of light among old elders and willows. "We are each the child of God—but he is the Eldest Son."

He lowers his eyes from the sacrament of sun among the wet forests.

"A reminder," he said. "He is a Demon; he is a Saint. And it must be remembered that when he grows a beard and is able to spurt seed, he must not be given a pony to ride, as are most boys—"

"What, then?" breathes the woman in her thrall of wonder.

"Only a dolphin," says Mr. Judah Samphire, whanging mightily on his tinny Salvation Army, drumlike, bladdered timbrel. "Only a dolphin will do."

And then? asked Adonis McQuestion, fingering my ancient ring.

And then Mr. Judah Samphire is gone up the road. Vanished. Until Sweeley's death draws nigh.

Adonis let his eyes mix with the stars beyond the tinted bus window; he mused at the moon, now at the first silvery sliver of newness.

And did he really know Jesus?

117

Yes. Haven't you? He's in all of us—you, too, you know.

I mean—you know what I mean. I mean did he—brush shoulders with the Man himself?

O, yes.

What was he like?

Do you really want to know?

Sure. I see him in the MGM version. H. B. Warner or maybe Charlton Heston. Something cloned not out of the Almighty but out of Burt Reynolds.

He wasn't like that. His face was not long and ascetic and sad. It was round and pug-nosed and jolly.

Really?

With a tooth missing in front, like his Poor. Hair crisped and curled and tousled. Cocteau said the hair is always crisped and curled over areas of generation. The cock and cunt. The mind of God. You know.

I paused, regathering my father's image of the Criste.

It would seem to me, said Adonis McQuestion, that this image—this appearance—would damage the gravity of his message, the dignity of his appeal.

What gravity? What dignity? I laughed. Criste is a Clown. He is a Fool. A blessed Fool! The Fool of the greatest King!

He is now, you mean?

Lord, he always *was!*

You make him sound more like a small-*g* god than a capital one.

O, that he will be again—and dwell amongst us.

Go on. What does your father say of Mary?

Criste's mother? O, her. Adorable. Absolutely adorable. Small, rather plump—*zaftig,* as the Jews say—round and sweet and juicy as an apple.

I paused, treading cautiously upon the Catholic stones of his mind.

And she was a harlot.

O, come now.

It is true. Not a whore—a harlot. Not a whore—not a good one, that is, because she was always too kindhearted to take money. She lived to give pleasure, to stanch tears, to ease, to please, to warm, and to soften. Above all to soften. Not a thought in her dear little country mind, really, but giving pleasure. Not a brain behind her large, dear eyes. O, Sweeley says you could hear Criste's little troupe coming for miles back in the country. But loudest you would hear the dear little voice of his mother—singing and dancing and twisting in the light, her ragged garments wreathing like a conjurer's clothes—and the blue lights of pagan mysteries winking in the soft, whorled hair beneath her arms, between her sweet, unstinting thighs. Mary. Great Mary. Grant Mary, Gramarye. Grammar. Glamour. And she had a tambourine she clanged, too!

He took each of the fingers of my left hand, the one with the ring, and kissed the tips.

One thing, he said, which I don't understand.

I waited.

If your father's Criste was always clowning, as you say, when was there time for the serious things he had to say?

O, you don't really understand, do you, Adonis? Poor baby.

What?

You don't know that the most serious messages of all invariably make us laugh.

Come now. Suppose that serious message is a sober, realistic, scientific formula?

Pliny tells of a dancer in Aristotle's time. In fifteen minutes of mirthgiving mime he explained the entire Pythagorean Theorem.

We were coming into the really atrocious Thomas A. Edison Plaza on the Jersey Turnpike. The McDonald's there features four-day-old hamburgers, reduced in price, as Oldies But Goodies. We disembarked. I thought for a moment I glimpsed Soleil, ravishing in an Alaskan wolf jacket, getting into a racy Corvette. Adonis helped an old couple down the steps. In mid-career, the octogenarian paused, turned to his dear, doddering mate, and inquired, falsetto: Got your pills, mother?

We had coffee and an English muffin.

How did it get lost?

I understood.

The image of the hilarious and huggable Saviour? O, you know, dear. The Old Men got hold of it. Changed Joy to Tears. Changed Passion to Power. Changed it to the Bruce Barton Madison Avenue Jesus in the Hickey Freeman—gladhanding the Born Again into the affluent Heaven, the open sesames to easy gospel gold. Power is what quenches the Criste Lite. That Lite is a candle in the lamp of One and One alone.

Back to Samphire—this Judah Samphire, he said then. Was he there—always? From the Beginning?

Well, what do you mean by Beginning? I said. Where is Beginning? Where is Ending, love? I can tell that you believe in something you call Reincarnation. It is not like that, lover. There is no Beginning, no End. No Middle. It's all a Spiral. Thinking as you do, a person who dies in the twelfth century would be reincarnated into the thirteenth and later die and move on into the fifteenth. Don't you know, love, that I could die this night and come again to life in a garden in a ravine beside the roaring Aragon in the last year of the Inquisition? When did Sweeley Leech begin his round in the Universe? 1919? Then backtracked through the hallways of Time and Space to a term in the French armies and death at Austerlitz. On into a time ahead of us, even—and then back to Provence in time to stand among the Albigensians against Simon and Saint Louis and the Devil called a God.

I am glad I did not waste you, Fifi Leech.

I am, too, love. Starting life over after death—particularly an unfriendly one—can be tacky.

He laughed again, bowing his tawny face so that a fetching look dangled into his eye.

Mère de Cézanne swears you are a goddess, Fifi. She says she would like to make love with you.

O, I adore her. How old is she?

Some say a hundred and twenty. You say your father played drums in the Paris Orchestra the night of *The Rite of Spring*. Mère de Cézanne was there—in her fifties. She threw a copy of Voltaire's *Zadig* at the detractors. She wants to continue havocking among the Pharisees until her death. What shall I tell her? Will you go to bed with her?

Of course.

I love you, you know, Fifi.

I know that. And I, too. Like a thirteen-year-old in the first sweat of things.

Mère de Cézanne wears the most tiny frothy pink lingerie.

Have you fucked her, dear?

The only article of the Macho Code I still cling to is never to tell.

Bravo. It is an immortal one.

Fifi, he said, I've been trying to ask for hours now—why does the scarab in your ring twinkle and give off lights?

O, is it doing that?

I lifted the great green stone and stared hard into its deeps, searching for a small white dolphin. It would be, when I espied it in my ring, frolicking in the Aegean near Paxi, in the Echinades. Four thousand years from here. The stone was, of course, enchanted. The ancients often substituted glass paste for precious gems—this often to secure a desired color. The paste of my scarab, which is really a greenish-golden aquamarine, if you are able to envision that hue, is imprinted with a dolphin leaping. There is a nude female figure on it—lithe and graceful as the sleek white mount she adorns and not in the stark geometric line of Greek gems of the eighth century before Criste. Sweeley always told me that if my eye were pure and deepseeing enough, I would discern the features of the tiny etched woman and see my own. I think I was always afraid to see that. I know only that at times of peril—mostly when someone I love is imperiled—the figure spurs the dolphin and together they arch and strut and plunge through the infinity of green and unfathomable bottoms of the tiny scarab sea. Atlantan wrecks strew that bottom, doubtless: I have never dared lead my steed *that* deep, but I know that when I take that mad and *enivré* tour within my tiny gem, someone I love is in peril. And I know strangely that I shall make that plunge again—within hours.

Fifi?

Yes.

I felt I had lost you. What is it?

He reached up to my hair, damp with morning mists, and plucked something out. A sprig of sargasso weed, with a tiny seahorse wriggling in it. He dropped both into the water glass and eyed me in frank wonder.

You are a mermaid, he said. A kind of myth. Who are you, Fifi Leech?

That was when I saw Sweeley Leech by the cigarette machine, lighting up a thin, black, Cuban gambler's stogie and tilting his raffish black hat and studying me gravely, through a blue, philosophical curl of smoke.

On the PA they were announcing that passengers on the New York Express should reboard immediately.

Nodding with an ingratiating wink at my lover, Sweeley came to the table, sat down, and took my hand.

I want you to come with me—briefly, Beurre. It is a mission I have to make to a place near here. It is vital. And I want you along. It will take no more than three hours at the outside. I have the other chopper nearby—three minutes' walk. There is a New York Express from Washington every hour. I'll get you on the first one in the morning.

On which, sighed Adonis McQuestion, I shall also be riding.

Good. Beurre needs friends and lovers just now. It is a time trembling on the brink, as it were, of worlds which must make fresh starts.

He turned again to me.

But this concerns us, Beurre—you and me. It seems that Rinsey has been seen. She is alive. She is still beautiful. But she is—

—in danger, I finished for him. Yes, I know. I saw it in the tides of my Minoan ring.

Mortal danger, said Sweeley Leech. Somewhere near a little Maryland river. That's where we're flying.

We are always saying good-bye, Adonis McQuestion.

O, I know, Fifi. But only so we can say hello again.

Righto, cherub. And always remember it.

There was a moon. It seemed we tucked New Jersey under our arm and flew clean into it.

# N✦I✦N✦E

If democracy has disappointed you, do not think of it as a burst bubble, but at least as a broken heart, an old love affair. Do not sneer at the time when the creed of humanity was on its honeymoon; ... For you, perhaps, a drearier philosophy has covered and eclipsed the earth. The fierce poet of the Middle Ages wrote "Abandon hope, all ye who enter here" over the gates of the lower world. The emancipated poets of today [1910] have written it over the gates of this world. But if we are to understand the story which follows, we must erase that apocalyptic writing, if only for an hour. If then, you are a pessimist, in reading this story, forgo for a little the pleasures of pessimism. Dream for one mad moment that the grass is green. Surrender the very flower of your culture; give up the jewel of your pride; abandon hopelessness all ye who enter here.

CHARLES DICKENS, Proems—G. K. Chesterton

Jasper Mayne, an obscure Restoration poet, wrote in 1648: "Time is a feathered thing."

Sweeley Leech calls that line a scientific statement. Time—

winged, feathered, plumbed, its hawk's eyes never sealed—darting both forward and backward, soar and swoop, dive and spiral up-ward—Time always moving. That is Time—that is life—and it is the core of the Criste Lite. Energy moving toward the core of the universe.

O, shit, here I am treatising when you're panting to find out what happens to Rinsey. And who the hell is Rinsey, anyway? *Attendez-moi.*

Rinsey is my mother: Sweeley's true love and darling and mi-gnonette. She is his appetizer and his main dish. She is folly and sa-pience, delight and despair. And she ran away six years ago, on a ravishing spring night, with a fourteen-year-old boy who said he would die unless she went with him.

Something in the smart tang of the Maryland astrosphere made us hungry. In 1990 a new rage swept the country—Mama Lapidus, the first coast-to-coast kosher fast-food network. Part of the almost festive popularity of the restaurants among local outlanders is the chain's colorful High Holiday policy. For starters, they close at sundown every Friday for the weekend. At Purim they close for four days, at Hanukkah they close for a week, at Rosh Hashanah they close for ten days, and then at Yom Kippur they burn the place down.

Here we sat, Sweeley Leech and I, enjoying scrambled eggs with onion and lox and heaps of hot, beaming bagels at our elbow. The air was, it is true, faintly scorched from the last gesture of devotion. But it added its faint hickory zest to the atmosphere.

Now the incredible happened. My wristradio buzzed. It was Lindy.

O, my God, Lindy, it's you. It's Lindy, father.

Of course it's Lindy, Feef. Lordy, don't always come on so emo-tionally! cried the thin, tense voice in the radiophone.

Lindy, are you safe?

I'm with my friends.

Friends?

The women of the—the Group.

Friends. Shit, Lindy, they kidnapped you.

At first I was kept here by force. Now it's of my own volition. Feef, these women are truly into Christ's work. Christ, I said. Not Criste. I abhor that blasphemy of father's.

Lindy, where are you?

Silence.

Lindy—I said, where are you?

In New York City. That's a big place, Feef. That's all I'll say.

Are you happy? Are you safe, love?

Safe in the arms of the finest group of Christ-fearing women I've ever known. Women who have the key to the world's travail.

Which is?

The Jewish role in the collapse of Christendom. Beginning in 1914 at Sarajevo with the Jew Princip, who shot—

Lindy, he was a Serb. Read your Rebecca West.

He was a Jew. But no matter.

Pause.

Perhaps you will allow me to ask father one question. Is he with you?

Yes.

Hello. Hello, father.

Hello, Lindy.

Father, I must ask you bluntly. Do you feel because of the Holocaust in this century that the Jews are exempt from any cavil call or criticism for the rest of time?

Sweeley pondered, but only briefly.

Certainly not.

Do you believe it is proper, then, *occasionally* to say—to speak out about the Jews? Isn't that guaranteed in our Constitution?

I agree, said Sweeley Leech. But that does not give you the right to shout "Ham!" in a crowded synagogue.

O, God, I suppose that's your eternal, infernal Kindness Principle again. Why must you always—in whatever situation or dilemma—be kind?

Kindness is best, said Sweeley Leech. Kindness could save the world—your world, Lindy.

O, fudgy darn.

Lindy?

Yes, Feef.

Are you safe? Are you well?

Safe? Yes. Well? O, a few aches here and there. But I'm all right. There's this divine mentor here among the group—a kind of ancient guru. Mère de Cézanne is her name. But there—I mustn't be giving away clues.

Does she have a protégée named Soleil? I asked.

Silence.

I'm going to come to New York City, Lindy, I said. I'm going to rescue you.

Save your strength, my dear. I am in God's hand.

Lindy?

The tiny speaker fairly winced as she pinched off the conversation at her end, and the tiny receiver rested silent in the lace at my wrist.

Shall we? asked Sweeley Leech then, and paid the check, and we wound our way out through one of the many fire exits, making our way across the state highway toward the chopper in a cornfield.


Again Rinsey filled my thoughts as the air wrenched us up and away and southerly. The image of her: rotund and lavish and ample, all breasts and smiles and comforting hands, a strong tree with branches for many birds. O, she was wild and she was wanton and she was free in Criste's strength!

A few days ago, I saw a flutter as of splinters of living wood upon a sundrenched rock at Echo Point. I bent and peered close: it was two daddy longlegs in amorous dalliance upon that unthinking stone: a ballet of dazzling, dizzying sex upon stilts, preposterous passion enacted upon thin, unsteady ladders, a rickety porn film upon the iris of Thoreau's bald, blasphemous eye. I knelt in prayer before this trash-heap sacrament. My legs felt swollen and ungainly before such spidery elegance: this limber, eight-legged loving. The daddy longlegs seized the lady longlegs and fucked her in pinpoint pyromania whilst the universe sent rays out from these minuscule orgasms infecting the whole cosmos with its lightheartedness.

My eyes lifted from this holy comedy to the Apple County cross. The federal government, after its grateful merger into TRUCAD, quickly relinquished its off again on again fight over the age-old problem of capital punishment. For a while the states dealt with it, and then, with TRUCAD's sanction, they turned the issue over to individual counties and parishes. It makes for some confusion but great local color and festivity and, it must be said, regional enthusiasm. County-parish capital punishment seems to encourage the Christian passion of every small district in the land. Executions are truly religious occasions in which the platitudes and falsehoods of the Christian ethic are imposed in full folk panoply. Some counties or parishes have gallows, some have Lazy-Boy electric chairs (to eliminate the "cruel" in "cruel and unusual" punishment), and a few, such as our Apple County, West Virginia, have an electrified cross. It is about fifteen feet in height and eight feet across. It is powered with current provided (as is the structure itself) by the Valley Power Companies. Death is (they avow) painless and instantaneous. The cross is, of course, computerized and approved by Underwriters; it is fail-safe. It doubles as a Christmas ornament during the United Appeal. The body is—at painful long last—incinerated completely, which, it is admitted, removes some of the festive fun connected in old times with the rite of viewing. The viewing of the ashes now takes place at the Echo Point establishment of Peace the Undertaker. The air—the wind that wafts the smoke of the burning malefactor over the county orchards—bears some taint of scorching and the staining tang of burning, which occasionally reminds the employees of nearby Dow Chemical and Mobay of the parent company in far Europe—and the smudging stench of I. G. Auschwitz charcoaling the orcharded skies over south Germany in another time-interim.

I recollect this because it had brought Rinsey to my mind. Premonitions of death cause what Edmund Wilson might have called, had he been a Believer, the Shock of Precognition. I had such a sense one October day when I was five—that my beloved mother, Rinsey, dear and adored wife of my father, Sweeley Leech, was surely going to die. It was a day of falling leaves. Green substance staggered down the livid, moving light of the sun: it was as if the world were afflicted, greenblushingly, with a magic and enchanted jade snow. One could imagine the sky filled with vertiginous butterflies collapsing and staggering down the luminous air to earth like falling death-green warplanes. Rinsey was ill. She was surely going to die. My adored Rinsey, wife of dear Sweeley—Rinsey, mother of almost Everybody: I thought of her as that when I was small. She was not fat, though she was ample—she spread and divaricated in her pretty clothes—a heave of happiness and giving. She was like Chaucer's Wife of Bath. She was girthproud, flaming red of hair, and ruddy of cheek. She smelled sweet always. On washday she smelled of carved homemade soap and bluing. She was always extra clean—hence her name.

Have any of you best-seller sensualists, devotees of chapbooks to orgasms and the stopwatch ecstasies of the paperback clinics, ever delved into this: the turn-on of smelling sweat on someone you know to be habitually immaculate? Rarely, this happened with Rinsey. At the great bungalow bedroom at Echo Point we all slept together in one huge twenty-foot-square stack of featherbed ticks. It filled half the enormous room, upon the streaked wallpaper of which guttered thick, scandalous candles. They viewed everything intimate about us. If a couple—Sweeley and the great featherbed-bodied Rinsey or perhaps lithe Loll—copulated deep in the ticks of goosedown, no one spied or tittered or developed a hidden neurosis which would afflict her adulthood. All of us lived inside each other. We endured and adored. We smelled the sweet reek of one another's periods and wet dreams alike. We were warm. Warm in common love and warm with foods from the hands of Rinsey.

Walking gravy was one of her specialties: chicken gravy, generally, thickened judiciously and lovingly with cornstarch and chilled until it came out shivering across the Haviland platter from its mold. Custard, yellow and sweet as a smokehouse apple from a bitten, frost-smitten Appalachian orchard. Hams injected with port wine through a veterinarian's hypodermic for weeks before they were Christmas-baked; and so filled with liquor, so drunken with intoxicating gravy, that they literally basted themselves.

In the pantry, where the morning sun calicoed in and splattered the west wall with stains of quivering morning, stood the pie safe— a Fort Knox of finger-dipping serendipity: lemon meringue and custard and butterscotch, deep and gowned in crusts that crumbled like Pharaoh's bones upon the tooth. Rinsey often made her own tomato juice—straining out the center and seeds, which Lindy could not abide, and then thickening it to a hot, sweet, tangy paste to be poured on biscuits. Or quince honey—from the quince bush by the Labyrinth—gritty and tanged at first, then milled and mortared to a thick gold which inched globby from the pitcher onto biscuits or cinnamon-strewn toast points. Ah, sweet, dear Rinsey. Milking the cow's three gallons down to the strippings, as she called them—the last two quarts or so of the old cow's letting-down—and all of it the rarest of creams. Rinsey used to thicken the strippings with cornstarch and sugar and a smidgen of vanilla, and this, too, was poured on hot biscuits, and she called it thickened cream. From an ancestor she culled this recipe—the crushed flesh and juice of staining red raspberries whipped into egg white or stripping cream and served on a blue platter like a blushing snowbank in January. A trifle, she called this. She smelled like all the things she cooked, all the things she rinsed.

She seemed to bear wild flowers in the crannies and crevices of her flesh. A sweet shrub bush grew in the courtyard at Echo Point—in summer it bore small, dusty, purple blossoms which Rinsey used to crush in her fingers and deposit into pockets and plackets about her person. She wore small sachets of pink and honeysuckle, dried and redolent, in her bloomers and in the cornices and pantaloons between her thighs. I remember when I was very small, nursing at the choking, generous flow of her breast, a sweetness and nourishment which seemed to stem from earth's own lavish larder. I sometimes slept between her breasts in the great bed even when I was a teenager; but when I was very small I fought to get to sleep between her great, warm thighs—breathing my dreams in along with the soft, malty odor of her lifegiving cunt. She always smelled of both flowers and the flesh. The Flower and the Flesh— that is the smell by which I always remember Rinsey.

As I say, when I was five, I was sure Rinsey was dying. She did not die. Thanks to me. I heard Dr. Bone name her disease. "Tuberose." I heard the word unmistakably. I ran downtown in a blur of childgrief. I passed Spoon's Confectioners', with its hateful popcorn and caramel breath. I passed suddenly into a fragrance. I looked up in my stunned, special sorrow. I saw the open-air flowers of Saltshaker's Dead Flower Market. Slaughtered blossoms were the *spécialité de la maison*. Slashed iris, guillotined forsythia, castrated calla lilies. And then I saw them—the tuberoses—the flowers that Rinsey was going to die from. I ran to the baskets in the bins. I tore them out, rending them, killing them—the tuberoses in poor, dear

Rinsey's dying chest. I saved her life. While poor Mr. Saltshaker, the florist, ran about trying to stop me, I tore the tuberoses to shreds and scattered them among the cobblestones of Camden Street, in front of where the baker's shop huffed its cinnamony breath of hot cross buns at Christ-tide.

I remember a Thanksgiving party she gave for a small group of Echo Point friends and relatives. It was an exemplar of her good taste—her class. We were rather poor then; Sweeley Leech was either the richest man in West Virginia or the poorest. The maid came through the dining-room doors with the turkey—small but sweet—on a platter. She tripped on a small Oriental rug. The turkey flew off the platter and skidded across the floor. Without raising her eyes from her Paul Revere gravy boat, Rinsey smiled. "Simmy," she said, "would you take that turkey back to the pantry and bring in the other one, please?" Taste. Class. The need—the absolute spiritual necessity of making other people feel good. She had it.

And her humor. I remember the August morning a small boy crept to her in the apricot light of the pantry and hemmed and hawed around for a long while before he could tell her his woe. His Uncle Charlie had told him that if he played with himself he'd go insane, blind, and deaf by the age of thirty.

O, yes! cried Rinsey. Insane as Van Gogh, blind as Milton, deaf as dear Beethoven. Now go, dear, and jack off to the praising strokes of God!

In that sullen, sexy April—lurid as a black eye—a teenage Echo Point boy fell madly in love with Rinsey. She attended him. The need deepened. He decided to ask Rinsey to run away with him and settle upon the island of Timor, somewhere east of Suez. Rinsey consulted with Sweeley, who, after great meditation, acknowledged that the boy did need the experience. And so Rinsey ran off with the boy—six years ago, come hot cross buns—and no word of her till now. Now—in the merciless grip of what Sweeley describes as a time-bend.

The night Rinsey left—but it's almost too painful to recount. They sat deep in the middle of the bed, discoursing, making desperate decisions, agreeing to the painful but necessary. The teenage boy had threatened suicide if Rinsey did not run away with him into the Maryland moondusk that night. Sweeley Leech, who possesses many arcane secrets, took Rinsey into the Gallimaufry, and they talked until it was decided she should go with him.

She was a cornucopia of a woman, who poured out her bounty spendthrift and heedless because of the glow of love in her; she was a woman without price because no price was greater than her cost of giving which was free. The teenage boy needed her, and so she went. Went. Went away from security and safety and the love of a demon-man like Sweeley Leech.

Hagerstown, Maryland! she used to exclaim. I don't know which sweet child is prettiest—Linda or Fifi!

"Hagerstown, Maryland," for some reason, was her choicest expletive.

I can see her now in the great mold-reeking basement of the bungalow, putting up blue stone jars of pickled green peppers and slaw in vinegar—or making kraut with cabbage and brine and sugar and horseradish that would eat the skin off your fingers if you touched it.

I remember the night she left: a long hour or two in the sack with Sweeley Leech, and then a walk in the Gallimaufry, where—unfortunately, perhaps—he taught her the time-bending Druid sneeze called the Screod. It is to be used on occasions of great personal peril only. It is a sneeze which rends clouds and splits oaks with its violence. It splits Time, too. It casts the sorcerer—or sneezer—into a pellmell past or future, he knows not which. It propels him into Time and Space. But it may deposit him (or her) into the most importunate Time. Or Space. Which is apparently what had now happened to Rinsey. She had got herself into a corner, and sneezed—sneezed the old Druid sneeze—and taken her chances, And now—?

Rinsey was the main inspiration for almost all the gardening around the bungalow, save for, of course, the Labyrinth, which was archaic. She planted and arranged the fabulous Flower Clock, an arrangement of strange, special blossoms in sequence which told the passerby the time of the day—within ten minutes—by his observation of whatever blossom then was in full flower, beginning, of course, with bold morning glories. She planted the scent-dripping, color-festooning wisteria, and beneath it, clownlike blossoms of the adorable impatiens. Phlox and baby's tears and lilies of the valley sweetened the air of Echo Point because of Rinsey Leech. Wild

English mint and wintergreen and sage made mad spice beauty in the air above our gardens. Smells fucked the senses around that place. And hollyhock and sunflower ruled above the kingdom of the solar majesty there. While nasturtiums clotted the green hush of leaves with ruddy fabric, and the wax begonia uncoiled a Fabergé elegance. The wild Appalachian dwarf iris was there, whose mentor was Rinsey's green hand, and the bird's-foot violet and the sweet william and the dallying dahlia.

Dear Rinsey. Have you bent Time and gone awry?

I can see, as I fondle it yet, the paring knife of her grandmother's mother, worn thin as the last crescent of the old moon; her silver batter-beating spoon bent double and crutched like a beggar's silver back.

In the helicopter Sweeley was restless, sweating.

My mouth filled with saliva as I remembered and tasted again Rinsey's classic winter recipe—from an Eastern Shore Cresap ancestor—macaroni and tomatoes and cheese with oysters lacing through and sanctifying its juices with oyster breath and broth together.

Rinsey. In danger! I ached with the cold dread of it. Sweeley Leech in the helicopter beside me was mainly silent. Far below, the Maryland ghosts winked their artifacts in the moonlight among the Mingo Mungo of the obfuscated ruins. I think often when in or over this part of America of our past: of the grieving Indian, grieving over lost and stolen lands—grieving and ashamed, that is, over the lands he stole from the Adena Mound People a thousand years before, in the time of the three moons.

The moon was savage in her failing brilliance. A slice of cool pale melon in the deeps of night—dripping and somnolent with mystery. The stars danced round the dying moon like satyrs at a fairy wake. The clouds were like the dessert with which Rinsey used to enthrall us: Eyetalian cream.

Down deep on the land, colors and lights argued and bit the black mists like ghosts of dead quasars. The Potomac shone like a whore's satin belt on the sexy waistline of the Piedmont.

I switched on the Library of Congress channel on radio. Mama Cass Elliot—I adore her name—was singing "Dream a Little

Dream of Me." My mind was like a bee tree—but no honey, only golden, stinging, singing little memories and worries over Rinsey.

Lindy was four the year I appeared, through my own nine-year-old connivance, at what is now officially called the Echo Point Richard M. Nixon Memorial Presbyterian Parish House at a Missionary Fund rally. I sang "Love for Sale," by Cole Porter. Lindy seemed to sense the Disgrace, just as Rinsey sensed the Victory. Lindy got Religion early—we all do. The great moral options are determined on the rag rug in the nursery. Criste or Satan—we embrace one or the other among the gawdy and bewildering painted wooden alphabet blocks, as important to our lives as once were the building stones of Chartres or Amiens or Coventry. Here is solidified forever the Great Pantry Creed.

The night I sang "Love for Sale," Lindy cried all the way up the sunken road to home.

Poor, dear Lindy. As a small child she was forever hiding small objects in her vagina. Why? I don't know. Maybe she thought things were safe there—that it would be the last place any really Christian thief would look. Pebbles and peppermints, acorns and jacks and small rubber balls, postage stamps and parts to Rinsey's old sewing machine. Her little bottom fairly rattled as she scampered around the candlelit halls of the bungalow. I remember many's the night Rinsey would fetch her wicker sewing basket, pluck out needle and thread it, and then rummage about anxiously for her thimble. A moment later she would upend the screaming, furious Lindy and shake it out of its damp little strongbox. Lindy mainly inserted stones, though. I think, even back then, she was building a kind of barricade before her hymen, erecting at the mouth of her cervix a veritable Church Militant—God's granite and Grace—in case she ever had to meet, and put in its place, the first intrusive, presumptuous, butting, bullheaded cock that entered there.

I compare women like Lindy and my poor unfaithful Dorcas Anemone. Dorcas is always anthropomorphizing her body in one way or another—imagining it as a kind of continent or world of places. The summer I first loved her, Dorcas declared that her body was the moon and that I, her lover, was Neil Armstrong. We played the moon-landing morning, noon, and night on the great bearskin on the bed in the bungalow at Echo Point. I would be giving her head—or maybe just licking and kissing her thin little hips or flat, dimpled belly. She kept up a kind of Walter Cronkite commentary throughout, as the lovemaking moved toward climax.

O, Feef, my darling—now you're in my Alpine Valley. Into the Sea of Tranquillity. Yes. Yes. Now the Sea of Rains!

I was getting down to business, her solo narration scarcely audible now as her thighs pressed close against my hair and ears.

Sea of Rains! Sea of Clouds! O, now you're moving from the Sea of Rains to the Sea of Clouds and back to the Sea of Rains again! O, God, how lovely!

In her passion a tiny salty spurt sprang free from the clasping petals.

Back to the Sea of Rains, my love. Into the Sea of Nectar. Now you're in the T-Taurus Mountains. O, God, God. Ready for contact. Countdown to touchdown. Neil. Neil! O, Neil, you made it!

Her body clasped and twisted and worried my head and torso as my lips closed at last round her clitoris. I felt the flood and wonder of her come mounting then and her amazing cry as she achieved it. My face was burning and slippery.

*One giant step for womankind!* she screamed, and the landing was effected.

Dear sweet perfidious lady that she was. I mourn her. I shall be more cautious in the future of such souvenirs tender as freckle transplants.


Sweeley murmured something. I turned to him in the glowing amber light of the dashboard. On the radio the LOC channel was playing Miles Davis with the Benny Carter tune "When Lights Are Low." We both hummed.

The helicopter tilted, tossed, bounced against cumulus, and skimmed down free. Hagerstown was a tiny phosphorescent pie on the black velvet breakfast table of the Cumberlands. We clattered on, southeast.

Where are we going, father?

You'll see.

But where?

To find Rinsey. Maybe in time to save her.

What has happened to her, Sweeley?

I told you. She gave the Druid sneeze at the wrong time. Snapped herself into the wrong time-fold.

Is she in danger, really?

He said nothing.

Is she?

Perhaps in death, Beurre.

But where?

We're getting there. Momentarily. You'll see.

I listened to the LOC record plan for the morning. Now it was Mabel Mercer singing "By Myself." I crooned and watched the slow, frozen firework of traffic down below.

Rinsey, my mother. Lindy, my sister. Both in dark travail. Idiot Lindy—welcoming her kidnappers. How like her. And poor, dear Mother Rinsey—she would be so lost without her *Golden Rule Cookbook* and her batter-beating spoon, curled like a sterling silver autumn leaf heavy with frost.

The LOC Music Library was on the radio now. "Over the Rainbow." Judy—who else? It kind of suited my mood. Hurrying south to somewhere in Maryland; something that mattered passionately to my father, Sweeley Leech, and therefore passionately to me: something involving a mortal peril to my mother—darling Rinsey Leech. "Why, then, Oh why can't I?" Somewhere. Beyond a prismatic chromatic effect caused by sunlight through minute droplets of condensed moisture. No, more. O, God, such a lot more! The Wizard of Oz, you see, is America's holy grail, holy Bible, declaration of individuality, credo, faith of our fathers. You see, Criste—according to Sweeley—is our Pal with Influence against the harsh, farting, belching, warring, drawing-and-quartering God. And that fake God is the really kindly-at-heart old Wizard we go through hells to find, and when we find him— pursuing relentlessly that Yellow Brick Road of affluence-is-next-to-godliness—we find him and he's what Uncle Will Blake always said he was: a belching, farting Nobodaddy who "loves slaughtering and drawing and quartering" now as much as ever he did. And Criste?—which is what we were yearning after all along? Why, Lord save you, children, he was with us all along! The Tin Man, the Cowardly Lion, the Scarecrow—and Toto—Lord love you, children, they were Criste with you alway! And you didn't guess— you never knew—until the golden journey to Oz was almost over.

As it is now. In 1992. But cheer up—even if God is dead, Criste is alive and well in you. And Dorothy is back safe in her trundle bed in Kansas. With Toto. And three astonishing metaphors—ideals which have become the secret Bible of America. "If happy little bluebirds fly beyond the rainbow, why, oh why—" And, love, you can. Like Sweeley Leech.

These days the air is cluttered with choppers. Fewer small planes than back in the eighties, but infinitely more choppers. And the new Lockheed-Datsun is really a marvelous little craft; all during our flight through the woolly midnight velvet, pricked by stars and slashed once through by a blazing tinselmoon like a wisp of child-hair on a barber's black floor, all throughout this mysterious pilgrimage southering, many craft were around us. Now I became aware of one chopper, lavishly civilian, which was, therefore, obviously a government, or TRUCAD, reconnaissance craft. Following us. Suspicious. Probably no more than that. Sniffing around. Keeping its eyes on Sweeley (and me) and wondering what could draw us southering like a hot, autumn, stargripped lodestone. Toward what? And for what reason did we go tunneling down the stardredged night?

The recon craft kept what they thought was a discreet distance, hopping and bobbing behind mountain ranges, skipping and skimming up valleys along the coal seam known as the Sewickley Vein.

Martinsburg, West Virginia, glowed below, like a campfire that's been kicked out by the big boot of two centuries: embers, coals, pinpoints of dispersed flame—blackhole black cinders. Glowworm automobiles inching errant up the ebony night. Shepherdstown. Even fewer glowing coals in the charred dark. We were setting down. The TRUCAD chopper seemed to have lost interest in us. We were alone in the shimmering, terraced darkness—lowering through a fluff and flocculence of thousand-foot-ceiling mists. Beneath it the windows of small-town houses blazed like sunlight through the tiny slots of a black computer card.

I opened a fresh pack of Galacticas—Lorillard-Gallo's contribution to the legal pot market. They were better than most of the government-approved brands. I lit up and toked, thinking, and felt the faint small rush like a gust of wind, and thought some more. I fantasize Rinsey again; her dear face rises before me, ageless and laughing and mortal—doomed, it would seem, to judge from the

drained, strained pallor of darling Sweeley Leech's own face in the
ruddy Coca-Cola glow of the chopper dashboard. Mel Tormé and
Maggie Whiting were dueting an old song by Brother John
Mercer—"Bobwhite."

In my fantasy it was a white blaze of a winter's night at Echo
Point. We were all deep in the ticks of the great common cradle in
which we, all the loving Leeches, shared our dreams o' nights. That
enormous, Rabelaisian bed, gay with gingham and calico and dimity
and lawn: huge patchwork quilts Rinsey and Loll and sometimes
Lindy and I had helped to sew, like dainty-fingered surgeons stitch-
ing up the sundered flesh of a gigantic cloth toy. The bed is stained
with wine and love; the gigantic sheets are cold and kiss the flesh
like winter's own chilled lips. The bedclothes are strewn and mined
with hot-water bottles. Army blankets—some bearing the logos of
kingdoms long fallen in the glittering dust of battles limned in dim
histories. Great feather-filled cushy cushions and bolsters. A naked
foot, seeking warmth, encounters something warm, silky, and quite
resistant. A friendly growl, and the living footwarmer scurries off to
a more secluded quarter of the giant bed: it is Eru, the Lhasa apso
who sleeps, along with several other animals, in our palacious pallet.
I learned reverence for flesh early—how else would I (or anyone)
learn reverence for the soul?


Below the cloud curtain, our chopper circled now two thousand feet
above a thick stand of timber, some fields, and a church steeple,
about whose pristine spire the mists toyed annd toiled, wraithlike,
like dreams before they go forth to seek out the dreamer.

Do you think Rinsey is—dead, Sweeley?

That would sadden me, he said. But I wouldn't grieve. You know
old Death, Beurre. He's just as big a fake as Nobodaddy. If Rinsey
died I would just find the key to that room and visit her whenever
either of us needed it. The other room. The upper room. I would
climb the long staircase to the room called Death and tear down the
For Rent sign. You know. We would shack up in the shambles.

Then what do you fear for Rinsey, father?—it's like map lines in
your face tonight.

That she sneezed the Screod at the one moment—the one day—
when it would blow her into a really terrible time-bend.

Such as what?

We shall see.

The chopper came to rest in a swirling cup of blowing leaves and mountain dust a hundred feet from a small river shore.

You mean into the future, sir?

No. I think, into the past. Past, future. Why do you discuss time in those archaic terms, love? You know as well as I that they exist in that huge, crazy spiral called Now.

You sound like a fucking Heinlein character, I said softly.

If Heinlein and those guys really believed what they wrote, it would scare them to death. But they're right. And they blow out a healthier gust of air than the Bellows and Updikes.

His eyes dreamed round the land, lambent with the watery, filtered moonshine through the hovering host of mists.


I think of Rinsey's adorable person. I remember how, when she was carrying Lindy, she would let me holler through her sweet, puffed-out navel. I would get very close, Rinsey shaking with love and laughter, my hands on her naked hips, and I'd shout: Come out, sweet child. Your first breakfast is waiting! But, naturally, sleeping, thumbsucking, fetal Lindy never heard. Or perhaps ignored me. In the way she still has of doing when she's bugged.

Time. I realize that what Sweeley Leech said about it back there did sound like science fiction talk. And this may be science but it's not fiction. Heed this. Your life—and afterlife—may depend upon it. But Time is a thing which you, me, and everybody—unless we had a Sweeley Leech father who could explain—think of as Past, Present, and Future. And it's not that way. Not at all. Sweeley was right. Time is a spiral, that favored form of nature, and it envelops Everywhen.

We have an old busted, broken-down, scratched, and squawky RCA table radio, and wouldn't take the world for it. Late at night, when the channels are clear and virgin out there in the ether, the little tanktown stations in the West start coming in loud and clear. Meridian, Mississippi. Corpus Christi, Texas. Once we got the radio operator of a large dope boat coming up the Atchafalaya River into Morgan City, Louisiana. We listened in throughout an escape from the TRUCAD Coast Guard. But stay up a little later,

stay up into the hour when the meadows of timothy and Queen
Anne's lace begin to glitter with spiderweb diadems and the fairies
set up little jewelry bazaars in the clover. Stay up past midnight and
into what Loll calls the Fourteenth Hour of the Sun. This is the
time when the San Diego and Belize, British Honduras, stations
have signed off. And then—and I swear this is true—that's when
we start picking up time-bent newscasts. I can't explain it scientifically; I can't even do it as well as Bradbury or even Cousin Davis
might. All I know is what Sweeley says: that every imaginable al-
ternative to history is happening within that spiral of Time and
Space. "Anything capable of being imagined is an Image of Truth"
is something you may remember from Uncle Will Blake. That's
why we do not think it strange—though we do consider it fascinating—when, somewhere deep in the Fourteenth Hour of the Sun,
we hear an announcer gravely discussing the implications of the recent attempted assassination of the President in Miami. Only the
President is Roosevelt. And there is chaos on the land; the scared
American skies hang motionless. And then monstrous armies of
American invaders come streaming up from Louisiana and out of
California. They meet and head for Washington.

I know this. I'll never let them repair that radio. It doesn't have
hi-fi or FM or eight-track stereo. But it gets ghosts. And I remember the unusual fidelity of voice the night Hitler made his first address from the ruins of the Lincoln Memorial. O, it's all innocent
and fun—so much more fun than *Policewoman* or *Bowling for Dollars.* I loved to be scared, as a kid, and the old Victor—its Magic
Eye pulsing in the blue dark—never let me down. Lindy, naturally,
couldn't abide it.

I think, too, that that old radio really helped me to understand
this time-bend thing Sweeley talks about. That's why I was as worried as he was about our Rinsey.

We left the radio on in the chopper. Ronnie Milsap singing "April
Girl–November Man." Sweeley led the way toward the river—like
a stream from a silver spoon of blackberry jelly coiling and misting
streamily up into the moon.

I followed Sweeley through the high grass of a grown-over pas-
ture toward the great stand of trees. I kept thinking I was seeing

the white dotted-swiss dress and pale-blue lace apron of Rinsey in the wisping mists among moonbeams. There were no fairies in evidence. Soon we were within feet of the thickest and tallest of the elms and sycamores and beeches upon the copse of the rise. There was something of compressed frenzy in the tilt and swagger of Sweeley's broad shoulders. His blond hair caught the wind and dallied with streams of it. His eyes glittered their fair blue—a wild-geranium tint. Sweeley always excites me sexually when he gets into this almost astral state. I know that he is with me, but I know, too, that he is with me on more than one level. I thought I saw Rinsey again, up ahead in the dim dappling of moon upon old oak leaves, splattered with autumn blood.

That was when I glimpsed the first row of tiny old stones. Little tablets of sandstone and quartz, and a few of marble and native granite, and each with a rank and a name and a number. I moved forward and touched one.

Got a cigarette, love? I asked Sweeley.

What?

Got a cigarette? I forgot mine.

He held out his pack of Salem Lights. I took one and punched around in search of my lighter. Shit.

Got a light, love?

What?

Got a light?

Sure—here.

He stared at the moon a spell and then was gone from me once more. We moved on among the stones—the tiny stones—row upon row of them, like silly little cakes on some monstrous baker's shelf. I caught the glint of something blue-gold and stooped and touched one little stone. The blue-gold glitter ran through it in divaricating veins in a way which, among such moon, was stunningly beautiful. Sweeley saw me and stooped and touched the stone himself.

There is hardly any Criste Lite in here tonight, he said softly, stroking the strange golden streaks.

The wind honed a sharp blade against some stone, and owls blew in the deeps by the creek. I looked at the golden-smeared stone and wished for a nice silver cake knife from Rinsey's racks to cut myself a mouth-watering slice.

Corporal Sheeny Strasserman.

What, father?

He was my friend. A queer, scared little Jew from the slums of Antwerp. He rode with Hood's Texans that September seventeenth.

What year, father? I breathed.

I rode with him.

What year?

September sixteenth, he said. And the bloody seventeenth.

He stared at me gently. Yet so many of him was on other dimensions, it was blurred a little.

It was 1862, he said. O, yes, Beurre, and it still is. It will always be 1862 in this place.

I spied my first fairy then—a small German immigrant one. He seemed frightened for Sweeley and me. He was frantically gesturing at us with a sheared-off buttercup, which caught the moon in occasional yellow flashes. A few feet away sat a group of interested fairies—Irish ones, obviously. And, O, the Irish fairies are the best! Fallen angels, to be sure: pharies and Pharisees once. But now?—angels with Deirdre faces!

O, he was a dear man, Sweeley rhapsodized softly. Fair of face, and eyes as blue as double washwater. I loved him truly. But he had this letch, this lust—this infernal lust—for gold. It possessed him. I met him in the spring of 1861 on the Bowery. We had a round of drinks and went on up to Overton and Blair's fine restaurant on Tenth Street, one door west of Broadway. There we got drunk with a fine Confederate spy. His name was Stephen Foster. This is in none of the history books, Beurre, but, by God, I was there. By Criste, I know. Stephen Foster started out a Confederate spy, met Walt Whitman on Broadway one night, went to bed with him, made love, listened to Walt talk about Lincoln awhile, and the next morning Foster defected. He was still drunk when he died, but he was a Union drunk. Anyhow, Sheeny had spent every year since 1850 prospecting for gold in the Sierra Madre. He never found it. Till now.

He patted the stone.

In his tombstone. Poor darling.

Sweeley, we're being warned. By the Seely ones—the wee ones.

Yes.

The place is full of earthbound dead, Sweeley said. Poor sons of bitches who died here on the Antietam, by the Dunkard Church, along with my darling Sheeny—

It was Sweeley's way, when warding off Evil, to sing a jolly tune. He hummed and whistled awhile.

Earthbound souls. They are so loath to let go. Think of it, Sweeley, hanging to these bones since 1862.

Since is a nonword; 1862 is Anywhen.

O, I know.

He began to sing and chant now, my lusty Druid avatar, dancing his way like Fred Astaire among the tombstones.

> Do you remember an inn, Miranda!
> Do you remember an inn?
> And the fleas that tease in the high Pyrenees.
> And the tedding of the bedding—

The dead were among us, all right. I was standing by the massive, gnarled roots of a pin oak; the sweet, forgiving brawn of the tree was covering the name bitten fatally into the surface of one stone. Corporal Adam and no last name and no dates. Just *Corporal Adam. Lover.* How thankful must be the soul who once toiled with worms hereunder. Free now. Freed by the spirit of the loving tree! But something had a soft, hot grip around my ankle. Fairy? No. Too hard, too hot. It is common to think of ghostly touch as cold, as it usually is, but there is also heat from the tomb. I could see them now, like mushrooms lifting from the starstrewn lawn of the Federal Cemetery: fingers—pale, invalid, feeble fingers. And hot. And voices audible now, as if the fingers were playing sentences upon the keys of a voice machine.

Come down here. Aw, come down here with me. Aw, come down here. Come on down here, see?

Come die with us, they meant. It was really awful.

I could see that not all the stones were so afflicted. Many were blissfully still and deserted and giving off the fragrant breath of ground moss and tiny pinks and forget-me-nots. A faint, dear glow of all-saving Criste Lite lingered numinous and glowing round those stones. Many of these stones had had their sad legends blissfully obliterated by the big barky fingers of the tree roots.

But the others' voices became even sharper and more poignant and—and here is the thing that scared me—more persuasive, seductive, and logical in their bid to bring us down among their bones and moldering finger rings and lockets dangling into rib cages, more enticing than ever to make us die beside them.

Come on down here, see? Aw, come on. Come where my love lies dreaming.

How I loved Sheeny, Sweeley was saying, stroking the gildered stone again with his longer, remembering fingers. Like a woman, I loved that little Jew. And he had this mad scheme of joining the Texans and making enough money so that when the Confederacy took over he could go prospecting out West in real style. On his Confederate pension. Find gold, find gold, was his beckoning voice.

The clamor of locked and lipless mouths was growing deafening. It is hard to make a fitting human sound in a throat which is now filagreed through and through by the roots of sugar maples and old, deep, rose-vine tendrils. It gives a particularly dreadful timbre, if such it can be called. Roots instead of vocal cords, if you understand. And spirit moving through matter never makes the same sound that air does. Sweeley's face was fixed and staring as if in heat of battle. God knows, Criste knows, what he was reexperiencing.

Do they ever let go of their bodies, Sweeley Leech?

He did not answer. He and his dear Sheeny were arm in arm on Pike Street in Shepherdstown. Before the bombardment. That hugged-in, sucked-out breathlessness that's in a town just before the bombardment. Shepherdstown. Fredericksburg. Sevastopol. Leningrad. New York? Not yet. But was that not implicit somehow in the air here—history not so much repeating as plagiarizing and, both of them bad scripts, America at war again? Civil—the always worst war. Yes. There was the feel of it in the air here—the Future overtaking the Past and merging into the Sameness that they always were, always will be.

Do they ever let go of their bodies?

Eventually. They must. There is infinite life in the universe but it must always be reused.

I remember, he said a moment later. On the sixteenth. In Shepherdstown. That's down the pike a ways.

I know, I said. I was getting your thought. Tell me, though.

Sheeny and me. In the room in the back of a saloon. Drinking. We were the last two people in the town—everyone else had fled.

143

McClellan's batteries were about to open up. Well, maybe we weren't actually the last two. There was one other. An old drunken butler with a bugle. He had blown the charge under Winfield Scott at Matamoros in the dirty little war with Mexico. It was the same bugle. Now he was walking up that deserted main drag of Shepherdstown with his fly open and his pecker sticking out and playing "Lorena" and the Union be damned.

The really terrible thing, I said, about the hot, clammy touch of these spirits is that absolute absence of sexuality in them.

Naturally, Beurre. The essence of human life is unbearable to them now.

When they touch my cunt, I said—and one of them just managed that—the touch is not amorous.

The grave's a fine and private place, but none I think do there embrace, said my father, Sweeley Leech.

The moon sailed like Wyatt's barque charged with forgetfulness across the sky behind the trees. She curved like a mouthful of white, shining teeth. Death whined around my left ankle, crying piteously with its dry-rotted throat. I got away from first one and then the other. When one touched my clitoris, my whole genitals froze in a kind of anti-orgasm which was heartrending. And I was growing more tired by the moment.

My dear Sheeny! cried Sweeley. How I loved you. And you died that seventeenth in the Bloody Lane, and after the battle I saw to your burial just—just here, I think. Yes, I remember. This is your stone—a small tablet of quartz with tiny streaks of the gold you hungered after right off the rim of Life.

Lord, I felt weak with tiredness. The hugging clutch was so strangely persuasive. I knew then that we were in danger.

I turned to Sweeley.

Father, what about Rinsey?

He was kneeling now, frantically ripping away vines and leaves from the face of the tiny, gold-flecked stone. He had a Bic out of the breast pocket of his Italian suede jacket. The flame spurted light out into the fingersome darkness. Fairies, hugging their knees, tiny caps clutched in their hands, sat round in the moonlight, watching.

Sweeley, what about Rinsey?

And then I saw what he was seeing—the thing that had drawn

him here on the tenuous thin strings of instinct: the little tombstone with its lichen-stained, root-clasped, and rainwashed legend:

Susan "Rinsey" Leech
1839–1862

I tearfully read the rest of the inscription:

In the disguise of a boy, this incredible woman won the hearts of both sides here in the frightful battle before Sharpsburg. Running back and forth at dusk and dawning she hustled her sex to lonely men in Gray and in Blue. Greater love hath no woman than to lay down her ass for her fellow men. For services above and beyond the Call of Beauty—Rest in Peace, Rinsey Leech.

I clambered away from the grasps among the stones, wrenching loose from them in tears and anger—one after the other—and everywhere, like platoons of insane owls, the voices gave up their ghost-litany:

Come on down, eh? Ah, come in with yer. Come on, I say— come down here where it's bony, won'tcha? You're tired, don't yer see? Tired, tired, tired! So come where yer love lies dreaming.

The moon was gone then, snuffed out by the pewter cup of a cloud on a silver stick of late autumn lightning. I made out the shape of Sweeley. And his head was thrown back, and he was chanting that song again as a shoulder against the dark things there.

Is it old Jack or a rabbit that I see upon the lane?
Will we ride at old Manassas or at Malvern Hill again?
No we'll cross the damned Antietam in the Horse Cavalry
And into Pennsylvania with Taliaferro and with Lee!

He seemed joyous in his battle with the hosts of the landlocked, did Sweeley Leech. And he sang on.

So it's up the road to Darkesville.
Follow the new of the moon
And we'll hang old McClellan
Ere there stands another noon.

So it's up the road to Darkesville,
With Banks and Pope and Lee
And the Union moon—we'll see it soon—
A-drowning in the sea!

He broke off, laughing, and rambled off into another song. But it was plain he was winning. We were approaching the large boulder with the bronze commemorative plaque bolted in stone. The rain pattered like old blood against our faces: stale and warm still with that carnal September day. When we came abreast the stone, Lee's shadow an implicity in it, the lightning gave one great shivering sheet like an exploding mirror. All the grief and stoppered anger in the earth spoke in terrible colloquy. Lester Young in the draft army screaming in a GI box. Billie Holiday screaming Stein and Cahn lyrics out of Alderson Penitentiary. Black impertinences such as these upon the place of their issue. But most terrible of all was what we read—by brief thunderflash—in that bronze:

To the brave defenders of the Republic
The 13th Arizona Chemical Warfare Unit
The 23rd Armored Unit from Puerto Rico
The Alaska Rangers—18th and 19th Divisions

I began to scream even before I came to the four numerals of the date, of which the first two were 1 and 9. I never saw. Nor would I tell you if I had. Love, why should I make you cringe in whatever year—perhaps this very lightning-lit one—you may now be cuddled with your children or your love. But know that it is coming.

O, yes! cried Sweeley Leech to the storm as we fought the crystal rods of the rain toward the waiting chopper. Yes. Yes. Know that it is coming. Coming again to America. As the old landlords give in and the new landlords take over. World without end. Amen.

He was laughing.

Is Rinsey free, at least?

O, yes, Beurre. Free as a baby's fart. Free, thanks to Criste. Free at last, just like Saint Martin Luther King called it.

We clambered inside. The radio was still playing, louder than the now-subsiding rain. A Gershwin prelude. Two, I think. The one that goes dum-dum-dum-de-dum. O, hell.

146

Sweeley, father?

Yes, love.

Then Sheeny Strasserman was Rinsey all along? Retroincarnated?

In a way, he chimed in a way he had when correcting or teaching me.

Then what?

I have had a love follow me since I began. In every lifetime I have loved that spirit—always in a different flesh. Sheeny was that spirit. So was Rinsey. And I am looking forward to guessing who it will be up ahead. For we'll always be together.

Then both spirits were—

You know, Beurre. Whomever you love—that is God.

Behind us in the Federal Cemetery the ghosts were sulking satanically. They were slowly—like snails into shells—pulling back into their dust-crumbled sleeves; sobbing nasally among the root-claimed ribs and vertebrae; airless and with spirit only making sound upon their spurious, green vocal cords. It was a din as of expiring toy balloons. Yet another sound made me freeze, my fingers on Sweeley's sleeve. A tambourine. Yes. Unmistakably. Jangling in forthright jollity. And yet with that undertone of gravity and solemn injunction which marshaled before it the inevitable vision of Mr. Judah Samphire.

Sweeley did not see him at first. I did. And shuddered. He was undamped and unruffled by the rains and winds. His black bowler hat rode prime-ministerially upon his placid, civic brow. He had a ledger under one arm and he was fiddling with a Pentel ball-point. Ready to record another Sweeley Leech Passing Over, I supposed.

Get in the chopper, father! I cried, pushing him.

Sweeley was shaking with laughter. He had seen Samphire now.

Samphire's eyes met his own. They held, locked, and it was like invisible laser beams cutting through Time like a rope and splicing it into new dimensions.

Mr. Samphire, it is not time, yet. I happen to know.

Samphire smiled. He smiled that apologetic and relieved smile which a clerk gives us when he finally admits he's out of our size.

He opened the ledger and searched up and down through thick tortoiseshell spectacles. He smiled. Closed the book. Diddled the ball-point back into its hard steel foreskin. He put it in his shirt pocket—a really rather lovely shirt of lavender brushed Egyptian cotton.

We couldn't hear his voice. He has such a low, soft voice, Sweeley always says. But we could read his lips.

You're right.

He banged the tambourine once more and stumped stodgily off through the mist and leaves. We could hear his shoes kicking through them. And then the moon was back. Cleaner—polished by the harsh chamois of the storm clouds—blazing like a piece of Christmas silverware on Grandma's black-velvet table scarf. It painted our faces with pearl. I kissed Sweeley on the mouth.

I turned, and Samphire had turned, too, and now smiled again. And again I read his lips, though saying nothing to father.

But soon, he said.

And the tambourine was lost in the roar of the gesturing blades of the rising chopper. Sweeley tapped the digital clock.

I told you I'd get you back to catch that fucking bus, he said. Since you must be off after Lindy.

I had an hour to get to the Washington Greyhound Terminal. But I felt a little sick at those last words I had read on Mr. Samphire's ruddy, country-squire lips. O, I know as our Thomas Wolfe told us, Death is our proud brother, but, O, no. No. Criste, spare my Sweeley just a few moments more!

# T · E · N

I was on the Greyhound New York City Express out of Washington. It was nearly daylight. I was filled with mixed emotions. Directly across from me, in the aisle seat, was a poor, really dreadful-looking, old, shapeless woman, and she kept watching me. Whenever I caught her at it, she quickly returned her eyes to the speeding landscape. A moment later I stole a quick look and found those strange, mean, spaniel eyes on me again. On her lap she held—really clutched—a string knit shopping bag, inside of which were pint jars of watermelon preserves. She was plainly one of those peregrinating, really homeless mothers who spend eleven months out of the year visiting with their children and grandchildren. Her slip was showing—ragged and dirty, with a greasy hem like the lace around a fried egg. Even across the air-conditioned aisle she gave off the odor of Ben-Gay, old cleaning fluid, and stale pee. A most impossible creature, poor darling. Because I knew she was not what she had so artfully arranged to appear. Her clothes consisted of utter mismatchment: a really awful green blouse with an off-purple jacket. I thought a moment; it was a color combination which a really daring dresser might have brought off with perhaps a flash of yellow somewhere, or the cool relief of blue. A daring dresser, but this poor soul was daring in nothing she did. Unless—she were color-blind.

I said nothing about this to dear Adonis McQuestion, who was in the window seat, nestling me against him tenderly. Dearly as I loved him, Adonis seemed somehow remote this time. I searched his tawny face for reassurances. It was like Warren Beatty's, but really prettier. But this time, distant and strange somehow. So that when his hand stole over to my left breast and did nice things with it for a while and then moved down my abdomen to my lap and obviously was beginning equally nice things there, I smiled and took his fingers away. Turned him down.

You're on edge tonight, darling, he said.

A little.

You saw the *Times* front-page story?

About father? The unrobbery?

Well, yes. But mostly about you, darling.

I know. "A young woman is thought to have been the central terrorist."

"*She* is being sought," he added. Nothing about the man.

That means, Adonis, that I'm being—perhaps tailed at this moment.

Why do you imagine, he said into my ear, that I am here with you?

I know, love—to take care nothing happens to me. And I know I'm being a kind of bitch, turning you off like I just did. O, Adonis, I haven't been nervous for years. What's wrong with me? God knows, it's nothing wrong with you.

He was craning his neck out the window as the bus moved through the infinite squatting suburbs of Philadelphia.

There's nothing wrong with you, love. You're lovely to look at, delightful to know, and heaven to kiss.

O, but what's wrong with me, Adonis? I love and adore you, but—but—but somehow I can't imagine fucking you again.

Well, that's normal.

Not for me it ain't.

I glanced at the old woman. She was leafing through a new copy of *Spotlight,* the John Birch journal. I tore my eyes back to Adonis.

It's that old woman, I said. She's a witch—or something. Maybe a TRUCAD agent.

Not a chance, he smiled. Not a chance, love.

The Greyhound was hissing and phissing and insinuating its great hulk awkwardly through the narrow, Colonial streets of Philadelphia.

Suddenly I felt a little nausea of panic. Something not yet visible to me was drawing closer to happening.

The old woman had folded her John Birch paper and put it into a large beige purse on the floor. She was looking at me again. I waited for her to flush and turn her eyes away to the damp gray wall of the bus-terminal driveway, along which we were passing. But she didn't. Not even my frightened eyes would drive her stare away this time.

I clutched Adonis's hand and turned to him, my face close to his neck.

That woman, I whispered hoarsely (I was sure she heard me). She's a member of—

She's no such thing, he intervened. And by the way—did you read the statement in the *Times* story about your unrobbery that TRUCAD has long anticipated a new and extremely dangerous crime to break out? It regards your father's act as the signal gun, so to speak. It is a new crime in our law. Ecumenical Subversion. The subversion of the Church, and through it, the State. I have a feeling TRUCAD will suppress the Criste Lite idea. That's one reason I stay so close to you, love.

He smiled.

To protect you.

He chuckled, and I don't know why, but his voice gave me what the French call a *frisson:* a grue, a shiver.

Maybe it escapes your mind, he said, that I love you. The way you look, the way you smell, the way you move and dress and—

The old woman had tucked her shopping bag full of mason jars under the seat. She had half risen, her eyes fixed almost madly on me, her body, gross and shapeless, inching out across the aisle. The bus was almost at the landing deck. Lights flashed from outside—checkering the old, raddled, overpowdered face.

I think maybe the thing that grabs me most about you, Adonis was saying, is the way you dress. No, I mean it. You could take any color combination and make it say something.

The old woman's liver-spotted, fat hand snatched down into the deeps of her purse for something.

Adonis chuckled.

You could take that old woman's pink blouse, he said. And her navy-blue jacket—

The old woman was standing up, poised. My God, hadn't Adonis seen her? Or did he merely imagine her, as she might have been, on the way back to the tiny toilet?

You could wear those colors, he said. And make them work.

I nodded, grinning idiotically.

The pink, I said. And the navy blue.

Right, he said, and then realized he'd said it and there was no unsaying it and his mask was gone.

You're color-blind, I chanted softly, like a boy in logic class. Adonis McQuestion is not color-blind. Therefore you are not Adonis McQuestion.

In a way, he said, I am. I really am. But you're right. I'm really not.

Well, I'm glad we got that settled, I said. When someone as pretty and cute as you turns me off, I know something is afoot. Where is Adonis McQuestion?

I am sorry to tell you.

Tell me. Is he dead?

Let me build up to it.

The *Bhagavad Gita* says: "Weep neither for the living nor the dead." Don't plan on wiping me out, therefore.

You know he is, or *was,* an art thief?

I turned my face away. The old woman was flexing her fingers. They looked like obscenely dancing sausages in an evil kitchen.

Did you know that?

Certainly I shall say nothing on that. If you should be holding him, my saying I didn't know will not release him.

He is not to be released.

He is being held?

By a higher power than TRUCAD.

Dead, you mean.

Undoubtedly.

O, I am sorry. Sorry. Sorry.

He died in the pursuit of his—er—uh—trade. I understand he was quite brilliant. He died here in Philadelphia. Last night. Or rather, only a few hours ago.

How? I asked, brushing away a tear I did not fight.

(It is said that Gandhi was distraught when his lady died.)

He fell from atop Billy Penn's hat on City Hall.

Stealing what?

The Great Rizzo Forgery.

I think I read of it in *Time.*

After he was dethroned, explained my companion, Frank Rizzo, in a mad gesture of Sicilian panache, stole the Calder bronze of William Penn atop City Hall and replaced it with the so-called Rizzo Forgery—a piece of bronze the aging *paisano* had commissioned, identical in every respect to the Calder Penn except that where the treaty juts forward from Penn's hand, Rizzo with a fine dashing honesty is pissing on the city.

Are you by any chance Adonis McQuestion's brother? I asked. And what are you going to do with me?

Which question do you want answered first?

He scratched his pretty ear.

I think before I answer either, I should tell you of something new in TRUCAD. That is the seriousness with which it takes this crime of Ecumenical Subversion. There is talk of resuming federal capital punishment to arrest it.

I am not surprised.

But you don't really take it seriously, he said. You don't understand that subtle relationship between Church and the economy. It is an interdependency which has increased since the Closet War and the Great Depression of 'eighty-nine. Splinter groups have sprung up in America espousing this really preposterous and harmful primitive Christianity. And you have doubtless heard their claim: Religion is not the opiate of the people—it is something worse. It is their Angel Dust.

Angel Dust, I said. A pretty phrase for hell. And you won't tell me.

Which? What I'm going to do with you? Or who I am?

Either. Or please fuck off, dear. And soon, love.

If I told you the really complicated method the Soviets developed more than twenty-five years ago of duplicating a person—and I don't mean something primitive as in *The Boys from Brazil.* Gosh, if I told you that, Feef, I'd be telling you all about the assassinations of the sixties—the Kennedy brothers, Martin, Malcolm, and a few dozen unsung martyrs—and how the original Lee Harvey Oswald not only was *not* the one killed in the Dallas jail but lived to mastermind all the others and is now in a fairly remunerative TRUCAD job in Lahore.

You were cloned out of Adonis McQuestion. Is that the asinine thing you are saying, love?

Not really asinine. And not cloning as you're using it. But an instantaneous and virtually total cell duplication from any size adult animal. You know, in Bulgaria now they're duplicating members of endangered species, like certain Himalayan bears. And the white Siberian tiger.

Philadelphia Greyhound Terminal, shouted the woman driver in the loudspeaker. Passengers here change for Allentown, Harrisburg, and York. New York City passengers remain on the bus. There'll be a twenty-minute rest stop.

I'm going to have to take you off the bus, Fifi, love, said the fake, the beast, the awful, awful person beside me.

He had taken a hypodermic out of a small snakeskin case. Fake, of course—the snakeskin, not the hypo, which was cute and small like in a little boy's Christmas-present doctor's kit.

You're going to kill me.

No, he said. This will make you very drunk, love. You will have to be carried. You will sing. Your eyes will wander like mad moons. You will slobber. You will expose yourself. The bus driver will understand. She will know that I am your husband or lover and am taking you for assistance to a hospital.

Where I shall be killed?

No. Simply kept in this not-unpleasant state of advanced intoxication, in entirely comfortable if not luxurious surroundings, until the Nobel Prize Contest is over.

The old lady seemed to be leaning over us, listening, not missing a word.

I don't understand everything, I said.

You see, TRUCAD *wants* your father's book to win, said the person. TRUCAD wants it to be published, praised, rave-reviewed—and then forgotten. As every book of these times is forgotten. Snowed under in a few years by glaciers of trivia and remaindering.

O, how beautiful, I said. They don't suppress books anymore. They bury them in apathy!

Now, hold still, love. And bottoms up, so to speak, he said.

The tiny hypodermic glittered like a blue glass flame in his attractive fingers, which held it against my thigh. The old woman came alive. Her huge, muddy, flaccid fingers darted out of the frayed, soup-stained coat sleeves and grabbed hold of my captor's wrist. The motley, mottled body became electric and dynamic in a twisting, parrying movement.

Ouch, cried the fake Adonis McQuestion as the turned-round little needle jabbed his left testicle. He glared up at my strange and terrible rescuer. Eyeball to eyeball, the faces held for a moment.

This! hissed the old woman in a kind of grating gasp. This is for the Mickey Finn you gave me in Vladivostok, old ripper.

And then with a strength which surprised me—who was this incredible woman?—she held the stricken man in her fist for a moment, thrusting him up like a hand puppet and watching as those fine Warren Beatty features melted and dissolved like a candle into driveling, blithering, boozy idiocy.

A cowboy and his Indian girl friend were doing Custer's Last Stand in the aisle with large Sears suitcases from the rack. We ducked under them. The old lady whisked me past a hip pocket that reeked sweetly of good sloe gin and down the relatively-empty-by-then aisle. We were past the driver now. Back in the shadows a drunk was waving a .357 Magnum. It went off into the bus ceiling and fell from the nerveless fingers which had held it. Quickly, we were out onto Market Street.

Somehow this amazingly strong person no longer smelled to me of liniment and benzine and dirty lingerie. Her various pieces of clothing did not seem so dismally at war with one another. Her eyes not quite so malevolent. My complete salvation from such cynicism was to be, in a moment, achieved. The great, liver-spotted hand seized my wrist more tightly, and we darted under the awning of a tiny novelty store. False faces made of the new organic plastic, Styron, stared like a jury box of mad children from the dusty window. On a fly-specked glass counter lay plastic hands, noses, penises, and boobs. A gallery of life-size figures stood in the shadows of the dusty-curtained and peeling walls. The proprietor nodded.

How'd it work?

Fine.

Worth the five hundred, eh?

Every bit of it, said Adonis McQuestion, already down to the last few bits and pieces of his disguise. I'll remember your service.

Talk it around, will ya? said the proprietor.

His voice fell.

With what I feel in the wind in this country these days, he said in a low whisper, disguises is going to be a big business before long.

I was breathless, as much with astonishment as with renewed love. Adonis peeled off the plumpish hands as if they were ugly gloves. His own dear hands shone forth.

He whisked out a five-hundred-dollar bill and an extra fifty and laid them with grace and elegance on the thumb-smeared glass.

There was an early Philadelphia fog, in off the Delaware. A great boat uttered three lorn bloodhound bayings somewhere south of Society Hill. I stared up at Adonis McQuestion's unquestioned face, with questions in me.

What color is my blouse?

Fuchsia.

What color are my high heels?

Black. Even color-blind people see black, love. Go on.

What color are my eyes?

Deep, deep brown. Chestnut eyes. With cat pupils.

What color are my nipples?

Rosy like in Herrick, Suckling, and Lovelace. Also Carew. Rosebud nipples.

What color is my vulva?

Like a seashell inside. With moss and the fragrant samphire all around.

Samphire? Darling, if only you knew. But go on. What color is the polish on my toenails?

A kind of persimmon orange.

You are my Adonis McQuestion without question. I love you.

And I love you.

You do? How presumptuous of you! Who said you might?

You did, love. You did, my chestnut puss.

O, I'd forgotten. Then, of course, it's all right.

Adonis drew me into the shadow of a sweating, steaming popcorn stand by the penny arcade and kissed me. I riposted his tongue again and again. But he slew me with it in the end. I melted, listening as he launched gravely into strange statements.

You are off to find your sister, Lindy—right, darling?

Irrevocably.

Yet if you knew—

Don't tease.

—if you knew what other incredible and marvelous and terrifying things are going to be involved in your search—

He smiled.

What are you getting at, beloved?

This, he said, thrusting a crisp, black-embossed business card into my hand.

And this.

And he kissed me tenderly, felt me for a moment, and then dashed off into the mists, his Aquascutum beating like a pale tan moth in the fog of a rain forest.

The card—a most official sort of Philadelphia-style, old-fashioned, black-letter Bible business card—began to blur in the light rain and run in black Rorschachs that couldn't fold or be anything but rivered onto my fingers. But I clearly read the name and address:

### Jonathan Thomas Bigod and Sons, Limited
#### Wonderists
#### Number Nine Mole Street

At the very bottom of the card, now beginning to run in rivulets of ink, was written the date the firm began. I did not catch the numerals before they were obliterated by the fine mists—was it *Established 1889,* or was it (no, it could not have been—or could it?) *1389?* No matter, I was soon to know. Indeed, it seemed at that moment as though I were about to know All—if that is not what Death consists of. For even before I heard the muffled choke of the silencer, I heard the big bullet tear through the awning against which the crown of my head was resting.

I turned in time to see the drunken Greyhound passenger—the

157

spurious Adonis—staggering and falling and rising again, with the big blue .357 Magnum in his trembling hands pumping shot after shot at me through the murk of Market Street. I began to run. And I was laughing—I am always laughing when I pray, as I am always praying when I laugh. I knew that I was as close to Sweeley's World Elsewhere as I had gotten in years—that I could at any moment cease materially to exist and be whisked off into either paradise or hell with one of those deathly, fingerjoint-size slugs.

Why was I being so molested? Was it TRUCAD? Had they taken so seriously and so malevolently this new faith of Criste, which seemed that morning not to be the sole property of Sweeley Leech alone? I ran. I stumbled once and cut my knee slightly. I could hear the staggering clump of the drunken fake Adonis on the pavements. A delivery truck turned suddenly up a street in front of my pursuer, momentarily obscuring me.

Molest. Molest. Molest, screamed my laughing mind. I raised my eyes and saw that word MOLEST printed on the fog. No, it was printed on metal—an iron oblong attached to a rusty telephone pole. *Molest*? Why, no, you little fool, it says *Mole St.* I glimpsed pleasant cobblestones leading through a narrow little archway and into a small, meandering street, misty as the rest of the city at that moment but lined with tiny and mostly abandoned shopfronts. The truck lumbered up the street behind me. I heard the curse of my pursuer and sank back against the streaming red brick of a building, exhausted and joyous. O, missing death by such inches makes us always hug life so hard afterward!

I leaned back, catching my breath, miraculously still clutching my two pieces of luggage from the bus. I stared at them stupidly. I did not remember taking them down from the overhead bus rack when my dear old lady, Adonis McQuestion, dragged me down the rioting aisle to safety. He had seen to it, however. Adonis McQuestion sees to everything. O, I desired him with every inch of my fear-quickened body in that moment. I stared back toward the end of Mole Street, where it empties timidly into brawling Market Street. In that little rectangle of white mists I saw the angry, besotted, staggering figure pass by—the big gun fisted in his furious fingers—and disappear, craning his head through the fog, into the pavement leading to City Hall Annex.

I began to look about for shop signs. Most of the little stores—

almost 1840-ish in their simplicity—were abandoned: an old toy store with one dusty doll face staring forlornly through the smudged and dirty panes; an old candy shop which, as I approached it, seemed to exude the odors of ghostly Christmas popcorn balls and the fading tang of unremembered saltwater taffies. Then I spied the old and weathered wooden sign—black it had been once and with gold leaf lettering, but it was unmistakable:

### Jonathan Thomas Bigod and Sons, Limited
#### Wonderists

And the address—Number Nine. And that ambiguous phrase: *Established 1-something-89*—what was that second numeral? A 3? Or an 8?

When I pressed against the single, quartered, paned door, a tiny bell spoke like a bright sparrow beside my ear. The wrinkled old panes seemed to give off a frail but friendly nimbus, and the door itself opened in the friendliest of manners. With surprise, I glanced down at the wet fragment of business card in the palm of my hand. It was self-destructing like a wafer of goldfish food into a soft, small wad of mush. There were lovely beaded curtains leading, I supposed, into the back of the shop, and a tiny golden bell—very ancient-looking and quite tarnished and worn from the touch of many hands—which I rang sharply. I heard a rustle, a soft susurration behind the beads, and presently there appeared through them, rather like an old Aphrodite emerging from bubbles of Aegean surf, a charming white-haired woman of perhaps seventy years of age. She was not matronly; she was, in fact, curiously voluptuous, like an orchard flourishing amid the ruins of a cathedral. She gave off a sweetness that seemed almost dear and familiar to me. I could not place it to save my soul. She laid her hands on the edge of the curio-packed counter in the most shopmistressly of manners and smiled a smile of heartbreaking, birdwing sweetness.

May I help you?

Yes, please.

I held out my upturned palm with the gob of quickly dwindling gook on it and scowled a smile.

This was your business card, I said. It seems to have—gone to nothing.

O, yes, it is supposed to, said the sweet lady. We don't want our cards lying about in gutters. The ink is designed to run, the card itself to self-destruct, as they call it these days. One has enough time to read the message, the challenge, the address. Someone who does not wish Wonder is handed the card, throws it on the street; the rains come, the card vanishes—as it should. We do not wish to be pushy with our services.

Well, I said, you have been most kind, darling. And would you be even more gracious and permit me to meet Mr. Jonathan Thomas Bigod.

The birdwing mouth curved in the gentlest of smiles.

At your service, she said.

You are Jonathan?

Yes. Does that distress you?

O, no. I think it's marvelous.

I bit my lip.

Will you tell me? I asked timidly, when you were established? I can see that the place—even for old Philadelphia—is somehow even older. What year, please?

She answered me as she turned and beckoned me to follow her through the beaded curtains. But for the life of me I could not hear her reply.

We moved in curious twinly single file through a pleasantly lighted little flat and came at last toward the glimmer of French doors which opened, between grape-colored damask drapes, onto an absolutely breathtaking Breton garden. At the doors Madame Jonathan paused and fixed me with her great green eyes. She smelled like sweet shrub and tangerines.

You are worried about someone dear to you, she said.

You are a soothsayer?

O, no. Nothing like that, dearest. It is simply that I read a concern for physical safety in your face. And I also read in your face that you are the kind of soul who would not be concerned about your own physical safety.

O, I'm not all that brave.

You are braver than you know, she said. Come into the garden. And please give me the sum of our small service fee.

O, how much, Madame Jonathan.

Fifty cents, she said. I hope it does not seem exorbitant.

I laughed.

It is most modest, I said, and fished out a Kennedy half-dollar—the famous 1988 Dallas Commemorative with the Zapruder film in silver relief on the obverse. I handed it into the soft fingers of Jonathan Thomas Bigod, whom I adored already.

I am worried about my sister, Lindy, I said, my lip a little trembly. She has been kidnapped by the women of the Cazzo Nostra.

O, horrors, smiled Madame Jonathan. How awful for her.

Yes, that's the worst part of all, I cried. She wants to be with them. That makes her rescue all the more impossible. She does not want to be rescued. She does not know what they are.

I paused. O, Madame Jonathan, what *are* they?

Come into the garden and I will answer your question, said the lady pleasantly, and she unlocked the French doors with a small and lustrous, though somewhat tarnished, brass key. The garden was as small as ours. And as large. I mean it had that curious way of seeming larger than, in fact, it was. Even though that Seeming, as Sweeley always reminds me, is Reality, too. The air was not damp and foggy, as it had been on Market Street. I don't mean to imply that it was one of your stock, fantasy, make-believe, magic gardens, either—though, in fact, it was, somehow.

There were small olive trees lining the walls, and little tables to sit and drink and rap at. A ray of early-morning sunlight had fingered its way through the clumped purple overcast and shone down now like a bar of light in a movie. The garden, I swear, was warm as midsummer. And the air was full of bees. They did not light on you; they did not strike against your arm, gather themselves, and sting. They seemed oblivious of everything but the route to their hives (and from them), which occupied a large corner of the charming little garden. The flowers were faded and dusty with Indian summer's recent killing kiss, but I could imagine what the place must be like in spring and summer. The bees barreled back and forth in the soft, liquid air like tiny golden fishes in a yellow sea.

Come, said Jonathan Thomas Bigod. We shall have tea. There is a nip in the air this morning.

Do you know anything, I said, that may help me find my sister?

Madame Jonathan reached into her low-cut bodice and fetched out a tiny, tarnished silver whistle, worn bright around the mouthpiece. She blew on it—a soft, birdlike note. Almost at once there appeared a small boy—perhaps six years of age—with a great bushy head and a turned-up nose and a livid, though small, white scar like an inch of butcher's twine lying upon his plump, freckled cheek. And most astonishing of all, a black patch over one eye. He smiled cheerfully and set the steaming tea platter on the little table between us. He looked at Madame Jonathan and then at me.

May I join you? he asked with charming politeness. I am of a generation which is often helpful in times like these.

He cleared his throat. I hope I don't seem pushy.

He held out a small grimy hand which was, at the same time, almost elegant. I am the other son of mother here, he concluded. May I pour, mother?

Please do, she said.

He poured tea into three cups, passed the yellow, glazed bowls of crushed English mint and honey, and settled down into the third chair.

He sipped his own with a coarse, sweet gusto and licked his adorable upper lip.

Madame Jonathan stared at me, her slant eyes darkling and fiery.

I know the Cazzo Nostra women well, she said. And to understand them you must understand what is called the Women's Lib Movement in this year of gracelessness, 1992.

I do, I said. I am of it. But I don't understand all of it.

You see, there are two Women's Lib movements, said Jonathan Thomas Bigod solemnly. The first—and there are many branches of it, including this Cazzo Nostra—the first kind of Women's Lib is intended to make women Masculine. The new kind—the kind blessed of the Lord—is to bring out the Feminine in all of us. I said Feminine—not ef-feminate. When I say Female, I mean not heterosexual or homosexual or asexual, but multisexual. You see, Fifi Leech—

I felt that *frisson* again—the gathering of tiny hairs at the nape of my neck. Was I in the presence of friends or enemies?

How do you know my name, Madame Jonathan?

I am sorry. I did not mean to frighten you.

But how? You *are* psychic.

No. It is not that. You see my son—my *other* son—spoke of you to me last night.

Do I know him?

I think you would not want to, said Madame Jonathan. Because of his two dark trades.

Which are? Perhaps I shall remember—

If you have made his acquaintanceship already, my dear, she said, eschew it at once, I beg of you.

What does he do? What are his, as you call them, dark trades? I asked, although I had already guessed.

I am so proud of my *other* child, said Madame Jonathan, tousling the child's hair and kissing his honey-daubed mouth.

How—how was he hurt? I blurted, and then seized the small, sticky hand.

His wounds suddenly appalled me: the scar, the patch.

O, how did you get so scary a scar? I asked. How, child, did you lose your eye? Do you mind too much my asking, dearest?

I don't mind at all, said the boy, like a little man. I was imagining myself on a pirate cruise last summer between Baranquilla and a vanished seaport, called Mudados, on the west side of Baja California. I imagined it too—too real, see?

I felt a shiver and understood the tigers I had imagined into Reality back at Echo Point and how I had left poor Sweeley to redd up, so to speak, my loose, wild dreams.

My other son, said Madame Jonathan suddenly then, tears shining in her gracious eyes, is not only an unregenerate TRUCAD agent—

She paused for a beat, in which the bee-loud golden air hummed like tiny mouthharps at the breath of fairies' mouths.

—he is also the most accomplished art thief in the Western World.

At once I confirmed those small foreguesses.

Angrily she shook off the memory of that unprodigal and turned her eyes back to me.

Back to what I was saying, Fifi Leech. The Cazzo Nostra is a representative of the darkest in us all, she said. The Macho. It is not confined, you see, to men. Nor is the Eternal—the Feminine. The Macho male is, indeed, the most effeminate of creatures; the Macho woman—that woman trying to be what she imagines is Man—is the most androgynous. Nor do women possess exclusivity in being Feminine. In being, that is, Sexual. Because the Sexual—the freely given, unbought, unsold, unforced Sexual—is, if you must be told,

Fifi Leech, the essence of what someone somewhere has called the Criste Lite.

Again that grue of cold, like centipedes under my collar. I smiled, though. I trusted this woman and her son. The trouble was, I also trusted her other son, Adonis McQuestion.

What, I asked softly then, is a Wonderist, Madame Jonathan?

Her other child—not my adored Adonis—did indeed have a most amazingly powerful imagination. I eyed the graceful hama-dryad he had fancied into reality on the dewglistening flagstones of that charming garden. I did hope it would not be imagined to bite any of us, though it did seem (perhaps the boy was tired) rather sluggish.

A Wonderist, said his graceful, white-haired mother (she must have been in her late sixties when this child beside us was born), a Wonderist is one who opens the Wound.

I don't think I should much like that, Madame Jonathan.

I realized that this comment had been facetious and ill-mannered, for my great friend's eyes were quite solemn.

I think you know what I mean, she said. I mean the Wound of Wonder.

I do know what you mean, Madame Jonathan, but I would like you to reassure me that I understand you.

It is not in the skin, as you jokingly hinted, she went on, lighting a low-tar cigarette and inhaling thoughtfully. It is in the spirit. It has a most disagreeable habit of healing over, this Wound of Wonder. It is then that it becomes dangerous. It has become a scar underneath which such infections as Piety can flourish and ultimately destroy their host. Yes, this Wound—especially before times of great excitement and peril such as are facing you, Fifi Leech, my darling—this Wound can actually save us from death.

She smiled, as a drone bee—glittering with male pride—lighted on the back of her graceful hand and supped a freckle of honey she had spilled there for it.

The incidence of cancer, measured professionally, she said quietly, watching the tiny, yellowdusty creature, is lowest among beekeepers.

The Wound of Wonder, I breathed. It must bleed that blood which is called, in the Bible, the Wine of Astonishment.

Continuously, she said, but only when the Wound is kept open.

Doesn't it hurt? O, of course it does. I shouldn't ask. The ache one feels during the "Ode to Joy" or looking at a burning Turner seascape or catching a glimpse of someone you adore at his or her most helpless—

Which is? she smiled.

When they're sitting on the john. O, I know what you mean by the ache of that Wound of Wonder, Madame Jonathan. The pain, the sweet, dear, adorable pain you feel—and someday I shall feel it—of a baby's wild, angry, astonished mouth tugging at your nipple.

Exactly.

The Wound of Wonder, I said. But why does one really need it as protection from danger?

Because Wonder, she said, is the exact opposite of Fear.

Of course, I breathed. O, I always knew. Of course, of course. And people come to you, Madame Jonathan, to get this Wound open?

We can help, she said. Even in the most healed and stubborn cases when the Wound is covered with the cicatrice called Religion. O, yes, we do help marvelously.

And in my case, I asked, you feel the Wound is closed?

O, no, it's quite happily open, my darling, crooned Madame Jonathan. But in cases like yours we must merely take precautions that, against the most deathly and Satanic forces, it shall remain so.

Satanic? Deathly?

My darling Fifi Leech, you would not believe what lies in wait immediately ahead of you—in Manhattan. Tonight.

It's already been pretty far out, Madame Jonathan. I sighed.

You have no idea, however, she said, of how much farther out it will become.

You know, of course, I said, toying with her really lovely French teaspoon on the flowered cloth, that I love your son.

He is a great little guy, she said, tousling the violent pirate's mop of ruddy hair.

I mean your other son, I said.

O, I am glad, she said. For his sake. Not for yours, necessarily. Because the remedy against being the two dark things he is may rest in being loved and in loving back. You know him, then?

You know that, Madame Jonathan. Don't tease me so disingenuously.

I'm sorry, she said. That was not fair. We Wonderists do put on airs of mystery and fake magic sometimes. It is an old guild—the original was in a tiny office on old London Bridge.

In 1389?

She smiled and sipped her tea. Perhaps you would not believe when, she said.

Why is he named McQuestion, not Bigod?

Why should people be named after their parents? It is absurd. Is your father named after his, for example?

That is different.

Yes, Sweeley Leech is different.

I smiled now and sipped my tea.

You know a great deal, Madame Jonathan, that you do not let on.

In the days that are coming, she said sadly, we shall need to learn once more the great arts of dissembling. It is sad, I think. Don't you?

I don't know exactly what times are coming, Madame Jonathan.

Glorious, fierce, hiding times, she said. When the followers of the new Criste come to light their tapers at his flame and then go stealing back into the alleys of the earth to carry the candle to others.

A yellow bird—almost tropical—sang in a small lime tree as if it would burst its little breast. I wondered where my drunken pursuer had gone to sober up. Had he lost his pistol?

I caught a glimpse of yellow fire on a small table against the vine-thick brick wall.

Why, Madame Jonathan, do you have a candle burning out here in your little garden in the early morning? And so bright!

That is not a candle. Come see. And touch. And feel. This is part of your treatment. This will thoroughly ensure that your Wound of Wonder will not heal over during the perils ahead. Perhaps never. Come.

She rose, and I saw a ring on her finger—an ancient topaz in a dull, rich, archaic bezel—catch the yellow flame from whatever lay on the little table and give it to the morning.

We stood at last beside it and I saw.

You see, she said. It is a tear-shaped stone.

Of the most amazingly yellow and luminous paste.

Not paste. It is a diamond, she said.

She reached out her fingers to it, and the stone seemed to answer by kindling its fires more ardently.

It is the diamond known as Face-to-Face, she said.

It is a diamond with a history, I said. I sense that. Like the Hope, perhaps?

The opposite of the Hope, she said. The very opposite. This stone has no history of murder and accidentally fateful death, or of theft—

I would think you'd worry, I said. Its lying out here in your garden—even walled as it is.

The stone lies here day and night, she said. No one has stolen it.

She smiled again, her full, unpainted lips flashing back like wings from the lark song of her voice.

No one *can* steal it, Fifi Leech.

You must explain.

Face-to-Face—and I know it's a curious name for a great gem, but it is a truthful one, as you shall see—Face-to-Face has two thousand years of history. According to legend—which is Truth, of course.

Where does it begin?

At the Last Supper. His Last Supper.

I think I know.

The Supper—as certain seers may have explained to you—took place on the second floor of the Holiday Inn.

In Weirton, by chance?

I thought you would know.

In the room called the Steel Room.

Yes, it was rented by Judas Iscariot for the occasion.

And Criste suddenly realized something and a tear fell off his cheek.

A great yellow tear. An enormous tear.

As we spoke, parrying thought back and forth, it was as if we were speaking with one mind.

Which became the diamond—Face-to-Face.

Yes, Fifi, but do you know where?

No.

167

On the side of the big plastic cup Criste was drinking Diet Pepsi out of.

And after his death——?

Yes. He was crucified on the hill above the big Dow chemical works. (Blake's own Satanic Mills.) On the hill called recently by the Ecumenical Council, in its desperate drive to popularize the false faith, Cross Patch.

After his death the stone passed on to other hands.

By no means. It was lost, my dearest.

Lost?

It has always been lost. It is destined to be lost. Ultimately lost, that is, by all who possess it——save one final owner.

Can't it be sold?

Never.

How is that possible?

Because a minute or two after the buyer has taken it——no matter what precaution he may take——it is mislaid.

And found again?

Always. Perhaps by a poor Arab child, or an old Ashanti woman, or a rich explorer——someone who holds it, glories in it for a little while or treats it as a toy, and then loses it.

It has never been willed to anyone?

Or inherited.

And you say everyone who has ever had it has lost it?

Until now. Part of the myth is that some ultimate possessor will keep it for always. And find that it is the key to the Kingdom of the Criste.

I mistrust God——I laughed——but I trust Criste with my soul.

You will understand the riddle of *that* mystery someday, my dearest, she said, powdering her pretty nose in a small Revlon compact mirror. She did her lips. She licked them and smiled, looking about nineteen. But I was into deeper desires just then than sexual ones. Adonis *did* have her nose, something of her gay laugh, her infectious good-heartedness. She smiled, and her face went sad, like the sun going down on a lawn party.

My poor Adonis, she said. I hope you mean it when you say you love him. A love like that might save him.

She sniffed.

And imagine, she went on, there being such ugly fortunes in fakes. O, the times.

I said, But I want to say that I think I know Adonis in a way that might surprise you. No, I have put that badly. I think I know a beautiful side of him you may never have noticed.

Do you think so? she cried, rapturous on two cents' worth of Hope. O, do you believe that, my dear? If I thought—

She shook her head. Sometimes even the most cunning and skillful of Wonderists can be blind in one eye or the other.

She cast me a quick look.

Do you have a sense, she asked then in a low voice, do you even have the faintest intuition—*déjà entendu,* so to speak—of the violent, strange things which lie ahead for you in Manhattan—I even see Long Island—and somewhere in England, Fifi Leech?

I am rapidly gaining that sense as my Wound of Wonder opens wider and wider.

I reached out my tingling fingers to the great tear-shaped ray of sunlight.

And Criste wept, I said. Grieving at the Last Supper in that Weirton motel two thousand years ago.

Wept for grief? O, heavens, no. Criste never was *seen* to weep for grief! That was a tear of *laughter.* Which is, of course, man's deepest-rooted cry.

Laughter? I said, marveling. At being betrayed?

O, no, she said. He *knew* he would be betrayed. Lord, he knew men so *well.* He had long ago known *that* would happen.

Then why did he cry?—laugh?—both?

He laughed at the saddest realization of all—the worst one of his life—the one that broke his heart so that he almost laughed himself to death.

Not at being betrayed, I said. Then why?

I waited.

I think I know.

Of course, you know. The worst thing that happened to Criste was not surely when he was betrayed, not even when he was killed. It was when he was *organized.*

She fairly roared the word.

And then the little candles were snatched out from under the faithful bushels and made into a church candelabrum to light the ledgers of the businessmen in the temple.

O, I do adore you, Jonathan Thomas Bigod!

And I you, darling—if there were time I would teach you ways of love I learned in Serendipity—

Ah, Ceylon.

—more years ago than you have lived, Fifi Leech.

She touched my cheek.

O, I think I will have you give my share of your lovemaking to my son—he needs a girl like you. I think you may be something he needs more than he can guess.

Yes, she went on presently, the flush of roused passions fading slowly, like winter roses, from her cheeks. Yes, the death of what men have called Christianity—the takeover by Satan—began when it was *organized* and the individual, the lonely, Criste-crazed individual, was banished to the deserts of the human spirit.

May I touch the stone? I asked, reaching out my fingers toward it and feeling a light steal up them as coal fire steals up the iron of a poker.

You may *have* the stone, my dearest.

Have it? O, my—I thought you said it could never be given away.

Once only in each century.

Given away.

Once. And once only. Every hundred years.

And is it lost by the one to whom it is so given?

It always has been, she said. Although one hand will possess it always—one heart, one daring, unflinching mind. And he or she will find it the golden ball that an old uncle of mine named Will described as leading in "At Heaven's gate—built in Jerusalem's wall."

Or Weirton. I laughed.

Or Anyplace, she said. For Criste is in Everywhen.

And you are giving Face-to-Face—to me?

Believe me—so long as you possess it, no one can really harm you.

Frighten me? I chuckled.

O, yes, they can frighten you. And god knows, they will tonight. But while you possess this stone—well, you will see—

From an apron pocket she produced a small and worn gray-blue-velvet jewel case. She opened it, and I spied Cyrillic script in the silken lining of the lid—the jeweler's hallmark, I supposed, and intended to check it out before I caught the bus.

She lifted up the stone—Lord, it seemed to bounce in golden light in her palm—and, fitting it into the little jewel box, handed it to me.

I am frightened, I said, holding the box awkwardly against the silk corduroy of my trench coat. A thing worth so much—

In money? Nonsense. In actuality it is worth nothing. It is, you see, uninsurable. Unbuyable.

But yellow diamonds, I said, the rare canary-yellow of this stone—they are priceless.

Face-to-Face is priceless. She smiled. No one can buy it. No one can sell it. Stone and money both vanish shortly after the transaction is so preposterously acted out.

She looked at the beehives at the back of the radiant little garden.

If the stone were, shall we say, unattached, a yellow diamond of this size and flawlessness would fetch perhaps thirty million in times like these.

She turned to me again, and I knew her services were about to be professionally concluded.

I walked across the flags toward the open French doors, barely noticing that I had stepped on a small yellow-and-white mess on the nearest stone.

Of course, she said, her hand on my arm, there are times when you may imagine you have lost Face-to-Face, when, in fact, it is still with you.

How can one know, Madame Jonathan?

One can never be sure, she said, shaking her head. But now you must hurry and catch the bus to Manhattan. Surprises await you. O, my, yes. I could not begin to describe how open you must keep that Wound of Wonder. O, yes, my lovely child, you must. And you shall. My treatment of Wonderism has, I think, been worth every bit of seventy-five cents.

I gave her another quarter from my purse.

She smiled and kissed me on the cheek.

And then she stood in the quarter-paned doorway of the shop, looking out into the persistent foggy mists of Mole Street and the sad, laggardly midden of trash that lay upon the cobbles. A hungry stray dog came rooting, staggering, panicked with need. She smiled and let him in the shop and got a dish of food from under the counter and set it down before him.

Nothing surprises the world anymore, she said. No book can be written that shocks, no play that astounds, no tune that will make men dance as did the archaic people. Apathy and boredom and the blasé, stunt-stunned mind of modern man. And yet, and yet—something is *coming*, Fifi Leech. Something is on the wind of 1992.

I know, I said. It is as if the tinder of the human mind these days is dead and barren and apparently finished—like a hillside of brush that was once green and yellow woodland. And yet—and yet—that tinder is as dry as Mojave sage—so dry that the tiniest flame of one man's small, brave, Wonder-Wounded idea could set the whole world aflame.

O, yes, I know you are right for my poor lost boy, she moaned against me, and I felt she should not have let herself go so—a woman of her vision and insight. We are so blind to our own children.

I was gone then, after a quick meeting of our tongues in loving sisterhood. Yet I was not gone; a moment later she called to me. She was waving a man's handkerchief.

I returned, and she knelt.

You are so chic, she said. So absolutely smashing in every aspect. I noticed you had something on your black pump. Let me wipe it off.

A bit of dog dooby?

Nothing like that. It was on the floor of my garden. A broken egg.

A broken egg?

Yes, she said, smiling. A friend of mine—very dear to me—who fancies himself an amateur magician.

My ankle literally trembled as I stood watching her clean the tiny spot from my Gucci shoe.


I was back on Market Street in a moment's long, easy strides. I felt a great protection from the treasure in my trench-coat pocket, but really, there seemed no sign of danger about. I knew there was another bus to Manhattan in half an hour. I did a moment's figuring. I was suddenly on fire with curiosity about the Cyrillic writing in the skyblue silk of the stone's jewel box. And I knew I was taking chances in planning what I did. Shyly, yet strangely without fear, I took the faded little blue box out of my pocket and into the light. In the glare of a neon-spouting record mart I opened it. The light flamed out like a micro-sunrise. I closed it and headed down Sixteenth Street toward the jewelry store of Bailey, Banks and Biddle. I remembered an old jeweler at Bailey, Banks and Biddle who, years ago, had fixed a small Byzantine cross Sweeley Leech had given me, with a ring and chain. If that man was still there, still alive, he would translate the jeweler's Russian words in my box.

The store, at that yellow, slanting morning hour, was almost empty. I saw my old friend almost immediately. I explained to him who I was and gave him the little jewel box without fear.

He took it into the bars of sunlight in his show window and smiled, shaking his head with wonder.

It is indeed beautiful, Miss Leech, he said.

He screwed a tiny glass into his right eye and squinted, shaking his head and crooning.

It is a beautiful stone, no? I said, laughing with joy.

All the stones, he said. All the stones.

I felt uneasy.

*All* the stones?

It is a Fabergé. He smiled. Unquestionably. Remarkable. Extraordinary. In fact, unbelievable!

Stones? Fabergé?

He reached into my adorable little blue box and lifted out a huge ornate Russian ornament of some kind: swimming with garnets and rubies, topazes and aquamarines, and set in the most incredibly intricate gold-and-silver niello.

Face-to-Face? I squeaked.

I beg your pardon. No, don't speak. Let me translate.

I felt a little saddened. I knew that Madame Jonathan had not fooled me. I knew that she had given me the great stone in the faith that no one else had done so in this century. I knew I had not been betrayed. And I knew, too, that perhaps I had not lost Face-to-Face at all. Yet—what was this?

Mr. Higgs—that was my jeweler's name—was staring at me above the object in its box, his face contorted with an almost apoplectic puzzlement.

I do not understand, he gasped, passing the closed box back into my hands. I do not *understand.*

It's a mystery to me, too, Mr. Higgs.

No, no, he said. You do not grasp the *import* of this matter.

Mr. Higgs, you look ill. Sit down. Can I get you a glass of water?

No, no. Thank you. No. I'll be all right in a minute.

What did you see?

What do you see? he said. You can see as well as I. An authentic, beautiful example of the work of Nikita F——, a craftsman in Fabergé's great St. Petersburg shops. It is unmistakable. And yet. And yet—

And yet what, dear Mr. Higgs?

It is a key, he said. As you can plainly read, if you read Cyrillic—

I don't.

Then I forgive you. If you did, you would be as shocked as I.

Why?

Because this is the key to locker number three-eighteen in the Manhattan Port Authority Bus Terminal.

A silence buzzed like a golden fly in the space between us.

Really? I smiled.

I kissed Mr. Higgs sweetly on the lips. I ran down Sixteenth toward Market again, toward the Greyhound station. I was happy. I knew this key to a New York City bus locker would lead me to Lindy. And perhaps save her from death.

# E·L·E·V·E·N

The perception of Power is Power.
—David Garth

When a man's friends become his followers, he is doomed.
When they become his disciples, his work is as good as dead.
—Sweeley Leech

The longest, coldest journey of your life? Either the ascent of a small child up staircases into unknown, upper-chambered darkness. Or the ten feet you race tiptoe across the cold, broken linoleum to light your tiny gas fire on a cold, cold winter's morning. Yet the last lap up the Jersey Turnpike seemed the longest, coldest trip I'd ever taken. O, the Greyhound was warm enough—overheated, in fact. It was an inscaped coldness. I think of a saying reported by Jung's beloved comrade Laurens van der Post. He told in his loving, lovely chronicle of that master's life of a Stone Age man in the South

African veld who said to him once, "You know, there is a dream dreaming us." That pinpoints it. It was that kind of feeling—that I was being dreamed. Dreamed by the myriad motley sleepers in the predawn dark of the cutout city skyline up to the left, its far, diamond windowpanes beginning to winkle from the lipping up of the adorable sun over the Atlantic rim.

I felt sad and tenderhearted as I lugged my twin bags down the impossible steel stairway of the bus and onto the iron-fenced loading zone. I pushed—was half pushed—through the junk-food-sticky glass doors. I stood staring, fascinated, at a Budweiser poster in Spanish. I turned and bumped my nose square into a crucifix—worn by a big, black-vestured, black-hatted clergyman. He excused himself, I excused myself, and our eyes caught and kindled for an instant. His face was absurdly asymmetrical—with a dimple on the left cheek only. It gave his gray-eyed solemnity a kind of frivolous affability. There are some faces I see and know I shall never forget—his was one. And I was right.

I pushed toward the escalator. A pre-Columbian face, like one of those recently uncovered at Michoacán and Tabasco, loomed up ahead of me. The carmine Toltec mouth opened and I caught a glint of a steel tooth in the rotting slum of its neighbors. His breath was a fanfare of green, cheap wine and garlic. I don't mind green wine and I adore garlic. But this script for them was horrid. I pushed against the Mylar fabric of his open jacket. His hands reached out while the steel tooth flashed his smile like a heliograph on the rim of some crumbling mountain range. He had little tufts of hair on the backs of his dirty thumbs. His fingers were like eight thick penises tipped with broken horn. I panicked; I thought to myself how Sweeley Leech had raised me so that in a twinkling I had taken the situation all apart and put it together again. I giggled; I sighed; I moaned. I pressed my hips hard against the big machocist's thighs. I groaned and ground, my absolutely unerect nipples pushing against the carnival rayon of his impossible sports shirt. I reached lips to the tufted ear upon whose greasy, scorbutic lobe a dark brass earring was clinging like a hand loop in a dingy subway car. I could feel his already taut cock begin to rise against the Korean corduroy of his pants, against my dress. I crooned again, as I saw a reassuring face in the crowd behind me.

If you only knew, *amigo,* I said, in flawless Nahuatl, how marvelous it is to snuggle up against a nice man and not have to feel that simply impossible pressure against one's sensitive breasts—

He was licking his lips—grayish, cracked strips of sweetbreads—and his eyes were stoked furnaces.

—that awful, hard .357 Magnum; I mean, like my boyfriend wears in his shoulder holster. Closer, closer, my heavenly bullock.

I paused, timing it impeccably even as I felt his tumescence begin to subside in his unspeakable pants. Poor baby—maybe if he bathed and sobered up, I would find him charming and desirable. I saw his black peach-pit eyes begin to dart, to flit from face to face until they settled on the one at whom I stared myself. That absolutely splendid and capital left-hand dimple was like the incipient sunrise. He was six or eight layers of people away, but he was moving toward us. My poor lousy Latin Lover. He was standing, hands at his sides, fingers flexing and unflexing.

I must note something at this point about clergymen in our time. Knowing the Church to be now the bastion of the Anti-Criste, I pity all clergymen. And not merely because of the fact—now that the great spiritual showdowns are approaching with the speed of light—that almost all men of the cloth these days carry guns. My pre-Columbian admirer knew this, too. He decided against going for the simple weapon I saw glinting in its winecork at the mouth of his frayed, satin shirt pocket. It is the sharpest of defenses. One takes a razor blade and breaks out a crescent of it with a pair of pliers. The resultant edge would lay open rhinoceros hide. Still—as the square, honest, faintly amused face of the churchman bobbed nearer and nearer through the Muppet balcony of marvelous heads—I wondered, meanly, how I should be able to bring myself to express gratitude for anything to a man of the Devil's own black-and-white cloth. Yet, surely, any moment that would be expected of me.

In a moment he was through, ignoring me entirely, sweeping me gently aside, and standing eyeball to eyeball with the startled neo-Toltec. I was aroused to hear his voice for the first time—not the sweaty gladhand howdy of the evangelist or even the BBD and O unctuousness of Norman Vincent Whoever. Just a nice kind of strong, pleasant voice—like maybe Richard Burton would have had it he'd been a miner in Pennsylvania instead of Wales. But it was what he said—in plain English—that truly astonished me and made me want to know this pastor better.

The voice itself was, I knew—well, hell, darlings, *you* know Fifi—going to make me want to fuck with him soon. I had never been fucked by a preacher—and I don't count my father as a preacher, you know. And I was just yellow with curiosity. And he was saving me from being dragged, only dimly aware, back into a corridor between Port Authority lockers, there to be raped. But what he said—

He said: My friend, this lady isn't the one you want to fuck. Because this lady doesn't want to fuck. Leave here and go out into the beautiful morning city and find her. She is waiting somewhere—the one who wants you to fuck her. And that will be beautiful—a glory to God—a sacrament of the living Criste.

And he stood while the big Mexican melted into the motley of faces and leather and rabbit-fur and loden-cloth shoulders around the little iron purgatory of the escalator. He turned, stared levelly at me a moment, fingering the crucifix low on its beaded necklace whose tip he had employed as if it were the muzzle of the snub-nosed revolver he probably actually wore somewhere among his black serge vestments. I opened my mouth, smiling, to thank him, but he reached up, touched me simply on the forehead with his two cool fingers, and was gone.

Why, the darling. Was it conceivable that there was a splinter of the Criste still smoldering vaingloriously deep in the midden of Methodism, the Reason-felled rubble of all the Coventrys of the man's mind? The thought thrilled me—that there were brave spies of God termiting amid the rotten phosphorescence of the rooftree of religion in 1992. O, the dears. I had never taken that possibility into account. And Sweeley Leech had never spoken of it, though I am sure he knew.

I thought ruefully of the yellow treasure I had apparently lost. Face-to-Face. O, I felt ashamed to think that I perhaps was the owner who had possessed her for the shortest time. Her? O, yes, her. I am certain of the fact that the light of yellow in the great stone had been the light of the eternal Feminine. Face-to-Face was so sweetly gendered. But I had the gray-blue scuffed velvet jewel

box, at least—with its Romanov colophon in the stained and Sara-
jevoed silk of the lining of the lid. And the lovely Fabergé key to
locker number 318—somewhere in the bank of little vaults that
stood beyond a group of befezzed Shriners and their portly misses
in the mass of people hurtling back and forth in the garish laser
light of the waiting-room level. I moved through them—smelling
sweet, sad wisps of Canoe and L'Oréal and stale McDonald's box
lunches—and sought out the number. I took the jewel box out of
the big pocket of my silk corduroy trench coat. I opened it. I
winced as the rock-racketing of a tiny hi-fi portable rioted past me
in the ear-to-shoulder of a stonefaced black. 322. 320. Ah, yes. I
reached out—it was the second locker from the floor. I held the
glittering platinum tip of the carved key before the hard, tiny slot of
the keyhole. Would it really work? Could a key fashioned in the
snowfallen dusks of St. Petersburg nights in faded, crumbling years
before the temple lights of Cristendom began winking out—could
this fine instrument, fashioned by tsarist Russians long gone to
bones, open a locker installed in 1985? Naturally. I say naturally
because it did. I didn't say supernaturally. Because, as Sweeley
Leech taught me, there is no such thing as the supernatural—there
is only the unknown, the undiscovered.

I opened the locker. The light flamed on, illuminating a caver-
nous and empty interior. Apparently empty. Yet not quite. Something like a tiny croissant lay at the bottom of the locker. I picked it
up, turned it over and over in my fingers. Damn. Damn! O, there
was only one person on earth capable of perpetrating such an elaborate hoax on me. I stared at the object in my fingers and, despite my
impatience, I laughed. It was a Chinese fortune cookie. Sweeley
Leech, you are incorrigible. For who else could fob off on me such a
mad illusion? I broke the cookie open and nibbled a sweet crust of
it—faintly tangy with a hint of Rinsey's darling red raspberry preserves. I unfolded the tiny legend on the paper. I giggled. Incorrigible. It made no sense whatsoever. And yet— And yet—

"Stanley Cohen never got past PSC102."

O, Sweeley, my priceless fool. I tucked the tiny slip of cheaply
printed paper into my pocket and nibbled a bit more of the really
delicious cookie.

I thought so gratefully of the strange black-frocked man who had saved me back there. In 1992, rape occurs in the Port Authority on the average of twice daily. Arrests rarely are made—the dockets are overflowing and plea bargaining always has the rapist back on the bricks within hours. I remember my thought as my great, smelly admirer reached for me, his talons pressing into the delicate small of my back. "O, God, I *do* hope you're clean" had flashed through my mind. Silly. And spider silk is so precious the way Loll weaves it—I hated to think of my black lace panties torn.

I smelled steak cooking. I repeat—standing there with all kinds of that wonderful waxworks shoving and pushing past me toward impossibly far exits—I smelled a good piece of steak cooking. With mushrooms. I looked around the phalanx of shops and fast-food marts that lined the level. Nedick's. A good fifty yards away. And whatever Nedick's smells like it doesn't ever smell like steak. It's seldom enough these days that steakhouses smell like steak. T-bone. No—maybe a nice little shell or Delmonico. And then I saw the locker beneath the one which had held my particular booby prize for the day. The steel door was slightly ajar. Wisps of smoke vined up into the air above it. Startled, I quickly knelt before this locker and drew the door gently open. I drew back with a peal of quick laughter. Within the locker space, larger than mine—big enough for at least two good-sized bags—a small family of really charming Jewish gnomes had set up pleasant, if transient, housekeeping. I say pleasant but I must add makeshift. There was a microscopic mezuzah epoxyed to the metal wall by the door. An Endicott Johnson shoe box filled with Charmin toilet tissue served as a bed. A small piece of steak and tiny mushrooms sizzled and bubbled temptingly in a frying pan cleverly fashioned out of a Diet Pepsi can. A Dr Pepper container had been sheared out into a really effective little stove, with a taped-down Bic lighter for a burner.

The little man was about a foot high and his wife a few inches taller. He had a merry, Slavic face but with lights of mischief winking in it. He obviously had a hard-on. It was clear he wasn't getting enough loving from his sweet-faced but independent-appearing little wife. I espied the tin box of Band-Aids against the rear wall and immediately I knew. The tiny soul was having her period. How persnickety little Jewish lady gnomes can be. I watched as the lady gnome went and adjusted the Bic's flame length under their meal. The male gnome stared at me with that New Yorker's first look that almost always softens soon into a hometown smile. But it hadn't begun happening yet.

*Nu?* You wanneh *shtup?*

I smiled and shook my head.

I really haven't time for sex or small talk, I said. And with me the two go together. I happen to be in a great hurry.

We know, said the small one. You are Fifi. Leech. Fifi Leech. My name is Moishe the Bissel and my wife's name is Sadie. You are looking for your sister.

You do know everything, I said softly.

I know what every enlightened Jewish intellectual gnome knows these troubled days, he said.

I am waiting.

We know that Stanley Cohen is a *shmuck*—

Who never got past PSC102?

Yes. How did you guess?

I didn't, really. To me it doesn't matter, when it comes to helping me find poor Lindy, if Stanley Cohen never went to public school at all.

Public school has nothing to do with it. As a matter of fact, Stanley Cohen has about five degrees. That's why he should know.

Know what, pray?

Know that there is a principle in the universe which is swifter than light. More powerful than atomic energy!

I see. Irrelevant. Totally irrelevant to what's on my mind.

Look at her, he suddenly said, turning to face the back of the locker.

Sadie had taken supper off and set it out for them. She had gone back to their Charmin box and lain down naked and was now merrily masturbating with a tiny birthday-cake candle for a dildo. Moishe shrugged.

When she's horniest, he said, she won't let me touch her.

I know, I said sympathetically. Women are prisoners, too. Poor baby.

His slant eyes kindled, and I let a sweep of my words brush the sex from his mind again.

My sister, I said, is somewhere in this city. Being held. By enemies—enemies who may do something dreadful to her.

A fact which has not yet reached her.

I know.

It will, he said. And you will be the one to reveal it to her, I think.

O, can you give me a clue?

Yes. A clue. And only a clue. And that clue will lead to yet another clue. And another, and so on. Until—

Till what?

One of two things must happen.

Like what?

You will find her, he said, or you will not find her.

He tucked up his tiny belt a little smugly.

You see, I have a logical mind. The kind of mind that yet accepts the being of the Invisible. Apropos of which, I declare: Fuck Norman Podhoretz!

Men like that can't help not believing, I said. They are truly the Bad News Bearers. But don't involve me in such partisan reviews just now. I am really half-sick with concern.

I told you—Sadie and I will give you the clue.

Maybe more than one.

I am a poor man, he said. If you could spare a bit of small change.

I gave him fifty cents, with a blessing and a smile and a pat on the groin.

He mused.

There is an old Jewish gnome's proverb, he said. There are three great Lies. First, it's easy to be poor. Second, it's easy to be a Jewish gnome. And third, just let me put the head in.

I love you, Moishe the Bissel. And if I had time, I might show you how much!

I'm very easily smuggled into a Ramada Inn, he said, leering little-ly. In any good-size purse or makeup kit. And there's one down Eighth near West Forty-eighth Street.

Thank you. O, thank you, but no. Another time. I do find you most attractive.

Sadie was astride a dolphin of lone joy on the shoe-box bed.

Besides, I said a little coyly, I'm afraid. Why only one clue? If you know where my sister is, why not just bless me with a whole bouquet of clues?

Unfortunately, there are realities, he said. And Art does not work that neatly.

Art? This is Life.

Ah, but Those in Charge insist on injecting Life with Art. And Art with Life.

It sounded—despite my feelings of utter frustration—completely logical. Someone was slowly—and I hoped surely—guiding me, clue by clue (the amusements surely of a madman), toward Lindy. Logic of this kind usually appeals to me. And I am a logical person. I think it grossly fair, for example, that football won't let them have a fifth down.

Moishe the Bissel smiled, not ungently, up at my face, reflecting the glare of a nearby Barton's—a bonbon bonfire of gold tinsel.

I wonder, he said softly, if you can even guess at the incredible adventures that lie ahead of you tonight?

I turned, startled, back to his face. I had been ogling a cute Vietnamese sailor by the newsstand who was leafing gloomily through a new *Penthouse*.

It's strange, Moishe the Bissel, I said. You're the second one who's said that to me today.

He handed me a small white envelope, perhaps half his size, and slammed the little baggage locker door in my face.

You must leave off looking at things obliquely, Fifi Leech, I heard him call through the riveted portal. And see them, at last, face-to-face.

I adored him instantly. I kissed the little envelope he had given me and praised Moishe the Bissel as a tiny Jewish prophet of some luminous latter day.

I fetched out two quarters from my purse. I had no intention of leaving the Fabergé key to be examined, misunderstood, and perhaps thrown away by Port Authority officials. I looked. And looked again. It was quite manifestly gone. I ran my fingertips up to the number to be sure I was not mistaken: 318—the same. But the key in it was a dull, flat, creased disk where I touched it. My hand flew to the gray-blue Russian jewel box. I opened it an inch. There was nothing there.

I went to the Person Room and had a good post-bustrip pee. I hastily blotted my curls, rose, adjusted my panties and dress, stared back at my stocking seams to see if they were straight. I hurried toward the Nedick's for a coffee and a quick perusal of the contents of the small white envelope nestling in the silk-lined pocket of my coat. Nedick's was impossibly jammed with nascent morning winos and construction workers waiting to grab a dog and coffee and then subway off to the job. I don't hate nascent winos or construction workers, but there was no stool. I got out onto Eighth Avenue and walked with the morning winds, which whipped my coat around my good legs and made heads of both genders turn. I walked up Eighth in the city and under the ceremonies of the new moon, which lingered, a survivor, in the vapors of sedition and foulness against which the young sun strove. Criste was in faces all around me: in faces that were scuffed and hurt and perhaps hating; in faces burnished and B-vitamined on their way to highrise, carpeted jobs. O, I wanted to shout to them, he is not *coming,* he is *here*—in *you*—waiting. Imprisoned. The One who is coming is the Strange One who will release the Criste from you. If you want to see the Criste, though—and face-to-face—dare to lift up your bushel and look: that tiny, gust-battered flame is he! Or see him glowing and Christmascandle-shining in the eyes of some buddy or child or beast you adore. I took the white envelope out three times and always put it back. Even when I was dining on a chopped-liver sandwich for breakfast (better than Crazy Cow!) and sipping dense, gritty black coffee in a joint near a Forty-second Street BMT entrance—even then I somehow did not have the gumption to tear the thing open and get it over with. Was it a note from Lindy? Was it a threat? None of these, I knew. And finally with a laugh I realized and acknowledged the basis for my reticence. I had bit before. On a fortune cookie. I somehow didn't relish another of my ubiquitous father's gags. I paid—tipped the bad Hispanic waiter an enormous amount—and went out into the light-splashed morning of the waking city.

An ancient bearded Kent State–type hippie confronted me at Forty-second and Broadway.

Will you give me twenty dollars for breakfast?

Doesn't that seem like a lot, I asked, for breakfast?

Lady, I'm a manic depressive. My lithium ran out last week. Can I help it if my expectations are grandiose and inflated?

I gave him a fifty and pressed on into the wind and quaking light of a holy, holy morning. O, I felt as if I were a tiny goldfish swimming back and forth within a tear on the cheek of the Lord. I wanted to do something terribly indecent—flaunt what I had, stick

it out to be adored in return. And I suddenly realized that the saddest thing about Times Square is that nobody notices anything. Except money. Death, sex, love, hate—all go unnoticed in that vast
neon nebula and universe; everything is ignored save money.
Maybe when Whitman and Poe meandered that tract and felt the
old telluric tugs through the cobbles, there was something else they
sought. Maybe back then it was love *and* money. But now it was
only money.

I walked up Broadway. I felt the fungus of money crusting the
pavements, the walls, the shopwindows I passed.

Impatiently I ripped open the white envelope. I yanked out a
cheap, magenta-tinted card—cheaply photocopied—of a solicita-
tion to a fundamentalist religious gathering:

> Children of Chinatown, the Day is nigh! Repent,
> O Mott Street sinners, before that Night (which heralds
> the longest Day) is come. Are ye washed in the tears of
> the Lamb? Can ye drink of the Styrofoam cup, ye Doxies
> and Denizens of Pell and Doyer? Are you prepared to
> welcome again the Dyer? His Coming is almost here!
> Meetings twenty-four hours without appointment.
> Donation gratefully accepted. Gospel Feedback Tabernacle,
> 16 Chatham Square (in old Venice movie theater),
> New York, New York 10001. (212) EN9-1348—
> —Right Reverend Jimbo St. Venus, pastor.
> All you need to face the Coming Darkness,
> that Dark before the dawn!

All I needed, indeed. All I needed to face the darkness before *his*
dawn, you mean. Some fool preacher's darkness, some hypocritical
pastor's false dawn. Would I go? Not hardly, I said aloud, tossing
the card and envelope into a litter basket. I walked on, frowning,
chewing my necklace lightly. Was it just another of the counterfeit
Moseses, the spurious Jesuses that choir continuously from out the
open, mad synagogues of Southern California: a million warring
creeds, spilling across the Rockies into New York City, which adds
its own hectic-voiced mistakers to the chorus? Was it just another
poor tiny frog glee club scritching Security to the lonely bog? I
walked slowly back to the trash basket. Somebody had dumped wax
paper with egg salad on it on top of my card. I wiped it free and

read again, with increasing curiosity. Besides, whatever sort of wolf's den of false prophecy it might be, it was part of the mad game I was being forced to play, amid such Jungian synchronicities, as clue by clue was handed to me to be accepted and followed, however strange-seeming and fraught with mysteries, to some new point of arrival and departure in my quest for the lost Lindy.

I walked on, rereading and then re-rereading that little magenta card. Are you washed in the "tears" of the Lamb? That was strange. I walked on. Tears, not blood. "Styrofoam cup"—curiouser and curiouser.

I listened to the click of my heels along that curious sidewalk. I fell in love with a young Parisian lady-secretary with an Air France tote bag. Or was she an American book executive just in from Paris? I adored her on sight. She possessed the most exquisite small mole above her left ankle, just before the ankle sweeps gently out to make the taut, firm calf. The mole spoke to me above her simple gold ankle bracelet. She was holding something before her. I drew abreast. The wind quickened as her fingers deftly flung up. A spray of something tingly and sweet sprayed across my lips. I licked and tasted. Nectar. Bubbles. I saw the open UnCola can in her fingers. The spray had risen when she snapped off the ring opener. We smiled. A little communion between women had happened. Some sacrament of sweetness shared in that bitter avenue's chill wind. I watched her good and happy hips bouncing off into Time, speaking joyously about all past hip ecstasies.

I felt that morning as if I were walking on unbreakable toy balloons that lifted me up and ever up! I took stock of myself as I perused that strange magenta card. Pancreas in fine working order. Liver likewise. Thank you, dear Lordy. Lungs all clear and in working order. Pineal gland has secreted its sacred infinitesimality into my organism. O, my thanks, loving Criste, for these blessings. Stomach not complaining and feeling sweet. Thank you, thank you, Seigneur. Bowels just grand. For these things, dear Saviour, the thanks of your loving Fifi Leech.

I knew by now—deep in the heart of the Diamond District, in the Forties between Sixth and Fifth—that I was going to catch the IRT down to the Bowery, to the Gospel Feedback Tabernacle. In a moment.

Again the "Styrofoam cup" came tilting into my haunted fancy.

Well, after all, I mused, considering how stuffy all preachers are, must there not be something remarkable in this prelate who refuses to change that frivolous name "Jimbo" into just "J"?

"Are ye washed in the tears of the Lamb?"

Already I half liked this Right Reverend Jimbo St. Venus. St. Venus, indeed! What a bawdy honeymoon of Christian and Pagan *that* name was! Had there indeed ever been a Saint Venus? My knowledge of hagiology was such that I could only speculate delightedly.

The Diamond District east of Sixth in the Forties is really a district East of Everywhere. It is so far East it is out there underwater somewhere in the breakers a thousand feet above Atlantis's moody ruins. Old Rouault Jews move to and fro like divers under deep, green water—glittering and sepulchral and sacrist are these ancient Rembrandt visions fetching gems of unspeakable brilliance to and fro from one dolphin-shattered casket to another. Rubies brilliant as fresh lung-blood. Emeralds inside of which green was first seen, a green older than grass or leaf; blue-midnight lapis streaked with the gold of spoiled and scattered stars; opals exploding with the Druid flames of burning wicker men all full of screams. These marvelous old Hebraic Neptunes bearing fire to and fro on their tritons filled me with awed love. I adored them. But I hurried on. Toward the IRT entrance I knew I'd find over at Fifty-first and Lex. I could smell the deli smells of the district. The smell of small china pitchers filled with chicken fat to be spooned out onto roast beef and thin onion on Levy's rye. Celery tonic smell. Dairy smell. O, I breathed in all Israel and exhaled impromptu psalms. I clicked past Mère de Cézanne's little shop, and images of Adonis and Soleil pressed into my mind. I stared through one dusty, quartered pane. Her tiny rocker of cunning Provençal wicker weaving, with its small, placid pancake of a cushion, was empty. Her Delft spittoon winked from behind the stoked fires of a Pascin nude—an original, alas, and not for sale, for it was virtually worthless. A neatly lettered sign hung in the door: CLOSED FOR DAY.

A boy pushing a rack full of Korean dresses paused, heard me, and, coming over—leaving his rack unguarded—gave me a feel and a kiss and billowed off singing a Fats Waller hymn.

I turned. I don't know why I turned. It is as if—on the brawly wind that cut down the canyoned Babylon—I had heard a chord of unearthly music. Just one chord. Which, when we are wiser, more remembering, will one day chime through Alice Tully Hall. I knew the chord said: Turn, fool Fifi. So I turned. And I saw it. The window was fully protected, shatterproof, bulletproof, antitankgun-proof—everything but proof against the mind. A Shah's ransom in diamonds and gold shone on small price-cards ranged all over the window. A. SILK & SONS—BROKERS IN PRECIOUS GEMS AND METALS. Everything on the little numbered cards—every price and kind of gem. Except the Priceless One. Then I saw it—crestfallen and dust-covered and all dingied under the left-hand bend of neon and alarm-tape—in the corner of the window, a dried-up dead moth partially obscuring it. Face-to-Face. Others came, looked in, looked *at* it, didn't see it, passed on.

I went into the store.

I approached the salesperson. She was a thin, cautious, gracious woman in a silk print dress that looked as if it came from Nan Duskin's, in Philly. Around her neck she wore a necklace of big beads of amber. Her hair was yellow and worked so well with the amber that I wanted to say something nice.

I decided something else about her which I immediately liked. Her air was one of cautiousness, as I have said. Yet she was not so much conscious, I knew, of the pirate's trove of precious gems from which she rose, like Venus rising above the seafoam; she was cautious and terribly self-conscious, I knew, about something entirely alien. She was flat-chested. I knew that was it. O, my dear darling, does it matter?

Might I speak to Mr. Silk?

Mr. Silk has retired. I am Ms. Apthorp. May I show you something? Or did you come for an appraisal?

There is a diamond in the window—

Many, said Ms. Apthorp. Which one did you mean?

She steered me toward the window to which I had pointed.

There are so many, she was saying. What price range did you have in mind? And is it for a gentleman, a lady, or perhaps some intermediate?

I smiled.

Neither. Or rather none of those three. It is a stone which is, in fact, not in any ring at all.

Ms. Apthorp frowned courteously.

I'm afraid I don't understand. All the stones in this window are mounted stones.

It is not a ring.

What was the price on it?

It had no price.

Perhaps it is a stone which fell from a setting.

I don't think so.

It would be quite unusual.

It is that stone, I said, trying to point, and the rays of yellow which it reflected burned so that Ms. Apthorp herself was startled.

Under the dust, I said. There's a dried-up moth— There— your hand is just over it.

Ms. Apthorp grew very quiet. After a moment she smiled.

Yes, she said. I see it now.

I waited for her to lift it out and hand it to me.

She stared, waiting, at me.

Well? she said, raising her brows.

Would you mind just reaching it out to me? I don't want to disturb the window, perhaps trip the alarm.

The alarm is off. And you must reach the stone out yourself.

She drew away from the window and turned her back to me, pressing her linen handkerchief to her nostrils. A breath of amphetamine reached me.

After all, she said, it was you—and not I—who found it.

Yes, but I lost it— I began, but she had hurried off toward frosted glass doors, behind which, in thick security, doubtless sat the experts. I reached in, without the slightest fear, and picked the lovely stone up in my fingers.

I could not understand. Madame Jonathan had told me that one owned the stone once, then lost it. And another found it. But I had found it twice! Was I therefore the One who would possess it forever? I brushed this vainglorious insanity from my thoughts.

Two people emerged from the little glassed-in office. A small, snowy-haired Sam Jaffe type with a loud Jones Beach T-shirt led the procession. Ms. Apthorp and two studious-looking Hunter College–type sons took up the rear. There were tears glistening in Ms. Apthorp's pretty eyes.

The little old man looked for all the world like the Dalai Lama holding out his fat, sensitive small fingers.

Say hello to Abe Silk.

I looked around.

No. That's me. Abe Silk.

He paused. He felt behind him for a Jensen chair and lowered himself thoughtfully, wearily into its wicker bottom.

So you have found it, he said at last, tapping his fingers into temple shapes.

I held up the flaming gem.

This, you mean, of course.

Yes. That. The goal of sixty years of hunting among gems in flea markets and emporiums where only those above the rank of English dukes are admitted to browse. Sixty years' search from Djibouti to Devonshire and back to Timor and Macao by way of Molucca and Samarkand. The hoped-for climax to a great life among gems I had hoped it to be. And you have found it—Face-to-Face—yourself.

But *you* found it, sir. It was in your window.

What *window*? You found it. I was—t-t-too blind.

But I must deal honestly with you, I persisted. I must tell you that only this morning the stone was given to me.

Where?

In Philadelphia.

Philadelphia. I never guessed. My agents are this moment in a small warehouse outside of Tashkent. And in Angora. I would have never guessed Philadelphia. It is the last place one would think to find a treasure.

You think it strange to search in Philadelphia?

What search? Who searches? I did not search. *You* did not search. You did not find—*twice* find—this treasure by searching. One simply puts oneself in a place where it is possible to find the gem—and one prays.

Oh, you're delightful, Mr. Silk.

*Nu,* I'm delightful, he chuckled. You are delightful. To the gods the delightfulness apparently is all yours. It was they who deigned that you twice find this stone.

I will not contest ownership, I said staunchly. If you think there is the shadow of a doubt as to its being mine—

Please. Don't tempt the hog that is in us all, young woman. The stone is yours—for a while—

For a while?

Yes. Didn't he (or she) who gave you the stone—and it can be given but once in every century—didn't this person explain to you all the terms of losing it?

Perhaps not all—

Did she not tell you that each owner eventually loses it?

Yes.

Inevitably loses it—

Yes.

Did she explain, however, that he who loses it twice—if he should recover it for the third time—can never lose the stone again: it is his (or hers) forever? The stone—this stone—

He leaned forward. His voice fell to a pleasant, grating sibilance. I caught the scent of Dutch cocoa on his breath.

—it came from the Cup. Do you hear? The Cup! Not just any common cup. *The* Cup!

He held out something that gave off a Coney Island tinsel glow. I took one. I unwrapped it. It was a chocolate candy cigar. Mr. Silk tapped his chest on the left side and coughed.

My doctor, he said, took out a lung two years ago. Since then, these seem to appease the craving—perhaps only because of their shape.

He laughed, chewing the chocolate as if he were a child.

I was a zeppelin crewman for the Kaiser, he said. Over England in 1915.

I stared at Face-to-Face as if it were a sunset come into my fingers.

I shall guard it this time, I said.

Mr. Silk shrugged.

Guard it! It won't matter at all if you have a Brink's truck to carry it around in all the time. When the time comes to lose—or not to lose—one cannot help it.

He looked at the gem in my palm. He licked his lips. His poor eyes shone.

I could take it from you. I could grab your wrist, break it, and snatch the stone. I could knock you down and run for the subway. You would never catch me. I would leave the store. My wife. My sons. Take a plane to some African city. Disappear. The stone would be mine—the quest of sixty years' impassioned searching—

I watched the vision collapse in his face.

The thing is I know that I would never get past Sixth Avenue with it. I would lose it. I could not help myself.

He paused a beat.

This is the one treasure on earth which cannot be coveted.

He fixed me with the most earnest, sweet look in his eyes and stared at me with tears of passion in his gaze, while he solemnly chewed up the last of his Dröste stogie.

Tell me, young woman, he said. It is a very personal question. Will you answer frankly?

Anything, I breathed.

Are you washed in the tears of the Lamb?

I could not answer. I was silent partly because the reappearance of that curious metaphor startled me so.

I kissed Mr. Silk on the forehead, kissed Ms. Apthorp on the cheek, kissed each Silk son on the lips, and wended my way back out onto the pavement.

Now I was jostling along toward Lexington Avenue and the last subway lap of my journey to the Gospel Feedback Tabernacle.

I had a curious hunch, which got even curiouser, that I was soon going to be looking across a strange and perhaps barbaric pulpit at a charming face with only one dimple!

# T✦W✦E✦L✦V✦E

"Astonish me!"
—Sergei Diaghilev

Saint Paul was no more a Christian than Christ was a Baptist.
—George Bernard Shaw, Preface to *Androcles and the Lion*

I headed for the Gothic hood of the subway at Fifty-first and Lexington. I was walking along Third, window-shopping and loving the day, when I spied—across the street and laying down a tray of steaming bagels at the sight of me—the abominable Adonis McQuestion. I say the abominable one and mean, of course, his meretricious double, whom, for no particular reason, I shall refer to as Chaz. Chaz reached through the window of the bagel truck and flashed out a midnight-blue revolver, which, I suppose, was a something-blah-blah-hundred Magnum or even worse. He came across Lex at a gallop toward where I stood before an out-of-place *botánica,* which featured a display of blood-dribbling plaster Jesuses.

I ran for the subway kiosk and darted down the steps. I heard a veritable wingding of popping New York State champagne corks behind me and stared up, with a giggle, as a hideous graffiti of bullet holes splashed a neat diamond pattern in the middle of the left cheek of a Johnny Cash poster. I darted down, fumbling out quarters as I skidded in some poor drunk's vomit, and drew up at last at the token booth. I could hear Chaz puffing and cursing down the steps; I could hear the curses of others as he thrust them aside in his maniac haste. I flung myself toward the turnstile and thrust in the token. I pushed and pushed and it would not go, that worn and rugged old crucifix of wood. I relaxed and pushed, and it clicked and opened.

There was no train in sight. And to make matters worse I observed the signs UPTOWN EXPRESS and UPTOWN LOCAL. Chatham Square was the other way. I heard the thunder from afar of a downtown train and saw the amber glimmer of it way down the tunnel. I turned and saw Chaz. He looked sad as he fired again and a tiny crystal earring disappeared from my stinging left lobe. I ducked down, took one look over the concrete edge, and dropped myself almost lazily to the tracks. I sucked in my breath as I gingerly made my way across the lightning-charged third rail to the Downtown side. The Downtown Local was whistling like mad, though not beginning to brake until it was only a few yards from me. I flung myself up onto the far platform and jerked my coat hem free in the split second that the train divided the air with its thunderous approach and hurtled checker-windowed past me.

For the moment my pursuer was blocked off. As I got on the nearest car I saw him. He did not chance another shot through the crowded car. And then he did a thing that chilled me to the marrow—he bowed and saluted. O, worthiest of foes, I have learned to feat you! Because, after that, with the muzzle of his smoking pistol, he made the sign of the cross.

When I've just passed through extreme peril, or even while passing through it, I get terribly horny. I was horny now on that dear old suicidal rattler, the underground Toonerville Trolley racketing and rolling south down lovely, lovely Manhattan. While the St. Louis–made car rocketed and bored like some gigantic eel through the stony fathoms of the city-sea, I closed my eyes and saw an Arizona sky.

I am not a death worshiper—except to the extent that all Americans are. I had driven a 1982 Mercedes SX1000 out to Phoenix to be with a love named Gerónimo Serrasalmos, a golden, gorgeous Indian from somewhere down in the rain forests north of Antifagasto, Chile. It was, I think, the first time I had coupled danger and sex.

Because on my twenty-fourth birthday I had made Gerónimo's other lover, Mario, take us up to 45,000 feet in his Cessna-Mitsubishi jet trainer and let us sky-dive. We were nude except for our parachute straps and packs, and it took us the fall of nearly a mile to maneuver into coupling position. Morning was aborning in the east, and far below us lay the wrinkled labia of the dear old Sangre de Cristo Mountains, and all of it rimmed in rosy gold. We fucked. All the way down—or nearly. In that absolutely splendid and pure rosy sun of the desert morning, you could see everywhere, yet I could see only him. I cannot remember such a fuck ever. We had to move in and out of each other using space for purchase. We dug our asses deep into clouds. Our bare feet kicked infinities loose. New Mexico was our bedside table; the Sierra Madres our headboard. I knew that if we did not both reach a lovely come before long, we would plunge into the earth together, locked in each other for eternity. I hated that, but I didn't think of it. I felt as if the nascent sun were plunging in and out of my vagina. My clit was the morning star, glowing more brightly with that solar caress. O, dear God, the joy out there in a cradled Nothing—I felt we probably were making a graceful vapor trail across the big azure dish of the sky. I felt as if my dear Lord held us, sharing, enjoying, in the sweet big waterbed of his palm. I could see the tiny reflection of highways and roadside fast-fooders in my lover's widewatching eyes. It was touch and go—but I didn't care. O, lovely! It began to happen. O, yes, dear Lord. It seemed as if a scarlet silk parachute were unfurling in my vagina and would presently, pleasantly boom open in the astroaltitudes of my womb. That precious instant then, when I felt my good girl lightning flash down around Gerónimo's gushing cock, I reached for the brass ring, then released it, remembering to maneuver free of him (O, tender parting as he slid out of me!) so that our shrouds wouldn't tangle, and I yanked then and my come was still subsiding when I landed.

Now, on the Lexington Avenue Local, hastening down the earth beneath East Side Manhattan, I picked up a copy of the London *Times* from the seat beside me. A few stories caught my eye. Plenty of oil coming in from China—the poor, darling Arabs so forgotten now. A flurry of executions reported carried out during August in the U.S.—most of them (alarmingly) for the new crime (more incriminating than Communist membership used to be) of Ecumenical Subversion. Then my eye caught an editorial discussing the serious religioeconomic (they are One in our time) impact of Manhattan's recent unrobbery. Similar crimes had been reported (said the *Times*) in two dozen cities in fourteen other countries all over the world. Something had been set in motion whose repercussions could not be immediately evaluated. Mr. Moto, the current President of the U.S.A., had been reported as saying— But then you must be told about our President.

The 1988 conventions were a shambles as the three major political parties jockeyed into a position which would give the electorate the illusion that it was choosing. Moto—Mr. Hamurai Moto—was the first foreign-born presidential candidate ever. This natal inconvenience had already been annulled by passage of the ill-fated Constitutional Revision Act of 1988. Moto, born in Kobe of missionary parents, had been educated at UCLA and took three years of postgrad at Princeton's Institute for Advanced Study. His hookup with Brzezinski and the late Henry Kissinger *and* the Rockefellers—including Jay, with his half-nelson on my own West Virginia—led to his being chosen for the people. The two other candidates were, respectively, a black man and a white woman, and you know well and good that America would elect a foreign-born man any Election Day rather than either of those hateful alternatives.

Moto is entirely pleasant—and entirely the instrument—or rather, *one* instrument—of TRUCAD. He is an impassioned born-again Christian. He learned colloquial American speech from old books in his parents' library—Sut Lovingood, Artemus Ward, Josh Billings, Kin Hubbard. He sounds like something out of Bret Harte. "I swan," he's likely to say on *Meet the Press*. "I calc'late as how this is flush times we're a-having now." (My God—tempura and soup beans!) He even says "hari-kari" instead of "hara-kiri," although nobody has any hopes that he would ever commit it. His lingo (as he calls it) hasn't even caught up with the latest vernacular of Mark Twain or James Whitcomb Riley, let alone the fingersnapping jive talk of the thirties. But his main importance is the way he succeeded, while president of the Bank of Yokohama, in causing a veritable landslide of mergers between huge Japanese corporations and companies abroad—particularly in the U.S. He isn't much, really, but he is kind. The trouble is that he is a member of that most terrible group called TRUCAD, whose aims for life on earth are anything but kind.

Anyhow, here he was in my subway copy of the London *Times*, saying that vast new police measures were about to go into effect regarding this strange crime which TRUCAD had labeled Ecumenical Subversion or, occasionally (and to the dismay of Edwin Newman), Illegal Ecumenicity. What did it mean? Well, its meaning was becoming clearer to me with every passing hour in New York: one's religious attitudes were becoming very interesting to the international government. I envisioned the even-more-darkling blossom of a really repressive administration in which, as in the Reformation, dreams would be the kindling pyres upon which martyrs burned. In myriad counties—and quite a few foreign countries—this was the only capital crime. Well, it had to come, I guess. The state, the ruling group, had to finally recognize that the thing which kept the masses in line was that Religion which is not so much the opium of the people as its Librium and Valium. It didn't put them to sleep totally but merely paralyzed certain vital instincts toward social ambition. (TRUCAD knows too well that sleepers have *Dreams*). It blurred and diffused the boundaries between Religion and Property into a kind of washy Rorschach that immediately had extreme meaning for the mass eye. They didn't know exactly what this ink blot meant, and their TRUCAD shrinks were busy convincing them that they didn't really want to know.

There wasn't a German in ten thousand who knew what the swastika meant—but, by Goebbels, he knew what it stood for. He knew it was a Symbol. And people accept symbols like that without really concerning themselves with what is being symbolized. It's as if Charlie Wilson had said, "What is good for General Motors—and therefore the Church—is good for America." Because this is true. Good for the only America that TRUCAD cares about—the one that makes money. And let Welfare and Worship be the Valium.

I glanced through the inside pages of the *Times*, feeling that good, thin paper—almost onionskin. I found a small box with a most curious ad in it—in almost diamond-point type. I squinted through one lens of a pair of tortoiseshell reading glasses from my bag.

"The outward ceremony is the Anti-Christ," read the ad, and then, with this sublime quotation from Uncle Will Blake, it began something quite different—a phrase of lyrics which already were growing quite familiar to me:

> When the night wind howls in the chimney cowls, and
> the bat in the moonlight flies,
> And inky clouds, like funeral shrouds, sail over the
> midnight skies,
> When the footpads quail at the night-bird's wail, and
> black dogs bay at the moon.
> Then is the spectres' holiday—then is the ghosts'
> high noon!

There was a box number for an address in Cornwall.

I put the paper down and slipped my spectacles back into my purse. It was Gilbert and Sullivan. That plagued song I had heard sung or played or hummed or drummed or accordioned in half a dozen remote places between Echo Point and Central Park South. If you are concerned with what used to be called coincidences as you hear this tale—forget about them. *Causal Liaisons,* the genius Pauli called them. *Synchronicity* was divine Jung's word. They happen so often these days as we approach in Time and Space that joining in the Precession of the Equinoxes which is near. And this is science, love, not soapbox solicitations. And so I racked my mind to place this strange and ubiquitous air from Gilbert and Sullivan. *Iolanthe. The Yeomen. Pinafore. Patience.* O, shit, impatience. I couldn't reach out and grab it yet. But I knew it was trying to tell me something.

I got off at the stop below Trinity Church. My period was late, and this was making me edgy. On the other hand, my periods never make me edgy. On the contrary, I feel my petals falling redly and I bless them each. What, then, was giving me that curious feeling like sitting in a hotel room and, having heard the second shoe drop in the room above and having forgotten it, then hearing a *third?*

Dear Lord, what *thing* is up there? Three one-legged men? A man with one foot and a woman with two? That kind of feeling. I have a relative buried in Trinity Churchyard: the Cresap connection—that's what relates me to Cousin Davis (rest his soul, I suppose) and Zelda and Dos Passos. What a crazy family!

I walked on to the Bowery, humming.

> When the night wind howls in the chimney cowls,
>     and the—

I just adored that tune. Which was just as well, because even as I hummed it, an old chicken-flicker wearing a face showing all the sites, craters, seas, and landing sites of the far side of the moon came jogging around the corner from an alley playing it plaintively on a harmonica. We looked at each other for a moment; he winked, and we passed each other by.

Sixteen Chatham Square. It was a literally ancient movie palace—a small one, but a palace nonetheless. You could read the old name VENICE molded in stale ice cream up under the coping of its pigeon-warbling eaves. As I stood there before the grotesquely marbled ticket booth—rounded and rosebudded with cake-icing stucco into the appearance of a U-boat's conning tower as Fritz Lang might have directed it—as I stood there feeling the fine, slow rain of flaking gilt and stardust glitter, I could almost imagine that the shot glass full of flies behind the window had last held liquor pushed by Legs or the Dutchman. The place kind of cursed at me, like an old bawd screaming imprecations through one lens of a broken lorgnette. Or maybe that was the voice of Stanley C. Ridges back in the movie, offering popcorn (and a fuck) to Barbara Stanwyck in *Interns Can't Take Money*. No, it was neither—it was the voice of my friend Jimbo in the Port Authority. Low, insistent, and yet—somehow—broken and in agony. I pushed into the darkened auditorium.

It was all lit up—like a Chinese joss house, I guess—with low-hung paper lanterns of every imaginable hue. The place was a shambles between the seats. Derelicts with wine bottles giggled in the pews. Young black hookers finger-snapped over an eight-track deck blasting out Ronstadt. There were more snorters than in the Seven Sleepers' Den that Donne dinned into our memories. Old

*Playboys*, *Wisdom's Child*s, *Mister Natural* comics, *Penthouse*s, *Screw*s, *Village Voice*s, and *Soho News*es. Everybody seemed to be doing his thing. And rather happy at it. But the sound I heard was that of my dear Knight in Armor—Jimbo St. Venus.

I hurried between blue wisps of good cannabis and very bad Honduran cigarillos toward the narrow, flake-pastry doorway with the sign over it: DRESSING ROOMS. I didn't move into a passageway so much as into a sense of *toujours vu*—I sensed I was in a very special alleyway of Time. Tiny doors with peeling brass-foil stars on them marked my passge on either side. The light bulbs over the doors had gone out. The stars had gone out—for the Long Lunch, I supposed. Ghostly Claire Trevors, Mayo Methots, and Isabel Jewells glowered out from behind rotting powder puffs with eyes mascaraed dark as death. The place smelled like fermented Chanel—with a dusty layer of sloe gin over it.

I saw the yellow crack of an open door up ahead. I hurried on. And then I saw, in a perfect welter of scarlet gore, the body of poor Right Reverend Jimbo St. Venus lying jammed down between his small desk and the body of a young redheaded female whom I took to have been his secretary. They appeared to have each been stabbed once with a long stiletto, the thin blade of which was bluish-green steel—though now bedabbled with blood—and the handle, of extremely ornate and probably Oriental craftsmanship. It was a curiously *feminine*-appearing weapon, though I could not pinpoint exactly how. I took it remarkably well. I mean, I loathe blood-shed, and this was the first time in my twenty-six years that I had been so confronted with it. I didn't faint, nor did my vision suddenly go blank. My heart beat a little faster than usual. I began to think what I must do now. The pale-yellow telephone stood in its cradle. Yet I perceived on it—vivid as the lips of a child—a fingerprint. In blood. I knew I must not use that phone. And why any phone at all? Except maybe for a hospital, for now my poor baby was trying to speak to me.

Incredibly, he took his bloody forefinger and painfully made two spots on the cracked yellow linoleum. As he spoke, obviously with great effort, he pointed first at one spot and then at the other.

Time, he said, does not travel from here to here. Time *is* from here to here.

It was a last-breath utterance so incredible that I began to laugh.

He seemed closer than ever to death as he spoke on. His voice was a passionate whisper, so that I had to incline my head to catch the words.

Don't you see, he cried in a hoarse, bubbling croak, that a poem such as *he* has written down needs only *one reader*? That poem is like a spark which sets that reader afire—and the reader runs out into the darkness, torching the whole earth with his newfound fire!

But if everybody reads it? I protested, insanely arguing with a man who was obviously on his last pins.

If everybody reads it, he grated out in the hushed, deathly air, lit only by the Tiffany shade with two broken panes, if *everybody* reads it, then the love in the poem is *organized*. And when Truth is organized, it becomes a Lie. There is no bigger Lie than organized Truth. There is no greater Hate than organized Love. Remember Guyana. And Synanon. And the Church Militant.

Why should that be so? I protested to the dying man, as if I could extract Truth from him with the last drippings of his poor brave blood.

Why? I cried out again, so that the rotting old movie queens in the queue of darkened dressing rooms all moaned the chorus of a Harry Richman tune.

Aren't a thousand people believing better than one? I said.

He laughed, sat up, and reached for a crumpled pack of low-tar cannabis. He tapped his trim secretary on her ass, and she also got up.

Only if they are a thousand *Ones,* he said in a soft, even voice, picking the pools and ribbons of plastic "blood" off himself and the surroundings. The only place where Truth can survive is in the spirit of the Individual.

O, dear, I exclaimed. I couldn't agree with you more.

I stared at him as he went about the room whistling unconcernedly and removing the evidence of his murder—which, apparently, he had used before or planned to use again, because he packed all the glistening, icky-looking rivulets and puddles of gore into a Marsh Wheeling stogie box and put it in his desk.

But why, I asked a little stupidly, this rather elaborate legerdemain to make me think you'd been murdered?

Because I had to test your mettle, he said, before taking you into my confidence. And because—at any moment—what you have seen may not be any trick of legerdemain but all too real.

I sympathize.

You mean someone is trying to kill you, too.

Apparently. Unless I've been wandering in and out of *Policewoman* sets all day.

I paused a beat.

Do blank cartridges make ugly holes in Johnny Cash's subway face—O, maybe half an inch in diameter?

Most definitely not.

Then it wasn't a *Policewoman* set. I've been shot at.

Charming.

What is? Me?

You. At any rate, I apologize for the deception. And by the way, this is my amanuensis, Ms. Algood. Ms. Samantha Algood. She has the best recipe west of the Eastern Shore for chicken fried with ham.

With rice—curried rice—and gravy, intervened that charming, lissome creature.

And cold chutney—gobs of it, added my dear and very much alive Jimbo St. Venus.

And I would suggest fresh lime juice and a sprig of green English mint, I put in silkily.

Both of them beamed.

Your addition to our recipe—older than Cresap's Maryland War, in case you're interested—gives me, at least, said Jimbo St. Venus, even greater proof that you are in possession of the Criste Lite. And therefore utterly trustworthy in matters arising out of the coming struggle. Ms. Algood is my only sister.

What *is* the coming struggle? I asked then. A relative of mine hints of it. I've heard it bruited round the town. I've been given evidences of it in assaults against my self. What is this gathering storm, Jimbo? Or would you rather I call you Reverend?

I dislike it if you do, he said. I do not wish to be revered.

Are you a preacher?

Not if I can avoid it.

Were you so educated?

Boston Theological Seminary. Union Theological Seminary.

Five-year fellowship at the Sorbonne. Three years Biblical research in codices discovered subsequent to the Dead Sea and Nag Hammadi Libraries. Associate pastorship of Riverside Memorial—

Is that all? I chuckled.

You laugh. Miserably for me, it was not all. I came back here and became associated with a woman missionary of exceptional courage and extraordinary spiritual power.

He turned to the waiting Ms. Algood.

Samantha, would you go into the chapel, please? See that those who want beer and ale have it. And I think there's some good zinfandel for the winos. It's beside the hymnals in the rectory. Give those who want it some sticks of grass—legal, honey, not the strong underground.

When *do* you preach to them, you delightful spirit? I crooned.

Rarely, he said. I let anyone preach who has something to say. Which is, of course, everybody.

You never preach?

O, once in a while.

You said you were a missionary, I interposed.

With this amazing woman, he said. She had gone into the jungles of Ecuador. Back in the fifties. Her husband, also a missionary, and five other men were killed and devoured by Chivarro Indians. Fierce, cannibalistic, archaic people—but living their lives, nonetheless, in a kind of Eden. All Rimas out of *Green Mansions*.

And so?

This lady went back, with her child on her back, and converted those murdering, cannibalizing Chivarros. Every one. To Christianity.

And?

I went back to Quito ten years later, he said sadly. I went among the Chivarros.

Did they have Christ?

O, they had Christ, he said. And they had—new things.

I think I can guess.

Yes. I suppose you can. Syphilis, drunkenness, crime, alcoholism, drug addiction, murder, greed. And they had the most important ingredient of all to make these other things work properly together.

I know.

Of course you know. They had the Christian Free Enterprise

203

Principle. They were being readied for the investments of world business.

The Kingdom of His Satanic Majesty.

Precisely.

What did you do, Jimbo darling?

I fled the Church, he said, and discovered Criste.

I studied Jimbo fondly. And you think this woman missionary was an agent for the Powers of Darkness?

I know she was, he said, because, for a while there, with her, I was such an agent myself.

Do you have a bathroom?

Of course, he said. My quarters are in the back.

I simply stink, I said. I haven't bathed since yesterday evening and I can't abide being dirty.

You'll need a change of linen.

I'm afraid I can't. My bags—

—were in the Port Authority Bus Terminal, he interposed. In a locker.

You know who I am, then?

We know why you're here in New York City, he said. We know your name. Yes, we know.

Why am I here?

Let me put it this way—

But what about my change? Could your sister possibly—? I mean, she's just my size.

No need. He smiled, leading me into a large library-bedroom. He pointed to the side of the enormous bed. My two bags stood there.

Samantha fetched them. The moment we found out you'd be here.

O, I love it—but, tell me, Jimbo, why *am* I here?

To stop the submission of the most important manuscript on earth to that infernal Nobel Prize Selection on Madison Avenue tonight.

I've heard rumblings of it, I said. The Nobel Prize Event. But that *isn't* the reason I'm in New York.

He watched my face.

I'm here to find my sister, Lindy, I said. I love her very much. She has been kidnapped. I calculate I'll find her, too.

God, how our great Christian President is corrupting common speech.

I'm very serious. I have no plan to try to stop the submission of the manuscript.

But you must, he said.

Must what?

Must help stop its publication.

Do you know surely that such a manuscript exists?

Yes. Unequivocally.

How?

Tales. Rumors. Legends aborning everywhere. The candle flashes shyly out from under the bushel and burns like a Fourth of July sparkler in the darkling night. Other candles emerge, without fire, and find fire from that first candle. And soon that coming together of little individual fires turns earth's darkness into a firmament. It happens only once in a millennium.

He bowed his face into a rosy Renoir shadow, away from the curtains, away from the pieces of daylight which blew through them gauzily and stirred the tender spitcurl of ivy beyond the ruddy brick sill with its orange-glaze vase spilling blooms of laburnum.

And what we must prevent is this, he said. That all those little flames be organized into the candelabrum which hangs in the temple of the money changers.

He mused.

The single candle of man's imagination, he said. That is all the light that is left. It is the last star in heaven. Because it was the First.

You are talking, then, about a Second Coming of Christ?

No. Not really. He is here. Under each bushel. The Second Coming is not the coming of the Criste—it is the coming of the Dyer with the Key. The Key to unlock all that imprisoned splendor!

Why do you foresee such an Apocalypse, Jimbo?

Because the Powers of Light and Darkness are becoming ever more clearly defined. Lordy, even the blind must see something! And after all—since our century has already experienced the coming of the absolute avatar of all darkness, can it not expect the arrival among us of some exemplar of human light?

I had ducked into the bathroom with my luggage and purse and was getting out of my absolutely terminally filthy clothes. I stood naked by the door crack, listening to his voice above the hot, good Niagara of my bathwater.

By the avatar of all darkness, I said, you of course mean Hitler.

Yes, he said. But not beginning with Hitler. There was another—who carried blackness, like a dark torch of inky flame, from out of the East to Germany. There it kindled into the black flame that was Hitler—and the Anti-Lite which almost consumed the world.

Who was this other?

*Is.* She is still alive. Very much.

What is her name?

Mei Ling.

The name means nothing to me.

It would if I told you the name of her father.

Why don't you?

Because if I did, you would laugh me out the window.

Don't be a tease. I'm a remarkably credulous creature.

Before I tell you her father's name, he said, which you will instantly recognize, let me tell you what he and this girl did.

Where are they from?

Lhasa, in Tibet.

I understand. One of the few places on earth where consummate Good or Evil—either one—can be focused and brought to be.

Exactly. Only it was Evil—the dark star—which was in the ascendancy first.

And this evil wise man and his daughter—?

Organized regiments of dark priests and took them to Berlin. And there began the subtle kindling of the waving black flame over all Europe.

Hitlerism.

Yes. But more than just Hitler and more than just ism. The threat of the black triumph of total Evil in the world. Through one man.

Yes. But brought there by that man and his daughter.

They couldn't have brought what wasn't there already.

Evil is everywhere. So, thankfully, is Good.

Was she—were this creature and her father—were they astrologers?

Of the most inner and archaic order. Astrology as the world

knows it today is the relic of a great archaic science. Astrology today—as it survives—is about as capable of explaining the universe as a beginner's Gilbert chemistry set found in a time capsule two thousand years hence could explain quantum physics. Yet Mei Ling and her father, in total possession of star knowledge, foresaw something in 1933 of which they devoutly informed the new Führer.

Yes?

This thing was the approaching juncture in the Precession of the Equinoxes, which could mean but one thing.

What?

The birth—sometime in the 1990s—of a Saviour.

And they warned the Führer of this?

In the most passionate and poetic of Oriental phrases. Mei Ling has—when she chooses—the most dulcet of voices, and the eloquence of her father was often remarked upon by Nayland Smith.

I stared down at my sleek, slick, gleaming body amid the happy, spicy vapors of my hot tub. I wiggled my pink toes and finger-flicked my nipples and peed goldenly, luxuriantly into my bathwater. I lay melting in it for a happy phase. Pee is grand for the all-over complexion. That's on the authority of a gorgeous Maharani I lived with for a summer in Kuala Lumpur. And on the testimony, as well, of countless milkskinned country girls who slept as kids in pee-soaked beds.

And so Hitler came to imagine his thousand-year reign of Evil as being challenged, Jimbo said. And that image, obsessing him as it did, was constantly fanned by Mei Ling and her father. A Saviour to be born. In the 1990s. That must not be. His Kingdom of Evil must last a thousand years!

And he launched World War Two.

We all launched World War Two. There was a Hitler in us as we marched off to fight, too.

He lit a cigarette and blew smoke—a pleasant riposte to the sweet jest of the blowing widow.

Hitler, who was intuitive rather than creatively imaginative, naturally supposed that in the 1990s, as in the year 5 A.D., the Saviour would be, as usual—

I laughed and understood.

—a Jew.

Of course.

And so Hitler, like Herod before him, set out to destroy not just the babies but the whole Holy Family. And didn't pause until he'd killed six million.

He flicked a tobacco crumb from his lip.

Have you ever heard this fact?

You mean theory. Really, it's almost preposterous.

Yet it is fact. It is, if you will, a preposterous fact.

Is there evidence?

The bodies of Orientals, not Japanese, in Nazi uniform—a whole division of them—were found by the British in 1945 near the bunker Hitler is said to have died in.

It is interesting. But then Hitler did die in that bunker.

Did he? Some of him came marching home with the victors, love.

In all of us. Yes. I couldn't agree more.

We sounded like a Nichols and May routine. The old Liberal gush.

He was restless now, pacing the only rag rug and staring at a framed motto of William Blake's above the coal fire: THE ROAD OF EXCESS LEADS TO THE PALACE OF WISDOM. And beneath it, ibid.: THE TYGERS OF WRATH ARE WISER THAN THE HORSES OF IN-STRUCTION.

What has all this to do with tonight—I mean, with the Nobel Prize Contest?

You must know first that Mei Ling is an integral part of the world religioeconomic order.

Of TRUCAD?

Yes. And she is exerting that same power on TRUCAD—power latent in all of us—that she and her evil father exercised on Hitler.

And his people.

The people through Hitler.

That is implicit. That's why you saw the most perfect destruction of the Individual—the most absolute rendering in the big I. G. Auschwitz soap kettle of everybody into one big Ivory bar of hate.

And what is TRUCAD's reaction?

Well, for starters, the pushing through both houses of Mr. Moto's controversial Ecumenical Subversion Act.

Yes, that certainly—

And now TRUCAD has gotten wind— His eyes dreamed out

the almost-Dürerlike window to a sky of small, hastening October clouds. Can't you feel it in the wind, he said—the Coming of the Dyer?

Of the Stranger with the Key, I said.

Yes. Criste is in us each. The Dyer comes with the Key to let himself out.

But you say TRUCAD is aware.

And scared.

Scared of this—this approaching Coming?

Yes.

And scared of this—manuscript. This short, amazing, gospellike work.

It is not gospel*like*. It is *the* gospel of the Criste.

How do you know?

I feel it. Everyone feels it. If not this manuscript, another one. Somewhere. They must be writing gospels on every continent in a time like this. But I know it is this one single manuscript—on its simple pages of ruled yellow paper such as Stallone wrote his *Rocky* on.

How do you know that, Jimbo?

About Sylvester Stallone?

No. About the—about this sacred document being written on a ruled yellow notepad.

Samantha saw it in a dream, he said. It was definite.

Did she dream anything else?

O, yes. The dream got wild then—really unbelievable. The sacred document is in a Red Apple shopping bag. On a Greyhound bus. In a helicopter. Among the graves of the dead in a vast graveyard somewhere south. All absurd.

Absurd, I said. But all true.

How do you know, love?

I'll tell you in a while. Meanwhile, I want to know all about this Nobel Prize thing.

I'll try to be brief. TRUCAD has transformed all world publishers into a single group called the Publishers' Union. They know that a very great and very dangerous manuscript is abroad in the world.

But wouldn't they want to suppress it?

O, good Lord, no. Not these days. Not on your life. Suppressing a book—and they learned this well—is like kicking a bonfire under a bed. And then lying down on it. Not on your life.

Somebody else told me this, I said, drying myself and skipping naked all around the big room. He watched me as if watching a child playing and listening to some grownup fairy story.

Somebody else, I said again, told me that the new way to obliterate a book is to publish it.

Of course.

With luck, I said, this condensation of Truth could be even shorter, more succinct—a jiffy beatitude—in the pages of *Reader's Digest.*

Beautiful.

And so—?

And so you and I, Fifi Leech, must go out after this manuscript and save it from the anonymity of bestsellerdom.

They don't have to burn it! I cried. O, wonderful. Delicious.

O, but they *are* burning it. They are burning it with chemicals in the self-destruct, recycled pulp paper that in a decade will be crumbly as a burned leaf. We burn books chemically now.

And buried beneath tons of Barnes and Noble remaindering.

A stone no angel is strong enough to roll away, he said.

That is awful. I think I shall have to help you.

Heaven will adore you.

It does already, I think. But I can use a little more. Would you like to make love to me?

He smiled.

Would I seem almost too ideally sexist if I suggested first things first?

I'm sorry, love. I am sometimes too persistently the earth woman.

Your skin—it's so lovely. What do you do for it?

If I told you, you wouldn't believe me.

A hint.

It is a lotion the color of the first yellow sunlight.

Anyway, he said, back to the affair tonight. TRUCAD has decided to assign to its arm of intellect and the spirit, the Publishers' Union, the task of producing for the masses the absolute, final, total ultimate Best-seller.

A popular book.

*The* popular book.

Like the Bible.

The Bible was only penultimate. This is to be ultimate.

Sex?

Of course.

Violence? Money? Yoga? Conservation? Women? Men? War? Peace?

All of these.

How are they going to manage that?

Well, of course they're not searching out and producing the world's greatest book for that reason. They're searching it out because they know it's here and they want to corner it, kill it with money, smother it with public relations, and finally bury it under glaciers of praise. Where are the best-sellers of yesterday? Every really important book in American literature had to sneak in under a disguise. If the public had known what Mark Twain was really saying in *Huckleberry Finn,* he'd have been pilloried. *Huck Finn* made it in the side door as a kid's book. *Moby-Dick* as a sea story. Maybe the next big American classic will be a porn book. Or an underground comic. Anyhow, for the past two years, since the plan was conceived in the Bilderburg Hotel in the Netherlands, the Publishers' Union has acquired the old CBS building on Madison Avenue and proceeded to construct there the largest computer, outside of planetary business, in computer history. It is being programmed with every recorded human value. It is being cycled to every whim about himself that man—both archaic and modern—ever bothered to record. And when that computer bank was completed early last June, the Publishers' Union widely advertised its plan and announced the coming choice—in cooperation with the Nobel Prize Committee—the coming contest to pick the best book on earth.

The best?

The best the computer can select from among thousands—probably millions—of otherwise unsolicited manuscripts. They have been pouring in at the rate of several hundred a day since last July. The computer will read, copy-correct, and do galleys on the winner. It will then publish it in an inexpensive Styron-bound, recycled-pulp-paper edition. It will review it in all the metropolitan papers. I have heard rumors that they are working on a unit in the computer to do an Academy Award movie of it, but I can't be certain of that.

At any rate, tonight, October twenty-ninth, is the gala night. At nine o'clock a chute on the Fifty-third Street side of the CBS building will open. At nine-oh-three, huge brown paper bundles, taped with steel ribbon, will come hurtling down the chute. To a breathless—and soon forgetful—world of readers.

O, God, how awful.

I was completely dressed now. I was sweet and fresh and wearing an old St. Laurent Rive Gauche straight-collared beige poplin jacket over high-waisted, baggy, ocher-pink poplin trousers from Greek Islands Limited, and a custard-yellow Irish linen shirt.

But the manuscript—the one you know, the one we both know exists—how can we be sure it will be submitted? And how can we know it will win?

Fifi, don't tease me, either. I don't know your connection with the great person who wrote the new gospel. Maybe you will never tell me. Maybe I don't need to know. But we both know that the manuscript was taken from its author only a day or so ago—near a small town somewhere north of Kentucky, we think—and taken to New York to be entered in the contest. The first thief was kidnapped—

Yes. The first thief, as you call her, is my sister, Lindy, I said a little hotly. You could have phrased it more kindly.

I'm sorry. But we know that she has been kidnapped and is being held by a group who are probably concerned only with the fifty-million-dollar Nobel Prize money and not with any true value the document might have.

All of that is so, I said. But what can be done now? If the manuscript—along with the hundreds of thousands of others—is locked up in the old black CBS building, how can we get at it? How could we even find it among all the others?

The place is guarded, he said. Doubly, triply guarded.

That's what I mean.

And anyone detected there who is unauthorized would probably be shot on sight.

Yes. Then what—?

There is a double reason for this macrosecurity, he said. I want you to know all the dangers involved, Fifi.

Someone—

Yes, someone is on hand very carefully supervising the entire operation.

This mythical Mei Ling?

She is not mythical.

I meant mystical.

She is there, Fifi.

For God's sake, Jimbo, stop jockeying. Who was her father?

Fu Manchu, he said abruptly, and turned away as if he could not bear it if I should laugh.

I laughed. I felt rotten afterward.

Fu Man*who?* I burbled.

You mustn't laugh.

The Yellow Peril of the 1930s comic books? Of Sunday-night radio? The MGM mandarin? O, really now, Jimbo.

Fu Manchu, he said again.

That makes an obscure but really very good British author named Sax Rohmer into a kind of H. G. Wells.

Fifi, does *fiction* mean that a character isn't *real*?

No, I said, amazed, and walked away nodding slowly. No, I said. I guess it doesn't. These also are the avatars.

I whirled to face him then, hands on my hips.

What kind of preacher are you, Jimbo St. Venus? I asked in a low voice.

A terrible preacher of the gospel, he said. Really, one of the worst. I know that today the Church is dead. Its wood's full of rats and termites and downfall. Yet outside it never looked more prosperous and full of light. That is an illusion. It is the light of decay! There are a few preachers like me—among the rebuilt, shopping-mall Coventrys and Hamburgs. We try to talk of the Bible as little as possible. We tend mostly to temporal, social change. That's all that's left to us without being false prophets in sheep's clothing like the rest. It is very, very sad.

Still, I adore you, I said. And I wouldn't have the slightest hesitation in going with you on this quest for the manuscript, except for one thing—

You have to find your sister, Lindy. You love her best. Therefore she is God.

Yes.

Then seek you first the Kingdom of God, and all these things will be added unto you, Fifi.

I guess that's right.

There *is* a danger I haven't told you about, he added.

Yes?

I'll try to explain, he said. There are, as you know, two ways of reading.

More, I would think.

Let us think, though, of two. What the line says. And what is said (and yet not visibly said) between the lines.

I have read those lines. In the Bible. In Blake. In Thomas Paine.

Well, there is now, Fifi, in TRUCAD's Chinese and English labs, an instrument which, by virtue of an extraordinary and unique kind of lens, is capable, it is said, of splitting light and then splicing it like rope, and which can scan a work like this and determine if the lines between the lines are unbearably dangerous.

Unbearably?

Yes.

So that it would then be suppressed—the pages burned.

You must get that old idea out of your mind. No. If the group found a work with dangerous lines between the lines, it would merely publish it in larger and larger editions—until it became, to the people, like mere litter.

Who developed this instrument?

Actually, Mei Ling's father—he was an extraordinary man, even though poor Rohmer was so frightened of him that he wrote of him, back in the thirties, in that kind of raffish code we know in the stories. The old Chinese was a wizard at lenses—optics in general. It was he who invented the deplorable police arm of TRUCAD known as the League of the Red Green Confusion. It was he who found and for a time possessed the singular lens for this truly amazing instrument.

For a while?

Yes. You see—he lost it.

Lost it?

Yes, incredibly. He was such a painstaking man, you know.

I listened as my radiophone clicked and then hummed faintly under my poplin sleeve. Someone was trying to reach me. My heart leaped. It might be my poor Lindy. But my heart tensed at something more. Something he had said.

What was it that Fu Manchu lost, Jimbo?

An enormous canary-yellow diamond. Maybe thirty carats. And shaped, it is said, like the great fallen tear of a god.

I was still a moment.

I imagine Mei Ling would move worlds to get that stone back.

Yes, he said. Worlds. And all the people on them.

# T·H·I·R·T·E·E·N

Debs, slouching his wobbly way all over the young, American Century, planting cabbages of Pluck and hollyhocks of Hope among the mulch and muck of Man—and then, abruptly, like a woodsman plunging through cat ice into a river, debauching himself on ten-cent whiskey from Terre Haute to Gary, and ending up in a warm, good bed, being sobered up with Chicken Soup and Socialism by dear Jane Addams at Hull House.

How I yearned for an uncle like that instead of the really detestable Mooncob! It was he who was frantically beeping me into outrage and shame on my radiophone.

O, darn, uncle, it's you. I'm so terribly tied up just now. I suppose it's money you're after.

Jimbo smiled and nodded at me. He rose and approached the door.

I'll leave you with your call, he said, and was gone, closing it softly after him.

I heard a girl's scream somewhere out in the tenements and the curse of a man and a blow and a crash and sob as someone went pitching amid wood and glass. Indeed, when I look and listen to this macho world it makes me ashamed as a woman that women have raised such men. Mooncob was rattling on in his rapturous, Rotary-religious voice that the money he wanted wasn't for himself but for the Lord's work.

I have to see you, Boodyboo, he said.

O, don't call me that, uncle. I'm not your nursery girl anymore.

You're still my Winnie the Pooh, he crooned, and I could see his big, polished Baptist face—like the face of Edward Andrews, the actor who does those commercials for Ma Bell.

And you, I suppose, are Christopher Robin?

If you want!

Hush, hush! Whisper who dares. Christopher Robin is buying his prayers.

You can't buy Salvation, honey. But a little money sure brightens up that place where you're waiting for Salvation to arrive!

Uncle, I'm really tied up.

His voice dipped—he was, I knew, giving a lewd wink.

*Laid* up'd be more like it—eh, Pooh?

Just remember you heard it from me first, I said.

Really, Pooh, I have to see you. I'll only take a quarter of an hour.

Can you tell me a little bit about it?

All I need is plane fare. One way. Tourist. To Denver.

What's there—a majorettes' and baton twirlers' convention? I remember the time back home they caught you in the day-care center with bubble gum on your fly.

Don't be unkind, dear. Nothing of the sort.

Well, uncle, I grew up to womanhood with respect, if not downright terror, of your absolutely unappeasable appetite for baton twirlers. Up to the age of nineteen.

Pooh—

Stop calling me that, you abysmal, baptismal beast.

Sorry.

And I'm sorry I cursed you.

Fifi, I—

Why do you have to go to Denver?

It's the Convention of the World Gospel Business Men and

Women's Foundation. They're meeting to vote, unanimously we believe, on a roll call of support for the Government's new Ecumenical Subversion Act.

You think I would give you money for that?

His voice smiled oilily.

Yes.

Why? I squeaked helplessly, for he had trapped me, I knew.

Because I know it is a principle of your nature to give to anyone anything they ask you for.

That's not so, I pouted lamely. Just this morning a lovely big pre-Columbian Indian in the Port Authority asked me for a fuck and I turned him down.

As you have always turned me down, my dear.

Since the age of nine.

Fifi, every man has his weakness. That is why we need Salvation.

I hadn't even menstruated yet.

Let him who is without sin cast—

Twinkling little buttocks, upthrust wire-framed titties—

—the First Stone.

—that almost hairless crease winking deep down in the silver-satin valley of Love—

Fifi! Don't, *Pooh*!

Dallas Cowgirls!

Boodyboo, I—

Don't you see, uncle? America's macho turn-on sex symbol isn't the Farrah Fawcetts, the Angie Dickinsons, or the Raquel Welches. It's the little drum majorette. It's your brother's kid up there with the sparkling nylon ass leading the Marching Band of Herbert Hoover High School. She's what every middle-aged Good Old Boy wants most to fuck.

Incest isn't all that common in America, Fifi.

Even if that were true, I'm not talking about incest. I'm talking about downright pederasty. Darling, if you want the honest truth, the Rita Hayworths and the Marilyn Monroes in *your* youth didn't give the male adults half the hard-ons that Shirley Temple and tender little Judy did.

I dislike talking on the phone like this. Can't I have a quarter hour of your time?

Sure, uncle, I can manage that.

A bird—red as a droplet of pigeon blood—flashed down and lighted on a sere bough of the little poplar in the courtyard beyond the window. Beyond it I could see the white clouds racing like the caravels of Sheba down the deep, dark Mare Nostrum of the mid-day West.

There's a kosher delicatessen a few doors from where I am now. I'm at Number Sixteen Chatham Square, so that must be about Twelve Chatham Square. Where are you now?

Uh, up in the Sixties.

Well, where?

He hesitated, and I could imagine his Ed Andrews mask adjusting and readjusting itself.

The Hotel des Artistes.

The Ho— Oh, *really,* uncle!

I know it's expensive, but let me explain. I keep this cubbyhole of an apartment here permanently. As a matter of fact, I'm months behind in my rent.

O, I'm sure everybody who lives there is years behind. Snotty, hardnosed New York apartment realtors are like that!

Well, think what you will, Fifi—I need that money to get to Denver tonight. There's a check for—an amount running to six figures waiting for me there.

What for?

I'm about to sign a ten-year contract with World Wide Satellite Television. Spreading His word. To the suffering, godless masses. Maybe even in space. You know—*Outer Space*: the Home Office, eh?

O, when I consider what I am helping you toward, uncle.

I looked heavenward, winkingly.

What's the place called? he asked then.

Hmmm. Rosenwasser's Dairy Deli, I think. Rosen-something. "Wasser," I'm pretty sure.

I'll be there in twenty minutes.

He buzzed off, but my wrist kept on itching, as if his voice had soiled it. Poor baby. He was really trying.

Jimbo, when I told him I had to leave for half an hour, thought, or half thought, I am sure, that I was going to run away from him and not have any part in our strange coming encounter in the Publishers' Union Building that evening.


A moment later I was seated at a window table in an ornamental-tiled, turn-of-the-century eating establishment under the out-of-character neon sign: RABINOWITZ—STRICTLY DAIRY.

There was a chill outside. Leaves were falling. Bums were bumming. I reached in my purse and took out some marvelous Gallimaufry rosewater and put some behind each ear. A radio in the back was playing a talk about the Yiddish theater at the turn of the century. Twelve dozen repertory companies, all going at once. A hundred and fifty marvelous-to-middling drama troupes dwarfing anything Broadway could ever be. I smiled and hummed "Dancing in the Dark." "Waltzing in the wonder of why we're here." O, my dear Wound of Wonder—how open and incarnadine with Wonder's wild wine it was this lovely autumn day! Even the sour prospect of the approaching avuncular encounter could not dull my pleasure.

I felt for Face-to-Face, in my suede bag. I put my hand inside and fumbled with the gold catch on the little jewel box, so that the diamond fell out into my fingers. I caught a glimpse deep in the satin lining of several degrees of sunset. My hand felt—not cold, but deliciously cool.

I kept an eye peeled for the absolutely Universal Man—the detestable Chaz. A Checker cab cruised along my side of the Bowery, the driver obviously hunting numbers. He saw the neon and sped up. I saw Uncle Mooncob—spiffy as the late Colonel Sanders—get out. I waved and rapped and waved. He saw me and waved back and paid the cab and hurried in.

He sat down without taking off his De Palma topcoat and glad-hander Stetson. His big, church-social eyes gleamed behind his glittering steel-rimmed spectacles. He seized my hand.

My dear Fifi, I have the most awful intimations of Death.

He was, I knew, the most atrocious hypochondriac; he viewed all the organs of his body—and those of the universe—with a kind of rabid, organic paranoia.

Who is plotting against you now, uncle? I asked. Your pancreas? Liver? Stomach? Bowels? The Food and Drug Administration?

It's probably nothing, he said with a laugh. You see, I bought this cigarette lighter. In Memphis. With a lifetime guarantee.

And—

I discovered this morning it was disposable.

I'd think nothing of it. You were taken.

I suppose so. Anyhow, you look—look—

He held up his thumbs and fingers to make a frame to look through.

—you look like a centerfold. In *Gourmet.*

Hmmm.

Absolutely mouth-watering, my dear.

Hmmm.

The waiter, a tall old John Carradine sort in a gray, once-black, suit came over. O, God. Mooncob had that light in his eye. He looked at the old man, who gave him back eyeball for eyeball.

How about a ham sandwich? Mooncob asked, rolling his eyes. How about some oyster stew? Or maybe a veal cutlet stewed in milk?

The waiter kept giving back eyeball to eyeball.

Just kiddin', Mooncob said, nudging the big man in the vest. I know Jewish dietary laws. *Trayf.* All that stuff. I'm a great kidder.

I could guess that, said the waiter.

I'm a Gentile, incidentally.

Really? I would never have guessed!

Have you ever eaten in a West Virginia restaurant?

The old man politely considered this. Once.

And—?

Did you ever see a place so filthy they had a sign up by the rest rooms for the help to wash their hands *before* they go to the toilet?

Come on.

From two boiled eggs I got salmonella.

Let me order, uncle, I interposed.

I ordered two bowls of the cabbage soup I knew would be dark and rich with the flavor of marvelous herbs and vegetables I could smell drifting back from the kitchen.

How much do you want, Uncle Mooncob?

Two hundred, he said. And it isn't just the money I wanted to see you about.

I'm waiting.

I wanted to warn you, he said.

The soup came. It was better, richer, sweeter, sourer—more *something* than I had expected.

Warn me?

About what's coming.

I know part of it.

You don't know this. A holy war, he said. A fight to the edge of Apocalypse—and beyond—for the living Christ.

Yes, I know.

You don't know all of it, my dear. Bloodshed, fighting in the streets, mass arrests, imprisonment in internment camps in Wyoming, Hawaii, Moscow, Alaska, Arizona. Fifi, we are on the brink of a period of holy wars on a scale not seen since the sixteenth century.

I did grow a little chilled at the intensity of his description. The waiter came back with an extra bowl of cabbage soup and a large spoon so we could help ourselves. He started away, but Mooncob grabbed his coattail.

Let me tell you a parable, my good Jewish friend. A Christian parable.

The old man waited, his slitty, black, pleasant eyes smiling, waiting, waiting.

You know my state of West Virginia—with the help of the Rockefellers and the Mellons—sent a marvelous Christian man to sit at the head of the TRUCAD Senate last month.

Yes, said the waiter. I read about this man in a book by Buckminster Fuller. I read a lot. Have you read Buckminster Fuller?

No, said Uncle Mooncob impatiently. I have not read Minister Fuller. But let me continue. This great and wealthy man came to power—was born again both materially and spiritually—because he accepted Christ.

I read this.

Did you read how, one languid, cloud-strewn, moonlit night at Rehoboth, Delaware, two years ago, this now-powerful world leader was a penniless bum combing his way along the beach? Suddenly this worthless derelict stumbled on something moist, slippery, cold, in the sand. He looked down and perceived a large black mass and, a few feet away in the surf, the enormous head of a sperm whale. This man knew at a glance what he had stumbled upon, what

Christ had led him to, and as the enormous seabeast turned and made its way groggily back out into the Gulf Stream, this wise man seized up the enormous lump of stuff and drove into Wilmington with it that night on a Trailways. He sold it to a perfumer, made a small fortune, made an investment in Appalachian power, realized that Christ had touched him in the person of this whale and, with the ambergris which it had produced, had set him forth on a new track in life.

A most interesting story, *chaver*.

And what is the moral, please?

Moral? Let me think.

It is a Christian moral, so you will probably have trouble with it.

I really will, kind sir.

Well, listen. The moral is this: when a man puts himself in God's hands and God makes him walk by the simple sea where His Son Jesus performed miracles, he is bound to get rich. Rich as every good Christian should be.

I see another moral, said the old waiter, adjusting the clean white towel on his arm.

Another moral?

Yes.

What is the moral, then?

That it isn't every man who can make a whale vomit.

Mooncob ladled up his good soup, enjoying it expansively. The waiter slipped on off to the kitchen, plaintively humming Debussy's *La Plus Que Lente,* which he could presently be heard playing and singing on a concert Steinway tuned to 440 pitch.

In this hour of decision, dear Fifi Leech, when the old world slips perilously toward Apocalypse, have you no apt religious motto on your lips?

Yes. It is better to fuck than to burn.

That's not what Saint Paul said!

No. It's what Sweeley Leech said. And Uncle Will Blake before him:

> Was Jesus chaste or did he
> Give any Lessons of Chastity?
> The morning blush'd fiery red:
> Mary was found in Adulterous bed.

Time will deal justly with poor, misguided Sweeley Leech, Mooncob intoned sonorously.

O, uncle, Time *has* dealt with my father—wondrously. Now he is *outside* Time forever.

I understand why you protect him—he is your daddy.

As he is your brother! O, *really*, uncle—I *knew* I'd find you trying!

I'm sorry, my dear. The two hundred? Did you say I could have the two hundred?

I laughed and picked four nice new fifties from my purse. I laid them before him.

Heaven adores a cheerful giver, Pooh Bear.

O, I do thank heaven for adoring me. Thank you, uncle.

He scrape-chaired closer. He put his hand, thick with lodge rings, inside my blouse, fondling my left nipple.

I took it out and patted it—his hand, I mean.

Fuck off, dearest. Fifi's not having some today, thank you. She will not play Czechoslovakia to your Panzers.

Why have you never let me, Fifi? Why? You've done it with everyone else in the family.

Except Lindy, I said. You and Lindy. I can't explain.

I mulled it over while he watched me, licking his dry lips, his eyes like bright black insects within the glass cage of his spectacles.

Maybe I'd have let you screw me years ago, I said, if you hadn't smelled like Aqua Velva.

He looked a little hurt; I repented.

I suppose we're all victims of TV advertising, I said.

Don't attack TV. He chuckled. O, my goodness, no. TV is going to cover the Big Event.

Which big event?

Why, the Second Coming of Our Lord and Saviour, Jesus Christ.

And doubtless—shortly thereafter—his crucifixion, uncle. With seven sponsors for each station of the klieg-lit cross. And when the poor boy complains he's thirsty, the soldiers will lift to him not a sponge of vinegar but a Dr Pepper. So that his dear teeth can rot and throb and ache like those of his dear little children.

The Anti-Christ will die in such a manner, said my uncle, but not the authentic, copyrighted Lord Jesus.

He kept me in the reading glass of his eyes.

What would you change about TV, then? The commercials, I suppose.

No. Not the commercials. Commercials are the Parables of the God of Getting. I like them for their unabashed dishonesty. So much dishonesty these days is disguised.

What bothers you most about TV, then?

I don't know. Dick Schaap's upper lip. O, I would change *nothing* about TV, really. I agree—it is marvelous! Who can resist Armageddon by Home Box in eighty-seven-inch, three-D color?

Sweeley Leech, said Uncle Mooncob, is in the gravest danger now, Fifi.

From whom? O, tell me, uncle. I know father has enemies—but who *are* they, really?

The government of the living God. That is, of TRUCAD's Central Congress. They have him atop their Most-Wanted List already.

For what?

He paused, his eyes kindling with curiosity.

Haven't you *heard*, Fifi? Really?

Heard what?

The announcement has been made. Just now. Over all major satellites.

*What* announcement?

The Nobel Prize Contest News Board has just spun out in a tapestry of golden letters above Fifth-third Street the winning author of the contest.

O.

Sweeley Leech is now famed from Baffin Island to the Balearics, from idea banks cratered on the moon to the tape recorders on our latest space probes.

*Why?* I cried. Why does he have to endure this thing—Fame—which is the last thing on earth he wanted!

What *does* Sweeley Leech want, Fifi? Maybe you can tell me.

He wants to help people.

Who did he ever help?

Okay. Last year TRUCAD passed its new Equal Rights and Opportunities Act. That meant, among other things, that the West Virginia Ku Klux Klan had to take in, annually, two blacks. One of them a woman. The Kleagle in Ripley is a knobby, gnarled, horny Good Old Boy with hair on his thumbs and a dangerous falsetto and a "You Picked a Fine Time to Leave Me, Lucille" kind of loose-limbed walk. His name is "Kill-a-Kike" Kallikak. And he like to had a stroke the night the ERA representative brought the two new members over. And the thing is, the two blacks can't get out. You see, nowadays, the government doesn't just make openings for two token blacks; it picks out the token blacks and they *have* to go in. Like the old gag about the boy scouts helping the old lady across the street when she didn't want to go. Okay. It's like Tom Sawyer was running things—like the whole comic nightmare of Nigger Jim in the fake French prison was a precognition of Things to Come in America.

I laid my cold, scared fingers on Uncle Mooncob's hand.

It is coming, Uncle Mooncob, I moaned. The worst tyranny in human history!

Yes? What tyranny do you foresee?

The tyranny of the Liberal.

Nonsense. It is the Coming of the True Word.

I squeezed his fingers, hating it.

I'd sleep with you, I said, if I thought it would make you help my father.

He blushed like a little boy and pulled his hand away.

I'm not a whore, child, he said. I'd never want to feel I used influence to—to get you into bed.

I don't believe you would, I said gently. With me.

It so happens, he said, glancing at his manicured nails. He frowned at a tiny chip. It so happens, he went on, that I may *be* in a position to say a word for dear Swee—if he ever comes to trial.

Trial? My God, is he going to be arrested?

Uncle Mooncob's face showed the passage of a dark thought, like the flit of a summer cloud across a great, coarse field of grass. He clammed up. And that scared me even more.

I stared at his turned-round collar, which bit into the doughy fold of his red, red neck. I looked into his deathly, vacant eyes, his resolute, mistaken mouth.

You won't make it, uncle, I said. You and your Christian Kingdom!

Why, whatever do you mean, child? We are in total control of that Kingdom.

You are bound to fail.

How, pray? How?

Because you overlook one eternal.

And what might that be, child?

That we must forget Worship and take up Love.

And what about worshiping God?

You *are* God, you old fart!

I rose then, my eyes aswim with tears, my chair scraping back with a ragged cry upon the scrubbed, drysudsy floor.

*I* am, too! I said in a whisper-shout.

He was silent, an aghast beat.

*You? God?*

Yes. So let us leave off crucifying one another.

I turned my eyes from him then.

Any time you name, I said, in a firm, steady voice. I will go to bed with you *now*.

He snorted, his own chair crying out on the still tiles as he rose.

My dear, he said with a dirty iciness in his voice. I never sleep with women of the enemy.

And then he stalked out into the lemony light of the street.


I cried. Not hard but hard enough. I just sat there racked with sobs. A huge fat girl in the back who had been eating bowl after bowl of bran and dishes of prunes, paid her check and swept up the violet afghan she was knitting.

Nothing for me! she chimed joyously. Everything for the bowels!

I stopped crying. Didn't laugh but stopped my silly sobs. And I thought about uncle and Sweeley Leech and me and Lindy and all of us. What is my faith, anyway? I self-quizzed angrily. Okay, it's simple. I say "Fuck you" to any religion which says, "I'm Something and you're Nothing because you're not like me." And here I had been coming on that way with uncle: abominably, and feeling so guilty about it I couldn't sit still now, and shivering—because it had almost landed me in bed with him. Because, you see, my religion is the one with the big bunk of tangled, sweet quilts amidst which anyone—yes, anyone—can play house and be beloved of God. And the hell with the trundle-bed trash who want to include you or me out.

I sat listening through the window to the new moon, an early-afternoon moon, in its ninth descant.

I switched to Public Channel VII on my wristradio. A minisermon by Dr. Norman Vincent Peale, sponsored by ITT. Ah, the Reverend Doctor likes a little Chile on his holy wafer. I switched to Channel IX.

Ah, God. Back in the seventies a few spoken-word political records won Grammys. Encouraged by this, politicians had tried ballads. So now this: Richard M. Nixon's plaintive "McArthur Park." I switched again to Miniphone. The channel was silent. Not even Lindy's ubiquitous voice to plague me and sting me with the knowledge of her peril. I thought of her. The radio clicked.

"The advance of locusts across Cambodia progressed unrelentlessly."

Huh? Unrelentlessly? Not relentlessly or unrelentingly? O, fuck. O, my dear sweet mother's tongue—they're cutting you out.

It made me think of uncle again. Poor baby. Uncle Will Blake says it is wrong for us to love our enemies, that only betrays our friends. I don't know about that. I do know it's better than pitying our enemies—because that gets us into bed with them.

I snuffled and blew my nose on a small paper napkin.

And what is holiness, anyway? The Bible has somehow created the illusion that Guilt and Wisdom are the same thing. And they are not. Either the evil intent of false prophets or the disastrous error of a translator is to blame. But—okay, well, you know me—in view of men like Uncle Mooncob, I suspect the former.

Across the street, a stuttering neon sign over a gourmet invasion of the district: COUSINE CUISINE.

I lit up a high-tar legal-grass cigarette called the Universal Joint and wandered out to the pavement. A hungry old dog stared at me and tried to wag his tail but couldn't quite make it. He wished for a purse full of burgers, but I gave him my heart instead to take away and chew for an hour or two.

A truck full of lawn-decorator merchandise grumbled past. In the bed of it were a half-dozen small, painted, cast-iron statues of Lou Rawls in a jockey outfit, holding out an iron ring to Ed McMahon.

A headline on a page of the *Daily News* under my shoe tips: CONGRESS PROMISES INVESTIGATION INTO ALLEGED MAOIST INFLUENCE IN DAR.

I peered up the Goyaesque alley full of drunken men and women. I saw the face of Uncle Mooncob everywhere, cold as a rooming-house toilet seat. The avuncular image faded and I saw Sweeley Leech. I blinked, rubbed my eyes the way they do in bedtime stories. It was he—large as life and lovable—standing in front of the New Bowery Brentano's across the street. I started across. En route I bumped face-on into a poor Bowery woman who looked like Trevor Howard, spoke like Tiny Tim, and smelled like banana brandy and Preparation-H—both of which were on her breath.

I staggered up, nauseated, to the figure of my father.

And then I saw.

O, those ass-wipes, how dare they do this thing!

The day was warm. There were record racks in front of the store. I caught a snatch of conversation between two buyers at a stall of pop discs.

The biggest thing, someone said, since Newton-John discovered gravity. And, O, dear, she is that—so *grave.*

Was that not Sweeley Leech standing nearby, big as life? No—it was one of those fucking holograms: a new dimension in sidewalk advertising. The figure of a best-selling author that you can walk up to and look at from every angle—and then walk completely through. I was dreadfully confused. Why was father being hologrammed in space in front of the New Bowery Brentano's?

I looked more closely for any visible clue as to why father was there. Of course—a book. The book. The Criste Lite. But how could it be out now? Was this an advance copy—sampled out of the gigantic computer bank? Apparently so. But more, I read the writing at the foot of the shimmering time-pedestal of the hologram. It wasn't an ad for the book at all. It wasn't a Publishers' Union hologram at all—it was a police image. A kind of three-D crime poster. O, yes, it was that. Because it said very clearly—and terrifyingly:

SWEELEY LEECH, WANTED
DEAD OR ALIVE

# P·A·R·T
# T·W·O

# F•O•U•R•T•E•E•N

But these words that you speak to us are laughing-stocks to the
world and sneered at, since they are misunderstood.
—Thomas the Contender
(from the Nag Hammadi Gnostic Library)


I am into sighs. And humming. But especially sighs. So few people
sigh anymore. And a sigh can be like a phrase of music, can be like
a whole short symphony.

I remember a woman in an Ethical Culture Society meeting back
in the mad mid-seventies. She had outlived WW II and the camps.
She never spoke of those smudged, fiery heights, though she did
talk to me incessantly about bargains in Bloomie's basement. But
now and again she would sigh. And, O, that sigh! It was full of all
Europe and all old Asia, and of breaths and whispers of the saddest,
wistfulest winds of the world.

As I stood outside the New Bowery Brentano's, staring gloomily
at the hologram of my poor father, I heard such a sigh.

There was something familiar to it.

I turned.

It was Dorcas.

I moved toward her lovingly, forgetting what she had done to me and reaching up a finger to trace gently the tiny scar beside her beautiful, though now saddened, mouth.

Fifi, I was with them, she breathed hurriedly. But I'm not now. Fifi, I betrayed you, but—well, I'm back.

I always knew you would be, love.

And, Fifi, you must trust me now. So much hinges on your trust.

I know that. And something inside me says I always did trust you—even when you were what you call betraying me. Love, do you think I could have been with you in the way I was with you and still not know you?

And, O, I could see the approving moon over her shoulder in the polished shopwindow, tangled in new night, and curled upon the soft magenta shoulder of the east like a tendril of frozen smoke.

Dorcas's funny little nose burrowed like a nursing lamb in the hollow of my shoulder. I could count her breaths.

Feef, terrible things are happening tonight.

I glanced toward the glimmering, shimmering hologram.

I know it, dear.

And, O, I'm scared, Fifi!

Dorcas, love, take hold. You aren't in half the danger my father is.

I indicated the quivering column of light and dark which was the obscene imitation of Sweeley Leech.

My God, I whispered. Dead or alive. I wonder what they want him so bad for.

I think I can answer that, Feef. It's still happening.

What's happening?

Feef, I can't describe it. You'll have to see. If I told you, you wouldn't believe—

But what—?

Do you have cab fare? The smallest I have is a hundred.

Yes, where—?

Just come, she cried, seizing my hand and streaking me through the quavering, winy light of the Manhattan dusk. I turned my face, smiling, and winked at the lover moon for luck. She hung low in the tinctured sky like the highlighted curve of a full breast and help-lessly dripped stars of milk upon the bib of the sea. No cabs in sight. I sought the dusk for a Checker. I waved a fifty. He had good eyes. His Off-Duty light flicked off and he darted toward us.

Lincoln Center, cried my lovely companion as we sprang in and sprawled out in the roomy seats. I can't tell you—Dorcas went babbling on again—you have to see. And it's still happening.

For heaven's sake, love, what's happening?

The book. The Criste Lite. It's lost forever, I'm afraid!

Whatever it is that's happened— I began.

*Happening*, Fifi.

Whatever is still happening, I went on, does it have anything to do with the Nobel Prize Ceremony tonight? That's scheduled at the New York State Theater at Lincoln Center?

Yes.

At nine o'clock?

I thought anxiously of my dear Reverend Jimbo, whom I had so indecorously deserted.

It *was* scheduled for nine o'clock, said Dorcas in a whisper, glancing anxiously at a cluster of women at the corner of Sixth Avenue and Thirty-fourth Street. There was a curious light—a kind of nimbus—around the shapely ankles of each. The Checker stopped for a light, and one of the women ran over, thrusting through the window a luminous, white, plastic New Testament. She was looking grimly at me. She was pretty in a hard, Latin way, except that her tough little mouth was too small for her round, flashing face—like the steely drain of a washbowl, mercilessly sucking in everything around it. The glowing Testament brushed my nose.

Are you washed in the blood of the Lamb? snapped out the rich Italian contralto.

Yes. But then I seldom bathe alone.

The woman cursed and swung the Bible at my nose as the cab sprang forward.

That was one of *them*, Feef.

Agonized, I thought of poor captive Lindy.

Dorcas's face brushed mine. I thought she was going to kiss me and began to melt again, but no—she brought her mouth close to my ear, and I could feel the agony of tension and fear in the quiver of her breathy words against the shell of my tinseled ear.

I think they're going to strike, she said. Tonight, Feef. I think New York City is next on their list.

She brought her face, a little crazy with sheer scaredness, around to mine, searching my eyes for some sign of understanding—which surely was not yet there.

Fifi, those women, she whimpered, with a drawn grin. They've been experimenting for months. And now they've begun to do it.

I waited.

Raise the dead, she whispered. They've begun to raise the dead. Not much. The simplest of dead things. But they're raising them from the dead—unmistakably. O, Feef—

Take hold, love. Tell me what's happening up at Lincoln Center.

I had no sooner said those two words than we were there—swimming out of traffic in front of the Hotel Empire. We sprang out and I gave the driver the fifty. A few hundred people, in clusters, some laughing, some angry, milled around in the central plaza. Fanfares of jeering children sprayed down over the walls and onto the open square. A huge banner, already splattered with fruit and vegetable missiles, proclaimed the event:

THE NOBEL PRIZE COMMITTEE AND
THE TRUCAD PUBLISHERS' UNION
ANNOUNCE THE WORLD-WINNING BOOK:
THE CRISTE LITE BY SWEELEY LEECH.

I caught a glimpse of a luminous high heel, a finely turned gypsy leg, the flash of a dazzlingly white Testament—obscene as leprous tissue.

The pavement was littered with books—small books, pathetically scattered and trampled like dead leaves. I picked one up. The violet air around me was shivering with canned music from the top of Alice Tully Hall. The "Gloria" from Beethoven's *Missa Solemnis*. Abruptly—so abruptly that when the change in sound came, the light itself seemed to change, deepening into a foggier, autumn twilight—abruptly the music began to lag and deepen: someone was letting the record run down. The tenor became more bass with every phrase until he sounded like the computer, Hal, dying in *2001: A Space Odyssey*. The "Gloria" ended. It was an invisibly malicious act by some turntable operator—a way of quickening the crowd's simmering anger. Instantly the needle skipped into—yes, it seemed by now inevitable—the all-too-familiar chorus of The Dead's "High Noon"—the song which had plagued Sweeley Leech and me in stunning synchronicity. I opened the wet, ornate, tasteful little volume I had picked up. I stared closer, my eyes yearning into its good rag paper. But my first look had been true. The page was *blank*. All the pages were *blank*.

The air was staining slowly to the reddish-violet of twilight, like the water round the shark-slashed limb of a hapless swimmer. And like sinister stars stabbing stilts into the rain-reflecting paving stones of the plaza, I saw pair after pair of those marvelous, almost perfectly vulgar, luminous French heels. They appeared to be made from some kind of clear plastic, each with a powerful small light bulb in it. Dorcas caught me staring.

A sound wagon out on Broadway, in front of Fiorello's, began to pierce through the music from Alice Tully Hall.

> Rockin' in his arms. Rockin' in his arms.
> Yes, I'm rockin' in my lovin' Criste's arms.
> O, I love my Lord like I love my man,
> Rockin' in my lovin' Criste's arms.

One of the high heels glimmered in the corner of my eye. No, it was one of those white, luminous New Testaments. Held inches from my cheek.

Are you washed in the blood of the Lamb?

I stared at the hard, sweet face—like something turned out of rock sugar on a lathe.

Are you washed in the blood of the Lamb?

The query was a grating scream.

O, fuck off, love.

I reached up and swept away the hand holding the livid, limp Testament.

Dorcas stood with her jaw dropping, fingers creeping to her mouth.

The woman's lips shaped a curse and she slapped me hard across the lips with the white Bible. It seemed to leave a wetness on my skin. I fell back and watched the stilted, reflected high heels stabbing off in the dark to join the others. I was too stunned over the blank book I held in my fingers to feel any hurt.

Dorcas sighed one of her great, beautiful sighs.

Isn't it a pity, she said, that he would go and do such a thing to his book?

Who?

O, Feef, you *know* what I mean.

No. No, I don't know what you mean. Though I suppose you mean Sweeley Leech. What is he supposed to have done?

Well, can't you see, Feef? The books. Everywhere. This was to be the setting for the appearance of the greatest best-seller in all world history. And look.

I looked. I felt like throwing up. Except that I hadn't anything to throw up—not a bite since breakfast at the bus terminal.

But what is my father supposed to have done?

Sabotaged the computer, Feef.

But how?

Nobody knows how. They only know it was sabotaged—and everybody knew he didn't want his book to be chosen to be published, and so he killed it.

O, Dorcas, how can you think like those fools?

Well, what else is there to think?

Dorcas, how can you?

O, I know, Feef—I'm not very pure, am I?

There'll come another explanation, I said. Father would never use force to stop this thing.

O, I want to believe that, Feef.

Well, you can. There's another explanation as to what happened—a good reason why these books came out blank. It could be the big computer just broke down on its own. Why must they blame father?

Fifi, the whole world is kind of paranoid these nights.

Another high heel at my left—scorching the night with its plastic fire.

Are you washed—?

O, really!

I clutched my little book and, grabbing hold of Dorcas's elbow, propelled us both forward along the pavement.

It happened around seven, Dorcas was saying. The computer began to register all systems wrong, and about five minutes later, the brown bundles of books, steel-taped and wrapped in heavy stock, began to abort from the chutes.

About two hours early.

Yes.

The air seemed to tremble. Big drops of rain, large as flower petals, began falling. The books looked sad and sodden as the pavement began to glisten like patent leather. The droplets wet my lips, tasting faintly of chestnuts, which were roasting in a pannier on a vendor's fire a few feet away. I bought a bag and ate ravenously.

Let's get out of here, Dorc.

O, Feef, let's. Are you hungry, Feef?

Am I? Do you know where they're serving horse rare?

Le Pot Noir?

No. I'm not into seafood tonight. Fiorello's, maybe. They have great chicken with bitter-chocolate sauce at Fast Forward. And Joe Albany's playing there.

We left the arena of this vast discontent and crossed Broadway against the light. I stared at the precious, worthless little volume. Printed in black and red and white on the sturdy Styron binding was CRISTE LITE BY SWEELEY LEECH. But the pages were still innocent of any imprint. My eyes filled with tears, thinking of the fate of the original yellow-ruled-pad manuscript in its simple little Red Apple shopping bag.

We found a parasoled table on the sidewalk and listened to utterly improper yet delicious dissonances coming out of Joe Albany's piano back in the restaurant's murky amber interior. There were no glowing plastic high heels to be seen. Yet. I ordered two margaritas and sat back a moment later, licking salt from my upper lip.

I reached across and squeezed Dorcas's fingers.

Love, I'm so glad you've come back, I said. Welcome home.

O, Feef, I *feel* home.

I know. And stick with me. I really need you tonight, what with all the family I have in the world living on borrowed time: my sister with those women, my father being hunted like an animal.

Dorcas was curiously silent, looking at the candy-stripe pattern on Joe Albany's shirt sleeve inside by the clump of shadows and stabbing lights all round the glistening, mellow Knabe grand.

Dorcas, what's wrong?
She chewed her lip.
Dorcas, what is it?
Fifi, I've seen your sister.
Lately?
Yes.
How is she?
Fifi, I swore to her I wouldn't tell.
She's still held captive?
Not really.
You mean they've released her?
Not really.
O, Dorcas, don't be a dumb-ass.
She began to cry.
I glared at her, and then everything softened.
It's all right. Dorcas, it's all right.
O, Fifi, I gave Lindy my word I wouldn't tell.
But can you tell me this much? Is she still being held by the
women of the Cazzo Nostra?
No. Yes. Not really. Well, I can tell you this—she's *with* them.
And O, Feef, I shudder inside with shame when I think that a few
hours ago I would have said "with *us.*"
Is she—all right?
That's what I can't tell you.
All right.
The waiter came with another brace of margaritas, and I ordered
the aspic with anchovy and Roquefort dressing. I watched a pair of
blazing French heels traverse the glistening, wet, moonlit pavement
of Broadway. I had noticed that each of these women wore, slung
around her shoulder, a strap holding a small yellow wicker basket
of some sort. I swore, even at that distance, I could see a flash of
grayish-brown fur through the woven lattice and hear the chitting,
chilling squeal of something with ravenous ivory-colored front
teeth. I shivered and turned back to Dorcas, who was eating salad
like a demoiselle in a Boucher print. She smiled weakly at me, her
upper lip gleaming deliciously with olive oil, and a morsel of carrot
shining like a jewel in her own white teeth. She swallowed.
Of course, now, she said sadly, now that Sweeley has sabotaged
the publication— O, Feef, I'm sorry. Don't look at me that way.

I'm sorry, darling. What I was trying to say is that now that Lindy won't be getting her hands on that fifty-million-dollar Nobel Prize money—well, she's not worth ransoming anymore.

Lindy wouldn't have gotten it. Sweeley Leech—to his bitter dismay—would have gotten it.

And paid every cent of it to ransom Lindy.

Every cent.

But now—well, financially, Lindy is worthless.

So she has been released.

I didn't say that.

She has chosen, I asked, to remain with the Cazzo Nostra on her own?

Something like that. O, Feef, I can't tell you *all*.

I respect that. But can you tell me one thing?

Yes. I think. What?

How can I find my sister? Tonight.

Dorcas's eyes narrowed earnestly; she nodded. I'm going to tell you, she said. In a minute.

She took a deep breath. I want you to find her, she said, even though I know how hurt you are going to be when it happens.

I won't ask what that means. I assume it's part of your vow.

Across the deepening blue of the sky now came the sweet trash of the stars: the lovely litter of the Loftinesses. I saw the tip of the cheap old moon caught in the hair of a lovely girl a few feet away at the bus shelter. The rain was done. But on the pavements still stood glistening pools—placid and reflective one moment, then wrinkling to splintery little waves by a huff of city wind the next. Stars lay enmeshed in the shuddering rainbows of oil slicks. A few high heels shone across Broadway like evil tapers.

The air was vintage. On high, a stratoliner trundled down the dark with a sound like insane and enormous skateboards on a floor above. The neon atop the Hotel Empire was a Medusa wig of golden wires. I could smell that pannier of roasting chestnuts somewhere down Broadway. It smelled more appetizing than anything I would order at this really first-rate café.

A stately silver-haired woman strolled past, leading a prognathous pug with smoker's bronchitis. She was reading a then-raging best-seller.

Fifi, Dorcas asked suddenly, do you believe in sex after eighty?

Definitely. Though I would never invest in large-type pornography.

I paused.

Anyway, I said. You said you would tell me.

Yes. To get to Lindy. O, Feef, I wish I could spare you this.

Spare me nothing, I said. My job is a heavy one. To find father and to find Lindy. And at the moment it is Lindy.

Well, I want to help.

If you can. O, if you can, love.

She took a postcard out of her purse and held it out in the throbbing, embered light of the table candle. It was mimeographed rather crudely in three colors—yellow, green, and lavender. It was an invitation to a séance that night on Sixty-third near Central Park West.

Nelson Rockefeller, said Dorcas suddenly, as if reciting, had a lavish home overlooking the Hudson. And the Hudson, you might say reciprocally, overlooked Nelson Rockefeller.

I smiled.

What's that?

It's Mark Twain.

At the séance.

Yes. O, Feef, she gets in touch with *everyone*.

You've been to other séances there?

Two. They were mind-blowing, Feef. She contacts everybody. Tonight it's Herman Melville.

Was Lindy at the other séances?

No. But I know she'll be there tonight.

Can you tell me how you know?

Feef, I was a member. I belonged to the Cazzo Nostra.

I keep forgetting.

The moon was sensuous now to the point of indecency. It hung like a circus queen's bauble in the puffed-voile shoulder of a lady wearing an Yves St. Laurent Rive Gauche frock. The air was so splendid. Everyone was promenading around as if it were May Day Eve. The stars lay like great splatters of golden rain, on earth and above. There is an hour after sundown which the Chinese say is when midnight is born. I think this was it. I wondered excitedly what lay ahead of me between now and that newborn midnight.

Harry Truman was there on the first night.

242

Did you enjoy him?

Not really. He sang some Harry von Tilzer.

Are you into Truman? Everyone seems to be these days.

I guess so. "The buck stops here." I always liked that. It's a swell epitaph.

Not really, I said, because that's not how the Truman epitaph goes.

How, then?

"The buck *starts* here."

Here? Where?

Hiroshima.

I was playing with the postcard invitation. It shook in the light like a moth's wing courting the candleflame.

A wind gusted, worrying the placid brows of rain pools. A skirt flew up like a birdwing. Men laughed.

> Ain't no semen on ma mustache,
> Ain't no 'gasm in muh beard.
> Ah'm a macho baby,
> Nothin' need be—

It was now settled in my mind that somehow that night I would find my dear sister. I put the card into my purse and zipped it.

You say the medium is a she?

Yes.

Dorcas paused and lit up a legal joint—one of the new brands out of Hawaii: Dole's Kona Lights. She toked and winced and then exhaled. I shared it, toking, exhaling. We sipped our cappuccino and raspberry honey.

She's Oriental, too, said Dorcas, and my heart caught its sleeve on a nail of awareness.

Is her name Mei Ling? I asked, smiling.

Why, yes. How did you know?

I guessed.

Anyway, Mei Ling is the daughter of a famous Tibetan mystic. I think his name was Chandu the Magician.

No. Fu Manchu.

Yes. That's it. A great guru.

I have heard variants.

Bad things?

I never pass on bad things.

More coffee? asked the pleasant waitress. Before the brownout?

What brownout? I queried.

The waitress glanced at Dorcas; their eyes met and nodded.

Doesn't she know?

You *do* know, Fifi—about the big-city brownouts this autumn?

No.

Well, it looks like there's going to be one in New York tonight.

What are they?

Dorcas nodded toward the golden stilts of a dozen blazing high-heels making their pious way up past Fiorello's.

Ask one of them, she said in a low voice.

Who are they?

They call themselves the Goody Two-Shoes.

Is it a terrorist arm of the government?

Not really. Though TRUCAD looks the other way on nights when the Goody Two-Shoes strike.

Who is back of them?

Well, the Cazzo Nostra, certainly. They're all mob widows since the WASP takeover in the early eighties. And most of them are former nightclub and Broadway gypsies.

Dancers?

Exactly. The best of their breed. The cream at the top.

The waitress smiled as I asked her to continue with this incredible tale. I should mention that, at that moment, six pairs of high heels—blazing like blowtorches on the wet, wind-dimpled pavement—were gathering in a menacing circle around our table, and began now to tap on the stone with an accelerating, and somehow Satanic, tattoo.

# F·I·F·T·E·E·N

The moon was a melting orange Popsicle on the universal pavement of the stars. It dripped, suckling, amid torn, racing cirrus, which were gliding like small, vainglorious caravels of Ericsons and Magellans. O, it was a night. And our little waitress was a jewel of beauty and charm. She unbuttoned her little apron and folded it.

I'm off duty now, she said. May I join you?

Right on, love.

She sat, folding her long, black-sheathed dancer's legs.

I have to be sitting down, she said, when I begin to talk about—

She tossed her silken, tawny head toward three more of the light-heeled ladies. Nine. Ten of them now. In a more or less perfect circle around us. On the leeward side, toward the street, where there were no tables at which they could sit, five of the luminous-limbed lounged on the curb, their heels impatiently tapping and thereby seeming to scatter showers of light all round them in an unholy aureole.

—them, finished the girl in the leotard. The Goody Two-Shoes.

She sighed and smiled as if whipping up courage.

I think this is their night in Manhattan, she said softly.

The Goody Two-Shoes, I said. Who are they? How do they strike?

They are militant Christians, said the girl. They cause brownouts in major metropolitan areas. Then they strike.

Strike how? Against whom?

Against those whom they regard as the enemies of the True Christ.

How do they strike? You say they cause brownouts?

In sections of the big cities—Los Angeles, Houston—

O, interrupted Dorcas. I do find Texans so—so Austintatious.

—and tonight it will be Manhattan. Yes, I am quite sure of it. I've never seen so many as I've seen tonight between Columbus Circle and Seventy-second.

She offered each of us a cigarette and then took one, tapping it reflectively before she lit up. Her tawny scarf of clean hair shone against her damask cheek.

My name is Toni Falconi, she said. I'm with the New York City Ballet.

She nodded, and her mouth made a vermilion *O* as she blew smoke.

So are a few of the sisters out there, she said. The Goody Two-Shoes.

You say they brown out metropolitan sections. What sections do they pick? Those with bookstores, I would guess.

Right. And districts with porn parlors and theaters and massage cribs.

Are they armed?

With the deadliest of weapons. Can't you see them shine?

Their shoes? They attack with their shoes?

Viciously. Accurately. Superbly, I might add.

She paused.

Have you heard of *Tae Kwon Do*?

It's an Oriental unarmed-defense system.

It employs what the Japanese call *deashabirai*—the sweeping foot.

Is it used against persons?

It is the Korean foot-fighting. It is used against objects or persons. It can shatter the plate-glass window of a bookstore. It can kick over a bin of offensive books. It can wreck a newsdealer's kiosk in a matter of minutes. It can lay open the cheek. It can rupture the spleen.

Whom do they attack?

Those whom they claim the Light of Ages has pointed out to them as enemies of the Coming.

What is their power? Fear?

That, but far more.

What is it?

If I told you, you would not believe me—yet. I must give you a little background first—some scenery to back the stage of this incredible period of religious convulsion we are entering.

She pointed. Some persons were putting together a small sidewalk theater. Its miniature proscenium was charmingly rococo: the set looked incredibly old, possibly Genoan. Presently the Punch and Judy show began. A Chinese couple eating tacos, a boy with a Doberman, and an old Jewish couple watched the ancient drama. A boy wearing a yarmulke with the colors of the Cuban flag came over with a portable eight-track. Judy's raucous voice penetrated the sound barrier. Punch bellowed. The old puppet brandished his stick.

They are with us, said Toni Falconi.

Pardon?

Those persons, she said. What you see is an authentic sixteenth-century miniature street theater. The proscenium was carved and gold-inlaid by Benvenuto Cellini. The puppets are probably older—maybe fifteenth century. Those people—they are ours.

By "ours," you mean *not* members of the Goody Two-Shoes?

Correct.

What do you call yourselves?

The Children of the Remnant, said Toni Falconi, chain-lighting a joint off her cigarette and flicking an ash impudently toward one of the by-now-fifteen pairs of luminous legs surrounding us.

What do you do?

We do nothing—but we do it creatively.

How does that scan?

We offer totally passive resistance in encounters with Goody Two-Shoe women. It's an art, too—our art—avoiding the stab of an *ashawaze* maneuver.

*Ashawaze*—foot technique?

Yes. That's all they use. I mean, in physical encounters. They are deadly. They are ladies of the chorus, remember. Ladies of the line in cheap lounge floor shows in South Bend and Laredo, Texas. They're all great dancers, but nobody pays for great dancing anymore.

She swept a lock of fragrant hair back from her healthy, glowing cheek.

We're great dancers, too. You've never seen a great ballet moment until you've seen one woman in flaming high heels trying to destroy another. And the other prevailing ultimately through sheer endurance—by feinting, dodging, weaving, ducking, parrying. Never striking back, mind you—just defeating violence by never letting it touch you. By wearing the enemy down. And then by teaching him about his holiness—as an individual.

How? How do you teach?

She pointed to the ancient little puppet theater, now a virtual music box of excitement, with ever larger and more enchanted crowds gathering around it.

Punch is Pontius Pilate, said Toni Falconi. Judy is Judas Iscariot, you know.

I think my father told me.

Your father? she asked, raising perfectly linear eyebrows.

Yes. He's a mystic.

I rather sensed so.

How?

I don't know. From your eyes, love. Anyway, let me go on. What you see out there—the primitive Punch and Judy show—really forms quite a complex code. We use it to transmit messages and sermons. We battle the vanguard of the Anti-Criste wherever we encounter it.

Messages? Sermons?

Entirely in pantomime. Which the government can never read, and so can never be certain that we are—what do they call it?—Ecumenical Subversives.

That is apparently a deadly charge these days, said Dorcas.

248

The deadliest. Far worse than the label of Communist was, back when nations mattered and money had not yet come into its own.

What is your message—your ciphered cause?

Why, it is simple. It is the gospel of the New Redeemer, Sweeley Leech.

O, dear.

O, dear, said Dorcas, too.

I managed not to reveal my feelings—though, I must say, I had good vibes about trusting this person.

It was the new gospel—his book—said Toni Falconi with passionate tears glittering in her eyes, that, on this night which will live in infamy, TRUCAD and the Publishers' Union have denied us.

Poor Judy's baby was dead. But it would be raised from the dead presently by the tiny, carved fingers of a fifteenth-century Florentine puppet. A police siren bawled blue ruin farther uptown.

How can they be sure that this—Sweeley Leech, as you call him—?

Beloved Sweeley Leech, she corrected.

How can you be sure that your—your beloved Sweeley Leech is really a Coming of the Lord?

There are those among us, she said softly, staring back with amazing sangfroid at the glittering ring of Foster Grant lenses which shone all round us.

Each of the women wore a tight black skirt, slit at the side. Each wore a man's jacket and a man's fedora turned down at the brim, like in an old Joan Crawford film.

There are those among us, Toni Falconi resumed, who have seen the original manuscript of the Criste Lite.

I tried a bold ruse.

Is it by any chance on a ruled yellow legal pad, stuffed into a large Red Apple shopping bag?

Why would you ask a thing like that? No. It is on hand-milled rag paper, as a book of its import should be. It is bound in full calf.

The golden calf, I mused. The fatted calf.

You sound like a doubter, said Toni Falconi. You sound like one of *them*.

Well, whatever we are, we're not that, love.

Then I believe you. Though I must say you are brazen, if not brave, in coming out together like this.

Why?

Well, you're so obviously lovers.

And the Goody Two-Shoes—is that why they're glaring at us so?

Undoubtedly. The women of the Cazzo Nostra are extremely sexual but they do not put up with deviations. I was to dance tonight, the girl went on. They're doing Bartók's *Miraculous Mandarin* over at the Vivian Beaumont at eight.

It's nearly that now, said Dorcas. O, I cherish Bartók.

I got cramps about sundown, said Toni Falconi. Anyhow, I wasn't dancing a lead.

She smiled at the moon, her white teeth flashing like snowdrops in her redwinged mouth.

We're interpolating, she said, a whole sermon about the Assumption of the Virgin. There will be those in the audience who are Children of the Remnant and who will understand. The police agents, luckily, will never guess. They are so literal.

She flashed me a quick, burning stare. Aren't we deliciously brave?

Yes, I rather think you are, I said. But what is this power you speak of the Goody Two-Shoes having?

Well, maybe you're ready to be told.

Try me.

The power to raise the dead.

Only the simplest forms of life, interjected Dorcas. I know that much about them myself.

Not so simple, said Toni Falconi, as they were at first. In the laboratories at Oral Roberts University they began by killing one-celled organisms and then raising them from the dead. They have been working feverishly for two years and have made amazing progress. Apparently the method, although extremely ancient, requires an arcane power of the human mind which is not ordinarily developed. But the power can be elicited by means of certain drugs. Yes, make no mistake about it: the rats in those yellow wicker bags they are carrying—they were dead recently.

Rats? whispered Dorcas, sinking down in her metal chair a few inches.

Rats, said Toni Falconi.

White rats?

No. The large brown Australian variety. The alley rat. The riv-

erfront rat. They are surprisingly responsive pets. They do anything they are instructed. They are wise beyond the very lip of
Death.

I had the sense that all the rats in all the wicker purse-cages had
suddenly grown still as we spoke about them. I had the feeling of
bright, lapidary-hard eyes glittering at us through the interstices of
the Macao-manufactured cages. I could almost see a bright, rusty
crust of blood upon one of the cruel yellow incisor teeth.

Yes, but I don't understand, I said, shaking my head. The power
to raise the dead—I had thought of that as the exclusive power of
holiness.

You were wrong, said Toni Falconi.

I could have told you that, said Dorcas. Okay, Feef, you know
how these unholy television evangelists are always healing with the
laying on of hands. Well, it's real. Christ, Feef, they say Charlie
Manson could do that.

But no matter, said Toni Falconi. The power has become theirs.

Yes, but from what source? Surely not God.

You mean surely not Criste, said Toni Falconi. Though certainly
from God—who is capable of the utmost mischief, as you must
surely know.

She paused. Your father sounds remarkable. What is his name?

Sweeley Leech, I said abruptly, cleanly, bravely. Though she did
not believe me.

We must each think of Sweeley Leech as our Father, said Toni
Falconi. Who art in heaven. I'm glad you put it so literally, Fifi.

And Echo Point, I whispered.

What?

Nothing. It was the wind.

At any rate, the government laboratories, the church clinics, they
gave the women of the Goody Two-Shoes these rats.

Are they—special rats?

The most special, she said. They are rats who died of chemother-
apy—or cancer—at clinics like Sloan-Kettering. And surely these
*are* the Least of These—dumb, low creatures assigned to slaughter
in the medical establishment's cruel, theatrical masquerade of
cancer research. And then thrown out dead on hospital dumps in
Queens—and the Goody Two-Shoes raised them from the dead.

How?

Through prayer.

What prayer? What themes spawned from hell itself?

Prayers written down in a document—on papyrus—by the father of Saint Dymphna—

My hagiology has its gaps.

The patron saint, said Toni Falconi, of the insane. Her father was a sixth-century alchemist. He left the incantation for raising the dead in a series of documents called the Brinkley Codex. Discovered near Youngstown—

Ohio?

Yes. A codex discovered in a sixth-century urn.

And the Goody Two-Shoes possess this formidable power?

Only up to the level of rats—so far.

What is the purpose of all this—other than terror?

For these persons, said Toni Falconi, there is hardly any purpose other than terror. Terror to stampede man into the Kingdom of God.

I understand. Then it's open war.

Yes—and tonight is its Sarajevo.

I raised my eyes to this heavenly autumn night. With a moon like a child's first spoon. And clouds like spinning bowls of raspberry trifle.

Yes.

It was at that moment that the lights on the Upper West Side of Manhattan all went out. All save the somehow pathetic lights of cars on the gleaming streets. And the lights, like evil burning wings, on the plastic heels of certain menacing shoes.

I saw a scorch of curved light flame like Halley's Comet down the moondrenched dark. It was aimed at Dorcas's left breast. I sprang athwart, and hurled her back in her wire chair, scattering legs and flailing arms and satiny hair across the wet stone by the pavement railing. I took a sharp, stunning shoe blow behind my right ear—though the lights which flamed in that moment were all behind my eyes. I was on my knees, then up and running across scared, lovely Broadway toward the Vivian Beaumont. Toni Falconi had hold of one hand and Dorcas the other, but Toni, being a dancer, was loping a little ahead of us. We seemed to witnesses, I am sure, a trio of madwomen leading what appeared to be a chorus

line of even more insane women whose shoes were miraculously—
or perhaps just from sheer wrath—on fire.

Inside—stage door! Toni gasped and swung me effortlessly
round an iron railing. I skidded and dove, dragging Dorcas behind
me. We were inside the Vivian Beaumont and backstage. A few
feet away, intense lights gleamed—floods and kliegs: the Beaumont, like all state buildings, had its own power supply. Behind us
in the wings thundered the solar heels of the Goody Two-Shoes.
Beyond us in the enthralled arena stretched the audience, like dimly
outlined rows of trees, while in the foreground the cast of singers
and dancers, fabulously, extravagantly costumed, were acting out
the queer Hungarian fable of the wondrous Mandarin.

Toni's red lips flashed close to my right ear. She grinned and
tightened her grip on my hand. We'll have to cross the stage, she
whispered. Fortunately, I know all the positions. I can lead a path
through the dancers, but they'll only stumble and collide with them.

The orchestra—the Philharmonic, led by Previn—was frenzying
the whiplash of music near the ballet's climax. Trombones flashed a
sensuous snarl of sound snaking round the rainbow brocade of the
costume of the dying Mandarin. Naked flesh gleamed like milk in
the split Chinese skirts of the holy whore. I felt incredibly horny
slithering through the dancers, blinded and gasping beneath the
bombardment of carbon lights and sound. There was a faint and
universal breath of delight from the audience as the darkened aisles
were candled into flame by the high heels of twenty or more rein-
forcements racing toward us. We were free then, and the red silk
ribbons symbolizing the Mandarin's merciful flow of blood twitched
into the light. The whore fell back in ecstasy. The snap and blare of
French horn and trumpet split the incandescent dark. We were
through a fire door and out into the limpid autumn night once
more. We had left most of the Goody Two-Shoes stumbling and
tangling, to the audience's childlike delight, among the members of
the cast and chorus. The music was in full orgasm behind us,
splashing great comes of finale on the ambient air. The moon was
sublimely indifferent to the power failure beneath it. The stars were
swinging on their eternal hinges. But clouds fled down toward the
harbor and the open sea as if they, too, were fleeing from the hell-
heeled ladies.

We've lost them, I think, said Dorcas—a moment too soon, because there immediately followed a fusillade of plastic heels like a drumroll behind us on the concrete by the stage door. We sprang off into the pink and violet of the city night. In the glow cast by our pursuers, we could make out our own shadows faintly. We were crossing Columbus a moment later, and I was frightened because I only had hold of one hand now and I was pretty sure it wasn't Dorcas's. Men and women and a charming five-year-old girlchild were drinking wine at three little checker-clothed tables under a small café awning. They were making do with candles and they beamed at us like holy pilgrims as we clattered, panting, past. The Goody Two-Shoes were amazingly fast. I was terribly distraught about Dorcas. It seemed we had hardly touched before she was off among the world's mysteries once more. But, O, I knew the only thing permanent in life was Love itself. And as for possession, even the presence of loved ones was not needed so long as they dwelt as tenants of our spirits in whatever attic room of memory.

Uncle Will chanted audibly in my ear:

> He who bends to himself a Joy
> Doth the winged Life destroy.
> Who kisses the Joy as it flies
> Lives in Eternity's sunrise.

Somehow we had gotten as far as Eightieth and Amsterdam. A group, as though crayoned on gray, coarse paper by Goya, clustered together on the brownstone steps of a rotting tenement. They were a small orchestra of street musicians. Shards of ardent moon glinted on an empty olive-oil drum, bottles, and percussive Nedick's silver knives, a flute, flashing colored sticks and flying grimy fingers, the coarse whisper of a gourd filled with sibilant pods, and a scuffed but gorgeous old cowskin-headed tomtom. In the splash of moonlight was a *botánica* window alive with white-cloth voodoo dolls sprawling in deathly threat among the fake relics and impedimenta of a dozen fake creeds, Christianity predominant, and Christs bleeding silently before the aghast Barbie-Doll Madonnas. The sounds breathed in joyously through my ears: eight men and young boys standing about the shadows and glister in poses of infinite and ancient grace, making the same kind of raw, feral sound that lashed the ears of Balboa's men as they waded through the hot sands up the peak at Darien. Someone lighted a rag torch, and instantly there sprang into view a small, sad child on a marijuana-roach-littered stoop. For a moment I paused and prayed before her young, dangerous face: a light was in her eyes which was the flicker one sees in the windows of a slum room amid whose flammable debris a person is dangerously playing with matches.

Vermilion shadows weltered and flapped like bandages of war on flagpoles. Somewhere a thrilled rat squealed. The young dancer seized my elbow and led me into the awninged shelter of a tiny cigarette shop. The Goody Two-Shoes were chanting in unison in the near-darkness. Plate-glass windows exploded under molten heels and tinkled broken music on the weary stone.

> Kill—the—Children—of the Remnant!
> Death to the Children of the *Remnant!*

The last word caught and shook in the dark the way a knife quivers when it strikes through flesh and hits bone.

> Death—Death—*Death!*
> Death to the *Children of the Remnant!*

A young hooker screamed and cursed and then screamed again as her body quailed under kicks somewhere back of the night.

I'd like to be out there helping, I said.

So would I, said Toni Falconi with a wistful smile and a slight pressure on my arm. But it so happens I was assigned to you tonight. Okay, I'd rather be out there fighting their Hate with my Love—somehow defeating their violence with nonresistant ballet. But I can't, love. The Children of the Remnant have told me to see you through this.

Thank you. When it comes to violent retaliation I simply run out of ideas. I guess that's a nice way of saying I'm a physical coward.

That is good, she said. It saves you for that which you were meant for—courage of the mind.

Thank you, love. I don't believe it. When I was a tomboy at Echo Point I always used to run from fights.

You didn't run from a fight on that Greyhound, she said softly. In Philadelphia.

I did, too, I said. The bastard was shooting at us.

Us, smiled Toni Falconi. Ah, that "us."

Besides, I said, how do you know about Philadelphia?

It was a member of the Remnant, she said, who saw you there. In fact, love, was *with* you there.

A man?

About whom I am completely mad.

O, I think I know, I said. I am, too. I hope you don't mind sharing.

I haven't decided.

She shrugged like a boy, and kept looking anxiously at the dark street for a glitter of danger.

He is divine, though. Okay? Right?

You could only be talking about Adonis McQuestion.

I knew you'd understand.

She sighed. Perhaps you're wondering, she said slowly, why he and Soleil haven't been watching over you personally. As they promised.

Not really. My mind is too happy with the memories of the love we shared.

You are a very strong person, said Toni Falconi. With the strongest force in the universe—the force of Love.

I suspect—I don't know.

Love is the strongest force in the universe because it is not Force at all. It is Strength.

What a queer night to be discussing philosophy.

What is happening out there now—that's philosophy. It is the flowering of any philosophy—even the most humanistic. It is the fist that even the gentlest fingers always form when they clench together.

But why haven't Adonis and Soleil been—as you put it—watching over me? I said.

They've been too busy watching over someone you love.

Sweeley Leech?

You really are his daughter, aren't you? But no—it is not the Master they are watching over just now. It is someone you love, but someone who is in even greater danger than either of you.

Lindy?

Yes.

I've been told that she's no longer wanted by the Cazzo Nostra.

That's correct.

Because she's not worth the ransom money any longer.

No. That is not the reason.

What is the reason, Toni?

I can't tell you.

That's beginning to sound familiar.

There was a Greek deli next door. Despite the Hispanic predominance, it endured. A slightly drunk customer was paying for a bag of sandwiches.

You Greeks are great people.

Thank you.

Great restaurant people. Greeks, I mean.

Silence.

I was married to a Greek once.

Pause.

She left me for a sixty-two-year-old Carvel ice-cream franchisee.

Pause.

You know what?

Assenting silence; the whisper of a nod.

You Greeks are great people—great, great restaurant people—but know what you're no good at?—you're no good at staying with people.

The screen door slammed with a small-town sound.

The dark leaned in closer. The night twitched like a predator whisker sounding the air for a death bite.

This is the longest raid they've staged, I think. The lights have been out nearly an hour.

How long have they lasted in other cities, Toni?

Thirty, forty minutes. Forty-five in Cleveland last spring. They killed a few hookers and beggars and pickpockets. Injured several dozen others.

A half-dozen kids came past on skateboards, reeling bright luminous plastic yo-yos in and out. A trio of Goody Two-Shoes women rounded the corner and for a moment there was confrontation. Then they passed, their flashing light a pretty spectacle amid such Stygian dismay. I listened as two rats encountered each other in the humped blackness of the street frenzy and fought with shrill, ra-zored squeals.

I tried to make out the shape of Toni Falconi's face in the dark of our shelter under the awning. But at that precise moment, as if some curtain had flung up and exposed us in a glare, we were dis-covered. And the attack was swift.

Toni sprang lightly between me and them—five tall black-clothed figures like mod Furies—figures with illuminated ankles and calves above fiery winged heels which soared out now from the smudged violet and crimson dark. I felt Toni's gathering power as she crouched for an elusive spring before the specter of the ten ad-vancing flames of the attacking Goody Two-Shoes. I could smell the excitement in her sweat, the flowerlike essence which she ex-uded—now soured and stained with the sweat reek of wrath.

Death to these two! Death to these two Children of the Rem-nant! Praise God!

The voices echoed a cappella in the street, now misty with sum-mer ghosts, and almost immediately—with maracas, tomtom, flute, and the clink of pilfered flatware on empty Pepsi bottles—the street orchestra mocked and repeated their savage announcement.

Now I could see the eyes of the leader of these five—a figure taller than the rest and with certain polished, angular, and terribly beautiful eyes and nose and mouth and cheek-ledges which com-prised an image long familiar to me. It was unmistakable. It was Loll. It was my father's lover, Loll. O, what a little earth this is, I thought as Loll and another woman leaped forward in arcs of fire, their lithe limbs pistoning out like instruments of deathly steel and springs. I got past Toni Falconi, who was going down, outnum-bered. I careened on my own quite lightless high heels and fell to the pavement beside her. I saw the bright heel approaching my face like the headlamp of a one-eyed, runaway trailer-truck. Toni flung up her thin arm and took the blow, and I heard the brittle bone snap.

Fifi, run! Fifi, obey me. Run, I say!

I won't leave you, love.

You're holding me back now—

A cool wind caressed my cheek as a blazing shoe went stunningly past—and near.

Run, Fifi! Up the stairs of Number Four thirty-eight A.

What?

Two of them had my arms pinned behind me now, and the limp, blazing Bible played like a punishing strap back and forth across my face.

Get the dancer! Praise God! Death to the Remnant! came the shout from somewhere behind all this tangled, flexing knot of women.

Number Four thirty-eight A! Top floor! Someone needs you, Fifi! Run!

I heard one of my captors curse a holy oath as Toni wrenched my left arm free of her grasp. The other let go, too, coming to the dark avenger's aid.

I heard a whisper then, from a voice I had known since old Time began. I am going to tell you something, Miss Fifi. It's dying time. Yes, it has come round. Dying time, Miss Fifi. Praise God!

Another flock of kids with nodding, flamy yo-yos racketed past on skateboards. A dog barked furiously amid the lustrous garbage of a neglected stoop. I felt craven and weak from running, but run I did. I felt rotten leaving the adorable dancer who was, in so many ways, my guardian angel. But then, one does not disobey the commands of angels. Number 438A. The top floor, where my angel had said someone waited, needing me. The sting of shame at my ragged desertion of the battle was assuaged by a hope that a better good might result from my obedience. I saw the green, rusted numerals hammered into the gangrenous woodwork of the doorframe at the top of a nearby flight of stone steps. A hand closed on the tail of my corduroy coat, and I heard the silk lining rip.

—to the Remnant. Death to the Remnant. Praise God!

And Loll's voice—so far from home, so far from Truth or Grace: It's dying time, Miss Fifi. Dying time. Come, little girl. Praise God thy wrathy spirit.

And as I half scrambled up the funky, reeking stoop toward the frosted glass of the slum door, I could see my own shadow cast before me in skittery silhouette from the light of four pairs of blazing Goody Two-Shoes inches behind me. Then I was through the door and into the thousand smells of the hallway. Behind me plastic fire thundered on the rotten carpetless floor. Roaches scattered like broken sequins across the moonshadowed landing of the Pisa-tower of the stairway. I felt the sweat on my hands as I swung myself swiftly as I could up the narrow, haunted passage. The graffiti were like a mindless ivy up the sweltering, unpapered plaster walls. A cat flung itself ahead of me, squawling.

Dying time, honey. Dying time, little Fifi!

I ran till my breath was like tight, unloose blood in my throat.

Instinct guided me in that little space of time, I think. At the top of four flights—in that old habitation of poor humanity, a structure without that spirit which all houses should possess—I saw a door, painted over and over and over, through decades, until it resembled a grotesque and decaying icing upon some obscene pastry. In the middle of the door on a roofing nail hung a tiny wreath of immortelles made of plastic.

Loll was almost upon me when I snatched for the doorknob, praying it would turn.

Dying time, honey! Don't fight it! Dying time, love! Praise God!

Every atom of will took over in me then, and through a series of movements I cannot remember, I was unscathed, a hair's breadth away from the flaming kicks of eight legs, and inside the small room. After all that dark, the light of a hundred candles stung my eyes. I flung home the bolt and fell back against the door as the tough thunder of shoes against the fainting wood filled my ears. I stared at the strange spectacle before me. I prayed to Face-to-Face, the great yellow tear of Criste in my handbag. Eight small children watched me with enormous, liquescent eyes as they paused in their game around an enormous, carved-pine and gilt coffin. Since it was immense it stood upon not two but four sawhorses, wrapped round with garlands of garish plastic blossoms. In it lay the body of the fattest woman I had ever seen. She was painted like a mannequin. Upon her deserted and somehow plaster face there was an expression of pique which said to me that she had, at the moment of her death, resented not having had time for just one more mouthful of junk food.

The room was surprisingly clean. The sleazy pathos of its decoration told me that the fat woman had probably been a hooker and the eight children were her orphans.

She was, as I say, the fattest woman I had ever seen. She was naked, but that was not the point. Her vast body lay like an open public garden in the box. It was obvious that the woman—an enormous, moonfaced doll—had been properly clothed by some cutcorners-cheap undertaker, but that, by candlelight and perhaps by illuminations even more ancient, the children, with great effort, had undressed their mother so that she would appear to them as they most remembered her. Unable to lift her gigantic body, they had simply scissored off the cheap satin of the obsequial robe. Then they had decorated the body with flowers—probably stolen from some Amsterdam Avenue florist's—into a kind of fleshy shrine. From the deserted *botánica* down on the corner they had filched small religious figurines of the Christ and the Madonna—figures in every size and color—and stood them around like mourners on the promontory of the enormous cadaver's rolling, hilly flesh.

They had loved that body. They had loved lap and breasts and cunt and womb of that strange, ever-hungering flesh. The breasts—upon which lonely men had fed milklessly through who knows what strange Dominican nights—the breasts, I say, each bore figures of saints standing upon them like sentinels, their painted lids quick in the quivering candleshine. The poor dead woman's great bush was intertwined with forget-me-nots and African violets and had been combed and anointed with aftershave lotion from the peeling dresser, whose top was littered with cosmetics. The cunt was like an Eden—a garden fashioned by children; it having fashioned them. These small sojourners upon the crowded earth had appreciated everything of which this strange, furry organ was capable. They knew, with the early sexual knowledge of the very poor, that they had found life in it, each. They knew, moreover, that this cunt was the livelihood of their small, unmanned family. From it had issued food and shelter and what ragged clothing they wore—and a rare, rare toy. From that cunt came all the Pepsis and bubble gum and pinto beans and rice and cornbread in their universe—a universe which was very, very small. They loved the great bushy thing. It had given them everything; it had given them themselves.

Those children, they were worshippers there, and if there had been grief and tears at the death, they were past. Even as I watched, even as the door sagged and glimmered phosphorescent under the splintering fists and shoulders and flaying heels of the Goody Two-Shoes, even through this huggermugger, the children still moved back and forth around the great white body, arranging a flower—here under a black-bushed armpit, there upon a nipple which had once flowed sweet, or perhaps there was only a forget-me-not to be arranged ever more tastefully, ever more gratefully, in the cunt. There was a butterfly tattooed upon the gigantic left forearm. It looked as though a painted piece of a lost summer had fluttered by and lit there, upon a vast white stone bathed in sunlight.

The naked, enormous woman had a faint mustache on a pleasant, round Mayan face. The line of dark hair was like the wing of a resting hummingbird. Her nipples were like great tarnished pieces of eight glowing with an indefinable sweetness in that poor room. In that half-light the body was flattered into the aspect of a miniature mountain upon which, in the thrill of some ancient rite, stood toy saints and toy gods and toy wondering disciples. The corpse was an enormous toy shrine.

Ceremoniously, the eldest of the children—a solemn-eyed and strangely blond-haired child who looked no more than six—went to the dresser and searched restlessly in the litter for a very special something. She found it and came back with it, a little business card, and placed the card between the big woman's rolling, heaved-up thighs, tucking it amid the blossoms in the cunt—a card like the stone which once closed up a tomb. Upon the card in gay red, white, and blue candy-stripe letters was the slogan GOD BLESS AMERICA! Now the child plucked yet another gay blossom from the wilting little bouquet in her fist and tucked it into her mother's navel, working it in till it stood upright like a tiny, blue-haloed angel. She adjusted the card again and then turned and stood looking at me, her face working suddenly like ferment in a wine vat and about to blossom out into tears. I did not hesitate. I dove into my purse and fetched out the great yellow diamond and gave it to her.

The children were thin—meager is the word. But she had kept them clean and she had not been dead long and the open cans of cat food on the cracked enamel table in the adjacent kitchen showed they had eaten recently. The candles burned with something that sweetened the dark. But the walls were covered with wild and joyous graffiti—all of them involving a fat and obviously smiling figure in various acts of love.

Behind me the old door sang on its tired, frozen hinges under the barrage of kicks and fists against it. Light shimmered like darting, golden lizards under the space between door and threshold to the dangerous hallway beyond. The children stared—a little resentful that I had interrupted a game they had been playing. And it was a game more of Joy than of Grief. The door was beginning to give. I searched till I saw it—a barred window to the long expanse of watertowered roof beyond in the bleary panes of the night. A heavy, rattling lock held the gate secure. I sobbed with frustration as Loll's voice chanted my death paean sweetly beyond the barricade. And I had the wild, maddening sense that, once the Goody Two-Shoes saw this childish irreverence in the face of Death and the X-rated graffiti on the sweating plaster, the children's lives would be endangered.

Someone needs you, Toni Falconi had said.

The door split, and light streamed through the crack in the lower panel.

I will die with little children, I thought in a sudden flush of queer pleasure. I will go with them to Criste.

Dying time, devil Fifi! bawled Loll through the splintering wood. I grabbed the chair and propped it fatuously under the knob. Might as well staunch a burst dam's flow with straw. Something heavy must bar the crumbling frame. And I must find a way to get these children out the window and to the escape offered by the roof. I caught a glimpse of light amid the litter of Avon and Estée Lauder jars and bottles on the candlelit bureau. I caught at it. It was a great ring of keys. The dead mother had apparently been some sort of building superintendent. I fumbled them up to the lock on the window gate, and the children resumed their game in the deathly light—plucking flowers from small bouquets and wreaths and decorating the dead woman in every imaginable way. It was a panorama of Grief more deep than I had ever witnessed. Everyone was making a gay game out of catastrophe. The fat woman had doubtless been a kind and loving mother. She was dead. Shall we cry? asked something inside the children. And the answer came back that the first tear would unleash upon them the fury of oceans. Better make a game of it.

I was trying keys insanely. I got the keys mixed up and started all over again. If only there were something heavy to push against the slowly failing door. Maybe the bureau— A chunk of wood sprang out of the splintering door and skittered across the floorboards; light from the hell beyond blazed craftily through across the candleshine.

Miss Fifi? bawled Loll boldly. Are you about ready to die? Praise God!

The bureau would not budge. I dropped the keys and caught them up and began trying them again in the heavy old lock. I felt like laughing hysterically when one of the silver-leashed rats, his halo somewhat askew, came squealing through the fresh break in the wood and sat upon his glowing haunches, cleaning his whiskers thoughtfully and looking at the candles, his black eyes gleaming like the heads of hateful hatpins. One of the children was eating handfuls from a can in the kitchen. I found the right key at last and the lock pried wearily open. I fumbled for the iron gate. But I knew in my heart that I needed another full three minutes to get my precious wards into the mood to dare desert their home and race with me out across the dangerous roofs of the city.

Two things happened then. The door began to show inch after inch of light under the kicks and blows, and Loll's voice trumpeted on like doom's bugle. The children quickly grasped the problem and dealt with it with an ingenuity of which I was incapable. In unison they ran to the enormous death box, got behind it, and shoved. When I saw what they intended, I gasped. The great coffin began to teeter and rock. The children grunted and giggled. This was part of the great new game, too. The fat woman's face was beatified by the weltering candleshine to a sweetness which was at the same time cosmetic and, in these circumstances, presumptuous. The reek of sour cat food, the smell of old semen and old perfume and tired men's yellow feet padding across the rugless gloom toward the bed—these haunted the atmosphere. The children gave a great happy cry as they shoved once more and the enormous coffin, slipping at last from its center of gravity, began to move like something in slow motion. With a crash that must have been heard in the street below, it went down in a cloud of plastic flowers and crashing wood. For a moment the corpse rose and hovered, in a kind of parody of resurrection, and then, with a thump that rattled the windows, it rolled and settled like a vast dam against the door. The woman must have weighed five hundred pounds. The weight was sufficient to give me the time I needed.

I looked at the children questioningly and drew two of them against me, stroking their curls.

It is time for us to leave, I said in a contained, soothing voice, and

pulled open the iron window gate and racketed the cracked window
up, breathing in as I did so the welcome freshness of the autumn
night. I winked at my lady moon, then lifted the smallest of the
children out into the night. And helped the others over the sill. I
looked at the dead mother, who had never before served her loved
ones so well. Her faintly smiling head shook a little under the impact of the blows behind it. The rat sat on her breast, nibbling at
the sweet smear of the painted mouth's lipstick.

Get you yet, honey! cried Loll somewhere back in the Death beyond the door. I'll get you yet. Because it's still dying time for Fifi
Leech. Praise God!

Now we were running, and the moon was in my ears, and I felt
the soft wet breath of trees from Central Park, and the stars were
tangled, it seemed, in the hair of each child I herded gently, yet
firmly, down the fire escape.

There was a flurry and respite in the alley at the foot of the fire
escape. I saw Toni Falconi. She was holding her broken arm tensely
against her well-rounded breasts. Her face was drawn with pain in
the moonlight—but with something more. Four other members of
the Children of the Remnant were with her.

We'll take them now, she said. You did great, love. Right on.
But you, love—

I'm all right. We'll take the children. Make for the park. We
must split here, it would seem. Later.

All right.

The children were game as scuffed small saints in the moonlight.
I glimpsed them being raced off to a waiting Volkswagen bus, and I
began to run again. A rag-and-oil torch was flung round the corner
of the alley like a dirty flag. It lit up Loll's face. And the others.
And I was running. And as I ran, thinking foolishly of games Loll
had played with me when I was as young as these children were.
But times had changed. Times always change. I was running and
there was a rustic wooden archway over one of the entrances to the
park and I headed for its silhouette against the smeared chalky
blackboard of the sky and trees beyond. I ran till I saw a clump of
brush, and I flung myself under it, my face pressing against the
earth so hard that I could taste the mushroom of that tired loam's
crumbling summer grasses. I lay very still as the bright thunder of
fiery heels went past me down the black, glistening pavement.

But the night was not done with me. Through clenched lids I could see the orange glow of one final and infernal pair of these Satanic slippers. One last pair. Surely fatal this time. Because they were planted in the broken grass no more than ten inches from my forehead. I sobbed, spent, tasting earth. I lay a moment waiting for the terminal blow. And then I lifted my eyes to meet the gaze of my conqueror.

The face—dusted with gold from the shine of the shoes—was the face of Lindy.

# S·I·X·T·E·E·N

In that queer, cursed twilight the shadows were stacked dominoes which, from time to time, slithered and fell in soundless riffles. The only illumination betwixt me and heaven were those two last, infernal shoes. Even as I watched, Lindy stooped and tugged them off. She flung them, falling planets, down the heaped dismalities all round us, where, equipped with certain self-destruct devices, the slippers exploded in mauve tendrils of soft rocketry against the gloom. I had seen in that moment's glare that Lindy was neatly and prosperously dressed—austerely, as always—in a tailored navy-blue suit and faintly mannish blouse, with the pale, wrinkled camellia of a Windsor tie blooming under her round, brave little chin. She dipped into her duffel bag of unborn Bavarian chamois by Cosima di Turin and took out a pair of new buckskin Tretorn loafers, which she slipped on.

At that instant, the city lights bloomed boldly back on, filling the somehow daunted world with light.

My sister and I stared at each other for a moment.

267

And then, with little cries, we embraced, and for an instant it became a night back in Echo Point some twenty years before, in childertime.

Lindy sought my fingers and pulled me to a rustic bench which was lovingly historiated with the initials and pleasant obscenities of old lovers.

Tonight there was something new about my sister which was, at the same time, incredibly old and familiar. It was as though some conflict deep within her had finally reached perfection.

She flung her head back and stared at the show-windowed heavens. Feef, sing for me the lullaby Rinsey used to sing us when father was gone off somewhere in the world. Do you remember it?

Yes, I think so.

I think if you sing me that bedtime song I'll stop being afraid.

I curled an arm around my beloved Lindy and drew her closely near me.

> Sleep, child—star-child
> Now your head is nodding.
> Dream, child—lovely child
> Daddy's gone a-godding.
> Though the sky's a vasty land
> Bereft of moony peace
> Sweeley shall wrest from God's hard hand
> Criste's starry fleece!
> Dream, child—moon-child
> Men's weary feet are plodding
> Go and tell them in their dreams
> Midst patchwork heaven's stitches and seams
> That Joy's as holy as it seems
> And Sweeley's gone a-godding.

As my voice—just loud enough for us to hear—trailed off amid the sounds of the reviving and somehow titillated city, I could feel Lindy's shoulder still tensed and quivering like the flank of an overridden mount.

Didn't it help? I whispered.

It's not like Rinsey, she said. That's all. O, Feef, it all seems so long ago. Everything seems long ago tonight. And sweet as your singing was, it wasn't Rinsey.

I know.

What else have you been up to? she said after a moment.

Finding you, mainly. That's been my job tonight. Running up and down this silly island—looking for you.

I touched her hand.

Are you still being held for ransom?

No. I'm—well, you see—I'm not worth anything to the Cazzo Nostra anymore.

Why?

Well, I suppose you heard. Tonight. What happened to father's book.

I saw it. I didn't quite believe—but I saw, Lindy. And I know as well as I know my name that he did nothing to cause the publication to abort the way it did.

But do you know what really happened?

I have several guesses.

Still, I don't think you'd be guessing the answer. The real answer.

What did happen, love?

Lindy stood up, a little unsteadily, a movement filled with a vast, ineffable weariness.

Maybe I'd better let father tell you, she said. Besides, we can't really talk here.

Then let's find a place to talk and maybe a joint and a sip of something cool.

We must go to the place called Le Pet au Diable, she said, a little more mysteriously than I felt was necessary.

What is it?

A charming combination lingerie shop and club. A really terribly wicked place, I'm afraid. But it's downstairs from the flat where the séance of Mei Ling is being held tonight. And, from what I've heard—and I think it's reliable—father will be there.

Séance? I have an invitation to it.

I checked the contents of my bag and found the mimeographed card. Lindy had one that matched.

Actually, she said, I've not been the captive of those women for several days now. I've had privater quarters.

Where?

The Algonquin Hotel. Where else?

Why "Where else"?

Well, Feef, you know I've been a subscriber to the Book-of-the-Month Club for years.

We rose and moved together toward the rustic archway silhouetted against the bright lights of Central Park West. The streets, after the brownout and the lightning assault of the Goody Two-Shoes, were curiously alive—even gala.

There were a dozen or more *botánicas* and porn shops along Amsterdam which were ravaged and windowless. Shards of glass crunched like ice beneath our innocent feet.

To answer your question, Lindy said. As to why father's book is lost—I shall try, briefly.

She lighted a Winston.

When did you start smoking, love?

Lately. I've started several new things lately, Feef.

Why?

Maybe there's a new urgency. Okay, that's not a full answer. O, I can't talk about it yet, Feef. Anyway, as I was saying—

Let me fill you in on what I know, I intervened. Thousands of manuscripts went into the computer.

Father's book, naturally, was chosen, said Lindy.

Why "naturally"?—somehow you seem converted.

I knew it would be chosen. I knew it would be the best book in the world.

And yet, love, you did the thing father deplored, the one thing he feared—you cast it to the world.

Feef, I wanted its message to reach people. Many people.

And you wanted a share of the money.

O, yes. Up until—up until lately I was the world's greediest witch.

Lindy, stop these vagaries. Stop the veiled hints. Is there something wrong you're not telling me?

Yes. Nor will I tell you. Not yet. I have too much to do. Somehow I have to be a part of the restoration of a work of genius which I helped abort.

You aborted the computer?

No. But I involved father's book in it. The computer aborted for the most natural and scientific reason in the world.

It failed. The computer failed.

Why, no. In a funny way it *succeeded*. It was more honest than the men who shaped it.

How?

Feef, that computer—in order to equip it to choose the absolutely most important book on earth—was programmed with every known, and perhaps some unknown, human value. At the same time it was programmed with a complete pattern of the way we really live.

And?

It drew a blank. The machine, faced with what we say we believe in—the things men for centuries have died for and been afraid to live for—was faced, at the same time, with what we actually do. Darling, don't you see the machine simply selected, edited, and printed the logical reaction to those two disparities—what we believe and what we do—and came out with thousands of blank pages. The machine, you see, was more honest than the men and women who made it. Who programmed it with these pompous and pious platitudes, which, in fact, have literally nothing at all to do with the way we actually live.

O, I am so glad.

Glad that father's book is irrevocably lost?

No, glad to know that my hunch was right—that he would never have done anything to stop the publication.

O, but how can you use the word *glad* about such a tragedy? Fifi, maybe we'll never know what the book had to tell us.

Yes, we will know.

How? It was made clear from the beginning that all manuscripts would be shredded after the selection was made—including the winner.

I still believe.

Believe what?

That father will remember what he wrote—and write it again.

He's tried.

He has? And what happened?

He has half of it. The other half completely eludes him.

You know this?

Yes. He told me.

Is he trying to get it down again?

Yes. He has—as I say—half.

Did you ever look at the manuscript before you submitted it, dear?

Yes, I took it out of that cheap Red Apple shopping bag. I'd never have been able to resist the temptation to look—to peek, at least. There was light coming from it. I know that. I saw that light—like a conclave of glowworms and fireflies—amid the shadows of many different strange places through which I carried it before I submitted it to the contest.

You believe now that it is a very special book.

Yes, now.

I mean really believe that father's book may turn out to be rather holy.

Yes. And, funny—now it's too late for my belief to matter.

Don't say that.

Thanks to me, Feef, the book is lost beyond recall.

I paused a beat.

Is father unhappy? Is he on the rack over this?

Lindy's face brightened a little, though she looked unhealthily pale and nerveworn. Oddly enough, he isn't. Really, Feef, I sometimes wonder if Sweeley Leech has any ego.

Any what?

Ego. The book is his, after all.

What does it matter who gets credit for it?

Well, after all, it was he who saw the Lite.

And it's Sweeley Leech now who knows that in certain times of history when the Lite is seen, it is made visible to several people at the same time.

You mean—you mean then that father knows that the time for the Criste Lite is here? And that if he doesn't bring it to light, someone else will?

Exactly. I would bet on it.

Lindy smiled. Something *is* astir, she said, in the world these nights. Something does seem to be moving toward its Time. Maybe Sweeley Leech is right—maybe his fame doesn't matter at all. Maybe the glory will appear somewhere else on earth.

O, it will, Lindy.

I switched on my wristradio. I suddenly realized I knew Paul Harvey intimately. I knew him as a child. He was the third cousin at Presbyterian Church picnics who always talked too much.

It seems so odd, Lindy mused as our shoes scuffed along the leafy autumn pavement of West Sixty-third. The relative simplicity of the book. I mean, how hard can it be to remember thirty or forty pages on a ruled yellow pad?

The simple stories are always the hardest ones to remember. People I could mention remember page after page of Old Jewish Bible hatred and vengeance and heavenly wrath—and forget the Sermon on the Mount.

Lindy strode on with long steps, pacing ahead of me nervously. She skipped through a couple of hopscotch squares chalked on the unremembering stone before she caught herself and turned her face to me, colored up and embarrassed. She glared at the little labyrinth some dusky Dominican child had drawn there on the sidewalk, and then grimaced.

Graffiti, she snapped irritably. Children have no respect these days.

That was Lindy, somehow—Lindy through and through. Halved and twinned inside into Someone who loved Fun and another playmate, huddled there in the steepled and well-bishoped Star Chamber of her Conscience.

For example, she still wore a little band of black crepe around the stiff serge sleeve of her suit jacket. That was the last surviving souvenir of the grief she had gone through at the sudden death of her most recent husband—a mean, pathetic little numbers writer from East Liverpool. He had been shot in a Cadiz, Ohio, voting booth for trying to fix a machine. With an ax. Lindy had gone in for grief in a big way. And crepe. Crepe—black as her Bible—was everywhere. Crepe in the dining room. Crepe in the kitchen. Crepe in black, weeping billows around the Colonial arch of the front door. And (dear Lindy!) on the bedside table an open volume of *Crepe Cookery*.

Lindy, how many pages did you say were in the yellow manuscript?

Thirty-some. No more than forty.

And how many words to the page? Or did you see?

I peeked. Feef, there were no *words* at all.

No words?

Pictures. Designs. In the most fabulous colors. I just caught a glimpse.

How could you resist reading it all?

I was frightened, she said. Frightened out of my wits. I told you that.

Why?

Because—well, because I just knew I was reading the Word of God.

But there were no words, you say. Only colored designs?

Yes. Colored designs which, if read in sequence, would give you the Word of God. Yes. O, I think if I had carefully gone through the manuscript—I mean absorbing it all—I think I would have *died* when I finished it. I tell you I was scared of it, Feef. I might have died.

You might have lived, I murmured.

What, dear?

Nothing, I said quickly. I didn't myself quite understand what I had just said to my sister. The most awful feeling of foreboding came over me.

We ambled on. The night air was mild and spiced like wild-rose honey. Windows had been flung open and equinoxes of heavenly stars entangled themselves like fiery briers in the washed, blowing curtains of the poor.

There was a message in everything this night, and it was directed at me. I could not catch it, but it was there, all around me. It was a message about my darling sister, but it was a message about more than just that. Things, I knew, were coming to a kind of furious orgasm in that moment of Time and Space through which we moved. I sensed a fabulous night still ahead of me. I mean ahead of *us*—for now my beloved sister and I, I knew, were closer than ever before in our lives.

O, Feef, sometimes I feel like—like such a—a crumb.

Why, love? I asked, though I well knew.

I aborted the appearance of a very great book is why. Maybe the greatest of books.

But, as you say—as father himself explains—if it is not he who brings it, it will be someone else.

Half, she said again. The outlines.

I don't understand.

He has every design on every page outlined—from memory.

And that's not enough to carry the Word?

No. He says he can't remember the colors. And the colors are what give it its deepest glory, and meaning. O, I could tell that from the page I peeked at. Lindy, it gave me the strangest feeling—just that one page. I really *wanted* to go on.

We all want to—we're all afraid to, I whispered.

The colors—O, God, the colors, Feef!

Heavy, huh?

I felt the brush against me of that strange Message, wafting invisibly through the perfumed autumn night air.

What were the colors, Lindy?

I don't know, she said. I can't describe them. Colors you see deep in the flames of glowing coals in a grate on a deep winter's night. Colors you sometimes see deep inside the pagan quiet of a Christmas tree. And something—something dangerous, too—like the tints you see flaming in sorrow within the wings of a murdered jungle butterfly imprisoned in a Lucite paperweight. I was scared, Feef.

I understand.

God, maybe somewhere on this earth tonight, someone really *has* the secret of the lost half of the Christe Lite. The colors. Do you believe that?

O, I believe they do! Yes, Lindy. We must believe.

We'll know tonight, she said. They may be coming toward us now. Bringing the secret to Sweeley Leech. At the séance we shall—

Was it my imagination, or did Lindy stagger a little?

Getting over into the Golden Time, she murmured softly.

That's a beautiful phrase, I said. Where did you get it, Lindy?

It's how father describes the experience of getting the Word on paper. "Getting over into the Golden Time."

Time, I smiled. Not place but Time. Yes, that would be Sweeley Leech's heaven.

Yes, Lindy had staggered, because now she leaned, her fingers cupping the black cast-iron knob of a balustrade by a brownstone, her face bent and her gray lips gasping, her eyes pinched closed in pain.

I rushed to her side; she sat on the stoop, a sick child, bent and hugging her knees and giving out soft, clenched little moans.

Lindy, love, what is it?

Ah, God, Feef?

Lindy, what——?

Lindy, stay here. I'll get help.

—let me *alone,* Feef!

Lindy, you're sick.

I tell you, let me *be!* I'm *all right.*

Her words slid into a tight little whimper of pain, and she was scrabbling madly inside her chamois purse for something. I saw a glint of glass—the twinkle of cold steel. I shrank back, watching as Lindy, with great effort, struggled out of her jacket and ripped up her sleeve, a mother-of-pearl button bouncing like a child's lost tooth on the damp pavement. I could not believe this thing I was seeing: my sister, Lindy, doing this thing she was doing. My proper, Christian, conventional Lindy with a neat, disposable syringe and an ampul from which she now drew a few cc's of color-less fluid. Her knuckles clenched white as chicken bones as a fresh spasm of pain hit her, and the hypodermic crumbled and splintered in her fisted hand. She sobbed bitterly and plunged into the chamois purse once again, feeling furiously around as if—horror of horrors—there were not a replacement there. But there was, and that seemed to calm her some; she managed to fill the second syringe, then plunged it into her arm, inside, above the elbow. She huddled like a praying pilgrim till the rush reached her.

Somewhere, beyond an open window, an Art Tatum piano solo was happening. My eyes fixed on Lindy's shadowed little figure in the trembling light, and I thought, foolishly, about Art Tatum, thinking how queer it must have been in there in the dark, knowing you were being hurt for something called Blackness and not having any real idea what Blackness looked like. Lindy moved; her dark sil-houette began to unfold from the damp, butt-littered step. She stood, unsteadily at first, and then with firmness, her neat Tretorn shoes planted apart, her hands on her hips. Something in her face, now stoned and somnolent with inner whispering wisdoms, fixed on me with the flag of defiance snapping in her transformed, pinpoint eyes.

So now you know, Feef, she said in a voice I couldn't quite place. Your holier-than-thou sister Lindy is a junkie!

Have I uttered one word of condemnation? Lindy, surely you know me.

I know you, she said. And I know you're shocked shitless.

I laughed. Why, yes, I guess I really am surprised.

She picked her purse up from the stone and slipped back into her jacket, holding the buttonless cuff closed with her fingers. She walked on ahead of me.

I ran ahead, trying to peer round into her face. Lindy, did they—the Cazzo Nostra women—force this on you?

No one forced anything on me. I'm a free soul, Feef.

Why, yes. I know you are, love. But—

Maybe I just decided I'd lived too—too sedate a life. Maybe I just decided to come over a little into your world, Feef.

Lindy, my world isn't heroin. Or morphine. But still—I think I understand. Yes. Maybe this will be good for you. For a while.

Yes, she smiled. Only for a while.

How long have you been using it?

Fifi, suppose I don't want to talk about it? Suppose this is my one little fling in life and I want to enjoy it alone? Okay?

Okay, love. I just don't want *you* to worry about it.

*Okay?* Is it a deal? No more questions, dear sister?

Yes. It's a deal. But I am a little breathless. I remember you would never even smoke grass.

That's different, she said. That's—that's self-indulgence. This is something else.

O, I'll bet it is, I chuckled, my eyes searching her dreamy, half-smiling face in the streetlights. Something else. Yes. I've heard.

I dug my hands into my pockets and swung along, feeling the rhythm of my shoulder purse against my hip.

Don't you know? asked Lindy.

No, I laughed. I don't know. I've never used hard drugs, Lindy. I know that surprises you. Heroin for me is dumb. It *numbs*—it doesn't illuminate.

Yes, I confess it does. I thought you did everything, Feef.

No. Not everything. I want to sharpen the Vision, not alter it. Heroin is like codeine to me—dumbing.

I thought you said we weren't going to talk about it, she crooned wearily.

We were passing the open window of a tiny basement apartment, where, with no one visible watching, a sixty-inch face of electronic evangelism was flaying sinners and calling for the new Coming, its authoritarian face thrust back, bullying grace from heaven.

I paused and stood watching with a merry laugh. Stop looking for him in the skies, Billy Graham, I shouted. Criste is alive and well in Everybody!

Lindy frowned and shook her head dreamily. No, she said. We mustn't make fun of that man's salvation. He may be right.

Do you really believe *that?* Believing as you do—or as you say you do—that father has somehow captured the *real* Word of God?

O, Feef, I'm not sure. Half of me believes. But half—

I know, love. And bless both halves, for they are my Lindy and I love her dearly.

I caught her by the shoulders and swung her round. I searched her stunned, half-happy face tenderly. Is there anything you're not telling me, Lindy?

About what?

Something connected with your becoming—as you call it—a junkie.

She backed off, wagging a forefinger at me.

Now, Fifi, you promised. You agreed we'd let it drop.

I walked on, silent. I saw the golden iteration of neon somewhere up in the chalky smear of skies amid the buildings. I knew we were approaching our destination.

Can I beg of you the answer to only *one* more question? I pleaded.

On my junkiness?

Yes.

All right. I suppose. One only.

Are you buying drugs off the street?

No. I'm not. Now it's closed. Okay?

She glared at me, really glared at me, for an instant then.

God, she said. You're really the last one I'd have imagined would have sat in judgment on me for some little habit I may have acquired. Maybe I just wanted to change my life-style.

You do want to. Badly. And you will. And as for my sitting in judgment on you, that's not so, Lindy.

O, you are. You! Such an exemplar of the sexual revolution and all.

As far as I'm concerned, I said, the sexual revolution never touched you, Lindy.

And never will!

O, there may be surprises up ahead, lover.

I'll never spread myself around the way you do, Feef.

It hurt and she knew it, and she turned then and kissed me quickly on the cheek.

I'm sorry, she said. Didn't mean that. Forgiven?

I kissed her softly on her soft, dry lips and hugged her close and breathed in deeply, trying to capture the Lindy smell, the dear childtime Lindy smell I had always smelled, but it was gone this night and another had replaced it: the redolence of a dangered and deep despair, acrid and somehow clinical. I pulled sadly away and searched her drawn, wan face. Her hair was bound back blackly in a chignon the size of an apple and her glasses gave her the look of a truly austere Geraldine Chaplin.

Forgiven? Her voice was the singsong of a frightened child.

O, you know you are, love! I tossed my head in a carefree laugh. Besides, you're right. I do fuck a lot.

I paused, thinking how long I had been without it, wanting it, almost wanting poor Lindy. And I am happy. Nearly all the time. And the reason I am happy, I think, is that I always fuck for love and never just to get sex off my mind. You know, that's the reason most people fuck, poor babies. "To get it off" is their phrase. To get it off their minds, to forget about it. I considered it solemnly. I fuck to remember.

To remember what, exactly?

Why—Joy, I suppose. Yes, Joy. That's it. I fuck to remember the Joy I came from—to remember the Joy I hurry to meet.

No Guilt, Feef?

Why, bless you, dearest. Haven't you learned yet that Guilt is the Original Sin? Guilt is what came and drove poor, dear Joy out of the Garden.

I kissed her again quickly. Original Sin is not poor Adam's curse, love. It's that he has forgotten Original Joy!

✦

We had reached a brilliantly illuminated astonishingly ornate Gothic brownstone on West Sixty-third, around the corner from Central Park West. The brilliant illumination came from a pair of baby spots on the curb which played a moving light on the building's lovely cloak of English ivy. Every window was alight to show the baroque interior of a small, and somehow very naughtily decorated, Parisian bedroom. Cut-glass oil lamps glittered on tiny doilied tables. Cherubs with gilt laurels in their baby hair looked down, blushing, from the canopies of Alençon lace and Breton linen. Faces, flushed and joyous, flickered and flirted amid the glowing curtains. Wineglasses glowed like tiny cups of ruby, and the soft autumn night air whispered with fumes of good marijuana. Somewhere a small string orchestra with cembalo was playing Bartók's Rhapsody No. 2. I often fall in love with places as I was falling for this place, as I have loved dear Echo Point since my mind woke, stewing in wet diapers in my childertime.

What captured my eye next, though, was the elaborate neon sign atop the tall, dark, fudge-cake opulence of the building itself. If the sign was not designed by Marc Chagall—and I suspect, looking back, that it was—it was fashioned by his most ardent pupil. It is somehow inadequate to call it a sign at all; it was more a volcano of color, captured in writhing, weaving tubes of molten glass. It was a creation of really intoxicating beauty and (as was clearly intended) of enticement.

Central to the phosphorescent glass arrangement was the name of the establishment, LE PET AU DIABLE, and beneath it, in a lovely parody of a lady's handwriting, one was able to read: *Madame Aubade and the Fabulous Monster, Footit the Chichevache.* O, this was getting richer by the minute! Above these words two figures were pictured in a fiery scribble of light: Madame Aubade, her beautiful legs giving off light as they danced, like a rhythmic aurora borealis, and off to her left, limned in scary luminosity, a fire-breathing creature which was, I supposed, the Chichevache, an obviously dreaded creature which resembled one of those nine-foot-tall lions one sees at the gates of Chinese temples.

I was like the child Sweeley Leech used to take to the Gentry Brothers' Circus when it came to the old Indian field near Echo Point in the zesty, hot summers of the cotton-candy past. I glanced at Lindy. Her mouth was thinning to a hard line. Even with the drug, lights of conscious rejection were flickering in her vitreous, teddy-bear eyes.

Do you have a pad, love? Lindy asked.

Are you—? You mean a Tampax?

No. No. Don't be nasty. Must you always be thinking down there? I mean a pad to write on. And a ball-point.

Sure, love.

I had a spring-bound notebook and a Bic in my bag. I gave them to her and turned back to the sign, a great chromatic peacock lashing its blazing rainbow tail against the star-pinned latitudes of heaven.

What are you writing, Lindy?

I'm taking notes. I'm writing a book.

I smiled and fed my eyes and senses with the spectacle candied out before me.

Lindy was squatting on a step at the foot of the sweeping, graceful stone staircase which led up to the wide entrance that was crowded with pretty, laughing people. The cembalo thrummed a chord which wept with the sorrows of old Buda and Pesht. Leaves danced on the pavement in little circles, amid which I spotted the tiny figures of old, small elves, mottled with liverspots and beady-eyed with lust, darting and dodging among the whirling leaves and candy wrappers. I could well imagine how old and degenerate fairy folk might be drawn, like moths to a candle, to this palace of Joy. I did hope they wouldn't be tiresome and spoil the night ahead for Lindy and me. My nose delighted to the odors and wafted enticements which drifted in the intervals between breezes. Succulent barbecue with Mediterranean overtones; roast duck and fragrant capon weeping with gravies uncaptured by Escoffier. The scent, too, of excited fresh perspiration counterpointed the rare perfumes of at least five continents.

A girl of no more than nineteen, with cinnamon-toast hair cut short to give her face the look of a purring Manx cat, came lilting down the ten stone steps on the arm of a simply heavenly boy whose silver face might have been profiled on the sea-god coins of Syracuse and Carthage. The girl kissed me on the mouth. Her breath was rich with the smell of fresh semen and a wine that was Château Simard, Saint-Émilion, and 1973, at least. I adored her instantly. The cembalo crashed and sobbed somewhere above our heads; the violas were maudlin with sensuous lament. I felt a little stab of false, tinseled grief as she swept the boy off to the open door of a glorious and venerable Daimler at the curb.

I turned and looked for Lindy. She was still bent over her writing on the stoop. Really! She was utterly untouched by this sensuous extravaganza lying open, like loving legs, before her, these sights and sounds and smells that had my young body singing songs. It came over me how long I had gone without loving someone. O, feckless, fuckless Fifi, you have been unfaithful in your love of God's body inside you! My lips were dry but, inside, my mouth was moist as a fresh fig with the excitement of anticipation. O, Lindy, really! You are a woman, too! How can we both be Sweeley-fathered and Rinsey-mothered and be so unlike? I turned by back impatiently on her again. What sort of book would she write? Perhaps she would surprise us all with one of those diaries, unearthly in its intellectual sexuality, which austere, bespectacled, troubled ladies occasionally produce.

*Nu,* you wanna *shtup?*

I felt a cold, small hand reaching up to my calf and, looking down, saw my Port Authority Terminal friend, Moishe the Bissel.

He gestured toward the throng of revelers who crowded in the doorway of Le Pet au Diable.

This is all a buncha hoors, he advised me. Come on, baby, let's you and me go someplace private.

No, thanks, Moishe, I said, reaching down and unfastening his bony little fingers from the grip they had on my hosiery.

*Nu,* this is it. He shrugged and slouched away in macho-miniature into a cloud of dancing scarlet maple leaves. A tiny girl with a great moonface under a gray-velvet bonnet with silver-wire embroidery caught a leaf and ran to me, laughing, holding it out to me.

Flower, she said and placed it in my hand.

I knelt and kissed her and watched her run away after another leaf.

I kissed the leaf and tucked it between my breasts the way movie whores tuck away tens and twenties in John Ford Westerns. Lord, the night—the night! I was *enivrée* with this winy, winsome night!

I felt a droplet of moisture, like the cool, kissing track of a snail, coursing slowly down my inner thigh.

I caught sight of a very ancient woman a few feet away. She seemed to be watching me. I smiled at her, and she smiled back and lounged against the carved stone balustrade, drawing thoughtfully on a dark Greek cigarette in a long teak holder. Lindy had stopped writing and was chewing her Bic, her eyes dreaming off into Central Park mysteries. At that very instant the sounds of revelry were scattered, like small fish by a shark. They were drowned out, in fact, by the most horrendous and unearthly of roars—an enormous growl which instantly triggered one's imagination as to the size and ferocity of any creature capable of such an outcry. I flinched and smiled, my eyes flashing with this new excitement—the wormwood of danger now fresh on my tongue.

The old woman moved. I would say she walked toward me, but that would not be adequate. She moved slowly toward me with a walk that was slow but rolling and voluptuous in a sense that I had never seen in a mere walk. It was as though she were inching her way up the sweet, smooth back of a dolphin just before it plunged with her into an Aegean dream. Her face was ancient and incredibly jolly. As she walked, a curious and not unpleasant whirring sound accompanied her: the kind of sound which a withershins old clock makes just before it strikes. Hers was the face of a Yeats "Minalouche," the cat's eyes that change with each phase of the moon. Her amber pupils, in eyes dark as the ash of Gallimaufry hashish, showed the thin crescent of the first phase of late October. It was the face of a scarred old Maltese: one who has survived all the world's dogs and brooms and hateful, teasing children. I fell in love with her. It was not a sexual thing I read in her face, but it excited me somehow. And I admit her first question did startle me a little. Her accent was a maddening challenge: something between Lautrec's Montmartre and the alleys east of Suez.

You are not, by any starcrossed chance, a virgin, are you?

I smiled. Then I broke up. The music had resumed. The merrymakers were moving slowly around one another, drifting like white bits of snow in a water-filled bauble. Le Pet au Diable was their plaster castle.

Perhaps I had better check, I said. It's been so long since anything really exciting has happened to my cunt or to me that my hymen may have sealed over again.

I like you. At once I like you. You are welcome to my establishment of Joy.

I could not keep my eyes off her legs. She wore a short evening gown of sheer Shantung, within the slight bodice of which her poor, purselike breasts dangled wickedly in remembrance of past and glorious caresses. Her arms were bare and thin and clamorous with jingling, chinking bracelets of gold and jewels. Around her neck she wore a large pearl pendant, which now she fingered. She sucked in brusquely on the cigarette holder and blew out a pale cloud of smoke, which hovered like a thought on the air before the impish winds tore it away. Everything about her looked old except the legs. I could not see them clearly in the poor light, but I could make out that they were incredibly shapely and that they were clothed in some strange kind of mottled stocking which looked like a fabric designed by Klimt. She undulated and whirred an inch closer, and I smelled the rich sting of attar of roses. She took my hands.

I am Madame Aubade, she said. And my question was a practical one and not the impertinence of a very old woman who still has a fuck or two left in her.

Again the joymakers fell hushed and even the wind seemed to catch its breath as the fearsome growl once more thundered down into the street.

That's why I asked. That roar you hear is Footit the Chichevache, she said with a smile, though her eyes glittered with emotion in the wrinkled old mask. She licked her thickly rouged lower lip and winked at me.

He's the monster, she said, famed in old French fable as a creature who feeds only on virtuous women. Hence his thin and meager look. Chaucer introduced and changed the word from the French *chichifache* into *chichevache*—lean or meager-looking cow. You see, Footit is—as you might say—my adored pet. Of course, as you may guess, there isn't the slightest danger of Footit's eating *me*, though occasionally, when I have become pious or sanctimonious, he gives me a good admonitory nip. But, you see, I screen everyone who enters my establishment. I allow no S and M couples, and bondage

284

is a no-no. Gay couples are welcome—or gay threesomes—though I manage, with some effort, to prevent Le Pet au Diable from becoming a resort for them exclusively. No children are admitted. Dogs and cats and certain well-mannered pet monkeys are always welcome. Rooms are provided upstairs for couples—or threesomes (frankly I have always regarded more than three in bed together as vulgar and distracting)—and the rule of the house is Love Whom You Will. Disturbances are quickly dealt with. Each waiter has at least five black belts. When someone becomes unpleasant he is not hurt but he is quickly and firmly ejected.

Have you had any close calls? I asked, in a teasing way, from an occasional virtuous woman?

Well, she shrugged, not often. I saw one on the step down there awhile ago. I was afraid she might be coming in.

Oh?

She was sitting on that step down there, writing in a notebook. Writing a Church tract, I would surmise. Feh! What a wizened, mean little soul in a really rather pleasant woman's body.

Where—?

I whirled and stared.

But thankfully she has gone away, said Madame Aubade, chainlighting another cigarette; this time it looked like Algerian hash.

She meant Lindy, of course. I caught sight of something white fluttering like a summer moth toward the pavement. Lindy had tucked a note in the mouth of my purse, and now the wind had dislodged it. I caught it up.

Excuse me, Madame Aubade, I said. I must read this.

She nodded, her silhouetted head showing the broadbrimmed fedora she wore jauntily: the sort men wear in lovely old Manets. She moved, whirring charmingly in that lilting gait up the steps.

Please bring it inside, she said, where the light is better.

She motioned to me.

Besides, she said, I have a table waiting for you. And who knows?—it may be someone you already know.

It was rude of me, but in my anxiety to read what poor, frightened Lindy had written me, I merely waved a flappy hand at her and began poring over the funny, unsteady words with the *i*'s dotted with little circles.

*Dear Fifi,*

*I know you thought, Well, old Lindy's coming over to my life-style, when you saw me shooting up. Lindy's starting to unthaw. Lindy may not be a swinger but at least she's a junkie. Well, I suppose I am a junkie by now but you don't understand why, love. I couldn't tell you when we were together. And the sight of all that un-Christianlike display of flesh at that awful place where I'm leaving you—well, it proved too much for me.*

*Well, let me come right out with it. I have terminal cancer. Uterus, tubes, ovaries—the whole kit. Three weeks, maybe a month to go, kiddo, and I'm scared. I still believe in the Church, and in many ways it, and the strange, but essentially Christian girls of the Cazzo Nostra, are keeping me alive right now.*

*Well, that's about it. I love you, Fifi—strange and puzzling to me as you are. And now I am—as Uncle Mooncob would so bluntly put it—down the tube. I won't go back to Sloan-Kettering, where the girls sent me. I had trouble enough getting enough morphine to go out on a pass tonight. I feel somehow cheated by Life. I know that's an un-Christian thing to say—*

Tears came as I read. I snuffled and brushed them away and blinked in the amber twilight beneath that flashing peacock sign up in the sky. Once more the air shook and ran for shelter as the Chichevache's thunder poured out upon us.

*—but I know, too, what I have given up in my rather short life to keep myself pure for Jesus. I have made mistakes. But I have never had intercourse with a man I wasn't married to in His sight. I do have one confession to make—one thing I would do again but about which I am a little ashamed. A few days ago when I found out I had Big C, as the girls jokingly call it, I went to a photographer on East Broadway. I had him take the enclosed nude photographs of me. There are a dozen of them. They may offend even you, Feef, because they are lascivious and really dirty. I showed everything and I did everything I've always wanted to do in life. I had these photos taken, as I give them to you now (in strange penitence), because I wanted them as reminders of what I have sacrificed in life to be with Jesus—*

286

I stripped a rubber band from a little deck of photos. They were the most innocent poses in the world—a five-year-old's parody of porn. Legs not opened to show the tiny furred oyster or its pearl. All of them with her tongue stuck out impishly as if—even now—she were mocking her body and her sexuality. But her eyes above it were sad beyond belief, as if they knew what Dying makes us leave.

*I want you to go to the Pet La [sic] Diable. It is your kind of world. Maybe you are right. Judge not lest ye blah-blah-blah. Don't try to follow me. I am staying at the Algonquin no longer. They were horrid last night. I needed quick cash and when I asked them to cash a share of Tao Chemical (Remember how I invested when the Chinese-American conglomerates came? Smart, huh?) they refused. You can't find me. You can't guess where I am living. I didn't want these photos found on my body when it is over. I have left sufficient identification. I want my body buried in the shadow of the Labyrinth at Echo Point. I love you.*

*Yours Truly in Christ,*
*Appassionata.*

I thought: O, love, you got lost in the maze once already. That is how you doomed yourself, my darling. Even a fool like Loll would know that much. O, God, I am dying with sorrow. I must find you, darling Lindy!

As I was reading I had slowly climbed the steps to the volcano of light and laughter which was the entrance to Le Pet Au Diable. Laughing couples brushed past me, and again I smelled on the air the strutting spurt and spill of fresh semen. I couldn't define the perfumes which sweetly assailed my nostrils. I was heartbroken. O, we can never understand death well enough to forgive it. Except perhaps Bach, who beckoned to its sweet coming—or Blake, who drove it back up the black alleys of hell with his fiery tiger. Lindy dying. Three weeks—maybe not that much. She would lie a little (asking His special permission for a white one) to make it easier for me. I tucked the note and the photos back into my purse. I turned to move back down the steps and off toward Central Park West and the arbored entrance to the park. Instinct suggested she might have gone that way—to lose me. O, my dear Appassionata. I think her use of that name—that souvenir—was what really broke my heart.

Back in the dusky amber evenings of a high-school spring we had played in a production of *Lil Abner*. I was Evil Eye Fleagle. Lindy was the prematurely voluptuous and overpowering Appassionata Von Climax. Now I was really in tears. I moved to the step beneath me and felt a hand on my arm. I turned.

It was Adonis McQuestion. On his arm was a slightly tipsy Dorcas Anemone. He had a little of her lipstick on his white, broad collar.

Hello, loves, I sobbed.

Fifi, what's wrong?

Don't ask, Dorcas. Just don't ask. And don't hold me back. I have to go find her.

Adonis grabbed me by the shoulders and shook me loose from my sobs.

Listen, Fifi. It's Lindy, isn't it?

Yes. She's— O, darn Life, anyway. How could old God have slipped this into the story? O, darn.

She's in trouble, isn't she, love?

Yes.

And you love her?

Yes. Yes. O, please, let me go find her.

Do you love Sweeley Leech as much, love?

I snuffled—not to consider my answer, because I already knew it—but to catch my breath.

Yes.

Well, then, come inside with us, love. Have a joint and have a taste of wine and calm down. And then get round to the real point of the evening.

I don't understand.

Helping Sweeley Leech, love.

Is he—?

He's somewhere in this wild and crazy house!

# S·E·V·E·N·T·E·E·N

Do you think there's going to be a war?

More than once that fabulous evening did I hear that question voiced throughout the otherwise gala dining room.

TRUCAD is resolving again into envious nationalities, said one.

There will be war soon. The religious orders are behind the Machiavellis of these times.

It will be an exchange of nasty interoffice memos in the form of nuclear missiles.

The Time is close. The New Saviour is coming soon.

Like a sentimental idiot I had fainted in the doorway over my concern about Lindy. My darlings, Dorcas and Adonis McQuestion (not the spurious Chaz), had managed to get me back to a pleasant corner table with real Irish linen and sterling silver and a tiny lamp of dolphin oil burning in the center. The room was packed with lovers. The air fairly reeked of good food and the tiny, acrid scents of various grasses and the yeasty smells of consummated love. If rooms can be said to possess souls, the soul of this room was pure

Joy. There didn't seem to be a mean thought anywhere in the atmosphere. Nothing possessive or jealous or aggressive.

I was alone at the dim-lit little table with my hostess. Dorcas and my darling Adonis were off under the arch, at a booth with persimmon-colored velvet upholstery, drinking tea with honey and fondling one another. O, I was so happy for them and felt the thrill of my two lovers sharing with one another and not just with me.

I looked at Madame Aubade. She was studying me with those great, first-quarter-moon eyes.

The thought of Lindy had now changed from panic to a kind of numb, unsolaced grief. I was past tears. And I was thinking of Sweeley Leech.

Where is he?

Madame Aubade smiled, the crescent moon flickering in her dark, rich eyes. Your father, you mean?

Yes.

Then you admit you are his daughter?

O, yes.

You are not ready to see him yet, dear.

Why not?

You are far too distraught. The fear of Death has filled your mind and heart tonight. We must drain that fear away.

And she reached into the litter of the table and picked up something: a flat ragdoll. She handed it to me.

O, how revolting, I exclaimed, examining it.

Yes, isn't it? But it seems to help the Faithful.

The doll was stuffed with batting and had a photograph of Sweeley Leech's face printed into the cloth of the head. It looked like a tiny Sweeley Leech elf which had happened in the path of a steamroller. I sobbed, despite the grossness of the thing, and held it against my face. I felt something warm against my chin and looked down with surprise. Then I saw it: the tiny plastic halo—perhaps two inches in diameter—which projected from two tiny dry-cell batteries on a kind of prong protruding from the doll's back. I pressed a button. The halo came alive. With dismay I looked around the room and saw similar dolls, one on each table, like curled glowworms.

Even sainthood, said Madame Aubade, requires a certain schlock promotion. This is 1992, dear.

Sainthood?

Sweeley Leech has been canonized.

O, really. This is too much. By whom, may I ask?

By revelation, primarily. But, actually, by a vote of the entire world membership of the Children of the Remnant.

O, this is absurd. I know my father. He would never consent to such aggrandizement. He is modest to a painful degree.

Unfortunately you are correct, said Aubade (I feel familiar enough with her now to drop the "Madame"). He is modest out of all proportion to the gift which heaven has seen fit to bestow upon him.

He is a saint now?

By popular acclaim. Actually, we do not consider him saint so much as archangel. You must consider this matter soberly, my darling, because the end of present-day civilization is approaching.

I have heard talk of war. But I don't want to discuss that now. I really would like to see my father.

You might not recognize him, said Aubade, rather self-satisfied in her tone.

Why?

He has been drinking, said Aubade. He is taking the honor of the living God really quite badly.

Archangels are appointed by God, not small committees.

That is so. But God is surely acting through the Children of the Remnant. That revelation has been made plain to us.

May I see him soon? O, may I? First Lindy, then father—!

After we have talked awhile, she said, you and I. I have so much to tell you. I want to know you.

I am afraid, I said, that sex is out of the question. I am much too distraught, Aubade.

I am glad you call me by my name, she said. And I am simply cluttered with love affairs as it is. I am not hitting on you.

She opened a small platinum-and-niello cigarette case—obviously Russian and pre-Revolution—and took out a joint wrapped in dark paper. She selected another one and held it out.

Smoke this, she said. It will relax you. O, my dear, I have so much to tell you. It has been so long since I have met anyone I felt like telling about myself. And I really am a kind of miracle, considering all I have been through.

Two tokes and I was feeling better; three and I was considering sentimentally a small golden mole on Aubade's wrinkled neck.

My national origins, she began, are as irrelevant and undiscoverable as those of my dear old friend Yul Brynner. Let me begin by saying that I was a young demimondaine in that sweet period of Parisian history just before the World War began.

World War One?

One. Two. Three. What does it matter? They are all the same war. And it is about to begin again. Man is inconquerable in his desire to destroy civilization so he may, in the middens and rubble of destruction, rediscover lost wild flowers and begin again.

Why must there be war?

Why, I suppose because an Archduke of low character and his morganatic and distinctly unstylish little wife were murdered at Sarajevo. In the spring of 1914. Ostensibly, that began it. Those two shots marked the beginning of the end of Modern Times. They cracked the great rooftree of Christianity. Which, as you know, encompasses all Business.

I inhaled another toke from the darling little weed, then broke off the coal with a slowed, happy smile and tucked the roach away between my breasts.

O, she sighed, it will be so good to witness the end of Christianity—to make way for the Coming of the Criste!

How old are you, darling? I asked, rather imprudently.

Aubade abruptly became Madame Aubade. She colored a little and smiled as if she had just ingested a fat mouse. She fetched out an exquisite little gold-link reticule, took out lipstick and mirror, and began doing her already over-Revloned lips.

In 1914 I was beautiful, she said. Lovely as a wild flower amid the wormwood and windmills of old Montmartre.

She made a moue and it was all rather glorious.

Toulouse-Lautrec, she crooned, once went up on me.

She eyed a rather loud blond lady named Betty, according to a silver pin on her lapel.

I ponder, she said, whether I should have admitted her.

I raised my eyebrows.

She is a Liberal, you know.

What *is* a Liberal, Aubade?

A Liberal, said Aubade, is a girl like her, who wore a black armband when the CIA killed Allende on the same day she stiffed a little immigrant from Santiago out of a dollar tip at lunch.

The walls of the dining room were covered with racks, among rather unstylish but wholly charming originals by Mondrian and Matisse. I could tell that Aubade was not as rich as she pretended because there was not a fine forgery among them. On the racks hung clusters and clouds and puffs of black and pink and seductive blue. I turned and reached up to those nearest our table and fondled them. Delicious! They were articles of lingerie—divinely silky and rapturously bordered with the most seductive handmade lace. I found a little tag. "Solange Claudet, La Pyramide, Algiers," I read. I found another—on a simply mouth-watering little black chemise—and read the tag: "Kiki, Le Sphinx, Paris."

You are admiring? asked Aubade, grabbing a brassiere of jonquil-yellow and holding it across my breasts. This is heavenly against your skin, my dear.

The whole room, I said, is hung with lingerie.

Not just lingerie, my love, she said, patting my hand. The lingerie of very special ladies.

Famous women?

And some men. But not famous in the sense you mean. These are the underthings of women famous only to their lovers. And there are so many of them. This explosion of Chantilly and Alençon which you see about you is the intimate wardrobe of the most beautiful and seductive courtesans since the turn of the century.

Are they for sale?

Nothing, she said, is really for sale at Le Pet au Diable. Some lucky girl—or perhaps chap—finds an article of lingerie here which obviously was meant for her. Or him. And it becomes hers—or his.

Do you charge for—for the entertainment here?

Not really. She mused. There are many of us in this world, she said, who will never be quite the same after the great unrobbery of a few days ago. Money has assumed a new aspect for us.

The profit motive, she went on, which is the backbone of the Church, of course, is about to destroy civilization again.

O, I don't think mankind will ever end, Aubade.

No. Of course it won't. It has always been here.

But Professor Leakey and Carl Sagan, Aubade, I began. They tell us—

Every day comes news that mankind is older than was once thought. One day soon it will be found that mankind's end is as impossible to mark as its beginning. Kingdoms have risen and fallen and been buried or burned or drowned since the aeons began ticking away. That is the meaning of Eternity. Man is eternal. So are all the animals and plants. Even this rather foolish little doll has a spirit.

We had a dollhouse at Echo Point, where I was born, I sang, softly remembering. And it was haunted.

How charming. By the ghost of a doll?

Yes.

A sad ghost?

O, utterly. The doll loved a tree which cast its leaf-shadows through the window into our nursery. I can see the calico greens and golds upon the beautiful rag rug upon which the dollhouse rested.

The doll ghost was languishing with love for the tree?

Yes. Because within the tree—an adorable old Royal Paulownia—was imprisoned the shape of a wooden soldier.

I am intoxicated with the tale already, Fifi!

Father—Sweeley Leech—soon came upon a solution.

I do so love surprise endings.

He cut off a good stout limb of the tree—and with his Tree-brand whittling knife he carved out the toy soldier. Released it from its prison in the wood.

And put it with its lover in the dollhouse—the wooden soldier and the ghost of the doll? I am fainting with Joy.

Yes.

Aubade threw back her head to laugh and instead farted resoundingly.

Most of those who heard it laughed approvingly. The girl named Betty turned her head slowly and looked hard at the old woman. Aubade soon felt her stare and turned her withering eyes to the girl.

I farted, she said, and you expect me to say excuse me, I suppose. Well, I shall not. I am a very old woman. I am filled to stuffing with the winds of many lands and seas. Occasionally, one must escape.

But *really,* said the girl named Betty.

Really, nothing. Fie on you, my darling. And what of a fart? What is a fart, historically and philosophically speaking?

She closed her great, patchwork eyes and smiled, reflecting. A fart is the wandering ghost of good food, lovingly prepared and tastefully served. A fart is the banquet Banquo. It is the poltergeist which haunts the fanciest of lace panties—even yours, my dear. The belch is officious and somehow utterly Turkish in its insolence. I never belch. The fart, on the other hand, is a soliloquy upon the good life, a gaseous apostrophe to Joy, a cheeky riposte to Death itself. It is a leveler of all, like Death. It makes instant friends out of stuffy, uneasy travelers. It breaks the ice between young lovers, perhaps being considerable as a small, golden bugle rallying the way to the adjacent, forested field of honor. The King farts, though I suspect Preachers seldom do—wanting to hoard the gases for their exhortations. A child's shy fart in church is often enough to restore humanness to these proceedings, having a far sweeter smell than that of Piety. The peasant farts in pleasant fluttering flatulence by his country hearth; the rich man, in his air-conditioned Rolls. Old couples in featherbeds often discourse in farts, each little pop or whine or quack reminding them, like phrases of music by some trouvère, of the glories of the past, when the nearby playgrounds were ringing with Joy and children. The French say of a stuffy woman (which you are, I fear, my darling): *Elle pète plus haut que son cul.* And this is fair and just, for indeed some do, as the proverb avers, try to fart higher than their behinds and the behinds of other people. The fart is in fact one of the greatest of natural lyric art forms. It provides the unwitty diner with a suitable rejoinder when he has just been told he must foot the dinner check. It can be an ode by Pindar or it can be Homeric. It makes of the body's humblest and second-most-maligned aperture a troubador. I say, why this onus on the anus? In short, the fart transforms an orifice into an oracle; the asshole into Asphodel.

So saying, she shifted slightly on the geranium upholstery and farted again.

And you may tell them, dear, she said, that for almost ninety years Aubade's farts have been *quoted.*

The girl named Betty—without escort—had not waited for these parting shots but had caught up her suede jacket and hurried away.

Poor baby, said Aubade. Perhaps I should have been kinder. Was I too grim, Fifi, dear?

But I was a little stoned and lost in other thoughts.

The cruelty of the Church in these times is proof of its approaching death, she said then. O, how heartless they are—filling as many troubled people as they can with more fear—dread of damnation, of hellfire, of heavenly vengeance—ever more fear in their little fearful lives. How utterly heartless! When it is known by the Wise Ones that we are all moving toward Criste—and shall one day be him. He shall utter Thou shalts and not a single Thou shalt not! O, the hideous Church today!

She flung back her head, radiant with disapproval and hope.

Preacher, thrash the sinner! Priest, kick poor lonely fools! Nun, butt the lonely heart!

O, I adored this old lovely soul!

That poor girl, I said, is somehow a fit product of the so-called Sexual Revolution—an insurrection I was spared, being free from birth.

Aubade blew out a long cloud of aquamarine smoke. So far as I'm concerned, she said, the Sexual Revolution came full circle in 1985—with the news of Truman Capote's vasectomy.

I reached over and squeezed her dear hand.

I stared across the room at Dorcas, now utterly enfolded in the charms of Adonis. I glimpsed the rosy flash of a nipple, heard the crisp whisper of a zipper; soft gasps, sighs, moans, the sibilant rustle of underclothes disarrayed.

And then, for the first time, I began to recognize some of the faces there. O, it was a gallery of portraits from my adventures of the past few days. Madame Jonathan Thomas Bigod with her charming little son, Mère de Cézanne with Soleil, holding hands, and O, there was darling Reverend Jimbo St. Venus and his agreeable assistant. I had settled my gaze now on a plump, pink pair of shoulders and a fat back pouring out over the confines of a tight black-velvet gown by Valentina da Genova. A red wig of improbable Titian hair hung down the freckled red neck against the glitter of small black pearls. Tiny crystal earrings like Roman empyrea glittered in the lampshine. Somehow I knew who it was and yet dared not admit it. And then the coquettish, great creature felt my stare and turned.

Heavens, I had been correct in my first instinctive surmise! It was he—Uncle Mooncob, in high-fashion drag—a kind of Art

Deco queen. Fortunately, Aubade had turned to the little waitress, who had returned with a high-heaped platter of ham.

Uncle Mooncob, do I dare believe my eyes?

He bent, desperate, the gardenia corsage wilting and browning as it bobbed against his anxious neck. His voice was a grating whisper.

For heaven's sake, Fifi, don't betray me. It was the only way I could gain admittance. She—she wouldn't let me in as a man. And I assure you, I am man—all man!

O, I am sure of that, alas, uncle.

Don't give me away.

He reached in his tissue-paper-tucked bosom and pulled out an amethyst pendant.

Pretty, don't you think? he tittered. I'm really not bad. Not bad at all. But don't get any ideas, Fifi.

I know, I said. You have come out of the closet and into the cupboard, uncle.

Don't be nasty, Fifi. And, for heaven's sake, don't give me away. I'm doing—

His whisper darkened, deepened.

—I'm doing special research into Sin for the Organization.

Already he had begun to fondle my knee, his lodge-ringed fingers beginning a slow ascent up my damp but sleepy thigh. I closed my legs and gasped, pushing him away. Aubade returned her attention to me. But I was shaken. Shaken, indeed. Heavens, was no place immune from such invasions? Uncle Mooncob in high drag had somehow the effect of Chuck Barris reading from the *Song of Songs*.

Blushing, fainting Dorcas had slid down under the tablecloth and was doing naughty, delicate things to Adonis with her pretty mouth. I remembered the nights at Echo Point when, in the haymow with some adorable farmboy, I had instructed her. It was all very nostalgic, and I was thankful for them. Still, it must have shown in my eyes: the shadow of a sorrow concerning two lovers and a trust and a freckle removed, with love, from one to the other. Aubade read these feelings.

You love that pretty girl with my dear Adonis, she said.

Yes, I agreed. But then, Aubade, I love so many!

Still, she is somehow special.

We were—we are lovers.

I told her then the full account of the surgical transplant from my darling's damask cheek to the warm, soft, damp spot so near my heart. Aubade smiled, her cat eyes smoking with memories.

I do not intend to demean the gesture, she said. All love tokens are, of course, sacred. Nor do I deprecate the generosity of your lover.

She smiled and the smoke curled out of her green, bright eyes.

But I think I once gave something rather more, she said.

O, tell me about it, Aubade.

She winked a worldwise eye at me and looked dreamily off into the haze and shine of laughter in the room.

I shall, she said, but first I must speak of Art. It is connected with Love, you see. And when Art is endangered, then Love is in gravest peril. When I first learned Love—more than ninety years ago—Art was alive and well, everywhere. And so was Love. But now—

Now, Aubade?

Now Art is utterly immoral.

She sighed.

No Artist gives a fuck about morals these days. The Artist is against every pulsating gesture of the human body or spirit. He is Loveless, as well. He has lost his good Paganism, you see. His guidelines to the Cosmos are tangled and fallen.

Tell me of your loves, I begged. Tell me of the love-gesture you made which was greater than Dorcas's with her freckle.

Don't rush me. I must talk of Art for a moment. For when Art is sick, so is Love. Did you hear about the Albee business?

I admitted I had not.

Albee, the playwright, was visiting in a West Side flat one night last spring. He had a copy—the only existing copy—of his latest—indeed, his last—drama. The phone rang. It was late. His host called him. When he answered he was informed that the copy of his play was needed at once. By important people. On the East Side. The Eighty-sixth Street crosstown bus had stopped running. Indeed, all transportation had stopped.

Taxis?

Don't you remember, Fifi? There was a cabdrivers' strike.

Yes. I seem to remember—

There was no choice for Albee. He had to cross Central Park, at three in the morning, afoot.

A dangerous journey.

Nay. A fatal one. Didn't you read of it in the papers?

I never read papers.

Albee was, of course, mugged. Murdered. The manuscript of his play—a bitter little revue he had concocted with Stephen Sondheim—was taken by the muggers.

Ah, so it was. I seem to remember. *The Golden Catheter*. Based on the life of Otto Rank. Hmm.

Let us make no value judgments. Merely observe what happened.

What, pray?

The muggers found the Albee-Sondheim play so accurate a reflection of their philosophy that they took over a small, abandoned amphitheater which Joe Papp had once built, and went immediately—and secretly—into rehearsal.

I seem to remember the reviews.

Which were raves. Sondheim fled to Granada. The reviews were, however, simultaneous with thirty indictments for first-degree murder.

How was it decided? Were they prosecuted?

Naturally not. The case was thrown out with the news that the company had won a Pulitzer Prize for drama.

Poor Albee. Poor Sondheim. I suppose he is moping in the Alhambra waiting for someone to bring in his clowns. O, how in love we all are with despair!

It is like this before every great revolution.

You see an approaching revolution for us, Aubade?

Don't you? It is here.

It began, I suppose, in Vietnam.

Nonsense. It began two thousand years ago when Paul and the rest organized Christianity and made it into the lie which is the modern Church. Give a laurel to Augustine, as well, with his despicable mother and his poor, machoed concubines. The Church, I think, is the counterrevolution to the revolution which was the credo of Criste. It is married to money and they are an old and loving couple.

She sighed and ate a bit of ham. Again she offered me some. I had a crumbly, delicious piece, which she held out to me with her fingers. It was fragrant with some rich and unknown flavor.

It is smoked for six months, she said, in a smokehouse.

Not hickory.

Of course not. That ham is smoked reverently in the vapors and fumes of Algerian hashish. It's a recipe I brought from Zagreb in the twenties.

I had another mouth-watering morsel.

Revolutions are the creation of Individuals. Counterrevolutions are the work of organized man. Think, if you will, of this: the violence man does to gain power is never so terrible as the violence he exercises to keep it. The Church today keeps Criste prisoner within its walls. He mourns there today in the dungeon dug beneath every pulpit.

She poured us each a thin-stemmed, diamond-bright glass of Tokay.

It is fashionable, of course, to say that the fault is not with the Church but with the people in it. That, you see, is a lie. Criste is in the people; he is in us all. It is the Church which shackles Criste inside—using shackles of Guilt and Fear and faith based upon negation. We must help our Lord escape.

Poor dear Albee, I sighed. How dreadful for him. And Stephen must be drowning himself in good Málaga.

If you would look for the most truthful moment in American Art, you must look to California. One artist has made that moment live—and that moment sums us up, surely, here in America.

Who was the artist?

Jack Benny. It was on his radio show.

Aubade, I wasn't born till 1966. I never heard him on the radio.

Then you missed the greatest moment of silence in all of American Art.

I had some more ham—and began to feel it like a luscious ruddy glow creeping up the Tokay in my veins.

People loved Jack Benny because he made fun of our most fatal weakness—the love of money. He blended it with an audacious and barely implied effeminacy, which appealed to something else hidden within us. But he mocked Greed masterfully. And he never illustrated it more masterfully than in the famous (what do you call it—skit?)—in the skit wherein he encounters a holdup man. The man has a gun on him and demands, "Your money or your life." And Benny pauses. And pauses. And pauses. It is a pause full of the most fateful stillnesses of our time. "Well?" asks the holdup man at last. "I'm thinking, I'm thinking!" cries Benny. Ah, my dear Fifi—that silence, that pause. No pause—no silence—in the American theater can touch it for pathos. It is immortal, that moment. It echoes along with Vietnam and the Closet War and the oil-embargo crises and ultimatums. It is full of the gathering counterrevolution of our epoch. It is the most eloquent apothegm yet uttered in American Art on the subject of Why and How this country is going to vanish soon. That silence of Jack Benny's is the wave of the future; it is the indictment of one moment's fatal and insane hesitation—as the fingers of Preachers and Presidents and Pentagon madmen hover above Doomsday's little button.

Uncle Mooncob gave me an unlovely leer through at least six layers of eye makeup. He pursed his absurd Cupid's-bow lips and blew a kiss of gratitude that I had not exposed him.

There is an old, old law in Anglo-Saxon jurisprudence, said Aubade then. It is called the Right of Ancient Lights.

Dorcas and Adonis both waved at me and moved into the hallway leading to the staircase that rose to the upper level of boudoirs. I waved back.

Are you really interested? Aubade asked with a little pucker of impatience. It is vital, you know—the knowing of this.

Yes. Yes. Yes! Go on, please, darling Aubade. Please.

Ancient Lights, she said, on a notice board in England meant this: if for at least twenty years uninterruptedly, a certain window in my dwelling has admitted light, no building may be erected which substantially cuts off that light.

Her green eyes sparkled with passionate tears.

Fifi, my dear, that Lite has been obstructed—not for twenty years but for almost two thousand. The window of man's house is blotted from the Criste Lite. It is a lifegiving light and man will surely die without it. It is blocked, my dear, that lovely Lite!

By the Church, I said, by the factories, brothels, temples, prisons, and the Satanic Mills which shadowed dear Uncle Will's New Jerusalem.

Yes, said Aubade, a little grimly. And those obstructions must be brought down.

It was a gloomy observation, and I thought: Well, I don't need any more gloom just now, though darling Aubade had touched my mind with her parables. But I had somehow, for a happy spell, tucked into some cupboard of my mind my grief for the dying Lindy, my fears for poor Sweeley Leech. Now I rather wanted to hear something Romantic.

Will you tell me now of your great love and its great gift, Aubade?

The tears seemed to glow then and grow brighter. Her eyes quavered and moved liquidly, like tiny jade fish in the wise and tranquil pool of her old, old face.

Yes, she said. Now I can tell you.

Were you much in love? O, I know you and I know it was a great love.

A Great Love, she said. But "in love" is not the right phrase.

She smiled and stroked her motley, shining, shapely calf. She stared down at her modish, foxy shoes.

You see, she said, in Russia—old Russia—in a winter more than seventy years ago, I gave another girl both my legs.

# E·I·G·H·T·E·E·N

POLONIUS: The actors are come hither, my lord.
HAMLET: Buzz, buzz!

—William Shakespeare,
Hamlet

There are phrases which, once uttered, take wing and silence whole rooms full of other speakers. Aubade's astonishing, and rather shocking, revelation cast a hush over the tables of merrymakers, caused the faces of lovers, sticky with adoration, to rise from kisses and other intimacies and turn to her in rapt attention.

Would you repeat that please, Madame Aubade? came a clear voice.

I gave my sister both my legs, crooned Aubade, a little overcome with emotion, her fugitive, Slavic eyes narrowed and smiling in her high and fine-boned face. And she rose from the sumptuous, soft upholstery of her seat and, with a few rearrangements of wine bottles and glasses and the ham platter, she sprang with astonishing alacrity onto the table and stood smiling at us.

Shall I tell you of it?

Yes. Yes, Madame. O, yes! choired fifty voices at once.

She raised her neat, lacy petticoats and showed us her legs. Now I saw them clearly—limbs as shapely as those of a tree-spirit but without hosiery. Her slender ankles tapered down like flower stems into the sexy clasp of high-heeled black pumps with hammered silver buckles. I leaned forward into the luminosity from the dolphin-oil lamp to see the legs more clearly. They were, for all their beauty, unearthly curious. And when I bent forward—as did a few others, including Uncle Mooncob—I could see that Aubade's legs were even more beautiful—and curious—than they had at first seemed. They were the legs of a breathless, dewy virgin of twenty. But there was about them a certain luster which was not that of flesh. They were plainly not the legs with which she had been born. It seemed as though, instead of skin, they were sheathed with small plates or scales of incredibly beautiful color and design. The legs looked like—or at least suggested—those of a Dresden china harlequin. Or like the ceramic serpents of Gustav Klimt. The overall design was exquisite; their appearance was somehow enhanced by a light which seemed to emanate from within—such as one sees in certain small, precious stained-glass windows in thirteenth-century cathedrals, such as those ancient suboceanic, coral-clasped chapels discovered by Jacques Cousteau in 1986 off the coast of Brittany. The legs were miracles of the jeweler's ceramic genius, and, I must admit, for a moment I was jealous of them.

Have you all seen them? asked Aubade then. Have you seen my legs?

There was a group murmur of Yes from the transfixed throng. Aubade paused, slowly lowered her skirts, and ranged her gaze slowly, wistfully around the room.

My sister's name was Villanelle. I worshiped her, although she was a year younger than I. From infancy we shared everything. There were no toys possessed by either child: each doll, each tea set belonged to both. There was no rivalry. We adored each other— seeing Krishna in our mutual worship. Yes, each of us was our Lord to the other. We were of that race of which, in Europe today, the language has almost totally vanished. We were Slavonic.

Our father was a disappointed poet who had had three hopeful years in Paris at the turn of the century. He imagined that he was the reincarnation of the exquisite medieval poet Christine de Pisan. He had had a slim, blind-tooled volume printed of fifty of his own verses, these in the manner of Villon or perhaps Charles d'Orléans. They were lovely: triolets, villanelles, aubades (from these, obviously, our Christian names), ballades, double ballades, rondeaux, and rondels. But the edition vanished in the pyrotechnic explosion of Verlaine and Rimbaud and was forgotten. Father was heartbroken with disappointment. At his death he possessed the sole existing copy of his little book—its leather limp and scarified and fringed with age like the ear of an old water spaniel. The volume was buried with him in the little churchyard at Brno. I rather think my father may have been what he said—the reincarnation of the woman poet—as well as a very great artist in his own right, for this same little volume, with a bit of his winding sheet as a bookmark, showed up in an auction at Maggs Brothers in London during what men refer to as World War Two. It was ceremoniously destroyed as blasphemous by the Bishop of Leicester in 1945. Bitterly, my father devoted himself to his only remunerative trade, that of bookkeeping. He defined a bookkeeper as a miser who absentmindedly counts the coins of others.

But the legs? exploded a stunning, cunning little blonde from a far table. Tell us about your legs.

My dear, replied Aubade with a patronizing look, would you hasten your lover there to his orgasm? Or would you prolong the ecstasy? I see you blush and look at him now. Let my story build thusly to its excruciating—and, I think, exquisite—climax.

She bent from the waist, with a slow whir, silver as the susurration of a hearth cat, and plucked up her cigarette case. She took out a thin, magenta-papered smoke and lit it, toked five times, and then passed it down to me.

It was clear by the time we had reached nubility, she went on, that my sister was the more gifted of us two. At nineteen, I was somnolent and brooding as a Russian winter; Villanelle was a born mimic, dancer, chanteuse, raconteuse, comic, who, with incredible instinct and skill, could have an audience one moment crumpled and limp from laughter and the next moment in full tears. She was exquisite in every way save one. Her legs. They were bowed and gnarled and hairy as those of a troll. She looked, in the nude, like a tree-spirit perched on top of a twin-limbed tree of incredible hoariness with a bird's nest tucked between.

Poor Villanelle. She became tubercular with sorrow and disappointment. Moreover, she was passionately in love with a rich St. Petersburg toymaker named Farfelu. Farfelu, I realized, could give my adored sister comfort, joy, security, and the impetus to a brilliant music-hall career. Security! Comfort! What hollow words those material considerations have become to me since. But, believe me, back in 1915 I would have given my life to bring precious Villanelle these things. I was young, I was foolish; and my sister was, as I have said, the image of God to me. Now I come to the point. Plain as I was, my legs were the most beautiful between the rolling Ural Mountains and the flashing boulevards of St.-Germain-des-Prés. If only Villanelle had been born as she was, in every respect—but with my legs! I was rather plain. I told the simplest story falteringly, as opposed to my present talent to hold you, as I sense, in fascination and breathless silence.

Aubade bent and took back the magenta cigarette with an impatient motion and stood puffing happily, one hand on her hip—her aged body erect and somehow more richly feminine in old age than that of any demimondaine capable of making an old queen at some literary causerie wish he were young again—and heterosexual. She flashed her gaudy, almost candy-gay limbs and passed her glittering, gemmy hands across them as if in the nostalgia of a phrase from Ravel's *Valses Nobles et Sentimentales.*

No one hurried her now; no one dared interrupt the hush that had fallen over them like that which falls over a kindergarten class during story time.

My father, she continued, deep into laudanum and absinthe by now and still wincing from his Parisian rejection, had begun to dabble in alchemy. This brought him into contact with many denizens and heroes of the Secret World, including the most gifted (and dangerous) of them all: a certain wizard high in the confidence and favor of the Russian royal family. I say wizard and I should perhaps say holy man. At any rate, he included among his gifts the amazing power to staunch bloodflow—even the most acute—instantly.

An enormous, bearded man in a caftan and with pupils the shape and color of the eclipsed moon, he came to dinner at the little family flat in Brno one wild March night and, after plum brandy and tiny cakes which my mother had baked that night—little sugar cookies with glitter on them and bits of ginger and candied fruit—he listened, patiently and with rapt attention, as father told him of his daughters and of their dilemma and sorrow. The giant toyed with the curls of his great tweedy beard for a few moments, murmuring Byzantine incantations into his beard, and then flourished a big butcher knife, which he produced from his caftan. I tell you it took us all off guard. He did what seemed an incredible series of juggling passes. The great blade spun and hummed and glistered in the dark of our little dining room like the wings of the Firebird. And then he cut off his left hand. Yes, cut it off and—before any of us could recoil or reject it—passed the severed member round the table for us to examine. I shall never forget its feel: still warm from the body, the great Scythian rings blazing like Fabergé Easter eggs. It was Villanelle who held it last, and she boldly kissed each fingertip and gave it back to him. I did not see him join it again to his body, but the blood which had spilled leapt up from the white, flaxy tablecloth, gathered and hovered in the air before it returned to the veins and disappeared under the sealing of the flesh of the wrist. I tell you it was a dinner scene which did not soon vanish from one's astonished recall. I can see it yet. I can hear the chant of Slavonic choirs which seemed to fill the small dining room. Within an hour I was alone in my bedroom, where I wondered if it were possible— though the wizard had never attempted such an ambitious transmutation before—for me to give my legs that night to my beloved Villanelle. It did not take me long to make the most serious decision of my life.

The operation—and though I hate the word I can think of no other—took place in a small church dedicated to Saint Nikita. I felt no pain. The wizard assured me that, within a week, he would return with a pair of perhaps equally beautiful legs from St. Petersburg—for all I knew, those of some dead grand duchess—and that I would soon be walking and dancing again. I shall never forget staring up at the Novgorod icons which blazed in aery Cyrillic frenzy from the dark, sacred walls of that chapel. I shall never forget the moment when Villanelle rose and watched the frightened village priest gather up her ugly old legs and bear them away in a sacred shawl to be buried with the full rites of the Orthodox

Church. I shall never forget the exquisitely comical and joyous dance which Villanelle performed through the streets of Brno on that moonlit March night—though pale with Tchaikovskyan sorrow was the wintry land.

Well, you can guess the next. The Revolution was erupting. Lenin was back from exile. The Romanov was doomed ostensibly to death in an Ekaterinburg cellar and the wizard was villainously drowned two nights before he was to return to Brno with my new pair of legs. There was, of course, no one known to us with powers like his.

Spring came to the land like a shower of young kisses. Villanelle married her toymaker. Within a month she was being auditioned in London for a Cochrane musical with score by Ivor Novello and P. G. Wodehouse. By winter she was the toast of Paris. And I was both legless—and pregnant. Yes—and O, I do not condemn him for it—when they had all gone that fateful night when Villanelle led father and mother and the village priest pirouetting out into the incandescent and holy moonlight of the Russian winter, when I was a mere stump alone on the cold flagstones of the old church, the dark giant stayed behind and took my maidenhead. He reeked of smoked fish and slivovitz. His beard tasted of cabbage soup. And I remember how cold his great cock was as it plunged in and out of me and how, when his seed came gushing out at last, the affrightened stillness was again filled with a great choir singing the "Missa" from the *Glagolitic Festival Mass* by Leoš Janáček. The child was stillborn, and although mother spared me from seeing it, I know it would have frightened me with the instant awarenes that it was not a creature of this world.

Somewhere in the streets outside Le Pet au Diable a hand organ was playing the Dance of the Ghosts' High Noon.

I do not intend to discuss Krafft-Ebing here, she went on, but I think he made it plain that there are men in society who, in matters of sex, as the young succinctly put it, dig distortion. I knew already I had something rather special—or rather that I lacked two things which, taken along with the rest of me, which was comely enough, would make a *specialité de la maison* in almost any great brothel in Paris. But there were many legless women in the brothels of Europe. I needed something else.

I wanted to dance. I wanted mobility. It was so trying to have father carry me in like a shattered statue, a mangled mannequin, to be set in my chair at dinner. I was an object of pity, or at least of patronizing condescension, which, save for the attentions of my ardent lovers, was suffocating.

At that moment Aubade smiled and bowed her head with a knuckle against her mouth, suppressing a giggle, it seemed, as the thunder of great feral growls—as of some firebreathing Minotaur—rattled the dishes and silverware in the dining room.

Yes, dear Footit! shouted Aubade. Yes, beloved Chichevache! We shall join you presently. Bear with me a moment more.

Footit, she said to us then, is so impatient. And why would he not be?—a creature which feeds upon female virtue in such a virtueless world as this. We shall be with Footit after a moment more of my story.

She paused and gave the revelers a chance to order fresh wine or hashish or such delicacies as wouldn't require too long to prepare in the marvelous kitchen. After a moment she went on.

In one of his essays Montaigne once encouraged young men to seek amour with lame or crippled ladies, suggesting that the sexual energy flees from deformed limbs into the regions where they join and creates a veritable furnace of pleasure. If this be so, it is doubly so when both limbs have vanished and left behind the aura of their fresh, fragrant, yielding, sensuous shapes. There was, indeed, those summer nights, it seemed to me, a furnace stoked down there between the ghosts of my limbs. It was as though my cunt, as well, had become a ghost and all the dewy curls of it become a blaze of religious lights and yearning energy.

I was lonely. I had many lovers—but I was lonely. I wanted mobility. I wanted legs.

And Villanelle heard of this; perhaps heard me tossing on the rather vulgar Empire love seat in the library one night as I masturbated and, at the moment of each rapid-fire climax, yearned for limbs to leap lovingly round a lover's loins.

She told her kind, rich, skilled toymaker of a husband.

One night in August, a night murmurous with the rumble of lorries and shouts of Revolution, while I lay alone in my little bed, weeping and feeling my melancholia alternate with waves of passion that sent my fingers flying to my shelterless cunt, I heard the song of a bird in the little lemon tree outside my window. The little lemon tree was the despair of my mother, who pruned and tended it constantly in the hopes of enough fruit for a pie. It had never borne fruit. But this night, I swear, as the little bird trilled mindlessly on, it seemed that the bitter fragrance of lemons blew and drifted among the blustery curtains of my bed. I lay very still, my hand still wet with the honey of passion, and listened very closely to the small bird's song.

Farfelu. Farfelu, it seemed to be singing.

I lay quite still. The sound of that bird filled the long-empty champagne glass of my heart with bubbles of joy, which spit and fizzed in my head with each heavenly outburst of song.

Farfelu. Farfelu.

It seemed to be hopping from branch to branch of the lemon tree, drawing slowly closer—as if held back by shyness—to the sill itself. At last I dragged my torso up and leaned across the bed, my nipples brushing on the sill, and saw the little bird. It was on the branch closest to the painted sill now—on a branch from which full lemons stood, like the breasts of Chinese dancers, in the cold arc light of moon. The bird was a toy—perhaps the most incredible toy since Galileo scooped up Time and all the stars in a golden ball and made it dance for a child. The bird was incredibly filigreed—each feather, like that of a swan on a Fabergé Easter egg, was intricately carved or cast. It had eyes of Javanese fire opals and a bill of knife-bright platinum. It was—long before the airplane itself had been fashioned into a flying toy—airworthy and, it was plain to see, had flown from the hand of Farfelu to my lemon tree, a full six kilometers' distance. It paused in its song, its opal eyes glowing, and ejected a bird dropping of carved jade onto a lemon below it. It hung shimmering like a glowworm in the deeps of the starstrewn night.

I was pleased: it was a sweet and pleasant gesture from dear Farfelu—and, through him, from my adored sister herself. It was nice of them to think of me, I thought, a little bitterly, and breathed in sadly the sensuous, fugitive sweetness of the lemon tree. The night seemed alive with stars: they seemed never to have burned so brilliantly, like daubs and smears of golden paint from the divine Vincent's brush, radiant as sunflowers. I reached out to take my toy bird, but suddenly it pecked me sharply on the hand. I giggled, charmed by this added touch of verisimilitude, and looked more closely. One opal eye winked merrily at me, and I knew the toy bird was trying to tell me something. It was then that I saw the tiny rag-paper envelope around its neck. It hung there on a thin, sturdy chain of golden links. I lifted it off and opened it, glowing with anticipation. Was it an invitation to be lifted by father into our droshky and carted off, like a sack of turnips, to see Villanelle in her latest music-hall triumph? Instead, I found in the tiny envelope—which looked like an invitation to the Mad Hatter's tea party—a tiny note and a tiny golden key. I read the little note while, with fingers still sticky from my honeycomb, I dallied with the little gold key.

*Go at once to the Room of the Pskov Samovar,* the tiny scroll of words instructed me imperatively. I slipped into a short night robe and thumped onto the fur rug beside my bed. I recognized the key. It was to the door which father had locked immediately upon hearing of the Bolshevik coup. It was—that room—a kind of shrine to Russia's great past.

I knew it well. Jewel- and gilt-framed portraits of every Tsar since Ivan glittered anciently from the walls. Priceless Novgorod icons cast down their muted flaming faces. Against the wall was a lacquered Manchurian cabinet of precious inlaid woods and lapis lazuli. Upon this furniture stood the Pskov Samovar—an enormous contraption of solid platinum. The ghosts of Nicholas and Alexandra sobbed from their quaint pearl-and-silver frames, along with those of the little murdered Tsarevitch and his sisters.

It is perhaps indelicate to note this here, but I must at all costs report that the friction of my legless torso on the cool, sensuous tiles aroused me to an incredible pitch of sexual lechery. Mother complained that I was constantly leaving a small track of honey in my wake—like a lame bee. By the time I had reached the great latch of the door I was panting with desire. I fumbled the gold key up to the keyhole and thrust it in. The key turned; the ancient lock-parts chattered; the door swung open.

I could make out the dull, blue-silver gleam of the great Samovar of Pskov. I could make out the figures of maman and poor papa, much the worse for drugs and strong drink, and the figure of my sister, Villanelle, as well, and close beside her the affectionate Farfelu. Two others were there, with bald heads gleaming like large ivory billiard balls.

It was Farfelu who went to the great carved table of fifteenth-century fruitwood and lit a small lamp. Shadows sprang free and performed a dance of death which flickered along the sullen gallery of dead kings and queens. Ivan the Terrible never looked more awesome in his lapis oval. In that whole room, at that moment, there was one pure touch of beauty and of hope for me. It came from an astonishing pair of legs, propped in a teakwood case beside the great table. The legs were clearly creations of a genius who rivaled Cellini. They were more than mere prosthetic adaptations. I fell in love with them at once and eagerly fisted my way across the Astrakhan carpet to where they hung in their polished wooden case. These legs, as I examined them more closely, seemed the legs I had been born for: more truly an extension of my torso than those which I had given away to my darling Villanelle. They let me alone—as parents let a child alone in those first moments under a Christmas tree.

She lifted her skirts again and passed her glittering, jeweled fingers lovingly across the magnificent artifice of her limbs.

On that magical night they were as you see them now—marvelous, intricate, fluid, fabulous as the Roc, clearly enchanted. In the side of each—ranging down from the blazing enamel plate of wine-colored material to the blue and canary-yellow plate which makes up the slender, sexy ankle—in the side of each, as I say, are three tiny keyholes. And for each a key, which hangs inside the case from its velvet lining on a richly brocaded ribbon of watered silk. The top keyhole has an inscription. It reads: *Pour Promener.* The second inscription says: *Pour Danser.* And the bottom one—in the calf—reads simply: *Pour l'Amour.*

I began to thump around in circles with sheer joy and aching to try on my new *raisons d'être.* It was Farfelu who lifted me onto them and adjusted the slender, strong straps of Siberian musk-ox hide to my small hips and waist. He stepped back. He watched me as I swayed a moment or two, getting the feel of them. And, O, I could feel their beauty flowing through me like the surges of a great, loving Orgasm: they were mine, mine, mine—I was sure! Farfelu, with the dispatch of an engineer about to launch a new locomotive for the Siberian railroad, stooped and wound the first two mechanisms tight. Then he looked back and smiled at me.

In a moment I shall bid you take your first steps, *bublitchki,* like the Child of God first learning to walk, to dance, to love!

My father glowered and slobbered a little in what I hope I may be forgiven for describing as absinthe-mindedness. My mother wept into a tiny, scented lawn kerchief. The two bald men, technicians from Farfelu's shop, stood by with small tool kits, ready to make any last-minute adjustments.

*Bublitchki!* cried the adorable Farfelu. You have made the greatest gesture of Love of perhaps this whole century. And so I have made for you my greatest creation—my utmost labor of Love and a lifetime of skills. The legs will last forever. They are motivated by a series of powerful springs. Never was such a series of spring motors constructed. The enamel is indestructible, having been fashioned as were the shield and tinted armors of Genghis Khan from formulas long vanished. You shall sensuously stride through the salons and bedrooms of Europe. You shall dance perhaps more fantastically than your adoring sister, Villanelle. And as for the mechanisms of Love—I shall leave it to you to discover their enveloping affections.

I fell to the floor twice. Not a third time. Not ever. I determined with something iron in my spirit that never should I fall again. That night I sprang to the table on my fabulous new limbs and danced a voluptuous and frenzied Danse Slav such as I shall presently demonstrate for you. I leaped down from the table and spiraled ecstatically out into the moonlight while the loving assemblage followed. I led them to the little lemon tree, and there I danced a kind of faery dance to the tinkling, liquid serenades of the tiny, jeweled bird which still hung there, singing out its frenzied clockwork heart. Soon everyone was drinking from the big rush-covered bottle of Vishniac which mother fetched from the library. All but father. He was off moping under the mimosa and grumbling that his friend Chekhov, the playwright (and once our family doctor), had three times refused to base a character in one of his plays on him—objecting that father was too gloomy. A moment later he was bemoaning the failure of his career as a poet. And finally he was nose to nose with Farfelu in the fiercest fit of fury yet. Farfelu did not love him as a son-in-law should! Farfelu had brought rare, expensive toys to his lame daughter! Farfelu had not brought a toy to *him!*

It was a fatal juncture in the evening. Farfelu was at a loss for a moment and then his kind, rubicund face lit up. He had just the thing. A toy for father, indeed. It was, he assured him, as unique as my marvelous legs, and he went on to say that he had fetched it all the way back from Topeka, Kansas, that spring. He motioned to one of his assistants, who thereupon—huddled in the blaze of Russian moonshine—fetched a heavy object from one of the small leather cases. Farfelu held it out to father.

Father stared through his bloodshot eyes. What the hell is it? he asked.

I am not quite sure, said Farfelu with an apologetic chuckle. But it is a toy. And since it is from the United States it is surely most remarkable.

It looks like a fucking discus, said my father, handling it. And it's heavy as sin.

The Americans are now making them out of pig iron, said Farfelu, even more appeasingly. They say they someday hope to make them out of something much, much lighter.

It hasn't any fucking moving parts, shouted father, getting more worked up by the moment. It's a fucking discus of pig iron. And you compare that gift to the ones you have made to my daughter?

Not really, said Farfelu. Still, I would keep it if I were you. Someday you may discover how to play some kind of game with it.

Well, fuck it! cried father in a perfect fury, and, running to the end of our little garden, he hurled the heavy pig-iron thing into the nascent moonlight. He turned then and was on his way back to Farfelu to give him, it is most likely, a punch on the nose, when, with a soft whir, the damned thing returned. It struck father—poor baby—in the back of the head, killing him instantly.

Well, what more can I tell you? she concluded. I escaped the Revolution with mother. Farfelu and Villanelle fled to Valparaíso where the great Cellini of toys created his last, and somehow anticlimactic, work of art—the Mickey Mouse wristwatch. In the East Indies—specifically, on the island of Timor—I made friends with the remarkable daughter of the late Dr. Fu Manchu. And it is she who awaits us tonight in the séance room.

As if to underscore this pronouncement, the truly fearsome thunder of the Chichevache's growl set swizzle sticks to rattling in glasses like chattering teeth.

I do think we had best be getting upstairs, my darlings, cried Aubade. Footit, you are so impatient!

She whirled in a pirouette on her astonishing limbs and, springing to the carpeted floor, led the way, seeming to float upon that whirring duo, beckoning to us all to follow her up the grand staircase to the upper rooms.

I felt a hand upon my left hip and turned, with an expectant smile. It was the detestable Mooncob—his really impressive bosoms pouring out of his improbable décolletage like buckwheat batter over the rim of an ironware crock.

When we get upstairs, my dear, he leered, with breath smelling of Scope, what shall I take off first?

O, dear one! I crooned, patting his cheek, at least twenty years!

He wilted in a fatuous simper and faded away as an even more blood-chilling series of roars came pulsating down the richly carpeted staircase.

Poor Footit, laughed Aubade, outdistancing us up the steps. Perhaps there is indeed a virtuous woman here tonight—and at last he shall feed. Shall we hope for that, my darlings?

# N·I·N·E·T·E·E·N

What must we strive for—now that he is coming again? I over-heard, on the staircase, beneath five staring Stuarts by Van Dyck—all, sadly, originals. We must strive against that thing in us all which causes us to choose, not Joy, but Despair and Greed and Death. That nastiness in Man which, I believe, has best been described by Dame Rebecca in her *Black Lamb and Grey Falcon.*

We moved down a hallway which was like some beautiful-peopled allée in Versailles. We came at last to a towering pair of deeply polished doors of solid ebony with great knobs and lock plate of burnished silver. Aubade paused with her hand on a knob.

Prepare yourself for astonishments, she murmured sweetly.

Before she opened the door, I pressed forward to her side and took both her hands in mine.

Aubade, I said, I know this is not of paramount interest to any-one here save me. But I am torn—I am utterly splintered—by two gnawing fears. My sister, with perhaps days left to live, is yonder in the city with her cancer—running. My father, Sweeley Leech, is

threatened with arrest, or death, or both. Somehow I don't think—
on top of these anxieties—I am up to a séance.

Hang on, dear, she said, squeezing my fingers and kissing my
cheek. In dreams begin responsibilities. Before this night is out you
may see both of these horrors vanish and become pure Joy. Have
faith. Believe. *Try* to believe—only *try,* as Uncle Will Blake has our
dear Lord bid us.

For some wild reasons, flying memories of Lindy and of darling
Sweeley Leech in the halcyon days at Echo Point came crowding,
unbidden, into my thoughts. I remembered, foolishly, vagrantly,
Lindy's lifelong and recurrent dream: that she has lost her purse.
Lindy has chased through millions of dream-miles after that fugitive
purse, and now she chases it down the last bleak corridors only to
find inside it—her death. O, my darlings!

I shook myself back to the reality of the room in which I now
found myself. Room? Chamber, Chapel, Theater, Salon—which is
the best word? For it was both enormous and intimate, that room. It
was, it seemed, older than the house itself, which was a brownstone
in the manner of Stanford White. Usually, counterfeits have none
of the precious charm of originals (the current Fake Art vogue
notwithstanding). Yet this room was preposterously—and heart-
warmingly—an imitation. The overall motif was Oriental in flavor—specifically, Pekingese. But it was not a room designed by
some Chinese artisan for the pleasure of the Pekingese. It was an
imitation of that style as it had been remembered, and then re-
created from memory, by some long-dead Commodore, back in
Gotham to count a fortune made in the opium trade.

Our Commodore had had both taste and humor. The dark, paneled walls were decorated with Eskimo masks and spears, and the
blunt, gleaming nubs of walrus-ivory scrimshaws were clustered on
the little tables of lacquered black bamboo and gold. In the midst of
these hung the Devil Masks of the Manchus; and gorgeous robes of
brocade and spider silk, the hues of Shanghai sunsets, hung on the
walls. There were, in addition, small, framed Currier and Ives prints
of the first contacts of the Western merchants with old China. And
some marvelous Szechuan watercolors hung, as scrolls, from small
teakwood brackets. There were drapes of silk the texture of plum
butter—as rich and deeply purple as throbbing Negroid genitals.
Gold and lapis lazuli, strewn with starpaths of yellow mica, glistened

and glowed everywhere. Hand-painted paper lanterns provided the chamber with a lustrous dusk of warm yellow—an atmosphere in which muted sunlight and the vagrant pollen of wild poppies seemed to intermingle.

It made me remember a dusk at the edge of the Gallimaufry in our dear childertime when Sweeley Leech had taken Rinsey and us girls for a picnic. I remembered his small miracle at suppertime: gathering a few blazing coals from a wild river-sunset to build a campfire for us. It was so touching—his inability to abide content with his Powers. And, afterward, he had plied us with half a dozen corny magic-store feats of legerdemain—none of which came off. But, O, I can remember, in the deep dark wool of the night which followed, drowning my eyes in the sunset rainbows of that fabulous campfire. And when, come morning, we had trod and splashed it safely out, it had felt as though we were quenching the splendiferous heavens, scrubbing away the stars, trampling Saturn and Venus and Neptune.

Astonishments, Aubade murmured again. No one knows what spirit may come tonight. We shall introduce the divine Mei Ling presently, and she shall be our astral pilot, so to speak, our Magellan across these unfathomed Pacifics of Time and Space and the Imagination. Before we do, I shall tell you first that the dread Chichevache must be faced by all of us—by everyone here—and he or she must somehow survive that and absorb the lesson of the experience into his or her spirit. All things, you see, are not always as they appear, and if our encounter with the firebreathing Wiwi shows us nothing else, it will leave us with that moral. The encounter afterward—with the great Mei Ling—who can say what it will hold? Surely, the purpose of this séance is to discover one thing.

We know, she went on, that the divine Sweeley has, at this great juncture of human history, brought back to man the message of the living Criste. Fate tore that adorable document from our grasp before any of us could scan its marvels with our incredulous eyes. It was destroyed, we presume. And now dear Sweeley Leech has managed to recall half of it—the bare outlines. But half is yet lacking. And we know, because we know that the imagination of man, like the Criste Lite, is totally and utterly universal—we know, as I say, that somewhere else on earth, other mortals have discovered that missing half and are, because the spirit of man cries for it, has-

tening toward us for a divine union of those parts. And, O, we
know that then shall come again the Golden Age. I know I sound
like some electronic evangelist, but I tell you this is true, my loves.
O, when the parts of the messages of the Criste Lite are married,
their child comes—and with it, the Age of Gold!

She turned and waved her hand toward a small carved proscenium arch, hung with curtains of rich, radiant silk, the hue of indigo
smoke—done in the manner of an old Chinese theater—perhaps
fifteen feet high and forty feet in width.

Hardly had Aubade turned than the room—even the ivory
scrimshaws on their exquisite lacquered tables—chattered like
teeth: the thunderous roar of Footit the Chichevache was closer and
more menacing than ever. Small puffs of steam, like hot, vanishing
cotton, huffed out from under the curtains and where they met in
the middle of the stage. Every mouth was dry with anticipation—
and with fear. Every charming woman searched her pretty spirit, as
she might search a beaded purse, for some incipient wisp of damn-
ing virtue, some shred of piety or hypocrisy about her loves and her
loins and the sweet liquids of her passions. Was there a virtuous
woman there that night to feed the voracious and longstarved beast,
this golden lion of some old French (or was it perhaps Chinese,
too?) fairy tale?

I think we have waited long enough, Aubade declared then. The
night hastens on and we must hasten in its starry wake. The lamps
of the Lord are hung out to light our way. The Chichevache is a
danger which—once passed—leads to yet another danger: the
menace which may come—in spirit—upon this room and upon
ourselves as the séance progresses. Aren't you scared, my loves?

Yes Yes Yes cried everyone in delicious unison.

O, let us face the dragon and get on! cried a young girl in a smart
man's suit with a bit of lace and organdy twinkling from her half-
open fly.

Aubade raised her fingers and clapped her hands sharply. Somewhere off in the wings a gigantic gong sent a shower of bronze
noise across the room, like the opening of a J. Arthur Rank movie.

Everyone cringed as the most violent and menacing of utterances
yet decibeled forth from the Thing behind the curtains, and steam
shot out in gusting billows like scathing, hot fog from a locomotive's escape valves.

I blinked as the curtains began to quiver in that moment before—with a nasal holy man's chant and the whir of prayer wheels like a thunder of butterfly wings—they swept back into the wings. I stared even harder, seeing nothing but a luminous little orange tree in a gorgeous, fire-glazed urn of the Tang period, nothing else but— I blinked again. Everyone blinked.

Downstage from the little orange tree, before a rather fabulous contraption of dials and pedals and blinking lights, and with its behind facing us, stood a rather roly-poly and very hairy dog—a Lhasa apso, perhaps ten inches high, and about as broad. From time to time it would lift a paw and press a pedal and steam would come sneezing out of vents along the footlights and in the wings. Then the officious little creature would growl furiously into a small Sony microphone and the sound, recorded on tape and slowed intimidatingly, would come out of loudspeakers. Someone applauded. Then everyone began to laugh, not with derision but with relief. At which the little black-and-white dog glanced furiously over its shoulder, its huge, luminous eyes staring at us with what I can only describe as defiant embarrassment.

Aubade's voice calmed the laughter. Nice, isn't it? she said. It is known as our Oz Effect.

The little dog no longer stood like a miniature, animated haystack, its impudent plume of a tail twitching and its anus winking with indignation. O, but such Oriental dignity was there. Because suddenly this Lhasa apso—for this was clearly all there was to Footit the Chichevache—trotted over to the little orange tree, lifted his leg, peed, scratched furiously with his hind legs, and then rolled huffily into the wings. Was this gesture one of pure theatrical contempt for both the show and its audience or was it something more? Evidently, it was the latter—for no sooner had the little dog vanished, growling in its small, normal and rather charming manner— than the wet place around the base of the trunk of the little tree began to smolder and then leaped into flame like naphtha, and presently the whole tree—oranges and polished, jade-colored leaves and all the foliage—was wrapped in a flame of the most beautiful rose and saffron color.

The chant of holy men rose; the whir of the prayer wheels somewhere off in the shadows was like the flutter of fairy wings in some grotto or folly deep within the Gallimaufry. A leg appeared from the flame—one of the most sensuous limbs I have ever seen—and then two breasts, and then a face of loveliness. A beautiful Chinese woman emerged, and flames and tree and the great Tang jar all vanished in a flash as swift as the leap of spilling quicksilver on an alchemist's bench or of moonlight when casement windows are thrown open to the adorable summer solstice.

She stood a moment, seeming to brush fragments and bits of starlight from her stunning cheongsam, and then she moved quickly to the table where a huge ceramic samovar—rather Mongolian in style—steamed, full of fresh tea. She fetched a cup and smiled round her at the people who came, rather timidly, closer.

This tea we shall share, she said, is two hundred and fifty years old. It is from a tiny house atop a cliff above a thousand-foot cup of space. The house has bright green jalousies in its tiny windows. It has a roof tiled with glazes the colors of a moonbow. It is the house in which, long ago, Sweeley Leech was born into his Yangtze period. In that life he came near to achieving the yearning goal of his two-millennial span—the getting down on paper of the Criste Lite. The tea was stored in a tin-lined little casket in the hour in which he leapt "into the dangerous world," as old Uncle Will put it. "Naked, helpless, piping loud—Like a fiend hid in a cloud." Yes, this was probably so because the peaks and highest reaches of the cliff were usually swathed in a bunting of mountain mists. And for some reason the sun never seemed to set, but bathed the cliff, the cottage, the whole valley with an ozone-sweet glow of eternal blue-and-golden Morning. "Naked, helpless, piping loud—Like a fiend—" Yes, because if Sweeley Leech is archangel he is surely fiend as well. How else would he be so powerful and yet so gentle, too?

She filled a tiny Tang cup and came to me with it as though holding forth in her delicate lacquered fingers a vessel which sent up fragrant, spicy steam from the hollow of half a nightingale's egg.

Thank you, no, Mei Ling. I am incredibly corrupt in matters of tea. I adore it, of course, and drink simply gallons of it when I can, but—

But what, darling? she asked, the little cup like a glowing blue-clay bubble in her fingers.

I take cream, I said. And sugar. The thought of which, I know, makes most Asian people feel ill.

Not wholly, she smiled, the fragrant, spicy drink still in her hand. There is an old custom in the Joy Houses of Kiatchiou. It used to charm the sailors off the Kaiser's yacht when he sailed there to twirl his waxed mustaches above this fragment of China stolen by heathen Teutonic kings.

She reached up and undid the mandarin collar, her fingers, for a moment, toying with the tiny black jet button. She undid another button. The robe fell open, exposing the beauty of naked flesh the tint of rich hollandaise. A small nipple rose from the globe of a custard-mold breast.

This, she murmured, I think, will please you.

She grasped the breast and held the little cup close to it.

It is both cream, she said, and sugar.

She gave a slow and rather rapturous milking movement to her fingers, and a thin, rich stream of mortal cream jetted out from the flower-petal nipple and mixed, swirling, into the tea.

She held forth the cup. I stared into the dark tea at the small pale clouds, like the Milky Way above us that moment in the strange house: the marbling swirl of Mei Ling's milk. I closed my eyes and smiled, and I know she saw the flutter of my clenched lids. It was almost too beautiful. I tasted it. I could taste this woman's soul, and I knew that, whatever came, whatever astonishments were ahead of me—of us all—in that room that night, it would change the lives of us each until the very candles of the stars should burn away.

My feeling for Mei Ling was more than just the wish to have sex with her. Somehow, with her tender gift of milk, I had experienced more than sex with her already. It had been a living communion of women—that act, I think. I felt safe with her. I remembered the fearful legends of Fu Manchu, her Hollywood ogre of a dad, and I wondered if she herself had not just come out of makeup. She was incredibly beautiful and had, like Aubade, one of those faces which are ageless. Yet the flush and fume of youth was still in her flesh, and I could almost taste it as I looked upon her there, next to an enormous dark globe of the world—in relief and perhaps twelve feet in diameter—which stood on its incredibly old-looking brass-and-iron axis supports. She fingered Popocatepetl. She flicked a mote of dust from a valley in the Pyrenees. She blew a frosty circle of breath upon the seas south of Java and polished them with her sleeve.

How long have you known Aubade? she asked me, with the slightest of Southern California accents.

Since now, I said. O, I think I would be willing to die young if I could be as full of Joy as that marvelous woman.

She is full of Sorrows, said Mei Ling. She prays to Criste every night in a perfect anguish of tears. There is little Joy in her.

What?

It is true.

Her legs, you mean?

She weeps for them every night—weeps herself to sleep.

I searched Mei Ling's face.

Of course—we have been lovers, she said. Many's the night she has wept herself to sleep in my arms. Her adored, her beautiful legs!

Why does she weep? Does she regret her gift?

Regret it? But no. She gives them again, in a sense, every waking hour. And in dreams as well. Yes. And Aubade's responsibility—the chief one of her life—has been those legs.

What is wrong with them? Uncomfortable as hell, I suppose.

I don't mean *those* legs. I mean her *real* legs. I mean she is heartsick over what has happened to them.

What?

Villanelle, she said, has been in an actors' nursing home since 1923. In Menton.

Drink? Madness?

No. Something which almost drove her to one and into the other.

What?

Polio. Villanelle was able to enjoy Aubade's exquisite gift for only half a decade. Glorious years, they were. But brief as kisses.

And Aubade prays for her—for Villanelle's—legs every night? Still?

Yes. It is the only totally mad thing about her. Mad, she said again. As the March Hare. Mad, with visions of Villanelle in the flowering of her youth, dancing again—dancing everywhere like some vagrant fairy in the meadows of the moon. She keeps seeing this young body restored, a Lazarus risen from the fetid tomb of wrinkles and gnarled pain. Youth. Youth for Villanelle again. That is Aubade's nightly prayer.

Nothing for herself, I said. That is strange. I don't know if it is beautiful or not, but it is strange. I think we should love ourselves, too, not just plug our egos into others and make them—or try to—into ourselves.

This is true, said Mei Ling. But it is Aubade. It is as if she has as little ego as Sweeley Leech himself.

She adores him. O, I know she adores my father!

And she should. For all good reasons. Not least of which is the Criste Lite, something which Sweeley Leech may unloose in her.

A miracle?

A miracle.

To set Villanelle curtsying and mincing among the footlights and arc lights of the great Joy Houses again?

Yes.

Broadway, this time. And Hollywood.

She speaks of these places, said Mei Ling, in her dreams.

O, she worships that sister of hers as though she were God, I said.

O, but she *is* God, laughed Mei Ling. What is God but the Ying of Me clutching close to the Yang of Thee? How often do we go marching through life over the bodies of others as we reach for what we are told is God? And find that, all along, God was those others.

Yes, I know, I said. That, too, can be called the Oz Effect.

Now there was something menacing in the air, and it seemed to be headed straight for Sweeley Leech. It was, I should say, halfway between Menace and Panic. You know the feeling you have at night in a city, lying alone or with someone else, listening to the effeminate yodel of sirens out in the million-millioned dark? Well, then, think how you feel when one of those sirens stops at your door—you listen as its scream winds down to a growl out by your stoop and footscraper. You know that feeling? That's how I felt just then. I reached into my bag for the great yellow diamond.

I smiled. It was there. Obviously, my child-friends had played with it for a lazy spring while and then tossed it away into the midden and man-marks of Amsterdam Avenue and it had returned to me—for the third time.

Where is my father, Mei Ling?

She smiled. He has the most adorable birthmark—shaped like a lichee nut—at the bottom of his spine.

She shook her head as if casting off a sweven, or dream-spell. What did you ask? I was lost in thought of him.

Where is he?

Upstairs, she said. I believe Aubade put him and Loll in the Mistinguette Room. Or perhaps it was the Mata Hari. At any rate, he has instructed me—all of us—to divine what we can from the séance. And after that, he has promised to get himself back into shape—

Into what shape? What's wrong with father? Loll! You say Loll is back with him?

He's been drinking. Popping pills. Smoking too much. Reading. Only Loll can handle him.

Reading Uncle Will Blake, I suppose.

That, said Mei Ling, and scandal sheets such as the *Star* and the *Enquirer*.

She chuckled. He's like a little boy in so many ways.

Just then I felt a nibble at my left foot, specifically my left great toe. I looked down and met an eye—a single eye—glaring defiantly at me up through a fall of lustrous, silky black-and-white hair.

Footit, you must behave, said Mei Ling over a wagging finger directed at this tiny dragon. Lhasa apsos are so gregarious. He's pouting now—he does it every time we expose him in our show. But that doesn't keep him away from ladies' toes.

I can feel! I laughed, pulling my foot back, and even as it retreated, feeling the pursuit of wet whiskers and a tongue.

Footit can be actually said to devour ladies—and not virtuous ones, either—for he is an incurable toe freak.

I can tell! I yelled again, running around the great bronze world with the furious Footit in pursuit.

Presently, snatching a well-chewed Barbie Doll up from the carpet, the little dog bounced from the room. From the doorway, the shaggy face and one eye indicted us silently. He ducked back again behind the curtain, growling and grumbling in his whiskers. The effect was of a small boy playing with a flashlight inside a small haystack.

I think we should be getting the séance under way, Mei Ling said, and again, as she raised her fingers gracefully above her black, loose hair, a gong sounded shimmering shivers of deep brass all across the chamber. Everyone fell silent.

This globe, said Mei Ling—and it was amazing how she did not have to raise her voice to make it heard everywhere—this globe is thought to have been cast and carved and hammered and shaped some ten thousand years before the Pyramid of Cheops. No one is certain of what metal it is cast—perhaps (and we have never had the impudence to test it) it may be that rarest of the ancient metals of the alchemists, electrum. It does not matter. The globe is enchanted. At the completion of a properly conducted séance a star should begin to flash and spit golden darts of fire somewhere on this globe, which, as you can see, is slowly turning and is—if you come close to look—constructed with microscopic accuracy. When that flame on the globe appears, it is indicating a location. It is pointing to where the spirit-journey has carried us. And then we know the location of the spirits in touch with us.

She put on a pair of heavy-framed spectacles and looked even more sexy.

These spirits are not, as in most séances, the spirits of the dead. They are the spirits of living people somewhere on earth—someone, or ones, yearning desperately toward us with some message of vital, vital import. Actually, the séance is already in progress. I am no fake. There is no lowering of lights, no joining of hands. We are all joined in other ways. Any one of us here could begin it—could tell us.

I don't know why, but I did it. I began to hum a bar of music and then whistle the rest, and then go back and begin to hum again.

Mei Ling flashed to my side in a blur of watered silk.

What is that tune?

I don't know, I said. I really don't. I heard it—or rather, Sweeley Leech and I heard it—in New York, the morning of the bank unrobbery. And I have been hearing it again and again since then. But I don't know the name of it.

It is a synchronicity, said Mei Ling. We must follow it. Something in this clue out of Time and Space may give us the place whence the spirits have departed. Does anyone here know music really well?

Madame Jonathan T. Bigod stepped amiably forward. Juilliard, 'ninety-three, she said. English music from Purcell to Vaughan Williams and Britten. Fifi, whistle or hum that tune again.

I did, blushing furiously as I always do when I am called upon to perform anything but sex in public.

Red Herring, said Madame Jonathan.

Red Herring? everyone murmured. Are we back to That again?

No, Rederring, said Madame Jonathan. It's a sea town in Cornwall. And there has been publicity on the wire services lately about a convention there.

I know, I interposed. A great meeting of men and women who are trying to save the planet. Biochemists—

Physicists!

Musicians!

Poets!

Conservationists!

From all over the world, chimed in a last voice.

Then, said Mei Ling, Fifi has brought that missing piece to us. The party left, by ship, from the south of England. But when did they leave? And where are they now? We must know that if we are to meet them when they land.

She turned now to me, her dark hair brushing my own. We must be quiet now. And wait. We know that our spiritual pilgrims in the night are at sea somewhere—presumably in the Atlantic. Though for all we know they may have chosen to go round the world with their great secret—letting what light it has already acquired shed itself on the coasts and islands which they pass. We must wait.

I went and sat in a deep-cushioned love seat, unmistakably early Empire—Chinese Empire. I reached into my bag and took out the small velvet box and pressed it into my lap. I could feel the light of the thing through layers of silk; I could feel stars fall from it like the last Roman candles on an old, innocent Fourth of July; I could feel it against my clitoris, the pearl of my Andes, and the lips and daffodil curls of my honeycomb.

I waited. The room was unearthly still. Yet there was some sound: a new sound, a susurration which seemed almost liquid. It was not like the lap of tides against a quay; it was like the movement of water high-piled and fathomed down, eardrum-bursting deep. Yes, I have expressed it: it was as though in a flash quicker than Time, Mei Ling had caused the very room we were in to go down like a Jules Verne diving bell into the deeps of the Atlantic, tossing and wild now in the tug of moon and autumn equinox and the cherub-blown winds at the four corners of the earth. It was as though we were many fathoms beneath the ocean, and it was not all fancy that made me think I heard the creak and gasp of the great, lacquered walls, the linseeded panels glowing brighter than a barrister's walking stick, the deep, rubbed wood casting out sundown of amber silence. I swear I saw a single spurt of spume shoot out from the boards beneath my feet, and in the little blob of seafoam that it left there glowed a rainbow seashell and a tiny seahorse, kicking like a great spermatozoon.

And then we began to hear them approaching: the ghosts of the great whale, the slaughtered dolphin, the baseball-bat-slain baby seal, the walrus and the dugong and the poisoned porpoise. I had heard recordings back in the seventies of the great whales singing in a deep place off Bermuda on a breezy tropical night when the trades go fingering the curls of blond waves between the legs of the latitudes. I knew those voices. But these were different: they were furious—faint but furious. And I sensed that from whatever meridian they had departed, we, in this floating nautilus chamber, were now their target.

Soon we could hear the chomping of their great ivory and the bulldozer snap of the great tail flukes; O, they were close.

Aubade cried out for Joy and kicked her motley, marvelous leg in the toy-lantern shine when they struck. And they struck hard. As the high paneled room began to buck and creak with the impact as of great, smooth, tiny-teated bodies, I thought of that passage in *Moby-Dick:*

> With the landless gull, that at sunset folds her wings and is rocked to sleep between billows; so at nightfall, the Nantucketer, out of sight of land, furls his sails, and lays him to rest, while under his very pillow rush herds of walruses and whales.

Thus it was for me during that siege beneath the sea. The cries of the beasts were the most haunting and menacing part of the experience. We heard them coming from afar—baying and lowing in queer sopranos and basses in the golden, shadowshot sea. The choir of them grew louder then, more imminent and more threatening. And then they were upon us in a veritable deluge of decibels, while with their great, astral hulks they slammed and caressed the limits of our room in fury. It was deafening—and very frightening. Because you know in the heart of you, in the place where the light always shines inside you, that it was not faked—not the Disneyed-up effect of some cheap, Art Deco thrill-parlor. You knew that, quite literally, and quite materially, you were somehow bubbled inside the chamber of a strange house in the West Sixties of Manhattan—deep beneath some sea—a bubble! A bubble which, at any moment, might pop at one more sullen battery from the flanks of a ghostly behemoth—surrounded, as cherubs surround a god, by clusters and conclaves of tiny murdered seals, a spume of mirth frosting their inquisitive whiskers—might burst and hurl you, hapless, into unknown oceans!

I thought, as we ponder in such twinklings of our lodestar, about Life and Death: When I leave this body it is as though I set sail from a tiny island in search of another island—or (at last) the Mainland. I wasn't afraid—yet I was scared.

The entire room seemed to creak and to twitch under the weight of piled fathoms. I knew it was not a theatrical effect, as had been the deceptions of the Chichevache—he who ran around the room, ducking between legs, and barking furiously, like a tiny Prester John announcing Apocalypse. I say it: that room—removed somehow from that building—was now a mile or so down in some vast ocean. An ocean peopled with the spirits of legions of assassinated innocents: the great creatures of the sea. They beat, like great wingless birds, against the walls, the ceiling, the floor. Spurts of water—creamy with seasavor and glittering with rainbow shells, tiny and rare as gems—shot out and stained the precious rugs. The illusion was not an illusion at all.

I saw Mei Ling cross the quaking room toward me. A priceless Ming vase fell and rolled across her long, polished toes. She smiled and, picking it up, replaced it on the little table—lacquered red as the blood of pigeons. She came to my side. She sat beside me on the other cushion of a two-seating Himalayan fan chair. I could smell the royal redolence which hovered about her, like bees haunting a bower, in a kind of cloud. She passed her slender, painted hand toward me until it came to rest on my knee. Between her beautiful fingers was a tiny wooden object, rapturously carved, shaped rather like a golfer's tee.

I knew what she was going to do. I smiled and lay my head back against wicker lace and opened my legs, which were already wet with weeping. A moment later she searched out my clitoris and began the most astonishing act of masturbation I've ever known. My lids were already nodding in the faint of a luscious come when I saw her reach into a tiny cloisonné box and take out a sprig of green with a blossom on it. I opened my eyes and searched her face for instructions, my breath catching with rapture.

Eat this, she said, holding the little tangerine-colored blossom to my lips. Just the flower—not the leaves: they are quite deadly.

I laughed and tongued the blossom. She laughed, too.

Eat it, please, she said. It is necessary for what follows.

O—wait—please, I choked, in the fury of the maddest of orgasms yet: one which racked me till I thought it would blister my toenail polish. My legs relaxed their viscous, soft grip upon her arm and fingers and the incredible little mini-dildo, which she was later to tell me had been whittled, according to ancient recipes, from the dogwood tree near Steubenville where Judas Iscariot hanged himself two thousand years ago.

In the light of the candied paper lanterns her fingers and hand glistened with droplets of me. She took a silk kerchief from the head of a young girl nearby and wiped her fingers.

I ate a petal of the little flame of a flower. It was sweet and tasted of the memory of tastes. You know? It tasted the way exquisite country breakfasts taste when you remember them: that red raspberry cobbler, fat and swimming with butter, and the red raspberry herself, sister to the rose, fainting in blushes under thick, light biscuit dough that crumbles under the cream like springtime riverbanks in flood time. Remember a taste like those and you know what I mean when I say that the little flower tasted like memory: like, if you want, dear Proust's little madeleines. I wasn't afraid anymore of the thunder of narwhals and manatees against the last world I had left. Mei Ling and the marvelous thing she had done to me had burgeoned such Joy in me that Fear ran out, much as the Chichevache now made for the curtains as a small netsuke bounded off a shaking, seasoaked side table and ricocheted off poor Footit's nose.

The din was like all the stops out on a great carved Baroque pipe organ: the beasts—the murdered millions, their harpoon gashes all healed by the Criste Lite—vomited their many-toned torsos, like hashish-maddened mermaids, upon our tiny lamplit world. But wait.

Was it that the concert of concussion and of whalewails was beginning to lose both heart and volume? Or was it that another sound—a single, held chord by a choir of simply immeasurable numbers—was approaching and somehow quelling the Pan-driven passions of the great beastghosts, was it that this pervading, insistent Yahhh, like the Yah of a Hal-Lay-Lou-Yah, was appeasing the juggernaut Yahweh spirit which drove them to the assault on the seasunk room?

Or was it the effect on me of the flower I had eaten? The center of it was perhaps the most succulent part. It was gummy, chewy like a tiny wild caramel, and I could feel the effect of it on my lips and mouth and tongue almost at once.

It was opium, I said. You gave me an opium poppy to eat, Mei Ling?

No, love, she said. I will not tell you its name. It is a powerfully guarded plant from a certain West African country. The drug has nothing to do with intoxication. It somehow detoxifies the mind, the soul. This flower I gave you—this particular blossom—came from a seed, among a dozen or so, found in the Great Pyramid. How they got there is not explainable. Believe what the drug makes you see, dear, for it is more real than Reality herself.

I saw them then: a group of ten naked boys with musical instruments and a brace of gleaming old gongs. They looked as though they could have been Javanese. They were perhaps sixteen, maybe younger, with small, feminine bodies, slender as naiads, and with tiny fern-hair above their genitals. They sat cross-legged in the darkest corner of the room in front of something which gave off a leaden luster from the shadows.

Mei Ling took my hand. I lifted the fingers that had played such gay tunes between my legs and kissed them, with the tip of my tongue licking between each finger where a droplet of me still lay. She led me toward the ten musicians who now formed an aisle, the two rows of them fanning out from the center, in which shone a long, silverish oval. The choir, the spirit sound—whatever it was— had risen and been victorious over the souls of the sullen slaughtered spumedogs and had softened now to the sweetest of voicings. Mei Ling smiled.

That means, she said, that they are now passing overhead.

A ship?

A boat, she said. I think you would not call it a ship. Perhaps when you see it—

She laughed. Yes, you are going to see it, darling.

How?

She turned to the mirror, for such was the mercuried, blistered oval before us. I looked at us there. We looked like a gimmicky Irving Penn photo of two quite elegant ladies in *Harper's Bazaar.* A blister of Time obliterated my left shoulder; Mei Ling's knees— which peeked out now and then, like the ubiquitous Footit, from the slit drape of her cheongsam—her knees were a permanganate-colored blur.

The mirror is very old, she said. It stood in the cloakroom of the Holiday Inn in Tashkent two thousand years ago. It alone, and the Lord, saw Judas slip furtively into that cloakroom to count more carefully his fifty pieces of silver. It is a holy mirror. And it is also enchanted. It—

*Fifty* pieces of silver?

Inflation had increased the price of betrayal. It always does.

But Tashkent? I asked. Sweeley Leech always swore it happened in Weirton.

Weirton, Tashkent, she said, smiling as the ten boys raised their fingers and bows and felted sticks to strike their gongs. Everywhen, she said. O, it happened Everywhen, Fifi Leech!

The end of her sentence was like a signal to the musicians. They began to play. I shut my eyes, listening, enraptured. It was some-how pre-Chinese—hints and tinkles and twangs of the Oriental in it—and yet it was like the kind of a song a Leakey skull might be singing that night, to the last of the three moons, from his crevice in the crumbling bank of the Huang Ho.

We must be naked for this adventure, said Mei Ling gaily and, reaching up, began to undo the buttons of my blouse. Come, hurry.

The choir voices had faded away. It was indeed as though we had heard the multitudinous crew of some fabulous boat as it passed above us and it was now fading.

If you hurry and slip out of those divine black panties and undo your brassiere clasp and—O, do hurry, love. I am afraid they will be gone when we get there. And we must learn their location so we can judge where to meet them later tonight.

Is there going to be a later tonight? I laughed, quite naked now, as I kicked off my heels and stood feeling like a pagan girl at her first gym class—carnal and happy.

Mei Ling was smiling at me reassuringly. She stood now as naked as I—and perhaps more beautiful. Her small breasts were like cups of blancmange turned out of lovely bowls and, in the heart of each, the stained blossom of the redbud. Her belly was like the smooth flesh of a sunwarmed Grimes Golden apple, and her cunt was bearded by the barest wisp of seaweed black, a tiny pen-and-ink drawing between her slender saffron legs, a cluster of black thorns curling about the open rose. She smelled the way they say the seawind does off Zanzibar, cloyed with the clove groves of Kenya. Or did the smell of sea emanate in sweet vapors from the stunned and broken light from the mirror? I had divested myself of everything save one article, although I had taken it out of the gray-blue, velvet jeweler's box: the great, golden diamond, Face-to-Face.

Mei Ling's small flat ass turned to me as she faced the mirror.

Stare deeply in the glass, she said. Stare and try not to blink. And think with me: They must not pass. We must get close enough to see. We must get there in time.

Her fingers tightened their grip on my own. Was it my imagination, or was she actually leading me between the quickening musicians, the boys at the end beating on their tiny gongs with a frantic tintinnabulation, rising as the humors rise in the body to make the colossal come—yes, it seemed she was leading me toward the mirror as if the mirror were to be the gateway to wild wonders.

# T·W·E·N·T·Y

I knew it was happening, and it was not that the drug in the flower had made it happen—it was as though the drug had permitted it to happen. The mirror—as I looked more closely—showed its incredible age, even though it was set in a frame which looked eighteenth-century American. The glass was darkened by Time and the friction of many a moon and the gnawing aspects of the planets. It seemed stained in the midst of its silver, so that the stained areas resembled mold-green islands in the midst of a turbulent sea of quick-silver.

Why the tear in your eye? asked Mei Ling.

I am thinking how, I said, whenever a Joke was told in family or company at Echo Point, Lindy would lightning-swift sense if everyone were going to laugh so that she could laugh, too. Occasionally, however, the laugh would not be at a Joke at all but an Irony, and Lindy could tell from their constructions that an Irony was not the same as a Joke. And this panicked her; it really stampeded and spooked her when her senses or a quick glance around at the faces of the laughers told her it was an Irony they were laughing at. Irony always seemed an invisible threat—furtive, sneaking, unfair. And ultimately, you see, they would be laughing at her, she thought, because she was the greatest Irony in their midst. If—

Mei Ling stilled my babbling lips with her finger.

We really must hurry, love. Please turn your loving eyes from me to the mirror again. See? It has already changed.

And it had indeed changed; the mercury shivered and darkened even more, and the whole oval somehow suggested the pocked physiognomy of some enormous eggshaped moon. Light flamed, too, from the yellow, glittering Face-to-Face I clutched in my knuckles. And the two lights met and flamed as though we were in the heart of a Roman candle on a starry night, and the instruments in the busy, flying little hands of the ten naked musicians flamed like Fourth of July sparklers in a spice-bush sundown.

The mercury in the mirror was apparently an amalgam of quicksilver with some metal seldom used in mirrors—perhaps antimony or arsenic. And it was streaming and reforming now, like the rivers of incandescent fire in the meadows beneath a Vesuvius or Pelée.

The choiring was so distant now, like the sweet fruits in a slice of Debussy, fainting with Time and distance.

And now the mercury steamed into vapor and was gone. The gongs were crashing in a burnished ribbon of sound in the hands of the frantic, maddened musicians, each with a heartwarming erection bobbing like a polished poppy against his little navel. The swirling disappearance of the mercury took with it the Picasso faces of myself and darling Mei Ling. The gongs sang urgently, as if they were not yet cooled from the cymbal-maker's forge. I looked at the glass of the mirror. It seemed to quiver like liquid. I touched it; my finger came back wet. I plunged my hand in and felt water to my wrist. I looked deeply into the green, imageless phantasmagoria now and tried to understand that what I imagined could really be true. I saw the tinfoil glitter of a fish then, and I knew. Something—a prayer or the Criste Lite—was all that lay, in a thin, sacred sheet like glass, between us and the Atlantic Ocean out there. I tried to peer into the murk, which was unlit by any dreaming mermaid's moon. The sea—in deeps beyond the stretching fingers of the sun, the lacy labia of the moon—the sea sucked into an oval aperture where the mirror had been.

Hold your breath, dear baby! cried Mei Ling and moved toward the quivering oval of ocean. She kissed me on the mouth and then flung herself through the door of still, green water and took me in her wake. I don't know what it was about those depths, my slow movement up through those deep-piled fathoms, but it seemed to stimulate the precious stone in my hand. It was like a marvelous scuba diver's torch as I held it up and saw, a few feet above me, the body of Mei Ling, her flesh like a faint, subtle Chinese painting; her flesh and hair: I mean the tiny black goatee between her laughing legs, so like the tiny beard of some old Tibetan lama, and her body salmoning up through the bubbles and tendriled seagrass. My ears popped. I held my breath the most monstrously long time and kicked and strove up between schools of mackerel and flatfaced flounder, the soulful sole, sinuously rocketing up from the green, litter-strewn Atlantic deep—somewhere above Bermuda was my guess, for the water was heavenly warm, though laced with chilly freshets of other, westering currents. The light in my hand seemed to do something quite extraordinary to some of the larger fish amid which we plummeted airward. Mei Ling's red mouth bowed into a smile as she watched a great gray shark nuzzle my ass and rub himself lovingly against me. She held up a finger as though to say: Wait, a marvelous experience lies before you.

The ascent to the realms of the sun and air seemed endless, though I was not really uncomfortable. My body knows it came from the sea; all of my body knows this with a wisdom finer than any in my mind, and my body loves the sea as if it were the lap of Rinsey herself, which indeed it seems always to be. I saw the glint of great bodies to my left, and Mei Ling, excited beyond measure, was kicking and gesticulating for me to look. I looked. The yellow morning glow from Face-to-Face bathed the sea around me for perhaps two hundred feet. And then I saw the swerve of a great fleet of comical, looping dolphins just as Mei Ling and I both burst gasping and laughing to the surface.

I'm Jewish, you know, she said.

On your mother's side, naturally, I said.

Why only my mother?

Well, your father. Wasn't he Dr. Fu Manchu? I laughed.

Of course, she said. Both my parents were Jewish.

She looked round as we bounced on the very slightest of swells.

The sky was the blue of one of Rinsey's old housekeeping smocks—heavenly as the eye of a baby. The sea was an immensity upon which perched an infinity of gladsome daylight. The light was that of early morning, like the dawn light which Sweeley Leech always swore constantly bathed the ramparts of the City of God: the kind of lapis lazuli and gold light you see caught in certain marvelous Maxfield Parrish scenes. Gulls revolved in endless spirals above us, as if climbing the light on invisible ropes of sheer heavenliness and air; far to the east something glittered faintly, fabulously, like a tiny jewel glittering on the edge of a great, green glass disc.

We didn't get here in time to see them—whoever they were.

It's my fault, Mei Ling. I was holding us back with my own damned shyness.

It's all right, she said. We'll be there to meet them when they land. I can tell by the stars where we are—and where they are heading.

What stars? I see no star but the sun.

Fifi, said Mei Ling gently, someday you shall learn how to see the stars by day.

She sighed. She laughed and ducked and swam under the waves and then came up like a mermaid, laughing through fronds of hair and flashing her incredibly white teeth.

A tiny wave caught her full in the face and a tiny silver dace glittered flapping in her hair a moment before she caught it up lovingly and released it.

Your mother, you mean, was Jewish, I said again. Your father was Fu Manchu, at least, so I've been told. He was Chinese?

He was a Chinese Jew, said Mei Ling. And so was my mother. My father was a member of the first minyan in Shanghai. But then he was a member of the first Presbyterian Mission Church on the Bund, and the Islamic mosque, and he was a member in good standing of the Laughing Dragon Society of Sorcerers and Wizards. How I remember my father and the other old Chinese Jews. They made bets all one summer on bowls of Siamese fighting fish set up by a wandering band of Bangkok gypsies.

Was there a sail to windward, gainward the sun? Was whatever caravan of ship or boat we had missed perhaps returning? But no. It was a trick of sea light—though some sense in my eye seemed to bring to my receptors the clear, microscopic vision of an ancient

337

freighter, its deck aswarm with motley children, and being drawn in silver and gold harnesses by— But no, that was absurd!

Naturally, we adored Jewish American food, Mei Ling went on. There was a restaurant where Chinese Jews could get split-coursed American meals. Like maybe you get no Spanish rice with Item B. Or choose two from Dinner Number Six. O, I can vaguely remember.

Mei Ling, why are you telling me this?

She turned her face away, clearly troubled.

And the Chinese Jewish girls, she was saying, they have these incredible guilt feelings.

Mei Ling, what does it matter?

It does matter, she said, turning her gaze back to me. I know what you have heard about my father—about me, as well.

You mean about Hitler.

Exactly, she said. And it is not true. It is true that there were Jews who betrayed Jews, but my father was not one of them. Yet, it is true that he was close to the Führer.

Doing what?

Guiding him, she said softly.

Toward what?

Guiding him to that bunker where he died, she said. O, my father did much to hasten the end of the war. And the Führer hung on his every insight or augury. Please believe me, Fifi. For nine out of ten crucial battles the Nazis lost, credit Fu Manchu. Or me. We were behind both lines, you see. You write, don't you, Fifi? Someday you must write the last, the greatest of the Fu Manchu novels. Perhaps the TRUCAD beasts would let us see that incredible War Department secret file known as the Dacoit Portfolio. Enough, though. Isn't the sea simply glorious today?

Yes, love, isn't it. But now I must ask: what were we supposed to see?

An incredible boat, she said. Incredible in creation, incredible in its sources of power. I had longed to get here in time, because we can see—

She pointed to some strewn blossoms of frangipani, like broken leis, now suddenly bobbing in the spume and wasted spindrift all around us.

I sight from that planet, she cried, and pointed to the twinkling vapors of blue sky above. And that one over there—and she pointed out another Nothing. And I know we are a few hundred miles from New York City—specifically, near Montauk, at the tip of Long Island.

She breathed in and smiled.

Can't you smell it? All cities have their own smells for a few hundred miles out to sea. I remember the smell of Shanghai—long before the ship lay in sight of her.

What smell?

Opium, she said. And human shit.

I laughed aloud and clapped my wet hands.

O, marvelous. And what does New York smell like out here?

She inhaled again and shut her eyes, pondering. Valium, she said. And Human Greed.

Mei Ling?

What, my lover?

Who are the people on this boat? And what are they bringing?

They are bringing the missing half of the Criste Lite. Sweeley Leech can remember only half. These wise men and women are coming with the missing half. When they are put together, they will comprise a document identical to the original which Sweeley Leech captured and wrote down and which the really unconscionable Lindy Leech stole and caused to be destroyed.

She is my sister, I said. Please, Mei Ling. Let me love her—and mourn her—untroubled by meannesses from you.

I am sorry, my love. Yes. You are right. As a Mr. Agate once wrote: Judge not—lest ye be beside the point.

Where will they land, Mei Ling?

I can pinpoint it, she said.

Nearby floated a little mass of sargasso weed. Mei Ling reached into it, stripped off three polished green leaves, and formed them into a tiny, makeshift sextant. She worked it into the light and at last nodded.

She reeled off degrees and longitudes and latitudes and said that they would land in the hollow of a tiny cove about six miles up the beach, near an old seamen's boardinghouse called the Walt Whitman Inn.

Are you getting tired of treading water, dear? she asked.

Yes, a little. My legs are getting cold—and chilling the hell out of their very good friend and neighbor, my puss. What do you suggest, dearest?

O, something nice, she said, and, turning in the water, began to send across its spinning, waltzing waves the very strangest of soft love cries. I have never heard such a cry—it seemed not from the earth, or from the skies, either, but from the immutable and immortal majesty of the ocean. I shivered—and the water was not really cold at all. She kept up the cry until I spied a shape really nearer than the horizon and white and approaching us with considerable velocity. I thought perhaps it might be a boat put out from the ship we had missed seeing, come back to meet us and coordinate our common affairs. But then I saw an energetic spout of spume and steam and discerned the broad, white, and wrinkled brow of a right whale. I saw beside it, gamboling around its mother in frantic, happy circles, the whale's pup. When it was so close that I could hear loudly the rush of vented water and air from its blowhole, it checked its career and turned its side to us. Mei Ling made an "After you, my dear Alphonse" gesture. O, it was hilarious, climbing up the corrugations of that pleasant and friendly big back. The whale remained almost as steady as a little island as Mei Ling and I stretched out nude atop it, playing our fingers now and again in the Old Faithful of its steam jet.

Father was formally kicked out of the temple in his old age, Mei Ling said suddenly.

Because of the Hitler rumor?

Why, no. It was discovered that he had never been circumcised.

How was it discovered?

It was noticed one night in the toilet of a porn theater by a gay Vice-President of the United States, Jewish himself.

How come he was never circumcised?

Father spoke, you know, from birth. He had an extraordinarily thick Lionel Stander accent in his infancy, which changed through the years into the mellow mutter of H. B. Warner, who, as you know, portrayed him in the movies. Father had a very loud voice. It was most useful to him on that morning. The Mohel and the Chinese rabbi were standing by. The Mohel approached the babe. And suddenly, clutching its tiny, wrinkled hands about its genitals, the baby began to race about the room.

Don't cut *mein svanse!* You ain't cuttin' *mein svanse.*

Just a *shtickel*! roared the furious, thwarted Mohel, in hot pursuit.

No. No! thundered father in a voice which in time we found out to be a Mel Brooks impression.

You ain't touchin' a fuckin' inch *mein svanse*!

Frustrated and desperate, the completely religious and orthodox assemblage resorted to ancient (and quite obscene) paintings of famous penises, all of them quite unmistakably bobbed and, presumably, quite handsome. Father pored avidly over the erotic oils, each on its little oblong of wood.

Hoo hoo! he would croon from moment to moment. Is this a baby dolly!

Sensing a deeply prurient interest on father's part, the elders quickly snatched away the pictures, and the chase was on again.

Did they ever catch him?

Never.

He was never circumcised?

Never. And he swears Criste never was, either. And remember that in the Nag Hammadi Codex Criste swears that if God had intended no foreskin he would have removed it in the womb.

It was a painful youth for father, Mei Ling went on. He had to constantly conceal his rather overadequate foreskin.

Was it large?

Simply enormous. As was his cock. It was like trying to hide a circus tent from small boys.

She sighed and picked a sea leech of some kind out of the whale's ribbed hide and flicked it gently into the lapping waves.

The baby whale kissed our fingertips. The wind blew fair from out of the Caribes or where the remote Bermudas ride. Gulls circled and sang stark, windtorn epigrams upon the plaster skies.

Everything down dawnward was on fire, like certain heartbreaking Ryder seascapes.

Mei Ling plucked a seashell—a marvel of mauves and misty moonfires—from the creased back of the great whale, where it had been lodged, perhaps painfully. The great bag heaved and blew a grateful head of steam cloudward to the winds.

Why are you smiling so, Fifi?

I am thinking of the séance—the other guests—they must be gone by now.

No. There is no way to leave, save by sea, until we return.

Won't they wonder what has happened to us? Perhaps we were seen when we went through the mirror into the ocean.

The light is poor, she said. No one could be certain. It is a room full of astonishments.

She smiled at my smile again.

Besides, she said, you must understand—all of this adventure you and I are having is encapsulated within a split second. Ah, there, love. You will understand in full time.

An idea struck me.

After years China and America are friends, I said. Tell me—as the Chinese people discover America, what thing in our country do you imagine will shock them most?

I know, said Mei Ling.

Our sex habits?

No.

Our drinking? Fast cars? Drugs?

None of those would shock them.

What will?

Pearl S. Buck, she said. And I mean no offense.

I cocked my head, considering.

The Paul Muni–Luise Rainer image of a Chinese farm family in the thirties. With Walter Huston as an old Chinese farmer.

Have the Chinese found it yet?

Yes, she said. From Harbin to Peking it is the comedy hit of the age, showing to SRO audiences who simply adore it. You see in what strange shapes beauty takes form? For surely laughter is caused by the ultimate beauty.

She felt around her body absentmindedly for a smoke and then laughed. Suddenly her face sobered.

I don't want you picturing Dr. Fu Manchu as an old queen, she said—although it would be a fair, if sexist, charge.

Was he openly homosexual?

Put it this way, said Mei Ling, chewing on a frond of sargasso weed. If father passed a beautiful man and saw that he was masturbating, he would offer to help. I wouldn't say he was gay. I would call it a passionate neighborliness.

Oho, beautiful.

He had women, too, by the thousands. And they adored him!

Where is he now, Mei Ling?

What does one say? Where is he now—my father? The last we knew of him he was a valet to Franklin Pangborn.

She ran her little tongue across her teeth.

Pangborn was a high-heeled martinet, snapped Mei Ling. And then father is rumored to be back in the Far East—maneuvering an enormous opium deal.

A mixture of Good and Evil, eh?

A perfect amalgam of antitheses.

Is it really true that only a fraction of a second is passing back down there in the room?

Yes. It is so.

Tell me more of your father, Mei Ling, I said. He sounds not unlike my own.

At the height of his popularity with Hitler, she said, when he was busiest sowing the seeds of the Götterdämmerung, father suddenly dropped from sight. The next thing we know, he pops up in one of the death camps—Treblinka, if memory serves; he had been picked up during a séance in a Vilna whorehouse—and on a fateful morning he was led to the showers. The guards were preparing to abandon father and fifty others to the gas when father began pounding furiously on the plumbing overhead.

*Nu,* you call this plumbing?

What's wrong with it, swine? shouted the guard.

You paid twice the markup you should have, said father, for one thing. For another thing, I am a plumber and I can do it over cheaper and ten times more efficient.

They neglected to gas anybody that morning, and father was led away to a barracks where he was consulted by the engineers in charge of the camp—indeed, of all the camps. Within a week father had installed new extermination gas plumbing in the entire camp. At a rather handsome fee.

I think I know what happened, I said. He had the poison-jet pipes in the officers' quarters.

Not quite, she said. He had the jets in the officers' quarters, all right—but he pumped laughing gas into them.

O, he sounds mad.

And the first diffusion of gas coincided with a personal inspection tour of the camp by Hitler. The officers, of course, laughed the formidable little Austrian out of countenance. It was the first of two apparent epileptic fits which the Führer suffered. The personnel of the entire camp was promptly shipped to Smolensk and the bitter Soviet front.

O, I do adore you, Fu Manchu.

There was a sound in the wind, a sound like a chord of music—like the singing of winds through taut silver strands, invisible yet filled with light.

The sun, though it did not seem to have risen so much as a degree, was lovingly warm. I slipped back into the kiss of the cool sea, and Mei Ling slipped into the waters on her side of the whale. We laughed and splashed each other over the great living hump of the seabeast. Suddenly the great creature turned on its back and hung so—its great, smooth underbelly livid in the sunlight, and the tiny teats softly dripping milk in the nascent mornglow.

Instantly Mei Ling smiled and lowered her lips to the nipple and drank a sup and a swallow, in an act of moving, pure communion. I did likewise, while the whale pup nuzzled and bumped in loving frottage against my body. Mei Ling and I laughed at each other over the great, gleaming ribbed back—our red lips white with whalemilk.

Have you ever seen a mermaid? I shouted.

Yes, she said.

A merman?

She laughed. Ethel once, she said. At the West Side Café.

No, I mean it, I said. Are they real?

Of course. Why do you ask?

Because, I said, between bumps and kisses by this baby whale, somebody is down there giving me some absolutely incredible head.

I bit my lip and rocked to the rhythm of it, arching my legs into a perfect wishbone of excitement as a tiny tongue, hard yet swift as the wings of a hummingbird, was leveling a soft, insistent rhythm against my clitoris. I gasped, I winced and stuck my tongue out at the sun for utter Joy—O, it was divine. I knew a moment later, when, glass-eyed and shaking with passion, I ducked under with a swoop of breath and swam down to see my lover—I knew it was no mermaid or merman. It was a dolphin.

Mei Ling was laughing and plunging and coming up and gasping with Joy and laughter, and I saw the white arch of the body of another dolphin. Mine was busy darting and nuzzling in between my legs, his small, hard tongue finding again and again the open petals of my flower. I dove under and beheld him—my knight errant from the sea. He had the most delicious-looking cock, with no foreskin, and I thought to myself that dolphins must be Jewish, too. I dove and embraced him; I darted away and hung like a sunbeam in the lightquivering water half a fathom down. I suddenly had to pee, and let it go, and the laughing face and balding, domed brow of the creature darted in and out of the hovering golden cloud around my limbs, obviously excited beyond belief by the pheromones in my urine. I flung up from the surface, spitting spume and laughing. I was going to do it.

I had never been into sex with animals until now, and O, I thought, it is the fleeting chance of a lifetime, and he is not built too big to do you any harm. He seemed to sense when I sidled up to him with open thighs what I was going to do. A moment later my legs gripped him and with my free hand I reached down and grasped his cock and guided it into me. He began to move then and I felt the leashed fury within him. As he dove and plunged and leapt, taking me always with him, by body fisted round him in a lover's embrace. Besides his forward movement his great body was throbbing and pounding against my hips, his white, snowy cock plunging in and out of me. O, I came as many comes as there were fathoms beneath us; it seemed that as my cunt, and my womb, opened to take him, he had let in the sea; that all the seas were flowing up inside me through the open lips of my sex—the seas and all the moondrawn tides and the oceans reflecting the stars in a frothy glister.

It was an incredibly lovely fuck. It took what seemed ten, perhaps fifteen, minutes. And all through it I kept repeating in my head the Credo from old Walt's 1855 Preface:

This is what you shall do [O, sea lover, touch me deeper, deeper in my quicks]: Love the earth and the sun and the animals [What is your name, lover, whose male seed surges and gathers now to flood me?], despise riches, give alms to every one that asks, stand up for the stupid and crazy [And, I, O, I am half crazy with the seaborn joy within me!] devote your income and labor to others, hate tyrants, argue not concerning God [O, this is like the big finger of God's earthcreating and heavenhanging hand against the puckered glans of my cervix], have patience and indulgence toward the people, take off your hat to nothing known or unknown or to any man or number of men [And my womb opened and let it in, the teeming man-blooded oceans!], go freely with powerful, uneducated persons and with the young and with the mothers of families, read these leaves in the open air every season of every year of your life, re-examine all you have been told at school [O, my cunt is a Suez letting in all of Macao and the spice ships of the Khans] or church [I am coming coming— Ah, God, coming!] or in any book, and your very flesh shall be a great poem and have the richest fluency—

I turned and saw the body of Mei Ling flow fainting free of her sea lover and lie spent and rosy, floating slowly, languidly surface-ward, while the pale, milky seed of the dolphin rose like pale woodsmoke from her orchard belly. I lay on my back while the baby whale nudged me from either side and his great mother lolled in the sunny latitudes of water.

I hope I didn't hurt myself, I said to Mei Ling.

No—unless you are abnormally small. Are you?

No. Average. Rather small cunt but very deep.

Then what are you afraid of?

I think we had better be getting back, don't you, Mei Ling?

Wasn't it wonderful, though? Can any man—?

O, it was beautiful, all right. Passing beautiful. But I have to be a little careful, love.

Why, Fifi? Are you—?

Why, yes. O, I think I am, as they say, a little pregnant.

Are you sorry?

Oddly, no.

And I thought of what I had said as she seized my hand and pulled me under and we clasped our pretty *jambes* around our dol-phin lovers and they bore us deep, ear-cracking deep, toward the faintly discernible mirror standing in its swiveled oaken frame at the bottom of the sea trench. The mirror seemed to froth and fizz as we passed into it, and a moment later we stood dry and safe again on the long Afghan rug which lay before it.

The musicians had gone. The other guests and revelers and members of the Children of the Remnant were moving about in small groups, chatting or arguing or merely wandering around the museum which the room really was. Slowly we dressed.

I said I was not sorry I was pregnant. That was an understatement. I am really rapturously happy over it. I think I shall be a pretty and pleasant mother. I hope my child will like me.

You will be, Fifi—a loving, marvelous mother.

She cast me a sidelong and rather classically feminine look.

Do you know who its father is?

Why, yes. I said. I think it is the seed of perhaps two thousand men. I can't imagine any *one* seed making a baby in me. It is as though one seed would not be the right spark to my carburetor—the wrong mixture. It is as though many seeds have become one seed and are making an Everyman in me.

At that moment, I looked across the room. Straight into the eyes of Sweeley Leech.

# T✦W✦E✦N✦T✦Y
## O✦N✦E

Sweeley was a sight.

Hagerstown, Maryland! I seemed to hear dear Rinsey cry from the shades and shadows purpling behind me. Just look at Sweeley, for he is a sight!

Yes, father was a sight.

In one hand he had a can of Coor's and in the other a copy of the *Enquirer,* with which he was frantically motioning me toward him. He was barelegged, and since his legs are a little bony, they caused the short white hospital jacket he was wearing to look even more childishly skimpy. On his left wrist he wore one of those plastic snap-on bracelets with a number and the words BELLEVUE HOSPITAL. He tucked the *Enquirer* under his arm and, grabbing my hand, dragged me furiously out of the room and down the candleshine of the hallway toward the winding staircase. Then it was up the whispering steps to the hall leading to his room. When we were inside, he snapped the door shut, locked it, and stood a moment with his ear to a crack. At last he went over to the bed and, putting

the can of beer and the newspaper on the night table, sank with a
sigh onto the mattress.

He lay for a moment with the back of his hand across a lock of
flaxen hair which had fallen across his troubled brow.

Then he began to speak:

> The Vision of Christ that thou dost see
> Is my Vision's Greatest Enemy;
> Thine is the friend of All Mankind
> Mine speaks in parables to the Blind
> Thine loves the same world that mine hates
> Thy Heaven doors are my Hell Gates.

Uncle Will Blake? I asked. *The Everlasting Gospel,* right? From
the Pickering manuscript?

He brightened then and nodded.

He sat up, and color came back to his cheeks. You know, he said,
everything in me wants to run to you and kneel and clutch your
hem and beg, Feef, help me—help me! But I know I can't do
that—I know you can't help. I must go this road alone.

He got up and began to pace, glancing from time to time toward
the closed, gilded door. He shot me a swift look, his blue eyes blazing from under the golden forelock.

Did you see the ship?

No. We missed it.

Did Mei Ling ascertain its location?

Yes. Precisely. And, lining that location up with a departure
point in the south of England, she found an arrow pointing directly
toward—

Where?

A cove on the stretch of Long Island beach on the ocean side
opposite Montauk.

Sweeley Leech laughed and clapped his hands sharply and began
to pace again, declaiming:

> I am he that walks with the tender and the growing
>     night;
> I call to the earth and sea half-held by the night.

349

Press close barebosomed night! Press close magnetic
 nourishing night!
Night of south winds! Night of the large few stars!

He whirled on me then.

You know it? It is a Sign. I tell you it is a Sign. Montauk was
where Cousin Walt used to walk the wild, winded beach composing
*Leaves of Grass.* I mean that is a Sign, Fifi.

I shook away his boyish zest and stared disdainfully at the shimmering disc of light above his hair.

Father, take that fool thing off your head!

O, that. I was afraid you'd notice.

What is it—plastic? Like the halos on those very wild and crazy
dolls down in the red chamber.

I can't help it, Fifi!

Well, can't you turn it off?

No, he whimpered.

I was deeply moved. You mean—you have a real halo?

Yes. And did you ever try to sleep with one of those things
hovering over the pillow above you? Just out of eyeshot—just
enough light to keep me awake. You know how I could never stand
that little night-light Rinsey used to plug in.

It must be great, I chuckled, for reading in bed. Or for doing
work under a car.

You can laugh. It's not you that's been saddled with this thing.

What thing? I whispered.

Divinity, he moped. The nearly full possession of the Criste Lite.

O, father, you were always divine to me.

I am almost clean, he said. I almost got clean in this life. Now—
O, Fifi, wait till I tell you— Now—and I have this on authority
from none other than Uncle Will himself—now I am assured that
in my next incarnation I will be—well—Perfect.

I think you are Perfect now.

You mustn't ever say that. I am really awful. Here God has be-
stowed upon me his penultimate gift, and I am fumbling it.

But you will not fumble it.

Your faith will give me strength, Fifi.

There is no Evil in you, Sweeley Leech. Only Good.

He sprang to his feet then, as if shocked (perhaps by a short in his halo), and began pacing and declaiming from Will Blake again:

I care not whether a man is Good or Evil
All that I care is whether he is a Wise Man or a Fool.
Go put off Holiness—
—and put on Intellect.

He slammed his palm with his fist again, stopped pacing, and came to me.

I'm insane—right? Crazy as hell. Right? Tell me—O, please tell me that I'm crazy and that none of this is real.

O, you're the sanest mortal on earth, father.

Don't say that. Don't attribute things to me. I am a fake—see?

He snatched up the scandal tabloid and flapped it in the air.

A fake, see? I read this—

He hauled out a sticky *Hustler* and two stuck-together *Penthouses* and threw them in the middle of the carpet.

—and these. I smoke pot. I drink wine. I take Thorazine. I fuck like a rabbit—and therefore—

He pushed his nose up against mine, his face twisted into a grimace of simulated lunacy.

—therefore—

His voice rose and yodeled maniacally.

*—therefore I am not holy!*

But you are. You may as well get used to it.

Do you really think so? he asked in the voice of a two-year-old.

He padded over to his bed in his bare feet. He stood looking at his reflection in a small gilded mirror on the wall. He shook his head; the halo bobbed like a blossom on its stalk.

I laughed aloud for Joy.

There was a long silence as he made rapid, grabbing passes at his halo, which ducked and dodged each time. He laughed, and his face froze into a fixed, sad-happy smile. I might as well accept it, he said.

Is it quite painful, sir?

Don't call me "sir." "Sire," maybe. "Sir" sounds like a fucking TRUCAD official. But to answer your question, he went on, yes, it is painful. Like an open wound—constantly flowing—with the Wine of Astonishment, as the prophet called it.

O, in me, too, sometimes, I cried.

That's the difference, he said sadly. With you, Sometimes. With me, Always.

He paused a beat. Criste calls it the Wound of Wonder.

I know.

They have made me into a fucking archangel.

I think our Lord did that.

Fifi, it is unbearable. For I am such an unworthy—

Stop that, Sweeley Leech. You know you are full of the Criste Lite.

Not full—not yet. Half-full, maybe. Enough to make me an archangel. O, but next time—next incarnation. Wow! He glanced quickly at his Mickey Mouse wristwatch.

God, it's almost four a.m. Only a few hours of night left. Then he puckers his big lips and blows out the candles of the stars.

Don't be so rhapsodic, father. If I were any more impressed, I should faint.

Don't worship me, Fifi, he begged piteously. *Love* me! For I am at least half mortal.

Stop all this and think how we must arrange to meet this boat, I said.

Yes. You're right.

Have you the helicopter?

He pointed ceilingward.

On the roof?

He nodded.

Father, I must tell you some simply soulsearing news.

Nothing will depress me.

Lindy has cancer.

I know.

Have you seen her?

Yes.

He paused. I laid hands on her. I would have drawn the cancer out, but—

I know—she panicked, I snapped, suddenly furious at my poor sister.

She ran off. She is somewhere out there in the city night.

Could you have healed her?

He came over and put his hands on my shoulders. They felt marvelously clean and smelled deliciously of green, liquid soap.

Fifi, I was in Bellevue because I did something yesterday.

What, father?

I raised the dead. A man hit by a crosstown bus at Fifty-seventh and Fifth. He was smashed like a bug. I didn't know I could do it. I was on the sidewalk nearby. People were taking a look at the remains and throwing up until the TRUCAD men drew a tarpaulin over the poor debbil. Fifi, I just stared at him a moment—and he threw off the tarpaulin, lit a cigarette, and went into a delicatessen and had a pastrami on rye.

They arrested you for that?

What else could they do? It was, to them, an act of criminally insane heresy.

They took you to Bellevue?

I had been drinking a little green crème de menthe.

Sweeley Leech, you know you shouldn't drink.

I know. Because what good does it do me? Fifi, the Criste Lite keeps me so high that drinking is a downer. So is pot. So are pills. And—O, heaven help me—so is sex.

Really, father.

I ran around behind him and goosed him and sprang up on the bed and across it as he chased me, laughing.

Can't get it up anymore, father? I taunted. O, come now.

It's true, he said, subsiding into a lovely old chair. Sex is the greatest of physical joys, but there is a spiritual one that is just as intense, just as beautiful—and it is constant.

It's like you were in the middle of a constant big come?

Yes. Your cheeks are so pink, Fifi, he said. You are all rosy. What has happened to you?

Nothing, I said, but I knew I was blushing from toes to nipples to the crown of my hair.

Are you by any chance pregnant, my beautiful daughter?

Whatever makes you imagine that? I lied, and for the life of me I could not tell you why.

I lit a Salem Light from my bag, catching a glimpse of the furious glow of Face-to-Face as I did so.

How did you get out of Bellevue, love?

Well, after I had healed all the cancer in the terminal ward, I ran up to Psychiatric again and exorcised a few dark spirits from several people there.

But how did you get out of the place?

I met another archangel, said Sweeley Leech, one I had known in my fifth life. He is amazingly gifted mechanically. They had let him into Occupational Therapy, and there he had built a powerful motor which operates on rubbing alcohol. He installed it into a wheelchair which could travel like lightning—outdistancing a police car.

And you escaped in that?

Yes.

Was it a good trip?

O, in every way. At a hundred and sixty miles per hour in my wheelchair. I shot past three patrol cars on the Franklin D. Roosevelt Drive and lost them in Yorkville.

And then came here?

Yes.

Where did you see Lindy?

On the street. The Lite brought her to me.

But the Lite could not keep her long enough for you to heal her, I said.

Fifi, I—I don't know that I can do it every time.

Sure you can.

But my own daughter. I would feel the same thing if it were you, lover.

Yet we have been that—you and I, I said.

Yes, and it was mad—beautiful and mad.

His eyes dreamed into the little gas fireplace until I began to blush just at the thought of all he was remembering about that wild night in the fragrance of the great feather tick at Echo Point.

We must go soon, he said, biting his nails. We must meet them. I have each device of the forty pages of the Criste Lite half-drawn. From my poor, stupid, mortal memory. I have, as I say, half. The others are coming tonight. With the missing half. We must not fail to be there when they beach.

Won't there be other, curious ships, perhaps Coast Guard, who have picked them up on radar?

Fifi, he said, I am almost tempted to explain to you what the

Criste Lite really is. For now, suffice it to say that no boat full of such Divinity would be visible on any radar or sonar now known to science.

What really is the Criste Lite, father?

Well, I'll try to be complex, so you can understand.

It must be enormously complicated.

On the contrary, it is enormously simple. I got it down in forty hieroglyphics, as we shall call them. If I were the Criste himself I would have been able to say it in one. And in my next incarnation—

He sounded like a carnival magician drumming up his next miracle.

Anyway, he said, the Criste Lite is the greatest power in the universe. It is stronger than electricity, it is stronger than nuclear power, and it is found in its purest earthly form in the kisses exchanged by little babies and puppies. It is swifter than light, too—one hundred and eighty-six thousand miles per second seems a mere snail's pace compared to the swiftness of the Criste Lite. As vitamin C is found in cabbage, so the Criste Lite is found in loving smiles and kisses. It is in each of us. It is in everyone. And if you wonder how a thing as big as the Criste Lite can hide in something so small as the souls of some people, I say that no soul is small but contains the whole universe and the mind of God. The Criste Lite is—scientifically speaking—a force found in the Imagination, and is therefore of the utmost variety. It is, even more specifically, the intermagnetic relationship between the earth with everything upon it and the moon, the sun, and every particle or atom of matter in the whole universe. The death of any atom diminishes me, as Deacon Donne's island's death diminishes the main. I am part of everything that exists, that breathes, that loves, that hates, that dies and is born again. The Criste Lite was known to the ancients—far more sophisticated people than ourselves. The builders of pyramids and burial mounds knew how to channel and use it.

Does it have a sound? I whispered, remembering the choir of siren voices on the sea.

Why, of course, he said. It sounds exactly like—

I waited.

—it sounds exactly like the happy fart of a baby who has just finished nursing.

O, yes. Yes. All right.

A siren went looning up the dark avenues.

Did I fancy the faintest of little kicks within me? No. Too soon for that. But soon. Soon. My fingers stole to my breasts and fondled them, imagining that I could feel the firm little glands of milk within. I was feeling so—well, private. I had a little life inside me separate from my own, a yang and yin in the womb of me. I wanted to sing. I wanted to take off my clothes and fly like a bird. And was I beginning to feel, like father, that the old kicks simply wouldn't be enough anymore? Not yet. But wait. Wait, Fifi Leech, something inside me seemed to whisper. The new kicks will be from infant feet. O, pregnancy is a kind of death of self and the rising of something you, and yet new, from the tomb of the womb. It is a sacrament and I was deeply into it.

Sweeley looked a little sad. The Criste Lite is scientific, he said. It is even provable. And yet I have told you about it—I have described it so poorly. Let me ask you if this doesn't make you feel it. And he began to pace and declaim again.

Am I pretentious since this happened?

Why, no—dubious, if anything. Anxious to escape the hound of heaven.

But not pretentious?

Absolutely not. Was Criste himself always so unsure?

Always, he said. He was a man of Joys—and of doubts. And he was very shy.

He paused.

Even with—with this? he squeaked, fingering the little circlet of twinkling tiny stars above his head.

Especially with your very, very foxy halo.

O, Feef, I adore you. I wish I hadn't gotten out of sex like this. We might—

Father, it's been years since we made out, I said. I'm afraid the expertise I've gathered since then might shock even you.

Why are we wasting time jabbering like this? We must select nine people from down there and take off for Montauk.

Father, do you think I would make a good mother?

He looked at my eyes carefully. Feef, you *are* pregnant.

I turned away and began to leaf through a *Penthouse*.

Yes.

356

God, how marvelous. I haven't been a grandfather since 1682. You don't know what it means to me. And the father?

A cast of thousands, I smiled.

Even better, he said. It should prove a most remarkable baby.

I'm praying so. But you didn't answer my question.

I'm sorry.

Do you think I'll make a good mother?

Fifi, you were always my girl—but you are Rinsey's daughter. I can't believe it. A grandfather again. God, I wish I could be here to see it.

But why won't you be?

Was it the jingle of drunken coins in Sweeley Leech's pocket I heard? Or was it the *chinkachink chinkachink* of the abominable tambourine of the peregrinating Mr. Judah Samphire, who came only to announce the death (or the birth) or my dear, bimillennial Sweeley Leech? Get away, you atrocious black drummer!

Sweeley was humming a tune he had made up to some lines of Blake:

> Was Jesus chaste? Or did he
> Give any lessons of Chastity?

I felt within my dress for the nakedness of my belly. I caressed mnemonically my small, pert navel. O, I could feel the core and nucleus of the universe slowly forming into love and beauty in the catacombs of that cunning honeycombed bole in the slim tree of my body whose branches were shaping small, sweet buds.

Father, is there going to be a war?

Not in heaven, surely.

On this earth?

Yes. Many wars.

Soon?

Soon.

Russia will fight us?

He shrugged. O, yes. That. But we shall also fight ourselves. That is the worst of wars.

The edifice is crumbling.

Since that St. Vitus Day, he said. By the bridge. Above the Red

Cross hospital. When the Serb chauffeur took a wrong turn—so did mankind. And all the Ferdinand and Sophie in us is still adying— still adying.

He cupped his fingers under my chin.

Just as TRUCAD's computer failed because of inner confusion, he said, so the great computer of our world is grinding to a frozen standstill. It is too big to work anymore, that's all—too clotted with Greed, with Apathy. It must come down.

He lowered his face to mine and kissed my forehead.

Time enough, world enough for babies, though, he whispered. Little debbils like I remember you, Feef, Beurre, heart of my heart, on my knee smelling of baby pee, Johnson's powder, and sour milk in the laughing moon in the boughs of the old Royal Paulownia by the maze at Echo Point. O, my love, man ain't going to die!

But a war would—could—reduce this planet to an ash, Sweeley Leech.

And what if it did? We cannot subtract one atom or molecule from this earth, no matter what we do to it. We can only rearrange them. But suppose that worst did come to pass. Well, there'd still be carbon and hydrogen and oxygen and nitrogen in that cinder. And God has his lightnings. And a thunderbolt would jazz life into being again. Just a blob. A striving, hoping, dreaming blob. And it would—Fifi, it *will* begin all over again. No matter how we batter this earth. It is eternal. We—man—life—we'll always be here be- cause we always have *been* here. And what's eighty million mere years but a clock's tick in the listening hallway?

I stared into his adorable face. He hadn't shaved in three days, but it still looked plenty adorable to me. He also smelled of green crème de menthe, rather like a huge dissolving peppermint lozenge.

It must be horrible, I said, being hounded by your enemies like this.

Enemies, hell! It's the hounding of my friends that's really dan- gerous. All my enemies can do is kill me and release my soul for its new Karma. But God almighty, my friends can *organize* me out of all countenance or sense. There are nine of them waiting to do just that on the roof right this minute.

I saw the pile of books beside father's bed and went and knelt by them, leafing through. There was his scarred and dogeared Nonesuch Blake, of course—and his Shakespeare from the original folios. And I shook my head at the stack of mischief beside it. You see, hard on the heels of the revelations of porn by those sterling avatars of life and heaven in America on the pantry calendar, Norman Rockwell and Maxfield Parrish—scarcely had the shocked Christian Endeavor whispers subsided over these than there appeared the Howard Pyle drawings for Mark Twain's well-known porn books. In the early nineteen-eighties had come along the Zane Grey Western porn classics, *Frontier Fag* and the even harder-cored *Cunnilinguists of the Purple Sage.* A score of semischolarly studies appeared in Americana booklists: *Sodbusters: The True Story of Early Group Masturbation in Lincoln County, Nebraska. Golden Showers in Kansas, or Pissing All Over Quantrill.* And the really rather revolting twosome: *Collective Peristalsis Among the Ute* and, of course, *My Mother, My Armadillo.* He had them all. Poor Lindy could never grasp the Irony of Sweeley's library.

Male lovers today, I said, going back to father's side, want a woman to smell and taste utterly devoid either of humanness or of her own sexuality.

Father was getting his stacks of yellow ruled pads together and stuffing them hurriedly into his old canvas totebag from Mark Cross. Then he quickly dressed.

Why do you suppose this is so, Feef? he asked.

So they can preserve the illusion of masturbation.

Have you had some bad loves lately, love? he asked.

No, I am blessed in that, I said happily. Almost all my instincts lead me to choose the right lover. And I thought happily of my darling Adonis, who, I somehow knew, I would meet before the rising of the sun, and my heart sang like a bird at the thought of him, of us: Cunnytongue me cunningly, O connoisseur among con men! Slip it softly into the sly and sunny south of my mouth!

I found one of father's ruled pads for him—it was behind his tousled bed—and looked at it briefly. It consisted of strange and lovely designs—almost Mayan, almost Chinese—one to a page. They were beautiful and there was rest for the heart in looking at them, but something was missing. Yes. It was the color. There was no color in any of the forms, and they seemed to beg for color— wild, glowing rainbow spectrums.

Suddenly I remembered a little microscope I had owned as a child at Echo Point. It was really a tiny miracle—consisting of two brass tubes fitted into each other and mounted on a tiny pedestal in which was an adjustable mirror. I think I first understood the stars through that little microscope. I learned both micro- and macrocosmos. I fell in love with matter in those halcyon hugging humming days because I knew it was the home of the spirit, that the habitation of the soul is rooted immutably in this darling earth! Of course, my microscope was really a rather cheap little toy from Japan, with badly ground lenses, so that as one looked at the pyramid cubes of salt or the microbehemoth of the ameba, one was aware always of a fringed rainbow in the corner of the field. Somehow I loved that rainbow border—product of some adorable and forever unknown slob of a Japanese lens grinder—yes, I adored it all the more when, long after the toy microscope was lost in the limbo of adolescence's junkyard, I looked through an expensive Bausch and Lomb in school and saw, to my dismay, that it had no rainbow. O, it seemed so sterile and banal without those lovely colors like curtains in this window to How and Why. O, cheap little microscope, where are you? O, blessed little slob of a Japanese lens grinder—you captured the rainbow in those tiny crystal ovals! I knew suddenly that once the colors were drawn into Sweeley's holy designs, they would comprise a document of earthshattering magnificence. I handed father the pad.

I mentioned that thing about men just wanting to use women to masturbate them with their cunts, I said, because I was thinking of poor darling Lindy. Father, we must find her. Men have always done that to Lindy, poor baby. O, father, where is she?

There'll be a synchronicity, said Sweeley Leech, which will guide us to her, and her to us.

Yes, father. But where?

I thought of the letter Lindy had written me. I groped for it in my purse.

The synchronicity simply wasn't to be found in anything Lindy said. I handed the note to father. Instantly he turned over the first page of it and read aloud to me.

She has written it here, he said.

Where she is?

An address, he said. Of a club, I think. Fast Forward—at Sixty-third and Broadway. That's across from Lincoln Center. It's a jazz club. Next door to Fiorello's.

Do you think she's there?

We can go see.

And she wrote it to guide us to her.

No, to guide her to us.

Can we help her, father? Can you do anything?

Such as healing her?

Yes.

Fifi, you must understand one thing. When I heal someone I am only bringing out the Criste in him—not healing him through the Criste in me. Remember what he told the blind man that day: *Your faith hath cured you.*

That's the Bible, I said. Father, is it true?

Bet your ass it is, said Sweeley Leech. I heard it outside Weirton. I was nearby in a hot-dog stand having a Coke. It was springtime. *Your* faith—not mine. And I can't heal Lindy—or anyone—unless that power in them is unshackled and let free. She *must* believe.

I smiled and chewed on a broken, painted fingernail. Lindy thinks I am a dirty young woman, I said.

No woman, however many lovers she has had, said Sweeley with a laugh, has ever been handled by so many fingers as the bank note I used to kneel and lick.

Lindy thinks she's— I began, but Sweeley stilled my mouth with his fingers.

Lindy will live! When the Criste Lite's tale is told!

But how, father? And by whom?

He seized my hand and galloped ahead of me into the hall, his totebag swinging in his big hand, and adorable locks of taffy-colored hair flying out from under the tall, black, and rather seedy silk magician's hat on his head. I covered my lips with my fingers as I eyed the indefatigable halo bobbing up there above the frayed silk crown, like an audacious dandelion atop a black flowerpot.

The hallway was blooming with flowers of candleflame—candles of aromatic tallow set in lovely burnished-silver sconces. We dashed on down the fairybook splendor of the passageway through a narrow entrance to a staircase to the roof. The door was painted with the most improbable flowers and leaves, with elves looking out from behind cabbage stalks and hollyhock leaves. A moment later we were on the roof, just a few feet away from where the great neon sign cast spectral, luminous static upon the misty air of the autumn night.

Father, do you really believe that you are the Criste?

Yes, he said brightly.

But father, there are madmen who believe they are, too. The airwaves are swarming with them.

But here's the difference, he said. I believe *you* are Criste, too. They think you're *vile!*

I saw the looming shape of the helicopter at the edge of the roof. Nine people were standing there, organized and waiting, their hair and scarves blowing like birdwings in the moonlight.

I caught glimpses of their adorable and familiar faces: Mère de Cézanne, in a heavenly paisley shawl and a Jaeger bodystocking; Reverend Jimbo St. Venus, fetching as hell in Manx tweeds; Dorcas, looking fabulously well fucked on the arm of my—of our—adorable Adonis; Mei Ling, of course, and in her arms the furious Footit, rumbling and glaring out from under Tibetan bangs; Madame Jonathan T. Bigod, in a perfectly resplendent Spanish costume, with a comb that scraped the stars with its frail black glitter, and feathery black Catalán lace that seemed to catch the moon like a fish; Aubade, in the short skirt of a coquette, and with a yellow rose between her laughing, flashing teeth; Soleil, braving the chilly abuses of the wind in a simply mouth-watering string bikini, so luscious that I found myself looking for the knot by which one could adoringly undo the wisp of a kerchief between her legs. Who else? Let me remember. O, yes, Loll was there, staring at Sweeley with mooncalf eyes, and I knew she had defected from the women of the Goody Two-Shoes.

That blessed courier of Life, the sun, had not yet begun to burn down the heart of darkness. It was about four-thirty in the morning. I could see the dull glow of lights inside the big helicopter. I saw the book in Loll's stunning ebony fingers—it was not the King James Bible—it was a Nonesuch William Blake. She bore down upon me and fetched back some of my recent fears. She waved the Blake under my nose.

I got it now, darling, she exclaimed. I have seen the revelation, and I was wrong when I fought Sweeley, the living Master. O, I found it all in Blake's England. Fifi, I am full of England now. O,

Will Blake's Jerusalem on Felpham Heath! I tell you, England is inside me, Fifi!

I patted her arm and fled; I had not forgiven her yet.

Aubade, with darling alacrity, sprang up the ladder and into the helicopter. We clambered up after her. In the close cabin they all smelled so good—the odors of their clean bodies and the smells of good wine and food and cannabis on their breaths—this mingling, interweaving of smells and pheromones they wove into a tissue of olfactory delight: that smell of mortality which always excites me sexually.

As the copter blades began to feel madly about in the pulsating dark and glow, we grew still. At last they swiftly accelerated and we clawed our way starward. The city lay like live coals raked from a campfire in untidy rows. As we began to descend I could see Broadway writing its fiery lines. That glowing confection—like a tiny heap of Rinsey's Turkish Delight at Christ tide—that was Lincoln Center. We dropped even lower. I could see a drag queen insinuating his way along past the New York State Theater. As he swept down into the subway I suddenly realized why drag seldom works for a man. It's because men imitating women can never dare throw in that pinch of woman's masculinity which is the basis of all feminine charm. If they threw that in, they'd backslide into whole macho maleness and end up just a funny boy in a dress.

Aubade had whirred over to me and opened her mouth to say something charming, I am sure, when Loll pressed between us.

Sweeley Leech is the living God, she said. Did you know? Uncle Will Blake has told me. O, England! I am full of England, dear Aubade!

Aubade was quite merciless. Really, she said. What's a nice place like that doing in a girl like you?

Adonis came over and kissed me, his tongue like a fighting thing between my teeth, his hand on the cheek of my ass and inching toward its heart. He smelled like him and maybe a half-dozen other hers. I rubbed my pelvic arch hard into his genitals. He laughed as I took it out. As I eyed his cock, he cocked his eye. Aubade smiled and reached for the hand of Jimbo St. Venus. I moved up toward the front, to the controls where Sweeley Leech sat, busy with settling us down on the plaza of Lincoln Center.

It was that hour before dawn when the whole world of birds and babies and eggs and trees speed up their dreams to meet the closing titles. A mist seems to lie upon the city in this hour—a mist which you know consists of far more than visible vapors. From the tunnel of shadows at the end of the street an early-morning garbage truck browsed from eatery to eatery. On the other side a gigantic street sprayer was wetting lengths of the curb like an enormous, furious Chichevache. And from an open nightclub came the haha of wire brushes and the Mingused meditations of an electronic bass. Then a flurry of piano and the warm-up of joining horns. And then a voice—more abrasive than any Piaf or Joplin—whining out a fingersnapping blues.

It was Fast Forward—the club whose name Lindy had scribbled on the back of her letter. I edged in, with Sweeley Leech's hand in mine, and searched the bar faces for Lindy. The singer was in her underwear—the lingerie black against the pallid cream of her flesh. And so thin. She was trying to do something dirty with her hips and it was only coming off sad.

"Your lips tell me No No, but there's Yes Yes in your eyes."

O, she was so loud. And I kept listening for Lindy's voice as we plowed through the pale smoke of the cutely lighted jazz room.

I kept searching—having left Sweeley Leech at the bar, watching the little singer with a tear in his eye. Lindy was nowhere. I went to the ladies' room, imagining that maybe she had gone there to get off. No sign of her. On the ladies'-room wall, above the perfumed john, and written in Helena Rubenstein Moonburn lipstick: *For a good suck, call my ex-husband.* And the phone number. I went back into the bar. Sweeley was still standing there, entranced by the poor girl.

"—lips tell me No No, but the-ere's Yes O Yes in your—"

She was doing so many things wrong at the same time that it was beautiful. I went to father's side.

She's not here, I said. Synchronicities don't always happen right.

O, but this one has. Beautiful, he said.

Have you found her, father? I cried, looking at the bar patrons to either side.

It's she, he said. Up there singing.

O, I looked more closely now and my heart really broke. It was Lindy—poor, dear, baffled, twained little Lindy up there trying to live, trying to be sexy, trying to let the Criste Lite out and not knowing how. I ran up between Joe Albany's piano stool and Ron Carter's bass amplifier and threw my arms around her.

O, Feef, take me home, she moaned, her face pressed into my neck and hot tears splashing on the two tiny moles of my throat. I led her down off the bandstand to father's side.

She looked at father. Hello, Master, she said, and fainted.

Father quickly knelt and lifted her head and shoulders while Joe Albany and the bartender got together a sniff of brandy.

Lindy's eyes fluttered open and fixed on father. O, Master, she whispered again.

Sweeley's face was stricken. He said, Even my daughter wants to organize me.

He got Lindy back on her feet and I kissed Joe Albany and goosed the bartender sensuously and we all swept out to the mnemonic nostalgia of "On Green Dolphin Street." The wail of TRUCAD sirens was nearing—catcalling down the catacombs of canyoned Time—as we got Lindy aboard the copter and climbed in after her. Sweeley cajoled the great four-armed contraption into leaving earth once more, and again we were spiraling out over the wretched wreckage of the South Bronx toward Queens.

Aubade came to my side. I never told you about the little chapel in which, with the aid of the old wizard, I gave my legs to Villanelle.

You said it was very old. And small. And very beautiful.

The pollution has darkened some of the stone, she said.

Pollution is bad in Russia.

Not Russia—Slovenia, she said. And besides, the little chapel is not in Slovenia any longer.

Where is it?

It is, she said, some five miles upriver from your Echo Point, four miles from the Gallimaufry—and only a few hundred yards from the well-known northeast, or Falcon's, exit from your father's enchanted Labyrinth.

I remembered. There *was* a charming old abandoned Eastern church up among those ragged woods and the scuffed, millscourged flats above Echo Point. We had played around it in our childhood. I remember what strange wild flowers grew there—hellebore and pimpernel and periwinkle and nettle and English myrrh. I had adored the old chapel, yet I had never dared enter it. For, sometimes in the sundown summers when the sulfur dioxide crawled like a yellow thought down the living flesh of the valley, sometimes when the bird choked on his songs and the frog fled air for the water and found foul solace there—sometimes in that yellowish hour, an old sound came out of the church. Or perhaps it did not literally emanate from the church so much as it was in the air, the winds, about the church—a choiring of many voices, deep and soprano and sweet as a beggar's sad old accordion—a choir of Slavic Joy and Sorrow as warp and woof of an enormous tapestry of spirit. Byzantine, Cyrillic, burnt-deep pagan fires, still smoking in its enormous voice. We had thought the place so strange that we had come to believe that it had been built by wise, sophisticated people in an era before the Adena mounds.

I squeezed Aubade's hand. But how did the little cathedral end up in Apple County, West Virginia, Aubade?

Because, she said, it was bought and brought there.

From Slovenia?

Precisely. By an atrociously rich mine owner's daughter whose maiden name was, I believe, Absolutington.

Not Ms. Cora B. Fiasco. That was her maiden name. *Née* Cora Belle Absolutington!

Precisely she, snapped Aubade. Lousy with money and acting the American rich bitch, she was flashing through the meadows of Slovenia on the Brno Night Train when she spied this little cathedral. She caught fire inside. She reached for her passport and her checkbook and, of course, a small American flag. She pulled the emergency brake. The train grated furiously to a standstill. The conductor rushed up to Ms. Fiasco *née* Absolutington. "What is the emergency?" he said.

"The emergency," said Cora, "is that I want that church."

"You want to worship in that church, you mean?" the conductor asked helpfully.

"No," said Ms. Cora B. Fiasco (and you know of her current affair with the Clarksburg Klan man and periodic barnburner and porno-fighter, "Kill-a-Kike" Kallikak). "No," she said. "I want *that* church *in* West Virginia."

"Ah, yes," said the conductor—refusing to believe. "You want to take a picture of this lovely church, of which I happen to be a member of the men's chorus. To take to West Virginia."

He tried his voice with a few quick tenor lines from Janáček's great *Mass.*

"No," said the stubborn and peripatetic Cora Absolutington Fiasco. "I want the church purchased! Then I want it disassembled."

"I believe you must be dissembling," said the conductor.

*"Disassembled,* you ass-wipe!" cried the bold Cora. "I want it taken down—brick by brick—"

"It is not made of brick, madam, it is made of stones which have been shaped with love."

"—and the stained-glass windows and all the icons and the fonts and the choir loft and the pews."

At any rate, the train stood on the main line for one hour while Ms. Fiasco, the mayor of Brno, the administrator of the district, and a large assemblage of mindless Ph.D.s and D.D.s argued back and forth about the amount which Ms. Fiasco would presently fill in when the Waterman's fountain pen she held poised above the blank check descended. At last it was agreed upon unanimously. Everyone in the town concurred that a far more progressive church, maybe something neo-Bauhaus, could be purchased with the really substantial sum the redoubtable Cora was prepared to pay. I say unanimously—but not quite. A few peasants who loved the old church resisted—and were shot, six of them, and twelve more jailed. In the spirit of true Methodist Christianity, Ms. Fiasco—after the sale had been put through—added an additional check, for a lagniappe, so to speak. She was giving the families of each of the slain or jailed peasants all the paperbacks of Billy Graham and a lifetime subscription to the *Spotlight.*

I glanced anxiously toward father.

That's a truly dreadful story, Aubade, I said. But why do you mention it now?

Because— She blushed. You'll laugh, perhaps.

She cocked her head at me. Or could the child of such a man as he possibly laugh at such a thing?

What thing, Aubade, darling?

A vision I had just now, she said, quite serious. Very clearly. Of the meadow below the old church. The desolate, bleak meadow, a kind of moor that falls down from the hill above. It is almost prehistoric in its starkness. And on it stands a cross—a cross made of aluminum, or perhaps stainless steel, with straps for wrists and ankles, and studded with all kinds of gadgety complexities. It is wired. It is obviously a place of execution.

The county cross, I whispered. Yes, it is there. The Apple County place of execution. Yes. You see someone on it?

Yes, she said.

Who?

She said nothing as she turned from me. She was crying too hard, as the helicopter began chasing the sweet blowing Pleiades up the seasky above Long Island and the first fingertips of rosy morning were tinkering with the horizon.

# T✦W✦E✦N✦T✦Y
# T✦W✦O

Lindy had collapsed onto a small cot hanging from the starboard wall of the copter. She slept with such a depth of intensity that I sensed that I should let her be—it was the first real sleep she'd had in nights aplenty.

I looked down on Long Island below. The lights were beginning to thin some as we flew northward toward the point of rendezvous. Aubade was still beside me, and on the other side, Dorcas. She reached a hand out and ran her fingertip across the lustrous surface of Aubade's ceramic left leg.

It feels cool as the face of the old Delft clock in my grandmother's house.

O, but it is quite warm within, you see, crooned Aubade, really getting something sensory out of the shy, exploring caress.

Somewhere out at sea, lightning opened and closed its gigantic shutters, silvering the sea and land. The sea rimmed the fainting land articulately with foam; the moon was like a heathen-hewn crescent in vast, blue armor which held back the sun. The horizon was

369

unflecked by craft of any kind but was slowing glowing with swirling yellows and azures and golds.

I switched on the radio. A Halloween commercial. O, really, this is too much! Razor blades guaranteed not to grow dull inside apples. I spun the dial. Billie Holiday singing a song she never recorded, and from guess where? The morning was latent and lovely in the level line of ocean. I smiled and felt the pretty lines of myself beneath my frock. Aubade looked pensive.

Does he know? Is the Master correct in his faith that others are coming? The sea looks so deserted.

Mei Ling lit a long Turkish cigarette and exhaled. Even the smoke seemed tinted, fragrant with lilacs.

They are there, she said. And they will come to the appointed site. We are no more than five minutes away.

She smiled at Aubade and laid her hand, with the cigarette extended, on Aubade's arm.

Just then Sweeley Leech called from the front, We're nearly there.

My ears popped as we descended. I ran to a porthole and looked out. The lip of the ocean was kissing the skyline into fluttering opals: she was blushing O blushing with the ecstasy of his touch. The sun was rehearsing his golden lines in the waving wings. Stars were striking their tents and heading, like circus caravans, down the west. Gulls made Michelangelo patterns against the diamond-strewn breakers.

There! someone said in a loud voice. There's the old tavern on the beach.

My darling friend Madame Jonathan T. Bigod was by me then. She smiled and touched my purse with her fingers. Face-to-Face, she whispered. He must be fairly blazing with volcanoes and sunspots now that the moment is so nigh!

I reached into my purse and plucked out the gray-blue velvet box. I opened it an inch and the nascent sun was pallid by comparison with the slow ardent flare of light that filled the cabin.

Tonight, said Madame Jonathan, you may be very thankful for the great yellow stone.

How? O, do tell me, Madame Jonathan. I hate surprises so.

But she said no more, only kissed my cheek and was gone just as I felt the big copter settle on a long stretch of dune. We came down the ladder into the sea morning. A soft wind honed its ancient legends against the driven sand. And from the open sea—was it the wind out there, too, or was it that choir I had heard which had come to still the assault of the behemoths against the bubble of our sea-drowned room?

The sea was polished and all shimmery, like port wine, ruddy, with rosy hints of morning, yes, like wine, with sheets and bits of mica floating on it. It was still not the full blush of dayrise, but this was hinted in the slotting, horizontal light, a thin, ragged ribbon of lacy flame and blaze, atop the cresting limits of the ocean. The wind was coming on in quick gusts and scattering the silvery sheets. Seabirds in terminal ecstasy rode the shoulders of the invisible trades, while the sea, with lisp and subtle thunder, came on in, drawling, to its spumed and hoary end.

I looked around me. At the sea. At the desolate beach and the gray, looming inn called the Walt Whitman.

Fear is so funny. There are so many kinds of danger. How do we ever know when we are in peril? How can we guess that that headache last Wednesday night at dinner, that slight restlessness through the night, that tiny fever—that these were the battle reports on a monstrous and titanic struggle within us. Against cancer. Or typhoid. Or worse.

The seawind tanged of tart cocks and jolly cunts. It was heavenlily miasmatic with the saline bite of the savory juices of the quahogs and oysters of Gardiners Bay. It had dollops of lobster mayonnaise in it. O, heavenly morning!

I was alive and in danger—these two things, I knew. We were all in danger in that strange, windblown place that darkling day. And didn't know why yet.

While I mused on the beach, Sweeley Leech had led the rest of the company up into the tavern in search of lodgings and to get things set up for the coming of the boat. There was a fine seamist on the air—chowdery and briny and dripping with ozone from the deeps.

The wind seemed to be produced by the seagulls—so closely did they come shouldering behind it, scrawling the seachanting air with chalky graffiti of sound. Water lapped against an old quay, now fallen into the kissing corrosion of the ocean, its black logs and slotted, spiked timbers standing against the slaty seasky like rotting lace. I kept scanning the glowing horizon for some sign of a boat. Was there not the smallest of dots upon the skyline? No. It was only a dark whale saluting the sun, darling of the morning. Yet—as the wind rose and fell—could not one hear that choiring vocalese I seem to remember as coming to appease the assault of the whale-ghosts during the séance? The air was twitching and wizarded that morning. Something—someone—was surely coming to us there! You could feel it like a whisper in the pulse of your wrist! But who? And how soon?

To my delighted surprise I saw Lindy coming toward me from the tavern. She had obviously slept deeply and bathed and had a fix. For an instant the slotted aureole of sun broiling on the skyline re-flected on the china smoothness of her cheek and the serious chest-nut beauty of her hair, like carved wood; yet a moment later the old weariness returned to her countenance and I could see Death, like a white, waiting wolf, behind her eyes.

O, my darling—my dear, dear Lindy!

I ran to meet her and we clung together. I could smell her per-fume and the wisping reek of fresh alcohol still evaporating from the scarified hollow of her arm. Still, she didn't seem stoned.

Memory rioted back into the funny papers.

I love you, Appassionata Von Climax! I said, through tears.

O, me, too, Evil Eye Fleagle!

And we held each other and cried a little and giggled some, swaying together like a smooth feminine tree and remembering the first night of a vanished Lil Abner.

Lindy looked up into my eyes. I know father is the Master, she said. And I know that he is filled with the Lite. But, O, Feef, it can't help me. I am beyond its help.

Lindy, the Lite that can save you is not in Sweeley Leech—it is inside you.

But she turned away, leading the way up to the tavern sign, as if oblivious to what I had said to her.

I grieved for Lindy in that moment, perhaps more intensely as the realization dawned in me that I was seeing her, perhaps for the first time, in relationship to Time and the earth and all other exist-ing things infinite in number, and therefore entirely deathless. It was an excruciating pain, that comfort, but it opened to its utmost limits my Wound of Wonder and I knew I would be able to live as easily with Lindy's death as I know I shall live with my own.

As we moved up onto the worn stone threshold beneath the wind-grating sound of the swinging sign, I felt the warm, sweet burn of the great yellow diamond in its blue-gray case. I knew that everything in the universe is related to everything else and that energy exists solely in the magnetic push or pull of things. And that this energy is the Criste Lite.

The holy, hoodlum wind swept up under my frock and played cool as a fool between my thighs.

I was horny.

Strange, that the realization of God should be erogenous. But then you see it isn't, really.

O, Lord, touch me there. Then touch me Everywhere. Rocking in my loving Jesus's arms. Yes, lovergod!

We moved into the ancient breath of the main room. There was a huge fire coughing on old iron dogs in the stone fireplace. The bloody light of it set aglow the flesh in old Revolutionary War portraits and kindled like candlelight in the gold-rimmed frames. The chamber was not, in fact, a room packed with antiques as much as it was an antique room. That bowl-charred clay churchwarden on its dusty cherrywood stand might still be warm from smoking. That battered and blackened silver tankard with the blunt, sweet Tudor rose bitten into its frosty side—wasn't there still an inch of foaming porter in it? The room seemed only recently quitted by its original occupants.

For the tavern—from the dusty registration book on the Duncan Phyfe table in the vestibule to the small (and rich) library in the back—was deserted, neither the proprietor nor a maid nor manservant to be seen. It had that curious feeling of waiting, watching Life in it that the Three Bears' house must have had to Goldilocks. Goldilocks set me to thinking of the Goody Two-Shoes, and I shuddered. But a glimpse of the swooning stars through a twelve-paned window—a window latticed like those in Howard Pyle pirate stories—brought me back.

Everyone was getting warm around the flickering, ruddy hearth, for there was autumn's ancient chill in the air. I saw Sweeley Leech staring in fixed attention at something which loomed dark and yet curiously living in the rear of the chamber. I looked where he was looking. I saw. I gave a laugh. It was Whitherhitherthithershins. O, dear, I must hasten to explain.

Lavishly littered with antiques though this charming hostelry was, it was nothing compared to the incredible clutter of History which Echo Point was.

As I have said, we were always either incredibly wealthy or grindingly poor. It was wonderful. The periods of poverty prepared us for the periods of *richesse;* made us appreciate Life and its very subtle relationship to Things. Sweeley Leech has always had this absolute phobia about Possessions. The more you have when you die, the more you have to carry on your back Out There. Can you imagine a Mellon or a rich Arab just recently dead and staring, stunned, at the pyramid of possessions he is now expected to move out through the stars? And so one day Sweeley had sold this wonder clock.

He had sold Whitherthitherhithershins one blowing April morning when the white serviceberry blossoms lay scattered in young trees like popcorn and the post-ramp sap-rise had cocks hardening from War to Weirton. Whew, what a beautiful day. But I was sure sad to see Whitherthitherhithershins go from our lives. O, ye of little faith! I wept. Lindy, on the other hand, was glad to see "that ugly old giant out of the house." I was really quite disconsolate when a gypsy (who looked like he had a gold ring through his cock to match the one in his ear) handed Sweeley Leech twenty-five dollars in ones (which Sweeley furtively passed out to the sticky, dirty little Romany kids with eyes like sweet sugar dates) and carted off the enormous clock at sunrise with the Caravanserai.

Think of things as having spirits, lovey, Rinsey said appeasingly. We never possess the Spirit till we get rid of the Thing.

Or, like Cousin Davis's mother once said to me: "We keep only what we lose."

But none of this is getting across what was so special about Hitherthitherwhithershins (and since it's a very old English word, you needn't bother about the order in which you place the Hither and the Thither and the Whither).

It was a clock, all right, but it was so many other things, too, like a good Swiss Army knife. Though the Clock was not made in Switzerland at all. It was an acutely Magical instrument, I will swear to that. Let me try to describe it.

The Clock is huge. It is perhaps eleven feet in height, ten in width and in depth—but how shall I explain a thing like the depth of Time? For this Clock was perhaps the only clock in existence which actually dealt truly with Time. It had what Sweeley Leech called a Time-Bend Escapement. I know what this means but I am absolutely powerless to explain it. I can, however, illustrate it. And maybe this whole strange tale explains it a little.

There was a recess in the base of the Clock, but not one of your customary pendulums. It didn't work on that principle. The recess in the Clock had a small, worn bench with a tiny old Norman tapestry upholstery. The bench was large enough for one adult or two children. On the walls were tiny metal engravings—coins and medallions and the prizes of old wars. The dark inside the Clock smelled queer and very ancient. It smelled like tonka bean. Sometimes it smelled like the evening wind during the harvest of clover hay. It smelled like Time.

The whole thing had apparently been constructed on a principle of such relative simplicity that, like a sundial, it would never wear out. On top was carved and whittled in microscopic detail a revolving black globe of the heavens, and it all looked down on a minutely detailed carving—maybe four by five by seven feet—of a medieval fortress town. All of it was carved in the most meticulous detail—it was like looking at a Dürer or a Brueghel. With the aid of small glass lamps of whale oil behind the pierced and star-fretted ebony globe of the universe the light came through—as sun or moon or star. I never seem to remember the little lamps needing to be refilled. The revolving of the ebony globe was, of course, coordinated to show the various phases of the moon and the aspects of all the planets.

There was a huge keyhole in the face, so I suppose the Clock must have been wound, though I don't remember Sweeley Leech's ever winding it, nor do I remember its key, which must have been very large. The Clock chimed faintly but almost continuously—almost like some delicate, though tuneless, music box. All kinds of bells and gongs were in it. Someone said (Sweeley, I suppose) that it developed a chime for every great moment in its history and would ring or chime or bong at the appropriate anniversary. So that we, deep in our huge common feather tick at Echo Point, would often be wakened by a most unconscionable carillon or perhaps be lulled back into our dreams by the faint whisper of bells as delicate as the waterchimes of the Balinese.

There was always a perpetual sundown back in the recess with the little, worn bench. And one would drowse and dream the most fantastic hypnogagic images, only to be startled awake as, from somewhere deep within, Whitherthitherhithershins would announce, in tuneless tintinnabulation, the fall of a kingdom or the lifting of a petticoat. Someone (and not Sweeley this time) said the Clock was built by Galileo and that it even figured as an exhibit at his inquisition. The Clock—Thitherhitherwhithershins—*was* certainly venerable. And, indeed, as I was to learn that night, probably immortal.

There was a tiny, carved, scrolled cabinet of fruitwood suspended on the back wall of the clock. It had the appearance of a small Low Country cottage. It had a small door with a brass handle, which Sweeley had repaired with a piece of invisible Scotch Tape.

Do you know who lives in the little house, Beurre? Sweeley once asked me.

I stared at it and scratched my behind. Yes.

Who lives there, Beurre?

The Devil, I said. He makes the big Clock run.

He is the proprietor, so to speak, of the little ancient village.

And the stars above? I asked.

He only contributes his blackness, said my father, so that we can see the light.

O, I said. I see.

I found a perfectly delightful place to scratch on my ass and paused, squinting and digging in.

I want to see the Devil, I said. Is he home?

Yes, said Sweeley Leech.

I opened the door. In the back of the little house was a very old and very wrinkled mirror in which I saw my face.

When I thought about it that night in the bed, I began to cry.

What's wrong, lovey-dovey? Rinsey called from somewhere off in the featherbed.

I want to see God, I blubbered.

Then go and look in the little house of Whitherthitherhither-shins, said Sweeley Leech. Because God lives there, too.

He yawned and scratched his day-old beard. He is the proprietor, so to speak, of the little ancient village.

And the stars above?

He only contributes his light, said my father, so that we can see the darkness.

O, I said. I see.

And I went that night and saw, by moonlight, God's round, sleepy face.

Above the amazing scroll hands of the rather small clock face on Whitherthitherhithershins there was a space called the Garden—a small cutout place backed by faded blue-painted tin. When a visitor was privileged to sit in the Clock, the most amazing thing would happen—a small, cutout tin flower would swing up slowly into the crescent space. And a different flower, it seemed, for each different sort of person. If a virgin sat in the seat, a white tin rose would appear. If a nonvirgin, a red tin rose. There was a pink tin rose which showed pregnancy. There was a yellow tin rose for duplicity and a green tin rose for sickness. But there was more to the Clock than perhaps even my father understood.

I have said it had scrolled hands: for minutes and for hours. Yet it had, in fact, three sets of hands and three dials—very very old and made of painted sheet tin that was faded and peeled. One dial and set of hands showed Time going forward; another showed Time going backward; the third was set at right angles to and between the other two and seemed not to be concerned with Time so much as with Space, for it was calibrated not with hours and minutes but with points on the compass and geographical locations.

There was yet another charming and remarkable feature of the Clock. This was a small, mechanical toy theater tucked away in a corner of the machine and near the floor. The theater consisted of a tiny, sheet-metal, painted proscenium and a stage (with real velvet curtains and wings and a safety curtain, which sometimes came banging down on your fingers, with the word *asbestos* on it. It also had twenty birthday-cake candles as footlights (with tiny reflectors), and a marvelous and surprisingly large entourage of painted, tin actors who popped up at the right moment or glided racheting out of the wings to meet one another for tinny embraces beneath the tiny cardboard apple tree by the light of a most entrancing mother-of-pearl moon. There seemed to be no end to the number of plays the tiny machine could produce—mostly melodramas and historical stories with religious overtones.

The little theater never produced a tragedy, though it was itself involved in one. It was, as you might imagine, intricate with gears and springs, and it was into one of these (I remember I was four when this happened) that a fairy, enamored of our tin Magdalene, fell and lost both legs. He is still to be seen—poor little soul—along the dusty river road below Echo Point in the sultry summer dusks, peddling tiny bundles of dried comfrey or feverfew.

The wood of Whitherthitherhithershins was like that of an old Cremona viola da gamba: rich, almost lapidary, almost confection-ary—so much so that, in certain evening lights from the stained-glass windowpanes in the parlor, the whole scrumptious structure of the Clock seemed to be the creation of some mad pastry chef, carved and tubed and spatulaed out of caramel and dark chocolate.

Now I stared at the dear old contraption, a bit puzzled. I looked at exquisite examples of Quattrocento woodcarving—tiny village streets and clinging battlements—held together with bits of wire and paper tape. Sweeley Leech had taken pains with the Clock—even after it had got broken, or at least lost its chief power. And that was all too long ago to be sensibly remembered.

Aubade handed me a platter of yellow English lusterware upon which was one of Mère de Cézanne's famous omelets—this one a marvel fashioned of eggs, asparagus, and black caviar. I munched gratefully on a crumbly, hot drop biscuit just barely held together with a smear of fresh yellow butter.

She watched my famished feasting with tenderness. The arrival of the boat, she said, is imminent. Come to the window.

I put down my empty platter and caught up a lovely Limoges cup of brawling hot sassafras tea sweetened with blackstrap. I fol-lowed Aubade through the cluster of us all—some cross-legged on the floor, some strolling about the beauties of the chamber holding their plates as they went, mingling Rembrandt Peale with poached egg, Chippendale with chives.

The window opened on an achingly lovely stretch of beach. The surf was tumbling like April lambs, and the heave and roll of the sea beyond was dark as raspberry jelly bubbling slowly in a great hot kettle. Dawn was now more than merely implicit. The fire on the sea line had spread, infecting a whole half of the domed heaven, upon which night still cowered tremblant. Yet prominent in the midst of this seaskyscape was a mountain of cumulus, like an island of meringue toasted on the edges with the dauntless flames of sunrise.

I see no sign of it, I said after a moment.

It is there, Aubade said.

I see only a huge pile of clouds, I said.

It is there, she said.

You mean in the clouds—?

There was no need for her to answer. Rays of light, of incredibly beautiful value and hue, shot delicately through a cloud in a fluttering rainbow moment, and then it became gray as an oyster shell once more. I realized that the light had to have some prearranged, human origin—it was more than just a natural phenomenon. What had Aubade meant? Was the ship lurking inside that motley cloud?

The wind blew my silver earrings back against my neck, under my flowing hair. The great cloud flickered on, ever changing, like a great revolving prism, jailing up light and then flinging out rainbows.

But what of the boat? I asked.

It is there, Aubade said again in that odd tone. It is still there.

The wind rose sharply again. The sea seemed to quicken its rhythms, too, and a moment later a shower of rain, like handfuls of pellets hurled through the open window, began to sting our faces and bare arms.

I stared and, indeed, at the point where the cloud met the ocean, a small dark spot had appeared. Not only had appeared, but seemed to be growing larger.

It doesn't look like a boat at all, I said, shading my face against the winds and rain and trying to see despite them.

It isn't, she said.

It looks like a man, I said.

It is.

Walking on the water?

Walking on the water.

Like—like in—?

Yes. The same.

Is it the Criste?

No one answered; my father stood smiling.

But who is that coming?

Wait. You'll know in a minute.

I waited. I would not have asked any more questions, anyway, for I was quite literally dumb at the sight which now unfolded. The lowest projecting cluster of the wispy cumulus behind the approaching figure began to dissolve. And as it wisped away, foot by foot, there became visible, in the interior, a boat—a ship, specifically: a battered, scuffed, rusty-keeled, pumpless, bilge-awash old freighter, probably christened long before what is called the First World War. In front of it came striding the unmistakable figure of a man, for his long mustaches were visible now above the luster of his Shantung silk robe and the beautiful jeweled pendant hanging from his throat.

The rain had abated but not the playful wind. On he came, on the water, rather boisterously, and carrying a red paper shopping bag. He stopped once, lifted his naked left foot, and took a small shellfish from between his big toe and the second, and lowered it gently into the water by his side. He had these long, Chinese-badman mustaches—nearly a yard on each side—and every few watery strides, he would twist and curl them wisely. He drew closer, looking more mad and enchanting by the moment—and yet, somehow, more sinister.

Behind him the old freighter lolled in the satiny swell. I could see small figures on it, but did not discover immediately that they were completely naked and no more than four years old, the rascally lot of them. They were, if it may be so imagined, the crew of this rusty old tub, whose peeling funnels gave off no wisp of smoke. How, then, had they gotten here, all the way across the pitching, pitiless sea? Then I saw the long traces leading into the surf, and these were connected to beautiful white harnesses which were attached, in turn, to dolphins. And here and there a small right whale, also harnessed and, to all appearances, having the time of its life. Closer and closer, upon the shimmering sea, came the feet of the stranger—moving away from this unspeakably beautiful scene upon the sea and toward the small, breathless cluster we now made upon the shore.

Against the sky the old ship appeared stunningly beautiful. Behind her funnels and scuffed, paint-peeling forecastle, the ardent sun loved the ship so fiercely that she seemed in flames. Yet she was alive with those small naked figures—daft, rosy little cherubs turned up unaccountably in a blazing, gold-leafed Turner. The sea seemed stilled with the arrival offshore of the *Anna Zelinski.* The cloud which had hidden the strange little caravel was now off gainward the sun. The children were all clustered around a large lifeboat now, while a pair of four-year-olds helped the three-year-olds aboard.

The stranger's beautiful feet broke the froth of the undulant and gentle breakers. He had scarcely touched dry sand when Footit, enraptured, ran forward, bumping and squirming against his feet and ankles as if trying to dry them. The venerable figure of the old Chinese stooped and affectionately tousled the little dog's silky mane. Then he fixed his black, twinkling eyes on our group and strode up the beach, his hand with its delicately long fingernails outstretched. I think we all expected some deeply religious greeting, but instead:

Say hello to Fu Manchu! he cried out, in a Mel Brooks voice.

In the midst of us, Sweeley Leech stood smiling, his own arms outstretched.

They embraced.

So glad to see you again, Fu! Sweeley exclaimed warmly. It seems only last week and not centuries since we held each other so!

They clung, in genuine affection, for a moment. Their haloes, almost gray in the livid light of the emergent morning sun, linked like rings in a magic act above their laughing, nuzzling faces. At last, each stood back and regarded the other gravely, suddenly all business.

Do you have the Criste Lite?

The old Chinese smiled and looked at the Red Apple shopping bag in his hand. The designs are here, he said. Forty-four pages of them. Was that the number in your original, Sweeley?

Exactly the number. Come, let me see.

There was an old beach table with an umbrella of gaudy colored stripes, now long faded by seawind and sun, and two wicker chairs. Sweeley Leech swung his own Red Apple shopping bag up onto the table and dumped out his yellow ruled pad with its intricate runes and symbols. The Chinese stepped forward with his own and shook his copy out onto the table, beside it. Each man stared, each riffled through the pages, comparing.

They are identical, said Sweeley Leech. And half is still missing—that half being the colors—the all-important tints and hues.

That, said Fu Manchu, staring out toward the sagging, lovely old *Anna Zelinski,* that is because the Dyer is not yet ready.

The Dyer, gasped Sweeley Leech. You mean that the Dyer— that he himself has come with you on your ship?

Yess. (The sibilant hiss was sweetly redolent of lichee nuts and rice wine.)

You see, said the old Chinese, stroking the lovely designs gently with his long nails, a gesture which produced the sharp, pleasant sound that crab claws make on seableached stone—you see, Sweeley, in the south of England (in Cornwall, in the village of Rederring, to be precise), six men and six women pitted their spirits and minds against the Darkness and came up with this much of the Criste Lite, the book of instant Salvation. But all we—yes, I was of their number—all we could manage to capture on paper was the outline, the bare linear design of the forty-four runes which make up the holy book.

Sweeley smiled.

I, he said, had it all. Including the hues. Once, long ago—

Yes, I know that, said Fu Manchu. But that was pure miracle, Swee. We in Cornwall had none of that gentle beneficence from the Dyer. Your vision, unlike ours, was direct from him.

Who is the Dyer? I asked, despite myself.

My dear, said Sweeley Leech, it is Criste himself.

And he came with you on the boat out there?

Yes, answered the object of my query, the old Chinese saint, whom I instantly admired and loved, not merely because Footit had greeted him so passionately, but for his marvelous way of switching from one character to another: the crass, funny shtick comic and the H. B. Warner wise man with the lapis lazuli silks he wore. O, I did adore him, and so did the darling Mei Ling, his daughter, who had been behind the tavern when he came and only now saw him and approached reverently, though trembling with emotion, her long white arms outstretched. They did not embrace—she knelt and kissed his fingers and then he knelt and kissed hers, and it was somehow more touching that way: each acknowledging the distances between them as well as the adoring, swooning Oneness. I found myself wondering if they had ever made love, as father and I had once done.

The children, whom I had last seen clambering aboard the sixty-foot lifeboat, had managed to lower it and push off. Their shouts and baby commands were louder now than those gull voices which skreaked and gabbled officiously above them in the morning mists. The boat was almost to shore and six or seven of the children had scrambled over the sides and were splashing up onto the beach.

Hardly had the work of us twelve been taken as far as you see it here, said Fu Manchu gently, noisily fingering the sheets of his tablet—hardly had we gotten this far when TRUCAD agents discovered us.

You escaped, said Sweeley Leech. And the other eleven?

Captured.

Killed?

Better if they were, was the answer. You know TRUCAD's torture methods in cases of religioeconomic heresy.

Among others, murmured Aubade somnolently, a spear of mornlight quivering in her lovely hair, the dreadful, hideous Orgasmus Perpetuum.

True, said Fu Manchu. Don't dwell on it, dear. It is so negative.

But go on, urged Adonis McQuestion, fetching as a country breakfast. What happened to you then?

A boat had been arranged, said the old Oriental. A boat had, indeed, been judiciously chosen. First, something on the order of a Viking ship was considered. Then a Roman trireme. And finally it was brilliantly suggested by one of us—it may have been myself—that we find a boat most rich in something which used to be called Romance.

Why Romance? I asked.

O, because, darling, cried Aubade then. Because that gentle emotion Romance is so close to the Criste Lite itself. I understand precisely. Is that not so, Mr. Chu—or how shall I call you?

Manny to some.

You are a Manny! You are, Dorcas Anemone crooned, and toyed rather seductively with the end of one of the old man's long black mustaches.

The children were hooting and lisping wildly somewhere up behind the tavern, where patches of late-summer wild flowers grew in profusion, their scent living now in the quintessence of the morning wind.

And do you mean to say, queried Madame Jonathan T. Bigod, that you navigated the Atlantic Ocean alone with those tiny children?

With the aid of the loving Dyer, added Fu Manchu.

I stared toward the ship, which was rocking gently in the cradle of the undulant waters. She was barnacle-crusted and rusty-hulled. From her cables hung garlands of flowers—clearly not from this hemisphere but from somewhere south of where the frangipani blows. Yet there was a light around her, hovering, Kirlian, and shimmery with color as if from the movement of waters within an opal. Surely the Dyer was there, and presently we would see him, too, come striding across the waters with his tint box.

Every eye was glued to the shifting, lovely outlines of the old boat riding the soft, dayrise swells.

What would he look like?

What would be his first words?

Or would he simply move wordlessly to the yellow pad—one or the other, it did not matter—and begin his coloring while we watched in wonder?

No answer, it was clear, would be immediately forthcoming.

And yet I found myself rejoicing in the ineluctable Joy the man Manchu radiated: like the first few tokes from the joint you've just rolled from a fresh country ounce of good Colombian. There was such an essence of Originality in this man that it made one immediately define Originality as a gigantic Simplicity. Sweeley Leech had it. I had been raised knowing it. I knew it now in Fu Manchu—that deliciously absurd figure in his silks that blazed rainbows like an oil slick lit by ardent moonlight, his tiny, outrageously loud yarmulke, his twinkling, slitty eyes which seemed narrowed, as it were, by a passionate and humorous affability.

Now, beneath the lollipop stripes of the faded beach umbrella, the two great men sat opposite each other in white-lacquered wicker armchairs. Not that they held our attention just then: we were still standing, we fumbling Seekers, with eyes fixed on the old rolling hulk with blossoms in her hair.

You know, of course, said Sweeley Leech in a voice so soft that it seemed his words were meant for the old Chinese only—you know, of course, that when the Dyer comes with his colors, we shall drive him away before he can finish.

We all heard the softly uttered pronouncement. Was that the wind we heard or the sucked-in breaths of our twelvefold conscience?

No, exclaimed someone—perhaps Aubade.

No, No, No! choired a half dozen.

Fu Manchu nodded agreement with Sweeley and then smiled palely at the rest of us.

It is true, of course, he said. The Dyer will come. With his lovely colors. And begin the task. It is so written, my dears. He will, yes, begin the task and come almost to the end—and he shall be driven away.

Not if we are forewarned! cried Lindy, in an astonishingly strong voice. Now that we know, we can be on the qui vive and avoid it.

It is written, said Sweeley Leech.

Yes, said Fu Manchu, smiling and curling his left mustache into lascivious and ancient patterns. It is so written—that e'er he be done with his gift, he shall be driven away.

But why, father? Why, dear Fu?

Neither answered.

O, I was no better than the others. I stared in hard determination at the decks of the old ship—my eyes peeled and unblinking to catch the first glimmer of his Power and Majesty.

Does he bring the colors with him? asked Madame Jonathan.

You will find Magic Markers of every hue inside the tavern, said Fu Manchu. Perhaps the two copies we have here should be there, too.

You mean he may come invisibly? May slip past us and go indoors?

He will come visibly. But he will undoubtedly slip past. And go indoors.

Sweeley took one of the two copies of the uncolored Criste Lite back into the room: we could see its table crystal laughing with light on the neat Irish lace.

Now, he said, returning to us. It is there. It is ready. It awaits only the genius of the Dyer—a genius old and venerable and wise with the cube roots of each of Time's sacred numbers.

The wind blew. Light caught in tinsel rags on the wires and sagging radio antennae between the stained, smudged stacks of the *Anna Zelinski*. The old boat rocked like a cradle in the inner limits of the Gulf Stream. Her flowers flashed sweet, fresh semaphores.

Suddenly I was aware of someone standing beside me, so near I could feel the warmth of that body. Fingers crept down and stole around my own, lacing in timidity and need. I turned. It was Lindy. I kissed her damp forehead and smelled the dab of alcohol and cotton she had clutched over a fresh puncture in the hollow of her arm.

It isn't true—is it, Feef?

That we shall drive him away—e'er he can finish? Yes, I think it will be, darling Lindy. Though I have steeled my soul against such a thing.

She was silent a moment, shading her eyes, staring at the ship.

No sign of him yet. While, back in the tavern, I could fancy the yellow, untinted pages with their lovely, queer Mysteries scrawled carefully on each. I could see the rainbow box of Magic Markers. And he would come from the ship presently and he would slip past us and into that room. I fancied the moment in my mind's receptors. I could see him, the Criste as I think Uncle Will Blake always saw him yet never dared depict. I could see his lovely hands filling in the colors. I saw then the ugliness of the moment when one of us—or perhaps all of us in a mob—would come yanking the doors open and driving this sacred old Spirit of God away. O, I knew I would not be one of the Guilty. I simply would not move—would not open my mouth to speak—until the Spirit of the Dyer had done its work.

Sweeley Leech seemed to be reading my thoughts. I squeezed Lindy's dear hand and smiled at him wanly, stubbornly, helplessly.

We all do it, he said. So don't feel bad about it, Beurre.

And then it was the voice of the old Chinese which spoke. Yes, we all do it, my tiny morsel of candied ginger. Do not grieve. It will be over soon. But it must come—his denial. For it is so written. And what is written must be read. And so—always. We will deny him and yet he shall come again and again!

Again I fixed my hard resolve upon the pregnant horizon. O, I felt impatient with the Lord. Why was he so long in coming?

Somewhere behind me—yes, in the teakwood room of the old tavern—a radio was playing. An old tune.

386

We're waltzing in the wonder of why we're here,
Time hurries by—we're here—and gone.

But what bothered me? What caught like a brier on the thick
wool of my meditations? The radio. It had not been on when mere
moments before I had walked the creaking floorboards of the teak
room. The faces of the Rembrandt Peale legends from my own past
leered luminously down the dark. Who had turned the radio on?
From the duskglow of an evening in 1848 Robert Delaplaine
smirks and licks a grain of snuff off his upper lip. Who turned the
radio on back there in the teak room? Had Whitherthitherhithershins come to life and done it? The fact was, the radio was on and
someone had turned it on and that meant someone other than the
twelve of us was now back in the room. With the precious document. With the tempting Magic Markers! Who?

Some thoughts are like a spark in dry moss—they blaze suddenly. I don't know which of us turned, but I know I got to the
door first and raced down the fragrant, echoing hallway and thrust
heavily against the many panels of the great door to the teak room.
All the rest, except Lindy, pressed hard behind me. I saw first the
dark, glowing, looming splendor of Hitherthitherwhithershins. And
then I saw the radio and one small naked child—his ringlets briny
with seafoam, his fingers gaudy with colored inks, his bare ass
sweetly twinkling—turning the dial on the radio. And then I saw
the rest of them—that infernal mob of babies. They were scribbling—yes, that is all I could call it—scribbling and daubing great
gouts of color on each of the pages of the Criste Lite.

Wait, kids! I cried, charging forward. You mustn't! You mustn't!
Those pages are waiting for the Dyer.

O, I wished them no harm. I did pray that the paints were non-
toxic, since I could see perhaps a dozen fat, paint-smeared thumbs
and forefingers pressed between sweet Rubens lips.

I don't know at what exact point we realized. I guess it was when
the children broke and scampered, their bare feet thudding im-
piously, their tiny penises waving like little sea urchins, their periwinkle vaginas twinkling like wee crescent moons. It was over in a
second. The radio chanted on. Now it was the air of the room full of
Charlie Parker—a sound which seemed to be laughing uproariously
at us each. *Confirmation.* Yes, it had been confirmed. I was the one

who went and gathered up the now spectrum-tinted manuscript and turned to let my soul face the others, in common shame.

Well, we did it, I said.

As it was written, said Reverend Jimbo, and Footit moped against the mauve davenport.

Maybe they finished it, said someone. I mean, maybe he finished it.

No, I said holding up the front and fore, back to back. It is not finished. There are two runes left undone.

The children were in their lifeboat now, drifting up the big, polished seaswells, on their way back home to shipboard like Morgan and his crew coming back from the sacking of Portobello.

But louder than our shame, louder than the talking oceans or the bouncing morning breeze, I heard a Voice of crumpling, wheezing laughter from outside, from the trembling sky, from the clouds, and I knew it was not fakery this time, no voice whored into computers by TRUCAD. No, this was the real thing. And It could hardly speak for laughing at the joke it had just now played on us.

Except ye—heehee—become as—harphharph—little children—!

But the voice fell to laughing too hard to finish. Yes, it was unmistakably the utterance of the great farting, belching Nobodaddy God!

—ye cannot—haha—enter—ohoho—the Kingdom of Heaven.

I felt something warm on my ankle and looked down. Footit was smiling up at me with his tiny, neat black lips, while with slow and accurate purposefulness he peed on my shoes.

# T✦W✦E✦N✦T✦Y
# T✦H✦R✦E✦E

Sweeley and the old Chinese were standing in the exit, watching, with faint smiles, the exodus of the angels. Their boat was caught up in the dragging tide now and it rocked and rode like a carnival car as a quartet of dolphins, innocent and joyful as the babies themselves, nosed and butted, with their smooth Socratic foreheads, the long boat toward the mother ship. I did not join father and Fu Manchu. I drifted away from the others and peered out in terror at the leave-taking.

I wanted to rush to the curtains and fling them aside and throw open the quartered casement windows and shout after these darlings: O, my loves, come back. O, lovely Dyer with the M & M chocolate and Tootsie Roll on your breath, please, please come back!

But the children were gone. They had clambered aboard the old patient hulk of the *Anna Zelinski*, and mists were rising again as they do in my mountains when the fog of morning toils and whispers in the sycamores and pine, and the miner, at his breakfast, observes, "The squirrels are brewing their tea."

I had the feeling as I watched these radiant clouds come clasping round the children and the old ship that in a moment it would be invisible to us again, drawn out to sea by some tide in the blood of that Greatest of Hearts, and into the Gulf Streams of the Infinite. And, true enough, in a matter of moments it appeared as if only a low clinging cumulus lay piled like Reddi-Whip upon the great, sweet pie of the sea. And moving, ever moving from our shore.

I was struck with a sudden incongruity in something and went over to where my father and his friend were standing. I turned my eyes to the old Chinese. I have a question which is really quite embarrassing to ask.

He waited.

I pointed to the undone—though marvelous—pages with their blazing runes. This vision of the mind of God, I said, could only come to one person—the Individual.

Yes.

Then how come you explained to us that it was put together by six men and six women? That's a middling-size multitude, in my opinion.

The old Chinese was silent for a moment.

It is simple, he said. I lied to you.

He paused a moment and walked away from the amused, twinkling regard of my father. I watched his progress. He stopped by the edge—near the tin children's theater—of Hitherthitherwhithershins.

The twelve—the six men and six women, myself among them— we did nothing, he said. Nothing but argue and form committees and panels and action groups. We could never come near to it.

Then how did the runes come to be drawn?

Let us at least be comfortable, he said, indicating the roomful of charming antique furniture, for it is a rather complex story.

I watched as Aubade lowered herself into a wicker chair. Dorcas and Reverend Jimbo sat cross-legged on an old rag rug, glittering with color like a fresco in Herculaneum. The others settled down comfortably on the old, graffiti-whittled bench against the wall and plumped up bright calico cushions to rest their tails upon.

As I have said, we ended up fighting, said the old Chinese, fingering his left mustachio. We began with the noblest of spirits and the most cooperative of dispositions. And we ended up in utter conflict. In fact, it was our conflict which led to our ultimate discovery and capture by TRUCAD. I rather think an Individual would have brought it off completely.

But who drew the runes? I asked again.

Yes, who? echoed a half-dozen other voices in the shady, cool room. The great Clock ticked somnolently on. O, whither are we bound, dear Thitherwhitherhithershins? I murmured.

A most amazing woman drew them, said Fu Manchu. Most utterly amazing.

We waited.

You see, we were a committee, he observed, as apostrophe. And did you ever hear of a committee producing a masterpiece? Even an unfinished masterpiece such as this— And he waved a handful of emblazoned yellow pages in the air and then laid them reverently back down and stacked them once more.

But the woman? What about this woman? Who was she?

He waved his long fingernails—like great goosequills about to scratch in ink a bar of immortal music.

I am coming to her, he said. Or rather I should say, she came to us.

Outside, a jetboat droned somewhere beyond the horizon, now clear of cloud and ship and not chick nor child visible upon the gull-dotted blue.

O, we were all eminently qualified—a biochemist, a nuclear scientist, a lady poet, a minister, a cancer expert, a dietician. We had everything. But it was not I—it was We—and so we failed.

But the woman, queried that O so chic Madame Jonathan T. Bigod. What of her?

A sudden gust of sea air blew through the distant pantry, setting into sound the iced-tea tinkle of wind chimes hanging from the ceiling on a bit of butcher's string.

We lived in an inn not unlike this one, he went on. Near the docks where the fogs always catfooted up on the dark each night. It was called Shadwell Stair and, like this place, it seemed to have no visible proprietors. Shadwell Stair was—or should be—well enough known, being named after another dockside spot of the same name in London.

The woman, we all moaned with curiosity.

She came one night, he said. Out of the mists. And not a moment too soon.

Why? What happened?

What didn't happen? None of the twelve of us could cook. The place was getting dusty. Socks needed mending. The pillows and quilts all wanted airing in the morning sun. There was no one to do these things—until she came. A most remarkable woman—in fact, totally amazing!

Do you mean to say no one of you was capable of making an omelet? Making a bed? Chasing mice out into the tool room?

Yes, of course we could have! he exploded. The astrologer was a gourmet cook. The lady poet was marvelous at making beds, having trained as a nurse. The astrophysicist was a ferociously neat person and could have dusted beautifully every morning.

But you were too busy—

We men were too busy being holy, sighed the old lovey. And the women too busy trying to be men. And we'd have starved and gone dirty, I suppose, if the woman hadn't come to us.

But there were six women among you, cried Soleil.

Not really, he said. There were six androgynes, creatures who had bartered all their carefully gendered gifts for Equality.

Well, what about this other woman, then? This strange, new woman?

She was a woman. She had given up none of her powers and mystic gifts for a handful of wages, a seat in high councils. She was a woman, proud of it, yearning after no more maleness than is necessary in the most feminine of women. And seeking out the feminine in every man.

She *was* feminine, then? asked Aubade, with my darling Adonis at her elbow.

Utterly, said Fu Manchu. She was, first of all, a most stunning creature to behold—not really young anymore, not really old yet, an anachronism complete within herself. Lord, she was a Joy. She smelled good—sometimes like fresh bread baking: clean and full of wholesome nourishment; sometimes like a garden: one of those old gardens you come upon in back of eighteenth-century country homes—rambling and briery and moonlit, with a sundial and ancient stone benches and wild, sweet, rambling roses everywhere in the glowing light and shadow. She breathed life all around her, this woman!

O, I bet you fucked her every night! breathed Dorcas Anemone.

Fu Manchu stiffened a little. How I detest half truths, he said.

He paused and smiled, remembering her. Every *other* night, he said brightly. After all, we were twelve—we had to share this delicious creature.

O, did the ladies sleep with her, too? asked Mère de Cézanne in her creaky but marvelous erotic voice.

In the mornings, said Lovey Manchu. She avowed she would make love with a woman only when the morning sun dazzled the looking glasses in her room in a certain way. Hours when the dayrise seemed so pure and ambient that the sun itself appeared to be only the moon in flames and the birds in the sky were like black, gritty stars anxiously searching out their proper positions before night should come again. Of course, she would strip for love in her bedroom only after she had changed all our beds and fixed us twelve succulent, happy, mouth-watering breakfasts.

Where did she sleep?

It's natural you should ask that, said the sweet Chink. And the answer is quite amazing. Actually, she had the last room in the tavern—and the smallest: no more than ten by ten.

And her bed? asked the dear Jimbo.

She brought it with her, he said, in a wagon. It was enormous. It filled the little room utterly. It was nothing more than a great feather mattress—a goosedown tick—gloriously soft and strangely fragrant.

I noticed Lindy stirring uneasily.

The old Chinese paused and reached for the small reticule of linked green jade rings which hung at his waist—the whole marvelous purse carved, it appeared, from a single block. He plucked out a rose-colored marijuana cigarette, lit it with his Bic, and toked four or five times. The fumes were like a sweet Colombian prairie fire. He passed it on to me. I toked a little and took wing with him.

You know, he said, how hotel mattresses—and particularly hotel pillows—always smell so sour and sad and pungent with the dreams lost upon them? It's as if they breathed out the ghostly despairs and aspirations of all the lonely salesmen and truckers and transient conventioneers who sleep alone and toss, or buy or barter love from pathetic little salesladies and cocktail-lounge waitresses. Love never given, you see—love which must be hidden and stealthy and invisible. And bought or bartered. Hidden love—furtive love—why must it be so? Why, because of Paul, surely, and Buddha and a handful of lesser Augustines and Thomases. So—you know the smell of such beds?

I remember such a bed, said Aubade, in Prague. It reeked of rapes by Gauleiters.

Imagine, then, he went on, a bed which, at the slightest pressure, the most casual plumping of its pillows, exhales a fragrance with something of sea in it and something of the clean wind above the chasing hills and woodlands within which flourish wild ginger and salsify and marjoram. Roses, too, and cannabis and such marvelous herbs and spices—mostly unknown to modern man—which thrive, I am told, in a mysterious region of the earth called the Gallimaufry.

Surely this discourse was moving ever closer to a region of adorable but menacing familiarity! But before I could intervene, Fu Manchu had regained the main thread of his yarn.

You see we were doomed to failure, we twelve. He sighed. We had everything we needed right there—knowledge, wisdom, experience, data, historical allusion and reference—everything necessary to create the Criste Lite.

Except Love, breathed Madame Jonathan T. Bigod obligingly.

Except Love, said Fu Manchu. We came there to do a loving task and failed to bring any Love among our supplies. The woman came then. It was the woman who brought the Love.

He knuckled a tear—quite genuine—from the Chinese fold of his right eye.

She did everything for us, he went on. She scrubbed our floors with the ardor and excitement of an archaeologist disclosing a long-hidden tile floor in some home in Pompeii. She did our washing—taking clothes foul with usage and returning them fragrant as morning in mountains by the Aegean. She cooked the succulentest suppers, mouth-wateringest lunches, happiest breakfasts. Recipes unknown to my palate—and I go back quite a way, dear Sweeley and my other loveys!

His eyes narrowed and he smiled, remembering the woman and her delights. Strangely, he said, whenever she was alone there was always the sound of small children coming from her room at night. The chuckle and tease of children's voices—small ones, mind you—and her cajoling them or teasing back or telling tales or perhaps leading them in some ribald nursery song. If one of us opened her door, the voices ceased and she'd be sitting there alone with a mischievous twinkle in her large green eyes and usually naked as the day she was born and the great mountains of the enormous bed all round her—and left on it the telltale stains of Mars bars and Forever Yours left by the small and now-deserted imps.

*Debbils,* corrected Sweeley Leech. The word which, in the new epoch, will come to signify what was once meant by the word *angels.*

I concur, said Fu Manchu, though I had intended to explain that in the next breath, my dear Swee. Do be patient with me.

And obviously, said Aubade, these were the children whom we—I—drove away. The children who comprise that soul once called the Dyer.

Fu Manchu seemed not to hear but plunged on in a perfect passion of self-disclosure. O, my loveys, as you shall soon discover, the Dyer can be quite anyone. Yes, anyone. Anyone, that is, with the soul of a child. The woman had the soul of a child, you see. Just as much as her debbils did.

And was she, too, captured by TRUCAD that last night? asked Adonis McQuestion.

Of course not, said Fu Manchu. She was a nobody to them. A servant, a menial. Obviously uneducated and without any gift. Moreover, she was a woman! She'd have been the last soul on earth they'd have suspected of putting together the Criste Lite.

And if she was not captured, then—? ventured Soleil.

We waited, while the old Chinese paced the length of a sunbeam on the enchanting old Persian carpet beneath him. He turned to us then.

It happened the night we came upon her in the kitchen, he said. He grew pale suddenly and then turned, standing with his back to us. You see? he said in a strained voice. I can't face you as I tell of it.

What did you see in the kitchen?

The woman was there, he resumed, his voice echoing curiously because it was not directed at us but at some receptor deep within himself. She had taken the yellow pad upon which we, the Council of the Twelve Wise Persons, had somehow come to a compromise after our six months of labor. It had been a long and tedious game—quite devoid of Joy (which was the lack that doomed it)—in which one of us would draw in a rune and presently another would complain about some detail and another pair would agree (with modifications of their own) and the big India rubber eraser would come out and two lines would be obliterated and three fresh ones put in. As I say, we had finally come to some kind of grudging compromise on the forty-four designs. And we *had* gotten them down in the pages of the yellow pad.

And the woman? murmured Aubade, as though she already knew the answer. What was she doing?

Why, she was impudently sitting there with a black Magic Marker of her own and her own eraser doing over our crabbed and penciled attempts. "Why, no!" she would exclaim, rubbing away with the big piece of India rubber. "That's not right. I know that much. Not right at all. It should be this way. And that—should be that way—not the way it is here. Wrong. Wrong. This whole design is wrong. And how do I know? Well, how do I know how to look after these twelve poor souls or take care of my debbils?"

Yes. Debbils, you see. The voices we never saw—the laughter we never witnessed—the small people.

The Dyer, breathed my father. Yes, they were he.

She had a most unusual exclamation, said the old Chinese. Hagerstown, Maryland! it was. Hagerstown, Maryland! That's what she always said when her keen, loving eye discovered some absurdity in the work of the Council of the Twelve Wise Persons. And so saying, she would reach up her pretty hand and cock back the worn, old—and unaccountable—fatigue cap she wore every waking hour. It was, I believe, a relic of the American Civil War.

O, dance, legs! O, stand up, goose pimples! O, sing, heart!

I turned my eyes to those of Sweeley Leech. He smiled. I smiled. He winked. I winked.

O, Rinsey darling, I knew, I knew that you would never die! I knew that your sweet restless wild flower of a spirit would never be content to lie unfertile in the root-plundered and still-bloodied loam of Antietam!

And the woman, said a voice then. What became of the marvelous woman?

I am thankful, said Fu Manchu. Hagerstown, Maryland! but I am thankful that you cannot see my face as I confess it.

You drove her away, chuckled Aubade, snuffing out a cigarette in an exquisite Burmese spittoon by the tiled hearth. Just as we—as I—drove away all those babies, all those debbils. It is comforting, however sad, to know that you—that I—always drive the Dyer away when we come.

One day we shall not, he sighed. One radiant, golden day to come. But it is true—I drove the woman out of the kitchen. There were others with me—all of us, in fact—who took up the chase. She had dared to tamper with our sacred runes. We could not know it then—but she had made them nearly perfect.

He straightened the silken slump of his shoulders. And so you see, he said, it is only the Individual who can do miracles. Only the Dyer. And the Dyer may appear in any place at any time and in any guise. As a lovely, bounteous woman. Or as a gaggle of ornery, shouting babies. Debbils.

But *they* were a group, objected Loll, and yet *they* succeeded in getting all of the Criste Lite on paper except for two remaining colors.

We are dealing here with perfect creatures, said Fu Manchu, spirits above the dog pit of competition and ambition and selfish egoism. The rules are not the same. Debbils are God's own little playmates. And they are Criste's cherished favorites.

And where did the woman go?

To her room, said the old Chinese sadly. To gather up her few patched shreds of clothing, an old Confederate tunic, and her feather mattress. Miraculously, I believe, a horse and wagon were waiting for her in the fog. She stuffed her bed and belongings aboard, clambered into the seat, and was off. And not a moment too soon. The hue and cry of her exodus—her forced and shameful expulsion—had not escaped the attention of a nearby TRUCAD patrol. Within  moments they had descended on the inn. Soon Shadwell Stair was a shambles. The woman—wagon and all—had clattered off into the woolly night, with myself hiding deep in the fragrant canyons of the featherbed in the back of the wagon. I know it was disgraceful, my using the woman for escape, particularly since I had led the expelling group. But I knew—I knew on

397

second sight—that the runes she had managed to limn out of our crabbed hodgepodge were the true Criste Lite. Without the all-important colors—but perfect in design.

How did you manage to get out of the bed? asked Sweeley Leech.

How did I? How, indeed? sniffed the mandarin. It was hours later. I could hear the foghorns and buoys close by and I knew we were at the waterfront. I remained hidden for a long time. I tell you I was shivering—not from fear so much as from the wisps of that plagued south English fog which searched out my very bones. I waited perhaps two hours. I breathed in the sweetness of the fragrant and somehow very feminine feather tick. At last I crawled out into the fog. It was everywhere. There was no sign of the TRU-CAD patrol, although I could hear sirens and Klaxons in the distant town and see the orange and yellow and black scorch of flames against the soft night sky. The enchanting tavern called Shadwell Stair was no more.

He paused and drew the curtain aside to stare out to sea. I looked where he searched the unblemished horizon, the cumulus resting upon the thin, almost invisible line where sea met sky, clouds like great whips of ice cream. He sighed again.

O, Swee! he cried in a breaking voice, would you have known better? Would you have known that the woman was the Dyer?

I least of all, said Sweeley Leech. I—was once married to her.

The revelation did not seem to astonish the venerable Oriental. No matter, he said. What remains now is for one of us to imagine and put in the correct colors on those two uncolored sheets.

Everyone looked at his neighbor. Eyes were lowered uneasily. Feet shuffled and strolled off into the yellow morning light.

That was when Loll appeared on the threshold. She was old again—the moon had fled and the stars had gone ascampering away, and Loll, as always, had grown old and gnarled and bowed with the first cool ray of morning sun. She looked at us all as she spoke, though it seemed her eyes were on me.

Someone is coming, she said. Someone on a motorcycle—racing up the clamshell road.

TRUCAD, several were heard to whisper.

Loll shook her head.

I don't think so, she said. It looks like a woman—a rather fat woman. Alone.

As we converged on the flagstone steps in front of the inn, the outline of the invader grew more distinct. On a Honda, with his violet silk headscarf streaming behind him on the seawind, and still in the tight strapless dress he had worn at Le Pet au Diable, Uncle Mooncob drew near, the rolls of back fat lolloping over the tight bodice of black chiffon, his face streaming with perspiration and his glasses steamed over too densely for us to make out his eyes.

He braked to a sand-spraying stop, swung his silk-sheathed leg over the YYxxx Honda, and came through the sand unsteadily, stumbling at least once on his sequined pumps. He came directly to my father, Sweeley, his brother.

Swee, I don't know why I bother so! he shouted, straightening his lopsided red wig. You've done precious little for me lately except cause trouble.

What is it, Mooncob?

First, said Mooncob, I want it understood that I am not joining your side of this tragic debate. But you are my brother. And I do owe you that! You must escape. But that is entirely up to you and, I suppose, this considerable body of people—shall I call them "disciples?"—you hold to you by one means or another.

He does not hold us, snapped Aubade.

Be that as it may, said Uncle Mooncob. If I were caught warning you here, in this place, it would mean arrest and trial for me, as well—and probably death on the Apple County electric cross.

He waved his hand, upon whose pudgy fingers glistened patches of peeling nail polish. At any rate, said uncle, adjusting his askew chestnut wig coquettishly, the hunt is on. TRUCAD has established its organized Church as absolute law. Members of your group, dear brother—

Children of the Remnant, murmured Madame Jonathan T. Bigod, with an angry tilting of her fetching Garbo fedora. That's what we are called.

Well, you are doomed, said uncle. And you might as well know it. And as for you, my dear male sibling—

I have been condemned, said Sweeley Leech. In absentia.

It amounts to that, said uncle. You are doomed most of all, I fear. Orders have gone out from the very highest level—

God?

They claim He has been contacted and approves, uncle went on. I'm only glad it wasn't I who made the call.

Do they know where I am? Wasn't God obliging enough to inform them?

The ladies of the Goody Two-Shoes reported on your last appearance, uncle said. In the West Sixties in Manhattan. They are the police arm of the Cazzo Nostra.

We've already encountered them, said Lindy, looking pale and valiant.

I suppose, said Sweeley Leech, looking not in the least perturbed by his prospects, they have ordered me taken dead or alive.

On the contrary, said Uncle Mooncob, orders have been quite specific on that.

Dead? whispered Aubade.

Alive, said uncle with a sinister glint of pleasure in his eyes, which gleamed like a child's marbles in the puddle of his mascara. They want a trial—a much publicized one—and a formal sentencing. And, finally, execution. They want to disgrace you in public, bring you to your knees, force a repudiation of all the things you espouse.

I espouse nothing save Love, said my father, and I can't renounce that. As for my execution, I look forward to it. It will free me for the next trip amongst us.

O, come, Swee, uncle snorted, you can't be yearning that much for what you imagine will be another chance at life.

Do they know where I am now? asked Sweeley Leech again.

They soon will. Precisely where.

How? Did they see us leave in the chopper? asked Dorcas Anemone.

Yes, but confusion exists there. Most of the Goody Two-Shoes said you headed southeast.

But they will find me, said father. That's what you mean?

Within thirty minutes.

How can you be sure of that? snapped Reverend Jimbo testily.

They're using, or beginning to use, said uncle, glancing at his digital lady's wristwatch, which gleamed in the fur of his dark wrist, a new kind of telepsychic radar. It is now ten-thirty. They were beginning the operation when I left two hours ago, at eight-thirty. They had located you then on the upper Atlantic seaboard. Within one hundred and fifty miles of Manhattan.

He glanced uneasily southward, where a thunderhead, purple as a cluster of ripe grapes, lay lowering upon the line of sea and land.

Actually, he said, I was in contact with them not twenty minutes ago. By teleradio. They had narrowed all possible areas down to northern New Jersey and Long Island.

Soon, crooned Loll, with a strange smile, they will know. Soon they will come. Soon he shall be dead so we can pray to him!

In thirty minutes, said Mooncob again. They have narrowed it down that much.

They will swoop down upon Montauk, upon this little tavern, murmured Aubade sadly. And the legend will be finished.

The legend, said Sweeley Leech, has hardly begun.

I took great risks, said uncle, contacting them while coming here to warn you. Great, indeed.

And I thank you, dear brother, said Sweeley Leech. I am really enjoying this, you know.

Well, I'm not, sniffed uncle ungenerously. And the sooner I see you all aboard that helicopter and off on your merry way—toward the Azores, I hope—the easier I shall feel. I tell you, Swee, this is asking too much. I could be tried and executed, too, you know.

How can we win, murmured Lindy gloomily, if God is on their side?

Because we have Criste on ours, said Fu Manchu, who had been silent till now.

A half hour, said Sweeley Leech, rubbing his stubbled chin thoughtfully and lifting a sandfly gently from his nosetip and setting it airily off into the glistering sunlight again. That's time enough to eat. And get a few things straight.

Lindy suddenly flung herself forward and clung, sobbing, to father.

O, father, how can you talk of food? she sobbed. Get us away from here. Save yourself. Make a miracle!

Even miracles have rules, said Sweeley Leech. They are really rather technical. That's why sleight of hand has always interested me.

What do you mean? asked Aubade.

I mean that we must not leave this spot, said father, until we know where we must go.

Go? cried uncle, almost falling as he remounted his Honda in a fury. Anywhere, that's where. Man, they mean to have your head on a mighty public platter before they are done.

There are rules, said Sweeley Leech. Rules even for miracles. We must not leave here helter-skelter—merely fleeing. We must leave with good reason.

Then what good reason would there be to leave—except to flee, brother? To save your life—and the lives of these people?

Why, to find the two missing colors, said my father, to the Criste Lite. We must go where they'll be found!

O, my fat aunt Hattie! cried Mooncob, flinging himself off his cycle and stalking unsteadily down the beach, his sequined shoes slipping in the sand. Swee, you are too much to be endured.

He whirled then. *What* two colors?

It was Fu Manchu who emerged from the tavern doorway then, holding the sheaf of childish, tinted papers in his hand. He pointed to the colored runes and then held up the two colorless, though exquisite designs. When the colors to these are discovered, he said, we shall hold the essence of Criste in our hands. And maybe—

Maybe what? snapped Mooncob.

Maybe save the earth, said Sweeley Leech, and all that lives upon it.

There was such pleasant, undismayed, even joyous zest in father's tone and manner that even his flustered brother did not protest.

We must wait, said Sweeley Leech, for the Sign that is surely close at hand.

Uncle Mooncob had sat down on the sand now and had a slipper off and was massaging a painful strap burn on his foot.

A Sign from what source, if I may inquire?

Why, from God. That dear old farting, belching Nobodaddy behind yonder sun, said Sweeley Leech.

I have already told you, said the sweating Buddha in drag, cross-legged and piously pugnacious in the sand, that God is on their side.

God is on every side, laughed Fu Manchu, fingering his jade. The old fool plays chess games with himself.

A Sign, said Sweeley Leech, and we knew he was speaking to all of us now, to us Children of the Remnant and not to his obdurate and forsaken brother. A Sign will come within the half hour. From the sky. From the sea. Perhaps from the earth itself.

What kind of Sign, Master? queried Loll.

A Sign which will be recognizable to one of us—to one of you, in fact—as to where the two miraculous colors can be found.

One of us? piped Dorcas. One of *us*? You mean one of us will finish the coloring of the Criste Lite?

It is so written, said my father.

What kind of sign do you mean when you say a Sign will come? asked Adonis McQuestion.

I can't tell that, said Sweeley Leech. It will come from the most unexpected source—and it will be a riddle which you must solve. When you have solved it—one of you—he or she will know where to find the missing colors.

Mooncob struggled to his feet then and wallowed up the dune toward us. And what, exactly, do you expect to have in that—that sheaf of childish scribbles when you have filled in the colors on those last two pages?

Something, said Sweeley Leech, which might amaze even you, brother Moon.

For example?

A book which will be full of the light of the world—and the Ancient Lights of heaven, as well. A book which will make you laugh. And sing. And dance. A book which will fill you with the utmost and totalest of Joys. A book which will heal the sick and the halt and the lame— It might even heal the blindness of eyes like yours, dear Moon.

Is that the thanks I get for coming here? For warning you? Your cheap, sawdust-trail insults!

I thank you, Mooncob, said Sweeley Leech. But things will be as they will be despite you. Or me. Or any of us. Still, we must do our best.

How much time do we have, do you estimate? asked Fu Manchu, before the TRUCAD planes and boats appear?

Twenty minutes now, said uncle. Certainly no more than that.

403

The telepsychic radar is new—this is the first tryout—but it is possible to predict with at least that much accuracy when it will reveal your whereabouts to the authorities.

Aubade whirred over and, with infinite sensuality, began to stroke the silk covering uncle's bosom, which overflowed the bodice of his dress like bread dough spilling from a brown crock. You know, my dear, you're really quite adorable in drag. I do hope you've come out to stay.

Uncle simpered, leering atrociously. It was a fancy, he said. At first, it was pure fancy. A means of gaining entrance to your absolutely irresistible establishment. But I met someone there—an assistant Presbyterian rector who was dressed as a French sailor. A dear, dear person. I have seriously considered—as you put it—staying out of the closet.

As I said a moment ago, said Sweeley Leech, I am hungry. I suppose all of you are. What say to an early lunch by the sea?

Do we have time, father? asked Lindy.

It is God's body, smiled Sweeley Leech. We must feed it when it comes begging at our door. There must always be time to feed God.

Christ, sniffed Uncle Mooncob. If you weren't so corny about all of it.

He belched.

Oooo, crooned Aubade authoritatively. How *à la Turc*!

She farted, in a tiny quack of riposte. I must confess, she said, my insides are *raging* for a bite. Great trade winds sweep my stomach and my liver and my lights. I am utterly empty. Still—where will we get food? The great icebox in the tavern pantry was, this morning, quite empty save for a few eggs. And we ate them at breakfast. Still, as I say—and I feel I speak for all of us—my guts feel as empty and wide as the China seas and my taste buds are teased by the most indescribable fancies and imaginings!

Fu Manchu looked at the sea, and then his eyes swept the small multitude. The hungry crowd by the ocean, he said. The sea. The situation seems to suggest a precedent. Eh, Swee? Saint Mark. Eighth chapter, right?

But father had anticipated him, and with a gesture not of competitiveness or jealous rivalry but of sheer Joy, swept the black, battered topper from his shaggy, dandelion head and, with a deftness that seemed to surprise even him, reached into it and drew out a delicious, steaming corned beef on fresh Levy's rye.

The venerable Oriental stared a moment, approached father, examined the sandwich on its platter from every angle, sniffing and savoring its odors, and then plucked a crumb of meat from the edge and tasted it.

Too much fat, he said, and, seizing father's hat, stalked off a few feet and stared out to sea. Besides, he added, turning his twinkling gaze again to Sweeley Leech, that was sleight of hand, not a miracle. And if I recall Mark's narrative, it was not a sandwich at all, it was loaves and fishes.

No matter, said father moodily. What I am feeling today can be found in something Camus once said: "Do not follow me—I may not lead. Do not lead me—I may not follow. Just walk beside me and be my friend."

O, I do agree, I cried, and turned to father. Still, I must ask a question, Swee.

Yes, Beurre.

Swee, how shall we know what the Sign means when it comes? And in what way will it be a riddle? And how can we be sure that one of us here can figure that riddle out? We have so little time.

We will make time in these last twenty minutes, father said, eyeing the figure of Fu Manchu, who had donned father's top hat and was now walking up and down the beach a few feet off, making passes and appearing to be building up to some sensational feat.

Father laid his hand on mine, and I felt the warmth of him with even greater love.

You remember, Beurre? In the Port Authority? That fortune cookie with the message inside?

Stanley Schwartz never got past PSC102, I said.

Stanley Cohen, corrected Sweeley Leech.

Stanley Cohen.

You see? That was a sign. A riddle.

I never figured it out, I said. I suppose it meant this poor Stanley Cohen never finished school.

Wrong, said Fu Manchu. It means that Stanley Cohen discovered the Recombinant DNA factor called PSC102. And that he never got beyond that.

What *is* beyond that? asked Dorcas Anemone.

The Criste Lite, of course, said father and the old Chinese in a single voice.

Fu Manchu—gripping the black hat firmly in his left hand—marched over to us. And it is that kind of riddle with which you will be confronted. And which you must solve.

I see. Yes, now I see. A Sign will come—from the sky, or from the sand perhaps, for Criste often wrote in sand. And we will ponder it. And we—

Not "we," said father. You. One of you. The riddle will be plain to one of you.

Now Fu Manchu began the bit which he had been rehearsing. I really have to give him credit. He had style. And as he moved from person to person, producing hot bagels with cream cheese and lox from out of the hat—father's hat, mind you—I really would have (if I had had one) taken off my own hat to him. But I began to sense his growing sense of competition with Sweeley Leech—yes, even rivalry—and I felt a little chill of dismay. Who would the Children of the Remnant look up to? Would it be, at the last minute, not Sweeley Leech but the much flashier Fu?

Enjoy! he exclaimed, handing the delicious repast to Reverend Jimbo. Enjoy. Enjoy (servings for Dorcas and for Mère de Cézanne and Loll)! Enjoy!

He looked like a Ratner's waiter on an acid trip.

I wasn't having any. No, not out of petty spite that it was not my father's miracle. I simply wasn't hungry. I wasn't tired, either, and that was a kind of miracle in itself, for I hadn't slept since those fitful catnaps on the Greyhound. I was dirty. O, God, I was dirty, and I felt the dirt on me like Grief.

I peeled out of my dress, slipped off my panties and pellmelled down the sand toward the kissing breakers. I lost both shoes on the way and was soon wriggling my toes in the cold, receding froth. The purple, swollen thunderhead down the coast was bigger now and piling cloud upon violet cloud as it ascended and began to master the valiant sun. I scampered out into the spindrift and seafoam and began to swim. I thought about it—the Sign. O, would it come? Was father right? Again I pondered the curious sense of unpleasant rivalry on Fu's part toward father. How would Sweeley Leech deal with this? And the Sign—would it perhaps be made manifest to *me*? Was I not surely one of the Least of These? O, the water was like ice! I closed my eyes and dreamed that the Sign would come to me, and suddenly, like a child, I would see it. I mean *see* it—the answer. And know, in a moment, where I should seek the two colors which the Dyer had left unfinished.

I could hear Uncle Mooncob bellowing back at the tavern.

You must take off now, he ranted. I risked my life to come warn you. And now you putter about this place where, in fifteen minutes or less, TRUCAD will surely find you. And me. You fool—O, you fool, Sweeley Leech. Wait no longer, I say. Leave!

Father's reply was blown ragged by the wind and sea, but I caught two words. The Sign. The Sign, he said again, and I felt my whole body tingle, and it was not just from the Popsicle coldness of the water. The Sign.

It is so marvelous to lie on your back with all the seas of the world under your legs and shoulders and ass and arms. Some of Rangoon wisps salty between your toes. O, a bit of algae from the Aegean is on the tip of your nose and, between your legs, you feel old tides off Zanzibar.

The sacred motherhood of the oceans was all around me. I exulted in it with a single, joyous cry that, too, was ripped soundless by the rising winds. The sea was quickening, too. The sky, the sea, the wind, striding like a great Criste across the quivering Atlantic—weren't these surely the Sign we needed? No. Because the Sign was a Riddle, and there was no Riddle in what lay around me—it was all so beautifully self-evident. The sea. The sky. The earth. The mind of God. O, praise him—praise him—and see him not as a petulant, sometimes cruel, sometimes loving deity, but see him as a God who, in the loneliness of light-years, created, in his own evolution, the conscience called Criste.

Of all the Children of the Remnant, Footit alone had heard my cry of Joy to the sky. Now he ran furiously up and down the beach like a sandpiper, just out of reach of the sea's icy lips, his entire hindquarters tucked under him, and cast wild, sidelong glances out of his large, bright eyes through the flowing silk of his mane. A thought which father had uttered repeated itself in me. The notion that God, after long, lonely, selfish ages, evolved a conscience whose name was Criste and who had tried a half-dozen times to live among us as a man and was destroyed. Because the God in man had not yet caught up with the God in the skies. O, those skies—how I drowned my eyes in them now. A nimbus of achingly beautiful fire. O, I have glimpsed this before in great paintings—especially those of that great arsonist, Turner!—a nimbus that made the half sky look like some great winestained cloth beginning, around the edges, to burn.

Perhaps the child unfolding now in my womb would bring the Sign—kicking out words in code, maybe. I giggled. He—or she, though I somehow wanted a he—was too small to kick. I laughed again, and again felt the arctic clasp of the sea like a sheath of glittering and fathomless deeps around me. I shouted again—that pagan, wild shout which the wind dispersed and which only Footit heard and understood.

I had been floating on my back, my long body rosy from the chilly kisses of the sea. Now I straightened, jackknifed, and thrust down my legs to tread water. Surely I was out too deep to touch bottom. I wriggled my toes, flexed my arches, trying to get the feel and purchase of my unexpected support. It moved. O, heavens, what new thing was this? I was not standing on the bottom, I was standing on something incredibly rough, yet worn smooth as old church stone and—this was what frightened me—moving in slow, strong pulsations toward the beach. For a moment, I thought to dart aside and swim ashore rapidly on my own. Was it perhaps my lover dolphin who bore me now like some kind of amphibious platform toward land and the sojourners gathered there to watch? I heard a great gasp of air as though through thorny nostrils, perhaps a gigantic beak, as my transport reached the shallows and surfaced, with me standing atop him, like a majorette on a football-game float.

I caught the astonishment in the eyes of my friends—and laughter in the face of Sweeley Leech—a full moment before I looked down and saw this enormous, dark creature who had become (I felt it was not the first time) my beast of burden.

It was a turtle: venerable, ancient, clustered with barnacles and missing one eye. His vast, doming carapace was a full thirty square feet of carvings—incredible and deep graffiti: it seemed that some of them were hundreds of years old. O, I remembered the custom of young country lovers in old times, the cruel stunt of carving initials and love mottos and the date on the backs of great tortoises and then discovering them a half century later with these now-heartbreaking and wistful legends still legible and clear. As I say, there was not one, there were literally dozens, perhaps hundreds, of the names and dates of old lovers and old liaisons long gone to churchyard dust. Some of them were in Greek, some in what looked like Icelandic, and some—but it was the look of the creature that overwhelmed me. There was something ageless and venerable in the lumbering, lubberly waddle, as it bore me, still standing and posing, quite nude, and the sea on my nipples and in the pert V of my bush where a tiny seashell clung like a jewel, bore me toward father, and Fu Manchu, and Aubade, and my darling Adonis, and all the others.

The turtle groaned and came to rest a few feet before the Children of the Remnant, who stood watching in wonder and expectation.

# T✦W✦E✦N✦T✦Y
## F✦O✦U✦R

An Empty Book is like an Infant's Soul, in which any Thing may be Written. It is capable of all Things but containeth Nothing. I have a Mind to fill this with Profitable Wonders. And since Love made you to put it into my Hands I will fit it with those Truths you Love, without Knowing them . . .
—Traherne, *First Century* (1690)

The wind blew. Like dark, lacy leaves, shadows seemed to be blown about by it. The great, weathered tavern sign flapped and spoke like the wing of a toy bird. The solar nimbus of the impending purple cloudbank blazed its golden fringe all down heaven, clean to the remote Bermuda's riding. Quite visible to all of us, quite devoid of shyness, a dozen sea-fairies, their little faces fawny and sunburned with summer, crept out from the high grass clustered in clumps about the rolling dunes. Here and there these little tufty wildernesses blazed with the blue flames of autumn asters.

Then, astonishingly, it cleared its throat. It coughed twice, like a bashful substitute Rotary speaker.

At that instant, the thunderhead parted and a single ray of radiant yellow light descended like God's own klieg, illuminating in vivid relief the astonishing carving and historiation of the great horn carapace in our midst. One almost suspected TRUCAD shtick, save that there was an expression of almost childlike sadness in the seabeast's huge amber eyes. O, those eyes!—one could read aeons in them. What envisioned memories they must have held of myriad maritime marvels: sunken Atlantises, Cornish wrecks and Malay typhoons, Balkan pirates and Pribilof sealers, Tasmanian tidal waves and Timor monsoons, black pearls beyond price and the fathomfallen garbage of piled, fathomless centuries. O, surely this giant from the deeps was incredibly old! He was like a great, carved netsuke of time-darkened ivory in whom a million untutored artisans had graven their diaries of shameless, joyful amour!

And then, with an accent which somehow suggested a Sir Laurence Olivier who had gone to an English public school, the turtle spoke:

My left eye, he said a little wearily. There's something in it—a bit of oyster shell, I would guess. Will one of you be kind enough to remove it?

Lindy was the first to his side: her frail, sunken little figure crouched valiantly beside the creature's head, while with a steady, clawlike little hand she gingerly removed the object.

Thank you, said the turtle, turning to stare at the offending object. Feh, he said. Not oyster shell at all. A Cuban cigar butt— tossed in my face from a Soviet whaling ship off Baffin Island last night. Thank you.

He fell silent then, musing, and quite relaxed, as if he had come a really long way and was now totally enjoying the respite.

All the while, I dressed slowly, watching and listening with the others.

After this brief exchange between the turtle and Lindy, I would have given anything for a Polaroid to catch the expression on the face of Uncle Mooncob. He stood up so violently his wig danced off his shoulders and fell to the sand. He stood a moment, staring with mindboggled eyes, and then darted forward.

It's a trick. A talking turtle. I tell you, it's one of TRUCAD's new electronic detection devices.

And he began to race around the poor big beast, rapping on its shell with his fists, and kneeling to lift a scaly dewlap, under the shell at the shoulder, and running round to stare up the poor thing's tiny asshole.

Here. Here, he cried. I've found it. The antenna.

Let go. Stop groping me. That's my cock, you ass-wipe! cried the turtle, squirming inside his enormous fortress.

Uncle fell back, his face as pale as buttermilk and his mouth working soundlessly. He sank into the sand in yoga position number eight and subsided into silence.

Now will all of you stop suspecting me? said the creature in a reasoning voice. I am real. I am a turtle. I was once a man—I am now a turtle. And I have traveled more than nineteen centuries toward this place, this moment, and to one of you.

A faint smile (I swear it!) crossed his almost lipless beak.

I am not a mock turtle, he said. Though, when I was a man, I fear I did considerable mocking.

He sighed, and O, it was the forlornest sigh: a sigh that I added to my vast collection of best-remembered sighs.

Nineteen centuries coming to you—and always by sea—nineteen hundred years of wandering the world's wide waters, waiting, waiting, for the moment, the signal, to come ashore—at what point in either latitude or longitude I knew not—and give one of you—

Lindy was still crouched, haggard and wan beside the seabeast's face, but her dear, dark eyes blazed pinpoints of excitement.

I know, she gasped. You have come with the Sign.

Why, yes. How did you guess? That takes half the fun away—I had so hoped to surprise you.

But he recovered nicely and continued to let his huge, luminous eyes wander first to one, then to another of us. O, I felt that if he could have clasped them together, he would now be wringing his great flippers in supplication! Again he sighed, but the wind came buckdancing in and whipped the fringes off the sound.

Nineteen hundred years ago, he said, I was a mortal man. A man with chances. A man with a future such as perhaps not twelve men in human history have held in their grasp. And I—I blew it!

Ten minutes till the hot winds of TRUCAD come blowing down

your necks! bellowed Uncle Mooncob. And for the life of me I can't think what keeps me here.

Of course you can, said Aubade. Don't be an ass. You're dying to know who this poor, dear, charming creature was nineteen hundred years ago. We're all dying to know.

She confronted the turtle then. Well? Who *were* you?

Madame, don't be a silly hare trying to hurry this old tortoise. I shall get to that in a moment.

Nine minutes! This last from uncle, now pacing up and down and staring back and forth, first at his Honda and then at the great, spidery hulk of our chopper, down the dunes a way. But, like every man jack of us, he was listening, and listening with fascination.

We lived together, said the turtle. Three of us. In a boardinghouse. In a place called Weirton, West Virginia. And the three were the man you call Criste and myself and the woman named Maggie.

The fairies—a few of them—grew bold and stole down the cloud-shadowed sand and squatted closer, their tiny, flossy scarves blowing like milkweed in the rising wind.

It is commonly believed that I never personally knew Criste, said the turtle, that I discovered him years after they gave him the hot cross. But that's not so. I knew him well and I knew the woman Maggie, too—Lord, who didn't know her?—and I loved her with all my heart and soul and flesh.

He grew still, though the wind did not, and a page of the *Daily News* blew up the beach and caught on the dome of the great carved shell, hung a moment over an inscription of lovers who had died in an autumn of the third century, and then went soaring like a kite toward the north.

It is true—I loved her! came the sob. And I always shall.

Was there a sound of jets coming in on the wind that blew from Manhattan down the earth ways? No, I thought, there is still time—there must be time: this is all too marvelous to leave unfinished. And he did say he had come with the Sign. I looked at Lindy, who was sitting cross-legged now—limbs thin as sticks, and with great circles under her eyes, but full of that legendary last spurt of energy with which the dying are often blessed. She was quite close to the turtle—closer than any of us, in fact—and was staring at his neck beneath the wrinkled, leathery, and salt-encrusted chin.

And O, the woman Maggie loved me back, I guess, he went on lugubriously. She gave me all her favors, I mean, just as she gave them to many—all her favors, I should say, save one. And that was the soul-love she gave to the man Criste. I would have traded all her physical gifts for that one; I dreamed of it at night—myself and the woman Maggie living alone in the cranberry bogs and never so much as touching each other's bodies and her loving me with that deep, deathless love she gave to him. I knew in the end that if I continued to live there with them, I would end up hating the woman Maggie, or even worse, hating Criste himself, who did nothing to steal the lass away from me at all— Lord, he did nothing but be kind and happy, he and his mother and the others—you'd hear them coming sometimes at sundown in the town when all the white clay houses are like sliced halvah in the crepuscular glow, which is somehow always filled with sunmotes and flowers bobbing in the wind like the heads of little children. You'd hear them coming, laughing and joking and singing a mile off, and the little bells that jingled in the scarves of his mother, Mary, and her delicate, strong little harlot's face laughing from under her shawl of cheap, dyed polyester—her son was always changing the colors of his mother's clothes to please her, since they could afford no new ones. And for a night there'd be Joy—Joy abounding in the village—and nothing, nothing, I say, but totally loving kindness. And Maid Mary's tambourine a-chinking in the country dusks.

A tiny crab, awakened by dry air, stole to the edge of the lower shell of the turtle and fell to the sand and scuttled off grumpily toward the distant breakers.

And then he seemed again to smile as he remembered that time, that place in Time and Space.

Love! It was everywhere that little band of holy fools and sacred clowns would venture. I remember something Criste said one day. It was in the spring and the new lambs were frolicking like little white hobbyhorses on the hillside and the sun was so golden that it seemed always as if the air were filled with some fragrant and luminous pollen. The bells in her clothes and her tambourine—I can hear them yet! And the campfire sweetness of the little songs she sang for us at night! O, she was a mother-lover to the world, you see.

Who were you? This soft, enraptured whisper from Madame Jonathan.

But the tortoise would not be hurried, not a bit of it. After they gave Criste the hot cross—well, I think you can guess what happened. The woman Maggie went away. In grief, I think. Though I never saw her after that. And I knew if I continued loving her memory—a memory, mind you, does not warm one's feet on cold Ohio River nights—if I did not, in fact, turn to hating her memory, I should go mad. Perhaps I did go mad. I heard—centuries later—a line of poetry from a sailor reading aloud on the forecastle of a British merchantman bound, I think, for Valparaíso or some such strange and lonely port down the trades and beyond.

Recite the line, please, asked Dorcas softly.

Again the turtle made a sound, and it was half a sob and half another clearing of his throat. "O, do not go—for I shall hate all women so when thou art gone."

He shed an oily tear, which Lindy, with a little gasp of pure empathy, reached up and dashed tenderly away with her Kleenex.

And now came a groan.

After the woman was gone I hated all women, you see, he said. I had to hate them or go mad with longing. And all that hate became entangled with all that love. And I went forth and preached a strange, strange, twisted version of Criste's words. Giving the multitudes everything, you see, but the most important thing of all, Loving Kindness. And Joy. These are the only two virtues that matter. Joy and Loving Kindness. All the rest spring out of these—but I had forgotten that. I had forgotten the nights with Criste and his mother, Marion (we called her that often), and Marthy and her brother, Laz, and Jack and Pete and Matt and good old Luke, who took care of us for nothing when one of us was sick. I had forgotten, as I say, those nights under enormous spring moons that hung in the chestnut trees and got entangled in the hair of river willows, like huge, costly melons—aching with love and singing till daylight with Joy and jokes and little traded wisdoms. We shared what food we had—an occasional real luxury like a can of pork and beans or spaghetti and meatballs. We had so much— why should we complain about these austerities?

The great beast moved his flippers, as if in impatience, so that his shell shifted an inch or two. All I remember of the man Criste was his Love. It was everywhere; it was for everything—for his enemies, even. For beasts and fish and birds. O, he had been a wild, mischievous boy and had led a hard, rugged life.

Was he a virgin? asked Soleil, and I have since thought that the question was a little impertinent. I have always wondered, she added with a wistful smile.

I have said he was a man, said the turtle. And I have said he gave Joy. We were all lovers in that little band. And the thing that saved us was this: we were not organized. O, had I remembered that fact after Criste was gone, after the woman Maggie was gone—if only I had remembered that organization means the destruction of Love. And yet I organized. O, I organized the hell out of it all.

He chuckled bitterly. Have you ever heard a turtle chuckle bitterly? Then you know how it pierces the heart.

I taught Love for all of humanity save half of it—women, he said in a high, rather nervous voice, as if even now he were uneasy in the presence of the feminine. I taught that the body—God's body, mind you—was vile and ugly and filthy. I presented the imponderable enigma—the unthinkable lie—that God's supreme act of Joy and Creation in the flesh of mortal men and women could belong to Satan. O, it cannot. Except in Greed. Except in Jealousy. In possessiveness, which is the archstone of marriage. How could I have taught that Love, sweet Love, could ever be vile except in the buying and selling of women and children—in the business, the commerce of Love which the Church I launched ended up creating? O, he sighed, it is a vision so tinted with antiquity, so rainstained and seasoaked with the centuries of my wanderings. Yet, I see it all so vividly.

Footit had found the turtle's rather small and ragged tail by now and was sniffing curiously under it. What he sniffed seemed to reassure him, for he crawled up, as if in shelter from the approaching storm, in the shadow of the giant carapace.

I remember, of course, that Last Supper, the turtle said then—in the rather dreary Weirton Holiday Inn and Motor Lodge dining room. Yet, even more starkly etched in my memory is the Last Breakfast. At the boardinghouse. The morning they took dear Criste away. There were three of us—Criste, myself, and another man—a strange, gentle, loving man, who for years had let us all live rent-free in his humble yet altogether delightful little hostelry. Of course, we gave him a few pennies when we had them, but somehow he always managed to give them back to us. He was such a strange, dear soul—not as *old* a soul as Criste, but as loving, I swear, as Criste himself and capable of quite a few miracles of his own, Criste having kindly taught him the knack of them. I tell you, we all knew that in a short time—in a few thousand years, that is—this man would give off as much Criste Lite as Criste himself.

Here our giant friend gave a chuckle; he was now deeply involved in his own narrative. It is strange, though—he could do almost as many miracles as Criste and yet this didn't seem to satisfy him. He wanted to do more.

More? What do you mean, more? Aubade asked.

Why, he wanted to do sleight of hand. *Tricks.* He was always buying them. And trying them. And failing to bring them off. Mind you, here was a man who, like Criste, could heal the sick, give eyesight to the blind, repair the legs of the lame—who would within a millennium or two be able, like Criste, to raise the dead—and he wanted nothing more than to do childish tricks of legerdemain!

Somewhere back in the teak room a self-deprecating cough was heard. Footit shut his eyes and scrunched up lovingly under his big, cool, shady friend. Thunder muttered and quarreled down the latitudes and the clouds blazed with flickers and flashes like a gigantic lamp with a loose bulb.

Here, the tortoise continued, was a man who could walk on the water (another, different masculine cough was heard—a very anthem of modest embarrassment), a man who could touch a barren fig tree and it would come alive and sweet with fruit in the orchard light—who could, as I have said, perform miracles he had learned from the hands of our Lord, and yet he was always journeying afar to magic stores in Athens and Bethlehem and New Kensington and Pittsburgh to spend money on wooden eggs that never hatched their scarves out properly, and for top hats that never produced little rabbits. Criste would laugh till he would have to lie down and recover his breath in his mother Mary's great bed—a vast goosedown tick which filled one whole room and whose mysterious fragrance enchanted the whole house.

Four minutes! sobbed Uncle Mooncob.

Criste laughed a great deal, the turtle went on after he had craned his long neck and Lindy had dabbed away a tear. Which is only one of the erroneous pictures we—I—gave of him. A man of sorrows, indeed. A man of Joys, it should read. A man who was, if anything, a kind of holy clown. But then our error is more easily understood if you reflect on how serious the business of laughter is.

O, I can hear Criste and his mother and the rest of them coming to a town. It is nightfall. Beyond the Satanic Mills, there is a patch of the land sunsoaked and green in the dusk, a place where the stinking, foul factory fumes have not descended and despoiled the wild flowers. The evening is violet soon and shot through with shadows of rose and deepsea greens. Fireflies stagger along the meadows drinking the winy dark. Then, as the river wind cuts loose a sliver of moon and lets it fall upon the clouds which hurry down the sky as in a Dürer landscape—then, I say, one hears the sweet *chinkachink* of maid Mary's clangorous tambourine. And her sweet contralto laughing and singing, leading the rest. And then Criste's voice—and the voices of Marthy and Laz and Pete and Jack the Bap and Lukey Boy. Laughter and Joy was on its way to town, and the people all knew and were glad! All, I mean, except the money-lenders and the landlords! Hadn't the County Medical Society joined the hue and cry after poor Criste that very summer for heal-ing sick people too poor to pay their fees? Hadn't the National Op-tical Society raised hell with him for restoring sight to the blind? And the county morticians—men of unspeakable undertakings—hadn't they resented to their very shoe soles the corpse of Marthy's brother, Laz, which Criste had snatched away from them—and it already stinking, and yet he had made it live and sing and have sup-per with them that night? O, I tell you this Criste was so beautiful. When you kissed him, your mouth came away with a sweetness!

A few cold raindrops came flinging against our faces. They glit-tered on the great seabeast's corrugations.

The Last Supper? breathed Aubade, in a trance, as were we all. What was it really like?

In what respect? asked the turtle.

Well, Judas, said Aubade. I've always felt sorry for him. I think, in his shoes, I might have done the same. He was so—so human.

Don't feel sorry for him, said the turtle. His bad Karma was ex-piated within a century of Criste's death. Mine has endured for *nineteen* centuries! His betrayal of Criste was an act of the moment. Mine, the studied act of two thousand years.

He hesitated then, as if carefully choosing his words. You see, Criste's ultimate agony was not from his hot cross crucifixion. It was from my hotshot Church. It wasn't dying that killed him for two millennia. It was organizing him! Away from the Individual!

The wind stirred a fringe of dying sargasso weed on his back.

I try not to remember the Last Supper, he said. I try to remember the Last Breakfast.

The Last Breakfast, murmured Soleil. O, you were telling us of that.

Criste was there. And that incredible landlord of ours. And myself. Just the three of us. Of course, in the other rooms there were dozens of small children—Criste drew little children the way honey draws baby bears. They were always in his quarters. They loved his jokes and small tricks and miracles and his little gifts to them and the pretty colored pictures he was always drawing.

On sheets of ruled yellow pads, murmured Lindy. Right?

The turtle cocked his eye. He smiled. But *how* did you know? Yes! On ruled yellow paper! He was always drawing pictures for the children, and though the children always lost these drawings, one knew they would remember forever the beauty of them in every detail.

But the breakfast—tell us about the Last Breakfast.

It was after the Last Supper, of course—the next morning—and we were all three of us a little hung over. Actually, we were broke, too, and the breakfast itself consisted of some stale cherry pie and some apples and a big bottle of wine and a few plastic cups from the night before. We had snitched them out of the Holiday Inn dining room.

The children in the other rooms were all hungry and they were clamoring to Criste to feed them. He opened the door and let them in, and since the cherry pie was all eaten, he made a miracle and produced not only a dozen cherry pies for the kids but as many apples as would fill their small pockets. He was always saying his funny little graces before eating, not thanking God for, say, an egg, but thanking the little hen that laid it. Not thanking his heavenly Father for a hamburger—but thanking the God in the little murdered cow. O, sometimes his graces—as on that morning—were little poems like Herrick's or Stevenson's.

The wind fell and the sudden lapse of its soughing, sighing sound was a silence like sound itself—audible, almost palpable. Low against the sky, a V formation of supersonic TRUCAD warplanes drew white staffs of sad music against the purple, brawling thunderhead.

When the children's hunger had been satisfied, said the turtle, Criste scooped handfuls of clay out of a window box, shaped them into small birds, and clapped his hands. The birds took wing and, with their wild songs and beautiful colors, led the children's way into the other rooms again. We were alone: Criste, the landlord, and myself.

The landlord, murmured Lindy, as though in a trance, her finger lovingly tracing a great yellow wrinkle in the turtle's throat. The lovely landlord, yes. Yes. Go on. I think I know—but go on. Yes.

We were silent—the three of us—for a long while, said the turtle. There were things to be said that we could not say. Criste knew he was going to be betrayed—by me as much as by Judas or Pete. But then, as always, he was thinking ahead. That was when he took the beautiful carved jade stone out of his patched and dirty rucksack. It was about nine inches in diameter and had a small hole in the rim with a gold chain looped through it. It was carved intricately with what appeared to be myriad, complex, and concentric circles, some of them interconnected. I tell you it was so very beautiful that I gasped when Criste handed it to the landlord, that strange and beautiful man, who stared at it a moment and then handed it back.

"Lordy, it is too beautiful," he said. "I couldn't accept it."

"You must accept it," said Criste, "for it is a Sign. It is the Sign which you shall carry into the misty centuries ahead. A Sign which will point a way to the words of mine, which by then shall be drowned out by hymns and hallelujahs."

And in the pearl-tinted light of morning which blew through the pantry curtains, he pointed to the words engraved on the bevel edge of the great jade carving: *Love Will Find a Way*. "That," said Criste, "is the name of the stone. Take this stone, Sweeley Leech, and keep it through your every life until the New Epoch has come.

And then give it to the one who can read it and restore the Criste Lite to man."

"But Lordy," said Sweeley Leech to Criste, "will it take two thousand years before people know you? What about now?"

"For me there is no Now," said Criste sadly. "I am about to be organized. 'Little children, love one another' is not loud enough to be heard above the stamping feet of 'Onward, Christian Soldiers.' Wars will be fought in my name, martyrs burned and hanged and electrocuted. But someday, some quiet evening—perhaps near this place—someone will look at this stone and, in truth, Love will then find a way, my dear."

Sweeley took the stone? gasped Lindy.

No, said the turtle. A moment later the police came and broke up that Last Breakfast. They killed Sweeley Leech and dragged Criste away to his own death on the county cross. I hid under the bed, and when I crawled out an hour later, I saw the stone called Love Will Find a Way on the small, food-littered table. I knew then that the task of delivering that sacred stone had fallen upon my shoulders. I picked it up and went out into the lonely morning street. The sun was dimmed by factory fumes, and police Klaxons were yodeling mournfully. There was another sound, too—the *chinkachink* of a tambourine—maid Mary's invariable announcement. I stood watching, waiting, staring at a certain street corner by the poolroom, as the sound of the tambourine grew louder. Perhaps he was free. Maybe they had let him go to wend his wondrous way beside his mother through the world's mean streets. But no. The person with the tambourine came around the corner then—a most dull and humdrum-looking man, portly and balding, with a bowler hat and a suit as black as an undertaker's, and he was simply beaming over something and banging the tambourine with all his might and main.

The turtle sighed. He flexed his worn talons. I went on through the years from that time, that place, he said. Keeping the stone called Love Will Find a Way always with me, on the golden chain around my neck. It was there that night on the National Pike when the cops beheaded me. They buried it with me—seeing no great value in it except the gold chain, which they stole and replaced with one of bronze links. No one could read it, riddle it, fathom its cipher—it was deemed worthless. And it helped weight down my body, which they threw into the river. And it was in the river that I became a turtle, with a big load round my neck and the destiny of centuries up ahead somewhere.

He moved his great eyes now, like amber beads around some Christina Rossetti's throat, from one to the other of us.

You may well smile at my ignominy. I mean, here I was a man who had turned his back on the pleasures of the flesh—God's flesh, mind you—turned his back on them, and therefore on God; and had been reincarnated into a turtle—a turtle, moreover, for centuries to come (almost twenty, if I may again remind you). And what happened to this turtle? God is the greatest of Wits, you know. It was from God that Criste inherited his absolutely peerless sense of humor. What happened to this turtle, for example, on soft Aegean nights when he swam in, exhausted, from the Mediterranean, and before that, the Bay of Fundy or the Malacca Strait? What happened as he dragged himself, groaning, into a shoal or small inlet along those romantic beaches? Well, what do you suppose happened, what with young lovers frolicking and—yes, I may as well say it—fucking adoringly along the rose-scented harbor? They took the turtle and carved immortal odes to their love on his own poor horny back. Often they would not be satisfied with their names and the dates but would inscribe painfully (of course it hurt, you fools) intimate details of their copulations. You will observe I am a walking men's-room wall of obscene graffiti. But you know?—I don't mind. O, I shall be another dish of tea in my next incarnation. Which I hope you will be instrumental in bringing to pass. By taking from me this great jade disc, this wheel of destiny, this veritable millstone of great Hamlet, and divining its mythos— its meaning to the human heart. The heart—as perhaps Sweeley in there will affirm—of only one among your midst. The one who understands this holy Sign!

You tell the tale beautifully, old buddy, said Sweeley Leech, stepping out from the tavern entrance now.

Thank you, Swee, said the turtle, but though I speak with the tongues of men and angels and have not Love—

I don't think Lindy would have moved aside for any other mortal but father just then. And she watched, intent, as he felt gently among the folds and creases and considerable turtle blubber of the great mottled neck for the jade piece. It was, not surprisingly, a long search; the stone was deeply embedded and the poor soul groaned several times during father's probing. At length, father grunted. I think this is it, he said.

We all bent close (though none so close as Lindy) and peered. The bronze chain had long since corroded, perhaps having been absorbed into the poor seabeast's system. The stone was virgin, intact, incredibly beautiful. It looked rather like a target, with literally dozens of concentric rings. Lindy cried out when someone quickly rose, the lovely stone in hand, and it passed from her sight.

Sounding brass! And tinkling cymbals! the poor turtle was declaiming in a sad voice. I am as sounding brass! And tinkling cymbals! Love, O Love—come back to me!

The rain came limping along the rays of sea light: a rain that one moment hobbled like a leper in white sheets, then seemed to stride forward for a second, then stumbled again, splashing wet droplets which pitted the sand, all the while with its shoulder jammed down into the wind's salty crutch. What was left of the blue of the sky ran fleeing from the purple, hulking cumulus of the lightscattering storm. The gulls had gone mad; in a joyous, panicked ballet of wing and flashing eye they labored up the livid air and turned on it to fall like black plummets and skim out in safety on the shimmery summits of the very spindrift and spume of the ever-aspiring waves.

And the great—and holy—turtle had turned now, slowly, laboriously, cumbersomely, absurdly, to make his lugubrious way back to the sea, leaving a swath behind him in the wet sand and scattered kelp and shells.

We all drew back from the wind and wet into the teak room and stood watching the scene through windows all awash.

Helpless we stood as there appeared a small blot upon the horizon; a shape very much like a figure eight soon formed and then, soundlessly, enlarged still more till we could make out the pilot's helmet under the flashing cowl of one of the latest TRUCAD fighters. It came skipping along the skies above the beach a mile or so upwind like a childflung Frisbee, though far faster, skimming along that nadir of nacreous light which remained between seascape and storm.

Against every Evil, the crawling turtle's voice reverberated among the rains, Love will find a way! O, Love *will* find its way!

The plane was gone in an instant, the tiny shape of it fading into the mists above Long Island and beyond. Like a tiny gnat it could be seen circling then, a hard arc against the troubled clouds, and then it descended close to the sea again and headed back, with something mean and intrusive about the very way it skimmed below the light.

The turtle was almost to the breakers, a few meters from where our chopper rested.

It had laid a great, flat jewel of an egg and was returning, or perhaps it should be said moving forward toward its fresh destiny, its happier Karma, the poor darling passing into a fresh-earned life of incarnation. Though its sufferings were not over.

Love will find a way! the voice seemed to thunder now—yet not a harsh voice: it was more of a prayer than a command. O, my dearies, love must find her way! She must, I say! I shall hold her back no longer!

The attack plane, approaching us again at about thrice the speed of sound, could not yet be heard as it ducked and swooped from dune to dune.

Forgive me! O, forgive me! cried the voice of the turtle. "O sweet and lovely lady be good—O lady be good to me!"

Had he, too, seen the plane, gleaming with hate like a twisting bullet set in invisible though hard trajectory toward that great turtle heart? Had he seen it and gone mad with fright?

"I'm just a lonesome babe in the wood—O lady be good to me." O, I tell you, Love will find a way, my dearies. I shall stake my life on that!

The plane flashed up from behind a dune now, as though it had been hiding motionless there, and bore down on the hapless turtle. From the blunt, Duralumin edge of the short wings came a flaming ejaculation of machine-gun fire. The V of concentrated fire was geometric horror as the bullets struck the poor, laboring carapace. O, only a few meters more and he would have gained the safety of the sea! But in a morning that had had its share of wonders, fresh ones were afoot. The plane was, of course, gone in a split second, its mission—to do some harm, to show some force, to let us know that TRUCAD now had us under its thumb—that mission accomplished. The plane faded amid cascades of ever-diminishing thunder.

The bullets had struck the hard, carved reticulations of the big shell as the chalked ferrule of a pool cue strikes the ball. The impact drove the massive creature up on end, and more bullets struck and set it spinning. The spin gained momentum, increasing long after the plane had disappeared from sight. It whirled upon the hard, wet sand like a child's great spinning top—a giant child, albeit: a child-god toying with a plaything by the sea. The skies were in the very greatest of ferment and movement. Down the horizon fled great, bloody rags of the burst thunderhead, and the sun came hemorrhaging through. The great thing spun more quickly. It was only a blur now in the rain; it turned like the very millstone of the stars! Mauve? Lavender? Apricot? What color can you conjure? Name it, and it shone in that sky just then. And the whirling top (clearly no longer a turtle) was growing luminous, eerily phosphorescent, as though the speed of its turning had caused it to burst, like a giant Catherine wheel, into flame.

As we stood on the sand in prayerful *témoignage,* the great, glowing, spinning thing—as blazing now as full moonshine—began to grow smaller, and at the same time brighter, until it was no more than four feet high. It came to an absolute standstill. We stared at what remained.

What is it? murmured poor Mère de Cézanne a little myopically. It looks rather like that little cherry tree dear Vincent painted once in Arles.

It does rather look like his cherry tree, I said, but it isn't cherry. It's a redbud. And I'll swear it is from my Gallimaufry.

It's a miracle, whispered Dorcas Anemone in flat, quiet wonder. This is October. They never bloom in October. Look. Look, the blossoms are like red, red fire.

The little tree literally blazed with light—an incandescent glow of its unseasonable fruition, like the flush of a great red raspberry on a plate of Christmas snow—and then from out this profusion of scarlet flowers came the strangest, the most beautiful, and the whitest raven I have ever seen.

O, Love did find a way! Love did! cried Soleil.

Almost as in an old De Mille, the black, bleak skies parted then to let the sun fletch goldenly down upon the little tree, spraying it with soft beams of luminous beatitude. The white bird cocked its dark eye for a moment and then—I swear it—winked. And then, in a voice utterly dissimilar to the turtle's rather arch dialect, it spoke to us:

> Oyster, oyster, in your forest,
> And little hermit named Clitoris,
> Why not plan a pleasant outing
> 'Stead of hiding in there—pouting?

An appreciative titter, both male and female, went round. The bird cleared its throat like a tiny bell struck once:

> Oyster, in your flowery thicket,
> Don't you think you're really wicked
> To hide your pearl from common view
> While playing sticky peek-a-boo?
> Oyster, oyster, burning bright—
> Do come out and play tonight!

And with this pleasantly pithy and rather nicely primitive prosody, the white bird flapped its wings, its white feathers almost iridescent with pearly tints. I say—*Dey's all debbils*! it proclaimed hoarsely, like a tipsy parakeet.

And leaving us thus with Sweeley Leech's own and often enigmatic pronouncement, the white bird leaped into the luminous air and spread its wings to go laboring up the now-doldrumstill sky and was off into the very sun.

At that very touching moment, as if in contrived bathos, uncle came running toward us from the helicopter, his face alight with evil pleasure.

That plane, he said, was here to confirm, that's all. Confirm that Sweeley is here. They knew it, but they had to see for themselves. Now they're sure. And in moments they'll be back—in force. You'll see. And they'll take Sweeley Leech. O, yes. It's in the stars. And they'll take you, too, all you poor slobs—slobs, I say, who have stood here for the past ten minutes being sucked in by my cornball brother's light show and ventriloquism and cheap legerdemain.

O, do hush, uncle!

I will not, Fifi. In five minutes—perhaps ten, if you're lucky—a half-dozen copters will be here. With the very cream of the TRU-CAD police arm.

He smirked, and an earring fell off. Have you figured how you're going to get out of this one, you old *soi-disant* archangel?

Sweeley looked at him, saying nothing, seeming (as he always did in crises) to be thinking elsewhere, elsething.

We have the copter there, observed Aubade with a scornful toss of her chin.

But you don't.

We don't? squeaked Mère de Cézanne, cupping her fingers against the tiny seashell of her ancient ear beneath her perfumed black lace veil. But there it is, my dear.

Yes, there it is, echoed uncle maddeningly. O, there it is, all right.

And no bullet touched it, said Adonis, walking forward, sniffing the air, for the gasoline vapors were strong now.

One bullet touched it, said uncle, smirking, and yet eyeing the horizon fearfully for the return of the planes.

One touched it. It punctured both gas reservoirs.

Adonis examined the chopper gloomily. It's true, he said. They're quite empty.

A pretty cul-de-sac we were in—for sure! For even as Adonis finished speaking we could see—low specks skimming the horizon toward Manhattan—the shape of the approaching TRUCAD copters!

# T✦W✦E✦N✦T✦Y
# F✦I✦V✦E

I don't think that one of the Children of the Remnant there on Montauk that strange morning, and at that critical moment, would have, given the choice, put his own safety ahead of finding the Criste Lite. I know this is so. As for myself, keeping my eyes lowered and away from those infernal wasplike birds which now circled the sky above the old tavern—as for me, I was trying to put my own priorities in order. Surely the issue now was to discover which one among us would be the one to interpret the Sign which both Sweeley and dear Fu had both assured us was already somewhere within our grasp. That seemed the most important thing just now. But where was the Time to achieve this? Surely the damned TRUCAD choppers would be landing shortly and sinister black figures would be approaching over the softlit morning dunes.

Whose life was endangered here? All our lives surely—and surely all our freedoms, for, were we captured, it would certainly mean trial and imprisonment in a TRUCAD concentration camp.

Whose life, then? Sweeley's? Lindy's? O, Criste, come to me now and enlighten my poor shadowed spirit. Show me whose life must be saved in these next few moments of this mad autumn morning.

If only we had a quarter hour's more time. Surely the Chosen One would discern the true features of that Sign for which each of us was praying at that instant.

I think we should go up to the shelter of the teak room, said Fu Manchu, and Sweeley agreed.

In a moment we were there—all of us, save one—staring at one another's faces intently, searching, praying, hoping that, at any instant, some one among those dear faces would light up with inspiration and announce the name of the Sign which would take us wherever we needed to go to complete the colors of the sacred runes.

Aubade strayed apart from us and wandered over to a white-curtained window and stood staring out at the figure of the one who had stayed behind within view of the choppers.

If only there were trees, she murmured, her legs whirring softly in the hush. O, I do so mistrust treeless spaces.

Me, too, said my darling Dorcas. I love trees. They're so—so deciduous.

Even the smallest tree would help, sighed Aubade. Even that little redbud we had a few moments ago. It would give him *some* shelter.

She was speaking, of course, of the one who had tarried on the beach by the very rim of the sea, squatting now like a Buddha with the tide lapping at his knees—my adored father, Sweeley Leech.

Why didn't he come with us? asked Mère de Cézanne.

Lindy said the strangest thing in reply. He is about his Father's business—that's why, dear.

Then she glanced again at the pale jade wheel in her fingers, handling it slowly and almost (for her) sensuously. There was the smallest of smiles playing about her face, which, until that moment, had appeared wan and drawn and ill—like a child's watercolor that has been left out in the rain.

I turned and moved recklessly out the door and down the beach toward father.

I turned and looked back once at the inn. Lindy was standing in the doorway watching me, the stone called Love Will Find a Way still in her hands. What was the new fire I sensed in her sick, sick eyes?

The thin spray of spindrift lashed me across the mouth with a salty flame as I smiled down at Sweeley Leech.

Sweeley, love, I said, if ever there was a time for one of your miracles, it is now.

I agree, he said, fetching something that glinted blue from out of his pocket. Perhaps just a little miracle—to give you all the Time you need.

Father, sometimes I don't understand you.

What, love? Speak up. The choppers are so noisy.

You! I cried. Sometimes you just infuriate me, Sweeley Leech.

O, I know I do. But tell me why, love.

Because you could save everything—but it would take more than one miracle.

One is all I can manage just now, he said, one to give you all the Time you need.

Father, I know that finding the rest of the Criste Lite is more important than our lives just now.

Still, the finding of the Criste Lite depends on your lives, he said. More certainly than on my own.

Don't say that, Sweeley Leech.

I must. I shall be going from you soon—well, sooner or later, eh? That can't be stopped. All I can do for you now is to alter a little the arrangements of Time and Space in this place. To give you the Time you need.

Why can't you just—just whisk us all away from this awful island? I cried.

I shall, he said, but it takes time. Lovey, even miracles need a little working at.

O, I suppose. But what are you doing? What is that little thing in your hand?

He didn't answer. He lifted the object to his lips—it was a small, cheap jew's harp—and pressed the tines to his teeth and began twanging away amid the racket of the still-circling choppers.

The voice from above, from the bullhorn in the lead chopper, was like the harsh voice of a god:

*Sweeley Leech, surrender. Only you will be taken prisoner. Your*

*disciples shall be allowed to go free. Give up your freedom now, Swee-*
*ley Leech, and spare your friends. It will not be the same if we have to*
*land and there is a fight.*

Father, do you hear them? O, father, don't listen to them. We're
all in this.

He didn't answer. He kept his gaze fixed queerly on the sea line,
but cast flickering little glances into the piled skies beyond it, his
face alive and excited above the grimace and the twanging jew's
harp, his eyes watching as if *for* something.

I waited.

I glanced again toward the tavern doorway. Lindy had been replaced by Uncle Mooncob. Uncle looked like a stale wedding cake
in his battered drag. I watched as he glanced toward the skies and
then, throwing up his hands in despair, scuttled back into the deeps
of the teak room.

I had the sense to let Sweeley Leech alone. His finger was a pale,
thin blur as it struck the leaping tongue of the jew's harp at his
teeth. Then something made me glance toward the sea. Was the
*Anna Zelinski* returning? Was that the pale, sunlit cloud I glimpsed
now upon the tangy air above the living sea? Still, I waited.

A vision of Lindy came stabbing back into my receptors. I remembered something Sweeley had said once: Only when the love
affair between body and soul is ended can cancer begin.

*Sweeley Leech,* brayed the bullhorn. *This is your last warning.*
*Give yourself up. Bring your followers—unarmed—into the light.*

The yellow cloud was closer now, and then with a sound of rushing which was no louder than the chopper sound but which somehow muffled it, it was everywhere above us. A cloak of yellow mist
was slowly gathering between us and the invaders! O, Sweeley, I
knew you'd miracle up something to save us!

Sweeley smiled and pocketed the tiny jew's harp. He looked at
the sky, at the shapes of the helicopters which were growing ever
more obscure beyond the cloak of gold which was enveloping the
beach.

In a moment, he said, escape will be possible.

But, father, I exclaimed, it's not just a question of going somewhere—it's a matter of going to where we can find the missing
colors.

That, too, he said, will come to pass.

431

O, Swee, you do madden me at times, I said. I sometimes think you know how all this is going to end.

I do, he said.

Can't you change it? I cried. A moment ago you were speaking of—of leaving us. Can't you change that?

It would spoil things, he said, if I did. Darling, didn't you ever hear the words: "It is Written"?

I stared upward into the golden shimmer of the cloud, shading my eyes with my fingers, trying to distinguish the particles which composed it. Then something bright-yellow and very tiny fell to the sand at my feet and lay there kicking before it regained its footing and again was aloft, spiraling up past my nose and into the chrys-. elephantine heights. I had had time to distinguish its shape—it was an elfin winged creature of gossamer frailty called a Nix, or water sprite. I strained my eyes into a golden cloud of them above as they inexorably crept between us and the choppers—myriads of them: tiny golden sprites swarming across the visible skyscape.

Sweeley got to his feet, stretched his stiff limbs, yawned, and then turned and moved back up toward the tavern. I followed, a little breathless, I'm afraid, and with the purest astonishment. The cloak of golden Nix Mist was between us and the enemy—that was Sweeley's latest miracle and really so very much more practical than moving a small mountain at a Presbyterian baptism.

Father, I said, as the sound of the choppers grew faint beyond the muffling protectors, can't the choppers get through them?

Do you see them?

I know—but they seem so frail.

The frail are always the strongest.

How much time do we have? Will they stay there in the air between us and the helicopters?

For a while, he said, sighing, as we reached the great flagstone stoop of the Walt Whitman. Twenty, maybe thirty minutes. That's the only problem with Nixes. They're creatures of whim and mood, and the whim or mood seldom lasts longer than thirty minutes. While they are around and above us they provide a shield stronger than the strongest stone or steel. I think these will go the distance. They seem in especially lively spirits.

I looked up and around. The air was yellow and iridescent as if it were filled with tiny flakes of pearl. Now and then one of the creatures would disengage itself from the mad, whirling dance of the others and fall to the sand, exhausted and fluttering with Joy. The air smelled faintly of ozone—mingled, of course, with the whispered scent of the sea, which was now quite invisible.

Have we Time, father? I asked Sweeley Leech. Is it, as you say, "Written" that we have Time to find the Sign and get away to wherever the Sign may lead us? Is it, father?

He looked at me with great tenderness and something of a piercing yearning to make me understand.

I mean, I said, I mean, all of this—

I waved my fingers round our little universe: that lonely stretch of Long Island sand.

—all of this, I said lamely. It seems like a kind of game.

Of course it's a game, said Sweeley Leech. And like all true games, it is sacred and has become, at last, a sacrament.

But what must we do, father?

That will become known, he said. Remember only this: That so long as we each hold faithfully to our pursuit of—

—the Criste Lite, I murmured. Yes.

Yes, he said. So long as we each hold faithfully to our pursuit of that, we are safe—we are the Chosen, the Adorned Ones. But remember: the moment we falter and seek after our own personal safety, we are lost.

He reached up and touched my cheek with his fingers.

I listened to the seawind and the whir of the tiny winged Nixes—like the tintinnabulation of ten thousand miniature wind chimes.

Phase by phase, said Sweeley Leech, we pass from Fear through Courage and out into the clear, clean light of Joy.

Then he turned and pushed ahead of me into the amber deeps of the teak room.

I was famished again. I wasn't surprised. You know how it is after Chinese miracle loaves and fishes by the sea—an hour after the miracle, you're hungry again.

Uncle confronted me for an instant and then, with a whimper of frustration, fell back into the gold shadows. His eyes, behind his mascara-smeared spectacles, looked like day-old oysters.

Footit passed beneath my legs—a silken blur—as he chased an errant Nix into the golden out-of-doors.

Uncle flounced forward, his face pressed defiantly up toward father's. He waved toward the golden windows, the golden doorway, the golden lights which fluttered ephemerally and lingered in our midst.

Sweeley, I swear I'd rather face TRUCAD than submit to your pagan magic, he said, adjusting his shoulder straps nervously.

Be still a moment, Moon, said father. We have a test before us. And there is little time.

He moved toward the circle of us who stood around the large table by the window. In the center of the table, glowing like a great eye, lay Love Will Find a Way.

There, said Sweeley Leech, is the Sign. It has come to us through centuries and aeons. And now it must fall to one of you—

He smiled as his blue eyes ranged the throng.

—one of you must tell us what the Sign means, he finished.

Madame Jonathan T. Bigod gathered her scintillating shawl around her pretty shoulders and stretched forth fingers to caress the corrugations in the jade wheel.

It is plain, she said. It is a map of the universe. One can even pick out the stars and planets.

Aubade whirred forward and pushed her own hand forth, brushing Madame Jonathan's hand aside.

Nonsense, she said. It is plainly a diagram—abstract, of course—of the human mind.

I kept my eyes on Lindy's face—held by it, fascinated by its wan, dark-eyed intensity. She said nothing as Mère de Cézanne creaked elegantly forth and laid her hand on the great jade stone.

It is plain enough to me, she said in her faint, quaking voice, that this is none of the things you have described.

We waited.

It is, on the other hand, she went on, equally plain what the stone does symbolize. It is a map of human progress.

And so each, in his or her turn—egos crackling—pressed forward with an interpretation of the stone's meaning.

Still, Lindy did not speak. Nor did she until every eye had fixed upon her expectantly and the silence was drawn out thin as a silver wire.

I make no claims to Divine Insight, she said in an astonishingly strong yet small voice, yet I think—in fact, I am quite certain—that this stone—

She let her eyes caress the whorled surface of the pale, liquescent jade. The queer yellow light from the canopy above the morn-wakened windows glinted on its corruscations. She moved her poor, thin, wasted finger to a small embossment.

Yes, she sighed, smiling. It is here. As I thought. As I remember. It has been so long, you know. I was only a child then. Yet I am sure.

What? chorused a trio of voices, though I remained hushed.

It is here, she said, pointing again to the raised place on the stone. The Lane of Spiders. And here is Montezuma's Folly. And here, most lovely of all, the very core of the thing, the very heart of it: the Chamber of Stars.

Swiftly I glanced at Sweeley Leech. His eyes were gleaming with pleasure; a faint smile played around his lips. He caught my stare and nodded.

Uncle Mooncob seemed all in motion, like a huge, spinning yo-yo. If all of you, he cried, would only stop this silly game and devote your thoughts to escape—I don't know what is happening out there in the sky, but I do know that in a matter of moments those choppers will land and the inn will be taken.

Hush, Moon! cried Loll, surprisingly, and cast him the most baleful of stares. Something holy is about to happen. Hark, now.

Lindy's face, despite the ravages of her sickness, had taken on a rosy glow of hope and expectation.

Yes, she said then, there can be no mistake. This stone is a map.

A map? exclaimed everyone except me.

A map, said Sweeley Leech softly.

A map of what? cried Adonis McQuestion in a tone which mildly irritated me.

Of Bebo, she said.

Of where?

Of what?

Of Bebo, said Lindy again, her eyes snapping with impatience, and looking a little irritated that she should have to repeat herself.

Outside, the tiny, faint bells trilled in the sweet tang of seawind. The clatter of the choppers was gone. Footit barked happily and nudged a fallen Nix with his nose until the creature recovered and spun off into the gold.

Bebo? someone asked again.

Bebo, said Fu Manchu uncertainly. Surely I've heard that name from your lips, Swee. Sometime—somewhere—I do remember.

Of course you remember, said father. Bebo.

But what is Bebo? asked Adonis McQuestion in a tone which irritated me even more.

It is the ancient Labyrinth, said Lindy, at Echo Point.

Her small claw of a hand was steady as it reached forth again and caressed the center of the design.

And there, she said, is where I—we—can find the missing colors of the Criste Lite.

The room seemed deathly silent, despite the sounds of fairy commotion that drifted through the curtains on the lips of the blowing breeze.

And where is Echo Point? asked Mère de Cézanne in a voice like the creak of old rockers on a well-worn chair.

It is, said Sweeley Leech, the place where you must immediately get to.

Your preposition, my dear Swee, said Fu Manchu solicitously, is dangling.

It is, my father amended, the place to which you must now get.

Bebo, said Madame Jonathan. Echo Point. Of course. The famous maze. At your home in West Virginia, Master.

O, don't call me that, exclaimed Sweeley Leech. The load is heavy enough without that onus.

The room, for all the golden light that streamed like yellow wine through the blowing curtains, was shadowed, and the shadows seemed to have lives of their own. From the paneled walls, in frames of crusted, flaking gold leaf, the oil portraits fixed their pigment eyes upon us. Again the curious sense that these faces, in this far and alien place, in this most strange of seaside taverns, were the faces of my ancestors. I could not escape this feeling.

Then that, said Lindy, is the place we must make for now. As father says.

But how? O, you fools. What is this game? cried Mooncob, moving now beyond the ring of us standing so intent around the pale, polished stone on the table. What is this insanity? We are none of us going anyplace—let alone West Virginia, let alone my poor brother's home. We are doomed, I tell you, doomed.

We are not doomed, said father quickly. We are in danger, but that is the very marrow of human experience—yes, danger is the thing that moves us forward. We are in danger. We must get to Echo Point. We must get to the heart of the Labyrinth and find the colors.

He paused.

When I say "we," he added with a slight twist of irony on his mouth—when I say "we," I mean *you*.

Lindy bent a little. I saw the flash of her even teeth in a grimace of pain. She poised a moment, eyes shut, and when she opened her eyes she saw the stone again, the goal, the end of the quest, and her face relaxed and took on color again. The spasm of pain passed quickly.

I seized father by the arms and searched his tranquil face.

What did you mean, Sweeley Leech, I said in a hushed voice, when you said that we and not you would be going there?

Beurre, he said a little sternly, this is no time for such questions. You have to do what you have to do. I have my own destiny. I must live this thing out to its end. But know that that End is only a fresh, clean Beginning.

But, father—!

Feef—Beurre, he said, don't try to unravel this thing yet. In time, it will all be clear to you. Help me now. I must consider how to get you back to the hills—by the dear, polluted river of streams—to the place where the golden string will at last be wrapped into a glittering ball. To the goal—that gate carved in Jerusalem's wall. It is up to me to think how such a return—such an escape from this place—will be possible.

The morning thrummed beyond the windows and the open door, creaking faintly, like an indignant bronze bird, upon its spear-shaped, handwrought hinges. I breathed in and, O, I could swear that I smelled the laburnum and lily of the valley which proliferated around the great maze's mouth.

Was it really so distant, so far? Was it actually hundreds of miles to the south? It did not seem so in that moment.

I looked at Lindy—at her confidence, her absolute assurance that she had correctly interpreted the Sign. I shared that certainty. Again I looked at father.

Uncle is right, father, I sighed. There isn't much Time. Can you—can you get us there?

I could, said Sweeley Leech, his brow furrowed with reservations. I could, if only—

He turned his gaze to the great time-machine which hulked and gleamed dustily in the shadows beneath a portrait which I would have sworn was a long-dead ancestor.

If only— he stammered softly, and his eyes saddened.

At that juncture Fu Manchu cleared his throat stentoriously. Without wishing to crowd you, Swee, he said, or to steal even a scintilla of your glory in this moment—

There is no glory yet, Manny, said father. Not yet, I fear. You see, we lack one thing.

Perhaps, said the great Chinese, I should take over.

Slowly, father's eyes rose to meet the slanted jet eyes of his friend. Take over? Lord, I wish you could. But you see—you can't. Not really.

But I can, said Fu Manchu. At least, I could.

No, said Sweeley Leech. I think this is up to me, Fu. Really I do.

I can handle it, said the mandarin a little huffily. Since you don't really seem—

It will come to me, snapped Sweeley Leech. Really, Manny, you are presumptuous. After all, it is my home that we—that you must get to.

And I can get us there, said Fu Manchu. I have at least five miracles in mind which would manage it in a matter of hours.

You don't have hours, you fools, cried uncle, pirouetting anxiously on the outer periphery of the circle we still formed round the great fruitwood table.

Hush, all of you! cried Madame Jonathan, rapping sharply on the polished tabletop with the great amethyst which she wore on her finger. Hush, I say. This is no moment for wrangling. This is the most dire and grave of emergencies.

She ranged us all with her grave gray eyes.

This is a holy moment—make no mistake about that, she went on in her attractive breathy voice. Perhaps the holiest of moments in any of our poor, small lives. Let us respect it. Now we are faced with a crisis. We need a miracle. And the dilemma seems to reside not in the fact that we have no miracle makers at hand but that we have a surfeit of them. Two wizards, two magicians, two holy men, if you will, of astonishing skill. Now who is to lead us into the Promised Land, my loves? Who? Shall it be Sweeley Leech or this venerable and greatly gifted Chinese guru? We must decide.

Decide? whispered Sweeley Leech in a kind of pale despair. You mean—I must *compete*? O, I loathe competing!

He left the table and skulked off toward the time-machine. Fu, old friend, I know the means of our escape, he said then in a clear, steady voice, his face dim in the shadows.

You do?

I do.

You're *sure* you do? asked the Chinese, somewhat pale.

I'm sure.

There was a silence.

Do *you*? asked father then. Do *you* know how to get us out of here?

Fu Manchu toyed with a silken tassel and then turned to the golden window. No, he said. It's got me completely stumped, Swee.

He still did not turn around to face us or father. Maybe you'd better manage this miracle, he said in a soft, defeated tone.

Master, called Aubade softly from the shadows by the lamplit table, what is the answer?

The answer, said Sweeley Leech a little gloomily, is only partly in our hands. That's where the miracle must come in to save us. We have almost everything we need—

Which is—?

Which is *this,* said father, his figure dim in the gloom of the far deeps of the teak room. This huge and ancient machine—this time-machine—this creation from the dim past whose name is Hither-thitherwhithershins.

Time-machine? snorted Adonis abominably. That old, battered thing? Really, sir!

Father ignored this interjection, though he was plainly unnerved by it.

Yes, time-machine, he said, as if to himself. And it could get us out of here, save for one thing—

Did the sound of the Nixes high on the piled, golden morning seem to be fading? I glanced at the hour and minute dial on the great wooden face of Hitherthitherwhithershins. Almost a half hour had elapsed.

Long ago, father was saying in his storyteller's voice, perhaps longer ago than even I can remember, this creation was the most miraculous of contraptions. It has, as you can see, a small curtained booth and a seat. Once—long ago—it was possible to seat a person in that booth, draw the curtain, make a few minor adjustments in the mechanism of the works, and Time did sudden, secret, magic things. In short, this great hulking piece of lovely woodwork and gears was able to whisk a person off into a time-bend which would deposit him anywhere on the earth or within the living universe to which the dials had been set.

Does it work so now? asked Aubade.

No.

Is it broken?

Not broken, said father, on his knees now and tinkering in the back of the great creature. But one thing is lacking—one part is missing: the element which the escapement of Time worked upon. It is gone—stolen perhaps by Barbary pirates or Indian Thugs.

What is that missing part, father? asked Lindy.

Was there a sound of golden flight in the wind now? Was there a noise as of myriad ephemeral wings of yellow gossamer and broken starshine fleeing seaward again? And the sound of the invading choppers—wasn't that becoming damnably audible again?

A great yellow diamond, said father in a clear, yet saddened, voice.

A *what*? I managed to gasp through my joy as I felt for my battered purse.

Its name, said Sweeley Leech, is Face-to-Face. It used to rest within the mechanism of this time-machine. It was its basic element. A great yellow diamond. And—if you care to come and see for yourself—someone has taken it.

I strode forward like the proudest pupil in the classroom. I held my handbag out to my father.

I think, I said, if you look in here, Swee, old lover, you will find the yellow stone called Face-to-Face.

He took the bag, looked inside among my smokes and love letters and makeup goodies. He smiled and shook his head and handed the bag back to me.

I darted my hand inside. I upended the purse, so that all my mischiefs and vanities poured out onto the great fruitwood table.

Someone has stolen it, I said.

For the great shining stone was truly gone.

I looked then into every face.

Strange, I said. It was here not an hour ago. I know, for I looked. It gives off a light. It was there. Now it is gone. And that can mean only one thing.

I know, said Lindy abruptly, brushing back a damp strand of soft dark hair from her livid, dark-eyed face.

Her eyes flashed fire.

It means, she said, that one of us in this room has taken it. And has it now.

Judging by the sounds from beyond the windows, we realized that the Nixes were tired of their game and were retiring again to the open sea. The air jangled tinnily, but the tinkle was growing fainter by the moment; once more the sound of the choppers beat the air as the great khaki-hued machines circled to settle on the beach and prepare for attack.

At that moment—oh, faithless one—my adored Adonis McQuestion snickered and stepped boldly forward. His hands had been in his pockets. Now they were no longer there. In one hand blazed the ambient yellow treasure called Face-to-Face. In the other, blue as a bottle fly, shone a .357 Magnum.

Now, he said, let us talk a little business, shall we?

I turned away with a groan from that distressing spectacle. O, damn! —I had been taken in again by the abominable Chaz.

Adonis—my true love—O, real Adonis McQuestion, where are you? I murmured half-aloud.

The sight of Hugh Downs running amok could not have shocked me as much as these repeated encounters with my darling's atrocious double. At what point had the switch occurred? It had surely been the real, the adorable Adonis back at Le Pet au Diable. But, of course, I would never know.

Now the hideous travesty of my love stood facing us with the critical diamond blazing in one hand and, in the other, a very authentic revolver. He smirked in a manner which suggested he had

441

watched too many TV thrillers, and dropped the flaming gem into the pocket of his loose Shetland jacket. His smirk widened to a cheap and insolent grin.

You—Sweeley Leech, he said, I don't much care whether we catch you or not. Religion and government really aren't my thing. No—

He patted the jacket pocket from which scintillating rays of light shone.

I have what I came after. And if you need it in your escape, that's just too bad. I've been after this prize for a long time. Face-to-Face is the prize of a lifetime.

I stared at father. O, it was maddening. He, too, was smiling, but this time the smile was golden. What was he smiling about? A glance out the window showed that one of the TRUCAD copters had landed on a dune and a dozen agents of as many nations were swarming out with laser guns to take their positions behind the sandy rise above the tavern. Surely he, too, could see these dreadful men inching toward the hospice which was our last and final refuge.

I have spoken a little of TRUCAD's brutalities. I haven't told all, for I am a lighthearted girl and hate cruelty. I haven't mentioned the *Daily News* exposé of an institution in Detroit—a doll hospital—which was taken over by TRUCAD doctors, nurses, and Ph.D.s. Dreadful as it sounds, it was there that cruel and painful experiments in the name of Science were conducted on well-loved but worn-out and eyeless teddy bears. Well, actually, does that sound any more absurd than most of the experiments done in the hallowed name of Medicine?

Chaz popped a mint into his mouth, and his smile returned.

So I guess it's so long, suckers, he said. I have what I want. I hope you get what you want—whatever it is. Criste? Okay, I hope you get him. Me—I'm staking my all on the luxuries of this world, not the next. So long, mom.

This last—addressed to Madame Jonathan T. Bigod—caused every head to turn. That lady had a curious light in her eye, a certain mocking set to her attractive bow-shaped mouth. She moved round the table and approached Chaz. Heavens, had even she been taken in by this counterfeit? I was dumbfounded that so sagacious a soul as Madame Jonathan could be so cheaply deceived. Where were her immemorially maternal instincts? Chaz was so patently a fake—even to me. And yet (I admitted) I, too, had been taken in. O, in whom could one believe in such devious times!

Chaz watched suspiciously as Madame Jonathan drew nearer.

What do you want, mother? he asked nervously. Remember— you're one of Them as far as I'm concerned.

Madame Jonathan's words came like a thunderclap.

Them! she sneered.

She turned and swung her hand in an arc, taking us all in.

THEM! she snorted even more contemptuously. I was never with Them. I am with you, my son. I am with my darling Adonis.

Chaz flushed a deep maroon and began to stutter confusedly as his mother put her arm around his waist and hugged him.

She leered at us.

Did you think I fell for your fakery, Sweeley Leech? she said. When the joys of this earth are so sweet, did you think I wanted to hear about paradise? Well, I—

You once believed in Sweeley Leech, Madame Jonathan T. Bigod! I shouted.

Perhaps I did, she said. Perhaps I, too, was once taken in. But I have more sense now. I have seen the clear light of that great diamond—

She patted Chaz's bulging tweed pocket.

—here in my beloved son Adonis's possession. Together we will share its fortunes—eh, baby? We will sell the great stone and travel!

She snickered like a true witch. Perhaps now and then, in memory of our old friend Sweeley Leech, we will drop a gold écu in the poor box. What say, Adonis? Will you share? Will you take me with you? I will be a great asset in your career in Crime. You know so little about your dear mother. I was one of the great counterfeiters of Europe during the nineteen-sixties. Before that I was a humble pickpocket—Big the Dip—famed from one end of Madagascar to the other, from Cairo to Cape Horn. O, Adonis—

Back, mother. I have no plans for a cut in this, snapped Chaz, pulling himself together and thrusting Madame Jonathan back into our midst at the table.

O, such shamed, guilty looks she gave us now!

Adonis—my own—! cried the once grand lady. How can you treat your mother this way?

Like this, cried Adonis, and, patting his blazing pocket once more, he darted out and could soon be seen running up to greet the approaching agents.

The silence in the room as we looked at Madame Jonathan T. Bigod was really quite ugly. You could feel it on your skin. I am sure she felt it on hers.

She smiled at us then.

Before you turn on me and tear me to bits, my dears, she said sweetly, will you show mercy by permitting me a moment's speech in my own behalf?

Well, I thought, she is a bold one. And she is making a rather good show of it.

May I, she purred, tell you an anecdote?

Aubade sighed. Mère de Cézanne teetered to the window and stood staring out at the ring of approaching men. In the distance, in the shadow of a small shed adjacent to the Walt Whitman, the despicable Chaz crouched for a moment, staring at the blazing treasure in his vile fingers, before dropping it back into his pocket and joining the rest.

I don't know why we should grant you this favor, Madame Jonathan, I said. You have lied to the others here as much as you have to me.

Wait, my dears, cried the lady, throwing up her fingers. A moment only. I beg it of you. I think you may learn something.

I was utterly confused. I remembered what Madame Jonathan had told me in her rose garden that morning in Philadelphia when she had first given me the stone. How it could not be stolen, sold, given away—except under the most stringent conditions. I had lost it twice. This would make the third time. Would it stay with me forever if I recovered it now? I doubted then. O, I doubted most sinfully, as I watched, through the blowing curtains, the figure of Chaz conferring with the TRUCAD leaders.

My anecdote—and I know we are pressed for time—she said, is about Wit. Or perhaps I should say Wits. Their use at the proper occasion. May I?

A murmur of uneasy assent was heard from most of us. Sweeley Leech watched with the broadest grin in the world on his beautiful face. O, father, really! You are sometimes as maddening to me as you are to Lindy. Or were. Lindy now was standing with her eyes fixed on father, an expression of absolute adoration on her face. I was in a maelstrom of misgivings!

One night in the nineteen-thirties, I was invited to dinner at the Governor's bungalow in Darjeeling, said Madame Jonathan in a leisurely voice, as if we had all the time in the world. It was a hot night and the jalousies were open and the air was filled with the most heavenly perfumes from the jungle. The moon was full. I remember that. Suddenly the Governor's wife did an astonishing thing. In a voice which would have wakened Buddha she addressed the native servant.

"Shari," she said in this stentorious, imperious tone, "go at once to the pantry and pour a saucer of rich cream. Return with it to the dining room and place it carefully beside those French doors."

Well, everyone winced at this apparent *cochonnerie* on the part of the elegant lady. But we waited. In a moment the sound of the servant's bare feet whispered on the rattan floor covering. She placed the saucer where she had been bidden. There was a pause—a pause which seemed to partake of the fear and suspense latent in that great full moon which hung like a ripe melon in the aloe outside the veranda. We could barely hear it at first—the faint sipping sound from the direction of the French doors. And then we saw it: the six-foot-long cobra which had been lured to the sweet saucer of cream—lured from the dinner table, where, for some moments, it had been coiled tightly around the Governor's wife's right leg. And now, harmless, it lapped the cream.

Nobody said anything.

The moral, said Madame Jonathan then, drawing what appeared to be a wedge of fire from a pocket, is that we must sometimes use our Wits to draw the Enemy away to other parts. Eh? What have I here?

I stared hard at the blazing object.

Face-to-Face, I said aloud, and then shook my head in confusion.

Don't be disturbed, my darlings, said that great lady. Once a dip, always a dip—eh? I brought it off rather well—don't you think? We now have the original and authentic stone. And my son's impostor—as if I had been for an instant deceived!—has the notorious Wolheim Forgery.

My laughter was the first to ring out in the silence. Wordless with shame that I had doubted her, I ran to Madame Jonathan and threw both arms around her.

Forgive me. O, please forgive me. I am so stupid, Madame Jonathan.

It's understandable. She sighed happily. I am really a superb actress. When I think what Truffaut could have done with me. But I'm an even more skilled pickpocket. Here, Sweeley Leech. Let Face-to-Face be restored to Hitherthitherwhithershins without a moment more of delay. Those buggers are getting closer by the minute!

In an instant Sweeley had the big stone in his hands and had gone to the back of the ancient time-machine and was stooping to peer within.

Yes, he was murmuring to himself, if I remember rightly, it goes here. And this small gear must be set so. And the pendulum set swinging. And this goes here—and so—and I think now we have it.

He stood up and came around the machine, beckoning with his arms.

Come, said Sweeley Leech. Each of you. One at a time. Take your seat in the little cabinet. Just so. Yes. You, Lindy. You with the jade wheel, and the wisdom to understand it. You must be first.

Lindy was smiling but pale when the old brocade of the curtain was drawn. Sweeley Leech touched a gear, tripped a lever, and we heard a faint sound as of rushing winds. He pulled back the curtain. The little embroidered cushion on the seat—it was empty.

I stood waiting my turn (I had determined to be last), with my fingers linked in those of my adorable Dorcas and the equally beloved Madame Jonathan.

The stone would have returned to you, said the latter, on its own. But it is a most capricious stone—it might have been hours before the restoration occurred. I could not wait. Look how close they are. Almost to the door's beleaguered threshold. O, what a perfectly divine adventure. I wish my littlest one were here.

Father was busy with the adjustments necessary for each projection.

When only Uncle Mooncob was left of the company of travelers, I faced him.

Uncle, I think this is it, as they say.

This is what?

It is the moment when you must choose. Do you go with Swee-ley Leech and us, or do you throw in your lot with those men who are already on the stones of the stoop?

He sighed.

Maybe, he said, I was with you all along.

He smiled and took his seat on the little brocade cushion. Swee-ley Leech drew the curtain. Again the tripped lever. Again that hollow, haunting sough as of the rush of autumn winds. Father drew the curtains. Uncle was no longer there.

I frowned, the sudden realization striking me that Sweeley Leech would be the last to enter the cabinet, and with no one left to trip the lever in the side of the great hulking Clock, he would be unable to escape.

There were just the two of us now. The hallway was clamorous with armed men.

Sweeley Leech, how will you escape?

Get in, Beurre, was his answer. There isn't but a minute.

But you, father— I am not going to leave you behind.

He glared at me then.

Believe, Beurre, was his shouted command, in a tone I had sel-dom heard him use to one of us. Only believe—and try, try, try, as Uncle Will bids us. Please, daughter—get into the cabinet. At once.

My life is not that important, father, I said.

His eyes softened now. His hand reached out and pressed against my abdomen.

It isn't just *your* life now, Beurre, he said. You don't have the right to a one-person philosophy anymore. There's a waiting life inside you—here. You must treasure it.

I don't think anything Sweeley Leech ever said to me had moved me so much. I nodded, like a dreamer, smiling, and took my seat in the little booth. Sweeley Leech drew the curtains.

From within I did not hear the sough of winds. I heard only the curse of Chaz and the others as they seized father. It was semidark. Suddenly the little booth seemed to expand to the size of a charm-ing little room, such as one would find in an Old World country inn. I saw a little blue bed and threw myself upon it, spent and rav-eled. I slept, the moon of an Appalachian evening on my eyelids.

# P·A·R·T
# T·H·R·E·E

PART
THREE

# T·W·E·N·T·Y
## S·I·X

I hadn't slept so deep a sleep in ages. I opened one eye and saw the unicorn rampant. I smiled, tracing it with one finger in the deep, soft brocade of the tiny pillow on which my head rested. I raised up on one elbow on the little bed and stared about me, my eyes focusing in the queer light.

I have no idea how long I may have slept. In one way it seemed the longest of naps, and in another it seemed but the blink of an eye. Wherever I was, it was night.

The room I occupied was small, old, provincial, and utterly charming. There was a little Colonial table of applewood, upon which rested a small bottle of wine and a polished glass. Above the table was a spacious, open window in which fluttered, like white dreams, clean starched curtains.

I looked longingly at the tiny bottle of wine glinting in the livid glamour of the full moon beyond the sill, caught like a great bag of glowing harvest honey in the bole of a giant Royal Paulownia which grew by the house. Somewhere a small dog barked furiously. On

451

the sweet, clover-smelling wind I could hear the tinkle of a mandolin, and I hummed along to an old Jerome Kern tune whose lyrics I
had forgotten. There was, along with the mandolin, the throb of a
guitar and the murmur of happy, casual voices.

I got out of the little bed and went to the window. I stared into
the moonmisted twilight of the rolling land, all chromatic and car-
mined with autumn, and saw what I mistook for at least a dozen
other moons—improbable lunar counterfeits, each of them no bigger than a child's balloon and glowing like a dozen different-colored
jewels within the rich fabric of the night. O, of course—not lesser
moons at all, but Japanese paper lanterns, each with a candle within,
polkadotting the dark. It was a lawn party, and through the evanes-
cent mists I could make out the familiar figures of Madame Aubade
and Dorcas and Madame Jonathan and all the others of the Remnant.

My mind was still a little misty about where I had come from and
where I was now, but the thoughts were crowding fast. Lindy.
Sweeley Leech. Of course. And like an instant replay on TV, the
images shuttered into place and I had it all together.

Father had been captured. He had not escaped, as we had, on the
tiny cushion with its unicorn of gold brocade.

I stared down at the little wine bottle. I picked it up and read the
label. O, heavenly. It was a good Verdicchio de Matelica and it was
already open. I poured the little crystal goblet full, raised it, sniffed
its goodness, and drank it all down.

Almost at once I felt rested after my sleep, of whatever duration,
in the time-trip. I put the glass down and turned to try to make out
the part of the room which had not been dipped in the spill of
moonlight from the fluttery window.

I saw an antique yellow bathtub resting on a gay rag rug on the
other side of the bed. I went to it with hope and cried out softly
with pleasure when I discovered that it was full of steaming hot
water, freshly drawn, with a huge towel on the wooden rack just beyond it. It was hardly an instant later that I saw, draped across the
arms and back of a little Appalachian rocking chair, fresh lingerie
and the most enchanting frock of dotted swiss and Alençon lace.

In a twinkling I had peeled out of my really disgraceful dress and
underthings and was soaking in the glorious hot tub. Floating in the
steaming water was a good bar of homemade yellow soap, and I

stood up, lathering my body luxuriously and looking round, my eyes getting used to the shadowy corners of the little room. Then I sank down again into the water with a blissful groan, feeling the clasp of the warmth again and wriggling my toes whorishly in the moonlight. Heavens, what a glorious night. And I was home.

Memory filtered back, inch by inch. Lindy. O, God, had Lindy gotten through with the rest? I scrambled dripping from the hot tub and raced to the window, my eyes straining through the phospho-rescent moonmists to the lights of the paper lanterns. There was Jimbo. There, uncle in his tawdry splendor. Dorcas. Aubade. No sign of my poor darling. I shut my eyes, feeling for the fluffy bath towel, and saw Lindy as I had last glimpsed her: clutching the white jade wheel in one hand and the sheaf of glowing yellow pages of the Criste Lite in the other. I dried myself and dressed slowly.

I felt the sensuous softness of the spider-silk panties as I drew them on over my steaming nakedness. How curious it all was. Where was the beginning and end of my journey? I pondered it. I stared round the little room, thinking, you were waiting for me. The wine. The hot bath. The clean dress. As if someone were watching it all happen—making things come into place, into focus. Someone. But who?

Buttoning the high collar of the dotted-swiss bodice to my throat, I shivered a little. For I could not escape the feeling at that moment that whoever it had been who had undertaken to look after me, he—or she—was watching me at this moment.

O, dear, I sighed aloud, watching the languorous, happy shapes of the far figures under the glowing paper lanterns. Why aren't you all looking for her? What about darling Lindy? Everything depends on her now! Why aren't you worried and troubled that she's not with you?

O, they will be, said a soft, small voice then—a voice that was somehow miniature in sound like the voices we sometimes hear as children and, turning, find no one there but dusk and moonbeams. They will be. Let them relax for a while after their long, hard jour-ney. Let them have some Joy.

I turned in a flash, staring hard into a shadowy corner of the little room which I had not yet explored. On a horsehair trunk, her tiny legs draped down over the tarnished brass clasp, I saw what ap-peared to be an antique china doll. Again the doll spoke.

As is the case with many on their first time-trip, she said, on arriving, the memory is sometimes slow in returning. Why, I daresay that if you went up there now—to the Indian Mound, where my party is being held—you wouldn't find one of your companions who would know you, or Lindy, or anything about the where and why of the place they have just fled. It will return. No fear. It always does. They will remember.

But *I* remember, I said to the doll—which I was beginning to realize with delight was not a doll at all but a charming tiny lady in a blue-velvet gown. I remember, I repeated. And I made the trip. How come I haven't forgotten?

Perhaps, she said in that frail little lilt like the striking of a silver spoon against a doll's teacup, perhaps because you are the daughter of a wizard. And so, you are probably familiar with such trips.

Once, I said, when I was very small. But that was so long ago.

As this night shall slowly reveal, said the little woman, the memories of childhood may sleep but they never die inside of us. Now, I must explain a thing or two.

I think you really should, I said. This room is plainly not one of the rooms in my father's house. Are you sure this is Echo Point and not just a place that remarkably resembles it?

I am quite sure about that.

And you— O, my dear, you are so tiny. I have never—

You have never seen any mortal my size, she said, a little bitterly. O, how used I am to that!

She sighed the tiniest of sighs.

It is at once my glory and my nemesis.

I can imagine, I agreed. What is your name?

Puddintame, came the answer. Ask me again and I'll tell you the same.

I laughed and then sobered—another bit of memory flickering back like a bird to peck at my wits.

Puddintame, I said with another laugh. Of course, my father spoke of you many times. You are the—you run the—

I am the madam, she said a little defiantly, of that notorious, awful whorehouse on the river road to Glory.

She stifled a tiny sob in the smallest of lawn handkerchiefs.

Nothing I do, she said, seems to erase my awful reputation. Well—

She sprang down like a puppet from the horsehair trunk and paced the small rag rug, passing now and again into the bar of blue moonlight, which enabled me to see her more plainly.

Well, to hell with them, she cried. At least Sweeley Leech knows me for what I am, heaven protect his beautiful soul!

She glared at me from the moonlight, her tiny fists clenched, a little sapphire glowing at her throat. And you, my dear, she said. I suppose you condemn me, too.

No, I said. I hustled for a year. In LA. I am quite beyond such value judgments.

Good, she said. Very good. Because I will be your companion on tonight's little journey into Truth.

I don't understand, I said. My sister, Lindy—

She waved a tiny hand at me, upon which—like Christmas glitter—flashed tiny finger jewels.

Let me talk about myself before we get to Lindy, she said. Myself. Me. All one foot nine inches of me. My why and wherefore. I suppose you *are* wondering—

Yes.

Let me make one thing clear, she said. I am not a fairy. I am all too mortal. And I can tell you a thing or two about fairies, indeed I can.

I heard a barking on the dusky hills above the moonstained river. The first bark had been Footit. I knew that now. But this bark was feral. Full of wilderness and weeds. I shivered despite myself.

O, yes, she went on, I am no damned fairy, let me assure you.

She pointed across the room. It was papered in old-fashioned green wallpaper. Quite close to the painted baseboard, I could make out the oval shapes of perhaps a dozen gold-framed oil paintings. Puddintame paced over to them, and I drew a little closer. She struck a match and lit a small oil lamp by the bed. She pointed to the first of the paintings.

Portraits, they were, of a very strange collection of people—little people, I realized, as my eyes grew used to the soft glow of the lamp.

Here, she said, indicating the first. This is Crachami. Native of Palermo. One foot, eight inches. Exhibited—

She cleared her throat indignantly.

—*exhibited* at Bond Street, London, in 1824. This one—O, what a jewel—she is known only as the Fairy Queen. One foot, four inches. Weight, four pounds. Her foot was less than two inches long—as is mine. She was exhibited at Regent Street in 1850.

She paced on.

Here, a family portrait. Strasse Davit Family, they are called. The man is one foot, eight inches. The woman one foot, six. Their child—at seventeen—only six inches.

She swept her arm toward the others.

I could tell you about the others, she sighed. The great dwarfs—like myself—of history. General Tom Thumb. Lucia Zarate. And the whole pathetic pack of us. Dwarfs. Freaks.

She strode to the window and glared up at the nascent, holy moon.

Well, she said, I long ago decided that running a whorehouse is a cut above being in some carnival sideshow. And I've done it. Successfully, too. The Jew's Harp House—for so my establishment is named—is a tiara on the brow of the Ohio River. There has never been a killing here. Never a robbery. I run the most respectable of brothels, I tell you. It has a bar and booths and bedrooms—of which this is one. And no one is ever turned away—

Again came the faint bark of the wild creature in the night, and this time Footit, close by the house, answered heartily.

—no one but one of *them,* she finished, biting hard on her tiny lips as she spat out the word.

Them?

Fairies, she said. This riverland is infested with them, I tell you. And they are drawn—the greedy and mean little mischiefmakers—by the smells of good drink and perfume and the sounds of merrymaking that are the custom of this establishment.

You seem particularly bitter about the fairies, I said.

As well I might be, she said.

She turned her tiny figure to the wall and pensively fingered the frame of the portrait of the Fairy Queen.

Yes, she went on, I know the fairies all too well.

She paused a beat.

I am in love with one of them.

Forgive me, Madam Puddintame, I interposed, but I am terribly concerned tonight. My sister, Lindy—

I know, I know, she said. But indulge me a moment more. That is only a courtesy you owe.

I am sorry, Madam—

Call me Pud, she sighed. Everyone else does. And I must say, you did pick a most inopportune moment to cut in on my confession of love.

O, I am sorry, Mad—Pud, that is. Can you forgive me?

She ran to my side and caressed my hand with her own miraculously tiny fingers, and I could smell her scent—like wild flowers and sage with just a touch of old roseleaf.

My lover, she said. Not my husband, but my lover—is a fairy. My husband—

Here she broke down.

—my husband, she sobbed, is named Clyde. He is six feet seven. He weighs two hundred and seventy pounds. And last year—last September, to be exact—O, I remember that sad day—

Your husband died.

Worse! she replied bitterly. They came and took him.

Who, Puddintame? I asked. Who came and took him? The police?

Worse than the police, she crooned through her tears. The men from the Home.

The Home?

She shook off my question with a tiny flourish of the little red knitted shawl she had thrown around her little bare shoulders, for the night had grown cool.

O, she was so small. And so plainly mortal. She was under thirty, I guessed, and in extremely trim condition. So many dwarfs and midgets are wrinkled, their faces wizened like old red winter apples—menacing and grotesque in appearance, and with unpleasant, quacking little voices.

But Puddintame was slender, well-proportioned, and lush with tiny curves. Her slightly slanting and somehow Amerindian eyes were ravishingly mascaraed and with natural lashes smaller than the fringes of a lady slipper; her mouth was impudently rouged, and beside it was a black beauty spot—a heart—no bigger than a speck of black pepper. She was rather like a miniature Sophia Loren, who, as research in the late eighties had proved, was actually a Minoan sea goddess. Her velvet and midnight-blue gown was scattered provocatively with tiny sequins and cut low round her beautiful and exciting breasts—each of which was no larger than a sweet Muscat grape. Her skirt was slit at the side, and from this fragrant aperture one caught an occasional flash of leg and thigh. She wore no hosiery, but her feet were clad in the tiniest, sexiest black pumps, each with a polished silver buckle no larger than that on an old-fashioned wristwatch. Her hair was chestnut shot with red gold and fell in lavish, glistening tresses around her slender little neck. I resisted my sudden smallgirl impulse to pick her up in my hands and dandle her on my knee like the china doll she so resembled.

Please don't, she said suddenly, shattering my reverie.

Don't what, please?

Don't pick me up and dandle me on your knee, she said, as I just read in your thoughts. Please, Fifi, try to treat me as an equal. It is written that we must be together tonight, and I promise you it is going to be a mysterious one. You must go on a strange journey soon—perhaps more strange than the one you have just made from the North. And I—yes, I—am going to be your guide and interpreter.

I am looking for my sister, Lindy, I said impatiently. Desperately, anxiously seeking her. You speak of a journey, Puddintame. Will that journey lead me to my sister?

She held up her little hand.

A moment more—of me, she said. I must talk to someone tonight—tonight of all nights—for it is a very special night.

What night is it, Puddintame? It's almost the end of October, I know—

Never mind, she said. I'll get to that in due measure. But let me backtrack for a spell as I speak a little longer of my own personal sorrows. Let me go back to me and Clyde. Our relationship, as the TV physicians call it.

I think I understand, I said. I don't see how you could have any—any relationship at all.

We couldn't, she said, her little lip quivering. O, heaven help us, we couldn't.

She sighed. I remember the night we met, she said, smiling ruefully. It was at a carnival sponsored by the Glory Moose and set up on the flats below the zinc smelter where that little circus, making its last stand of summer, has pitched its tents tonight. I had foolishly wandered off to the carnival alone, drawn by the sounds of the carousel organs and calliopes and the blackamoor in silks blowing marvelously on the battered brass cornet. I wandered there and was discovered standing near the Loop-a-Plane by a band of mischievous Glory schoolboys. They intended all sorts of meanness with me, I knew—if they ever caught me. I am quick and I ran. I ran for almost five minutes, darting among pizza stands and Coke fountains and even under the Ferris wheel. I came out beside a pitch stand which offered a prize for anyone who could knock down ten pins with a baseball. The prizes were dolls, of course, which were, providentially, all about my size—perhaps a little larger—and I quickly assumed a rigid pose among them. I escaped the eyes of the gang of boys, but I didn't escape the eye of a perfectly beautiful roustabout—Clyde, of course—who came, saw me, pitched a perfect game, and (I hate the phrase) won me.

And took you home? I whispered, enchanted and truly forgetful, for the moment, of my desperate mission.

Took me to a courthouse clerk for a license—that took some explaining!—and then to a preacher—we got him out of bed—who took one look at me, accused Clyde of child molesting, and ordered us out. We were finally married at the Apple County Courthouse.

And your honeymoon? I murmured, as tactfully as I could, but I had to know.

A fiasco, she said. A travesty. A little tragedy.

I know.

No, you couldn't know, she sighed, pacing the rag rug, which wasn't much longer than she was. She stared at the glowing miniatures in their peeling golden carved frames—the great dwarfs of history.

She sighed. Mad with passion for each other, we hurried to my little home and raced to the bedroom. We undressed. I remember—O, ignominy!—Clyde tossed his long underwear on the bed and completely enveloped me in it. I came out, with as much dignity as I could muster, through the drop seat. Clearly a bad beginning.

She shivered. I was a virgin, she went on a little breathlessly, but raging with desire. But desire for what? For Clyde's kisses? I had had them. For his embrace? He had hugged me a little too tightly the first time. For what, then? For his penis? Heavens, I could barely lift it—let alone accommodate it. He was enormous, I tell you, and I think even a full-size girl would have found him large.

So you did nothing?

What could we do? Little games. He got an erection and let me ride astride it while he walked me around the bedroom. What a strange, sad hobbyhorse he was! And then at length we both began to cry and ended up in a rocking chair, naked, with me in his arms, while he sobbed and rocked me to sorrowful sleep and truly tormented dreams.

She chuckled. Christmas that year was beautiful, though. Just for a few hours on Christmas Eve, Clyde agreed to get an erection and let me decorate his penis and balls with tiny tinsel and Christmas lights. It was rather festive, I must say. No one saw it but the two of us, and then the string of tiny lights must have been shorted by a pubic hair, for there was a flash, the acrid smell of burning hair and meat, and Clyde let out a roar which was heard, they say, in five river counties and interpreted, it is said, by many small children as an expression from Santa Claus of displeasure at the children who had been bad that night and were going to get coal in their stocking next morning. Poor Clyde peed three streams for a week because of the blisters, and the travesty continued into the New Year.

You are not still a virgin, Puddintame? I said then.

How do you know?

I know, I teased. Your walk. The way your body moves. The way you hold yourself, the way you smell—like miniature wild flowers. I know. I know the way a woman tells a man with her body that the body is now asleep but will waken joyful and ready in a twinkling if he has the Magic to make it so.

You know too much, she smiled, but it is true.

At that moment I was startled by a pair of large black and white spectacles fixed on me. I laughed. It was a rather small raccoon, which had slipped silently into the bedroom and sat up now, cleaning its whiskers and sniffling, by the corner of the horsehair trunk. Puddintame brightened a little and quickly turned to the creature. She pursed her little mouth and uttered the strangest little cries. Instantly, the creature waddled over to Puddintame's side and gave a grunt of pure pleasure as she began ruffling its fur and scratching its back with one tiny hand.

You mustn't be afraid of him, she said. He is—well, I won't say he isn't wild, but he is, at least, passably domesticated. His name is Seek. He is my almost constant companion, though I suppose a watchdog would be better. Still, I adore Seek. We understand each other.

You spoke with him.

I did.

They were not words.

They were not words you understand, said Puddintame, but all creatures have language.

She sighed. Once in the great library at Alexandria, they say, there were codices and dictionaries and grammars of all the languages of the universe—including those of the beasts. The library was supposedly razed in the fourth century.

How did you learn, then, Puddintame?

I said *supposedly* lost, she answered. It still exists.

Where?

She gave me the most inscrutable of smiles and with a tiny, shrill cry she hiked her skirts and bestrode the complacent creature, tugging his whiskers like reins as the raccoon bore her around a circle of moonlight on the pretty patterned rug. I could smell the harsh, wilderness odor of the beast mingling with the scent—fragrant and fresh—of Puddintame herself: rather like a thimbleful of crushed baby's breath.

At last she dismounted and stood a moment, pensively chewing her finger—she was a veritable pocket Venus. She flashed me a look. I lost my virginity— Again the bark racketed faintly among the pawpaws waiting to blacken in some imminent night of frost. I lost my virginity, she continued, five years ago this very night.

The barking in the meadow night seemed closer.

And I lost it, she said, to one of Beelzebub's very own—a scoundrel of a fairy named Didnt.

Didnt?

Didnt. That was his name. Not Master Didnt. Not Sir Didnt. Just Didnt.

He deflowered you?

Yes.

Was it pleasant?

Excruciating.

But the second time?

Interesting.

Was there a third?

Yes.

What was it like?

She paused and traced the smile on her tiny lips with one tiny finger. Rapture, she said. O, it was sheer paradise!

I thought as much, I said. I didn't want to seem to be prying, but I could not resist. How long did the affair last?

One night, she sang, dancing up and down the gay rag rug like a windup toy. O, one night of heavenly love! Five years ago this very night, my dear Fifi Leech. One night—and then, on the anniversary, another night a year later. For four years.

An exceptionally vociferous outburst of barks from the fringes of the Gallimaufry, where wild raspberries bloom sweetly among the wild copperheads, broke the night hush. Even Footit seemed submissively silent for a spell. Old hounds woke and bayed in the patchwork farms under the lovely old moon. Then they, too, fell silent—as if abashed at their own indiscretion at challenging the old voice of the wilderness. Up on the Indian Mound I could see my friends, under the soft light of the paper lanterns, which were bobbing gently on their colored strings in the autumn night breeze. Dear Dorcas and Jimbo and Uncle Mooncob and Fu and Aubade and all the other Children of the Remnant. And moving among them with drinks and trays of mouth-watering food, and strumming guitars and plucking deepbellied mandolins, were six or seven of the prettiest young country girls you could imagine. I judged these to be Puddintame's girls from the Jew's Harp House.

Again the barks from the river moonmists, and the cattails bobbed in the shoals as if trying to hide their rough brown faces.

That's his vixen, Foxy Jane, said Puddintame. They are married. He rides her through the woods and meadows on nights of the full moon. And on this—this very special night.

I thought he spends this night with you, I said gently.

She brings him here, said Puddintame in a clenched voice. O, it is all so beastly. She brings him here and sits watching while we make love. Unspeakable, eh? And I try—O, I try so hard not to want him. She sits and watches us and licks her foxy chops at the spectacle.

I guess it gets her off, I said.

I suppose. Anyhow, it is simply insupportable. I can't go on like this. It has already taken its toll.

How do you mean?

Clyde, she said. I mean Clyde. He was the first casualty of this unholy liaison.

They took him away, you said, I said.

The men in the white coats, she said with a shiver. From the Home.

What Home?

She was silent.

Can't you speak of it, dear?

The Home—the dreaded Home.

She cleared her throat and clenched her tiny fists. The West Virginia State Home for Agelasts, she said at last and only after the greatest effort.

I once knew, I said, what an Agelast is. Would you refresh my memory?

Agelasts are fucking Owls! Fucking blood Owls, she snapped.

You mean—owls?

No, of course not, she said. I mean they are simply people who never—cannot—laugh.

There is such a disease?

O, indeed. It is particularly prevalent among failed presidential candidates and Ph.D.s. It is endemic these days.

Are they really harmful—I mean, do they have to be institution-alized?

O, yes. O, yes. They are a menace if left to run loose in society.

How did Clyde's disease manifest itself? I mean, what were the first symptoms?

Clyde found out about my affair with Didnt, she said sadly. He took it rather hard. Began to spend all his free time reading *U.S. News and World Report*. Then he switched to *Grit*. After two months of that, he won a big-screen TV set at a Burger Chef raffle.

TV.

He became hooked. Watched it from six in the morning till sign-off. Week after week. And all the time growing more silent, more withdrawn, more—more *unlaughing*.

Is laughing so important?

It is the holiest sound we make, she said. And the only unholy laughter is the canned laughter on TV shows.

At last your poor husband—

Became a blood Owl, she gloomed. A bloody fucking Owl. Never a joke. Never a smile. Never a heart belly laugh. O, he was in bad shape when they took him.

And you?

I mourned him, of course, she said. And heaven knows, I had little enough to laugh about myself those lonesome days and nights after they took Clyde away to the Home. But I kept my ability to smile, at least.

And Didnt?

He got me pregnant, she said. O, how could I not have become pregnant after that mad, beautiful night of love five years ago this date! How not! At first, as I have said, it was painful. And then I became, the second time, aware of vaguely pleasant sensations. The third time, as I told you, was rapture. And I could remember the pain of the first time only as a rapture itself. Do you know? He was an insane little lover.

And your child?

It was born dead, she said in a flat, lifeless voice. Dead at birth. It is buried under the honeysuckle vine by the porch. O, it was beautiful though. Not mortal, of course—or only half-mortal, I suppose. Anyhow, it didn't have a chance. It was so tiny. Not much larger than a Flintstone vitamin pill and glowing with light like a tiny firefly. Clyde preached the little sermon at the funeral. O, he was so understanding. He even had a hearty laugh about it all. This, of course, before his—his—O, you know.

Before Agelasm overcame him.

Yes.

How pathetic. Is there any hope? I mean, do the authorities at the Home administer any therapy?

Therapy! snorted the pocket Venus. Hmmphh. Far from it.

How do the patients spend their time?

Watching *Gilligan's Island, The Brady Bunch, Welcome Back, Kotter*—that kind of thing. You can see, can't you, how this only serves to make them worse?

She sighed, shaking her head slowly. Yet you must understand the feelings of the people you think inhumane. Obviously, Agelasts can't be let loose to spread their Owlishness among good-humored people. They are really quite devilish and unholy when you get right down to it.

Joy being the norm, I said. Yes, I understand. Joy is the holiest state, and laughter the most sacred sound. Yes, I guess they have to be confined.

No more confined than I, she sighed. Imprisoned in this fucking house.

It is a lovely house, I admonished her.

It is lovely when it is night, she whispered. Lovely when it is the night and Didnt comes riding Foxy Jane through the Queen Anne's lace and meadow clover. It is lovely when Foxy Jane sits licking her jowls lasciviously on the hair trunk yonder—perched back on her haunches and watching as Didnt undoes my clothes and stretches me at last naked beneath him. Yes, that is when this house is lovely. And only then.

Would it not, perhaps, be more lovely, I queried gently, if your Clyde learned to laugh again?

She began to cry into her little kerchief, and the breeze tinkled windchimes somewhere down the long porch with its old honeysuckle vines.

O, you know, Fifi, I think I'd give my life for the chance to be happy with Clyde. I do love him. My thing with Didnt is only a wild, passionate fancy—I know that. He doesn't love me. After he fucks me, he beats me dreadfully, and Foxy Jane licks her jowls and smiles her foxy smile. Perhaps that is the moment she has been waiting for all along—to see Didnt beat me. Yes, I think that is so.

She sighed. I have only one hope, one prayer, she said then.

What is that?

It's not a What—it's a very beautiful Who.

Who, then?

Sweeley Leech, she said. He was once here and promised me a miracle.

A miracle?

He swore that before he left this earth he would make me and Clyde the same size.

He did?

Yes. It was a spring night and he couldn't stay long enough to make the miracle then and there, and besides, he said he was exhausted that day from moving a mountain at a Presbyterian picnic.

Baptism.

Okay, baptism. He was low on Criste Lite, he said.

But he promised you, I said. Isn't that enough?

I suppose so, she said. Someday—some way. But now—

Now he is a prisoner, I said. I think I know what you are going to say.

Yes.

Will he escape with his life, Puddintame? I asked in a voice which sounded queer and remote from me.

I cannot tell you that, she said. You would not understand. Suffice it to say—

She paced to the little window table and stared at the small, empty wine bottle. You drank my last bottle of the good 'eighty Verdicchio. Well, that's all right. I drink too much these days.

She wandered back to the bar of moonlight on the tiny puffed rainbow of the gay rag rug. She looked at me. Suffice it to say, she resumed, that I know you are fresh time-tripped from a place called Montauk to the north. You are in quest of your beloved sister, Lindy, who is terminally ill and who possesses—

—all but two colors of the Criste Lite, I finished for her, my heart beginning to pound again.

Yes, she said. Precisely. And she must find them.

O, she must. I agree, Puddintame.

I ran to the window and stared through the mists toward the gay throng at the lawn party. She's not among them, I said. I'd know her a mile away. She's not there, Puddintame. Do you suppose she—?

Suppose she what, my darling?

Suppose she got lost somehow in the time-trip?

No. She got through.

Was she here?

Yes.

How was she?

Astonishingly strong. Fervid. Passionate. She was determined to find the two remaining colors.

It is simple, I said. The secret to the mystery is somewhere in the Labyrinth.

Yes. But that is not so simple.

O, I know—but why, Puddintame?

For the simple reason that the mysteries of the devious and tortuous ways of the passages and chambers in that great, ancient maze are guarded and hidden and made almost impenetrable except for one kind of person.

What kind, Puddintame?

A child, she said. To conquer the secrets of the Chamber of Stars we must become as little children.

I have never found it hard to be a child, I said simply.

I know that, Fifi. Nor have I, said the little creature. Perhaps you and I—

You mean you're coming with me?

Yes. I know the maze reasonably well. I think I can help.

Puddintame, where's Lindy?

When she got here she was very ill. Bleeding a little. And weak. I put her to bed. Nursed her. Fixed her a kettle of mutton and barley broth with good tomatoes in it. And a pinch of an herb or two from the Gallimaufry with certain therapeutic powers. She recovered some of her strength. I let her sleep—

Where is she now?

Puddintame gestured toward the other small door in the room: its brass key glowed like a goblin's scepter in the moonshine. In there, she said.

May I—? I asked, moving toward the door with my hand outstretched to the latch.

Yes. We will both go in, she said, and moved in my wake as I turned the rasping key and set the hinges of the door to speaking as I swung the door open.

Moonlight flooded another tiny bedroom. I saw a small dresser and a narrow featherbed with a bright apostle quilt tousled and tangled across it. The bed was empty. On a small chest of drawers something shone pale and white as semen. I moved toward it. And saw. The jade wheel called Love Will Find a Way winked at me like a fallen moon from the crisp doily where someone had placed it. The ruled yellow pages of the Criste Lite, already glowing a little from the colors and runes already there—well, there was no sign of it.

I turned to Puddintame.

She stared at me with frightened eyes.

She has fled, she said. O, she shouldn't have. This means but one thing—

O, what, Puddintame?

It means she has gone into the Labyrinth alone, said the little woman. Alone. O, how foolish of her. I told her to wait. I told her you'd be here.

Maybe she wanted to go it alone, Puddintame.

We all go it alone, she answered, but that doesn't mean someone who loves us can't help. And she couldn't have picked a worse night.

Why, love?

Fifi, you said you were a child at heart. How could you have overlooked it?

I don't understand.

Tonight, she said, the anniversary of my encounters—my fatal interviews, as Miss Millay calls them—with Didnt. Fifi, this is Halloween.

I don't know what startled me first. I heard poor Footit howling like a small fuzzy coyote out in the spice bush by the tanbark walk, and at the same time, I saw Puddintame's tame raccoon pad silently up onto the table and out the window. I reached down and caught Puddintame's tiny, cold hand in my own as I stared through the moonlight toward the worn threshold of the door to the shallow hallway—the only apparent escape which my little companion and I had. But escape from what? I felt my throat tighten and the tiny hairs at my nape rise and tingle.

I was barely certain of it at first—the light which seemed to be cast from something—or someone—approaching our little room. A board creaked—like a small wooden voice speaking somewhere around the corner of the door.

O, Fifi, I am afraid, cried Puddintame, pressing her tiny body against my leg. Don't let him take me. Don't let him handle me, as Porgy's poor Bess said, with his hot hands.

Is it he?

Well, someone is coming, she said. There is a light. And, O, Fifi, this night of all nights I must not dally with him.

Why this night more than the others?

Because five is the charm, she said. If he manages to toss me in the sheets for the fifth year in a row, then—

I felt her tiny body shudder against my shinbone, her tiny arms clasped round my calf.

Then what?

The light was brighter. And could I not hear the stealthy pad of four furry paws beyond the corner of the door?

Beware of him yourself, Fifi, she said then. On Halloween, you know, fairies have the strength of twenty.

But you were saying, I interposed. If he spends the fifth night in five years in bed with you, what happens?

O, the pathos of that tiny sob. It merely means that he has achieved the Charm, she said in a plaintive voice. It means that he and Foxy Jane have the power to take me away to their little house under the big rock on Hangman's Hill. It means that I will become their servant—their slave, their drudge—working sixteen hours a day and being beaten every night for my trouble. Forever! That's what it means. O, Fifi, don't let him take me.

I caught the tiny lady up in my arms and cradled her against my breasts just as Footit howled again, a tiny, lorn lament somewhere out in the moondust. I heard a clap of freak thunder (the skies were cloudless and starstrewn) just as they appeared on the threshold. O, most astonishing of spectacles—a she-fox whose every hair was like an electric wire, whose fur and burning, jewellike eyes were tattooed in gold and evil light upon the flinching flesh of the dark. But the vixen was not what astonished me most. It was, rather, the malevolent and totally enchanting twist to the lips and bushy golden brows of the handsome little fairy astride his Foxy Jane. They were luminous, the two of them, in the dark hallway, which they made bright—painted like a picture whose pigments were crushed and ground-up glowworms.

I shuddered and hugged the little form reassuringly. And then as the vixen and her flaming burden made toward us with a sharp and most peremptory bark, I dashed with Puddintame into the other bedroom and out the moonwashed casement window to the garden beyond.

# T✦W✦E✦N✦T✦Y
# S✦E✦V✦E✦N

I saw a shooting star go dribbling down the dark, damask cheek of the dark skies and made a wish. For Lindy. For Sweeley Leech. For Puddintame. For my friends— O, that little star was bent down with the weight of wishes and lasted barely long enough for me to name them all. There were so many I cared about—and despaired of—in the heart of that curious night.

Having cleared the sill and made the short drop to the wild flowers below, I heard the quick patter of Foxy Jane's pads in the room behind me. I clutched Puddintame till she squealed and then made for the garden gate half-hidden in the late-blooming glory of a veritably ancient bush of tearoses and hydrangea. I unfastened the old brass latch and flung the gate open, racing out toward I knew not what.

The moonlight was like day but not bright enough to diminish the luster and crackling brilliance of the myriad October stars in their tiaraed aspects. There was a short flagstone path leading down

470

to the river road, and a sundial whose arrow cast a numb, dark moonshadow on the numerals. Late locusts were down in the river willows, sawing down the silence and racketing their sweet litany to winter's coming.

The pause by the sundial was almost fatal. I heard Foxy Jane and her evil burden coming through the shrubbery of the yard and cast my little companion an anxious glance.

That way! she cried. To the orchard over there at the edge of the river road. I'll tell you what to do then.

I raced out to the road and paused as Uncle Mooncob, tipsy as a Christmas reveler, roared past on a Honda, with one of Puddin-tame's prettiest girls astraddle behind him. Before I thought to yell for help, he was gone in a swirling tornado of dust toward the others up on the Indian Mound, under the paper lanterns.

Could I get to my friends in time? Surely even the daring vixen would not attack me or Puddintame with a lot of others around.

No! cried the little lady, having read my thoughts again. You mustn't go to them. You have something else to do now. Something that you must do by yourself.

But Puddintame, I gasped, upon reaching the tangled moon-shadows of the little orchard, upon whose boughs late apples glowed like fat rubies. I crashed in among the low-hanging boughs, feeling the cold fruit strike against me as I thrust the leaves and twigs aside.

Yonder! commanded Puddintame like a tiny captain astride the bow of my neck and shoulders. Yonder, quickly— O, Fifi, don't let him get me.

I remembered the orchard from my childhood and knew the trees were perhaps a century or more old. The crotches were low and devious and quite sturdy as I began to climb one, Puddintame hanging on gamely and, I am afraid, a little hysterically. I could hear her shrill sobs in my ear as she pressed her face against me at each yap and yip from the pursuing vixen. Moonlight streamed down through the leaves of the old tree, and something dark loomed up ahead—between Sirius and Betelgeuse, you might say. It was the most elegant of treehouses—which I seemed to remember from years gone by as well. It was quite commodious and even rudely furnished—a most proper and swell little treehouse indeed, and just the place for us in this crisis.

Neither Foxy Jane nor her mischievous rider saw our ascent, and they shot past in a blur of cold fire among the raspberry bushes and ironweed beneath us.

Puddintame cast me a grateful look, kissed my cheek, and relaxed her hold enough for me to lower her gently to the sturdy planks of the treehouse floor. We could hear Didnt chanting his evil little song in the moonshine, somewhere off toward the river willows:

> When Didnt does what Didnts do,
> It kindles fire inside of you.
> So come and join this merry game,
> You naughty little Puddintame!

(A pause here, and the vixen howled and made a little chattering sound as if she, too, were trying to join in Didnt's evil song.)

> And when our night of loving's through,
> A beating I will give to you!

Puddintame paced the rainworn boards of the treehouse, her tiny, blue-sheathed body barred with the moonlight which fell through the windy cracks in the walls and tarpaper roof.

We can't stay here, I said. Lindy isn't—

That's not the only reason we can't stay, said Puddintame. The little devil and his vixen will be back once they discover they're on a cold scent. They'll know we're hiding here in the old orchard. Foxes have marvelous noses. They're sure to find us.

Foxes can't climb apple trees, Puddintame.

No, but fairies can. And I tell you, I am afraid.

I won't let him take you, love.

Of course you wouldn't—willingly, she said. But fairies have a million devious little tricks and spells and passes. You are a bright woman, Fifi Leech, but I doubt that you are up to outwitting a fairy on such a night as this.

She sighed. And there isn't that much time, she said. We must get to your sister.

I had not noticed till then that she had been carrying something in her little shawl. She unwrapped it, and a finger of blue moonlight fell on the object within—the pale, liquid jade wheel. She proffered it to me, and I took the cold stone in my fingers.

There, she said, pointing to a spot in the outer ring of convolutions. There is the main entrance to Bebo.

I held the stone, tracing its lines with my own fingers. Lindy was right, I said. It is a map of the Labyrinth.

Puddintame was now standing at the little silled window of the treehouse and was staring off toward the white looming shape of the great Labyrinth in the plain below the Gallimaufry.

The Labyrinth, she said, has many entrances. Some of them are well known and rather obvious. They, of course, lead to hopeless culs-de-sac. That main one out there—

She pointed a tiny hand, and an even tinier diamond winked amid the starshine on her finger.

—that one—you can see it from here. See?

I crept over and looked, having to crouch a little because the treehouse was not made for grownups.

I saw the looming shape of the Labyrinth—a structure of ancient stone—and remembered it from childhood, when, without fear, I used to explore its winding alleys and secret chambers. It was perhaps ten acres in circumference, though it always seemed much more expansive than that when you were in it. What a strange, history-haunted place it was. No one knew who had fashioned it, or how. It was mysterious and shadowed—like Machu Picchu in far-off Peru.

Down in the smoking blue mists of the river meadows we heard the call of a bobwhite once—and then again. Footit howled unhappily up by the Jew's Harp House. A wave of distant laughter, like the tinkle of festive glasses, blew on the wind from the revelers on the Indian Mound. Had they not remembered yet? Would they merely stare back stupidly, without recognition, if my name, once loved and familiar, was mentioned, or the names of Lindy and Sweeley Leech? Would their memories return, so they could be of *some* help in all this?

Puddintame took the jade wheel from my fingers and carried it to the moonlit little window to study it.

Again my thoughts were on the Labyrinth and its wonders. Who had built it? Surely not the Mingo-Shawnee-Delaware people who managed well enough with a tepee. Not even the Adena—the

Mound Builders—before them. Who, then? Giants from other worlds perhaps?

I shivered. And I marveled at my own fears. Time was when I— or Lindy—would wander down the river road from Echo Point and spend hours, even days, alone in the maze. Rinsey and Sweeley never forbade us such expeditions. If there had been true danger, I think they surely would have. No—we went there as children in perfect trust and widest wonderment. We would explore its many entrances and go winding through its historiated halls and chambers. There were so many rooms full of marvels I have forgotten, wonders which come to me even yet in dreams. And there were menaces, too—places like the Lane of Spiders, which we knew not to explore. The maze, the Labyrinth, Great Bebo—it was a kind of nursery to us as children. I loved it then; I think I loved it even now.

And yet I could not help remembering the curious thing that had happened to us children as we grew older, wiser, more cunning and cautious. We began to fear the Labyrinth—to look with dread upon byways and alcoves and small rooms which had once held wonder for us both. I shivered again despite myself, and the thought of Lindy alone in that vast, forbidding stone maze brought terror to my heart. And Puddintame said she had been gravely ill—bleeding and faint. O, my love, my poor dear darling Love!

I strained my eyes through the almost hallucinatory gauze of mists at the main entrance to Bebo—just beyond the farthest edges of the Gallimaufry. Something glowed there and flitted back and forth ominously around the high stone portal.

Again Puddintame read my thoughts. In the drawer of that little table, she directed.

What?

You'll find what you want, she said.

I crept to the little table. The treehouse tilted and listed like a tiny ship as my weight shifted from one end to the other. I opened the drawer and saw a glint of old brass. I reached in and took the object out. It was an old miniature telescope.

See for yourself, said Puddintame, how well the Neptune Gate—that's the main one—is guarded.

I took the little telescope to the window and looked through it toward the large gate. Sure enough, the dandelions and rank iron-weed around the mouth were swarming with fairies, and each of them appeared more menacing and malevolent than the rapacious Didnt.

Were we to try to breach that defense, said Puddintame, the result might prove most dire.

How, Puddintame? They seem so small.

I can't impress on you enough, she said, the fact that things aren't the same on Halloween. Fairies have twenty times their usual strength. And the most docile and amiable of creatures may turn into a true ogre. No, Fifi. The Neptune Gate is not for us.

I sighed. How did Lindy get past them?

She didn't.

She didn't?

She didn't enter the Labyrinth by the Neptune Gate, said the little creature. I warned her not to.

Then how—?

Come, said Puddintame, beckoning me toward the ladder.

She paused. The vixen's bark was distant. And furious. Didnt's voice echoed from the far reaches of the river willows:

> When Didnt does what Didnts do,
> It kindles fire inside of—

Come, said Puddintame. It just so happens that the Neptune Gate is one of the false entries.

Where are the true entrances?

Don't you remember, Fifi? smiled the little lady.

I blushed. I knew them all once, I said. Strange how—when we grow older, grow up—the familiar ways are lost to us.

There is a true gate to the Labyrinth, she said. And I think the way is clear down there for us to try to make it.

Again we both waited, listening, and again the fox barked—this time even more distant and more angry—and Didnt's vile little chant was hardly distinguishable in the breeze which gusted up from the meadows.

Come, said Puddintame. Pick me up again, please. I think we can make it.

I caught her up—heavens, she couldn't have weighed more than five pounds!—and started down the boughs toward the rank high grass and weeds which made treacherous walking with their windfalls of autumn apples.

I paused when I reached bottom. I've forgotten the jade wheel, I said. Shouldn't we go back for it?

No need, said Puddintame. I know the way quite well. It is simple. Obviously—

She smiled at me, the moonlight glinting on her tiny painted mouth.

—obviously, it was simple enough for your sister to remember, she went on. She didn't take the jade wheel with her. Didn't need it.

O, Puddintame, why am I so frightened about entering a place which was once beloved and simple and enchanting to me?

She did not answer but climbed astride my neck like the tiniest of children and tugged at my hair.

Come, Fifi dearest, she commanded. Go up toward that grove of willows—above the river—where the creek winds down and empties into the Ohio.

I made my way a little breathlessly toward that goal amid a great cluster of lovely trees like grieving women. Their frondlike boughs were barely moving in the light kiss of wind which played up from the shoals of the great stream.

I put Puddintame down again, and now she raced on ahead of me, her dark hair streaming behind her. She was silhouetted in moonlight, and I marveled again at the beauty of the tiny creature.

The French have a lovely word—*pignocher*. It has two meanings: one, to pick at one's food, and the other—O, lovely language!—to paint with tiny strokes. That was how Puddintame looked to me—*pignochée*—picked out in bird's-peck tints on the tiniest of canvases.

And then I noticed something quite curious and stopped. It was Puddintame's shadow. The moon was high above the Gallimaufry and the hills beyond it; that meant it would cast shadows toward the west. But all was not quite right, you see. Puddintame's shadow fell *toward* the moon and not *away* from it. I filed this strange little bit of trivia in the back of my mind and walked on behind her up the narrow little path toward the towering cathedral of willows and elms and maples just ahead.

Far away—at least to the Devil's Elbow—I heard the yip-yip of the angry vixen. Again the bobwhite called from the Queen Anne's lace.

The night was truly perfect. There was a nip in the air, but frost had not yet come to kiss the pawpaws to Bible-black. Everything seemed so still that it was as if God had been so pleased with the scene that he had frozen it in a kind of Moviola, stopped it, and kept it now in a holding pattern. Even the revelers under the paper lanterns had grown relatively still. Footit was probably happily curled up at some pretty lady's painted toes, dreaming of a phoenixlike rise to manhood from the ashes of his present doggie existence.

It was the kind of scene which Samuel Palmer, that wild and beautiful friend of Uncle Will Blake's, used to paint.

We came up against a blank wall of high shrubs and low-hanging boughs of gnarled apple and craggy oak, and Puddintame turned and imperiously held up a hand for me to stop. Well, there was nothing else I could do save crash headlong into that really impenetrable wall of greenery. I studied her little eyes, my head tilted with curiosity.

She pointed.

There, she said, that aperture—see it?

Yes. Sort of.

Well, stoop down, Fifi. There. That's it.

She strode toward it and smiled back at me. I don't have to stoop, she said. I don't have to crawl my way into paradises such as this. See? Sometimes it's really nice to be a dwarf. Come, my love. And let your eyes and mind be prepared for something, something— Well, you shall see. Come!

I was charmed, being ordered about by her in this fashion. I got down on all fours and crept past an abandoned anthill and a clump of wisping white milkweed. I felt something sharp against my palm and looked down. Somebody had been littering. I picked up the arrowhead and dropped it in the pocket of my frock. My knees tickled in the sourgrass and groundnut leaves. The wind tossed the green boughs above my head, gesturing praise toward the moon. The bobwhite spoke his *bob* and then grew still. Where was *white?*

The aperture led to a kind of tunnel, like the runs rabbits sometimes make in shrubbery. It smelled divinely of wild sage and crushed mint. I felt daisies smashed to death under the juggernaut of my knees. I slew legions of bird's-foot violets under my flinching palms as I pressed on. O, forgive me, my darlings!

I came out into a soft sward of grass as silky as babyhair and spotted with dandelions. I stood up.

How can I begin to describe what I saw? First, there was a waterfall, a gushing stream which issued from under a huge rock and fell perhaps twelve feet into a pool below. I lifted my gaze to the huge sylvan cathedral in which we now stood. It was all quite natural, nothing man-made—or even fairy-made—about it. The simple fact was that it was an area perhaps a hundred feet across and maybe three hundred feet in height which was completely enclosed in greenery, a kind of temple nature had fashioned in that untroubled place. The waterfall descended into the pool below with great commotion, sending up a mist of glowing spray in which bits of moonlight, filtered through the boughs and leaves high above, fell flashing among the mists with rainbow tints and hues of varying intensity—a kind of moonbow, as old sailors used to call it. The pool was about forty feet across and wisping above it were curls of vapor like cream swirling in iced coffee.

I saw Puddintame then. She was calmly standing beside a cluster of lady slippers and peeling off her dress.

Come on, Fifi, she cried.

It's October, Puddintame, I said. Really, you shouldn't be swimming. You'll catch your death.

No. It's warm—deliciously warm. This whole place—don't you feel it, Fifi? Warm. Springtime warm. It's a hot spring. It's lovely.

Yes. It is. Yes. I fumbled for a button and laughed.

Springtime, crooned Puddintame. It's always spring in the Venus Grotto. Always spring! Come, Fifi Leech—out of your pretty clothes and be naked like me.

She had kicked off her blue-velvet frock and stood nude, one finger on her left hip and one small brow cocked high above an eye that regarded me impishly.

"In Xanadu did Kubla Khan/A stately pleasure-dome decree."

O, this place was that. The trees and their huddled covering boughs so high above me, like windows to the night which some mad glazier had done all in green glass. They glittered and shifted to and fro in the winds up there, and rays of moon shot through,

478

virgin and livid with moony urgings, tugging now at the tides of my womb.

I pulled the dotted swiss over my head and dropped it amid the grass and wild flowers: columbine and aster and the pale wake-robin; orchid and iris and the wild geranium with its workshirtblue flowers. I breathed in the warm, scented air and peeled off my panties. I wriggled my toes in the warm grass. Now and then a wisp of October river wind penetrated the warmth and puckered the skin pleasantly with its wintergreen kiss. My nipples were erect. I was wet. O, God, what a tense time to want sex. So much to be done before I should reasonably think of sex. But the glands have a mind of their own.

Yet how?

Puddintame was a bare foot and a half in height. She was miniature in every way, perfectly so. Tantalizingly so.

How? O, how could we make love?

Come, she cried, her shrill voice piercing the rush of the waterfall.

I ran to the pool's edge, masturbating a little.

I tried the water with three toes. It was deliciously warm—like a bath on a hot summer night. I held my breath and dove, coming up moments later with my head wreathed in wraithlike wisps of vapor. The water tingled my cunt like a Perrier douche.

Over here! I heard Puddintame shout.

I turned and saw her, lying on her back, floating, like a child's celluloid toy.

O, my little love, I want you so. I want to heal your wounded womanhood with my woman's kiss.

But how?

I watched as Puddintame—after all, she *was* able to read my thoughts—swam over to me. For a moment her tiny face and glistening shoulders were erased by wisps of vapor. Then I felt her— her tiny arms hugging close to my left breast, her hands and mouth doing perfectly extraordinary things with my nipple. She lifted her tiny, laughing face.

Nice?

Nice, I groaned. O, Puddintame, I do adore you, simply adore you.

Me, too, she said, and her face was merry. Come, she commanded again, and pointed down into the water, the deeps of which looked unfathomable.

She disappeared under the wisping, bearded water, and I followed.

There was moonlight even down there. In the warm, limpid deeps of the Venus Pool shone tiny sunfishes and waving fronds of mossy grasses. I lost sight of Puddintame as I dove deeper into the enveloping warmth of the water. The little fish darted amiably against me—nibbling at nipple and earlobe like tiny golden lovers—and the dancing, slow leaves of the underwater grasses caressed my belly and thighs.

I saw Puddintame then.

Was it the magnifying power of the water? I couldn't be sure, but I knew that as she swam toward me, sliding up a watery, shimmering moonbeam, she seemed my size. It was illusion, I know, but she came up against me, her oval face like a Da Vinci Madonna, her tiny nipples pert and erect, the little feathered wedge of her pubes black as an arrowhead against the creamy platter of her belly. I kissed her tiny mouth—like a raspberry against my lips, a tiny fruit set in the softness of her face.

I don't know all that happened then. But I know it was incredibly lovely, whatever it was we did to each other. It was not merely woman to woman—it was mortal against mortal: we were totally inside each other, each totally enveloping, with tenderness and love, the other. I could feel her, taste her, and even in the deep envelope of warm mountain spring water, it was as if I could smell her fragrance and sweetness.

It didn't last long.

I shall never forget it, though.

After that hot, sweet interlude we both bobbed to the surface and spouted water and laughed and blinked our eyes in the spray, each of us appearing and disappearing in the hairlike mists which coiled and writhed above the Venus Pool's surface. The moon shone down through the leaves.

I think I saw it first.

It was resting on the sward, amid columbine and tender little forget-me-nots: a most elegant Hammacher Schlemmer picnic basket.

I laughed out loud. I don't really believe this, I said.

Was Puddintame as genuinely surprised as I? Or was she merely pretending not to know the how and why of this most tempting provender?

Do you see what I see? I cried, clambering out onto the banks of the Venus Pool and going naked to the basket to stare down at it in total wonderment.

She still had not spoken. She came out of the water, streaming rivulets of crystal, and shaking diamond droplets from her wild, pretty hair. She watched me with a slow, wise smile.

Is it real?

Why don't you open it?

You think I should?

It is obviously for us. Someone brought it while we were— O, Fifi, you were heavenly.

So were you, my darling. But the basket?

I put forth a tentative hand to touch the latch of woven yellow reed, my nose wrinkling with pleasure at the delicious odors which wafted up to it.

It's Halloween, I said. Perhaps it's poisoned.

Puddintame said nothing, her tiny body still wreathed in vapors from the warm waters, her black eyes flashing with gypsy mischief.

O, she *did* know something. But what?

Surrounded by such prescience and miracleworking as I had been in the past day or so, nothing came as a surprise anymore.

Well, I said, grabbing the latch to the picnic basket, I don't know about you, darling, but I am utterly ravished with starvation. And whatever is in here, it smells mouth-watering.

Open it, said Puddintame softly, her tiny hands kneading her small breasts as if in a sweet reverie of our embrace.

In a moment the lid fell back and I stared inside.

Everything was wrapped in clean damask linen napkins, which I carefully folded as I opened each steaming delicacy. Fresh roasted Maryland crabs and a pair of sterling silver tongs to crack them open so as to feast upon their flaky, fragrant sweetness. There were Parker House rolls and little Potsdam cakes topped with Dutch chocolate icing and a brown pot—like a steaming frog—of savory, molasses-rich baked beans, the kind Rinsey used to bake on Fourth of Julys.

Rinsey?

The thought of her made me glance suspiciously, hope-filled, for some sign of whoever it had been who had brought us this charming feast.

Who? But *who?*

Who what, Fifi? Who brought our supper?

Yes.

Puddintame smiled and ate a little sandwich of watercress and cottage cheese, all crispy with thin slices of fresh cucumber. Why bother about such wonderment? she said. Just accept. And enjoy.

Enjoy, I said reflectively. I remember someone who said that once—on the beach at Montauk. Enjoy, he said, as you did, while he passed around food for the multitude.

Puddintame bent over the basket and came up with a little jar of homemade strawberry preserves. The berries were wild—tiny and sweet as perfume. I watched as she daubed them onto a small buttered roll with adorable gestures. O, she was my love, my love—a true little Venus.

The verdure, the flowers, the moonlight—they were undisturbed, motionless. There was no one in sight. Whoever had brought us the basket was gone. Yet I could not forget the swaying of branches and leaves as I first emerged from the water—a movement as if in the wake of some retreating mortal.

I looked again at my tiny friend. How did we do it? I asked, with a warm chuckle. I'm still amazed.

How did we make love?

Yes.

She stared toward the surface of the little pool, wreathed like the face of a satyr with its beard of tiny mists. The Venus Pool, she said. It is a most remarkable pool. There is a reason, also, for its name.

What is the meaning?

Its meaning is this: those who come here—however different they may be: beggar or queen, mortal or elf, giant or dwarf—will be united in its waters. You and I, for example. How different we are. And yet, underneath, we were already united when we first met. Don't you agree, Fifi, my dearest one?

Yes, I said, but how can I be your dearest one? Surely you mean just "dear one"? There is Clyde.

O, I suppose. But for a while there, you made me forget Clyde.

I was trying to make you forget that evil fairy, Didnt.

I know. And you succeeded.

And what about Clyde? You never could fuck together—correct?

Never.

Then why didn't you come here together—to the Venus Pool?

She sighed. Men aren't qualified, she said, to share in the joys of this grotto. Mortal men, that is. And my darling Clyde is all too mortal.

Then it was a woman who brought us the picnic supper?

Not necessarily. I said a mere man couldn't come here. I meant a really macho man. No, he would have to have a touch of the feminine in his spirit.

Not gay?

O, no. Just loving, gentle, warm. That's all.

And Clyde?

Clyde is more a survivor, she said, eating a crisp radish with charming tiny crunches. He is *almost* loving, *almost* gentle, *almost* warm. Yet at heart he is as macho as the next man. O, I hate the phrase "All men are beasts," but Clyde almost drove me to use it. But it is not his fault, she added. He comes from the most macho town in West Virginia—a small and rather hideous hamlet called Havoc. All the men there are macho to the nth degree. They whistle—

Yes?

—they whistle bass, she continued. Any man who whistles—you know, like a *whistle—shrilly*—is banished, driven out of town, sometimes on a rail.

She knuckled away a tiny tear. There are potholes on the sidewalks of Havoc, she said.

They drive on the sidewalks?

No. The potholes are caused by the men's bootheels. They all have hair on the backs of their thumbs, and those who have no hair there carefully disguise the fact with the aid of tiny finger toupees.

Drunken beasts, I bet.

Drunken? You have no idea. Their Bloody Mary mix is pure Tabasco—with a hint of tomato juice.

No, she went on, Clyde would not—*could* not—ever come here to the Venus Grotto. Perhaps if he had, our lives would have

blended together—closely, passionately, in tranquillity and connu-
bial joy. Yet it was not to be.

She stopped her chewing and pondered. It is strange, she said.
But all the men in the Home are macho. Machismo and Agelasm
seem to go hand in hand—or perhaps I should say fist in fist.

I felt my thoughts come to a sudden halt. The beauty of this
place, the charms of my little friend, and now this delicious repast
had drugged my mind to the urgencies of the moment. With Sweeley Leech in custody, with Lindy—God knows where, I felt a pang
of reproach for dallying here in the midst of this enchanted grotto.

As usual, the small eyes read my thoughts. Don't fret, my darling, she said. All will come to its fitting end. All will be resolved.

I know, Puddintame, I said, but with my sister lost again—and
dying. With my father—God knows where—

O, He does, my dear.

But I must at least do something to help Lindy, I said. Where is
she, Puddintame? Where has she gone with the jade wheel and the
almost-finished Criste Lite?

Where would you go if you were she?

Into the Labyrinth, I said instantly. O, I would. For she interpreted the Sign in the jade wheel. She knew, Puddintame. She knew
when everyone else guessed wrong. She knew that the missing
colors were in the heart of Bebo. And, Puddintame, much as I love
you and enjoy all this—I must follow my poor sister.

Be patient. You shall follow.

But the old entrance to the Labyrinth, the one on the road to
Glory. You said, didn't you, that it was a false one?

There are many false entrances, she said. But there is a true
gate—the Venus Gate.

And where is it?

Fifi, it is here. By the Venus Pool. In this little oasis in the polluted and ravished river bottomlands. It is in this shadowy, glittering jewel box of a forest retreat—where the moon has to bend
down and part the leaves with silver fingers that she may let down
her shining hair.

And can you show me—?

She came to me then, came to my nakedness and, mounting to
my thighs, huddled her small head close between my breasts.

Stay with me a moment more in this place, Fifi love, she crooned.
Moments like this don't come in every lifetime.

I sighed and bit my lip. O, she was a most persuasive creature.

Now she pointed to the picnic basket. Is there anything else to
eat inside?

I took a peek. Nothing else to eat, I think, but there's a good
bottle of wine. And what looks like a small package.

The devil with the package, cried Puddintame with a laugh. Let's
have some of that wine. O, wasn't the food elegant?

It was, I said, opening the bottle with a handy corkscrew I found
on a hemp string attached to the bottle's neck. Whoever had prepared it had thought of everything. Still curious about the package
in the bottom of the basket, I poured us each a small glass of the
wine and handed one to Puddintame.

You are my Pupu-vae-Noa—my tuft in the center. You are my
most adorable Maga-vai-l-e-rire—my little cunt with a lasso in the
middle! I crooned.

What language is that, lover?

Tuamotuan, I answered. I learned it five years ago. On a love-
trip to the Pacific. It was almost as heavenly as this. And my lover
used to call me by those names—as I call you now.

How beautiful!

You are, I cried, catching her up and dandling her in the moonlight like a doll, you are my Toke-a-kura—my clitoris bathed with
ecstasy!

Fifi, I think I could stay with you forever.

O, no, I laughed. No one is forever, dear. Love me—but promise to love others, too.

Don't you believe in lasting attachments?

I considered this a moment. Well, I said, I must admit I have
been thinking a lot lately of a certain unbearably handsome jewel
thief and onetime TRUCAD agent—Adonis McQuestion, by
name.

He sounds most elegant, said she.

O, he is, I said, and I think I have fallen in love with him.

On a permanent basis?

Yes. I'm afraid so. O, Puddintame, is that awfully dreary of me? I
mean, you do understand?

I do, she said. I can't get Clyde out of my system. Even though we've never ever really been together. I do understand.

Anyway, I said, I suppose you're as curious as I am.

About the small package in the basket?

Yes.

It might give us a clue as to who brought the food here in the first place.

Perhaps.

The blue ribbon undid itself like magic under my fingers; the tissue paper whispered like Christmas morning, and the package lay open.

What was this?

Puddintame raced over and peered into the tangle of ribbons and red paper. It was a heavy cardboard carton about six inches long, four inches wide, and two inches deep. It was a gun. On the top of the box was its picture—it was ugly, deadly. I stared at it with mild distaste.

Look, said Puddintame. There is an envelope attached to it with Scotch tape.

The tiny envelope contained a card, upon which was inscribed a sentence in a certain long-remembered and unmistakable hand. I read it aloud. "This gun, Beurre, will see you through an imminent confrontation."

It was not signed. But even without the adorable familiarity of the handwriting, how could I have mistaken the significance of the name "Beurre"? Only one person on earth called me that.

O, Sweeley Leech, did you make a miracle or scream a Druid Screod and escape from Them? I said.

Puddintame searched my face with a slow, small smile.

Remember what your Uncle Will Blake quotes dear Criste as telling us: "Believe—only believe—and try, try, try."

I was silent, listening to a faint susurration from beyond this little kingdom of the grotto.

Was there someone yonder in the moonlight—in the meadow beyond our little tunnel? I shook my head and covered my face.

What's wrong, Fifi?

Nothing, I—

I put the package back in its tissue and ribbons. I felt like a child who's gotten a practical present on Christmas morning when his little heart was yearning for the most impractical of presents.

Fifi, is there something wrong?

Yes, I said. Something very wrong.

What?

Father would never give me a gun for protection, I said. He is too—too imaginative for that. It would be something else—some-thing—something— O, Puddintame, I don't know. The minute I saw that picture on the box—well, something in me cringed. And then I saw that little note in father's own beautiful hand—and call-ing me "Beurre" and all like he used to when I was small and has ever since. But a *gun*, Puddintame. A gun from Sweeley Leech? Really, now. He is the very Master of Peace.

Puddintame had heard the sounds outside, too. She stared at the package and then at me. You may be very thankful to have a gun, she said, even one from such an unsuspected quarter. Shall we crawl through the grass to the tunnel mouth and have a look?

Could it be your fairy friend, Didnt, on his fox?

No, she said. The moon is full. It is Halloween. The fox would be barking and howling.

Couldn't we just ignore them? I whispered. Stay here and wait them out?

Puddintame scowled a little. I'm curious, she smiled. Aren't you?

Yes, I confessed, and together we knelt on all fours and crawled through the rabbit run in the high grass and out to its very mouth.

The moon rode high in full splendor, shedding her light like a sil-ver dew on the light-thirsting earth. Spiderwebs glittered in gemmy phosphorescence like the tiaras of sweet, dead queens gone to earth and dreaming in heaven of their lost jewels.

But that moonlight was not bright enough, not kindly enough, not all-obscuring enough in its brilliance to dim or lessen two alien sources of light in the high timothy and trampled aster. Yes, it was unmistakable and terribly, terribly imminent—the evil, phosphores-cent glare of two high heels. Down in the meadow, in the place where it dips gracefully and races to the river, other high heels glowed and sparked like moving embers.

The Goody Two-Shoes had come to Echo Point.

Yet I was puzzled. I could still see the lights of the lanterns on the mound and hear Strauss waltzes and Franz Lehár being thrummed on a mandolin; I could hear the laughter of Puddintame's girls and the singing, carefree voices of the Children of the Remnant. If the Goody Two-Shoes had come here, why were they not breaking up that gay moonlit lawn party?

She had a face as dull as a clean limerick, and small, piggy eyes set in a pudding of a face. She was enormous. I mean she must have weighed at least two-fifty or maybe three hundred pounds. She was dressed in an outsize pantsuit and wore small earrings in the form of the cross. She was eating a candy bar—a Forever Yours, I think— and the grass was littered with other candy wrappers, which blew and rattled faintly in the river wind. She held a cocked .357 Magnum.

I started to whisper something, but Puddintame held a finger to her lips for silence.

The mandolins and happy voices drifted on the breeze from the lawn party.

I had motioned to Puddintame to start back toward the grotto, when I noticed something else. It was on a steel chain leash and was tied to a bush next to the fat woman's feet—it was Footit. I paused in my retreat. I couldn't leave Footit behind; he was one of the Children of the Remnant in every way. He whined pathetically. Which settled it. Somehow—some way—I was going to rescue him from the Goody Two-Shoes.

The fat woman finished her candy bar and fished around in a small canvas rucksack which hung from her shoulder. She fetched out a bar of peanut brittle and began loudly munching on it.

This is unthinkable, I whispered to Puddintame. She's got the dearest, sweetest, loveliest—

I began to cry soundlessly.

Puddintame laid her hand on my arm and pointed back to the grotto, where a small and now perhaps indispensable carton lay in its wrapping and ribbon in the wild flowers by the pool.

The gun. Of course.

I was about to go for the weapon when the fat woman turned, gun leveled vaguely in my direction, and belched like a Turkish houri after a fifteen-course lunch. Puddintame scurried on through the run, after the gun.

Parm me, said the fat woman after her gassy comment, but, praise God, He has revealed you to me, Fifi Leech.

I kept very still.

I heard you whispering, Fifi Leech, said the Goody Two-Shoes woman, slowly rising from the stump on which she had been sitting. The big gun gleamed ominously in the moonlight. I did not move.

You are, praise God, within twelve or maybe ten feet of me, said the woman, walking slowly toward the exact spot where I was. Footit was furious, though doubtless—and in total innocence—he had led the Goody Two-Shoes to this spot. He barked and tossed the jingling leash to and fro, straining to be free.

The fat woman paused. She stood poised on the glowing heels of her malevolent shoes, the gun bouncing in one hand, the unfinished peanut brittle in the other.

Puddintame returned silently from the pool, lugging the gun carton in her arms. She laid it by my fingers. I reached for it. O, God, I couldn't. I mean, here it was within my reach—a gun—a way to handle the imminent danger the note had described, and I could scarcely bear the thought of taking it in my hand. The fat Goody Two-Shoes woman was silhouetted hugely against the full moon, the edge of a white plastic Bible gleaming from the mouth of her rucksack. I could have put all six shots into her e'er she could blink a greasy lash. Yet, I couldn't—yet.

Fifi Leech, praise God, you are going to be tried with your father. You will be convicted. You will be—

She stopped and bit off half the remaining peanut brittle and chewed as if the excitement of the situation made her even more ravenous.

I can make out your form now, she said, the gun still bouncing like a big, sinister toy in her pudgy fingers. Footit pointed his bushy black nose heavenward and addressed a lorn, low lament to the lovely listening moon. The fat woman came forward another step.

Are you alone? It don't matter. Praise God, it don't matter. This gun will blow a hole in this hill if I want it to. And besides, we don't want anyone but you, Fifi Leech. We have your father. And now we'll take you. The trial is tomorrow—here in Echo Point.

She took another step, her fat-encased little eyes twinkling as they strained to pierce the shadows by the grotto's entrance.

We don't even want them drunken, dope-besotted friends of yours over there on the mound, she snorted, and proceeded to eat the last half of the peanut brittle bar. Praise God, we only want the two of you, Fifi Leech. And I think tonight will see you both in a government jail cell.

And what if—God, the thought sickened me—I shot this poor fat fool in cold blood, there against the pale moon? Wouldn't the others come running? And wouldn't there be reprisals against my friends?

Take out the gun, whispered Puddintame, jostling my elbow frantically.

Puddintame, I can't!

I heard you clear then. Praise God, your voice is as plain to me as that bobwhite speaking down there in the mists. I can see you now.

But before coming any nearer, she paused and fished—at first casually, and then frantically—in the canvas pack. A last she came up with the treasure—a Heath bar—and unwrapped it, unprettily, with one hand and her teeth, while covering with the enormous revolver the general area where Puddintame and I cowered. She munched contentedly, grunting like a complacent sow, on the fresh candy. She advanced another step.

The gun, darling, the gun! Puddintame was frantically saying. It's too big for me to handle. O, Fifi, you must.

I reached for the box. I felt a little nauseated at the thought of what I must now do. The target of the Goody Two-Shoes woman—like a vast, dark meteor fallen from the merciless night—was etched perfectly against the moonrich, starspangled sky.

She engulfed the Heath bar between her massive teeth and crunched it down loudly, like some sort of rock-crushing machine doing away with a small, delicious boulder. She swallowed and wiped the back of her hand against her mouth with a dainty flourish of her fat little finger.

Of course, she said, praise God, this little heathen Tibetan dog of yours—he will be destroyed.

O, heavens, Footit! O, my darling, I will do anything to keep that from happening! I did not utter this last apostrophe aloud, though I might as well have. Footit began to bark victoriously, his face pointed directly toward the small copse where Puddintame and I were crouched.

With a sob I tore open the little carton and snatched out the gun. It was light—astonishingly so. My finger felt for the safety catch. The fat woman had heard it all and now sprang forward, the big Magnum booming in her fist. The enormous slugs tore through honeysuckle and gentle columbine. The bullets buried themselves in the Indian-haunted earth or bored cruelly into the bark of flinching old trees. She came upon me like a storm cloud—with that swift alacrity which some fat persons have—and came down with an earthshaking thud on the grass a few feet away.

Shoot! Shoot! screamed Puddintame, jumping up and down.

I was having trouble finding the safety. The gun was somehow not right. I stared down at it through dry, terror-stricken eyes.

Lord!

Incorrigible Sweeley Leech. Another of his little jokes on me— like the fortune cookie in the Port Authority locker.

It was a gun, all right.

But it was by Dröste: one of those foil-wrapped guns made of pure milk chocolate, the kind you put in Christmas stockings, totally incapable of causing any greater damage than a tummyache. The fat Goody Two-Shoes woman grunted with vast satisfaction and took the candy gun out of my cold, astonished fingers.

Praise God, she cried, my favorite!

And as fast as she could peel off the gay blue-and-gold tinfoil she began to eat it while, with her free hand, she held the big Magnum's muzzle against my right temple.

# T✦W✦E✦N✦T✦Y
# E✦I✦G✦H✦T

A little while and I will be gone from among you,
whither I cannot tell,
From nowhere we came, into nowhere we go.
What is Life?
It is the flash of a firefly in the night.
It is the breath of the buffalo in the wintertime.
It is as the little shadow that runs across the
grass and loses itself in the sunset.
> —Crowfoot (leader of the Blackfoot Confederacy)

Poor Dylan Thomas, dying as he did: trying to get his other wing into paradise. But he was obsessed by his fear of Death, the great Translator, and it almost spoils his work. Sometimes he pretends his view of Death is a poetic conceit. But underneath, always, lurks the real fundamentalist, hellfire phobia. That is why—and I often think of poetry when I'm in peril as I was at that moment—that is why, as I say, I am totally unimpressed by two of dear D.T.'s most popular lines:

> Do not go gentle into that good night
> Rage, rage against the dying of the light.

Not rage, certainly. Resentment, maybe, but curiosity is what will illuminate, I think, my moment of dying.

O, I know it's all there—all of *them*: the dear, lost ones, waiting. And helping us over into what my father called the Golden Time.

Notice he said Time—not Place. Because Life after Death is all Time.

And Space.

And so, crouched there as I was, cramped and uncomfortable enough without the hard, cold muzzle of the revolver against my head, I thought of quite a different line of dear Dylan's, and one that does him the service of immortality:

> The ball I threw while playing in the Park
> Has not yet reached the ground.

It was that ball, or rather that moon, in the corner of my eye, which sustained me. And I knew how wrong darling D.T. was—the light does not die. It merely changes into the Invisible. And, of course, the totally, irreversibly, absolutely Deathless.

O, my Wound of Wonder was open wide and flowing in that moment.

Errol Flynn, said the fat woman.

Pardon?

Errol Flynn, she said, through mouthfuls of my delicious candy gun. (O, Sweeley Leech, you've gone too far this time.)

Much as I hate real guns, I think that a real one at that moment might at least have given me something resembling a chance with my foe—though I am sure I could never have summoned up the Whatever-You-Need to shoot at her.

Errol Flynn, she said. Swashbuckling and beautiful.

Her small, bright eyes looked strange in the moonlight and star-shine. And her shots had surely signaled to her sisters down in the river meadows. I could see the pendulum motion of their moving, phosphorescent heels a few hundred feet down the slope.

The only one of them I could ever imagine doing it with, she said. Errol Flynn.

She ladled the two words out through the thick, dark syrup in her voice.

Them? I asked.

Men, she said, and choked a little, her face getting blotched and raddled with anger. *Men!* The nasty, hairy things.

What are you going to do with me? I asked. And my friend?

The Goody Two-Shoes woman eyed Puddintame with severe and distrustful intensity. I don't trust circus freaks, said she, and Puddintame seemed to grow an inch in fury and resentment.

O! Really. To be held prisoner—and be insulted on top of that.

The fat woman fought back a yawn, failed, and showed us a mouthful of solid gold and melted chocolate. She blinked and shook her head like a harried hound dog. I'm a swashbuckler, you know, she said, in a queer voice.

She rubbed her eyes with the heel of the hand holding the small foil-wrapped fragment of the chocolate gun. Yes, jus' like Er—Erl—Errol. Her head lolled and bobbed like a broken toy on the fat trunk of her neck.

You poor dear, I said, catching on. Your swashes are all coming unbuckled.

O, Sweeley Leech, how could I ever have doubted you? O, me of little faith. I felt a perfect ass-wipe of a girl. I knew what was wrong, knew as the fat sweating face plunged down onto the freckled breast, and the Goody Two-Shoes woman slumped snoring into the bluebells and buttercups with a thud that awoke every mole and fairy within a thirty-foot radius. Her face rested (symbolically, I felt) in a fresh cowpie, but that, after all, is a country remedy for freckles, so I didn't feel too evil about being a party to what had just transpired: the falling into a perfectly sound, smiling, snoring, dreamless sleep of somebody who had just ingested candy laced with a strong sleeping potion.

A movement in the nodding, diamond-tipped weeds startled me. It was the same huge pair of spectacles regarding me like those of an overworked Latin professor: Seek, the amiable raccoon who sometimes carried my little friend around on his back.

Naturally, I looked at the gun in the grass beside the outstretched, fat, candy-smeared fingers.

No, said Puddintame, reading me like a book of old, familiar poems. No, we won't need that now. Come. Quickly.

I turned long enough for her to mount the bushy back of the raccoon—long enough, too, to see, a few feet away, the flash of two heels and the blue metal of a small automatic in the hands of another of the Goody Two-Shoes.

There were six of them coming very rapidly up the rise of land. I was held for a moment, as if in thrall to my own curiosity, then felt Puddintame reach up and tug at the hem of my dress.

O, do come, dear, she cried. And she spoke a guttural squeak to her small mount, and together they entered the Venus Grotto again.

I followed. But they had seen me.

And now the ugly sound of those big booming revolvers and little cracking automatics broke the hallowed dream of the moon and shamed the stars. I could hear the bullets cutting, like little lead scythes, through the grass and flowers.

Come! Puddintame cried, and beckoned with her pretty little arm.

Again she lowered her tiny face and spoke to the raccoon, and it plunged into the warm, steaming, fog-tendriled pool and swam directly toward the cataract.

Is there room behind the falls? I shouted. Can we breathe back there?

Puddintame tugged a shaggy ear, and the beast stopped swimming and trod water. It is the entrance to the Labyrinth, she said then. The truest entrance of them all. It is the Venus Gate. It leads directly to— But you shall see. Come, lover. Through the Cataract of Venus. Come! Quickly.

I faced the pool and the scintillating, bombulating cataract ten feet beyond. I watched as the plucky raccoon thrust his pointy nose directly into the foaming commotion of it and soon, with Puddintame gamely on his back, disappeared from sight.

The spray of the waterfall caught the moon as a white spider captures a butterfly. It spun the water into tiny prisms, each one reflecting the gaudy gay hues hidden in the light, each breaking color out upon the misty air in ten thousand circusday hairribbon colors.

There wasn't a moment more to tarry. I snatched up my purse and held my nose and jumped. I sank. Bobbing up into the wisps of moonstruck vapors from the warm water, I was not visible to anyone on the shore. Still, I was aware of two shots fired aimlessly into the fog above my head and I heard the dark slugs bite into the stone above the cataract. I swam swiftly toward the tumult of the fall. I am a fine swimmer, having learned when I was ten years old, in 1976, a year otherwise memorable only for having given the world Jimmy Carter and his Vice-President, Walter Mundane.

Anyway, I swam directly into the cascade of warm water and came out almost immediately on new turf. I say turf, though it was, strictly speaking, sphagnum and that glorious, common golden moss that covers the gnarled, tired roots of old trees and venerable Pleistocene boulders. It was like that in there—a small, domed, underground entrance to a place I knew as a child but had now grown coldly to fear.

A few pale larkspur and a half-dozen nodding sprays of Dutchman's-breeches grew here and there, receiving, I guessed, only an hour or so of sun a day, and this through an aperture which glowed blue and glittery just over my head. The archway to the maze was most curious, being a true fornix—and I suddenly knew where the word *fornicate* comes from: the bricks of the archway formed the perfect long, tapered oval of a woman's vulva. The path beyond the arch was the first, simple passageway of the Labyrinth and, being open at the top, was all awash with moonstarlight. Faintly, from beyond the twelve-foot-high walls on either side of me, I could hear a medley of noises: the soft clamor of twanging mandolins and laughter from the lantern-glowing Indian Mound—a snatch of Victor Herbert—the inimitable laugh of Dorcas Anemone—the voice of my adored Adonis. O, heavens, I loved them all so.

I felt something against my ankle—wet, warm, soggy.

I looked down. It was Footit, drenched but game as a Havoc, West Virginia, fighting cock. He barked at me once, his black lips gleaming against his merry white teeth. Let's find Lindy, he was really saying.

Then I saw Puddintame. She was sitting on a rusty, empty Pennzoil can which someone had cruelly tossed over the wall from the adjoining river meadow. The raccoon sat on his haunches and begged. Puddintame stroked his pert nose and produced a single wild strawberry from her tiny dress pocket and fed it to him. She watched as he washed it in a small pool of clear water and then ate it with slow, whiskery gusto.

I stared at a pale, white, flat block of sandstone and mica at my feet. A red freckle, no larger than a dwarf poppy blossom, had spattered it. I knelt and touched it with my finger to be sure. It came away incarnadine, scarlet—yes, it was blood: a droplet my brave sister had dropped on her way to the Chamber of Stars. Brave Lindy! O, love, maybe your plain stubborn braveness will heal you. For there is a degree of Courage before which even old Death chuckles and stands back, pausing, in respect.

I—I am frightened.

Come, said Puddintame in her tiny voice, reverberant with encouragement.

She jumped from the rusty oil can and climbed aboard Seek. Come, she cried again, and spurred the small beast gently with her tiny toes.

And off we went into that incredible place. For a moment my thoughts went back to the Venus Grotto and its hateful invaders. Heavens, do you suppose they knew about the secret entrance under the waterfall?

No, said Puddintame, reading me again as if I were a first-grade primer. They will not follow.

I am thankful, I said. That poor fat woman—what an evil, selfish face she had. Poor dear. It saddens me to see God's body all ravaged by hate and sugar, doesn't it you, Puddintame?

I suppose, she said, though you are far more tolerant than I. I despised that woman thoroughly. She looked—well, you said it— mean. Yes, mean. Mean. Mean. The kind of woman—

She shook her head.

—the kind of woman who would have smoked cigarettes at Tony Randall's bar mitzvah.

Yes, she did, rather.

The inner walls of the Labyrinth were incredibly intricate mosaics with some peeling, ancient frescoes. Aside from the oil can, the place was remarkably free of litter. Wild flowers grew in jeweled profusion.

And that made me curious.

We wandered on, through passageways which never came to

culs-de-sac, and yet which were fearfully, maddeningly intricate. I watched the banded tail of the raccoon pluming up with brave panache over our little parade. And curiosity nibbled mousily at the fringes of my wits.

Why hasn't this place—in mid-America—ever been discovered or explored by archaeologists, Puddintame? I asked.

Do you want them to?

Heavens, no.

Then don't put the thought into your imagination, she said.

But why? I said.

Puddintame eyed me with some impatience. One might as well ask why botanists didn't chop down and study Jack's beanstalk, dissecting it in scientific amazement. You see, darling, the things of Fancy—the all-powerful and seemingly superhuman feats of the Imagination—are, sadly enough, beyond the scrutiny of almost every little Ph.D. and M.D. these days. That's why people like your Lindy still have cancer and heart disease.

You mean—we're imagining all this?

I didn't say that, said Puddintame a little testily. But don't worry if your heaven *is* imaginary.

I know, I said. That's what makes it real.

And so we prowled on through the honeycomb of moonlit and wild-flower-festive chambers. It was as though we were microscopic creatures—mere reasoning, one-celled organisms—prowling like tiny insects amid the whorled fingerprints of a giant of whose existence we were—or at least, I was—totally ignorant.

It was therefore in this curious, labyrinthine quandary—in God's own fingerprint—that I sought my sore-sick sister.

Irreverently, but all the same a little frightened by the silence of the place, I switched on my wristradio. It was the TRUCAD channel, and America's Secretary of Ecumenical Affairs was speaking a benediction for these troubled times.

I knew the sales pitch would wrap up the vespers in a bare minute. I switched the tiny radio off.

I smiled. Hush, hush, whisper who dares! O Sweet Billy Graham is selling his prayers.

We walked on through the sharp, angular shadows of the moon-starshine as the periodic wink and burn and dip of a firefly strayed in from Queen Anne's lacy lands beyond.

498

At last we came to another archway. Puddintame dismounted, fed her raccoon a tiny bite of crabapple, and looked at me with kind determination. Above her, on the moonwashed wall, glowed the peeling, muted splendors of a mural that looked excitingly like something by a divinely careless Cro-Magnon Picasso. Well, couldn't it have been?

I looked at the stunned, soft colors of it, loving greatness, praising it, on my soul's knees before the feet of genius. I thought of a game I used to play when I was thirteen. I used to think up famous questions in history I was glad never got asked. One of them: "Are you certain that you want this abortion, Frau Mozart?"

And so on.

Anyway, Puddintame was quite serious. Almost solemn. She pointed to something on the ground that glittered yellow in the spear of moonlight which kissed it. It was the end of a golden string stretching off among the wild flowers and sphagnum into the mystery-shrouded distances of the Labyrinth toward that strange place I remembered once hearing called the Quandary of Queens.

Take it, said Puddintame, proffering the end of the glittering golden cord to me.

Why, Puddintame?

Take it, she said again. Then I will tell you why.

I went over and grasped the end of the thin, threadlike golden cord in my two fingers.

I give you the end of a golden string, said Puddintame. And her words brought back memories of Uncle Will Blake and father. Only wind it into a ball and it will lead you in at heaven's gate, built in Jerusalem's wall.

That's him—that's Uncle Will, I said. But why are you giving me the end of the golden string, Puddintame?

Because, she said simply, yet kindly, because from here you are going on—alone.

I see, I said in a littlegirl voice, and shivering a bit in my wet frock and heels.

I shall miss you, darling, said Puddintame. Though it is surely written that we shall meet again.

I pray so. Meet again—and maybe love again.

So do I pray so, she said. And I think we shall—if I ever get through this benighted night without being kidnapped into slavery by that little fiend Didnt and his Foxy paramour.

It is surely written, I said, that you shall.

Anyway, she said gaily, *may* we make love again?

The voice was so honey-soft, the eyes so large and ardent in the tiny face, the little lips, gleaming like a red raspberry in the moonlight, so enticing.

I reached down and picked up my little lover. I kissed her face and then—gently, so as not to bruise them—each little breast.

Yes. She seemed to look at me enviously.

This time I read her like a primer. You are envious of me, I said.

A little, she sighed. Your freedom and all. I haven't any. Poor Clyde in the Home. And no other love but on this vile night—and then with a rapacious and S and M fairy. Once a year. Sigh. Sigh.

She studied my face.

You have the look, she said, of one who makes love often.

O, whenever I can, Puddintame. When it comes to lovemaking, I am a regular Little Often Annie.

Arbutus and some wild honeysuckle flourished at the top of the Labyrinth wall where we stood. The moon was caught in some leaves and blossoms for an instant and then wrenched free and sailed on, serene, in the Van Gogh skies.

I must leave you now, said my small friend.

She smiled at me. I'm afraid my face showed some of the dismay I felt at the prospect of going it alone.

Don't worry, she said. And she quoted Uncle Will again, "Only believe—and try, try, try."

Yes. O, I do try, Puddintame, but it's been ages since I've been here. If I were four or five years old—why, this would be a kind of lark, I guess. I would dare any corner of the Quandary of Queens without fear. But now—

She pointed to the gold string in my hand and smiled as she mounted the saucy raccoon again.

Only wind it into a ball, she said.

And with a spurring of her sharp little heels she was gone, not through the waterfall, but through another egress she knew of in her quaint little storehouse of memories. O, she knew the place—there was no doubt of that—and how I envied her that knowledge.

I stood a moment, smelling the crushed mint under my heels and the scents of all the flowers and herbs and spices in that enchanted place. I stared about me at the walls. To the left was a fresco of Criste—peeling like a stale gingerbread man but jolly and happy as Saint Nick.

I could hear them singing above the mandolin and guitar over on the festive eminence of the Indian Mound.

"Say not love is a dream—"

Lehár.

*The Count of Luxemburg.*

I smiled and began to walk slowly, watching the moon, watching the wink of the golden string as it lifted from the buttercups and moondrenched groundnut before me, watching the small ball grow in my fingers. I passed among sequestered shadows. Long bars of jagged moon lit the amazing walls on either side of me.

What's this? A Dance of Death series—each cartoon perhaps four feet high and (incredibly) in the unmistakable style of dear Cézanne himself.

But this was madness, and I stumbled on through that madness, noting each of the pictures as I passed it, a little out of breath at each pause.

> The merchant turns as Death touches his shoulder.
> Death beckons to the magistrate.
> The baker receives his summons from Death.
> Death taps the soldier, who turns in surprise.

And so they went—fifteen of them, in the style of those lifesize murals old Villon rhymed about in the *Grand Testament.* The last two caused me to cry out with Joy.

It was simple. Perhaps the most carefully painted of all the Dance of Death series: Death himself surprised and turning in fear as he feels a tap on his own bony shoulder from—yes, of course you know—the hand of Criste. And the final panel where Criste leads Death away.

O, Lindy, I love you! I cried aloud despite myself—and no one there to hear but Footit.

I love you, Lindy Leech!

And I ran on and on, past the Lane of Spiders, where all the moony night harmless arachnids spin silk which is gathered by fairies and a few favored others to weave with bones into the lovely fabric which now composed my lingerie, past the alley called Montezuma's Folly, past the sweet-reeking Chamber of Spices.

The decorations on the walls became, alternately, more modern and sophisticated and then more primitive. I finally decided that they were both at once.

I ran on, the moon caught in a curl of disarranged hair at my temple. The stars danced in their mad starry night above me. Footit ran on ahead like a valiant furry scout.

In fact, it was Footit who announced the end of our quest. He paused, looked straight ahead at a paneled and very ancient carved door a few feet ahead of us, and then ran to it and began scratching and speaking in soft, low gasps.

I wound up the rest of the cord (now a sizable ball) and paused with my hand on the latch of the door, which stood a few inches ajar.

Lindy?

The silence was somehow more eloquent than any answer, for I knew someone was there. I edged the door open, producing a great, woody groan, and stared inside.

It was, I think, the most amazing chamber I had seen yet, and suddenly—O, these memories never die in us!—I was there again and it was childertime and Innocence was everywhere and Fear was only shadows of trees on a midnight window blind. But there was no Fear in this place.

It was the nursery Lindy and I had shared as children.

With certain differences. O, the old toys were there, scattered about the rag-rugged floors like sunbathers on some beach in Atlantis. Slobbo, the teddy bear, and Mingo, the doll with the pushed-in face like the delivery man from the drugstore had when we were sick and he brought us calomel and chewing gum, citrate of magnesia and the latest Uncle Wiggily book. It was a charming room and there were no toys lying around which I did not instantly recognize. Including a few my father said had been made by Galileo.

I noted all these details only briefly, because my attention was riveted to what sat crosslegged on the rug before a tiny play table.

Lindy.

Lindy, looking very ill, but poised with a paintbrush in her hand above the last two runes of the Criste Lite and a glass of tinted water and a box of Art Crome watercolors open on the tabletop.

Slowly she lifted her gaze to me, not smiling.

Hello, Feef, she said in an amazingly strong voice.

Hello, Lindy love.

I wanted you to be here, she said, and the voice had grown hoarse and strange, when I finished it. I wanted you to see that it was really—me.

Finish it, Lindy, I said.

She dipped the sable hairs of the little brush into the gaudy waters and swizzled it around. Then she touched it to the pan in the flat metal box where a simple chartreuse was to be found. She filled in the green with gestures of heavenly, childlike carelessness which made me remember the children of the Dyer at old Montauk. Then she cleaned the brush again and tinted the remaining rune a clear, limpid magenta.

I don't know all the things that happened then. The air of the charming little room with its gay blowing curtains seemed to grow lighter, brighter. The dolls rose up and strutted, and the very shadows caught fire and curled at the edges like fine Bible paper burning, and the beams of moonlight which shot in through the quartered panes drew from the moon her very blood and glowed with it.

Lindy stacked the yellow sheets of colored paper neatly. She got to her feet and I saw the small mark of blood she had made on the gaudy, gay carpet, the crimson of it blending in with the faded calico.

Lindy held the sheets tight against her small breasts and stared at the moon, her face wan but transfixed. I have it now, she said. Once I destroyed it. Now I have brought it to life again.

She turned to me suddenly then, defiance and fresh fear all over her pale features. Her lips trembled; her eyes blazed.

I shouldn't have waited for you, she said. I can read it in your face, Feef.

O, what, Lindy darling? What?

I can read your mind, she said breathlessly and in a voice knotted with thick sobs. You don't trust me with the Criste Lite. You think I'll destroy it again.

She swayed a little, like a fine little tree in a great gulp of wind. You want to take it away from me now, Feef.

Lindy, wait. Lindy. O, I don't, dear!

You do. You do, she shrilled, and before I could move—and with a celerity which amazed me—she clutched the pages of the Criste Lite against her breasts and ran through the open doorway. I stood listening, helpless, as her irregular footfalls chattered and rumored past the echoing walls of the Labyrinth.

I leaned back, exhausted, staring at a box of toy soldiers and a pile of alphabet blocks, some of which had been chewed by a teething baby.

I was dismayed. Lindy *had* read my thoughts, God forgive them. I *had* been full of suspicion that she might—

But no. The thought was too grotesque, even horrible. Yet I could not keep that thought from returning to my perceptions. I could not escape the sudden feeling that I must follow Lindy quickly and rescue the precious bundle from her painracked fingers before she—

I scratched Footit on the head and hurried back out into the moonlight of the corridor.

In the dark the spiders worked silently. Spices and Ravel, *Dreams of Matisse* drifted in the dark.

The moon spun her dreams. The stars made merry.

I began to run toward the chiaroscuro of dark and shadow and arrows of thin moon from which, still echoing, I could hear my sister's fatal, fateful footfalls.

While both Time and Space hammered, like demons, upon my temples.

# T✦W✦E✦N✦T✦Y
# N✦I✦N✦E

I ran—not blindly, for the way was now familiar, but hard. Sometimes I think that it was Footit, not I, who found the way out of the maze for us.

But at last we were there, beside the river road, beside the copses of willows who sob a soft green scene by the river herself.

Something, up the road a piece, glimmered off and on like some enormous firefly, and I ran toward it, Footit leading in his utterly officious little way. I knew I was going along the Glory road toward Echo Point and the bungalow of Sweeley Leech. Somehow I felt that, whatever her intentions, Lindy would go there first. The place would be empty, I supposed, and echoing with shadows and the squeaks of old, familiar floorboards which creaked like the very gibbet of Montfaucon.

The meadows to my left were sparkling with fireflies and reveling fairies, and I could hear, beneath the dark sough of the moony wind, the twang of harps and the tweedle of elf pipes. Ah, many's the bluebell cup brimming with wild-flower wine that was lifted that

Halloween night. But I could no longer hear my singing friends atop the lanternlit Indian Mound. Had they seen the Goody Two-Shoes and taken refuge? No need—the fat woman had said that father's disciples were not being sought. Still, it made me uneasy. The night seemed to have grown tense, as the web grows taut at the spider's glittering crouch to seize its prey. Ah, Sweeley Leech, how I would love the sound of your voice about now.

I ran on along the dusty macadam until I was in sight of the intermittent light. It was a neon sign atop a rather flashy little roadhouse. COCKTAILS BROMPTON'S COCKTAILS BROMPTON'S COCKTAILS.

The light slammed off and on in scalding orange metaphors, as if consciously trying to soil the moon and the stars. I stared at the interior of the place from the roadside, standing with my legs apart and my hands on my hips, my purse dangling. The place was chic—even chichi—not your regulation roadside Appalachian river beer joint. And the bald statement against the pulsing, bruised sky: COCKTAILS BROMPTON'S COCKTAILS BROMPTON'S.

The name rang a strange, darkfeeling bell in the far, far interiors of my mind. There was an association between Brompton's and Lindy. But I knew not what.

Well, some hunch—some craftiness in the marrow of the bones—guided me into the little cocktail lounge.

It was surprisingly pleasant, beguilingly pleasant—I mean, it had the effect of making you feel you were being duped by its pleasantness. There were two bartenders and a waitress in attendance. There were no other customers, though I saw, and was drawn to, an empty glass and a fallen pigskin glove on the floor beside the bar. I climbed upon a stool, fingering the glove.

No one else, I said to one of the bartenders.

He was wax-mustached and slick-looking—like the horny dentist in an old-time smoker film.

No one else what? he asked me in a reedy, unpleasant voice. Or, as the case may be, who?

Nobody else around here wears this kind of pigskin glove. It's from South America. Comes from a big peccary kind of boar.

Ah, yes. That would be the young lady who just left.

Dark? I pressed forward then. Pretty? Green eyes?

Yes.

Wearing a nice Harris tweed?

Yes. Do you know her?

She is my sister, I said. She is very ill.

Yes, we know, chorused both bartenders, smiling, like undertakers who must constantly be pretending that kind of sweet, sympathetic sadness.

We know, said the first bartender again. He sniffed perfunctorily. He took the glove out of my hand and stared at it, shaking his head slowly. That's why it would be pointless, he said, to hold the glove for her return.

I stared, dumbfounded, furious and growing more so every moment.

Or even asking you to give it to her, he went on. Pointless to think of her ever wanting this glove again. She is so clearly terminal.

Give me the glove, I said.

He stared and for a moment I thought he was going to defy me. Then he sniffed as before and tossed the glove on the bar over by my hand.

There isn't enough time left, he said, for her to need it in.

How do you know so much?

Oh, tut-tut, he said, you must not question.

You are a bartender, I snapped, not a doctor. And, as such, you can pour me a drink.

Very well, he said. I recommend the house special—Brompton's Cocktail.

What's in it? I asked.

He leaned forward with a wet wink and began to whisper. Are you broadminded? he said hoarsely. Because you see—with them it really doesn't matter what's in the damned thing. I mean, how can you hurt somebody who is so mortally hurt already? See?

What's in it? I asked again, staring at the drink in his hand, a drink that looked about as appetizing as Sammy Davis's glass-eye rinse.

His voice dropped two decibels. Cocaine and heroin to begin with, he said. It's the British formula, you see. Then ethyl alcohol, 190 proof. O, we make the very best Brompton's. With a little Valium. And a really first-rate cherry essence for flavor.

Yes, I know. Yes.

You've heard of us, then? O, our cocktail is the very end, every-one says.

I would have thought it impossible, but his voice dropped even more while the other bartender went to the cash register and began to stack hundred-dollar bills.

You understand, said my bartender, this Brompton Cocktail, in addition to being a painkiller of sorts, it—well, it appeases those last upsurges of insurrection in the—the customer. I mean, it removes from his mind forever all sorts of notions which might strike his fancy about a—well, let us say miraculous remission which might embarrass accepted Medical Establishment opinion.

O, that would be unthinkable, of course. Like maybe one of them might decide to laugh his cancer out—we wouldn't want that, would we?

No. The word was purred—as if in from the silver throat of some huge, deathly cat.

Try it, he said, pushing the awful drink toward me in its slopping paper cup.

He and the other bartender began to move round the bar toward me. In that split second before I grabbed up my purse and sprinted for the door, I suddenly remembered. Lindy. Brompton's Cocktail. Of course. Brompton's Cocktail was the mixture given in cancer wards to suffering terminal patients. I felt a grasp of fingers at my shoulder as I skidded out into the night and began to run.

I ran breathlessly for perhaps a hundred feet before I paused and looked back. The two had not followed. They stood smiling in the doorway, and I could lip-read, by moonlight, their words. You may be back, they said. Remember that. At any time. You may be back—begging.

Never! I screamed, and pellmelled down the dusty ribbon of river road toward the blessed house of my father, in which there are so many, many mansions. Never!

Dimly, dustily, looming ahead I could see, beneath the shadow of the Indian Mound, the great scissored cutout of the bungalow. The slates were glistening under the moon's fine sifting radiance and a few kerosene lamps were burning in the windows.

My walk became more leisurely and my panic less extreme. And

I felt guilty. After all, sick as she was, how far could poor Lindy go with the precious manuscript? Certainly she was incapable of any distant kidnapping of it—like the one to Manhattan that had spelled doom to the first copy of the Criste Lite. I went slowly up the tanbark walk toward the veranda.

Fifi? a voice cried softly in the firefly hush.

Yes.

It was familiar. It was my darling Adonis. I smelled his scent and prickled.

Fifi, you'd better come upstairs.

Why? Where's Lindy?

Upstairs.

How is she?

Fifi, something is happening. Something very strange is happening. I think you had better come and join the others outside her bedroom door.

They were all clustered before the great paneled door to Lindy's room. It was shut. Beside it on a small fifteenth-century French fruitwood table stood a fine Tang vase in the preferable green with a sprig of bittersweet burning in its mouth like visual incense.

I looked from one to the other of the gentle, good, kind, concerned faces of the Children of the Remnant. They shifted their feet uneasily on the thick, patterned Araby carpet. There was concern in their faces, and that concern may have been the same as mine, for from within the otherwise silent bedroom where my sister lay—from beneath the door, through the keyhole, through the thin crack in the antique paneling—came the most exquisite shots and beams of quivering rainbow light. It was as though that ancient, carved door were not lovely maple but the iron gate to a furnace behind which breathed the spectral, flaming Unknown.

I was no help to the others. I stood and stared. I saw each of us illuminated by the quivering shafts of motley light—and more. Now, from behind the door came sounds. O, my God, such sounds—such a concert of sounds—such a medley of strangenesses. I say strangenesses because most bright light blinds, dazzles, bewilders the optic nerve. This light—though somehow brighter than sunlight itself—seemed only to expand the ability of the eye to see. Moreover, it did not dazzle, it soothed. And I say strangenesses because of the sounds—all of them from Lindy, all of them her voice, all of them very much alive and very much, I am afraid, under the stress of some enormous, fresh, and wholly original emotion. First, it was a kind of chant, but then it would stop and become laughter—O, laughter that bubbled up from the very wellsprings of her heart, that laughter so rare in all of us. And then the laughter segued off into a song and the song lilted and lifted with Schumann sweetness and then came the laugh again—rich and throaty and feminine.

We stood. We waited. We wondered. We pondered.

Should we go in? asked Reverend Jimbo finally.

I say no, snapped Aubade at once. Something very special—I might even say something very sacred—is going on behind that door.

Did she lock it?

No.

Have you tried it?

Yes.

Do you think she's in any danger, Dorcas?

I think she's in less danger than she was, say, an hour ago.

And you, Fu Manchu—what do you say about it? What say you, old soothsayer? Say a sooth about this, pray.

She should be left alone, Fifi.

But listen, now it changes—

And indeed it had—swiftly and remorselessly the chants, the songs, the laughter, bled off into groans and whimpers of the most piteous nature.

O, Lindy, I cried, my fingers outstretched to the knob.

Don't, Fifi love, said the old Chinese.

Don't, love, pleaded my darling Adonis.

But can't you hear? Have you lost your ears, all of you? She's dying in there.

The sounds of Death and the sounds of Love are—unfortunately—almost identical, observed Madame Jonathan.

I listened more closely.

Dear Dylan's face and phrase flashed in my receptors:

> The ball I threw while playing in the Park
> Has not yet reached the ground.

O, Lindy, what are you saying to us, to God, to the universe, with these gasps and groans and whimpers? For I suddenly realized that the sounds I had at first interpreted as anguish might as well have been bliss—the bliss of a young woman in the throes of her first physical liaison.

—has not yet reached the ground.

I opened my eyes.

The groans and other strange noises had ceased almost as abruptly as they had begun.

I looked at each of the Remnant in the weltering light of the hallway under the sweet, cool silver gleam of the oil lamps: Fu Manchu, Mère de Cézanne, Dorcas Anemone, Madame Jonathan T. Bigod, Aubade, Reverend Jimbo St. Venus, even Toni Falconi fresh and crisp from Lincoln Center— O, I adored them so. And I looked to each of them for some reassurance that what I had just heard was not my sister Lindy's death.

I think, said Fu Manchu then, his long nails rasping on the thick silver doorknob, I think we may look in on her now.

Is it—? I mean, is she—?

Fifi, said Aubade, her hands cradling my face. Fifi, something very strange, very secret, very personal and, I think, very sacred has been going on behind that door. But as to whether we find Life when we open that door, is something not one of us, not the oldest and wisest of us, can ascertain. We must see for ourselves.

It was she and not the old Chinese who pressed the door open.

Despite the fact that the sheets of the holy book had been tucked away in a fresh Red Apple supermarket shopping bag and flashed only intermittently by the bedside, the scene was filled with light from the moon. The great hussy was nailed like a gold salver to the sky and pricklets of silver light all round her showed the hobnails of the silver, hammered stars. On a table by the window a single rhododendron blossom floated in a tiny glazed Danish dish of water. The water wrinkled and shivered in the breeze from under the blowing, moonlit curtains.

Lindy lay on the bed. She was quite naked. She was asleep.

The ball I threw—

I have never seen anyone so transfigured, so—so *fulfilled* is the only word I can make do here.

She looked like a sleeping and contented woman after the first happy fuck of her life. And her color: all the old Harkness Pavilion pallor was gone; nothing now but roses twinkling in her cheeks and on the pert, remembering tips of her upturned nipples. Her flat belly rose and fell with her slow breathing.

She stirred and one hand brushed a strand of clean, curly hair into her mouth and chewed it sensuously.

O, my Lindy, I know you have not died. I have never seen you look so alive.

I've spent my whole life looking for closets to come out of, but I knew in that moment that Lindy was the one member of my family with whom I could never make love. She was now, at least, too utterly female. Not that I have a thing about incest. I do think it has been cheapened some since Orestes and Electra. I mean, I read a headline in a Philly paper the other night that illustrates this: MODERN OEDIPUS BURNS CONTACT LENSES AFTERWARDS.

Like that.

Anyhow, I have seldom seen anyone look so beautiful as did my sister, Lindy, in that moment.

I moved into the room.

And then I saw it—the Thing beside her on the bedsheet. And I could smell the aftermath of something—like ozone—in the air.

The Thing was perhaps the size of an order of sweetbreads—pallid and almost luminous with a curious, leprous glowing health. I touched it gingerly with a fingertip. It was still warm and still moist from Lindy.

She had given birth to it.

Her pale, leprous infant.

And now she lay, spent, but whole and glowing and all brand-new, on the bed; her dark hair, once so sharply chignoned and proper, now spilling out in glorious profuse abundance on the flowered pillows. Her lips were gently parted and moist, as in some kind of corny *Playboy* centerfold—I tell you, she looked simply *épatante*.

I felt a memory of a something. It was a TV show back in the early eighties by Kanin Garson or somebody about some of the old movie makers. One of them said this simply beautiful line, a line so full of the craft and genius of moviemaking: "Hurry—we'll be losing the light soon."

I couldn't get that weathered face, that line, out of my mind.

I went to where the precious, and now completed, manuscript of the Criste Lite lay bundled into its Red Apple shopping bag. I picked it up and led the others, single file, out of the room and closed the door upon the sleeping Lindy. Aubade had covered her with one of Rinsey's old apostle quilts against the chill of the moon's imminent fading.

We stood in the hallway a moment without looking at one another. And then our eyes rose and met, and each of us smiled.

The quest, said someone—and it could have been any one of us—the quest is fulfilled. We have the Criste Lite again. And from the looks of her, Lindy Leech is whole.

O, yes! I cried. Couldn't you just see it? And wasn't it a miracle, the way the roses came back to her cheeks? Yes, she is whole. And it was the Criste Lite.

I wandered off toward some moonlight which fell upon an arabesqued flower in the carpet and made it glow.

And yet I doubted her, I said. And I am ashamed of that. I thought she would run away again with the manuscript and it would be lost again.

Aubade laid her gentle fingers on my arm. We understand, lovey, she said. It was natural of you to think that. Any of us would have thought—would have done the same.

She squeezed my wrist. But hold on, she said. Do not relax just yet.

What do you mean? asked Madame Jonathan then.

I mean the tale is not yet told.

You mean Sweeley Leech, of course, I said. His destiny is not clear. As if it were ever. O, my dears, he has always been such a wanderer among perils. You can't blame him for this latest one.

The first striations of rose and saffron of a river sunrise flowered pale among the eastern hills. The autumn birds were waking with wild, high decibels of song.

Have the women been here after me? I asked.

What women? O, you mean the Goody Two-Shoes, Reverend Jimbo answered. They were here late last night and searched the bungalow—it was before your sister got here. Then they left.

There was a birdsong pause.

But they will be back.

Yes, I suppose, I said. And I am on their wanted list, too. Such illustrious company I am in.

Almost as if in confirmation, the sound began, plangent and silvery: the beating of a great bell. It rose and fell on the faint river wind from the dying west, where stars were growing watery and pale; in the growing eastern light the day had laid her soft fingers upon the river with golden praise. Raincrows fluted in the low, low willows. The lost ghost of summer ran grieving through the colored lands, whispering of old promises and August love affairs.

Where is that bell ringing? I asked.

Fifi, you must know now—there is no sense in keeping it from you any longer, said Toni Falconi gently, her fingers on my arm. They are summoning the people.

Who is? What do you mean?

Today, said Aubade, in the great church above the wasteland where the smoke from the zinc smelter blows—today they are going to hold the trial of Sweeley Leech.

And me, I said. I suppose they will be here for me soon.

I think not, said Fu Manchu, with some small sign of cheerfulness.

What do you mean, Fu?

I mean they are no longer seeking you, he said.

He held up a small, folded document with TRUCAD insignia all over it. Your pardon, he said, because you are pregnant. You should be very thankful. It's official from President Moto.

I want no favors! I shouted. I'll stand beside Sweeley Leech.

Of course you will, said Aubade, but think how much more powerful you can be here on the outside.

I don't want any special consideration, I cried. Sweeley Leech is the most important thing in the world to me now. I want to be tried with him.

Think, Fifi, said Dorcas then. Aubade is right. You can do more for your father in the freedom of where you now stand. Perhaps merely because you love him—if possible—more than any of us do.

For an instant the spiritual image of his face flashed upon my receptors.

The ball I threw while playing in the Park—

O, father, make a miracle and flee these awful people!

We have seen him, said Aubade.

Father?

Yes.

Here?

Yes. He—he came here about the time we came in from the lawn party.

Was he—was he well?

Yes. Very much so. But his powers—

They are failing, I suppose.

Not really. He is—he was as energetic as could be, said Dorcas. But he told us that his powers—

You mean his powers to work miracles?

Yes. He has three left.

Three?

Miracles. Yes. He says he has the power left for only three miracles in this life.

And I suppose he is saving them.

Yes, but not the way you might think.

One of them could be a miracle to save his life.

He would never waste a miracle on that, said Jimbo. He called it that—"wasting" it.

Then what—?

Let us go to the church, said Aubade, whirring past me like a charming mechanical *poupée*. Let us go and see for ourselves.

They are holding his trial today?

With a cast of thousands.

It's being broadcast on TV, Fifi.

O, how gross. O, that grosses me out!

I fear you have not seen an end to grossnesses, my darling.

We left the Red Apple shopping bag glowing faintly in Lindy's room in the closet where her clothes were hanging. It shone a faint, sweet gleam even after we had closed the sliding door.

Lindy was, to my surprise, not still asleep in bed, but in the tub, having a geranium-scented bubble bath.

Miracles—had there not been perhaps enough for one day?

The rags of the night were torn and purple in the west, where the moon languished, as if in final rites, upon the boughs of the Royal Paulownia. O, she was doomed to the glorious death of a sunrise soon. To the east the painted boughs of maples and elms burned with breakfast fires. Each leaf seemed handtinted with morning light, and the birds went about in the gay frenzy they always express when they discover that each night is not eternal.

We walked.

The November morning lay white as pieces of ice in the waking trees all round us. The moon languished, wan, a sleepy homebound reveler, lolling her head on the shoulder of the Appalachian ridges. The fairies, elves, gnomes, and other small creatures (including Didnt and his Foxy Jane) had lapsed off into drunken slumber. Along the river road, tall poplars spun their white coins in the quivering light.

At last we came to the barren, striated plain above which the old bell tolled its stumbling, bronze anthem in the belfry of the ancient Slavic church.

The church, as you may remember, was transplanted from Slovenia to West Virginia by the redoubtable Cora B. Fiasco, *née* Absolutington, and is one of the fading landmarks of the countryside. Below the church, below the plain, below indeed the river road, is the ferryboat landing, where a small boat, the *Magyar Lady,* shuttles back and forth across the Ohio, manned by two rivermen of Slavic extraction. Slavic people favor this means of crossing the river, preferring it to the bridge a few miles upstream. Hence—inevitably, I suppose—the little boat is known as the "Hunky Dory."

The light was queer. I can't explain it except to say that—the light was queer. Like heaven and hell at eternal war in some John Milton universe, the rays of morning were crossing spears with the last dark arrows of the night. It was like that peculiar light you so often see in the films of a certain director-producer who achieved early success in the mid-nineteen-eighties. By now you probably know him. As Hitchcock chose as a kind of hallmark his own appearance in one scene of every film of his, so this director has developed a trademark of his own. His films are as violent as early Peckinpah and full of death and mayhem. His gimmick is that in each of his films there is one death—a snuff—which is real. An actual death. A murder. His cast and crew, naturally, never disclose the victim, since they would thereby reveal themselves as accomplices. At any rate, that is his trademark—that and the curious light which flickers and fades and flames through all his flicks.

It was that kind of threatening light this morning in the riverlands.

We walked up the eroded, grassless plain toward the bombulating cathedral. The rich tones of the great bell rolled like great bronze balls down the slope, bouncing and booming brassily as they came, rolling past us and into the river and across it and against the hills of old Helvetia. And then echoing goldenly back. It was somnolent and rich, that sound. It came somehow from the strange Middle East, though, and brought little *frissons* to the small hairs at the back of my neck.

The birds in the sycamores and maples joined the carillon and did sweet and enigmatic variations on the "Gloria" from Leoš Janáček's great *Glagolitic Festival Mass.*

Aubade seemed curiously cheerful, but my adored Adonis was solemn, a faint smile upon his lips, as we approached the drama's end and prepared for a last play with the toys and then into the box with them until another day. Uncle Mooncob—well, how can I describe the change that had come over him since that revelation in Lindy's bedroom? He was sullen and pouting at first—as if reluctant to accept something so obviously divine. And then a light had come into his eyes—and it had not faded yet. Loll was full of flashing teeth and eyes—all smiles. Madame Jonathan T. Bigod had her hand on my left arm, and Reverend Jimbo was on my right. Toni Falconi, long-legged and lissome, strode on ahead like a boy, whistling softly through her teeth to the pagan melody of the bell. Mère de Cézanne hobbled along gamely beside us.

Toward what did we move so inexorably, like pawns upon a chessboard, like filings of iron drawn by the hungry currents of some gigantic magnet? It seemed somehow an act of obedience, of duty, of fulfillment. And yet I could see in the eyes of each of us a kind of flinching horror of something which was approaching faster than the speed of light.

I saw an arrowhead—a frail and lovingly fashioned birdpoint—and stooped and picked it up and pocketed it.

The ball I threw while playing in the Park has not yet—

Move on.

Uncle approached me now—poor, dear, transfigured darling.

Fifi?

Yes, uncle.

What is going to happen?

I wish I knew, uncle.

He paused and scratched the tip of his nose with his little finger. I can't help thinking of Uncle—of your grandfather, Fifi—Link Singletree Cresap.

O, that dodo!

I know. The family never ceases talking about him. His life. His death. Still, you must heed the lesson in the man's existence, Fifi.

O, dear. Here we go again. "Tenting Tonight on the Old Camp Ground" and all that bull. "Cheers for the—"

Shush, Fifi, uncle hissed. Picture the man. His last great charge. With Pickett at Gettysburg. Armed with a Sharp's fifty-caliber rifle and a Navy Colt. And charging up the hill. Surely you remember the rest of the story, Feef?

I am trying to forget.

The bullets are thick as honeybees under a shithouse. Buzz. Buzz. Buzz. Buzz. But Uncle Link has a copy of the Holy Bible in a pocket over his heart, and when the bullet-meant-for-him comes whizzing through—

I know, I know, I said. The Bible stopped it.

Uncle looked unhappy.

Why, no, as a matter of fact, he said thoughtfully. It went right through the Bible and killed Uncle Link—stone-dead. Fifi, what *is* the moral to that old family story? I must confess I can't make much of a Christian parable out of it.

I think we are approaching one, uncle.

One what, lovey?

Christian parable. Whatever is going to happen inside that church. O, yes, I feel it.

Me, too, Feef. Me, too.

And he hurried on ahead—out of drag now and sensibly and rather colorfully clad in khaki shorts and shirt with a gay scarf fluttering at his throat as if in commemoration of his exodus from the closet.

I heard a cry from behind me, and turned and saw—to my mild amazement—Lindy, dressed in one of my gay dresses instead of something from her own rather solemn wardrobe. Her face was rosy and flushed with health. She looked as if her little nap and bath had completely refreshed her. She was eating a raw carrot and talking between chews to someone beside her—someone small, very small indeed. A closer glance through the mists proved this to be none other than my charming companion of the night before, Puddintame, looking charming in a white linen dress and low-heeled oxfords no bigger than a cigarette snipe.

Lindy and the little lady hurried along and were soon at my side.

Where is father, Feef?

I don't know, Lindy.

I think, said Lindy, that if all this had been happening to me a few hours ago, I would be scared. Now I am not, Feef.

Nor I, Lindy.

I don't think you understand, Feef. I don't mean scared for myself—I mean scared for Sweeley Leech. Somehow I am not.

I know, I said. That's what I meant, too. They have captured him—he is their prisoner—and yet something whispers inside me that he will outwit them all.

Yes.

Come, darling. O, half my prayers have been answered, Lindy. I think I have so little left to ask Criste for.

I know, Feef. I have that feeling, too.

I searched her with my eyes—not just her face, which was radiant with health, but the contours of her body. Lindy had always had a good figure, disguise it as she might. Now she had more than that—she was lithe and petite and slender and yet wearing that curious voluptuousness that some thin girls have. And she looked whole.

Somehow, she said, with a strange little smile, I think my life began back there in my room tonight.

I know, Lindy. I saw it. I believe that, too.

My life is beginning on the night before the ending of the life of Sweeley Leech—for I am afraid, Feef, that this is what impends.

We had drawn close enough to the church to see, through the dwindling, wisping morning river mists, the white trucks of the TV crews and other workmen round the entrance.

Great movement was in evidence. Men and women bustled around, laying cables and setting up light reflectors. On the TV trucks were posters proclaiming two current TV mini-series based on best-sellers: Bill Cosby's autobiography, serialized in *Parents* magazine, and the much-heralded political memoirs of Henry Kissinger's life in politics, *Call Me Pisher.*

A red bird scratched down the brightening azure sky like a hard ruby glass cutter. The "Hunky Dory" hooted its little horn for a landing. Refreshment stands were setting up for the day's festivities.

Taking Lindy's strong, thin little fingers in mine, I entered the open doors of the great cathedral. A flurry of strings, a clamor of horns, a thrum of percussion came from the full symphony orchestra preening itself in the highest reaches of the choir loft. The windows glowed gay motley.

And then I saw it—below the pulpit and altar—a thing of steel bars and panels: a cage.

And in that cage—alone and naked save for his magician's top hat—my father, O, my adored father, Sweeley Leech!

# T✦H✦I✦R✦T✦Y

My impulse was to run to the cage, but I held back judiciously for father's safety. One look at him told me how he had already suffered, but the prevalence of Goody Two-Shoes and other TRU-CAD muscle made any rescue out of the question.

I will not say that none of us was armed: we were armed with that strongest of universal forces, Love, but this, as you know, is often powerless in the material world.

And was Force what we needed just now? I tell you, honestly, I had not given up, but I tell you, too, that I had come to accept the probability that one of my father's life spans was about to end. I think the others felt this, too—their faces were solemn and grieving.

Let me describe the interior of the church. TV and other film technicians were everywhere: on rigs and scaffolds and booms that looked like the prehistoric monsters which used to roam this very land in the time of the three moons. These men and women crawled around like lemurs on their ladders and scaffolding, adjusting lights and cameras for the filming of Sweeley Leech's celebrated trial. As I have said, there was a full symphony orchestra in the high pews and, in the seats immediately below, there was a choir. They were rehearsing fragments of the Janáček *Mass*. O, they were going to give father a right merry send-off.

The news of my own reprieve should, I suppose, have cheered me. As it was, I felt only a dull ache as I stared through the cold iron bars at father, at my darling Sweeley Leech. At least, I thought, Lindy is saved, and so is the precious document. And I knew Sweeley Leech would have given his life for either of these ends. So I was, to this extent, very thankful.

As abruptly as it had begun, the bell, high in the church belfry, ceased tolling. At that moment, the colors of the place seemed to begin to pulsate and throb. I stared about me.

The Eastern Christian churches never mastered stained glass and have concentrated therefore on the muted interior color of fantastic icons. There were dozens of them against the walls—glowing like Rouault Jews and gesturing in holy movements captured by the artists of Novgorod and Moscow six hundred years or more ago.

The colors burned like stoked coals in a furnace: they threatened; they cajoled; some were in the gay frenzy of early Christian ardor, when saints still walked in the gardens of man's estate. Some were ominous and full of foreboding against the judgments of Patmos's John. The beast with seven heads strutted and strove against saints on lightbathed golden mounts, wielding formidable spears and broadswords. Some were the green and gold of the lush world of the south; others, the cold ice-blue of the steppes of Central Asia. Wide-eyed as lovely painted dolls were Constantine and Methodius before the stark assaults of the pagan Russian world of eggs and sacred trees.

There was a TRUCAD flag over the pew which, I supposed, was to serve as the judge's bench. It looked so bleak and harsh there among those more ancient lights.

A wren, which had flown imprudently through the open-wide doorway, now swooped and circled in panic through the incense-fragrant air. It battered its wings against TV kliegs and artifacts from before Ivan the Terrible. I followed its flight in sad, musing silence and breathed a sigh of relief when it found the light again and soared out into the sun.

For such a trial, Aubade said to me then, of such a man—one would think there would be milling crowds outside.

Reverend Jimbo overheard and leaned close.

It has been kept secret, he said. It will remain secret until it begins and the TV cameras begin sending it the length and breadth of the earth—to tell the world that its religion is once more being made safe by murder.

There is still time, I said. If Sweeley Leech chooses to, he can save himself. He has that power.

He told the TRUCAD authorities that he is prepared to die and will make no attempt to escape illegally. And remember, he has also said that he has the power left for three miracles in this life. Three, and no more. I felt that was, well, almost pathetic. Don't you?

O, he must be so tired! sighed Madame Jonathan.

Was it my fancy or did I really hear it from the open door, upon the river wind, lifting and falling in the first rays of morning light—the faint, tinny clangor of the tambourine which always signals both the beginnings and the ends for Sweeley Leech? No—it was not my fancy. I could hear it, rising and falling as it came closer. I shivered in the fresh morning air.

I was brought back by the sharp, electronically amplified slam of a gavel and a loud, but rather pleasant, voice over the public address system.

Instantly the orchestra and choir softened to *sotto voce,* though they did not stop—providing, as was the government's intention, a subtle background to the proceedings.

Order. Order in the court, came the words, rising and falling on the wings of the music.

It was then that I became aware of other sounds in the church: a susurration of voices, a clamor of many feet, both old and young; and the mobs began to pour gaily in through the doors, like visitors to Disneyland. O, it was unspeakable! They were vending Pepsi and hot dogs in the aisles. They were selling small aluminum facsimiles of the county electric cross, the one upon which Sweeley Leech was surely doomed to hang. I tell you I could scarcely keep my seat, could hardly keep from shouting out against the floodtide of ignorance and cruelty in that place.

And then I saw the men clustered around the pew, the bodyguards of the judge, who had just appeared. He was small, Oriental, dressed in a smart Oscar de la Renta sports jacket and gray flannel trousers from Chipp.

O, TRUCAD had hauled out its biggest brass for this occasion. The judge was none other than the President of the United States, Mr. Moto, America's first foreign-born Chief Executive.

Without ostentation, but with an unmistakable flurry, the redoubtable Moto reached behind him, as if preparing for a ritual, and produced a large dove-colored Stetson ten-gallon hat and put it on his head.

Howdy, he said. The court is now in session. Where is counsel for the defense?

The court-appointed counsel identified herself.

It was then that I saw the jury, cloistered below the choir loft: twelve American Gothic types, by Grant Wood out of Norman Rockwell.

The two attorneys. Clad in full-length body stockings. The prosecution in white. The defense in black. Both youngish women with excellent figures, so that the effect on the jury and spectators was sensational. Each wore a mask the color of her costume. Neither spoke. The entire prosecution and defense was, it appeared, to be carried out in pantomime. Sensational theatre was what TRUCAD yearned for. It was evident that both attorneys were highly trained in both mime and the law.

The TV crews were motionless except for those operating the boom cameras and mikes. The eyes of every man, woman, and child in that strange cathedral on that strange morning were focused on the defendant.

I switched on my wristradio very low and held it to my ear. I could hear the voice of Dan Rather describing the progress of the trial. The smooth, unctuous commentary was interrupted for a commercial.

"With one finger and a Yamaha organ you can play like John L. Lewis."

I switched to Off.

I felt a tug at the hem of my dress and looked down. It was Puddintame, and though she was tugging at me, she was straining up to see Sweeley Leech. I lifted her onto the hard bench and seated her beside me like the doll she was.

He promised me, she murmured. Me and Clyde. O, he did promise.

I said nothing. There were so many of us there that morning to whom Sweeley Leech had made—and kept—promises. I searched his bearded face for some line of hope, of happy foreboding.

Naked in his cage, he looked so very tired. Wearing only his battered silk magician's hat and above that his maddeningly (to TRUCAD) undisguisable halo. It bobbled like a nasturtium above the tattered crown of the hat. He was chewing gum and occasionally made an *O* with his lips and blew a bubble.

O, darling Sweeley Leech, chewing Dubble Yummy bubble gum at his own trial. I knew the sight of that bubble well, and each time it came and went like hope and despair alternately, tears flooded my poor eyes.

But there was something about father which frightened me, too. And that was the unmistakable air he gave off of wishing the whole affair—from indictment to execution—were over. A weariness. A certain exuberant wish to be off and about his Father's business on another plane, where he would not be held back by these absurd physical impediments and judgments for and against. Sweeley Leech had been friends with the poet Sandburg long ago, and that grand, white-haired magician had written him, "We live in times when we don't know whether to say Give 'em Hell or Pax Vobiscum. Perhaps I could say 'The peace of Great Phantoms be for you.'"

O, how I silently wished that peace for father now.

The pale little globe of the Dubble Yummy bubble gum inflated enormously and burst against father's beard and his pleasant, snubby nose. He gathered it back into his teeth and ruminated some more. How wise. Yes, I knew now. The bubble gum—all of it—his air—his fine, steady nerve—they were all going to make fools of the TRUCAD tyrants before it was over.

I calc'late we're ready to proceed, said Moto then. Sweeley Leech, how do you plead?

O, every chance I get, your honor, said Sweeley Leech. Not a day passes when I don't plead with people to be kind, to love one another, to hate riches, to argue not concerning God, to give what they have to the poor, etcetera etcetera etcetera.

That is not relevant, consarn it, snapped Moto. I mean, do you plead guilty or not guilty.

To what, your honor?

To be specific, to three charges of Federal Heresy, six of Ecumenical Subversion, and four of Necromancy in the Third Degree—all punishable, as you know, by death under laws of the World Federation of Nations. You are aware of that?

Even a little impatient, said Sweeley Leech with a faint smile. Now, how can I help in such a way as to get these rather confining proceedings over with?

Don't be impudent, Sweeley Leech, barked the court stenographer.

I'm sorry, said father, but I must speak my mind. This is a free court where I may speak my mind, is it not?

It is!

Then permit me to say, said Sweeley Leech, that not only am I guilty of all the things imputed to me, but I am even willing to demonstrate my illegal powers with three more miracles.

In this courtroom?

You don't see me going anywhere, do you?

You wish to perform three miracles before the court? asked the white prosecutor in pantomime. (Somehow, everyone in the church understood her, a miracle in itself.)

Sweeley Leech answered with a mime gesture of his own: Yes.

At this point Moto intervened.

You wouldn't be trying to hornswoggle us, now, would you, Sweeley Leech?

How do you mean?

I mean, supposin' you do have the power to perform miracles.

The sharp, vivid bars of light from the kliegs illuminated the attorneys—the two contending dancers—in a livid, steady circle of black and white.

The music of the now somewhat sinister Janáček *Mass* purred softly in the background, soothing the scene and somehow adding enormous—even unbearable—drama to it.

I mean, Moto went on, supposin' you really do have the power to perform miracles—how does the court know that if it lets you testify by showin' off two or three—?

Exactly three, corrected father.

Very well, then, dagnab it, snarled the little Japanese, who was often—and, I thought, cruelly—referred to in the radical press as "the Sawed-Off Shogun." Three, he said. Very well, then, consarn it—three. But how does the court know you won't make one or all of them a miracle to effect your escape or in some way harm this court.

I am a man of violence, said Sweeley Leech. I am also full of mischief. But I give you my oath upon the love of the living Criste that I will do neither of these things, your honor.

There was a pause.

I like your spunk, Leech, said Moto then, and I think I believe you. Go ahead.

Father slipped into a pale-yellow caftan the bailiff handed him and stepped out of the cage, which had been unlocked.

O, Sweeley Leech, I wanted to cry out, why are you playing into their hands this way? Deny your power to work miracles. Don't demonstrate it further!

But I knew him too well—far too well—to hope for that. I reached for Lindy's hand on one side and Puddintame's little hand on the other. The choir caroled soft benedictions above the reedy murmur of the orchestra and the great pipe organ. The crowd was restive, but tense and expectant.

Sweeley Leech was led to a small platform illuminated by half a dozen varicolored spots. The effect was fantastic. The spots were pitched and angled to give him the shadowy look of some kind of cheap sorcerer. Yet he dominated the scene—his head thrown back, his top hat bobbing on his head, the halo unfaded by the luminosity of the spots.

May I ask the court a question?

Permission granted, Sweeley Leech.

What would happen—what would you do with me if I were unable to do these three miracles, as I have said I would?

It is an interesting question.

And the answer?

You would stand a good chance of being acquitted. All charges against you would probably be dropped.

Pause.

You would, of course, attribute this failure to your total reformation—to your conformin' to the principles of the State Church, of the noble television evangelists with their Godsell. You would swear upon this white Testament to eschew your old ways, to forgo the dubious pleasures of uncontrolled and promiscuous do-goodery. You would, instead, agree to do good as the *Church* prescribes. No more raising of the dead—

It was marvelous—and sinister—the way the music of the orchestra, choir, and organ all managed to maintain a *sotto voce* background to all that was being said. I shivered and drew my shawl closer round my shoulders against the chill of the morning mists, which stalked wisping through the sunlit doorway to the church.

You would, in short, recant, said Moto. Consarn it, man, it's never too late to reform, now, is it?

Yes, said Sweeley Leech, it is too late to reform. I shall not change. I shall perform my three miracles. And then the court may do with me as it pleases.

As most assuredly it shall, said Moto grimly, tilting his ten-gallon hat at a rather raffish angle and lighting up a cheap Tampa seegar.

A promise, said Sweeley Leech, is a promise. And I have promised certain miracles to certain people. So, may I have the court's permission to proceed?

Moto sighed. I wash my hands of all responsibility as to what this court may decide to do with you, Sweeley Leech, he said. But, dagnab it, man, get on with your own destruction if you must.

For my part, of course, I prayed that father's miracle would fail—that all his miracles would fail—that the court would see the absurdity of its charges against him and set him free. It was touch and go.

Sweeley Leech made a grave little bow, like a guest magician on the Carson Show. Aubade, he said then, will you come here?

There was no movement where the Children of the Remnant were sitting.

Aubade? called father softly again.

She rose to her feet. Yes, Master.

Please, said Sweeley Leech, don't worship me. Love me, if you please, instead of that. Aubade, don't help them organize me. That would be the death of all I mean.

I do love you, Sweeley Leech, cried Aubade, whirring elegantly up onto the platform where father, bathed in the accusing kliegs, stood in his yellow caftan. O, I do.

And please forgive me if I have forgotten the miracle you once asked of me, Sweeley said.

My sister, Aubade said in a choked voice. I want her to have her lovely dancing legs again.

You mean, said Sweeley Leech, like the dancing legs on which you are now standing?

There was a silence you could hear.

What do you mean, Master?

Aubade, look down.

And Aubade looked down, and, of course, her marvelous mechanical legs were gone and in their place gleamed two silk-sheathed, incredibly beautiful legs of flesh and bone.

She uttered a soft cry and touched one as if she could not bring herself to believe in their warm reality.

Your sister, said Sweeley Leech, passed on to Glory more than a decade ago. But you have proven the great principle of the Criste Lite that if we love enough we are blessed with Criste's rarest benediction, the benediction that has given you back what once you thought to lose. Don't you see, my dear, we keep only that which we give away.

Aubade pirouetted, her skirts held high above her twinkling, dimpled knees, and ran to Sweeley Leech and kissed him on the mouth.

Heresy, murmured someone in the crowd. Witchcraft. Treason. Don't let him continue with this mockery of the true faith.

But Moto hammered furiously on the bench with his little gavel—a plastic one from the Sands Hotel in Vegas—and held up his hand. Silence in the court. Order. This court has promised the defendant three miracles. Since he was foolish enough to accept, let him continue.

Aubade was back in her pew, her fingers fluttering like butterflies over her lovely, shapely limbs. And, O, Uncle Mooncob, that unregenerate rake, was already flirting furiously with her.

Could I have a sip of something cold? asked Sweeley Leech. My mouth is dry as a desert.

Pepsi had outbid Coke for the concession at the trial and proba-
ble crucifixion, and immediately a frosty paper cup was handed to
Sweeley Leech.

Clyde? called father softly, wiping a small line of foam from his
beard. Puddintame?

I felt the tiny hand in my fingers stiffen and clench and heard
the little creature's soft cry of pleasure. Instantly we turned at the
sound of suppressed sobbing as two attendants in white jackets led
in a large, sad-faced man with red eyes and a runny nose, at which
he dabbed occasionally with a Kleenex.

Who is this? counsel for the prosecution demanded in pantomime.

These two gentlemen are from the Home—the West Virginia
State Home for Agelasts, said Moto stentoriously. They have
brought in a person named Clyde upon whom the defendant pro-
poses to effect a miracle.

What miracle? asked counsel for the defense, also in mime.

Why, two in one, said Sweeley Leech. I promised Puddintame
there that I would make her husband laugh.

You what? asked both counsel in dumb-show gestures.

For years, said Sweeley Leech, Clyde here has been unable to
laugh. He has been an inmate at the institution for such poor
wretches. I am going to save him. I am going to make him laugh.

He stared thoughtfully at Clyde and Puddintame, who were now
standing side by side on the dais. Great tears rolled down the big
man's cheeks and dropped off onto the ugly gray of his institution
jacket. From time to time he sighed thoughtfully and shook his
head fatefully from side to side. Occasionally a muffled sob was audible.

O, Sweeley Leech, this would be one of your greatest miracles:
to save one poor wretch from the Home for Agelasts.

Moreover, said my father, at the same time I make him laugh, I
am going to make him and his charming, though rather petite,
spouse the same size.

The orchestra, choir, and organ fell to a whisper. Moto leaned
forward, the saucy Stetson tilted back on his head, the big seegar
clenched in his teeth.

Well, Sweeley Leech, have you not perhaps bitten off more than
you can chew?

530

Sweeley Leech pranced gaily over to Clyde's side and whispered in his ear for half a minute. Clyde listened politely. He nodded from time to time. Not a flicker of a smile passed across his lips. On the contrary, he was so racked with sobs at what Sweeley Leech was saying that he had to cover his face with his hands for a moment in order to go on.

Well, Sweeley Leech?

Father faced the court.

I have just told this man the funniest joke I know. To no avail. It is apparent, he said, that this is a most advanced case of Agelasm. It rivals the case that Dubin and Franciscus reported: a young Ph.D. who was so Agelastic that he was not known to have so much as snickered once in twenty-five years. I shall have to try an extreme measure.

He turned to Moto. May the prisoner approach the bench?

Permission granted.

Sweeley Leech caught up a full quart bottle of Pepsi from a vendor's tray and walked over to the pulpit where Moto was perched. May I borrow your handsome hat, your honor?

Moto looked startled, then smiled, took off the hat, and handed it to father. Father took it quickly and emptied the whole bottle into the hat. He handed it back to Moto.

May the prisoner request your honor to put the hat back on your head?

Nothing untoward will happen?

I have done the trick many times, your honor.

Moto stared at the sloshing, full hat and shrugged.

*Ala kazam!* cried father at that moment.

Moto put the hat back on his head and sat for a long while as the dark fluid poured in rivulets down his face, extinguishing his cigar. He sputtered and half rose.

O hell, said Sweeley Leech. It should have turned into confetti.

Sweeley Leech, dagnab it—

Your honor, wait! A miracle is about to happen!

And so it was. Clyde took one look at the hapless Moto and his face seemed to relax. The relaxation was the first sign. Then a slight quiver could be seen at the corners of his mouth. Something appeared to be bubbling—like a coffeepot—deep in his massive, macho chest and stomach. He giggled. He pointed at poor Moto, who was still dripping and sticky. Then he opened his mouth and the first laugh erupted like a volcano of sound. He rocked on his heels. He clutched his sides. He beat his knees like Sammy, Junior.

It was a miracle indeed, and even Moto, subsiding from his outrage, settled back, impressed.

Just then we realized that Sweeley Leech was only warming up. As Clyde's peals of helpless, joyous mirth came rioting out of his gold teeth, he began to shrink. Visibly. It was as if he were a noisy toy balloon getting smaller with each squeak of escaping air. The crowd was on its feet, laughing, too. And staring over one another's head at the final miracle—Clyde and Puddintame, standing hand in hand, and neither of them more than fourteen inches tall.

If there is a moral to any of this, said Sweeley Leech, it is this, your honor, and ladies and gentlemen of the jury: laughter is the great equalizer.

The moral is well pointed, said Moto. And the court will overlook the—the slight inconvenience—in view of its relevance here. Now, Sweeley Leech—

Yes, your honor.

Do you count the laughter and equalizing miracles as one or as two?

One, your honor. I still have one more.

He was looking at me now as I helped lift tiny Clyde and little Puddintame onto the hard bench beside me.

Beurre, said Sweeley Leech softly, coming to my side.

Yes, father. Yes, my darling Sweeley Leech.

The last miracle is for you, lovey, he said. The last miracle of my life. Once I have done it they can do with me as they please. I shall pass on to new essences, new realms, and then, propitiously, I shall come again—for the last time.

Father, I cried, don't squander your miracle on me. Use it to save yourself.

Tut-tut, cried Moto. None of that. You swore—

Sweeley Leech waved an appeasing hand.

Never mind, your honor. I shall keep my word. The miracle is for my darling daughter.

I waited.

Do you remember, Beurre, when you were ten and had the measles and it was in the dead of winter and you were a little delirious and kept calling for me to bring you one red red rose?

Yes, father. O, yes.

I promised you one red red rose that night, said Sweeley Leech, and something happened—one thing or another—I think Rinsey and I were making love or she was having a tea party or something. Anyway, I never got you that one red red rose.

Father, it's all right.

No. No, he said. No, it's not. A promise to a child is sacred. It is holy. It is most highly regarded by God Almighty and the living Criste. I promised you, Beurre.

Father, it was a whim of mine. A red red rose in a glass by my bed. But, father, I never really missed it. It is not important.

It is important, Beurre, said father, and with no apparent effort caused the most beautiful, long-stemmed scarlet American Beauty rose to materialize in his fingers. He handed it to me gravely as one would give such a treasure to a sick little girl lying beneath some ancient counterpane.

I love you, Beurre.

O, and I love you, Sweeley Leech.

He closed his eyes and sighed. The long, hard life of him—this one, at any rate—was almost over. He spoke so that Moto and the jurors all had to bend forward to hear him, though I heard him marvelously clear.

> With the red that's in this rose
> I give my life away.
> But both of us, dear Criste knows,
> Shall live another day.

He paused and his fine, clear eyes swept the throng. He changed meter.

> For we only keep what we give away
> And we only sleep that we may live alway.

He turned to the court and squared his slumped shoulders. I am finished, he said. You can do with me now what I am sure you have intended to do from the beginning. *Komm, süsser Tod, komm.*

He went to his chair and slumped into it.

The orchestra and choir soared powerfully into the "Gloria" of the Janáček *Mass.* The sweetest and yet somehow frailest of sunbeams penetrated a slit high in the eaves of the great church and fell across father's head and shoulders like the soft touch of a hand far greater than his own.

So you are finished, Sweeley Leech? said Moto.

Sweeley Leech nodded slightly.

And you will not recant?

As well ask me to stop breathing.

You are sure?

Certain.

Then the case now rests at that point where defense and prosecution will both present their final arguments. Let the trial proceed. Already it is growing tarnally late in the day.

The arguments by the two women attorneys were brief, pictorial, and extremely dramatic. Each would act out a statement for or against the defendant; the other would then outdo the first in mimic emphasis and argument.

I was raging, frightened through and through. Yet I somehow feel that for me to make my account of these proceedings, the trial and execution of my father, Sweeley Leech—to make it, as I say, longer than those other accounts of another trial and retribution and another death—a trio of them, if memory serves, and God rest ye, Saint Dysmas—for me to make father's story, in brief, longer than that of the dear Christ would be somehow gross and disproportionate.

The jury did not even retire to consider its verdict. Caught up in the excitement of the spectacle of the white and black dancers, they rose as a man at the end of the arguments and shouted, *Guilty*!


Father was taken away to the little hill by the river road, a few meters from the Indian Mound, where stands the county cross. It is not large. It is barely taller than the man (or woman) who is strapped to it. It is made of aluminum. At Christmas time it is uprooted and set up on a truck-bed float and ornamented with lights to serve as the symbol of the United Appeal. It is regularly examined and approved by Underwriters Laboratory.

It is fail-safe, O ye salt-free of the earth!

And father was strapped to it, his mouth still chomping on bubble gum, the black top hat in his outstretched hand as if he were about to perform (as indeed he was) another trick. They let him keep the thing, this last badge of humanity. They let him keep it, I know, because they thought it would make him look ridiculous in the eyes of the mob.

The sky was pellucid, blue as a desert sky, with birds crossing it like tiny shooting stars—blackbirds and ravens and a lone tiercel on the hunt.

The switch was thrown. Father disappeared in a flash of light that I'm sure illuminated the very ceilings of the earth. The aluminum cross disappeared in a puff. And when our eyes had become adjusted to the gentle light of day once more, we saw, where the cross had been, where Sweeley Leech had been, a perfectly lovely granite statue of Sweeley Leech naked as old Uncle Adam and holding his battered top hat.

But that was not the all of it.

Father succeeded, in death, with the trick he could never pull off in life. From the outstretched hat flew a pigeon, hopped a hare, clambered a raccoon: small animals in profusion, and blinking bewilderedly in the first light of their existence.

While over the heads of the demanding mob, over the helmets of the TRUCAD guards and the bouffant hairdos of the Goody Two-Shoes, over the hills and from far off, came the clangor of the tambourine as Mr. Judah Samphire led his ward to the foothills of the shining City of God.

535

# T·H·I·R·T·Y
# O·N·E

Yet none of us grieved. We missed Sweeley Leech sorely, we ached for a glimpse of him, for a joke by him, but we did not grieve.

The Children of the Remnant stayed on together for a week in his marvelous, sprawling old bungalow at the edge of the Gallimaufry. During this period we pored through the pages of the Criste Lite and absorbed its marvelous effect.

Lindy was a changed woman: charming, soft, sexy, and very funny indeed—a kind of miracle, I know.

On the eighth day the TRUCAD people heard about the document and came to the bungalow demanding to see it. As you may imagine, what with the light constantly pouring out of the thing, one might as well have tried to hide a sun or moon. We handed it over.

And watched in sorrow and loss as two Goody Two-Shoes tossed the leaves one by one into the blazing fire on our winter hearth.

They burned, as any paper would burn. But the flame changed and became rainbow-colored. It was inextinguishable.

The TRUCAD men and women, realizing that something holy had happened, poured bucket after bucket of river water into our fireplace, whence it vanished while the colored flames burned ever more brightly. They burned with this chromatic brilliance for thirteen days. During that period, pilgrims came from all over the earth, and perhaps beyond—came by night with candles and lit their wicks at the hearth of Sweeley Leech.

I remember that last night as Lindy and I stood on the Indian Mound looking down at the cottage, at the Labyrinth, at the river road and the great winding, gleaming river itself. From the cottage came—one by one—lighted candles.

Lighted, tiny candles everywhere, fanning out like a Busby Berkeley effect in a wonderful old thirties movie—tiny points of fire radiating out in a wheel whose spokes ran on till they were lost in the Pleiades and were scattered by the Milky Way.

O, Lindy, I said. It will last forever.

Yes, she said. The Criste Lite is now ten thousand little candles in the dark.

And it will light that dark forever, I said. Look at them—like the jeweled fan of the Queen of the Night. Like a rainbow—exploding slowly.

Lindy and I stayed up there till dawn. And the wind in my hair—I swear, it whispered the soft word over and over: Beurre, Beurre, Beurre.

Until it grew too cold and we went down and crawled naked into the great feather tick and slept the sleep of the Just, softly sure that Criste loved us after all.

# E ✦ N ✦ V ✦ O ✦ I

Now go, write it before them in a table, and note it in a book,
that it may be for the time to come for ever and ever . . .
                                                    —Isaiah 30:8

They say there will be general war tonight.

It is a year later, and I have begun to write down these fabulous
events in a kind of journal—perhaps like a Scheherezade against the
evil temper of the Sultan.

It is early evening. The November moon is like a great gold-
crusted Spanish galleon on a stormy, painted Howard Pyle sea.

The wind blows.

My baby plays on the clean rag rug with her curious new toy.
She fills the sweet, quivering air with the sound of it.

At sundown I had finished pruning the apple trees as I looked
ahead to fruit in the springtime of the new Eden.

My baby beats the painted floor with her new toy. She laughs
and blows sweet bubbles with her Botticelli breath. She teethes on a
great yellow diamond.

The Children of the Remnant? They are scattered to the far reaches of the earth—with tiny colored candles—shedding a little light in the eternal-seeming darknesses of the world.

Adonis McQuestion—the adored, the divine, the authentic, the non-Chaz, the irreplaceable—he is my husband now.

We are divinely happy.

I think I have mellowed a little with old age—I'm twenty-seven now. I never believed that I would— But no matter.

This night Adonis is off somewhere in the Gallimaufry, hunting. We live in the old bungalow, and we eat nothing which we do not raise or catch with our own hands.

Lindy fell in love for the first time in her life with an Armenian fortune-teller in a carnival and is divinely happy. She visits us in the spring—before the show hits the dusty roads. She brings a toy or a treat to Footit.

Aubade proved unable to resist the feverish adoration of Uncle Mooncob and they, too, were wed, and I must say my uncle is a changed character—charming and funny as a clown.

Back to this curious article, this odd toy which my baby daughter beats on the wooden floor. I have heard its sound so many times in the past few weeks that it is a wonder I was surprised when I heard it on the river road this very night—a little after sundown—when the crescent moon hung like a silver hammock between two boughs of the old Royal Paulownia.

Mr. Judah Samphire, on his way to announce Sweeley Leech's comings and goings, clanging furiously on his durable old Salvation Army tambourine.

The augury was clear to me. So that I was not surprised when, over the sassafras tea and dark honey we shared in the study, he bade me christen my child Sweeley Leech—informing me that the original, wild, terrible, naughty, improbable, and infinitely beautiful life of him was to begin again here.

With my daughter.

And so my baby, Sweeley Leech, plays on the carpet with Mr. Judah Samphire's tambourine—long after he has departed gainward the moon.

He left the thing with her for a toy.

You see, he said he wouldn't be needing it anymore.